# The Huguenot

# And

# THE HEATHEN

**The 3rd Novel in the Huguenot Series**

*The Huguenot and The Heathen*
is a work of fiction.
Names, characters, places, and incidents either are the
product of the author's imagination or are used
fictitiously. Any resemblance to actual persons, living or
dead, events or locales is entirely coincidental.



LIBRARY OF CONGRESS CATALOGING-IN-PUBLICATION
DATA

Force, D.C.
The Huguenot and The Heathen: a novel / D.C. Force

ISBN 978-1-7339762-5-1
eISBN 978-1-7339762-6-8

Published in the United States of America

*Book Cover Design by*
**The Book Cover Whisperer**

# The Huguenot

# And

# THE HEATHEN

By

## D.C. Force

The 3rd Novel in the Huguenot Series

# Books by D.C. Force

## The Huguenot Series

***The Huguenot***: *Flight From Terror*

***The Huguenot II***: *Building the Dream*

*The Huguenot and* **The Tower of Constance**
(an e-book novella)

*The Huguenot and* **the Heathen**

*The Huguenot and* **the Heathen II**
(release planned for 2020)

## Other Books by the Author

*Family: a Century of Blood and Tears*
released 2007

Visit our website to leave comments, ask questions, learn about the author, or catch previews of books to come.

www.dcforce.com

www.amazon.com/author/dcforce

This series is dedicated to all the men, women, and children throughout history who have suffered severely and cruelly because of their sincere and non-political beliefs in and love for
our Lord, Jesus Christ.

Significant Characters

**Early Hudson River Valley Frontier**

**Petre Lindstrom** widower
    daughter **Elka**
    son **Lars**


**Elka Lindstrom/Elk-woman** kidnapped and mated by **Anokyen**
    daughter **Naxàti** who births
        daughter who births
            **Singing Wind** who mates **Red Elk** (brothers – Bending Branch &
            Fleet-of-Foot)
            and births
                *Ajappawe Waseleechen*, **MORNING LIGHT** and **Son of Red Elk**


            **Bending Branch** is mated to 2nd wife, **Mist-On-Moon**
                **Yellow Rock** (son by 1st wife) is 1st cousin to Morning Light
                and Son of Red Elk

**Capture by Mohawk**

-Yellow Rock is adopted by older warrior whose son has died
-**Five Beavers** mated to **Little Smoke** and brother of Sachem/Chief
    takes Singing Wind as 2nd wife and adopts Son of Red Elk, names him
    *Wakuwéskwani Atatswvhsera* (**Wani** for short)
-Mist-On-Moon mates **Quick Panther**
    is 1st wife and by whom she has her 1st son and 2nd daughter
    has 1st daughter by lover **Tonoaki**
-Morning Light is given to *Atakenhrohkwa Okwaho/***Gray Wolf** who names
her *Ohronkene Hahser(Morning Light)*
    weds Gray Wolf, has son, **Gray Wolf's Son**
    weds Tonoaki, has daughter

## Logging Camp

**Sonya Olafson** widow of Sven
sons     **Sven Jr.**, wife **Clara**
        **Uland**, wife **Anna**
        **Bor**, wife **Sasha**
        **Regin**, wife **Kristen**
        **Peter**
daughters    **Freyja** (named for goddess of love, beauty and enchantment)
        **Snotra** (named for goddess of virtue and knowledge)
        **Skadi** (named for goddess of the winter and the hunt)

## Chartes Landing

**Jacques** and **Marie's CHILDREN** and **Grandchildren**

    **JOHN/Jack/*Sak***    weds Alana Huffsmeier
               weds Morning Light/*Ohronkene Hahser*/Ronnie

    **PHILLIP** weds Caroline Weaver
        **Charity**
        **Faith** & **Hope** (twins)
        **Grace**
        **Patience**

    **HELEN** weds Thor Boot
        **Thomas**
        **Sybelle**
        **Joseph**
        **Jennette**

    **LOUISE** weds Raphael/Rafe Bonchance (only recognized son of Richard
Bonchance)
        **Rebecca**
        **Sebastian**
        **Michael**
        **Josephine**
        **Frances**

    **RICHARD/Richie**
    **JAMES/Jamie**
    **ISABELLE/Izzy**

"We are shaped and fashioned by what we love."– Goethe

"There will always be about the same percentage of people capable of real love, and there will always be about the same percentage of people who aren't." – John Galsworthy

"Only People who are capable of loving strongly
can also suffer great sorrow, but this same
necessity of loving serves to counter their grief
and heal them." – Leo Tolstoy

# *Prologue*

## The Mahicanituk (Hudson) River - Mid 1630's

The young squaw sat keening over the still, quiet bodies of her two children; her young husband was powerless to ease her pain. Their sturdy son of less than three winters now lay stiff and cold, his body thin and disfigured from the battle he had fought. His sister, not yet a full year old, lay beside him, unnaturally quiet. Her plump little cheeks had withered. Their life force was gone. Their spirits had left. The Great Spirit had taken them to be with Him. The woman wept as she wailed, her tears not filling the empty hollowness within her. She wanted her babies back.

Only a short time ago these two had played happily with the trinkets the pale strangers had brought into their midst. The pale strangers had created a stir when they had suddenly appeared in the village. No one of the tribe had ever seen anyone like them. At first, they seemed fearsome with hair growing over their faces like the beasts of the wild. They wore strange heavy clothing and smelled odd. Their hair was of different colors, some brown as wet earth, others fiery red, and some like captured sunshine. They were a source of great curiosity and amusement. But they had come to trade. They paid much for common skins which they were pleased to take away with them to their home across the great water. In exchange they brought wondrous gifts. Bright beads to dazzle the eyes. Fine heavy pots which flames did not consume. Metal so shiny it reflected images. Iron knives of greater strength than flint. And so much more. Once their initial shyness was overcome, the children had taken great delight in playing with some of the novelties the pale strangers had possessed. But when one of their kind suddenly fell ill, the pale strangers had left.

Soon after, their children began to fall sick. One by one they were overcome with a strange fever. It was a sickness such as they had never seen before and they had no idea it was the beginning of a wave of death. Adults also began to fall ill. Some broke out in horrid red and white pustules but most simply languished with a rash while their life was burnt out of them with a fever so intense it was like being devoured in a living fire.

Several days after the young mother and her husband had built the small funeral pyre and watched it consume their children's bodies, the woman knew she, too, had the sickness and she decided it was a good time to die and follow her children into the after life.

The young warrior did not understand why he had been spared. When he finally revived from the daze that had overcome him after his family's death, he looked around and realized their village population was less than half of what it had been.

There had been so many funeral pyres and so few left to build them, that they had been shared. The bodies neatly stacked one next to another. Families were put together. And when it was over, the survivors moved on to a place of new beginnings. They wanted to leave the sickness and the memories behind.

Two Years Later

It was a habit to walk silently through the forest, listening to the wind stirring in the tree tops, the birds calling overhead, the buzz of insects flying around. In his moccasin covered feet, Anokyen's light tread could not be heard but he could hear the rustle of the small creatures who scurried along in the brush. He was looking for bigger game, however, and not interested in delaying himself with small creatures. The tall, sturdy brave detected the sound of water. He was aware of his own thirst and followed the sound.

Anokyen did not usually hunt alone but his hunting partner and closest friend, at least the closest he had left since the sickness had wiped out most of their village, had turned his ankle and was still recuperating. Anokyen had teased him that his friend must stay behind to tend the hearth like a woman, but he, Anokyen, would bring back the food to fill their bellies. Both braves were without women. There were no single women in their village. Every female over the age of twelve was joined and every one under the age of twelve was spoken for. Several raiding parties over the past two years had garnered them a half dozen females of child-bearing age, but Anokyen had not been one of the fortunate ones to find a woman.

He was lonely but he would not allow himself to think about it. Memories of his mate and his children still haunted his dreams. In his dreams, they were as alive to him as they ever had been and each awakening was a fresh shock of his losses, even now. But after two years of mourning, the natural drives of his body were asserting themselves in an ever growing demand to procreate, multiply, and survive.

The sound of the water grew ever louder, water bubbling over rock, coursing its way along a rocky river bed. And as Anokyen walked noiselessly, he detected yet another sound. Humming. The faint melodic sounds of a human voice. Higher pitched. Female. He halted and then, very slowly worked his way closer to the sound.

On a flat dry rock with water swirling around it, knelt a slender female form in a long skirted garment. She was scrubbing something in the water, working with a lather of bubbles, while a pile of wet cloth lay beside her. Several garments were spread out on a nearby rock, drying in the sun. But it was the long golden hair caught in a shaft of sunlight, shimmering like liquid sunshine, tumbling down her back in one thick, heavy braid that mesmerized Anokyen and made him catch his breath. A healthy surge of lustful desire rose up in the brave, tempered with the knowledge that he wanted and needed a life mate. He had no desire to scare off the girl or do her harm. He was not interested in rape and plunder, but in capture and relocate. As he crept closer, everything he saw was very pleasing to him. She was slender but sturdy, her face was turned away but a glimpse of her profile revealed that her features were even and pleasant. And her hair had the white gold brilliance of a high summer sun.

It was spring and as she worked, Elka hummed a song her mother used to sing. It made her feel closer to her mother and not so alone. Mama had died two winters ago and Papa had insisted on moving away from what he called the "unbearable memories" and relocating on the very edge of the frontier. Elka regretted leaving what little society there was in the small settlement along the river by the fort. There had been a few girls near her age. A few young men. Nobody she could imagine marrying but there was always the hope of an eligible bachelor making his way into the settlement or of meeting a newly transferred soldier at the fort who took her fancy. There were more men in the New World, after all, than women. At fifteen, she certainly was of marriageable age but with her papa only recently widowed and her young brother, Lars, to watch over, she really couldn't think of leaving them yet.

Elka finished her laundry and spread it all out neatly upon the sun-washed rocks to dry. Then, on impulse, she undid the lacings of her dress and slipped it over her head. She almost stripped off her shift but halted herself. If Papa or Lars, by some small chance, came running down to the stream looking for her, she didn't want to be completely naked. Stepping into the rushing water, she washed the sweat and grime from her simple knee length shift as she wore it. In truth, once the thin cotton was wet and stuck to her body, it wasn't much different than being naked.

The water only came up to her knees until she sat down on one of the submersed rocks. Moving quickly she lathered the cloth as it lay against her body, then pulled it away to scrub her skin beneath with the harsh homemade soap. She didn't want to linger in the water long. It was cold and chilled her quickly but she made certain she rinsed herself and the under garment well before she got out of the water to dry. The hot, sun-drenched flat rock felt very good now and she stretched out over it totally unaware of the pair of eyes that had been watching her every move from behind the underbrush.

Lulled by the sound of the rushing water and the gentle warmth of the sun, Elka dozed off briefly only to be startled awake when a powerful hand clamped across her mouth and another held her hands trussed together. She opened her eyes to stare into the black ones of a swarthy skinned brave staring down at her. His leg, spread across hers, pinned her, she couldn't move and she thought she was going to die. Her heart was racing and all she could think of was to pray, a prayer begun with the full expectation of being concluded in front of the Lord in person.

Anokyen looked down upon the female and when her eyelids flew open, he saw bright blue eyes that danced with lights and terror. He did not want to make her fearful but he could not risk her screaming and alerting her family to his presence. He worked quickly to tie her hands before she could resist him and he placed a gag into her mouth. And then, he stared again at those brilliant and astounding blue eyes.

After several long moments, Elka realized she wasn't dead. Her prayer was finished and she was still breathing although she now had a gag in her mouth. Only then did she realize she had been so frightened she had forgotten to scream. It was too late to scream now, not that there was anyone close enough to hear. She wasn't being raped, in fact, the body which had pressed her down was now lifting off of her and the air hitting her skin brought the goose-flesh up even in the pleasantness of the day making her nipples stand out hard and erect against the coarse cloth.

Anokyen knew he had to concentrate on the task of getting this female back to his village. It was very important to him that she trust and like him and he was wise enough to know this was going to require some patience and suffering on his part. As a matter of fact, he was suffering a little already. After watching her bathing and then being on top of her body with only his loin cloth and her flimsy garment between them, he was actually suffering quite a bit. Trying to be gentle, he hefted her up onto her feet and was surprised, standing face to face with her as he now was, to find that she was as tall as he. As they stood there facing each other, she with her extraordinarily vivid blue eyes wide open staring straight into his face and he holding the rawhide rope that bound her hands, he reached almost reverently to touch her hair and caress the loosened strands of silken shine. There was something in that gesture that bespoke of gentleness, affection even, and Elka's racing heartbeat began to slow back down just a little.

She made a sound when he began to lead her away coupled with a strange hopping motion with her feet that made him stop. She pointed as best she could with her bound hands and her head toward her shoes. If she was going to be walked away, she needed her shoes. He looked at her bare feet and understood. Elka was allowed to sit down and put on her shoes but when she next wished to pick up her dress, his patience had run out and he pulled her along with a tug.

Elka felt utterly ridiculous walking along through the forest in her loose shift and shoes, her hands tied to a lead tether, and her mouth gagged. A hundred thoughts raced through her head in no particular order. She had left a stew cooking for the evening meal. Who would mind it to make certain it did not burn? What would Father and Lars think when they discovered she was gone? There would be no biscuits for their supper. Would Father be angry with her when they saw her dress left behind? Would they think a wild beast had taken her away? Surely a wild beast would have left a bloody trail. They must realize she had been abducted. Would they come after her? But how would they know where to go? How far was this native going to take her? Why had he taken her?

Why *had* he taken her? Even though she was only fifteen and innocent, Elka realized there had been something rather intimate in that caress to her hair. Something in the native's eyes told her that. And she instinctively suspected on a level she could not yet acknowledge, that she had been captured to be made a wife. And on that same unacknowledged level, she found the prospect just a little exciting as well as frightening but she couldn't fully admit either point to herself as yet.

Elka found herself studying the brave who was leading her. He wasn't ugly. It was difficult for her to judge how old he was but his skin was very firm and smooth and she thought perhaps he wasn't very much older than she. His body was completely naked except for his loin cloth and footwear which didn't leave much to her imagination. Lean muscles stretched over his evenly proportioned frame giving him a look of wiry, flexible strength. He might not be ugly but his overall looks were strange, very different from the few young men she was accustomed to. His skin was quite dark, a brown hue different from even the most sun-tanned white man she'd ever seen. He had deep black eyes with a shape to the lids that made them appear wider and they were slightly hooded. High cheekbones widened his face, flanked by coarse straight hair so black it held a bluish sheen as it hung down to his shoulders. There was an almost hawk-like look to his face, gaunt, angular, raw but his lips were very generous and full.

The thought came to Elka that she was being taken away by someone with whom she could not speak and whom she could not understand. How would she let anyone know what she needed or felt ever again? She was no good at languages and the idea of spending the rest of her life with people she couldn't communicate with was terrifying. Perhaps she was mistaken in his intent. Perhaps he wasn't going to keep her. Perhaps she was only going to be a captive for a time and then ransomed back to her family. She had heard of that happening before. But ransomed how? Her father didn't have any money. They only had one mule to help plow and take out stumps and move logs. They, in fact, didn't have much of anything to serve as ransom.

Anokyen was focused on putting as much distance between them and his captive bride's home as possible before nightfall. Because of this, he didn't allow any slowing of their pace or give any breaks although he did stop after a time and remove her gag so she could breathe more easily. By then, she must realize screaming would be utterly worthless. By late afternoon, he was well aware that the girl was growing tired. That she made no noises of complaint nor did she weep filled him with a certain sense of pride in her. Neither did she fight him for which he was exceedingly grateful. Starting off their relationship with harsh discipline would make his progress in wooing her much slower. He had no desire to hurt her. He noticed she was stumbling more often now. Her body glowed with a sheen of perspiration and he heard her belly growl. They were close to a cave he had used the night before. It would give them shelter and allow him to build a fire without being seen. He kept his grip on the girl's lead rope and forced their march to continue.

He heard the sound of moving water and led her down to a fast rushing stream. She picked a spot with care and dropped to her knees. Bending over, she scooped up the icy water and drank from her hands. There was a decidedly feminine grace about her and he watched her every movement with continuing fascination. Then, distancing himself from her a little, he put his mouth to the water and drank deeply himself.

Elka splashed some water over her face and arms, careless of the droplets that fell on her shift. "I'm sorry," she spoke at last in Swedish, "farther tonight I cannot go and if I do not eat, I will not be going much farther tomorrow. Understand me you may not but I am tired, hungry, and ready to drop right here in my tracks."

The girl was talking her words and he didn't understand them but he could well imagine what she was saying although there was no whine in her attitude. He motioned up the side of a hill and told her there was shelter and they would soon have a fire against the night chill to come, and food. He knew she didn't understand his words any better than he understood hers, but he hoped she could understand something of his meaning.

Elka heard the brave. It was the first time he had spoken and his voice had a strange guttural timbre. He was pointing up the steep hillside and she did get the impression that it was their destination. She sighed; if it was not, she thought, she would fall over right there on the ground and he could carry her if he wanted her to move another step.

They began their trek upward and she was finding it more and more difficult to put one foot in front of the other carrying the weight of her own body ever upward with each step. Then, from pure fatigue, she caught her toe and almost fell to her face but his quick response in jerking up her lead rope saved her from hitting the ground. At this point she must have looked pitiful because he took her wrist and half pulled her onward.

She saw the cave. He led the way inside. It was a comfortable size and smelled of charred wood and ashes but didn't smell of animals. Elka saw the remnants of a fire and guessed that the native had used the place just recently. He said something again and motioned for her to sit and she did so quickly and gladly.

Anokyen was now uncertain what to do. He needed to hunt supper but he was afraid to leave the female unguarded. At the same time, he didn't want to leave her tied up to a tree as easy prey for a mountain lion. He decided he would build a fire at the mouth of the cave as a deterrent to animals. He re-tied the girl's hands behind her back together with her feet after which he left her on her side inside the cave.

"Please," she pleaded, "leave me not like this. Please, I cannot even relieve myself." It didn't do any good. He couldn't understand her. Anokyen left after throwing several more large pieces of dead-fall on the fire. He determined to return before the fire could burn itself down too far and started off silently in pursuit of supper.

Elka watched the brave disappear and felt like crying for the first time that day. Being trussed hand to foot and left alone and defenseless in the midst of the wild was demoralizing. She realized he had undoubtedly gone off to hunt some food but that didn't seem to make any difference. She wished she hadn't thought of having to relieve herself because now that was all she could think of. Lying on the rock floor was very uncomfortable, trussed up as she was so she could barely move. That was his intent, she was sure, but this now seemed cruel. Kidnapped, half-naked, starving, marched to the point of exhaustion, and now left deserted and unable to answer nature's call. Large tears rolled out of Elka's eyes across the side of her face and fell to the ground. Despite everything, she fell asleep.

When Elka awoke she could smell roasting bird. She opened her eyes and saw what she guessed was a small turkey hen roasting on a spit over the fire. She tried to move and moaned which brought the brave's attention to her immediately. He untied the bindings to her feet and helped her to sit up. As soon as she did, she knew she had to find a bush. The pressure on her bladder was painful. Elka stood carefully, allowing the circulation to return to her legs. She did a little jiggle dance and began to walk away from the cave. The brave stopped her instantly.

"Look, I know not how to make you understand this but wait I cannot," she said with a grimace and locked her legs together tightly while rocking back and forth.

Anokyen suddenly understood. Of course. He had voided just before hunting. She had had no chance. How thoughtless of him, he chided himself and nodded to the girl. He watched her walk into a thicket. Her footsteps and the sound of breaking twigs did not go far. He turned his back and after a few moments he heard the distinct sound of liquid falling onto the ground. He smiled and went back to the turkey, still listening to hear her footfall return.

Elka didn't even think of bolting. The forest was getting very dark and she didn't know how to get back home. There were too many wild animals roaming around out here to be traveling defenseless with her hands tied behind her back. And she was hungry. With her bladder emptied, she was careful to avoid the puddle she had made and dropped her shift back down into place but not before a few mosquitoes had fattened themselves on her tender behind. She shivered and returned to the fire.

"*Tack*," she said softly, hoping he would understand her grateful tone if not the words. "Much better I feel." Rather awkwardly, she sat down on the floor of the cave and pulled her legs up on one side. She thought of crossing her legs but her shift was too short and it would have been too immodest.

They sat in silence. The crackle of the fire had ceased as it became a glowing bed of coals better suited for roasting their supper. He slowly turned the spit. Each time a drop of grease dripped onto the burning embers, there was a small flash and hiss. Elka heard an owl hooting high up in the dark. Sometime later, a mountain lion's distinctive cry rolled through the night. She looked at the native in the firelight aware that he was watching her even while caring for the roasting bird. She looked back at the fire but she could still feel his eyes upon her and she wondered what exactly he was looking at and what he was thinking. She felt very disheveled and grimy. She could feel wisps of her hair sticking to her face and her mosquito bites were beginning to itch causing her to squirm a little, unconsciously.

By now, Elka's stomach felt so hollow she thought she was going to be sick. She was getting light-headed and her stomach rumbled again which set the brave to chuckling. His chuckling surprised her. Had she thought they never laughed, she asked herself? She looked at him and was equally surprised to see how different his face looked when he smiled. His teeth were very even and white. His eyes softened and he really was quite nice looking, in his own way. She smiled in response and then, realizing she was smiling at her abductor, her enemy, she stopped herself as if somehow it was traitorous and inappropriate.

He removed the spit and lifted the bird away. The fowl was done and needed to cool for a few minutes so they wouldn't burn their mouths eating it. Propping it up off the ground, Anokyen threw more wood on the fire causing it to blaze up again and give off more light. Then, he picked up the bird and bringing it with him took up a seat close to the girl.

Elka was aware of his faintly musky, earthy smell, like burning leaves mixed with cooked fat as he pulled a hunk of roasted flesh from the carcass and tasted it. He assured himself it was thoroughly cooked. Elka watched and unconsciously licked her lips in response. He saw this and instantly brought the remaining flesh to her mouth. She ate it quickly from his fingers, taking some care not to bite him. He pulled more flesh from the carcass and held it to her mouth while she again took off several bites; this time she actually chewed before she swallowed. He took another mouthful himself.

It didn't make a great deal of sense to her. Why he left her hands tied up behind her like he did, she certainly wasn't going to attack him. But he continued to feed her, watching those brilliant blue eyes catch the firelight and the red of the flames reflecting off her golden hair. The act made her look up at him. It gave him reason to be very close to her without frightening her. It was a universal act of caring, to feed someone, as well as a sign of utter dependency. Elka found herself responding on a multitude of levels.

At first, she thought only of taking care not to bite him and getting the food into her belly. She was so hungry. Then, as he continued to feed her, looking at her so intently and being so tender toward her, she began to feel something else. When his thumb moved across her lips, slowly and gently wiping the grease away, she felt a strange quivering go through her. And with the next bite she found herself licking the juice off his fingers. After his next bite he also licked his own fingers and when she licked them again drawn on by their somewhat salty taste, it somehow turned to sucking and it wasn't a big leap in tactile sensation to find him licking her lips with his tongue, sucking on them with his mouth. At that point, Elka felt such an overpowering feeling race through her insides she wasn't thinking about food anymore. Bracing herself with her bound hands caused her young breasts to thrust forward and then, suddenly, he was sucking there as well right through the material. She uttered a soft little gasp. It wasn't proper. Pa would never approve, but what could she do? She was defenseless and it did feel strangely good.

Suddenly, she had to be free of her bonds and half twisting around, she thrust her hands out to him from behind her back. He understood and brought both arms around her to reach her bindings. This brought him, his face, his chest, his body in close contact with her and she closed her eyes, feeling his tongue licking her cheek, moving on to her neck.

Instead of balking when his hands brushed the hem of her shift up toward her hips, she actually moved her weight to free the garment as she sat and in a second her hands were free and her shift was over her head and tossed aside. Everything was going so quickly now. His hands were warm as they continued with a gentle stroking that soothed and disturbed her at the same time. His body was warm as it pressed against her. She was flat on her back and certain that had he been white she could have never allowed him to do the things he was doing to her down there in her private places. She would have had to protest the indecency of it all but as he was a savage and she was helpless as his captive and in no position to protest anything, and couldn't be understood even if she had, she allowed herself to relax and simply enjoy all the stimulating sensations she was experiencing.

Those sensations were mounting and suddenly so was he. With frustrating patience he went about it, and she had no means to verbally hurry him along. She didn't know she didn't need any words, that the squirming, writhing movements of her body were telling Anokyen everything he needed to know. And still, wanting to minimize the discomfort for her, he held off until the path before him was completely slick and she was beating on his back and pulling at his hips.

When he entered her she met him wildly with a thrust of her pelvis. The momentary shock of the breaching caused her to stop suddenly with a muffled cry. He felt her stiffen and paused also, giving her a chance to catch her breath, giving her body a chance to adjust to his presence and size within her before his hips began to move sensuously between her legs and she discovered it didn't hurt anymore. Quite to the contrary, she had never imagined anything to feel so good in all her life.

Four and a Half Years Later

"You cannot delay any longer," said the sachem of the tribe, "Elk-woman has recuperated from childbirth. She is fit to travel and we must keep our word."

"The white does not keep his word!" Anokyen cried out in frustration. He and Elk-woman had been mated for over four years, they had three children, the youngest was just weeks old. He could not stand the thought of losing yet another family. "She stays of her own choice!"

The sachem looked long and hard at Anokyen, then his expression softened to sympathy. "We have promised her return, if she chooses to leave again, that will be her choice as well."

"They might keep her restrained."

"Enough!"

Anokyen left the sachem's hut grimly and returned to his own. Elk-woman had just finished nursing their baby and was putting her down to sleep. Quietly coming up behind his wife, he caressed her naked breast and held her.

"He said we must leave," he said quietly against her bright pale gold hair. She turned in his arms, fixing him with her intensely blue eyes. "You must return to your people but if you choose, you may come back." She understood his words better than she could speak them to reply and so she simply nodded.

The river looked the same but the small settlement around the fort had grown. Elka could hardly recognize it but it had been six and a half years since her family had left it. She was feeling very nervous. She wanted to see her father and brother again, she really did. Lars would be sixteen. She had missed his growing up. But wouldn't it be harder to leave after seeing them again? Wouldn't it be harder saying good-bye? Undoubtedly they had thought she was dead after all this time. Wouldn't it have been better for them to continue to think so? But someone who had chanced upon the village had seen her and reported it. A tall blonde woman with bright blue eyes had the tendency to stand out amongst the Indians. There was a treaty and it said all white captives were to be returned to their families. Her father sent her a letter. She had read it. He didn't understand at all. He thought she was a prisoner. That they were actually rescuing her.

Elka looked back at the figure of her husband growing smaller upon the far shore while the fort loomed up before her. She had her baby on her back and tightly gripped her two children by the hand as the boat landed.

Petre Lindstrom stood stiffly watching the boat make its way across the width of the river. He was a tall, gaunt man, his shoulders slightly stooped from the plow, his thick and once blond head of hair now snow white. He recognized his daughter by her light golden hair. If not for her hair he wouldn't have recognized her at all. She wore a soft doeskin tunic with lacings down the front, Indian moccasins which rose up her legs and she had a papoose carrier on her back. In each hand she gripped a small, dark skinned, dark headed Indian child.

"There she is, Pa," Lars said excitedly, waving at his sister.

"Stop that!" Lindstrom ordered.

"Stop what, Pa?" Lars looked at his father in surprise.

"No need to wave around like that and make a spectacle of yourself," Lindstrom growled darkly. He was embarrassed and ashamed.

Lars frowned and turned back to watch his sister. A soldier had helped her from the small craft and she was walking toward them, slowed by the pace of her children. Lars went forward to meet her.

"Lars," Elka cried. "Oh, Lars." She reached out to embrace him and started crying. He had grown taller than she over the past four years and already had broad shoulders but the face was the same. His blue eyes mirrored hers and a thick thatch of very light golden blond hair topped his beardless face.

"Good it is to see you, sis," he choked. After a moment he pulled back and looked at the children.

"This is *Kwëti, Nisha,* and the baby is *Naxàti,*" she introduced them proudly.

"You may have to repeat that a couple times before I can remember," Lars laughed.

"Just call them *One, Two,* and *Three,*" she smiled, "They are learning our language too."

"That I can remember," he grinned warmly.

Elka continued to walk up to her father.

"Hello, Papa," she offered hesitantly, not understanding why she felt guilty.

Petre Lindstrom nodded, his arms stiffly at his side. "I see you brought *them,*" he said through tightly held lips. "Hoping I was you would come back alone."

"These are my children, Papa. Your grandchildren. I could not leave them. The baby is only weeks old and still nursing."

"Good God, after almost five years he still cannot leave you be?" Lindstrom seethed. "Has to keep getting more bastards on you or do they share you around?"

"Papa, my children are not bastards. I am a married woman."

"Injun marriage," Lindstrom gritted out.

"I saw no Christian preacher about," retorted Elka a little stiffly, "but if I asked him, Anokyen would go through a Christian ceremony if it means that much to you."

"Are you saying he's a Christian?" Lindstrom asked gruffly.

"No, but..."

"Good Book says 'Be ye not unequally yoked together with unbelievers: for what fellowship hath righteousness with unrighteousness? and what communion hath light with darkness?'"

Elka felt as if she had been stung with a slap across her face. "I understand not, Papa. Would you rather my children *were* bastards?" she asked at the brink of more tears, but this time tears of pain.

"They are bastards, you just do not realize it. Bastards of a damned heathen. And if you lie with him willingly, you are no better than a whore."

"Pa!" Lars cried out.

"Papa!" Elka gasped. If this was how he felt, why had he arranged for her to come home to visit?

"Willing I am to overlook it, girl, that glad I was to hear that you were still alive. I ain't like Grady Johnson who turned his back and told his daughter he rather she had killed herself. I ain't that way. I understand you did what you had to in order to survive. All I ask is that you do not flaunt it. Have some sense of de-cency and shame. Now, come, home we will take you and you can change out of those heathen garments and into some decent clothing."

Elka was feeling so emotionally assaulted that she didn't know what else to do but obey her father as she had always done. Lars helped her put her babies into the wagon before she climbed in herself. Soon they were rolling down the deeply rutted dirt trail that led to their farm.

Elka sang a little song to her children to help them fall asleep. They had giggled and laughed at the fluffy feather ticking of the big, comfortable, soft bed their mother had tucked them into. Elka herself laughed, remembering again what it was like to sleep in a featherbed.

When she was sure they were asleep, she crept back down the ladder wearing the dress she had put on the moment she had arrived. It had been a little enough thing to do to keep her father from losing his temper. Now, Petre and Lars were sitting before the hearth.

"I had almost forgotten what a featherbed is like," she smiled, taking a seat before the fire herself. "The children have never slept on anything so soft."

"I would say there is a lot you have forgotten," her father said stiffly.

Lars looked up in curiosity. "What do Indians sleep on?"

"Animal skins, furs. Often pine needles we heap underneath for some cushion to insulate from the cold ground. It is warm, just not so very soft," she smiled. "In the winter fleas can get bad if you let the dogs in. This is why I will not let Anok..." her husband's name died in her mouth. The look she received from her father stopped her instantly.

"That's the way you've been sleeping?" her brother asked gently.

"It's not so bad, Lars," she recovered her voice. "Used to it you become."

Lars nodded and almost blurted. "You gotta tell us, Elka. What happened that day? We found the wash all dried out on the rocks. We found your dress. But you had vanished... what happened?"

Elka explained how she had decided to bathe and had been trussed up as she was, in her shift and taken away.

"Still learning the language I am. I understand it better than I can speak it. From what I have heard he lost his whole family to smallpox. In fact, most of their village died. There were many braves who were looking for wives after that but there were no free Indian maidens around. So, they took to kidnapping wives for themselves. And Anokyen found me." She paused, refusing to look at her father and patted her brother's arm. "Always he treats me well, Lars," she smiled. "When we got to his village, he declared to everyone I was his wife. The medicine man did something like what we might call a blessing and Anokyen took me to his hut. That is their marriage ceremony. I am his wife, I share his status in the village which is considerable. A very skilled hunter he is."

"And now ye got three little injun babies," Lindstrom broke in.

"Half Indian, Papa," Elka said softly.

"And you just had to come dragging them in here under our noses."

"Sorry I am, Papa," Elka said, evenly. "I thought you would want to see your grandchildren."

"Those are not my grandchildren," he contradicted sharply.

"Yes, they are! Half me they are and I am your daughter, am I not?"

"I see no blond hair, no blue eyes, no fair skin. All I see is three little injun brats, that is all," he added cantankerously.

"They may not have our coloring but they are still half us!" she said insistently." They all had blue eyes when they were born, perhaps Three will keep hers. And none of them have true Indian hair and Three doesn't even have hair yet, I look at her scalp and it looks blonde to me. It may come in blonde. Half me they are," she repeated insistently.

"Injuns is all the world will ever see," he stated firmly.

"I suppose you are right," Elka said quietly with a long sigh, "all the world is ever going to see is that they are Indian. To bed I go now," she added abruptly and climbed up to the loft to sleep with her children.

The next day Petre and Lars went to the fields to work and Elka stayed at the cabin watching her babies and baking bread. In a moment of quiet, she found herself drawn to her mother's old chest.

Unlocking the small keyed lock, she opened the heavy lid. The fragrant scent of cedar rose up and immediately she spied her old rag doll. Propping the lid up securely, she took up the doll. A flood of memories washed over her. She was a small girl again with her mother. Lars was only a baby. Her papa was handsome and full of laughter. Her mother... the smell of the chest brought the memory of her mother to her, arms that held her, soft lips that kissed away her little hurts. A gentle voice. She saw an old shawl and gingerly drew it up from the chest. Her mother's shawl. Why could she not clearly remember her mother's face anymore she asked herself, as large tears rolled down her cheeks? Then, her baby began to cry and she quickly brushed the tears aside and put the shawl and doll back, closing the chest again.

After changing the baby, Elka fixed lunch pails for her father and brother. Hot fresh bread and rich creamy butter along with a slab of cold meat. She took the children and carried the food to the men. She found her father and brother out in the far field, preparing the soil for planting. They stopped when they saw her approaching. Petre took his lunch pail with a stiff nod of acknowledgment while Lars grinned and gave her a kiss of thanks on her cheek.

"A man could get used to this!" he exclaimed cheerfully. "Whoa! It's still warm. Gosh, this is great!"

Petre looked at the baby on Elka's back in her carrier and frowned. He ate in silence. Elka spread an old blanket upon the harder soil of the unplowed portion of the field and set her children down with some fresh bread. When he had finished eating, Lars began to play with them. Petre ignored them and returned to the plow, calling Lars to join him. Elka packed everything up and returned to the cabin.

When Sunday came, they dressed and rode into the tiny settlement nearby which had sprung up since she had left. There was a church. Very few of the gathering congregation greeted her although more spoke to her father. Elka was aware of all the eyes upon her and her children. If no one felt they knew her or wished to speak to her, or were unsure what to say, she could understand. But she didn't understand the overt hostility she detected in many. She had spent four and a half years becoming very sensitive to what people communicated with their bodies and their faces. And she recognized the hypocrisy in some of the things people were saying, because their bodies were saying just the opposite.

As she left the stuffy, small, split board church after a service referencing Christian brotherly love, she overheard insulting whispers. Out in the yard she waited for her father and brother by the wagon and saw several young men leering openly at her, their expressions were coarsely familiar as their eyes raked over her body not even caring that she saw them doing it. And while she couldn't hear what they were saying, she saw how they were speaking to each other while looking at her. Smirking, sharing ribald laughter and for some inexplicable reason she felt dirty, like she *was* a whore.

Monday, Elka awoke determined to give the cabin a good cleaning. She fed her children and made breakfast for Lars and her father. As they ate she began gathering dirty clothing and linens together.

"It looks to be a nice day," she said brightly, "so I plan to do a wash and take the mattresses out for an airing. A good spring cleaning is overdue."

Petre grunted. "Woman's work it is and we have had no woman here."

"I know, Papa. Only saying so you will not be surprised. Best you take your lunches with you. I doubt I will have time to walk to the far field."

Petre nodded. "Wash tubs we have now. Lars will fetch the water you need before we leave."

After breakfast was over, he and Lars departed, lunch pails in hand.

The wash tubs were set up outside and a large cauldron hanging over the outdoor fire kept her supplied with hot water. *Three* had been fed and was sleeping in her basket hung up on a tree limb, *Two* was tethered to prevent his wandering off or getting too close to the fire and *One* was playing with him in the dirt.

Elka dragged the mattresses out to lay in the bright sunshine. She spread yarrow and other herbs over them to sweeten and drive away unwanted pests. She went to the washboard and with homemade lye soap she began to scrub the sheets.

She had the sheets wrung out and draped over the bushes to dry when she saw the two young men walking out of the forest. She stopped her labors and wiped her hands on her apron. She recognized them immediately. They had been part of the group who had stared at her so disrespectfully outside of church. Her first thought was fear for her children, her second was that she had no weapon with her. Papa always brought the musket with him in case of animals but a second much older piece did hang on the wall above the door. She didn't even know if it was loaded.

"What do you want?" she asked boldly as they walked straight toward her.

"Your pa around?" asked the shorter of the two. He had dark hair that looked shaggy and greasy. The beginnings of a beard covered his thin, sharp face.

Elka shook her head. "I think you know he is not. So what is it you want? Please, stay away from my children!" she cried out quickly as the short one hunkered down next to *One* and *Two* just watching and smiling. But his smile was cold. He brought out a pocket knife and began whittling on a wood stick figure. The tall one was looking at Elka. His hair was a little lighter and his features were coarse but he was still young and not ugly until he spoke.

"I think you know what we want, whore. Just stay calm and yer little bastards 'll be fine. I see you even got the mattresses spread out to advertise." He and the short one both laughed. He took her elbow to guide her back into the house. "I guess a table will do."

"No," she stopped; her heart was pounding. "I want not your smell in the house, we go to the barn." She pulled away and walked briskly to the barn on her own. He followed.

Inside the light was dim and she went to what was left of the straw stores from last winter. She turned and looked at him.

"Take off your clothes," he said as he removed his jacket.

Elka immediately took off her apron, then unlaced her dress and took care to set it off to the side, out of the way. Finally, she slipped out of her shift and was standing before him completely naked. She shivered. "I do whatever you want but please hurt not my children," she said softly.

"That's kind'a what we figured," he grinned as he approached her. As he fondled a breast, a shaft of sunlight streaked in through a crack in the wall. It highlighted Elka's breast and he saw a drop of milk ooze from her nipple. Without a word he latched on sucking on her painfully. She tried to push him from her breast. That was her baby's food. He had no right to it. He pulled away laughing. "I hear tell the injuns like their women to walk around naked, that true?

She said nothing.

"So, this should be nothing t' you. How many injuns have had you?"

"I am married to one man. He is my husband."

"Yeah, but I hear they like to trade their women to each other, even to strangers."

She shook her head.

"Ever had a white man before?" His hand had moved down to the apex of her legs as he unbuttoned the front flap of his breeches with the other.

She shook her head not trusting herself to speak as his fingers began to probe her.

"Hell, yer dry as toast," he grumbled. "Now get on your back," he ordered, then spat on his hand and rubbed himself before he entered her.

Elka leaned back on the straw. It didn't take long and she closed her mind to it and said not a word. When it was over, she closed her legs as well. He grabbed his jacket and walked to the door buttoning his breeches.

"She's ready for you now," he shouted with a self-satisfied sneer.

The darker one came in taking his time to look her over and waiting for his buddy to leave. "Get on yer knees," he ordered when they were alone.

Elka kneeled back upon her heels on the barn floor.

"Suck me. Hard! Til I say to stop."

Elka rose up off her heels and began to unbuttoned the flap on his breeches. Her fingers felt cold and stiff, like they didn't belong to her. She pulled the flap down and could see that he was very small and flaccid. Holding her breath for a moment, she reached in and did as he had commanded, trying not to gag. He smelled and tasted like old body sweat, soil, and urine. She concentrated mightily upon her children to keep from throwing up. In time, he grew rigid.

"Stop!" he growled. "Now turn around and get down on all fours!"

Elka obeyed and was startled when she felt him spread her open and push into her. She gasped, clenched her teeth, and willed herself not to pull away. It was very uncomfortable and disgusting. When she tried to relax she felt like she was going to soil herself. But he was small and it was bearable. She could hear him grunting and panting as he pushed her hips to and fro. It took what seemed like an eternity for him to reach his satisfaction and all Elka could think about was her children. They were out there with the tall one, was he watching so *One* did not go too near the fire? Was the tether holding for Two so he could not wander into the creek? Surely *Three* was still asleep but she would be waking soon for her feeding, would they hurt her if she cried?

Finally, the short one pulled her tightly against himself as he rammed her a final time, groaned, and finally withdrew. Elka grabbed a handful of straw and quickly wiped herself. She could not wait to pull on her shift and run out to see her children. She burst through the barn door and was out in the bright sunlight. Her heart was pounding. She squinted and shaded her eyes. They were there just as she had left them, playing in the dirt, the baby silently sleeping. Elka took a deep breath to steady herself.

"Please go now," she said flatly. "You got what you came for." She refused to cry in front of them.

The tall one laughed and tossed her a coin. It fell to the ground at her feet. "We'll be seein' you again real soon," he grinned and winked.

Elka stood silently watching them depart. She picked up the coin before one of the children should find it and swallow it. A penny! Two for a penny! Did that not make her the cheapest whore in the world, she asked herself?

She raced to the creek, kicked off her shoes and lifted her shift. Frantically, she cleansed herself with the icy water, so icy it numbed her so she could feel nothing as tears ran down her cheeks.

When Petre and Lars came back late that afternoon, Elka had supper ready and waiting. The mattresses were back inside, the beds were made up with clean, fresh sheets sprinkled with lavender. The children were fed and she looked neat and composed, her hair freshly combed and smoothly braided. She said nothing to her father or brother of what had happened that day. She would never ever tell them of her shame.

That evening after the elder Lindstrom retired, Elka and Lars went out on the porch to talk quietly.

"I want you to know, always welcome you will be, Lars," she stated firmly.

"But you can't be thinking to leave us already," Lars was objecting.

"I have to."

"You know Pa was hoping you were coming home to stay. I, too, am wishing it, Elka."

Elka smiled sadly. "I know. Part of me wishes so, too." *But if I do not leave those two will be back and their friends they will bring. They will turn me into a whore.*

There was a long pause while the sounds of night birds trilled and kept the night from being quiet.

"Do you love him?" Lars asked hesitantly.

Elka knew he was referring to Anokyen. "He is my husband. He has been kind. He takes good care of me, Lars, and he has never mistreated me. A family we are." *And never raped or sodomized have I been until I came home.* The silence that hung between them reminded Elka that her brother and father were family also. "I did not ask to be taken away, Lars."

"I know that," he replied sympathetically.

"No choice did I have. I knew not how to return. I had to accept it," tears had brimmed her eyes. *In this world there is much a woman must learn to accept.*

"I understand."

"I admit it is not like I dreamed as a girl," she tried to lighten her mood. "I mean I always thought I would marry some... some Prince Charming and have a little cottage on a farm near you and Papa," she half laughed and was quiet again for a time. "We cannot really talk," she continued more solemnly. "I mean *really* talk about things, ideas, feelings. I cannot understand the language well enough. Of course, this means argue much about anything we cannot do either," she tried to joke again.

"I guess that's one way to keep peace in the family," Lars grinned supportively.

"I admit I do not understand many of their ways but much thought I have given this decision today. I will never give up my children but I cannot keep them here. So there is no reason for them to become used to anything in the white man's world. They will never be seen as anything but savages so why should I put them through the hurt? I love you, Lars. I love Papa, too, but family of my own I have and my children must come first." She said that last with almost a touch of hysteria in her voice.

"Of course, they come first," Lars immediately agreed. "They should come first. I can understand that, but does this mean you cannot come visit us," Lars reasoned, his brow was wrinkled up in a frown, fearing he was losing his sister again.

"Much better it is that you should come to visit us. I will not expose my children to constant rejection, hatred, insulting words, the feeling that they are not quite clean. And Papa is right in one way. The white world will see them always as dirty Indians and treat them as something less than human. Even their own grandfather looks at them as though some kind of vermin they are."

"Awwwh, Elka, he's not that bad, he'll get used to them," Lars tried to reason.

"His grandchildren they are, he should not have to *get used to them!*" she cried out indignantly and Lars dropped his head in embarrassment. "This treatment they do not get in the Indian world. So, taking them back I am... tomorrow."

"Elka!" His head snapped up, his eyes full of hurt. "You only just got here."

"It is better this way. I want my children to know you, Lars. I want them to know they are part white but not the hate and the disrespect." Lars looked at her sadly. "Besides," she added softly, "I know over there he is alone, waiting, wondering. These are his children too, and he knows not if we will return," she said softly as she reached out to caress her brother's sturdy shoulder. "Remember, Lars, welcome you will always be."

Lars nodded and held his sister in a brotherly embrace.

# *Chapter 1*

## Switzerland 1713

Rain or sun, heat or cold, Herr Hendrick Huffsmeier left his home each morning at precisely seven-thirty after synchronizing his pocket-watch with the large pendulum clock standing in his foyer. He always walked into town much to the dismay of his liveryman whose horses stood idle. Huffsmeier always walked briskly and took the same path. The village only had one main street which he traversed from beginning to end and then he swung around and did an outer path, much like a huge circle that mimicked the old town wall. When he had finished he found himself back at the end of the main street and so he walked down it once again stopping at his favorite coffee shoppe. On even-numbered days that was the *Kaffee und Gebäck* and odd-numbered days found him at the *Pâtisserie céleste.*

Huffsmeier was a man of many good habits and he was a fair man. This was eighteenth century Switzerland after all and at any given moment on any given day one could encounter people speaking German, French, or Italian, whichever served their mood and their comfort level although Italian was not heard here as much as it was across the Alps nearer to the Italian states. Today, Herr Huffsmeier took his usual table at the *Pâtisserie céleste.* He liked his coffee served hot and strong with cream on the side. His friends and providers knew what to expect from him but he was not irrationally bound to constant sameness. He would always choose a different pastry.

Oh, the variety was tantalizing! But wisely, he restricted himself to just one. Today he decided upon a multi-layered tort, airy cake alternately layered between sweet chocolate crème and raspberry crème, sprinkled with nuts and upon serving, drizzled with a delicious salty caramel.

The coffee and pastry arrived and Huffsmeier smiled a nod of appreciation to the baker who always served him personally. Huffsmeier withdrew his pocket watch. It was exactly eight-thirty. He looked to the door and told himself he would wait five minutes but no more; the creamy goodness of the slice of heaven setting before him could be resisted no more than that.

A minute went by and a very smartly dressed, fair haired young man in his very early twenties could be seen outside reading the name of the cafe. He looked right passed all the delectable pastries in the front window to Herr Huffsmeier himself. The young man's large gray eyes lit up as they met the older man's, he nodded and his thin golden mustache twitched in a grin. He took off his hat and entered the shoppe.

Herr Huffsmeier noted the richness of his apparel, the handiwork of some Parisian tailor no doubt, but was much more impressed by his shiny blond curls, neatly styled, clean and natural, and certainly *not* the vogue in Paris.

"Doctor Huffsmeier?" the young man questioned with a distinct accent.

"Monsieur Power?" Huffsmeier replied and pointed to the chair across from him. The young man had introduced himself in a note as an American colonialist. Huffsmeier was not comfortable speaking English, he felt very limited with it but the note had been written in perfect French so he decided to see if the youngster could keep up verbally. "*Asseyez-vous s'il vous plait. Vous devez me rejoindre dans un café et choisir l'une de ces délicieuses pâtisseries.* Sit down please. You must join me in a coffee and choose one of these delicious pastries."

John Power bowed respectfully before the older man and drew out the chair. "Of course, Herr Doctor, and thank you so much for agreeing to meet with me," he continued in French. "I cannot tell you what an honor it is to speak with you after reading the paper you wrote on the life all around us we cannot see."

Huffsmeier smiled. The French was perfect with no accent at all.

Through the next hour and several cups of coffee, John Power introduced himself more fully. He was the son of Jacques-Jean Charte Power, a Huguenot who had fled France and settled in the colonies. And who himself was the son of a Catholic duke. At this Huffsmeier nodded sympathetically. John went on to explain that his father was now a very successful businessman and had sent his eldest son to France for a medical education. It was while in Paris that John had come across an obscure paper written years ago by Huffsmeier on his work with the micro-scope and the discovery of something called micro-organisms and the theory of their connection with disease.

"I cannot believe the medical world has not embraced this. It makes so much sense."

Huffsmeier smiled again at the handsome young man, so full of life, so full of energy. In John, Huffsmeier recognized himself and liked to believe he himself was still like this but now, upon hearing John speak, Huffsmeier felt he had given up somehow and accepted defeat.

"So you think it makes sense to believe a tiny, tiny little organism so small you cannot see it with the naked eye can slay a man dead in a matter of hours?"

"It may sound implausible but… Herr Doctor, I come from people who have always believed in a high standard of… of hygiene… is that the right way to say it?"

"Yes, yes, go on… how do you define *high standard.*"

"Well," John paused. "For example, my grandparents believed in washing regularly, insisting the servants wash themselves regularly, wash their hands when preparing foods, use only designated latrines, keep animals out of the kitchens and the spring houses, protect wells from fouling. And I believe it is no coincidence that through the years, they had no outbreaks of disease like plague or deadly fevers.

"My mother is much the same. We came in from our daily labors and were expected to scrub up before we ate; as children we were bathed every week and she and father believed in bathing so regularly that they had a large metal tub installed in a room of its own with a drain pipe that leads to the garden so the servants do not have to run buckets to empty it."

"And how was everyone's health?"

"Most excellent."

The older man laughed. "And so much for the fear of opening the pores to *evil vapors.*" He made a sneering gesture. "Not that I do not respect the idea of some micro-organisms being born on the air and thus entering the body through holes in the *dermus*. It is what makes surgery such a hazard for infection. I firmly believe our skin is a barrier to such invasions. Even the ancient Greeks realized this."

"But what happens when there are no cuts to be infected?" The younger man asked most seriously.

Huffsmeier having just put a modest piece of tort in his mouth pointed to his eyes, his nose and finally, his mouth. "We all have holes but we forget we have them," he said after swallowing. "I have looked at a single hair from inside a nostril, it was teeming with life caught by the hair before it could get any farther. I have also tested my theory in regard to the skin. It was my hypothesis that one could place the most virulent organism upon clear, unbroken skin and it would do no harm, could do no harm as the skin protects us."

"And...?"

"And in over three dozen such experiments, I proved my theory correct. The medical schools are so invested in the ancient writings of Aristotle and Hippocrates and the idea of 'the Humors.' You will soon discover… you take an elderly man who has believed in something all of his life, it is easier to move a mountain than to change his mind. But it is not Humors that turn milk to cheese or yogurt or sour cream. And from this I hypothesized that there are good organisms as well as bad, just like people, eh?

"My cook takes equal parts flour and clean water, he mixes it together and allows it to sit in a jar, covered but not sealed. In a few days something is happening, it is bubbling, growing and we call it *leavening*. You add it to the recipe for bread and it makes the bread rise and bake up fluffy and light. So, where did this leavening come from, eh? How did it appear? Is it magic? No, it is all around us, my friend. I can see the yeast already on the wheat grains, just like it is on the grape which causes the grape to ferment and turn to wine, eh? Your family knows something about that, yes?" With that Huffsmeier took out his watch again. "Oh, it has been almost an hour and I must be some place else. Tell me, would you like to see a micro-scope?"

"Absolutely," John said quickly, rising from his chair as Huffsmeier rose from his.

"Come to my home, at this address," he invited, producing a card from his pocket. "Shall we say five? We shall dine and talk."

"Thank you, Herr Doctor, I am honored." John bowed again.

"Do not be late," Huffsmeier said as he hurried out the door and took off down the street at his brisk pace.

John spent the rest of the day shopping for a good Swiss pocket watch. Finally he purchased one he found that actually had a minute hand and a dome-shaped covering of cut-out design through which one could see the time without opening the cover and exposing the vulnerable watch hands. One had to open both the front and the back to expose the place one inserted the key into the mechanism to wind and set it for the day. He received instruction from the watchmaker who assured John that on any given day the time piece would lose no more than a minute or two. Neither John nor his father had ever desired to own a pocket watch. Back in the colonies, pocket watches were notorious for losing several hours through the course of a day and considering that and the fact that they only had an hour hand, both father and son could not see the point in carrying one.

At four-thirty, John, dressed in a handsome suit of clothes, slightly heavier and darker in color than his day suit, and topped with fresh snowy white linens, left the only hotel in the village and sought a cab. He watched approvingly as a driver some yards away scooped up a fresh horse dropping and deposited it into a container. John handed the address to the driver and climbed inside the empty cab.

Watching out the window, John noted that they were traversing the main street, then they passed through what at one time was undoubtedly the town gate, but was no more than an arch over the thoroughfare now. For several hundred years the town walls had been in the process of disappearing, the stone blocks being reused in new construction. Ever since the perfection of the cannon such walls had become obsolete for defenses.

Outside the village some pleasant orchards grew, not yet blooming this early in the season and the Alps stood looming over everything, in every direction one looked, appearing so deceptively close and yet from what he had been told it would actually take a full day of hard riding to reach their base. They were truly magnificent, if formidably threatening, always snow-capped, and awe inspiring. Nothing like the mountains he had grown up near back home.

Contrary to what he had assumed, this little community was actually protected by the mighty Alps. The mountains sent cooling breezes all through the summer, he had been told, and yet blocked the worst of the weather during the winter making each season enjoyed by the little village surprisingly moderate. John had also heard the story that Eleanor of Aquitaine had passed through somewhere near here in her travels on horseback at the ripe old age of seventy-something going from France to Italy on behalf of her favorite son, King Richard, the Lion Heart. If the weather stayed so mild, John could understand how it was possible to travel through in the winter.

In less than five minutes the cab pulled up and stopped before a rather modest looking brick home. Some rambling extensions had been added on the side closest to town and to the back, with no consideration given to harmony of architecture. Was this it? But he was much too early!

Sticking his head out of the window he told the driver to go back to the town gate.

John drew his cape around him in the chill of the coming mountain evening. He dismissed the driver and did not make any arrangement to be picked up again. He was so close, he could easily walk back to the hotel when the evening was over, he thought. He proceeded down the road at a modest pace in the sturdy red heeled shoes that made all men an inch and a half to two inches taller. It was so common a fashion in Europe that to not wear them would have been to draw attention to one's self as a country rube.

As he walked, he was able to take a better look at the doctor's house and the extensions behind it, allowing himself to hypothesize as to what purpose they had been built. Obviously the smaller extension closest to him was the doctor's office; a handsome wooden sign hanging beside the door announced that. As to the much larger extension in the rear? A large dining hall, perhaps? Or perhaps a ballroom and/or musical stage? Or had it been built for an aging parent to live separately but close? Surely it wasn't for animals, he saw a barn and several other outbuildings some distance beyond the house. Perhaps it was the doctor's laboratory? Indeed, he now realized he saw only small high windows in the larger extension making any usual uses very unlikely.

John slowly walked on, finally reaching the garden gate. He swung it open, passed through, closed it. He had no reason to swerve onto the path to the office but approached the deep set portico of the main entrance where brick had been mixed with several slender marble columns. He took out his watch, it read two minutes to five. Just as he was about to raise the door knocker he heard the clock from within begin to chime. He let it chime its five times and then he dropped the knocker against its plate.

John suspected he had passed a test by arriving exactly on time. The door opened immediately and he smiled to his host who greeted him warmly while the butler took his cape. He was offered an aperitif and invited on a tour of the main house by the elderly doctor. John found the library extensive and most impressive, which frankly was to be expected of such a learned man. And behind it was his laboratory.

"Here it is," Huffsmeier stated proudly. Taking a dust-cover from an odd looking mechanism, he put a slide in place, adjusted it into focus, and offered John a look.

"What am I looking at?"

"That is a human hair," Huffsmeier pronounced.

"Amazing," John uttered.

"No-no, just greatly magnified. Now, if you wish to see *amazing*… allow me.

The older man took a clean slide and dipped his finger into a fish tank.

"Charlemagne does not mind giving us a bit of his pool," he said with a chuckle and dropped a single drop of water onto the slide. "Do you see anything in the water or do you believe it clean?"

"It looks very clear," John responded cautiously.

"Ahhh, but wait." Huffsmeier placed the slide into position, added lenses and established the focus. "Now look."

John again bent over the micro-scope and saw a teeming world of strange shaped creatures swimming about and bumping into each other. "Unbelievable!"

"You say that, but you are seeing it with your own eye, is that not so?"

"Yes… yes. Are these good or bad?"

"Well, I would say for Charlemagne and the plants he shares his tank with, they are good… but for humans, perhaps there could be a bad one. And what if you carefully dipped into the tank, then picked up a … let us say a bit of bread. The organisms transfer to the bread and you pop it into your mouth, um?"

"Does well water look like this?" John looked up in concern.

"A good well? No, not so populated. As you travel have you ever drunk the water and suddenly had an attack of diarrhea? Most likely you ran into some bad ones. Now watch." Huffsmeier put his finger into his drink and allowed the drop to fall onto the slide. He pushed it back under the scope and told John to watch.

As the slightly golden shaded liquid spread out into the drop of tank water, John saw the organisms go still and cease to move.

"What… what just happened? Did the alcohol kill them?"

Huffsmeier nodded, a self-satisfied grin on his face. "And if doctors would only learn to wash their hands and instruments in alcohol they would stop making their patients worse instead of better. Contaminating a clean wound with the pus of an old one, spreading the disease of one patient on to another, it is not so difficult to understand."

"Oh, my God!" John blurted in English and then apologized to Huffsmeier. "Excuse me, Herr Doctor. I just realized something. All my life I have watched my parents add water to their wine, my grandparents as well. But now I realize they were really adding wine to their water. I thought they were weakening their wine but they were cleaning their water. My father even told me that in France everyone has a rather healthy fear of plain water. Too many have become sick from it."

Huffsmeier nodded with a smile. "I think perhaps they were doing both depending on the time of day, hm? But it is true, if a cow stands in a brook and defecates, the water bubbles on a mile and mother scoops up a bucket of the clear bubbling brook and gives it to her babies, some very bad organisms are now within her children. So often we see the young, the weak suddenly grow sick and die… why? Could it be because the cow pooped in the stream? Or a dead mouse or bird or squirrel lies rotting in the stream. And the reason the babies do not always die? I contend it is the dose. Sometimes the organisms ingested are very few and the body is able to fight them."

John nodded his understanding. "Some time ago, I was part of a rescue mission with my father back in the colonies. We found that the man for which we were looking had fallen down a well in a struggle with an Indian. The Indian was dead and such a stinking ghastly sight I hope never to see again but our friend was still alive after two weeks in the well. Nothing was broken, he had no obvious wounds but he was in a raging fever." He saw Huffsmeier knit his brows. "Perhaps I should add the Indian was wedged and our friend was on top which saved him from drowning. I told my father it was unreasonable to assume he had not drunk the water after more than three days despite the putrefying flesh that was fouling it. We never broke the fever he developed and our friend died."

"And what might you deduce from this?"

John carefully replaced the dust cover over the micro-scope.

"The same thing I thought then. The fouled water had killed him, I just did not know how. I even was able to witness the autopsy. There were no other injuries. Now I see where the likely suspects might have been."

Huffsmeier nodded. "Lest I give the wrong impression, I might also say I do agree with the ancients on some things. They believed in treating the patient en totale. I do not approve of the way we have split the treating of a patient into three separate... for lack of a better word I shall say disciplines. The apothecary attends to his diet, his need for pharmaceuticals depending on his complaint. The surgeon deals with the external manifestations of the problem, while the physician waxes on in his learned way to diagnose what 'humors' may be responsible for the patient's complaint. Bah! Three heads are only thicker not better than one. They fight with each other on what is best and in the end it is the patient or his family who must decide on the treatment and they have not the education to do so." The older man tossed back the remains of his drink, then chuckled. "Come, I get so wound up, I forget my manners. Supper awaits us. It is a good thing my daughter is not here, she would scold us both for our topics of conversation before dining."

"I am sorry to have missed meeting her," John said politely. "Is she with Madame Huffsmeier?"

"No, I am afraid we lost Madame Huffsmeier when Alana was still a very small child."

"Oh, I am sorry."

"She had a disorder of the blood," Huffsmeier said quietly. "And that is the worst frustration of our profession, my young friend. Even a doctor, a learned physician, a contemplater of the metaphysics cannot keep his loved ones totally safe."

"What about child bed fever? I wanted to ask your thoughts on that." John followed his host into the dining room and took a seat as Huffsmeier sat down.

The elder doctor shrugged. "As you saw some villains can be slain with alcohol which can prevent infection but once infection has taken hold, once it progresses into the bloodstream…?" He shrugged. "Once an infection takes hold within the body, we have no means to fight it. Then, it is up to the body, so beautifully designed by our Creator, to fight it. And it becomes our job not to weaken the body by blood letting. My advice if you are to deliver a child remains the same as it always has, keep everything as clean as possible… and pray."

Dinner was served and the two men found it easy to talk with one another. Halfway through the courses, Huffsmeier decided to put the young American to a test.

"So, tell me now, it is only the two of us… what do you think of France? Not the politics but the people, eh?"

"Oh, Herr Doctor, we must be fair. I have met very few people to really know them and I have seen very little of France. My *grand-père* is an aristocrat and a member of the nobility but I suspect he is what we might call atypical."

"How so?"

"Well, for one thing, he married a Huguenot woman."

"Yes, I would say that is not typical," Huffsmeier chuckled and raised his glass to acknowledge the point.

"They are elderly now and I realize I was quite young when they came over to visit us in the colonies but my father often speaks of how his father and mother did not care for court life. I suppose one could say that is only sour grapes as *Grand-mère* would not have been welcome at court but I do not think so. They are quiet people, kind to their attendants, concerned for their tenants. I rode about with *Grand-père;* he is a most careful steward of all that is his responsibility. He never mistreats his workers. He speaks against the extravagances of the Court and the aristocrats. He knows the taxes are a heavy burden on the little people. I have even seen him pay his people's taxes for them if they had endured some unexpected hardship that left them short."

"That cannot endear him to any of them, the other aristocrats I mean."

"No, I am certain it would not *if* they knew. In Paris, I saw a coach full of them out on the town, up to who knows what. I suspect they considered themselves to be slumming. They came into one of the student haunts, a tavern in the Latin quarter. The stench of their body odor was overwhelming even in Paris. And the immodesty of the women, I found on par with a common street whore. Beneath the glitter is such grotesqueness. One of the women accidentally caught her wig on fire and tossed it down in fear. I saw it. It was teaming with lice, as was the matted greasy tangle of her real hair. Do they never wash their hair?"

"I should think it would itch them to death, especially with all the company within it." Huffsmeier chuckled, thoroughly enjoying John's critique.

"Frankly, I do not understand all the white powder and make-up. It certainly doesn't look attractive. And putting white flour in your hair all the time as so many of the students do… it is inviting insects, is it not?"

"But is not white a symbol of cleanliness, purity, and innocence?" Huffsmeier mocked.

John nodded. "At the risk of sounding like a complete prude, I find the widespread lack of morality a bit shocking."

"Of course, you come from Puritan country," the elder man teased gently.

John accepted another glass of wine. "Not really, Herr Doctor, the Puritans settled far to the north of us."

"And how did you find the Parisian medical school?"

"Quite honestly?" he looked to his host who nodded he should continue. "It is an enigma, monsieur. How can France claim to have some of the most prestigious medical schools in the world when the very doctors teaching at those schools live their lives flying in the face of basic hygiene and common sense? I do believe I learned more from the papers I was able to access and read. Papers that unfortunately just gather dust."

Doctor Huffsmeier's eyebrows shot up.

"I am sorry. I am being too brash… and honest."

"No-no, continue, please. So Paris as a whole did not enrapture you?"

"I am sorry but Paris as a whole is a cesspool," John replied mildly. "Filled with filth, garbage, and the stink of human waste. And the people fear to bathe and so they reek, even those with money and education who one would think should know better."

Huffsmeier fairly hooted with laughter. "Ah, my young friend. You have said it all. How refreshing. And money, do not forget, has never been a measure of intelligence. Just remember, London is no better. They copy the French though only the

Good Lord knows why. But the colonies are breeding men of honesty and true spirit, it would seem."

"Thank you, monsieur, I suppose in the colonies we do become so used to wide open spaces where the air is clean and clear… and perhaps there is a Puritan influence, I have never considered that. I like to think it is just… more… *honest* perhaps? In the colonies, we must work together against the challenges of an untamed wilderness."

Both men attended to their meal for a time.

"My mother has always set great store by the Native Indian remedies." John broke the easy silence.

"Ah, yes?" Huffsmeier nodded. He had always found the ideas and beliefs within folk medicine most interesting. Some could be dismissed as superstition but he had no doubt many had merit.

"My mother is an amazing woman. She has had seven children and against the common odds, we have all survived. Better than survived we have all thrived. My mother never miscarried but she became friends with a native woman who fed her plants and herbals that my mother swears kept her from child bed fever and in good health."

"That is a remarkable record," Huffsmeier agreed. "Many a woman has had to bear upward toward twenty children just to have perhaps three or four make it to the goal of reproducing adults."

"She even sells herbal tea mixes as remedies in her shoppe." John nodded.

"Ahh, and what kind of a shoppe does she have?"

"My mother owns what we call a *general store* in the colonies which basically means she sells a little bit of everything from herbal teas to plow blades. She built it up from a trading post at the edge of the frontier when her first customers were the natives," John said proudly. "Now we have a small settlement, not much smaller than your village here. Father continues his interest in the fur trade and has a string of posts he established with his partner but has also built a lumber mill, and harvests lumber off his own land. And of course, there is the apple orchard which produces fresh apples as well as ciders and vinegar as I am certain, you are familiar."

The server brought around the dessert and John declined so Huffsmeier did as well. "You are a good influence on me," the elder man smiled.

"May I be so bold as to ask you a question, Herr Doctor."

"But of course. Ask anything," the older man replied expansively.

"When I approached your house earlier this evening, I noticed several… what I would call extensions. I realize the one is your surgery."

"I call it a clinic," Huffsmeier interjected.

"Ah, yes, but I am most curious about the one to the rear. I thought perhaps it was your laboratory but you have shown me where that is. May I ask what is housed in the extension, for what is its purpose… or is that too personal?"

"Not at all, I will show you," Huffsmeier dabbed urbanely at his mouth, then set aside his napkin and rose from the table. "Tell Uphred and Aphalstay to meet us in back," he said in German to the servant clearing the dishes. He led John through a corridor and into another room where he lit a lantern before proceeding down another short corridor. "This is truly my *sanctum sanctorum,*" he said as he opened a door and led John into a most unusual room.

John felt the humidity immediately. As Huffsmeier went about lighting more lanterns of ancient design, John took in his surroundings and was reminded of drawings he had seen of ancient Roman villas. The room was constructed of marble with lounging couches and small tables scattered about. Graceful columns encircled a long and narrow retangular pool and in each corner of the pool a small fountain gushed forth water. The room was surprisingly warm. John stooped and put his hand in the water and discovered it too was warm or at least it was not cold.

"The ancients knew how to live," Huffsmeier said with a sigh. "They adored their bathhouses and knew good food, exercise, massage, and frequent bathing was the secret to maintaining a healthy body." He looked at John who was taking in the beautiful mosaics on the walls and floor. "So what do you think? Are you game for a massage and a dip Roman style?"

"I believe I would enjoy that," John replied.

They started in individual dressing closets where John was advised to remove all of his clothing. Huffsmeier told him Uphred and Aphalstay would soap them both down and rinse them off so they could enter the hot pool clean. What he forgot to mention was that Uphred and Aphalstay were both women... sturdy, no nonsense, strong, Germanic women. Wearing short thin tunics to cover their private parts, the muscles the two displayed in their exposed arms and legs were formidable.

The men sat on stools to receive a shampooing. Aphalstay motioned John to stand and with a soft body brush she started at his neck and proceeded down his back scrubbing vigorously all the way to his heels.

"They say if you give a German *Hausfrau* a bucket and a scrub brush she is happy," Huffsmeier said cheerfully. "Very clean people as are the Dutch. What they cannot scrub clean, they boil clean."

John's skin was tingling as Aphalstay turned him to face her. She had given him a wash cloth to wash his face but instead he was using it to shield his own private parts. Aphalstay smiled and said something in German.

"She says you are a very modest little boy," Huffsmeier translated. "Oh, do not take any offense in that, we are all 'little boys' to her."

"I take it, oh..." Aphalstay had taken one of John's hands and stretched it upward while she proceeded with her brush, down his forearm, then his bicep brachii and finally lingering in the pit of his arm. "ah... ha-ha," he laughed and pulled back. "I take it she speaks no French."

"That is correct. How is your German?" Huffsmeier chuckled as he was tickled, receiving the same treatment from Uphred.

"Practically non-exi.. ah-ha-ha...non-existant."

Aphalstay was going through the same routine on the other arm and John made a quick switch of the wash cloth to his free hand. He noticed his scrubbed skin was pinking out.

Finished with the arms, Aphalstay proceeded across John's well developed chest, down his muscular abdomen and then she heard a resounding *"Nein!"* when she tried to invade the sanctity of John's wash cloth.

When the front of both legs had received their scrubbing, both women had buckets of warm water at hand. Standing on the stools to be above their subjects, they gave each man a complete rinse off. John noted the water disappearing down a narrow grate.

"Ah, now the hot pool," Huffsmeier said rather gleefully and bounded off quickly, his small buttocks firm and very white. Into the pool he leapt which while much smaller than the long pool could have easily seated six grown men around its perimeter without infringing on their individual space.

John followed suit as Aphalstay snatched away his wash cloth in her last bid to assure no unnecessary contamination got into the tub.

"Ahhh," Huffsmeier sighed loudly. "Now could anything feel better than this? And the ignoramuses of our day believe it unhealthy. Everywhere the Romans went they built their bathhouses, even in England. People used to know what it was to bathe."

"What happened?" John asked with real curiousity. "How was the knowledge lost?"

"Hard to believe, is it not? But it does not take long to lose knowledge in an illiterate society concentrating upon self-preservation after the plagues wiped out so many. It takes only a single generation once those with knowledge die leaving only the young who know little."

"It is rather frightening to comtemplate. In the cities, of course, survivors would continue to school the young, would they not?" John asked as he took a vessel of cool water and poured it over his head.

"Yes, my young friend, but which young? And what would they tell them?"

John's hair was slicked to his head and he shook it. "I see what you mean but the bathhouse was still there. Did not anyone wish to use it?"

"First, we must remember that most bathhouses were actually heated from below. A team of slaves laboring in a small cramped sub-level, stoking fires to heat the floors and the water. That in itself would have been a very extravagant use of labor in a society suddenly in short supply of people. By necessity focus had to be on food production and civil order. Then, writings indicate that when men finally did begin to return to the bathhouses, it seems to have ceased to be a recreation enjoyed by both sexes. I am certain we can blame the more pious grip of the Roman Catholic Church for that. But the whores found bathhouses a most convenient place for business. The men were already naked, yes? And what better place to nonchalantly flaunt your own body and show it free of disease?"

"Could they not also look over their perspective customer for signs of plague?" John added with a grin.

"Exactly. But, of course, as we know, there are other diseases that can harry man less virulently. Perhaps this is where the rumors and fears began that bathing was dangerous. Perhaps it was with the spread of the diseases of Venus."

John nodded and they both lapsed into a quiet time of relaxed contemplation.

Finally, John spoke again.

"Where does all the water come from, Herr Doctor, and the heat? I am almost certain you do not have a bevy of slaves beneath us stoking fires."

Huffsmeier looked very pleased with himself. "Some years ago I discovered I have a hot spring on my property. And so I built my dream… a duplicate of the Roman baths of the ancients. There are pipes running under the floors which are filled with the hot spring water. The system is all rather ingenious."

"And after our look at the things that can grow in water, I cannot help but wonder what might grow here."

Huffsmeier laughed. "Very good. You are thinking. The answer is *nothing*. The water is slowly leeched out via the drain system and pressure gauges while new water comes in to replace it, so it is never 'stagnant,' you see. And the minerals contained in this water inhibit the growth of things."

"How wonderful."

"It really is." He looked over at John. "I see the sweat popping out on your forehead again, my young friend. It is time to change pools." And with that, Huffsmeier emerged from the hot pool and plunged into the large cool one. John followed.

"Oh, my lord, this is cold!" he shouted and jumped up and down within the pool a few times in an attempt to adjust to the change in temperature. "I felt it before and it felt warm. How did you cool it down?"

"I did not. It is not really so cold but in comparison it feels that way. The small pool is wrapped in hot pipes, the large pool is not. And the fountains aerate it, there is an exchange of heat from the water and cool from the room air."

"Fascinating."

"Have you read of the Scandinavians who go from their sauna houses into a frozen-over lake or roll about in the snow?"

"Actually, we have one in our settlement." And John proceeded to tell Huffsmeier the story of his mother's difficulties with her sciatic nerve and how alternative forms of medicine including Chinese acupuncture and Swedish massage finally had given her relief. "To this day she gets a weekly massage and has talked my father into it as well. And she frequently goes to the sauna house on 'ladies night.'"

"Excellent! Excellent! Good for her. You sound more progressive in the colonies than the big powers over here."

"I think it is just our little settlement. I have never lived in New York or Boston but they are dirty and people get sick there all the time." He proceeded to tell Huffsmeier what he knew about Charles Town and how the residents have to leave their plantations in the summer to escape what they called the *Yellow Fever* while the black peoples seemed to have a natural resistance.

"I would love to see the Negroes' blood under a micro-scope," the elder doctor said.

John nodded and looked at his hands. "I think I am becoming what we used to call 'waterlogged' as children, Herr Doctor. I am ready to get out."

"By all means, as you wish. Aphalstay is waiting for you. I am going to swim a couple laps, then I will join you."

Huffsmeier began swimming the length of the pool and John had only just grabbed a fresh towel when Aphalstay patted a table covered with several towels in an invitation for him to lie down. He was going to beg off and then decided "why not?" He certainly didn't want to offend his host and Aphalstay had already seen his birthday suit.

John stretched out and under Aphalstay's surprisingly soothing hands he actually dozed off as she massaged his muscles, oiled his skin and turned every bone in his body to warm gelatin.

Sometime later Huffsmeier woke him with a nudge.

"Come, it is time for you to go to bed." He handed John a thick, soft robe. "You will stay here tonight, it is too late to send you out into the cold only to tense everything up after you have become so relaxed."

"Are you certain? I really do not wish to inconvenience you," John said sleepily.

"Not at all, now come this way."

Wearing their fluffy white robes and guest slippers, Huffsmeier led the way back.

Settled into a guest room, John lay wide eyed thinking about the evening. He'd had just enough of a nap to take the edge off his sleepiness. Suddenly he sat bolt upright in bed. He'd left all his clothes in the Roman villa!

Dressed in the robe, and taking a taper, he silently opened his bedroom door and found his way down the stairs and back through the corridors leading to the pool. The lights were still flickering in the lamps which he thought a little strange. Why hadn't Aphalstay or Uphred extinguished them?

He was in the little dressing room gathering up his clothing when he thought he heard the door close. Padding back out to the main room he saw a figure dressed in a white robe much like the one he was wearing. John was just about to call out to let whoever it was know that he was there when she dropped her robe and stood naked before diving into the deepest part of the pool.

John drew back into the shadows behind a column, mesmerized as he watched the young woman stroke gracefully, barely disturbing the water as her body seemed to slice through it to the end of the pool where she twisted quickly and began her way back. Back and forth she went, an almost hypnotic piece of motion, liquid grace itself until suddenly she stopped and began to look about the room as if she had heard something… or felt eyes upon her.

John pulled back deeper into the shadows and held his breath. He felt terrible, guilty of being a voyeur, what back home they called a *peeper*. He hadn't meant to be. He had been going to say something to announce his presence, but once she was naked, how could he? It would have been embarrassing to them both. Well, maybe not as much to him as to her? Or maybe more to him, he couldn't think anymore. What was that? He heard a disturbance in the rhythm of the water from the fountains and peering out from behind the column he saw she had resumed swimming her laps. He was very careful not to make a sound although he did dare to breathe once again.

Who was she? He had a sudden sinking feeling that this was his host's daughter. Oh, no, no - probably a servant or maybe a servant's daughter. Pretty enough to be allowed to use the Master's pool. *Nice try, John, what member of the servant class has ever had the time to learn to swim like a… a water nymph?*

Suddenly the laps were over and he saw her pull herself out of the pool. Bounding up on her hands with the strength of her wrists and arms, twisting her torso quickly as her legs came out of the water and around. She was up on her feet, just that fast. Now she stood twisting the water from her long, dark hair, an innocent tableau like Eve in the Garden unaware of lust or shame or prying eyes. She toweled herself briskly, slipped on her robe, and she was gone.

John fell asleep that night thinking of the young woman until he saw her in his mind's eye like a beautiful painting come to life. When he awoke the next morning he was half convinced that he had dreamt the whole thing.

It was past dawn and he dressed quickly, checking his pocket watch and winding it for the day. Thick carpets lay on the floors muffling his footsteps. He heard nothing in the house as he descended the staircase but as he walked by the door of the dining room, Doctor Huffsmeier called out.

"Good morning! Come, John, have some breakfast," he invited.

"Oh, no, thank you. I could not possibly. You have been most gracious and I have already..."

"Nonsense, nonsense, I insist. At least you will have coffee, yes?"

Coffee did sound very good and John nodded gratefully and took a seat as a manservant placed a cup and saucer in front of him with an accompanying napkin and table service.

"I trust you slept well?" Huffsmeier asked as he tried with his toast to scrape the last bit of yoke from a very soft boiled egg.

"Extremely well. I am envious, Herr Doctor. If I ever find a property with a hot spring, I shall try my best to duplicate what you have here. Do you have engineering drawings?"

"Yes, yes, but mostly it is in my head like so many other things. I know it is not the best methodology but life is too short to constantly write everything down," he chuckled.

"And the micro-scope, may I ask... did you design it?" He saw the doctor nod. "Where did you get the lenses? Who made the metal structure? It seems too fine for a common metal worker, perhaps a jeweler?"

"Very good, exactly. Now, my young friend, each day without fail I leave to walk to town at precisely half passed the hour of seven. If you would like to join me, you have exactly six minutes to finish your coffee and put on your cape. If you would prefer, however, you are welcome to stay, continue with breakfast, and leave when you are ready."

"Oh, yes. By all means, I will join you," John replied, trying to drink his coffee without burning his mouth. He added a generous splash of cream and helped himself to a small triangle of toast, already buttered. "I still have so much to ask you," he said before taking a bite.

At precisely seven-thirty, the two men left the house and John was quite surprised by the pace at which the older man walked. John had no trouble keeping up however. Although he was still trying to acclimate to the higher altitude, he was young and his legs were long.

As they walked they talked of the micro-scope and of the expanding theories Huffsmeier had regarding the causes of disease beyond a dirty water supply. He told John how he had been examining blood, comparing the blood of a healthy person such as himself and his daughter with the blood of patients who were ill, and of animals like dogs and rats, and even the blood of fleas.

He had formulated a theory that disease could be spread not just through touch or breathing the same air but also through the bite of an animal, even an insect such as a flea or mosquitoes. The time went by quickly, it all was so fascinating and without realizing it, John found he had walked the same path as the older doctor, up the main street and around the village until they ended up at the top of the main street again. On returning back along the main street, Huffsmeier led them into the *Kaffee und Gebäck* where John was served a most delicious slice of apple strudel, warm from the oven with delicate hints of cinnamon tickling his nose, just as Doctor Huffsmeier liked it.

After several more cups of rich coffee and the strudel, Huffsmeier offered to take John to the jeweler who had helped him design his last micro-scope. He left the younger man there with another invitation to dinner, this time with both himself and his daughter.

# *Chapter 2*

John met Alana Huffsmeier that night and she was indeed the water sprite of the bath but that distant, shadowy glimpse had not prepared him for a face to face meeting. Now, seeing her full on, in good light, he could not breathe. She was, John would later think with conviction, one of the ten most beautiful women who had ever existed. Allowing for personal taste, love, and bias, he would concede the possibility of there being perhaps nine other women in all the entire world who might be *as* beautiful but he could imagine no woman, living or dead, ever being *more* beautiful. He stood staring for several moments until even Huffsmeier felt the awkward pause and coaxed John's numbed tongue back to a connection with his brain and speech, with a few simple syllables of French.

John felt as though all the air had left his lungs and he had none left with which to speak but he managed a few small sounds which eventually became words, embarassed words, half stuttered words, and he flushed pink from the top of his curly blond head to the top of his snow white cravat.

She held out her delicate hand, slender and warm, for him to kiss, which he did as he bowed deeply. He stood upright again, feeling the brush of her gentle fingers as she retracted her hand. Looking into her eyes which were at the level of his chin, he said something about being pleased to meet her and then wondered dumbly with stupifying horror if he had not just said that already. Her eyes meeting his were a blue so dark, they were actually an indigo violet and rimmed with thick, long black lashes under perfectly arched dark brows.

John had to tear his gaze away and looked to the servant who was offering him an aperitif. He took the drink and looked to Huffsmeier who appeared rather amused.

*So, just how many young men have you invited over to meet your daughter, Huffsmeier, so you could observe and catalog their descent into blithering foolishness?*

With great discipline, John forced himself not to look back at the young woman until she herself spoke, at which time it would have been rude not to look her way and so by bits and glances he took in her remarkable flawless beauty: skin as poreless as porcelain, a nose neither too long nor too short, too thin nor too thick above full, soft lips no sculptor could have improved upon, cheeks, chin, and jaw line of such perfect feminine proportions as to make her profile exquisite. Her natural hair, shiny and clean, was so richly dark it glinted an iridescence like a raven's wing, and was piled upon her head and dressed simply with a few fresh flowers. He was grateful that the dinner gown she wore was exceedingly modest, the entire neckline filled in with lace right up to just below the base of her slender, swan-like neck. Around that lovely neck she had tied a black velvet ribbon. From the ribbon hung a single elongated baroque pearl. And from the lobes of her delicate shell-like ears two more baroque pearls hung.

She caught him staring again.

"I am sorry, I was noticing your pearls. They are unusual and very beautiful. They suit you perfectly," he managed to say with some sophistication.

"Thank you," she smiled graciously, "they were my mother's." She didn't finger the pearls nervously as his sisters might have but walked fluidly over to a wall and pointed out the portrait hanging there. "This was my mother," she said simply and John noticed the same pearl hanging from the subject's neck.

If Alana looked anything like her mother or perhaps better to say if her mother had looked anything like her, the artist had done the woman a grave injustice. It was not a good portrait but stiff, two dimensional, and just so much dead color applied to a canvas. In an odd quirk of thought John hoped Alana didn't see herself this way. He looked at Huffsmeier who was also looking at the portrait very tenderly.

"Does Alana favor her mother?" John asked.

"Very much so," Huffsmeier nodded quietly, "they might have passed for twins. Unfortunately the artist was not up to his task."

"Was he French?"

"Italian… but not the best," sighed Huffsmeier. "It was a disappointment." Just then a servant announced dinner.

John gallantly escorted Alana to her place on her father's right side and held her chair for her. Then took up his own seat across from her. He was feeling more comfortable now. His wits had returned and he was again in full control of his tongue. He wanted to know what interested the girl and how she occupied her time but he didn't want to be rudely forward. He wondered what kind of education she had had but one did not simply ask a woman how educated she was. It wasn't a commonly accepted feminine accomplishment. And why had she not been snatched up as some man's wife years ago? What was her flaw? Nature did not create perfection; the beauty of nature was often within the flaws... so what was hers? He couldn't detect a single one.

The meal began with a light soup which John barely tasted.

"Do you have an interest in your father's work?" he inquired, wondering if any talk of it would bore her.

"*Oui, monsieur,* I have an interest although I am not as learned as he," she replied modestly.

"Do not let her fool you, my daughter more than knows her way around common medicine. She is, in fact, a fully trained physician with a practice of her own and..." Huffsmeier chuckled, "she speaks four languages and reads six. That is one more than I have managed."

"Pa-pa, that is not important. It is your research that is important, and I think the medical community is filled with idiots who have turned their backs on you because they do not want to think differently." She spoke to John. "Since your arrival

I have seen a spark return to my father, and I am very glad for it. I hope your studies keep you here a very long time, *Monsieur le docteur* Power, so you can continue to motivate him."

John had not expected this at all. Had he actually been concerned that she would prove vapidly witless?

"Please, call me John and let me guess," he said in English. "You speak French, German, Italian and... English?"

Alana nodded her head.

"And you read all four of these plus Greek and Latin?"

She nodded her head again.

"That is truly impressive."

"I hope you are not threatened by an educated woman," Huffsmeier stated bluntly, having understood just enough of that exchange.

"Pa-pa!"

"I think not, monsieur," John replied with a smile. He looked again at Alana whose cheeks had flushed ever so becomingly. "I was telling your father today er... perhaps it was yesterday... that my mother has been running her own businesses... by herself... for years while raising a large family, running a home, and volunteering within the community." He was suddenly struck with the fear that he had just made his father seem like a lazy ne'er-do-well. "Be assured it has been her choice and my father has his own business interests which provide for us all very well."

"Hm," Huffsmeier grunted, "a strong entrepreneurial mother is precisely why I thought you should meet my daughter."

"Pa-pa, are you trying to play matchmaker?" she asked quickly in German.

"He is a very good looking young man, *liebling*, you should see him naked. And he is intelligent. And thinks like we do. What is the harm?" he replied in German. "Forgive us," Huffsmeier switched back to French. "My daughter was just chastising me for... well, it does not matter." He smiled.

Alana smiled.

John might not know much German but he thought he had picked up on the basic feel of that last exchange although he would never say as much. He smiled.

As the food and drink were served John found it more and more comfortable to look directly across the table without turning into a muddled half-wit. *So she is a doctor, my God...* not that he didn't believe a woman was fully capable of being a doctor but... *how did she get an honest pulse and heart beat from a male patient? The man would have to be half dead or unconscious.*

John smiled to himself and looked down at his plate. He saw that it held a thick and tender slice of roast pork with gravy and dumplings, and a sweet, purple sauerkraut. Instead of wine, he had been served a stein of beer. He had not noticed.

"Do you both practice in the village?" John asked politely.

"Our village is Pa-pa's responsibility although he trained me here. We have a sister village about an hour's distance by trap. I go once a week and stay the night so I am available to receive patients much of two days."

"That sounds like a rather grueling schedule," John said with concern. "Is it safe?" He looked to Huffsmeier.

"It has been safe for…. how long has it been now Pa-pa? Three years?" Alana answered quickly.

The elder doctor shrugged his shoulders in a non-committal response. He did not like his daughter returning late at night, on the roads alone after dark, but she was stubborn.

"But when you started, *liebling*, the clinic was not so busy. She had to earn the people's trust," he said to John before turning back to Alana. "You always were home before sundown, even in the winter. Then things became busier and now? I heard you come in very late last night."

"I am sorry, Pa-pa. Katya had her baby. I really should have stayed but I was worried you would be worried."

"I would not worry if you took Leopold. He does nothing when you are not here anyway but grumble that I do not require a carriage. If you took Leopold it would give him something to do and give me some peace of mind, yes?" The elder man looked at his daughter, all but begging.

"Very well, I will take Leopold but I must find him someplace to sleep."

"That is no problem. He is a driver, he needs not the Palace at Versailles... which I hear smells like piss anyway," and with that small joke the mood was lightened.

John had remained silent, observing the interplay which he had inadvertently started. In a way it reminded him of his mother and father, two people who loved and respected each other but might disagree on a point. And that thought reminded him that he really must write home and let them know that he was well.

After dinner, Huffsmeier suggested the two young people go for a walk in the orchard. The fragrance of the blossoms became stronger at night, he said. It was a nice excuse but very premature as far as any blossoms were concerned. The trees had not even begun to bud as yet.

Alana was agreeable and John helped her don a sturdy cape.

They walked for a minute in silence then Alana spoke first, choosing English.

"Thank you for not taking his side."

"What? Oh. You're welcome. My parents are very intelligent people, you would like them," he said striving to be casual. "They taught me that a wise person never inserts himself into the domestic quarrel of another family. As a doctor, I've found it a very important maxim by which to adhere."

He heard her chuckle. "Wisdom indeed. But it was not really a quarrel. Papa can be overly protective. We are a very peaceful valley, everyone knows everyone. The horse knows the way but I will admit after a particularly exhausting day, as yesterday was, having someone else to drive has its appeal." There was a smile in her voice. "So, we spent the entire dinner talking about me and my practice and

Papa's research, tell me about you. From your comment I conclude your parents are alive?"

"Oh, yes, very much so, and very healthy and happy I am pleased to say."

"And do you have brothers and sisters?"

"Quite a few. I'm the eldest and I have three brothers and three sisters. My oldest younger brother is already married and had a baby on the way when I left home. He works for our father at our saw mill and lumber yard. And my oldest little sister is being courted by the fellow who was the very first baby born in our settlement." John proceeded to talk easily about his parents and what they had accomplished in carving Chartes Landing out of the wilderness of the English colonies.

"It must be nice to have a large family on which you can rely. People who both love you and support you in what you do."

"Your father seems very supportive and very proud of you."

"I was not thinking of me but of him. It was very hard on my father when my mother died. I was just a small child, of course, but my memories are filled with his sadness. His peer group rejected his theories and then, he lost the love of his life. The one person who truly believed in him. And to double the blow, as a physician, he had also lost his most important patient. She had slipped through his fingers so young and to this day neither of us really understands what it was that killed her."

"Not that knowing would ease the pain… I imagine."

"No; you are correct, the pain would still be there but one deserves to know one's enemy by name."

They continued on in silence beginning to circle back toward the house.

"I often wished my father would have remarried… or at least had a serious lady-friend. I do not believe my mother would have wanted him to be so lonely."

"And what about you? Surely every unmarried man in the village has been at your door at one point or another."

Her laughter had a gentle grace. "I do not know about *every* but I suppose I have had my share of..."

"Suitors?" he supplied the word at her hesitation.

"I was going to say *callers*. Some were very nice, some were very arrogant. One even had the nerve to tell me outright that I must stop the vile, immodest practice of medicine immediately if he was to court me… but, in truth, I think they all had a problem with my vocation and..."

In a single move, John drew Alana close and covered her mouth with his. It was a warm, soft kiss, not entirely chaste but very gentle. She didn't resist but became pliant in his arms.

"Oh, dear lady," John breathed into her ear as he held her. "I can only be forever grateful there are so many fools in this world. Don't ever let anyone tell you to change who you are. You are perfect."

This time Alana kissed John and it was a kiss of intense passion.

Images of her, naked and voluptuous, appeared in his mind's eye and he felt the blood rushing through his veins as his heartbeat accelerated and his masculine appendage began to stiffen. He broke from her, keeping her at arms length as he tried to slow his breathing. "I am trying very hard to hold on to the last vestige of the gentleman within me. I think I had best take you back into the house."

When he and Alana returned from their walk, Huffsmeier was there with an after dinner drink and an argument insisting John move from his hotel and take up residence in their home as a permanent guest. The reasoning was sound. It made communication so much easier; it saved John the inconvenience and expense of keeping up a hotel room while spending most of his time in Huffsmeier's laboratory and library; and if they were to work long hours together, it kept John from squandering what little free time he had in just walking to and from the hotel for sleep and fresh clothing. John could not argue that those were not all valid reasons but for him the unspoken reason was simply that it would keep him much nearer to Alana.

Agreeable arrangements were made all around. Doctor Alana Huffsmeier agreed to take Leopold and the carriage for her two days at her clinic and upon returning, she began to see all her father's patients during the rest of the week, thus freeing him to work uninterrupted with John. Doctor Hendrick Huffsmeier saw his patients on the two days of the week Alana was absent and introduced them to Doctor John Power. John had time to read medical papers. Huffsmeier had time to experiment. And at least five if not six evenings of the week they all dined together, discussed interesting tidbits, and shared knowledge.

But Alana's presence was driving John to distraction.

That kiss. He kept reliving that singular kiss. But never since that one extremely passionate kiss had she agreed to walk again with him and in the past almost three weeks, they had not been alone together for more than two minutes.

He had written home. A letter even he recognized as rather vague and disconnected. What could he say? That he had fallen in love with the most perfect woman who he was sure would never leave her home village and so he would never see them again? Or perhaps, that he was doing all this independent study so he could become a much better doctor for Chartes Landing in the New Jersey Colony when she rejected him and sent him packing off as an embittered misanthrope? No, the main point of the letter was to tell them where he was, that he was well, and how they could get word to him. He knew his mother worried about his being in France, but he wasn't in France anymore. Perhaps he should also write a letter to his grandparents… but again, what would he say? Better he trust his father to relay his good health to his grandparents while John stay quiet until he knew what path his life was taking.

He had also written to the largest medical school in London and requested copies be sent of all the papers which had been presented over the passed year or two. Huffsmeier had little communication with England or Scotland, although John had heard some interesting things were being done there. Huffsmeier's weakness in English clouded his judgment.

One afternoon John was perusing the shelves in the library and happened upon a very old and somewhat delicate portfolio, wrapped in thin leather and titled in Italian. He took it to the desk, untied the old cording and opened it carefully. The leather was very aged and somewhat brittle but the pages of vellum inside contained fascinating illustrations of anatomy with notes bearing the signature of Leonardo da Vinci. Surely this couldn't be original, he thought, but who would copy a signature? He was deeply absorbed by the depictions of muscles, bones, ligaments, tendons, even blood vessels meticulously illustrated in a hand, a foot, different sections of arm, shoulders, the human heart, brain. Da Vinci had been a genius.

John turned over the next leaf and saw a very detailed drawing of a man and woman... were they? Yes, they were, no mistaking it. Pornographic pictures were nothing new. He remembered reading that the ancient Romans had drawn pornographic graffiti on the sides of buildings often in an attempt to belittle a public official. And the students in Paris had many sources for such dabblings but this was not pornography. It was drawn as a bi-section, like a lab specimen, as though one had neatly sliced the couple from waist to anus and split them precisely down the middle, exposing their insides to the eye of the beholder. They appeared to be standing for the act and their flesh and organs were depicted in great detail just as da Vinci believed them to be. In the drawing, the man had an extremely long appendage, better suited to a horse John thought, which filled an equally long vaginal corridor clear up to the female's very highly placed uterus.

"Well, that's all a bit off," he muttered to himself, hoping da Vinci had done other drawings more accurately and was startled to hear Alana's voice behind him.

"What is?"

"Oh!" he slapped the portfolio shut as he twisted around to see her standing right there. "You startled me."

"I am sorry. I apologize. I just closed father's clinic and was curious as to what everyone was doing. I found father in the cellar seeking a bottle of wine for our dinner. Cook is preparing lamb. Would you like to join us for an appetizer and drink?" She seemed to be talking inordinately fast.

"Yes, yes, of course. I'll just return this." He stood up, tying the portfolio closed.

"What was off?"

"Oh, nothing, nothing, not important," he shrugged as he slipped the portfolio back in its place on the shelf.

John heard the great clock in the foyer strike. He counted as it struck ten more times. Eleven o'clock already and he had yet to be able to fall asleep. He kept reliving that kiss and da Vinci hadn't helped. He tossed and rolled over again. The weather was mild and he had opened the window for fresh air. Perhaps if he closed the window drapes…? They were pulled back and bright moonlight was flooding into the bedroom.

When he was alone, he was always seeking to distract himself. At this moment he observed with metaphysical interest that moonlight turned everything black and white and shades of gray. There was no color in the world of moonlight.

John heard the faint engaging of his bedroom doorknob and sat up in bed to see a white clad figure enter and shut the door again quietly. The apparition paused for a few seconds with back to him, and he could just make out the sound of the lock tumbler being moved by the key. The figure turned around and fairly floated to his bedside.

It was Alana but not Alana. All the delicate colors of her skin and cheeks, hair and eyes, had all been removed and she stood like a work of marble come to life in shades of black, white, and gray. Shades of shadowing. Shades of stone. She said nothing and he sat naked in his bed, frozen like a statue himself, afraid to break the spell.

He saw her hands slowly rise to her shoulders, her delicate fingers push the loose fabric down until it tumbled to the floor, like a sculptor's drape during the reveal before an expectant audience of connoisseurs and art critics. Here, he and the moonlight were the only audience and far from any criticism, he could only venerate the sight of her.

She remained silent and still. He could not see her eyes, they were shadowed by her brow, but he knew she looked at him.

In the cool moonlight, John felt he was receiving a visitation from a goddess who had stepped down from Olympus and stood at the door sill of the world of common men. A goddess too polite to enter his world without an invitation. Wordlessly, he slid over in the bed, raising the covers in a clear invitation and she spread out a towel before taking a seat on it beside him.

Stories from mythology raced through his head. Far from cold, hard marble she was warm, so warm and so giving of herself as they kissed and caressed each other. Her hair, a heavy silken mass, fell about them like a scented curtain smelling of lilacs. Her soft, gentle hands moved over his body, exploring, caressing, with kisses to match. At last he carried her downward and covered her body with his own. There had been not a word between them but he knew when she was ready as the heat of desire radiated from her.

He felt the resistance and pushed his way passed before he realized what it signified. She reacted with a small sharp gasp and he stopped all motion.

"You're a virgin!" he said in hoarse surprise, his words although spoken quietly seemed to thunder in the room. Pulling back he peered into her moonlight washed face. He'd never bedded a virgin and here he held a virgin goddess in his hands and she had not told him.

"Not anymore…" she replied softly, matching his gaze, her fingertips stroking the hair back from his face, caressing his cheeks. He heard her soft plea. "Do not stop, John, please, do not stop."

He felt her move her hips beneath him and his mind went fuzzy. Now, he didn't think he could stop if he wanted to but he did strain mightily to slow down the process. He heard her breathing become ragged as she joined him in a rhythm he worked long at, slow and deliberate at first and then quickening until finally gasping, she strained and whimpered and cried out softly. And he let himself go with a groan.

After a few moments, John regained his composure and took stock. He could not believe he was still holding her warm supple flesh in his arms. Surely it was a dream. He began slowly running his hands over her firm body in pure wonderment, kissing, caressing, breathing in her scent.

"You are full of such surprises," he sighed at last. "My God, I can't believe this. I still think I am dreaming."

"It was exhausting waiting for you to make the next move," she said softly, her hands continuing to move over him, her fingers playing in the moon gilded hair of his chest.

"Waiting for…? But you rebuffed every invitation to be alone with me." He spoke in quiet confusion.

"To go for another walk in the orchard?" she smiled, running her hands over the muscles of his chest. "My father is right, you do have a most beautiful body… no, I would not have done this, my first time, on the hard ground in the orchard or up against a tree." Her fingers traced the ripples of his abdominal muscles. "How do you maintain your muscular integrity? In the colonies I can picture you chopping wood, digging fence posts, pitching hay, riding horses, perhaps fencing with your brother but here you do not do these things."

John was laughing softly. "Asks the woman with a body Venus herself would envy."

"I swim."

He almost said he knew but caught himself and said instead, "Well, it works. And I do push ups and sit ups and if your father invites me to the Roman Bath I swim as well."

He began kissing her again, slowly, lingering over every part of her like a man pacing himself at a banquet. Her slender neck, her silken shoulder, her high proud breasts, the enchanting dip of her navel, the swell of her hip, the tender pulsing flesh behind her knee. Finally, pleased with the sounds to which he had stirred her, he returned to kiss her mouth and judge if she was ready for another devotional swiving. He knew he was more than ready.

"You know what this means don't you?" he asked as he regained his breath for the second time.

"What?" she smiled and stretched, feeling totally wonderful and very primitive.

"You have come to my bed, you have had your way with me. Now you must make an honest man of me. It is a matter of honor."

She laughed softly with him and then he became serious.

"We took no precautions, Alana. I may have impregnated you."

She reached out in the moonlight and wrapped one of his silvery appearing locks around her finger and kissed it. "From just one time, I doubt it."

"I would remind you in case you have already forgotten, it was two… and you have the feel of a ripe and fertile vessel. You are a doctor, you know yourself it need only be once."

"I would not have you trapped into a… how do you say it in the colonies? A musket held wedding?"

John laughed again. "I've never heard that one before." Then he gripped her tightly. "I love you, Alana Huffsmeier. My God, I hope you know that. I could say I fell in love with you the moment I saw you, but that is not completely true. In truth, I fell in lust with you the first moment and I could scarcely breathe I wanted you so much but it was when I knew there was a brain inside your beautiful head that my heart became yours forever. I want you to marry me more than anything in this world. Share a life with me, Alana. I would ask that you be willing to visit my family at some point but I will never force you to move to the colonies if it is something you do not want to do. And need I say I will always support and encourage your practice of medicine."

"John," she sighed softly, deeply moved, "oh, John… I could not have given myself to you if I did not love you as well. You accept me for who I am and respect my work."

"And?" he prodded.

"Obviously we do have a great passion for each other," she smiled coyly.

He was quiet, still patiently waiting.

"You are a very generous lover... let us enjoy what we have now, for ourselves. We do not have to share it with the world. We do not have to rush into marriage, my love. It is too soon, too fast. In time you may change your mind."

"No, Alana, never." He felt a little hurt. "I know in my soul we were meant to be together," he said almost sternly, "and once we Power men lose our heart, it's 'til death do us part." He paused and looked searchingly into her dark eyes. "But perhaps what you are really saying to me is you are afraid *you* may have a change of heart."

"No-no, no, not at all!" She looked at him. He was so earnest, so vulnerable and she was now afraid she was going to break his heart. "How can I *change* my mind when I have not yet had time to consider what I think. I did not come to your bed thinking of marriage... oh," she anguished, "does that make me indecent? I thought only of my feelings and sharing this wonderful intimacy. John, I could not keep myself from you. Am I a licentious person? Immoral? I was drawn like a moth to your flame..."

He had to cover her mouth with his own to stop her. He kissed her again deeply and after a long moment he pulled back. "If you are indecent, there is no decency left in this world. But since I know my own mother and father to be very decent people, it cannot be so." He kissed her again. "And my mother and father have an undying passion for each other."

"I must think. Please, my love, I must speak with my father."

"Of course." He was disappointed but he told himself it was only fair. He hadn't asked Hendrick for his daughter's hand. He hadn't even asked permission to court her. But somehow he had thought Alana could make those kinds of decisions for herself. She had walked to *his* bed, he had not seduced her. She was no child; he judged her to be his age and as a fully grown adult and an educated doctor, wasn't she capable of deciding who she wanted to marry? But, he reminded himself, this was a different country, a different culture, and he must be patient. He pulled her close and together they slept until almost dawn.

She woke with a start. "I must go."

Groggy, he watched her slip into her gown and fold up the towel.

"What was that for?"

"It is only a small trace of blood, but it would not do for the laundress to find my blood on your sheet," she smiled and brushed the hair from his face before she gave him a parting kiss. "I will see you at breakfast, my love." And she unlocked his door and was gone while he was still recovering from his shock, confusion, and gratitude.

In what seemed like no time at all, John heard the big clock strike six and with it came a tap at his door. He knew it was the hot water arriving so he could shave and have a wash up. There was no need for a fire in the hearth so the servant would simply leave the container outside the door. John flipped back the covers and swung his legs over the side of the bed.

He stood and it took a moment for him to realize his nether regions held evidence of more than a trace of Alana's bleeding. He searched the bedding. It appeared to be good, but it did smell of sex. He pulled the bedding straight, covered it over and fetched the water so he could sponge himself off. By the time he was finished his waste water was obviously tinged with red. Was this normal? Having never been with a virgin before, he accepted that it must be within the range of normality. As a doctor, he felt certain that if Alana had suddenly begun her menstrual cycle there would have been much more blood.

Taking fresh water, John began to shave and when he finished he made the smallest cut under his chin allowing a few harmless drops of blood to spatter on the wash stand and the razor. Staunching the cut with styptic powder from his black bag, it quickly ceased to bleed. He finished dressing and went to breakfast. He knew while he was gone the house servant would clean up his room and the pink tinged waste water would be attributed to his shaving cut.

# *Chapter 3*

John found the next days difficult. He did not like keeping such a secret from Herr Huffsmeier and yet, it would seem, Alana had told him nothing. Each night she came to John's room and their passions boiled forth. Each day he was frustrated in his desire to kiss her, touch her, hold her in the little affectionate ways he had witnessed his parents behave with each other. It puzzled and hurt him that she did not want an open relationship with him. He understood keeping their nocturnal rendezvous a secret out of respect although if they were married there would be no need. But he could not understand Alana's reluctance to commit to him and to make their intentions public.

If Huffsmeier suspected anything, he said nothing but invited the younger man to the Roman bath on the evenings Alana was away. John tried to sweat out his frustration and swim away his moods.

Alana returned from the sister village but the moon was waning so John had drawn the draperies and had lit candles all around the room as he awaited her visit. The clock struck eleven, then half past. Then midnight and still she did not come. John blew out all the candles except one and crawled into his bed. He told himself she was tired, she'd had a busy day and she needed her rest. But somehow that did not ease the fear that she didn't love him, no longer cared, that somehow despite their recent passion, she no longer wanted him. It had happened to him before. Years ago a woman had used him for her own satisfaction and then ignored him to make a play for his father.

No. John could not believe that Alana, who had remained a chaste virgin for twenty years was now somehow enthralled with another. He bore his confused state of mind in the belief that she was indeed just tired. And John awaited the next day.

The following morning Alana was not at breakfast. John tried not to react too obviously to the revelation.

"Is she unwell?" he asked with restrain as his coffee was served along with bread and ham.

"Quite well I am told but a little tired. It is a rainy day. Few patients will show up. I told her to sleep on a bit more."

"Ahhh," John nodded vaguely. He knew Huffsmeier walked even in the rain and actually looked forward to the brutal pace the older man would set.

With umbrellas in hand and wrapped in their capes, the two men walked in silence shielding themselves from the downpour and gusting winds. It was an even numbered day and so they ended up at the *Kaffee und Gebäck*. John took faint solace from the apple strudel. By now he had tried every tasty delight this cafe had to offer but in the end, the strudel was the best. Today, he could barely taste it.

"What is it, John?" the elder man asked. "Something is not right. You are too young to be so sad. Do you miss your home, is that it?"

John looked across the table at Huffsmeier and directly into his keen, observant eyes. "I have too much respect for you to lie, Herr Doctor. I have not asked your permission, but I have fallen deeply in love with your daughter and I beg your blessing to marry her."

Huffsmeier screwed up his countenance and nodded his head. "I half suspected it," he said at last. "We cannot choose with whom we fall in love. I can see where being as well educated as she is, Alana would be even more irresistible to a man such as yourself than her mother was to me and I was totally bewitched from the moment I saw Anna-Theresa. Good luck to you, my young friend, you have my blessing but Alana makes her own decisions as you know."

"Then it would not upset you for her to marry?" John replied with a deep sigh of relief. "I know how much you depend on her but I assure you I would not take her away. Indeed, I envision us continuing much as we are only with many grand-children to fill the house." John was smiling with happiness.

"Upset me? Heavens, no! Alana deserves a life of her own, however she wants it. She does not need to stay to care for an old man."

"That is most generous for you to say, monsieur, but I could be happy right here with her at my side."


Alana came to John that night and all his doubts and fears were swept away in the maelstrom of passion and ecstasy they shared. He was overjoyed at Huffsmeier's kind encouragement and saw no impediment to their making a life together. He chose not to share this with her at that moment however. He had too many much more physical things to share. He needed only to get Alana to agree and perhaps pregnancy would give her a push. He wanted her pregnant.

They had just made love and now he knelt before his goddess and held her ankles up to his shoulders.

"What are you doing, John?" she giggled.

"Enjoying the sight of you with your legs open as an invitation to me."

"John, please, allow me some modesty." She pulled a sheet to cover herself and tried to sit up and he pressed her back down and began kissing the inside of her dainty foot, progressing along her firmly sculpted calf, working his way down along her smooth, tight thigh and finally pushing the sheet aside, he sought the seat of her femininity. "Oh!" She stopped struggling and embraced the action. It did not take long for her to cry out softly for him to return to within her. And he did with robust vigor which she participated in equally.

The next night she came to him again and he had the candles lit awaiting her. As he held her naked body in the glow of the candle light, he noticed bruising.

"Alana? What is this?"

"It is nothing." She tried to brush his concern aside.

"Did I do this to you?" He was filled with self-loathing and remorse. "Oh, my darling, I had no idea I was so rough with you. Forgive me, oh, forgive me." He kissed her bruised skin and held her as gently as a babe.

"You are not too rough, my love, I just bruise easily, that is all. Please do not blame yourself." She caressed his head, stroking his blond curls and kissing his eyes, one lid at a time. "You are a very gentle lover, but my darling, I also thrill when you are fierce and driven. I want it all. You make me feel things I never knew existed. I have known only a father's love. I would never have known the tender and fiercely intimate love of a man if God had not sent you here to me."

"Alana," he rasped softly, his heart full of hope and joy. "We can have all this for the rest of our lives. I'll give you gentle and fierce, dominate and beg, your wish shall be my command. Just let us agree to spend our lives together. Marry me, my love, be my wife."

A tear rolled down her beautiful cheek. "Yes, my darling John. I will marry you. I will marry you and be as good a wife as is possible for me to be and I promise to love you until the day I die."

"You make me the happiest of men," he sighed with joy. John thought his heart would explode. The goddess was forsaking the heavens and choosing the less lofty world of mere mortals. But John had forgotten that when a god or goddess steps down from the heavens on high, they too become mortal.


Mail was not entirely unheard of in the village but it was a rarity. Thus, when a letter arrived at the hotel addressed to Monsieur John Power and holding the seal of the First Bank of Zurich, it did cause a stir.

A messenger delivered it to the Huffsmeier home; everyone knew Doctor John Power was living there. John tipped the delivery lad handsomely.

Inside were two pieces of interest. The first, a short but elegantly written note on bank stationary stating, in French, that the enclosed had been received from the firm John knew to be his grandfather's lawyers. The instructions the bank received from the largest law firm in Paris was to please use the information in their possession, via the account John drew upon for his living allowance while in Europe, to ascertain his whereabouts and relay said missive to him at the behest of his father in the English colonies.

John immediately felt the hairs raise on the back of his neck.

The second piece was a folded letter addressed to him, rather soiled, rather travel worn, but the seal was intact. Breaking the seal and unfolding the letter carefully, he read:


*Chartes Landing*
*New Jersey Colony*
*Late Autumn 1712*

*John, My Dear Son,*

*As I write I know I must trust to Providence that this letter will find you and that you are indeed no longer in France. The news I send is much too important to wait. It is late in the season and traffic from here directly to France is non-existent. Thus, I am sending two letters on two separate ships whose itineraries vary and I trust at least one finds its way to my father's lawyers and to you.*

*It is a fact of our times that lawyers and bankers can almost always find someone with whom we lose touch. And the law firm has a most excellent relationship with the Zurich bank.*

*We have heard nothing from you since we received your letter saying you were leaving France to study in Switzerland. Then I received news that both my parents had passed away. It must have been very soon after you departed.*

*I am told your grand-père had a bad heart and he died peacefully in his sleep. He never mentioned anything to me directly but as I look back, I now believe he knew there was a frailty as he did express concerns over dying first and leaving your grand-mère behind unprotected. Perhaps you observed clues to his health on your visit.*

*This next was even more of a shock.*

*Your grand-mère has also passed. I was told she expressed a desire to live no more without her beloved Jean-Philippe. They wrote she simply died in her sleep three days after he. How is this possible? Unless she had help either by her own hand or from someone else. It grieves me sorely, John, to think my home and family and our love were not sufficient to motivate her to live. But there was no one there to encourage her to overcome her grief.*

*Now to the pressing point – Do not go back into France! Do not try to revisit the family estates or go to the houses in Paris. Do not try to contact the new duc de Pouvoir.*

*I have it straight from my father's own mouth that my cousin, who now is in possession of everything, is a rabid Huguenot enemy and France is no longer safe for you. I trust them not. Please heed my warning, son. Your mother is beside herself with worry and only a letter from you assuring us you are safe and will not again step on French soil will calm her nerves.*

*When you are ready to leave Switzerland, I would advise that you make your way through the German states, perhaps to Amsterdam, and depart via the North Sea. From there I am certain you will find transport to the colonies.*

*Please write as soon as you receive this. Set our minds at ease. May God bless and keep you.*

*With much affection,*
*Your loving Pa-pa*
*Jacques-Jean Charte Power*
*(sealed with the Pouvoir ring)*

John sat in stunned silence.

Huffsmeier observed his posture from a room away and poured a glass of his best brandy, slowly walking it in to John. The young man was quiet, he rubbed his hand over his face and taking the brandy, motioned for the older doctor to join him. Huffsmeier sat down, frowned and asked, "Bad news?"

"Life is so ephemeral, is it not? As doctors we know this, we encounter it every day. Only a single heartbeat stands between life and death. Herr Doctor, all this time I have been picturing my grandparents sitting in their chateau, perhaps looking forward to the next letter from me when in fact they have been dead ever since I arrived in Switzerland. In fact, they may have died before I even left France.

"Here," he tossed the letter to Huffsmeier. "You may read it. It was written last year. And my father writes in French. Tell me what you think."

Huffsmeier adjusted his spectacles and read. When he finished he looked up.

"So," John asked, "as a learned physician who does not believe in blood letting or the wisdom of tablets made of cow dung, do you think a healthy woman can simply *will* herself to die?"

"John, your father is grieving. Both his parents have died and he worries for his first born who is an ocean away from him. He lashes out in wild speculation. It is understandable. As a doctor you will witness things that have no explanation. How does a little 100 weight woman muster the strength to lift a 300 weight rock off her trapped child? Why does a mother's kiss make the hurt suddenly disappear? How can a man walk four leagues on a broken leg? We must simply accept that these things sometimes happen. And love? Is that not the most mysterious power of all?

"Write to your parents, John, your letter should go out on the next coach. Send it via this law office so they know you have been found. I have heard of this firm. Its reputation is impeccable. Give your parents the gift of at least not having to worry about you."

"I did write to them since I have arrived," John frowned.

"Excellent but… were you able to acknowledge your father's warning to stay out of France?" The older man went to a desk, pulled out writing paper and ink and brought it to John. "Just a note will do for now. Let them know you have received their warning and that you are well. Leave all else until you have had time to digest it." In walking away, he reached out and gripped John's shoulder for a brief few seconds in support and understanding.

John sent the simple note.


Later that afternoon when Alana had finished her hours in the clinic, John shared his news. And he posed the same question.

"Do you think a healthy woman can simply *will* herself to die?"

She came up behind him as he sat in the chair in the drawing room. Putting her hands over his shoulders, she tenderly stroked him. "John, my love, we have all heard of or even seen the person who against all reason holds on to the threads of life until that one person, perhaps a husband or lover, perhaps a child arrives to say goodbye. Is it not feasible to accept the reverse? The person so heartbroken, so tired of this life, so utterly bereft and disappointed that they simply give it all up?"

He reached across his chest to one warm hand, kissed it and held it fast. That it was too warm, did not register with him at first until it did. He pulled her around to sit upon his lap.

"John, please… I have not told Father yet. What are you doing?"

"I am taking your temperature, *Mademoiselle la docteur*. You are fevered," he said with concern.

"No," she smiled, "I am fine."

"You are fevered, you have caught a chill."

Just then they heard Huffsmeier approaching.

"John, let me go," she whispered frantically.

"No. It is time he heard." Raising his voice, John called out, "Herr Doctor, please, we have something to tell you. I have asked Doctor Alana Huffsmeier to become my wife and she has said yes."

Entering the room, the older doctor looked at his daughter curiously as she sat in John's lap, her hands held fast by him.

"I guess I should say congratulations."

"Thank you, monsieur. And now would you be so kind as to settle a small professional dispute? I say she is fevered. What say you?"

Huffsmeier put his hand on his daughter's forehead. "Child, you are burning up," he said gruffly. He called to the housemaid and told her to see Alana to bed. "I will be up to see you in ten minutes, precisely. I want to find you in bed."

What worried both men was that Alana did not argue.

"John, please go to the kitchen and ask Cook for a large bowl of ice chips and bring them upstairs with you."

"Of course."

Huffsmeier walked up the steps and looked at his watch. When it had been exactly ten minutes, he rapped on his daughter's door and opened it.

"Claire," he addressed the maid. "Thank you. Now if you will please wait outside and when *Monsieur le docteur* Power arrives, have him wait outside the door until I am finished."

Claire bobbed a little curtsy and took up her post in the hall.

Huffsmeier felt his daughter's forehead again and the lymph glands in her neck. He opened the neck of her nightdress and reaching within, he felt for the glands in her arm pits. Then, pushing up the sleeves of her gown he recognized the *petechiae* on her arms and bruising. "I am going to take a sampling of your blood."

"Do not bother yourself, Pa-pa, I already did," she said with a sigh and relaxed back against her pillows.

"And?"

"And my blood looks just like the notes you made of Ma-ma's blood. I am sorry to say I have the blood sickness."

He maintained his discipline not to react like a father but as a doctor. "So, fever, fatigue, swollen lymph glands, red spots on the skin, easy bruising… how about easy bleeding, what have your menstrual cycles been like?"

"Heavy."

"Nose bleeds?"

"Not yet."

"Have you been losing weight?"

"Not that I have noticed."

"So your appetite has not yet been affected. How long have you known?" he asked gruffly.

"I suspected six weeks ago but I knew for certain when I checked my blood about four weeks ago."

"About! About! Can you not be more precise?" he said sharply and then crumbled to tears. "Oh, my dear Alana, my precious girl, not you too! Not you too!"

She reached out to him as he sat upon her bed and they held each other. After a few minutes, he quickly wiped his eyes.

"And what are we to do about young Power, eh? It is not fair that you should let him fall in love with you."

"Oh, Pa-pa, I tried but *I* fell in love with him. It is not fair, I know. I should have told you so you could send him away but… I could not. I love him, I truly love him and I did not want to die a virgin, Pa-pa. I wanted to know the love of a man and he is such a good man. He is thoughtful and kind and gentle and giving. And he loves me."

Hendrick sighed very deeply. "How could he not?"

"He is the only man except for you who has ever supported me in my work."

"I know, *liebling*, I know," he said softly.

Huffsmeier stood up and cleared his throat before walking to the door. Opening it, he found John standing there as he knew he would be, hugging that bowl of ice chips and slowly turning them to water.

"Go in," he invited. "Claire bring some linens, please. John, see if you can get that fever down with some icy compresses on her head, neck, and wrists. Give her lots of water and hopefully, she will get some rest."

John stayed with Alana all night and in the morning she felt better but Huffsmeier insisted she stay in her bed. He had breakfast sent up to her and John both.


Alana was sleeping and John with the stamina of a twenty-one year old slipped out to his room, refreshed himself, and changed his clothes. On his bed he found a note from Huffsmeier requesting his presence in the laboratory.

"Herr Doctor?" John called out as he walked into the room.

"Here. May I present your micro-scope. It was delivered today." Huffsmeier announced and uncovered a beautiful black and silver instrument with multiple lenses in place and a series of fine lenses in a velvet lined box. "You will learn which to use and in what combination but for now I want you to look at something." He took John's hand and pricked a finger. As the drop of blood oozed forth, Huffsmeier smeared it on a slide. Bending over the scope, the older man brought the specimen into perfect focus and offered John a look. "What you see there is some fine and healthy blood and if you will notice there are two kinds of cells present... what I call the A cells which are very red and the B cells, which are more transparent. Do you see?"

"Yes, yes I can," John replied with some excitement.

"Now look here," he gestured to his own micro-scope. "Tell me what you see."

John looked into the scope. "The B cells are different," he said. "There appear to be many more and they look..." he pulled back from the scope with a slight frown wrinkling his brow. "They look misshapen."

"Now, John, read here my notes."

John looked at a notebook laid out to a page with a drawing very much like what he had just seen in the scope. The notes were in French and stated the observance of an over abundance of misshapen B cells. He flipped the page back and saw the name **Anna-Theresa Huffsmeier**.

"Alana's mother," he said softly and already his heart was beating faster.

Huffsmeier nodded.

"And whose blood is this?" he asked, knowing what the answer would be but wanting to hear it anyway.

"That is Alana."

John looked again and then at his own blood, and then back to Alana's specimen. "It is hereditary?"

"So it would appear."

"But not contagious."

"No, not at all," the older man said.

"What can we do?"

Huffsmeier slowly shook his head.

"How long?"

"Not long."

John stared at Huffsmeier, his eyes demanding more of an answer.

"Less than a year...months. She will seem to get better, have some good days and then she will decline. Each time she appears to be better she will then decline again even farther than she was before. She will need us, John. She loves you very much."

"And you are absolutely certain there is nothing to be done?" he asked, his voice had grown thick. "No one has found a cure?"

"I have spent years searching, researching, calling out to the far ends of our world in hopes of learning something, hearing something to hold against this day. From the day that Anna-Theresa died I feared for Alana and yet I hoped upon hope that she would remain healthy, that she would escape this curse."

Suddenly John had the overwhelming urge to hit something, he needed to hit something, he had to hit something and there was nothing in the laboratory to hit. He ran from the room, and out of the house. He went on briskly to the barn where he saw a freshly butchered hog hung up from the rafters. Good enough! He tore off his coat and tossed it aside and punched the hog again and again. He punched it and punched some more. He punched until his knuckles were scratched and bleeding and he was sweating profusely. He punched until he felt like he couldn't breathe and yet he punched again and again. He heard bones cracking beneath his fists until the carcass fell to the ground and he upon it, screaming every curse word he had ever heard in English, in French, in Swedish, even in German, and then he bawled as he continued to beat upon the fallen carcass until he had worn himself into complete exhaustion.

Leopold found him and the battered hog and reported to Herr Huffsmeier who told him to bring John into the house. Uphred and Aphalstay took over from there. They brought him to the Roman bath muttering consoling things in German that John was grateful he did not understand. He could not have tolerated hearing any-one saying consoling things to him. There was no consolation. What could possibly console him as he stood on the brink of losing the love of his life after what was to be mere months of knowing her? The Fates had led him to the most perfect woman for him, a woman of beauty and charm, a mate of intelligence and compassion who shared his vocation and they were cruelly going to take her from him, snatch her away. A sacrifice they were demanding as an appeasement for what? What reason? What had he done? What had she done? What?

The tears began to flow again as he sat or stood dumbly as the women stripped him, soaped him down and rinse him off. They brought him to the hot pool where they sat with him, one on each side, lest he slip beneath the water line. The minerals in the water soothed his aching muscles, the heat soothed his aching mind and the bowls of ice chips soothed his bruised knuckles. They pushed him into the large pool where he sat in the shallower end cooling down until they walked him out to the massage table. There they laid him out, face up and worked over his muscles, one set of magic hands on each side, using fine oils to replenish his skin. They flipped him over and continued on his backside, soothing and smoothing, massaging and stretching and oiling until he fell fast asleep.

When he awoke, Aphalstay was there like a mother hen. She had changed into dry garb and helped him into a big fluffy white robe and walked him back into the main house. He noticed absently that his knuckles were bandaged. Aphalstay left him but Huffsmeier heard and came out of the library.

"We are dining in Alana's room, if you would care to join us." He took hold of John's hands and looked at the bandaging without comment. "You might want to put some clothes on first."

"Of course, and forgive me, Herr Doctor. I lost control. I shall be happy to pay for the pig. I am certain it's ruined."

"Unnecessary and say nothing more, there is nothing to forgive. I just hope that is all out of your system now so my daughter can depend upon you."

"Of course. Excuse me, please, I shall dress."

They were married in the apple orchard on the very spot where they had shared their first kiss. A light breeze made the apple blossoms fall around them like snow. It was magical. Alana was feeling so well and looked as beautiful as ever, radiating happiness. John was proud and happy every time he looked at her. Perhaps Huffsmeier was wrong, he thought, perhaps God was listening to John's prayerful supplications for Alana's health. She looked as healthy as she ever had except for the bruising that never seemed to go away anymore.

It appeared to John that the whole village had been invited. Perhaps they had. Tables were set up under the shade of the trees with plenty of food and drink and music. There was no sedate courtly dancing but wild, high energy, swirling folk music that caused bodies to weave and jump and bob all over the grounds in celebration. They tried to drag Alana in but John ran interference while many muttered behind his back that he was selfishly protective of his beautiful wife, trying to keep her so completely to himself. They had no idea she was ill. But John and Hendrick both knew just one such exhausting dance could have put Alana into bed for a week.

Time was passing quickly. She no longer traveled to her clinic but confined herself to helping John in her father's office. Huffsmeier traveled instead as the compromise to keep his strong-minded daughter at home. John found her presence invaluable when a patient spoke only German or perhaps Italian and he treasured every moment of normality, every shared laugh or serious discussion of a treatment. Good days were followed by good nights spent in John's room while the bad nights which followed bad days, Alana spent in her own room being nursed.

John tried very hard to refrain from asking God why they could offer cures and treatments to so many but there was none to be had for his deserving wife. He knew he would receive no answer just as he noticed she was leaving more and more food untouched upon her plate. He coaxed her to the relaxation of the larger pool, the mineral water was good for her even if she didn't feel like swimming laps anymore. Surely it would help stimulate her appetite. John remembered the first time he had seen her diving into the long, narrow pool. Was that only four months ago? Such a short amount of time and yet time was flying. He tried not to compare the perfect body she had at that time to the one he saw now wasting away before him.

Huffsmeier warned that soon her bad days would outnumber her good ones. And John saw it happening. Blue shadows had become permanent under those vividly violet eyes, as though their color was spilling out upon her flesh. It was now a rare occasion for her to take a meal in the dining room.

Alana awoke and saw John. His chair was pulled up to her bed, as he sat dozing and holding her hand. She smiled and brought his hand to her lips, bestowing a kiss upon his long-healed knuckles. She did not rise.

"It is late," she said softly. "You need not watch me sleep, my love, but it is a comfort to have you near."

He gave her a slightly crooked smile as the question raced through his mind: *How much longer will I have you near?* "All I ask is to be a comfort to you."

"Take off your clothes and join me... unless... I now repulse you." she added hesitantly

"Alana," he shook his head, "you could never repulse me but... I don't want to hurt you."

"I miss your sweet body," she sighed.

At that, he kicked off his shoes, removed his stockings and stood. She watched him remove his shirt and breeches. She could have named every muscle in his body; every man in the village had those same muscles but his were packaged up so very, very well. Naked, he carefully crawled in beside her. It was a full moon whose light flooded the bedroom as he gently strove to honor her request. After a time she stayed his efforts.

"It's all right, my dearest, stop," she reached out to stroke his hair behind his ears.

"I'm sorry..."

"It is not your fault." She smiled sadly. "My body no longer responds but in my mind you are still the gentlest and most thrilling of lovers. Just hold me, my love, I miss the feel of your skin next to mine, the smell of you, your warmth."

He lie beside her, gently caressing her. "When you are better I want to spend my lifetime making love to you."

It was an innocent subterfuge, they both knew she was never going to get better again.

"Remember the first time I came to you?" she asked softly. "It was a night like this."

"Of course I remember. I could not stop thinking of how you had kissed me in the orchard. It had me tossing and turning, unable to sleep. You left me hanging for several weeks until you walked into my room that night, a volcanic goddess ready to erupt with such passion, I am still in awe." He stroked her cheek and felt the wet. "What is it, my darling? Are you in pain?"

"No-no. John, forgive me. Forgive me."

"Forgive what? You make me a very happy man." He continued to stroke her.

"I must confess to you." Her voice had become very soft and the tears were flowing faster.

"What is it, my love?"

"When I kissed you in the orchard, I knew then that I loved you - madly, illogically, undeniably, deeply."

He smiled in a silent response.

"But I also knew I had no right. From the time I was old enough to compre-hend, I knew I might be cursed with my mother's illness. I snooped in Father's pa-pers, I read copies of his inquiries. I knew he feared it as well. When I was seven-teen I took a sample of my blood and looked at it under his micro-scope. I was elated to see only normal cells and I convinced myself that I was safe.

"After our kiss, I tested myself again. I had been feeling a bit more tired than usual and the fear was coming back. I saw them. I saw the crippled cells. Not as many as there are now but I knew. This is why I tried to stay away from you but I was weak. I wanted so desperately for you to make love to me. I wanted to give myself and know what that kind of love was like. I was selfish, John, I am so sorry." She sobbed quietly.

"Alana," he rasped hoarsely, "I am only sorry we wasted three weeks. There is nothing you could have done to stop me from falling in love with you. I already loved you. I told you I fell in love with you at the dinner table. I can tell you the very moment, the very second... We had not kissed but I was already mere soft clay in your hands."

She chuckled through her tears. "Then you do not... you are not... sorry?"

"How can I be sorry? Some people live a very long life and never find such love as we have."

They held each other through the night and the next day the fever raged. The lymph nodes all over her body were very swollen and sore, her liver ached and so did her bones.

The days were getting shorter.

The apples were ripening in the orchard outside her window and Alana begged to be taken outside so she could pick one perfect apple fresh from the tree as she had been doing every year for as long as she could remember. The day was very mild but John wrapped her in quilts and blankets to carry her out. She seemed to weigh nothing at all. Huffsmeier was there, overseeing this foolishness but he said nothing. John lifted her so she could reach a favored choice and she grasped the apple but could not tug it from the flexing branch. Hendrick assisted as John held his wife. The apple was plucked free, red, shiny, and firm. She bit into its sweet-ness and smiled. He carried her back into the house. She did not protest. As they climbed the staircase, the apple fell and rolled down the steps unnoticed.

The day of the funeral was the first day since his own wife's funeral that Herr Hendrick Huffsmeier did not leave the house at precisely half past the hour of seven and walk into town. Instead at nine-thirty he was part of a solemn gathering at the village church. Just as many if not more people were there as had been at the wedding. Everyone was in shock. It seemed like only yesterday the handsome young couple had been wed.

They all knew *Mademoiselle Frauline* Doctor Huffsmeier who had never been exactly what they thought a woman should be, but they had liked her, greatly admired her beauty, and sympathized with her being left motherless to be raised by a father of metaphysical interests. But no one had had any idea she had been so ill. Those of her father's generation did remember that her mother also had died very young. Mothers of eligible daughters could not help themselves from casting appraising looks at the solemn but finely dressed young widower. He was obviously in need of consolation and, in time, a new wife.

John's bags including his new micro-scope were already packed. Parting was painful but staying would be even more painful. Huffsmeier understood. He thanked John. There was no need to explain for what. John understood but knew there was no need for thanks but it was too painful to speak of. Huffsmeier told John he would be splitting his time between the two practices with hopes of finding another young doctor to assist who was open to new ideas. He would write the Academy, he said gruffly, but in the meanwhile keeping busy would be his antidote to his own pain.

He handed John an envelope containing a brief statement written in German asking for assistance in seeing the bearer on his way to transportation and the North Sea. "Just in case you run into a *Dummkopf* who speaks no French or English," he muttered mixing a favorite German word in with his French. He had Leopold hitch up the carriage with instructions to take John to the nearest town with coach service going in the right direction.

The two men embraced and for one long moment they clung to each other knowing that in parting they were losing their last link to the incredible woman they both loved and had just buried.

"Do not become bitter, John." Huffsmeier stood looking into John's face. "Life is short for all of us and we are meant to live it as long and as fully as possible. She would not have wanted nor expected anything less from you."

John looked into the older man's eyes. He could not speak but swallowed, nodded, and climbed into the waiting carriage.

# Chapter 4

## Amsterdam, Early Spring 1714

The best thing about a whore is no emotional investment. A pro takes her money, leaves when you ask, and there are no regrets, no complaints, no expectations, no complications. John gave a friendly pat to the fleshy rump of the big, bouncy, blonde *meisje* which John now knew to simply mean *girl* in Dutch. He had just swived her vigorously for the last time and made a gesture for her to leave. The energetic and accommodating young miss put her clothes on quickly, flashed him a smile with deep dimples, took her money with her, and was gone before he rose from the bed to wash himself. Tomorrow he would be leaving.

He had wintered in Amsterdam. He liked the people who he found to be generally hard-working, good-natured, and stout just like their beer.

John had made his way by coach to Basel Switzerland where he had found passage on a river boat hauling goods on the Rhine. Eventually, he found himself in Amsterdam where he fell in with a local crowd of good fellows at one of the popular drinking establishments. He spoke no Dutch, they spoke only a smattering of rudimentary English or French all of which suited John perfectly. They could all enjoy the warmth and entertainment of the tavern, the comradery, and the beer without any deep philosophical conversations about life, its beauty, its ugliness, its meaningless waste. John was not interested in any deep thoughts on the meaning of life... or death.

It took no time for him to be introduced to two or three young working girls. Girls his drinking friends stoutly proclaimed *Schoon! Schoon!* Which was quickly translated to him as *clean*. Sturdy, buxom young women of accommodating temperaments who knew how to start and finish a job. And so, he had superficial satisfaction all the way around.

Despite the frigid weather, John had found himself walking a good deal. He had been conditioned to walking by Huffsmeier and Amsterdam was an easy place to walk. Flat as a pancake, so very different from the Alps. Different was good; John sought no reminders.

One had to admire a people who fought for their scrap of land and took it bit by bit from the sea, he thought. Huffsmeier had called them "a clean people." And even in winter, John observed housewives scrubbing the stoops of their homes right up until the canals froze over. And not once had he seen a slop pot being emptied from a window.

When the canals did freeze over, he was a little surprised to see the number of skaters out on the ice. As he stopped to observe them the first time, he couldn't help but notice how relaxed they looked, how carefree. Some fairly flying up and down the canal, others sedately circling making lazy figures on the ice, or playing games in teams. Men, women, children. So, why not him, he'd asked himself? That night in the tavern he asked in his own way, which was a combination of words, gestures, and pantomime if anyone there could skate and he received hearty laughter in reply. Everyone could skate, he had found out. One learned to skate in Holland just as one learned to walk. Once the canals were frozen, it was the quickest way to get around. And it was a source of an infinite variety of recreation. And so John had found an agreeable soul who took him to the local merchant to get the proper equipment.

The merchant spoke excellent English. The most desirable skate, John was informed, was a handsome boot built with attached steel blades. A more economic choice was a beautifully crafted steel blade attached to a slender wooden platform and sized to clasp the bottom of one's boot in a type of partial cage and then lace tightly over one's foot. And the most economical choice used exclusively by delivery boys and servants was a firm wooden platform with two small runners, designed for stable, straight-forward skating and quick donning and doffing as one went about their errands.

John remembered he had surveyed his choices with some hesitation while his guide said something in Dutch and the merchant nodded quickly and presented a sturdy attachable skate with a double runner, "for the beginner."

John had found his choice and remembered spending an enjoyable, if chilling, afternoon learning to glide across the ice. He also discovered it to be an excellent work out physically and within the week he had gone back to the same merchant's shoppe to purchase a pair of single runner skates. He now suspected that the large, roomy, almost barrel-like pants Dutchmen wore were designed to hide a great deal of winter padding against the cold... and the falls.

And so the winter had passed. John would not say quickly, but tolerably, and as soon as he learned ships were preparing to sail the North Atlantic route to the colonies, he had booked passage. On one last errand before leaving, he went to the skate merchant and requested he write a note in Dutch. John would give it to the tavernkeeper. The note read simply that his skates were to be given to the next winter visitor who wanted to try the sport. John couldn't imagine ever needing them in the colonies.


The trip over was a little rough but John did not mind it at all. In fact, the rougher, the more distracting. He was heading home because he really did not know what else to do. It was his home, they were his family, and for now he needed time to think, he needed time to heal.

Chartes Landing needed better medical care. He did not intend to put Doctor Ajax out of business, but he had to be advised of the world one cannot see, about microbes and bacteria, about the insanity of the idea of *humors*. The micro-scope would help and hopefully Ajax would be accepting of the new ideas but John didn't want to appear like a know-it-all. In reality, there was still so much they did not know. John had read all the medical papers he had received from England but Huffsmeier had insisted he take them with him. John planned to gift Ajax with them.

He thought again of home. There were bound to be questions. He had been gone for almost two and a half years and really did not want to talk about any of it. And yet how could he not? And how was he to respond without dredging up unendurable pain. He hadn't told anyone he had been married, not even Father. It was still a subject much too painful to even think about much less speak. Mother would sense something, he knew she would. It was uncanny how often she would make comment on a subject of which one had only been thinking.

He wondered what changes he would find at Chartes Landing. He was almost certain his parents would be the same. The businesses? Probably the same. His siblings would all be two years older. Two years could be considerable depending on one's age. The difference between a new born and a two and a half year old was astonishing, but the difference between a five year old... which is what his little sister had been when he left... and a seven year old, not really so amazing. And the difference between an eighteen year old Phillip - already married, settled, maturing, and expecting a child - and Phillip at twenty was probably not even noticeable.

Suddenly, John was struck with a realization. Two years as an adult could be nothing or it could be a very long time depending on what transpired during it. Indeed, he felt as if he had lived an entire lifetime already. It had been a lifetime. It had been Alana's lifetime.

John stood motionless at the ship rail for hours.

They landed in New York Towne and after securing his baggage, John bought passage on the packet boat heading out at first light the next day, sailing to points south, including Chartes Landing. He was arriving unannounced and decided he would go to his mother's store first. If she was there he would be fresh and more able to bluff a good face. If she wasn't there, he could find out how things were from Caroline or Lyndyn whom he assumed were still working there.

John walked up to the door of the Chartes Landing General Store, took a breath and opened it. His mother Marie looked up from some paperwork at the main counter, saw him, threw down her reading spectacles and fairly flew from around the counter and into his arms.

"John! John! It is you! You did not tell us you were coming," she kissed him repeatedly.

"I didn't want you to fret, Mother," he smiled and held her in a gentle hug as she clung to him with surprising strength.

"Ohhh, John. Welcome home! You have no idea how good it is to see you. How glad... how happy it makes me. You are safe. You are here." A tear was in her eye as her hands ran over his coat sleeves, his shoulders, his chest as if she was confirming he was not an apparition. Her gentle mother's hands went to his face, caressing his cheeks, stroking his curls as her eyes searched his face. He suddenly felt like he was being stripped naked, laid bare, as though she could see beneath the mask and would know everything. He could not move. She stared at him for a long moment and then, "Your moustache!" she finally said and smiled broadly. "You have shaved off your moustache!" She clutched his chin.

He took a breath and grinned. "Thought I would try a new look."

"You are very handsome with it and very handsome without it, makes no difference. Have you been to the house?"

"No, Mother, I came to see you first," he said projecting the implied innocence of a good son.

She pulled his head down to her again and kissed him soundly on each cheek.

"Oh, *mon fils*, I will sleep much better tonight knowing you are safe in your own bed."

Marie, who had barely begun her forties and could only be described as a very attractive bundle of energy, asked her assistant Lyndyn to care for the store and close it at the appropriate time. She led John out the back and had him put his baggage into the carriage so she could drive him home.

"I'll drive," he insisted and helped her up to her seat.

"As you wish," she smiled and began to tell him some of the current news. "I suppose the biggest surprise is your Uncle Richard brought home a son just after you left. His name is Raphael but everyone calls him *Rafe*."

Richard Bonchance was not really an uncle but he was Jacques' best friend. They had grown up together in France, were both bastards born of Huguenot mothers and aristocratic fathers. But Jacques had been his father's only child and his heir. When the Edict of Nantes giving French protestants equal rights under the law was revoked in 1685, jealous relatives sought Jacques' imprisonment and Richard chose to partner with his friend in a dangerous escape just ahead of the authorities.

"His ma-ma was a French woman," Marie continued speaking of Raphael as John allowed the horse to choose its speed which was barely a walk. "She was from the north and she died young, very tragic, a suicide... oh," she touched his arm, "but Rafe does not know this, Richard has never told him. We had no idea and when they showed up on our doorstep it was a complete surprise. Rafe and your sister took to each other instantly." Marie chuckled.

"Your pa-pa tried to make them wait until she was eighteen like Helen and sent Rafe back out on another trek. When he returned in the fall, the fire was burning so hot we were afraid... biology would overpower self-discipline."

John chuckled. "A very scholarly way to phrase it, Mother."

"Yes?" She looked at him. That he no longer called her "Mama" was a detail that had not escaped her. "Well, your pa-pa softened and it was a New Year's Day wedding after Rafe returned. They live with us. I insisted because Rafe leaves every spring to travel the route of the trading posts and returns not until fall to spend the winter, just like Richard and your pa-pa used to do when we first came here. Rafe is your age. And Richard has assured your pa-pa that he takes no interest in the Indian women and will be a faithful husband. I believe him. I like the boy. And he was here to welcome his new daughter... born eleven months after the wedding." Marie added contentedly. "Our nursery is filling up again, only with grandchildren this time. And this year your brother Richie has gone on the trek with Rafe."

"I remember Helen and Thor were married just before I left," John nodded. "How are they doing?"

"Yes, yes, and they now have a little boy, Thomas. I know not whose chest was puffed out bigger, your pa-pa's or William's, two very proud *grand-pères*." Marie laughed. "I think they are grooming Thor to take over management of the mill."

William Boot was a faithful employee from the very beginnings of the settlement, a huge, hulking Swede whose oldest son, Thor, looked much like him. But so did William's younger children, exceptionally tall, large, and blond. A gentle giant, William had gone from being a lumberjack to managing the lumber camp and then managing the sawmill for Jacques Power. After William's first wife died tragically it took him many years, but eventually he married an exotic looking Swedish woman who gave Marie her weekly massages. And together the couple also operated a Swedish *batstuga* or steam bath house.

"I thought Phillip was going to be groomed to manage the mill," John said looking at Marie and she laughed.

"I tease him he should have had a boy." She looked over at John who was looking very serious. "It is a joke, *mon fils*. I hope you have not left your sense of humor on the other side of the ocean. No, Phillip is already managing something. I am not certain what exactly but it takes him more often to the lumber camp. You will have to ask him what exactly he does. I do know he and Caroline are very happy. You remember they have Charity, and since, they have now twins, Faith and Hope. I believe she has her hands very full," Marie chuckled. "I told her I do not expect her in the store for some time but she can bring them to the nursery any time she needs a break. I cannot imagine keeping up with twins."

John couldn't tell his mother that all the talk of happy marriages and babies was like pouring alcohol on his lacerated heart so he just smiled and nodded.

"Oh, and little Martha... you remember Francois Nicholet's step-daughter, yes?"

"Of course." How could he forget their trek to the frontier cabin and finding Francois at the bottom of the well on top of a bloated, rotting dead Indian.

"We received a letter just recently. Evidently things are not going well. Your pa-pa is thinking of going to England. I told him if he goes, I go too. I could not bear to be left behind to worry."

John was only half listening.

As they approached the large French influenced and somewhat rambling three story frame house, Marie suddenly called out. "Look who I have with me." Donald Sims, their all around handyman and gardener of over twenty years, looked up. "Look who has come home," Marie smiled proudly.

With a steadying hand from Sims, Marie hopped down from the carriage like a woman half her age.

John came around and shook Sims' hand. "Hello, Sims."

"Good to see you, Master John. Welcome home."

"Thank you."

"Come, John, come... we must find your pa-pa." Marie led the way through the front door, pausing to wipe her feet as did John. "Jacques? Jacques, come, come see who is here," she called.

Jane Sims, Donald's wife and their housekeeper had trained them all to wipe their feet. She smiled and welcomed John just as Jacques Power, the family patriarch, entered the hall from his study. A fit man in his mid-forties, trim, well muscled with the graceful strength and balance of a man trained early with a foil. It was easy to see John was his son. They had the same build, the same coloring, the same wide gray eyes rimmed so remarkably in black, the same nose and mouth, and the same thick curly blonde hair although Jacques' now looked frosted in silver.

"Son!" Jacques approached opening his arms. "Welcome home." He kissed his son on each cheek and then grabbed him in a masculine hug. "You see how your mother beams? So, I take it all this study has made you an excellent doctor who can care for us in our old age, *n'est-ce pas?"* He smiled and slapped his son affectionately on the back.

"Father, I don't think you will ever be old," John smiled.

"I hope that does not mean you think we shall die young," Jacques teased and John flushed in embarrassment.

"Of course not, sir, you know what I mean." His voice became softer. "I was very shocked and saddened to hear about *Grand-père et Grand-mère,"* he added, looking directly into his father's eyes.

"Yes, yes, as were we all," Jacques nodded sadly.

Just then fourteen year old Jamie came flying through the door with their little sister Isabelle who had escaped the nursery and was not about to be left out of the excitement. They both had their father's blonde hair although Izzy's was much fairer, rather like *Grand-mère's* had been just as she had her eyes while Jamie's large brown eyes went well with his light caramel blond hair.

They ran up to John and hugged him in welcome. Then they began peppering him with questions. Izzy's chief concern seemed to be if her big brother had remembered to bring her a present.

"Enough everyone," Marie spoke, "allow John to go to his room and refresh himself. He has had a very long trip and I can see that he is tired even if you cannot. We will all gather together for dinner later. John, I shall have the cook make a light snack. I know those packet boats, if you do not bring your own lunch there is nothing. And I wager you did not think to bring a lunch. Did you even eat breakfast?"

"Mother," John stayed her gently. "I shall be fine until dinner. But I would like to go to my room for a bit. I am tired."

"Of course, of course. Jane, please see to some hot water for Master John. Children," she addressed the younger ones, "do not pester your big brother. Let him rest now."

Jacques, too, had seen something in his oldest son and he did not think it was just fatigue. There was being "travel tired" and there was being "world weary." John had not come home like a young man excited and ready to embark upon a new career, instead he appeared more like a man returning to his cave to lick his wounds. And what wounds might those be?

As John walked up the stairway, Jacques motioned to Jane who followed him into his study.

"Yes, Master Power?"

"Jane, would you be so kind as to bring this to John's room?" He gave her a small decanter holding about three or four shots of his best brandy with a glass.

"Of course, sir."

# Chapter 5

## A Month Later

"What is it, Jacques?" Marie asked as she walked passed his office and saw him looking sternly at a letter before him, an uncharacteristic scowl upon his face.

"Oh, come," he gestured her inside with a softer look and when she drew up close he put his arm about her waist and drew her in nearer. "I have here a letter from Martha."

"Martha?" Marie smiled. "She must be… let me think, why she must be thirteen or fourteen now, yes?" she nodded, her hand and arm gently embracing her husband's shoulders and neck. "How is she? Is it not good news?"

"It is most strange news. The child writes roughly which leaves much to interpretation, her education was short-lived, after all, but the feeling I am getting in my gut says she is quite frightened."

"Frightened? Whatever of? After living through a frontier Indian attack and sailing alone over a huge ocean with a mother who was more child than adult, what could possibly frighten her in the countryside of southern England?"

"*Ma chère amour,* you more than anyone should remember what evils the peaceful countryside can hold, *n'est-ce pas?*"

"You are right, my love, what does the girl say?" Marie swung around to lean herself upon the edge of his large desk.

"She says nothing good about her mother's father. She does write that her grandfather's second wife, Abigail, is a kind and gentle woman she is growing quite close to. But, she says, she allows her husband to dictate everything even the diet of her children. Martha says they get no milk. She does not think the children are growing as they should… at least that is what I interpret when she writes. 'They be small and poorly for their years.' And evidently the little girl has just grown so ill she cannot leave her bed."

"Does she say what the symptoms are?"

"Vomiting, stomach cramps, no appetite."

"We must ask John what he thinks it might be," Marie suggested.

"It sounds like a flux but she mentions no fever, and a flux kills much more quickly, does it not? It sounds like this has been going on with the girl for some time now."

"The flux I knew, when it came to our village, killed much more quickly," Marie nodded seriously. "And there is always most definitely a fever."

"She also writes her mother sees a lot of her old friend 'Emily' and that much of her memory has returned but she is confused as to where her sons are and wonders if they too became ill like Florence. She still doesn't remember marrying Francois Nicholet."

Jacques looked up into his wife's thoughtful face. "I imagine it would bring her too close to the events she does not wish to recall," he said quietly. "But this last is what bothers me the most. Martha writes she has not told her mother or grandfather of the coin she still has from the purse I gave her for fear he will take it away and she would be 'helpless'… that is the word she uses. And she cites as an example that she fears him finding out she is writing to us, fears he would not allow her to post this letter much less give her money for postage if she had none of her own but because she can supply postage, Martha can go to her mother's friend and ask her to post a letter for her.

"This hardly sounds like a healthy environment, does it?" Marie nodded to her husband. "Do you think the girl exaggerates?"

"I do not know, my love, I do not know."

Southern England - Three Years Earlier

They had just argued over the price of a coach ride to Penelope's home village. The driver was getting a stronger and stronger impression that something was not exactly right in the head with the matronly aged woman who acted like a rather vapid young miss until it came to shelling out coin that is.

Unfortunately, young Martha, who kept a wary eye on the purse Mister Jacques had given to her for their journey, had no idea what the prevailing costs of anything were. On the frontier, people didn't exchange coin for goods like they did in town. And even there, a small settlement on the coast of North America could not be compared to England. She just watched and learned not to take anything for granted.

Martha had diligently sewed most of the largest coins into the hem of her underskirt and discovered they helped to keep her skirts down in the windy sea breezes. The multitude of smaller coins she had divided into three purses, one she kept in her deep pocket, a much, much smaller one she gave over to her mother who insisted on being called her sister, Penelope by name, and the third Martha hid away in the most convenient spot on any given day. Today that was the bottom of her satchel.

Now, as the coach rumbled along a deeply rutted road bordered on each side by quaint stone walls, she saw a very pleasant little hamlet emerging from the rolling pastures of green. Whatever would be her grandfather's reaction, she wondered? If their places were reversed, she couldn't deny she might be a little shocked but more than pleased to meet a grandchild never met before.

If she had not been peering studiously out the coach window at the passing houses and shoppes, the change in the noise would have told her they were on cobblestones as they rode toward the market square. They came slowly to a halt and Martha stuck her head out the window.

"Are we at the vicarage?" she asked rather anxiously pulling at her bonnet.

"Sorry miss. Don't provide special service to a residence," the driver called down.

Martha thought quickly. She knew they wouldn't be able to handle their luggage alone which meant another fee to get transport to her grandfather's. And the sky was overcast which threatened rain.

"All right, then to the church. You see it?" she pointed sticking her arm through the window as well. "I can see the tower right over there. That's not a residence."

The driver sighed and decided it would be easier to drive on the short distance than to argue and try to force the American youngster out with the other one. *They certainly grow 'em up odd in the colonies,* he thought to himself and urged the horses on. *But then with the older one being ready to haggle over every penny, why should the little one be any different? They're worse than a bunch of gypsies.*

The horses headed in the direction of the hamlet church. To Martha it looked very cold and ominous. It was all made of stones, she observed. She had never seen a church made of stone before. Indeed everything seemed to be constructed of stone. The little houses, the market place, the shoppes, the church, the rectory. Martha wasn't used to seeing so much building in stone. Of course there was some timber, and stucco plaster, and thatched roofs that looked so even and thick they could have been carved from wood.

The coach pulled up in front of the church and the driver got down to assist his passengers out. He pulled their luggage down to set it in the street. He was trying to maintain a schedule and all the arguing over fare at the beginning of the trip had put him behind. As he pulled away and continued on, Martha turned to look at the vicarage next door. It too was constructed of stone and looked rather cold and un-inviting.

"Come, M- ah Penelope, we need to carry our luggage over to th' house," urged Martha.

"Surely Da has someone who could help us."

"Maybe so, but we don't know that fur sure. We don't even know if he's here an' we can't just leave it in th' street. I keep tellin' you, it's been a while since you was home."

"Oh, very well," Penelope capitulated and picked up her bags.

The two struggled slowly with the heavy luggage but finally found themselves standing before the large front entry. Martha pulled the bell. It took a minute or two but finally a pale young woman opened the door.

"Yes?" she asked.

"Well who are you and what happened to Tabby?" Penelope asked.

"Tabby?" the woman responded, a confused look on her face.

"Yes, Tabby, Da's housekeeper," Penelope replied. "You must have replaced her. I'm Da's daughter Penelope. Is he home?" She walked in without invitation, right passed the woman, leaving her luggage behind.

"I'm sorry but you must be confused. I'm not the housekeeper, I'm Mistress Richmond, Reverend Richmond's wife," she responded while Martha struggled to bring all the pieces into the hallway by herself.

At this Penelope stopped still in her tracks. She looked about in confusion.

"This is the vicarage, is it not?"

"Yes."

"And the Reverend Thomas Richmond is the vicar?"

"Yes, of course."

"But then, I don't understand, where is my mother?"

The new Mistress Richmond looked at Martha in dismay.

"We've only just arrived from the colonies, ma'am," Martha said quickly. "It's been a long journey an' she's very tired. Might there be someplace she can lie down fur a spell? An' I'll sort-a fill in th' details after." Martha spoke very maturely for a child just turned eleven years old. She was aware that she didn't have the luxury of being a child anymore.

"Oh, well, of course. I'm certain that will be all right. Come this way," responded Mistress Richmond and led the way up the stairs.

Upon reaching the top of the stairs, Penelope immediately took the lead and marched to her old bedroom.

"Here we are, Tulip. Oh, I see you've changed the décor in my absence. Why ever would you do that? I was perfectly happy with what was here."

Mistress Richmond said nothing. The décor had in fact grown very shabby and she had convinced her husband of the need to update it as the official guest room of the rectory.

"Come Penelope, time to have a lie down," Martha urged. "Yer plum wore out." Penelope sat as Martha removed her mother's capelet and shoes and helped to raise her legs up onto the bed. She drew a light coverlet over Penelope while Mistress Richmond pulled the drapes shut to darken the room.

As Mistress Richmond and Martha exited the bedroom, Martha felt compelled to explain.

"I am sorry, ma'am. I know this must all seem very odd. Penelope is the preacher's daughter and my mother but she thinks she's my sister and calls me 'Tulip.' Perhaps my grandfather can explain that one. My actual name is Martha."

"How do you do, Martha. Please call me Abigail. Would you like a cup of tea?"

Martha nodded. "Oh, yes, ma'am, that would be nice."

Martha followed the woman and found herself in the kitchen which surprised her because it was right there, a part of the main house, but then everything was made of stone. She was invited to take a seat while Abigail set up a lovely tea service complete with cream, sugar, and scones with little individual pots of clotted cream and jam for each of them.

"Shall I pour?" Abigail asked while picking up a delicately decorated teacup and saucer. "Do you take cream and sugar?"

"Never had neither one before, guess I could try 'em," replied Martha. In the Power family nursery they had had milk and water, apple juice and lemonade but never tea unless someone was being doctored for something. Then when her mother had been rescued and mistook Martha for her sister, the Powers had brought Martha in to the adult table where she found herself having to be the adult to her mother. There watered wine was most common.

"Ma went through somethin' fierce with th' injuns back in th' colonies an' it caused her to lose memory of everything back to when she were jist a girl. I have a letter from Mister Power explainin' it all. Ma needs… care," she added softly.

"I see," the young matron nodded not unkindly. "My husband should be home shortly. Rather than having to repeat everything twice, why don't you just relax and enjoy your scones."

"They are delicious," Martha grinned, trying to remember to use her napkin. "This here clot-cream is jist wonderful."

"Thank you." Abigail said with a little smile, "I'm so very glad you like it." She observed that the young girl appeared to be ravenously hungry, packing away the scones, clotted cream, and jam with gusto. She dearly wished her napping Allister and Florence ate with such an appetite. "You appear to be quite hungry. I'll fetch some more."

When Reverend Thomas Richmond arrived home, Martha was disappointed that he seemed indifferent to meeting her. She presented him with the letter from Jacques Power. After reading it through carefully, he set it aside and looked at Martha. They were seated in the parlor and Abigail had joined them.

"So you are my granddaughter," he began rather sternly. He was dressed all in black with a stylized white stock and very stiff, short jabot at his throat. "Your mother had written home about the death of your father."

Martha nodded. "I don't really remember him very well, sir. I was pretty young."

"So why don't you pick up the story from where you do remember and tell me in your own words what has happened to bring you to my doorstep."

Martha squirmed a little sitting on the fancy settee.

"Well, I kinda remember Ma sewing for some lady. She was always bringin' home pretty clothes but they weren't her's she jist sewed on 'em. Then she married Mister Nicholet. An' I remember all the singin' an' dancin' an' music in Mister Jacques' old barn. He were Mister Nicholet's boss an' threw him an' Ma a big ol' weddin' party."

Richmond inwardly cringed at the colonial accent and poor grammar but said nothing and continued to listen.

"Then we all went to th' frontier to homestead. We worked real hard but we jist had no luck 'cause th' injuns kept plaguin' us. Come th' fifth year, after suffering through a terrible rough winter, th' injuns attacked us full out. Pa... Mister Nicholet told us to call him *Pa*... Pa gave me a bag of food an' a canteen of water an' told me to run off an' hide an' then after two days I was to run to th' coast an' find Mistress Power what come from France. She's a real nice lady. So I did what Pa told me to an' I don't know what exactly happened back at th' homestead but when I got to th' coast, Mister Jacques, he headed up a rescue party to go help.

"When he come back, he an' some of his men were hurt; th' injuns had attacked them too. He said they kilt my brothers, left Pa near dead at th' bottom of our well, an' took Ma away for ransom. Pa died of th' fever but Mister Jacques got Ma back only... well, she don't recognize me as her daughter, sir. She don't remember my brothers, don't remember Mister Nicholet or even my real father. Mister Jacques said th' injuns done things to my brothers that weren't fit for any man to see, much less a woman. He wouldn't tell us what but Ma must'a seen it all an' she don't want to remember it."

"I see... so what does she remember?" Richmond asked.

"Well, she knows she's Penelope Richmond, sir... only she thinks she's still a young girl an' she kept telling everyone she wanted to go home so Mister Jacques he arranged everything an' sent us home... to here."

"I see and who paid for all that?" Richmond asked sternly as if he was expecting to receive a bill.

"Why he did, sir, paid for it all an' Mistress Marie... his wife... she outfit me an' Ma with a whole new set of clothes. I'd pretty much grew out of th' ones I had on my back. Even bought us th' luggage to pack 'em in."

"Quite a wealthy man, your Mister Jacques, I'd say. But don't expect that kind of charity here. We're used to hard times and simple living. Everyone must work for their keep here, *earn thy bread by the sweat of thy brow*, says the Good Book."

"Yes, sir."

"And what exactly is your mother capable of doing?"

"Well, I suppose as long as you treat her like she was sixteen an' think back to what she could do then, it would be about th' same."

Richmond stared. This young girl was entirely too brazen to his way of thinking. Didn't seem to know her place but then battling wild Indians must have had some effect.

"Could you answer me one question?" Martha asked frankly. "Who is *Tulip?* That's who Ma thinks I am."

"Tulip was a pet name for her younger sister. She died some years ago," Richmond replied.

"Oh… sorry to hear that."

"Yes, quite so," the older man replied gruffly.


Dinner that night was strangely quiet and subdued. It was nothing like the Power family table. Talking was discouraged and yet Richmond insisted his wife's children sit at the table as well. Seven year old Florence and nine year old Allister had learned to sit quietly under Richmond's judgmental eye. Martha looked at the children across from her. They were blonde, like their mother, extraordinarily pale and somber. Martha found herself wondering if they ever went outdoors to play. And they seemed so small for their ages.

"Come children, where are your appetites? You've barely touched your food," Richmond admonished. "Surely you're not shy. See how Martha attacks her food."

If the comment was meant to somehow embarrass Martha, it did not. She grinned broadly and turned to Abigail. "Best vittles I've eaten since we left Chartes Landing," she said nodding appreciatively.

Abigail gave a weak smile.

Penelope laughed.

"Oh, Tulip, you are so lucky you are still growing, you can eat whatever you please. Would you like seconds?"

"Don't mind if I do," Martha replied and accepted the serving bowl Abigail was handing to her.

"Well, if you are not going to eat," Richmond said roughly to his two stepchildren, "then put another spoon of sugar into your tea. At least it will give you the energy to last until bedtime."

"Thomas, I dislike seeing them have so much sugar," Abigail protested weakly.

"Nonsense! They must eat something," he responded brusquely and turned to the pair. "Now drink up, drink up."

Martha watched as under the iron cast gaze of the reverend each child stirred another spoonful of sugar into his or her tea and dutifully drank it down. It seemed to her that milk would have been the more appropriate beverage.

"What about you?" Richmond had turned his attentions to Martha. "Don't you like sugar in your tea?"

Martha shook her head. "No, thank you, sir. I tried it this afternoon. Too sweet for me. We're not use to so much sweet in th' colonies, cream is jist fine."

Richmond gave her a hard stare as if she was challenging his judgment.

"I wish to invite Beatrix and Emily over for tea tomorrow, Da, would that be all right?" Penelope asked brightly.

"Who?" Richmond looked at his daughter.

"You know, Beatrix Cummings and Emily Owens, they're my best friends. Mum always allowed me to invite them and it feels like its been ages since we've seen each other."

"Oh, yes, yes… might be just the thing to bring you into reality. The Owens girl married awhile back and is now Emily Billings."

"Emily married?" Penelope responded with a half giggle. "But why didn't she invite me to her wedding?"

"Undoubtedly because you were in America," Richmond replied. "As for the Cummings girl, she's out in the church cemetery."

"No! You mean…? Oh, Da, no, not Bea. Whatever happened?" Tears had sprung to Penelope's eyes.

"Complications from childbirth, I believe. Both she and the baby died. Married a fellow by the name of Cole as I recall, moved away but they brought her back here to be buried."

Penelope was sobbing and excused herself from the table.

Martha looked at Richmond. He seemed almost pleased with the shock his news had created.

"Might wake her up to reality," he muttered as he turned back to his supper.

"I'll go see to my mother," Martha said and left the table.

Martha found her mother in the bedroom they were to share, stretched out face down on the bed, sobbing pitifully. She approached the bed and stroked her mother's back.

"Please don't cry no more," she pleaded.

"They were my best friends," she wailed, "how could they both get married and not invite me?"

"Maybe they did," the girl said softly still stroking her mother's back.

"What do you mean?" Penelope raised her head. "I would have remembered."

"Mm...ah, Penelope, there's an awful lot you don't remember," Martha said sadly.

"What?"

"Your memory… it ain't all there."

"Tulip, whatever are you saying?" Penelope drew up to sit on the bed.

"You.. you were married too."

"What?! Why that's nonsense. Don't you think if I had been married I would remember it?" she almost shouted.

"Do you remember Officer Carver?"

"Who?"

"Samuel Carver… he was a young officer you met at a dance."

Penelope stared into space and then shook her head. "Maybe, maybe, I don't remember."

"You married him, Ma, an' I'm not Tulip… I'm his daughter an' your daughter."

"No. No. That isn't so, it isn't so. Why are you talking such nonsense? I don't want to talk anymore. Leave me alone, Tulip, you're being very cruel. It's a shock to hear that Bea is gone. I can't wait to talk with Emily," she sighed. "I want to sleep now."

Martha sighed as well and wiped a tear from her own eye before she left the room.

As she stepped back into the hallway, she heard Reverend Richmond say, "disruptive to the household they can at least do some chores."

"But I can't be ordering your daughter around, Thomas. She's older than I am."

"But you are the Mistress here!"

Martha diplomatically cleared her throat and coughed. Then she entered the dining room.

"Ma's gone to bed for th' night. Guess hearing that that Bea person has passed hit her pretty hard," she said quietly as she took her seat to finish her dinner.

"Oh, that's grown cold. Let me warm it for you," offered Abigail.

"No, never mind," she said cheerfully, "it's fine. We got used to eatin' what we could, when we could, an' however we could. Mister Nicholet, he never complained once," she added and looked to her grandfather.

Armed with a crude map and an address, Martha accompanied her mother to the home of Emily Owens, now Billings. They walked the crooked twisting streets with the houses all joined one to the other. At last they found the number they were searching for.

The woman who answered the door vaguely resembled Emily's mother.

"Hello, may I speak to Emily, please? Tell her Penelope Richmond has come to call."

"Penelope?" The woman gasped in surprise. "Is that you? Gracious, you look wonderful! Come in, come in. Let's go to the parlor. You're just in time for tea. Oh, tell me everything," the woman gushed in delight and steered the two toward the parlor. "Sophie," she called. "Sophie, put the kettle on and we'll have tea a bit early. One of my best friends has come to visit."

"But I'm here to see Emily," Penelope said in confusion.

"Oh, you're such a tease," Emily laughed heartily as they both sat upon the settee. "Surely I haven't changed that much… and if I have how naughty of you, Penny, not to pretend otherwise."

"Don't call me that, please. I've always hated that nickname. Thought it made me sound cheap," Penelope said testily.

"And who are you?" Emily asked looking to Martha who had taken a seat in a small chair.

"I'm her daughter Martha, ma'am, but Ma thinks I'm her sister Tulip."

The smile left Emily's pleasantly cheerful face. "Why Tulip died two years after Penelope left for the colonies. Surely her mother or the reverend wrote and told her so?"

"Don't know, ma'am," Martha replied softly.

Tea was soon served and as Penelope sat quietly staring in disbelief at Emily Owens who was now Emily Billings, the mother of six and a heavier set, matronly looking woman with laugh lines around her eyes, Martha told Emily everything she could of what had happened to her mother.

"Now that we're here, I've been trying to tell Ma I ain't Tulip, I'm her daughter Martha. I figure th' more she talks to people she used to know an' see's they aren't like they used to be, th' more it will start to make some sense to her. She avoids lookin' in th' mirror. An' keeps actin' like she was sixteen."

"Penelope," Emily spoke softly to her guest. "We were the same age, remember?"

Penelope looked at her girlhood friend and barely nodded her head.

"If we were the same age then, it only stands to reason we're the same age now, that can't change and I'm going to be thirty-two on my next birthday. And you are the only one I would ever say that to because a lady never tells her age," she smiled tearfully.

"Emily?"

Emily nodded and reached for her friend's hand.

"Oh, Emily. I've seen too much pain."

"I know, lamb, I know," Emily said sliding over to gather her childhood friend to her bosom and rock her gently.

Emily sent her oldest boy to the vicarage with a message that Penelope and Martha would be spending a few days at the Billings home with a request to pack a bag he could bring back for them. Martha thought it a wonderful idea. She was seeing progress being made with her mother, and it was encouraging.

A few days stay turned into a month with Martha going back and forth with updates to the Richmond household, updates she preferred to pass along to Abigail when the reverend wasn't there.

Emily brought out a small box containing old letters she had received from Penelope in the early years when things were exciting and new in her marriage to Carver, and they reread them repeatedly.

The two older women spent a good deal of time talking about the past and eventually that past including Penelope's meeting Second Lieutenant Samuel Carver. Their wedding, the birth of their first child, their move to the colonies, the birth of their second child, their move to the fort on the Delaware Bay, and the birth of Martha. The doors of Penelope's memory were starting to open.

"It's a sad burden you have been bearing, to see your mum so stricken," Emily smiled encouragingly. "But don't you worry, we'll soon have her sitting, right as rain." Emily invited the girl to go play with her children and be a child again herself.

The two older women spent a good deal of time in the gardens in the back of the house. Every square foot was cultivated and pruned into beautiful patterns of lush flowers and greenery. The gardens ran the full length of the row housing which curved about and lined the other side of the gardens as well. It was understood that this was commonly held ground and the gardener was paid by a contribution from every household. The two friends walked and talked, enjoying the beauty of the grounds away from the street and the privacy away from the outside world.

"I still don't understand why Da waited so long to tell me Mum had died. If we had only known sooner, Em, it could have been life changing. Truly. I think Samuel could have obtained Compassionate Leave. We could have come home, seen everyone and most importantly, Samuel would have never gone out on that final patrol that took his life."

Emily nodded. "But you can't look at it that way. There's no telling… could be the ship you took would have capsized and you'd have all been drown. You can't second guess the Fates. But I suspect your father's motives were very self-serving."

"What do you mean?" Penelope asked as she stooped to pick one perfect and brilliantly red hollyhock.

"Frankly, I saw the way he was looking at the widow from the moment her husband died. I'm sorry Penelope, your father may be up there at the pulpit raising hell fire and brimstone for everyone on Sundays but the older I get, the more I see hypocrisy. I am sorry. I shouldn't be saying that about my dear friend's father."

"No-no, go on, be honest. If I can't count on you to be honest with me, who can I count on?"

"Well, it's only my opinion but I don't think he wanted you to come home and get in the way of his plans. Your mother's body was barely cold and he had the young widow courted and wed."

"Did she have money?" Penelope asked as they continued down the path.

"Quite a bit, from what I heard."

"I thought so," Penelope nodded.

"I like Abigail. She's a decent sort. A little too meek perhaps but there's nothing she won't do for a body in need. Although I dare say he's clipped her wings a bit there."

"Her children seem so fragile."

"Really? They were a couple of chubby rosy cheeked dears before the wedding. I remember thinking they looked just like cherubs supporting their mother in her mourning."

"They're still rosy cheeked but they are so thin and subdued in his presence like they are afraid to make a sound."

"Oh, well, I suppose that's natural enough," laughed Emily, "after all he is the evil stepfather and children do stretch out as they grow."

Martha was happy to hear real laughter coming from the far end of the garden.

Penelope and Martha returned home a month later to discover little seven year old Florence was stricken with a stomach upset. Abigail was beside herself with worry. With abdominal cramping and vomiting, the poor little sprite was not eating at all.

Chartes Landing - Three Years Later

"Marie? A second letter from Martha," Jacques called to his wife as he waved the missive in the air.

"So soon?" Marie came hurrying in from the garden, wiping her hands on her apron. "What does it say?"

Jacques broke the seal and scanned the page.

"*Mon Dieu,* Florence, Penelope's little stepsister has died. And the little boy has now fallen ill in the same way and the doctor can not determine a cause… but he bleeds her as he did the girl." Immediately he muttered, "Surely that cannot be good. John would say it weakens one."

"What else does she write, Jacques?"

"She begs us to come and rescue them… before *he* has killed them all."

"He?"

"I think she was afraid to write the name but do you not think she means Richmond himself?"

"Oh, Jacques, how terrible! That is her grandfather! What a dreadful man. She is but fourteen, no one will listen to her suspicions or take them seriously, and if Richmond discovers how she thinks, he might kill her too."

"So you think John is right, that it is poison?" Jacques asked.

"When did he say that?"

"When I showed him the first letter," Jacques replied.

"Really? Then we should leave immediately."

"We?" Jacques arched a brow.

"You do not think I would let you leave without me, do you?" she asked wrapping her arms around his neck. "Sarah will look after the children. The mill and the store are both in good hands. And I think we should take John with us, he has been a bit at odds of late, this would be just the thing to awaken his spirits."

Jacques could not help but smile at his darling wife, always eager to help someone.

"Very well, my dearest," he agreed while holding her cheek tenderly in his hand, "you go pack some bags and I shall see to other details." And he gave her a soft warm kiss.

Fair winds and a fast ship saw the threesome to Southampton in record time but the black crepe on the door of the village rectory a half day's coach ride to the northeast had them thinking they were too late.

Martha opened the door.

"Mister Jacques!" she cried and threw herself into his arms as she hugged him fiercely. "And Mistress Marie!" she cried again and almost knocked Marie over. Martha had grown at least four inches since she had stumbled into the General Store at Chartes Landing. "You don't know how glad I am..." she almost started weeping.

She pulled the door shut and proceeded to walk them back down the path to the street. "Where are your bags?" Martha asked quickly.

"We checked into the inn on the square," Marie replied.

"Let's take us a little stroll while I show you the village."

"Martha, we really do not need a tour of the village," Jacques began.

A few steps on the street and Martha whispered hoarsely, "I only said that in case there were ears listening." She smiled at them fiercely and then her smile began to crumple into a sob. "You have no idea how glad I am to see you. Little Florence is gone... and I fear Allister will go next. And Abigail, that be the Mistress Richmond, has been looking rather poorly to me. It's like a house of death!"

"Then Allister is still alive?" Jacques spoke. "We saw the crepe."

"They keep it up a year and yes, Allister is still with us but he struggles. He's really a good little fellow," Martha murmured. "I'm gunna... going to," she corrected herself, "tell Abigail that Doctor John is here to offer a second opinion."

"How is your mother?" Jacques asked.

"Ma seems to be well, for now at least, but who knows how long that will last."

"So you think these illnesses are... unnatural?" Marie suggested softly also noticing how Martha had improved the clarity of her speech.

"I don't know about that, ma'am," Martha replied earnestly, "but I think they're being poisoned."

Marie looked at Jacques who looked at John. "Well there we have it," she said.

"We can go back now and act all normal. I'm sure Abigail will let you look at Allister, if *he* ain't... isn't at home. Often he sends his clerk over to spy on everyone."

Back at the house, Martha made awkward introductions and Abigail was more than glad to have Doctor John look at her son. John immediately recognized all the classic signs of arsenic poisoning.

"Mistress Richmond," John spoke to the mother, "I'm very surprised your other doctor did not recognize the signs."

"Signs?" Abigail repeated weakly. She was feeling a bit nauseous.

Just then Richmond himself stormed into the house. "Who are these people and why are they here?"

"Monsieur Richmond," Jacques spoke up immediately. "Allow me to make introductions. I am Jacques-Jean Power and this is my wife, Madam Marie Power, and my son Doctor John Power. We are long time friends of your granddaughter in the New World, and led the rescue of her mother, your daughter, from the savages. But we were especially acquainted with her former husband Francois Nicholet. The man worked for me for many, many years."

Richmond paused his bluster to nod and ask, "So what brings you here?"

"My son offered his services to Madame Richmond for a second opinion and has examined your stepson," Jacques said smoothly and looked at John, "he was just about to tell us his diagnosis, monsieur."

John nodded. "May I see your hands, sir?"

"What?" Richmond asked in confusion. John assumed cooperation and examined Richmond's hand. Aside from ink stains on his fingers there was nothing unusual.

"And your hands, Mistress Richmond?" John held her hands and looked at her nails. "Thank you. Do you have any servants?" John asked of Richmond.

"Only the cook," he replied.

"And has he… or she..."

"She," Abigail confirmed.

"Has she," John restated, "had any health complaints of late, or had flux like symptoms?"

"No not at all," Abigail answered.

"I am sorry to say your child has all the signs of long term exposure to arsenic and is being poisoned by it."

Abigail gasped and sat down heavily in a nearby chair."

"Arsenic?! How do you know?" Richmond challenged.

"I think the more important question is how is it your family physician did not know? It is as obvious as can be."

"So you think the cook has been poisoning our food?" Richmond asked.

"If that were the case," offered John, "you would all show signs of the poisoning and since only the child and Madam Richmond seem to have been affected then one can also conclude almost certainly that it is not from a source such as the drinking water or the soil in your vegetable garden which would affect everyone in the household equally."

"I have it too?" Abigail shrunk back.

"This is ridiculous. Who could possibly wish to poison my family? I want you out of my home," snapped Richmond.

"Not until the authorities have been called in," Jacques stated. "The lives of Madame Richmond and her son are at risk." With Jacques and John both standing square shouldered and armed with pistols and foils, Richmond became quiet.

Just then Penelope arrived from a visit with Emily.

"Whatever is going on?" she asked recognizing the Powers.

"Ma," Martha ran to her. "Doctor John says Allister is being poisoned by arsenic. Which means Florence was probably done the same and Abigail shows signs of it, too."

"Poisoned!" cried out Penelope and looked to her father. "Is there not enough killing and bloodshed in this world without taking out those we love with poison?" she all but screamed. "Did you poison my mother too, you bitter, stingy, hateful old man."

If looks could kill, Penelope too would be dead.

"How dare you accuse me you ingrate," Richmond snapped. "Why would I wish to poison my own family? How do we know it was not you who returned to us acting like a mad woman?"

"Penelope, it's important to remember that nothing has been proven yet." John said calmly as he looked at her hands as well. "There are tests to run and evidence to gather and for this we need the local authorities. Can you go for the constabulary, please?"

"With pleasure," Penelope nodded. "Martha, come with me child."

"Yes, ma."

By the time they returned with the local constables, John had run several tests on strands of their hair which indeed proved that both Allister and Abigail had ingested a goodly quantity of arsenic over a considerable length of time. And John had ordered the cook to contact the local dairyman and procure milk for Allister and Madam Richmond, as well as Martha.

Abigail turned to John. "Tell me, Doctor, would that have caused me to lose my baby?"

"When were you pregnant?" he asked.

"Two years after we were married."

"It's possible, I cannot say for certain but I doubt that you have been that severely dosed for all this time or you would have died by now. We need to discover the source. If it was not in your food then it had to be in your drink. What did you all drink in common?"

"Tea... but Thomas always drank tea as well," she sighed.

"But he never used the sugar," Martha popped up in the midst of their conversation. "He never used sugar, and you used sugar moderately because of concerns for your figure but he was always forcing sugar on your children. 'Here,'" she mocked in a low voice imitative of her grandfather, "'have another spoonful of sugar so you have the energy to last until bedtime. Now drink up, drink up!'" she growled.

"The sugar!" Penelope exclaimed. "You wouldn't drink your tea with sugar and I stayed away from it out of concerns for my waistline. Can you hide arsenic in sugar, Doctor Power?"

"Yes, of course, it's white, tasteless, and has no smell."

"The dining room," Abigail said and led them to the sideboard where a large sugar bowl sat. "We always had to use this particular bowl on the table, Thomas insisted. Test this, Doctor, I bet you will find your arsenic."

John set about doing tests that proved the sugar to be soundly laced with arsenic.

"Now the sugar in the kitchen," she said and led him into the kitchen where they found the cook's supply of sugar stored in a very large glass jar. It proved to be totally arsenic free. "And when he wanted lemonade," Abigail muttered to herself, "he always insisted the cook make it here in the kitchen and if it was not sweet enough, he sent it back to her to sweeten."

Abigail walked back to where Thomas sat silently upon his chair. Gathering all the strength she could muster she slapped him soundly across the face.

"You monster," she said steadily "day after day you shoved arsenic down my babies' throats as if it was harmless and all the while you knew you were killing them. My poor Florence. Too bad you can only hang 'til you are dead once. So tell us, just for clarity. Did you poison the first wife also? Penelope deserves to know."

"I think it's very convenient that this one," Richmond nodded toward Martha, "not only refused to use sugar but then knew precisely where to point to the source."

"Are you accusing my daughter?" screamed Penelope.

"With all the wild savage things she's seen in the colonies, why not her?"

"If you would allow us to exhume the body, we could put the matter to rest," offered John.

"Absolutely not," thundered Richmond, "it's sacrilege and I won't allow it!"

"But I will allow you to examine my little Florence," sobbed Abigail. "And she grew sickly long before Penelope and Martha arrived at our door."

Thomas Richmond looked at his wife and sneered.

Richmond was taken into custody. The contents of the sugar bowl was taken as evidence.

"Thank you, Doctor Power, sir," said the head constable. "Will you be around to stand as a witness?"

John looked quickly at his parents. "I don't know, Constable, I suppose that depends on how quickly the trial will be held. My parents and I are going back to the colonies in a week or two."

"Well, sir, if you don't mind coming down to make a formal statement. At least we'll have that on record."

"Of course," John agreed. "But first I must treat young Allister and his mother to a medicinal purge as quickly as possible."

Florence's body was brought up from the grave. John performed the autopsy and tests with the village coroner as well as the village doctor as witnesses. The evidence was conclusive. Florence had been poisoned with arsenic and over a long enough time as to preclude Martha or Penelope having anything to do with it.

Thomas Richmond was formally charged with murder, judged, and sentenced to the gallows.

"Must we exhume your first wife's body or will you tell us if she too was poisoned," John asked as the courtroom proceedings ended.

"Yes, as well as that insipid little Tulip who had no intention of ever getting married and getting out of here but planned to be a parasite for the rest of her life," Richmond bit out.

"Ohh," Abigail gasped, "Why, Thomas, why? Does money mean that much to you?" she asked with growing anguish.

He said nothing.

"Time to go back to your cell," said the attending constable. "Ain't goin' to be spendin' none of that money I'd say."

"So what will you do now?" Marie asked Abigail as they all sat in the dining room having a light dinner. The large sugar bowl that always used to grace the table was gone.

"I still am rather shaken by who I married and what it has cost me," Abigail said softly and shuddered. John had given her a mild sedative. "Allister must be my first priority. The poor boy. I think I shall take him on holiday to the seashore and perhaps Penelope and Martha would like to join us. And then on to Bath for the waters."

"Oh, that's sounds like fun. A seashore with no injuns to worry about," said Martha.

"Why, Martha, you did not have to worry about Indians at our seashore," smiled Marie.

"I guess I just feel better having them an ocean away," the girl replied and looked to her plate.

"You mustn't forget that you also need some recuperation," John spoke with professional attention to Abigail. "You were on your way to becoming as ill as Allister. "I shall administer another purge to the boy tomorrow morning and when he is settled we'll see how you feel."

"Whatever you say, Doctor," Abigail nodded submissively. John Power was entirely too young and good looking to be a doctor, she thought recklessly. Doctors should all be old and fat.

"What I was really asking," said Marie, again turning to Abigail, "is have you given any thought to how changed your circumstances have become? Surely a new vicar will be sought for this parish and this will be his house, will it not? Where will you go? And in what I presume will be mere days, Monsieur Richmond will be executed and you will again be independent. A widow of means. All of your wealth will return to you, and his wealth as well. I doubt not his accounts will be surprising."

"But anything that was not mine to begin with… really belongs to his children, Penelope and her siblings, does it not? I shall look for another house, but I should be happy to share my roof with Penelope and Martha… the rest have their own homes."

"I suspect that will all be for you to work out with the family lawyers," commented Jacques with a wry smile, "I pray they are better at their jobs than the family physician. As for us, I am most happy that Martha wrote and that we could be of service but we do need to return to our home. Summer shall be over before we know it."

Later Martha caught John by himself in the hall.

"Doctor John, when do you think Ma will get the rest of her memories back?"

"I can't say, Martha. Perhaps she never will, perhaps she never should. She has shown tremendous progress but perhaps your time on the frontier is just too painful. Personally, I would not encourage her to remember seeing your brothers killed. It was both bloody and truly savage and something no mother should see happen to her child. If forgetfulness is how the Good Lord protects her from the savageness, let it be."

Martha looked pensively at John who looked rather sad to her. "Yes, sir. I guess I can understand that."

"Now, if you're ever back in the colonies, be sure to look us up. And if I ever find myself back over here, I will do the same," he smiled weakly.

Martha was gangly and awkward but she was able to go up on tip-toe and kiss John's cheek. "Thank you for everything, Doctor John, and God bless you."

He said nothing, but nodded.

# *Chapter 6*

## *New Jersey Colony - Autumn 1714*

The sudden crack of thunder covered the howl of laughter emanating from Phillip as he slid from his horse and approached his brother. John was sitting in the very middle of a mud hole, his fine buff colored breeches undoubtedly stained beyond recovery, his gray, light wool coat splashed over with mud with its flared skirt wicking up water to its fitted waist. Dirty speckles dotted his handsome face which had drawn from startled surprise into a deep scowl.

"Brother," Phillip shouted as he extended his arm, "you look as though you could use a hand!"

"Damn!" was all John could utter as he grasped his brother's hand and felt the suction and heard the *urckka* as he left his muddy seating. Once on his feet he sought a clean spot on the simple linen shirt under his coat on which to wipe his hand before he gingerly wiped at a bit of mud too near his right eye. It wasn't easy to find an unsoiled spot.

"I thought for certain you saw that branch," Phillip said with just a hint of ridicule in his voice. It was not often that he was able to criticize his big brother.

"If I had seen it," John growled in reaction to the impudence of his younger brother, "I would have dodged it!"

"I think I saw a light up yonder," Phillip changed the subject, not wishing to push his brother's usually mild temper any further. "Do you want to seek shelter?" Phillip had to shout above the increasing sounds of the storm.

"Shelter from what?" John muttered, "I'd say I've already gotten the worst. The rain could only help wash me down."

Phillip snorted another suppressed chuckle. "Well, I haven't and could use a bit of shelter before I look as bad as you. Come, let's go this way."

John was not used to letting Phillip dictate to him but at the moment the practical streak John had inherited from his mother told him that being stubborn and catching pneumonia by staying out in the storm was not the wisest choice. He remounted his horse, cringing at the feel of the mud squishing beneath his rear, and followed.

The two brothers soon found their way to a crude farm house and after taking the liberty of leaving their horses unsaddled within the shelter of a small barn, they knocked on the cabin door. The rain was beginning to come down in hard sheets.

The farmer opened the door, musket in hand.

"We are sorry to disturb you, sir," Phillip said in a graciously cavalier manner learned from Jacques. "But my brother and I seek shelter until the storm abates. Please do not be frightened," he could barely contain his mirth. "My brother had a rendezvous with a very large mud puddle a bit down the road. Perhaps we could stay in your barn?"

The farmer thrust his lantern closer to the pair, studied them for a long moment and then stepped back and gestured them into the dwelling.

"Git t' the fire," he muttered gruffly, "'fore ya kitch yer death."

The brothers entered quickly, Phillip carefully shutting the door behind them against a gust of wind. John, mindful of the filth he brought with him, took care not to touch anything but went to stand by the fire, grateful for the warming heat.

The cabin was like many that had sprung up in the colonial wilderness. Crude split board construction dabbed with clay, a large stone fireplace dominating the singular room and a loft above, accessible by a small ladder attached to the wall. Dried onions and bags of beans hung from the rafters and a few shelves held crockery and utensils. The furnishings were sparse and mostly hand-wrought.

"You on foot?" the farmer asked.

"No, I'm afraid we have rather assumed your hospitality and settled our horses in your barn," John replied politely.

The farmer nodded a grunt and studied the two young men. Although one was filthy, they looked much a like, were probably brothers. He recognized the fine tailoring in their clothing even under the mud, and a refinement in their speech and manner. They wasn't common road tramps, certainly didn't look like highwaymen, and he weren't a mean man to not give a helping hand to a stranger in need.

"Git some hot water for 'em 'n' fetch a change of clothes," he said gruffly and for the first time the brothers noticed a movement in the darker corner. A young woman appeared from the shadows, her head bent in what they assumed was shyness. She was thin, almost bony in appearance as her simple calico dress hung unflatteringly upon her, held in place with a large white apron. Her limp fine hair was pulled back in an unbecoming bun at the nape of her neck which did nothing to hide the fact that her ears stuck out from her head to the extreme. With small eyes, sallow skin, and almost no chin, it was a kindness to consider her plain as opposed to downright homely.

"Actually, I have clothes in my saddlebags in the barn..." began John but he was cut short.

"No need t' go back out in that mess," the farmer said and they could all clearly hear the rain pouring in heavy torrents on the roof.

John and Phillip expected to exchange introductions but the farmer had no acquaintance with the niceties of polite society. In his mind, the girl needed only to go about her business which she did with amazing speed.

In a matter of minutes, she had strung a rope from a notch about midway over the mantel to the other wall, draped two sheets to create a privacy screen, positioned several buckets of hot water with a basin and wash cloth, and brought a clean homespun shirt and worn trousers for the muddy young man.

John accepted these gratefully. Then, when the girl retreated to her side of the privacy screen he doffed his filthy garments, sponged himself clean and slipped into the fresh clothing which was large in the waist but a bit tight in the shoulders. Phillip, meanwhile, had hung his wet coat up to dry and was drying and warming himself by the fire and watching his brother in amusement.

"Those aren't going to be worth the washing," Phillip observed, indicating the mud drenched clothing.

"Well, I have to make do, don't I?" John muttered in reply, "I only brought one other set. I just need to scrub them a bit."

"Don't do for no man t' be washin' no clothes," the farmer interjected from the other side of the hanging sheets. Then, he burst through and took the clothes before John could stop him. "My girl'l see t' these."

John was caught off-guard and relinquished the clothing without objection. With a look at Phillip, he began folding the sheeting up, leaving it neatly on the rope but clearing it from partitioning the room. The two brothers were not used to women being treated with such a lack of courtesy. Even the indentured servants in their parents' home were treated with respect.

"My brother and I thank you for your kindness," John said, managing to appear dignified despite his poorly fitting clothes. He stood before the fire looking from the farmer to the girl, obviously including her. "Please allow me to properly make introductions. I am John Power and this is my brother, Phillip. We are on our way up river to our lumber camp and were rather unexpectedly caught by this storm. We very much appreciate your hospitality."

"Name's Danner," the farmer muttered with a nod.

"And, Mister Danner, is this your daughter?" John pressed, not liking the way the man was ignoring the girl.

The farmer only nodded his head.

"Surely, she has a name."

"Gert," the farmer grunted and looked as if to say, *what is it to you?*

"Gert? Is that short for Gertrude?" John smiled warmly at the young girl.

"Yes," she said faintly, smiling shyly in response to him, her small eyes missing nothing. She was very aware that these two were, in fact, the most handsome men she had ever laid eyes on. Beautiful, was the only word she could think of. Tall, strong, healthy, well-made bodies, without sagging flesh or an over abundance of body hair protruding from every orifice, she'd never seen *young* men before. Even their faces astounded her. With long curling lashes, neatly arched brows, and smooth tight skin, even with their wet hair they were so pleasing to look upon that she was reminded of a story her grandmother had told her of when the angels had come in the form of men to visit Abraham. Might these two be angels in the disguise of young gentlemen? Might they be testing them for their hospitality to strangers? If so, it was indeed fortunate that her pa had let them in. Whoever they were, she was awestruck and totally smitten.

"Well, Maiden Gertrude, I want to apologize for the trouble I have caused you,"

John spoke with all sincerity, looking at her with friendly warmth in his eyes. "It is most kind of you to assist my brother and me on this inhospitable night." She was struck dumb for several moments mesmerized by his attention and staring at the black edge about his irises, black that matched his lashes.

"It ain't nothin'," the girl stammered at last, clearly blushing and the farmer was not looking pleased. Phillip was concerned that they would soon find themselves out in the cold barn, or worse, if his brother didn't leave well enough alone. It was bad enough that the girl looked totally besotted. The poor thing probably knew no one her age in the whole world, hidden away as she was, an only child on the frontier with her father, at least he assumed she was an only child. But if Danner suspected John of having any interest in her, they could well be tossed out into the rain again.

"How long do you think the storm will last?" Phillip asked, not being able to think of anything else to gain his brother's attention.

"With our luck," John said with a sigh of acceptance turning toward his brother, "all night. Oh, well, one more day won't matter."

"Did y' say your name was Power?" asked the farmer.

"Yes," John replied looking at the man pleasantly.

"Of *the* Powers?"

"If you mean the first settlers in the harbor," John's tone had grown a trifle stiff, "the answer is *yes* again. Our father and mother established the settlement with a trading post before any of us were born."

The farmer nodded. "I've heard the stories... how yer ma wrestled a bear by herself and the injuns made her some kind of princess and..."

"I'm afraid those are folk tales, more fantasy than reality, I assure you," John interrupted with a dry chuckle. "Mother never wrestled a bear. She stands barely as tall as my shoulder. But she knows how to use a musket and I remember her telling us the story of how she had scared one away when she was all alone. As for the Indians, I believe they were good friends. I vaguely remember them when they used to trade at her post, before they moved on into the interior. I have no idea how a story could have started that she had been made an Indian princess."

The farmer nodded again and scratched his bewhiskered chin. "Well, I know for a fact yer daddy's made quite a name fer hisself. Everyone knows its Power property all along th' river. And half th' businesses in Chartes Landing. Didn't think you two looked like no lumberjacks. When ya says yer lumber camp I guess you really mean *yer* lumber camp, don't ya?"

"Well, it is our father's," Phillip clarified while John was silent.

It was not easy being the eldest son of a successful man. No matter where one went someone was trumpeting one's father's successes. One could either try to compete and fail miserably just by virtue of being so much younger and less experienced, or one could decline to compete and walk away. John had chosen the second path. He had never shown any interest in any of the family businesses although he had always labored hard, but he did have a knack for medicine and he had brought his bag with him just in case. He wasn't certain what they would find at the camp.

In the light of the lanterns it was quite obvious the two young men were brothers. They looked and carried themselves very similarly only Phillip had dark hair and broodingly dark eyes which he had been told he had inherited from his mother's father.

Phillip had been rather hot-headed and impulsive when he was young which is how he ended up married at just seventeen to an equally young wife who was already pregnant with his child. And as fortune would have it, Caroline had been very good for him, a moderating influence, it would seem. They had lived in the family home while both Caroline and Phillip worked and saved to furnish their own home. Then, with lumber from the mill, a gift from Jacques, Phillip built a very nice two story home on an acre next to Marie and Jacques. When their *grand-père* had died and left a considerable amount of money to the family, Phillip had used part of his portion to purchase prime acreage further inland and build on to his house along with suitable outbuildings for his growing family. The young man had a lot of contact with the lumber camp as he was now responsible for how the logs traveled out of the area known as the "Indian Forest" and down the Iwiki River to the sawmill. The lumber camp itself had moved since the days when William Boot oversaw it. Under Sven Olafson's management it now penetrated more deeply into the old growth forest.

With trembling hands and under her father's watchful eye, Gertrude brought steaming bowls of a hardy stew to the two strangers along with tankards of frothy small beer. Seated at the crude kitchen table, the brothers thanked her before she quickly retired to the dark shadows of the corner where she could watch them unnoticed by her father as she scrubbed the muddy clothes she had been given.

The warm food did much to decrease the brothers' chill and restore their good humor. As they sat before the pleasant fire eating and drinking, they talked intermittently to each other about the state of affairs at the lumber camp, almost forgetting the presence of the farmer and his daughter, neither of whom were much given to making conversation.

Two days ago, a message had arrived in Chartes Landing from the lumber camp. Sven Olafson who had managed the camp for the Power family for years, had suddenly died. It had been a complete shock. A large imposing Swede, the man had always been in exceptionally good health. He had come to the settlement back in the early years but was younger than their father and the message had not said how he had died. Phillip suspected a fall from a tree although he couldn't imagine Sven being that careless. Still, accidents were called that because they happened without intent or expectation.

Phillip immediately prepared to travel to the camp while John had volunteered to go along. He had not seen the Olafsons in many years. Of course, everyone wanted to know exactly how Sven had died. As a doctor, John was concerned for disease. They also wanted to assure themselves that his widow and family were all right but from a practical standpoint, Phillip had the task of appointing a new manager to ensure the camp continued to run smoothly. The lumber business was a very lucrative side to their family holdings.

The brothers had lapsed into a thoughtful silence. The rain could still be heard falling hard outdoors but the thunder and lightning had subsided. The farmer went to the fire, tossing several more logs on it, and announced his intent to go to bed.

"Gert, git up in the loft," he ordered his daughter after she had finished hanging the wet clothing upon the same line she'd strung up to make the screen. "You two kin stay here by th' fire," he told the brothers. "Fetch'em each a blanket," he directed the girl as she was climbing up the ladder. Moments later she tossed down two blankets. "Now, you boys settle down an' mind, I'm a light sleeper so don't git no ideas," he warned before stretching out on his thin mattress upon a platform in the corner by the ladder.

John and Phillip each wrapped themselves in a blanket and, grateful to be warm and dry, they sat in the crude chairs by the fire and tried to sleep.

The rustic chairs of roughly hewn wood did not make comfortable beds. Hard and unyielding, the edges poked and jabbed and John and Phillip suffered a very fitful night of sleep at best. Early before dawn they were stiff and unrested and both were wide awake. They could hear the old farmer snoring in his corner as they signaled to each other. Standing with a soft groan, Phillip tried to stretch out his kinks and then, he stirred the fire and added more wood. John hobbled stiffly to his clothing and was glad to find it dry. It didn't look half bad in the light from the fire. What it would look like in full sunlight remained to be seen. He slipped into his own clothing as quickly as he could without losing his balance and left the borrowed shirt and breeches folded neatly upon the table. Still flexing to loosen up their muscles, they quietly left the little cabin stepping into the chill of pre-dawn. Then, as if of one mind, they headed straight for a large bush, each passing water before proceeding to the barn by the light of the setting moon.

The brothers found their horses content within the barn, threw their saddle blankets and saddles on them and were glad to be on their way. The animals may have wished for more rest but the young men had little sympathy. It was a good guess that the beasts were more rested than they. Riders and mounts traveled the rough path back into the forest where the air smelled strongly of rich, wet loam. The tree leaves were still laden with droplets and with each shudder in the wind, it rained down on the riders anew. The earth was sodden and springy under foot except where standing puddles and mud made the going slippery. The young men knew better than to push their mounts and allowed the horses to pick their way carefully over roots and slick surfaces setting their own pace.

"I think we would have been better off sleeping on the ground," said Phillip at last as he stretched yet again. "My back has so many kinks in it, it feels like someone tried to braid my spine."

John ignored the attempt at wit. It was too early in the morning. "I spent more time trying to find a comfortable position than I did sleeping. The fire was nice but we would have been better off with our saddles and the hay."

"Uffff...soft hay would have been wonderful!" his brother sighed and gave a shiver against the chill air. "If we were on our way home I could have Caroline walk on my back. She can do wonders for me when I get kinks like this but unfortunately..." he let his statement drift as though the whole thought was apparent and didn't need completing.

"You'll live," John chuckled.

"Don't you feel a bit ungrateful, slinking away without saying good-bye?"

"Not especially. I think we expressed our appreciation quite well last night. And I'm certain Danner will consider himself well rid of us."

"You were just afraid if you stayed around any longer the old man would have you betrothed to his daughter," Phillip teased. "I thought the poor girl was going to faint at your feet."

"Not bloody likely."

"What? That you'd be betrothed or that she'd faint at your feet?"

John only gave his brother a look that said he didn't think this line of conversation amusing.

"I actually feel rather sorry for that girl," John said thoughtfully. "It must be very hard to live off by yourself in a wilderness like this so isolated from people your own age. She did a very decent job on my clothing," he added smoothing his jacket down over his chest.

"I'm sure she would have pressed them for you as well, if we would have stayed a bit longer. And cooked us a fine breakfast, too."

"Not necessary. I don't want to be more beholden to them than we already are. We can eat in the saddle. I'm more concerned about getting to the camp and finding out about Sven."

"But that is supposed to be my concern, brother," Phillip smiled mischievously. He knew very well that John was trying to cover his real reason for haste in departing. He had seen the blatant besottedness of the young girl. And he knew John was well aware of it as well. It amused Phillip that his older brother was so uncomfortable with the feminine attentions he attracted everywhere he went. Women of all types and ages seemed to almost throw themselves at his feet. Phillip might have been jealous if it were not for the fact that he wore his wedding band proudly and made easy reference to the wife he loved dearly. But John acted as though a wedding ring were more like a slave band, to be avoided at all costs. He sought release from his normal appetites within appropriate quarters from women who had no expectation of marriage in return for their favors. But with the daughters of the respectable community, John never even flirted.

The brothers continued steadily on their way as the sun rose up out of the trees into a clear blue sky. By proceeding cross-country rather than following the river, they were cutting miles off their journey. Bird song filled the air above them and bittersweet was blooming out everywhere as if the rain signaled a show. Most of the trees were still fully leafed, shading them from the full force of the sun as the morning grew older. Gnawing on beef jerky for breakfast stifled conversation for awhile.

"What is it you have against marriage?" Phillip asked after a considerable span of time.

"Who said I have anything against it?" John replied with surprise, removing his hat and raking his fingers through his thick hair. "Mother and Father have a wonderful marriage, I can't imagine one of them without the other."

Phillip shrugged. "So why haven't you... well, I mean… you are the eldest but you don't seem to have any serious interest in anyone."

"How can I when you took the prettiest girl in town?" John replied lightly.

"True," Phillip agreed readily as he thought of his young wife with her large, dark blue eyes, copper colored hair, and skin like fine cream. Only he had the privilege of knowing first hand that the same soft, fine skin of her cheek covered every inch of the rest of her as well. "But there are others," he added encouragingly.

"None that have taken my fancy, little brother. You don't expect me to marry just anyone do you?" he chuckled again but without any real humor.

"Well, no," agreed Phillip, "but surely you want to start a family of your own soon."

"In time, all in good time. Despite the way I feel after sleeping in that miserable chair, I am a young man still... don't rush me," he smiled and with that he nudged his horse to pick up the pace.

The two brothers cleared a crest and the lumber camp set back from the river came into view below them. The largest cabin in the camp belonged to the Olafsons. It was a sturdy structure of logs and wood shingles. The main portion had two extensions added on, and each of those had been added onto again to form the structure somewhat into the shape of an E. The Olafsons had moved away from the coastline when it was decided Sven was to take over management from William Boot.

Glad to manage the lumber camp for the Power family deep inland, they had raised five sons and three daughters, adding to the main house as needs required. Now, there were several grandchildren as well and the wings had been added which were shared by the four oldest sons and their growing families.

Sonya Olafson saw the brothers ride in. She was a tall, big boned Swedish woman who looked like a lumberjack's wife, able to throw a side of deer on her own. Her large broad face was lighted by two cornflower blue eyes about which an array of laugh lines splayed attesting to happier times. She wore her thick mane of hay colored hair, now streaked through with gray, in a large massive braid coiled about her head which made her appear even taller than she was. As she stood in her embroidered muslin blouse and skirt with a half apron tied about her waist, large feet apart, big hands on her hips, she tried to look pleasant but her usually clear eyes were red from weeping and her face had a haggard disheartened look upon it.

"Master Phillip," she nodded in faintly accented speech, "Master John. Good it is to see you again."

The young men slid from their horses and each in turn embraced the woman they had known all their lives.

"We were shocked, Mistress Sonya, and deeply grieved. I still can't believe it. Mother and Father bid me to express their deepest sorrow and sympathy," Phillip stated earnestly, holding her by the shoulders. If not for the heels on his boots, the woman would have been taller than he.

"We would have been here sooner but the storm held us up. I apologize for my appearance," John said gravely and kissing her cheek, he added "I can't tell you how Sven's death has shocked us."

Sonya nodded and grimaced a smile, trying very hard not to weep again. The last thing on her mind or care was the appearance of anyone's clothing.

"Years it has been since last we see you, Master John. Ain't you grown to be the spittin' image of your papa now. Glad I am you came. Come inside," she managed to sound gracious and gestured them into her home. "We have some coffee first, good strong coffee. Then, we talk."

She ushered them into the heart of her home, her kitchen. It was a very large room, airy and light with clean lines and a hardwood floor that looked like it was scrubbed regularly. At the far end of the room was a massive cooking hearth and the floor turned to flagstone. To the side, a door opened to a pantry larder, and a spring room was constructed beneath, where cold spring water flowed year round.

The long table which dominated the kitchen was made of a solid slab of timber cut lengthwise from the middle of a massive maple found in the virgin forest. The cheerful table coverings were embroidered with pleasantly angular designs and bright colors. And the golden maple surface that shown around the cloths was hand rubbed to a deep luster stating clearly that the table had been made by hands that loved wood and all its natural beauty.

The kitchen curtains were embroidered in a similar manner to the table cloths, as were the cloth napkins and doilies and chair coverings. A large hand-braided rug softened the middle of the room and brought the wood and flagstone floor surfaces together. Hand carved little animals set about the fireplace mantel which was also intricately carved with figures and rich designs bringing old Norse gods and fables to mind.

Sonya poured cups of dark rich coffee and set out a plate of fresh baked pastries at one end of the table. She insisted the brothers take some and she sipped at her coffee until they had finished their sweets.

"I couldn't tell you in a message," she began, a quiver in her voice. "It was... it was not something what you can write in a message."

John and Phillip both looked at her expectantly and with full attention.

"We been having troubles for some time now with a band of renegades. Always they are stealing something from the camp. They come by night, late. First, it is chickens, then a tool or two turns up missing, then someone reports a musket gone. Tired of it, we all were. It got so nothing be safe. We was all concerned for our families, of course, but we get no threats, and no one harmed. It just a big damn nuisance.

"I tell Sven, 'Sven, it just nuisance, they go away.' But he was bound and determined to catch 'em red-handed in the act." She paused for a moment and choked back a sob.

"I think maybe if it up to him alone, he wait but the rest of the folks, they keep complaining. They give him no peace." She sighed deeply. "Well, last week Sven set up trip wire all around the camp. You know the kind. He strung wire from one point to another and hung spoons, forks, whatever, from it and if it is touched the metal would jangle.

"So, one night we heard jiggle jangle all over and Sven goes out in his nightshirt, unarmed, to tell the thieves he's tired of it all and for them to travel on elsewhere. That's all he wanted to tell them. You know Sven, he never wish no one harm his whole life. He just want them to go.

"He leave the porch and come face to face with little runt of a savage. He be no more but half Sven's size. Sven says, 'Hey, there! And just what you think you do?' and bang the musket goes off. The savage look surprised to see Sven crumple to the ground and he take off running like a pack of wolves is after him. The rest went with him. I ran to Sven and when I see what they do I could not help but scream after them. I guess I call them all sorts of names, perhaps some I should be ashamed of but my Sven's blood, all over the ground it is and I..." she stopped and hung her head.

"Good Lord, Sonya, he was shot to death?!" exclaimed Phillip. "We had no idea it was violence!"

She nodded. "In minutes he was dead. His blood drained from him so fast. We bury him the next day." She looked pitifully at John, shaking her head slowly, "I still can not believe he is gone."

Just then Sven Junior came in. He was a huge man, almost seven feet tall with a broad expanse of shoulder, a barrel chest and long thickly muscled legs resembling tree trunks. A thick mop of straight hay colored hair topped his head, cut blunt at the neck, a dark blond beard covered his chin, and bright cornflower blue eyes were set deeply into his darkly tanned face. He went to his mother and she grasped one thick, sinewy arm and clung to it sobbing. The brothers had risen.

"Sven Junior," Phillip acknowledged the large man with a warm grasp to his free forearm in a mutual arm clasp, "we came as soon as we heard. We're completely shocked. Your mother has just told us how it happened! I'm very sorry to have upset her like this."

Sven Junior nodded also shaking hands in an arm grasp with John. Then he gently stroked his grieving mother's head.

"The Bible says there be a time to weep and a time to laugh, a time to mourn and a time to dance. This is mama's time to weep, this is our time to mourn. You have done nothing to upset her."

John and Phillip nodded in understanding.

"We want to talk to some of the others," said Phillip quietly over Sonya's soft muffled sobs. "Perhaps this would be a good time. We'll be back later."

Sven Junior nodded his big head and turned all his attention to his grieving mother.

# Chapter 7

John and Phillip heard variations of the same story from all the inhabitants of the camp. The renegades hadn't returned since the shooting but everyone was on guard that they might at anytime. Some expressed concern now that blood had been spilled, it might continue to be spilled. What had started out as nuisance thieving, had taken a life. Murder could not go unpunished. The renegades needed to be hunted down. This plague needed to be stopped short before tolerance courted worse consequences. They should gather a search party and track the Indians down. Several men volunteered while several expressed concern for leaving the camp unguarded.

That night as the Olafson family began to gather around the huge table, it appeared not so very large after all. Sven Junior and his wife, Clara, had three children, his brother Uland and wife, Anna, had two, brother Bor and wife, Sasha, had one but by the size of her belly it was evident another was due any day. Regin and wife Kristen were newly married and brother Peter was only twelve. None of the three young sisters had married and left home as yet. That brought the head count round the table to nineteen with Sonya and twenty-one with Phillip and John added in. Of course, the babies really didn't sit at the table but they were there near their parents.

Talk was subdued. Sven Senior's place at the head of the table was left empty. Phillip remembered how proud the big Swede had been of the ever growing family filling that table and how lively the conversations had been, full of laughter and joking. Someday it would be that way again, perhaps, but it would never be the same for poor Sonya.

Sven Junior who was taking a seat at the end of the table nearest the empty head was making introductions for John's sake. It had been so many years since he had been up to the camp. As the eldest brother finished, John was helping to seat Clara,

Sven Junior's wife, next to himself and across from her husband who had just set their youngest on his knee.

"Oh, and you will remember Freyja," Sven said looking up at his eldest sister who had just placed a final serving platter upon the table. "Although the last time you saw her, John, I imagine she was still running with the boys in britches."

John turned automatically to his right, the direction to which his host spoke, a friendly smile on his face to greet the little hoyden he remembered rather well.

"Little Freyja, of cours...." the words died on John's lips as he faced a tall, slender maiden in the bloom of her eighteenth year standing a narrow chair's width away from him. John wasn't even aware that he had stopped breathing as he beheld her and everyone else in the room seemed to fade away for that moment.

This was no little tomboy but a vision stepped out of the swirling mists from the land of Norse gods and Viking ships. Instantly, he was drawn into the depths of two large slightly tilted sea-green eyes the color of a bottomless fiord and fringed in thick sable lashes while delicate golden brows arched at him quizzically. Speechless, he took in the golden mantle of gloss about her shoulders, hair so brilliantly gold it seemed to radiate light like the midnight sun. Her short, slender nose showed the barest kiss of the sun while her flushed, full-lipped mouth hinted at raw sexuality.

"Freyja?" he acknowledged, finally exhaling and finding his voice. She gave him a half smile.

"It is good to see you again, John," she said, her voice lilting, light and clear of tone but modestly soft, perhaps a little mournful.

She turned to take her seat, the soft muslin of her garments moving with her. John automatically held the chair to assist her. Her hair done in two magnificently thick golden braids, hanging low and she gracefully avoided sitting on them by bringing them both around to pool in her lap.

John began breathing normally again as a hundred thoughts of guilt and disloyalty raced through his brain. How could he have such an overwhelming reaction to this young woman? With Alana only just in her grave? No, not *just* it was actually a year now. He had survived a whole year. He remembered Huffsmeier's last words to him. Was fate actually offering him a second chance at happiness? But he was being foolish. He didn't even know the girl.

Sven Junior could not help but notice the eldest Power brother's reaction to his beautiful sister. "None can say we do not grow our women fair," he said cordially, but with an unmistakable note of guardianship. "She keeps us busy beating the suitors back with a firm rod, and Snotra and Skadi will be coming up next." With that he winked at his two youngest sisters who, at fourteen and eight, were rather gangly ducklings not yet transformed into swans.

John quietly took his own seat, fighting to maintain a mask of control and project a relaxed neutral demeanor. As one male to another, Sven Junior's message had been very clear. There would be no tolerance of anyone, not even a Power, treating their sister with anything less than the highest respect.

As John rather mechanically picked up his napkin he found himself wondering how it could be that such an elegant creation had been born out of this good but rough peasant stock. He next found himself wondering how it could be that she was not yet married. Suitors? Even tucked away in this remote place, he had no doubt they could well be coming from all over. How many, he wondered, and had she found one she fancied? Or, had her formidably intimidating brothers managed to frighten them all away? And then, quite unwillingly he discovered himself wickedly speculating on exactly what it would be like to kiss those darkly flushed, full lips.

He looked up and caught Phillip looking at him with a mischievous grin and twinkling eyes. John immediately looked in another direction.

Large plates of food were being passed around the table and each serving dish he received, he must pass on to Freyja who took them with careful poise. He was very aware of the grace in those long slender hands and delicate wrists. Twice his fingers brushed hers. They were soft, warm, delicately tapered with perfectly rounded nails of modest length that held no dirt. John felt a surge of excitement at each contact although she showed no notice. Once she looked up and into his eyes as he watched her, and in an instant he was helplessly drowning again in those incredible sea-green depths until her lashes swept almost to her cheeks and she looked down. His breath mercifully returned to him.

The temperature of the room seemed to be rising at an extraordinary speed. John felt his clothing binding him, stifling him, damn near choking him. He wished he could rid himself of his coat and stock but his manners forbade it. He looked down at his plate with a certain surprised dismay to discover mounds of food there. He didn't know why he had taken all that food, why he had taken any food at all. He wasn't the least bit hungry although, in fact, he should be. His appetite had disappeared. He knew he must try to think of something, anything, to take his mind off her presence so near to him.

"Your sisters have such interesting names," John said to Sven. "I'm sorry to say I don't have a great deal of knowledge concerning Norse names. Are they family names?"

"Naw, Papa liked to name his girls from the old stories," Sven replied.

"The old stories?" John asked.

"Skadi was born in the winter," Sonya volunteered. It took her mind away from Sven Senior. "Skadi is the goddess of winter and the hunt."

Sitting near her mother, young Skadi looked embarrassed. John smiled her way with a nod.

"And Snotra?" John prodded.

Sven had just washed a mouth full of food down with a half stein of beer. "Ah, Snotra is the goddess of virtue and knowledge, is this not so, little sister?"

"Freyja has much more knowledge than me," a faint and modest voice replied.

Phillip looked at John and would have loved to tease his brother about Freyja but was obliged to remember poor Sven Senior was cold in the ground in order to keep himself in a properly sober attitude

"And what about Freyja?" Phillip asked displaying an innocent frown of interest.

"Ah, Freyja," her mother replied, "she is a very naughty goddess but Sven loved the name so." Sonya began crying and stepped away from the table. "Sorry," she blurt as she hurried to another room.

Things had become very quiet at a table holding twenty people. Even the smallest children were quiet. John wracked his brain for something meaningful or comforting to say. At this moment he would settle for something to say that just made sense. His mind was a total and absolute blank. He could think of not a single thing until he thought of Sven sitting across the table one seat over. And this thought caused John to actually look at his host and damned if he didn't find the big man's eyes observing him which just made the room seem to grow even hotter.

Through diligent effort, John did think of the renegades but didn't think it proper to broach the subject at the supper table. Getting up a manhunt to track the savages wasn't really polite conversation and he decided against it. It was, after all, really more fitting for the men to discuss this amongst themselves. No sense in upsetting the ladies, no sense in upsetting... her. And so, he continued to try to eat, making a half-hearted stab at it in uncharacteristic silence while Phillip loquaciously conveyed the latest news and happenings from the coast.

Toward the end of the meal, John had gathered just enough of his wits to ask Sven if all the brothers might meet after dinner was over. Sven instantly agreed. After that, John was content to finish out his meal in a mute struggle to not feel so like an awkward adolescent or a shamefully disloyal husband.

Four large cherry pies and a huge pot of rich dark coffee disappeared neatly and the meal was over. Sven stood and announced the men would go to the parlor and the women were to keep the children from disturbing them. All the brothers stood then, and John and Phillip followed suit. Once the parlor door was shut, Sven turned the meeting over to the Power brothers.

"How long have renegades been a problem?" John asked finding it much easier to think now that Freyja was not in the same room.

"Off and on. You know how the frontier is always stirred up by the fighting between the French and the English," Sven replied. "Always we must be on our guard but the official warring is once again over. This party was just stealing. I think, maybe, they are a band which was displaced by the fighting."

"Or they have had their war paint on so long they have forgotten how to live in peace," Uland suggested.

"Does it matter?" asked Phillip.

"No, I don't suppose so," replied John, "except it doesn't appear that they are a warrior faction out to take scalps."

"I think that is safe to say," nodded Sven looking at Uland.

"There are many in the camp here that feel we should organize a manhunt to track them down," Phillip said. "They are demanding retribution for the crime. They think the killing will escalate if we do not respond and exact an eye for an eye. What do you think?"

The Olafson brothers looked at one another, their eyes communicating in silence. Then, Sven spoke.

"My brothers and I agree. If we do not at least make the effort to track this band down, we are going to appear weak. Weakness is despised by the Indian. They expect revenge and respect it."

"But won't that cause them to next seek revenge on you?" John asked, knitting his brow in concern.

"Not if we only exact punishment to fit the crime. One life for one life, preferably the same one who took Father's," replied Sven, and his brothers all nodded and grunted their agreement.

"Very well, I shall join you," said John.

"As will I," injected Phillip and John shot him a disapproving look.

"We'll speak of that later," John said in an aside to his brother and then spoke to everyone. "There are many in this camp who are willing to join us. Of course, we can't take everyone and leave the camp unguarded with only women and children. I think a party of nine or ten is enough but who is experienced at tracking? How do we even begin to pick up a trail now?"

"Tracking Bear can help us!" proposed Bor. "He hangs around the camp and helps us mark and track our timber cuts. As long as nobody gives him spirits and he stays sober, he'll be all right."

"Then, I suggest we make plans to start out immediately," said John with an air of leadership. "Undoubtedly the rain will have spoiled the trail. Someone talk to this Tracking Bear and see what he thinks. And someone needs to find out who is coming and who is staying here in the camp."

"Those who stay behind," interjected Phillip, "should be assigned work details to improve the defenses here. A stockade wouldn't be a bad idea."

"That's true," John agreed.

"A stockade?!" Bor exclaimed.

"You mean put a wall around us like a fort?" Sven frowned. "This is not how free people should live."

"Yet, from the first settlements, Sven, there have been forts to secure the inhabitants until peace was clearly established," reasoned John.

"We've been here over twenty years..." Sven began but Uland cut him off.

"It is a reasonable idea. Frankly, much happier I would be knowing Anna and the children had that protection." The other brothers nodded in agreement.

"All right, we shall have a stockade," nodded Sven. "When peace is well established, it can be torn down."

"We should be ready to leave tomorrow as soon as this Tracking Bear can be located. And Phillip, I need to speak with you privately," John added as he moved toward the door.

The meeting was over and the Olafson brothers continued to talk together assigning themselves the details. John motioned Phillip out of the room, out of the house and into the balmy night air.

"I don't want you coming along," John said bluntly as they stood away from the big log house.

"Why?" Phillip asked a bit defensively.

"Because you have to go back and report to Father."

"What do you mean *I* have to go back? Don't try and pull rank on me, big brother. This lumber camp has been my responsibility for several years now. You can go back and report to Father."

"Why didn't you warn me?" John suddenly blurted in a loud whisper and it took Phillip a second to follow his brother's sudden jump in thought.

"Warn you?" he asked with a puzzled frown that quickly changed to a placid grin, "Why what of?"

"I think you know perfectly well. You could have said something, given me some hint... instead of letting me... my God," he groaned in chagrin, "I was acting like a complete ass in front of everyone."

"Of whatever do you speak?" Phillip continued to pretend ignorance but was barely able to control his laughter.

"Not what but whom and you know... perfectly... well!" John gritted out while scowling at his brother. Then he added very softly, "Freyja."

"Ohhh. Well... yes, now I see. You were rather unusually quiet at supper. I suppose one might say... *dumb*-founded," he snorted a guffaw that would no longer stay suppressed. "She's grown up rather nicely, hasn't she? But then, I'm a very happily married man, brother, I really don't notice other woman," Phillip feigned a moralistic tone that was too nonchalant to be believed.

"*Rather nicely!* I've never seen..." John spun on his toes with the ease of a fencer, trying to come to terms with his feelings. But he had seen. Just a year and a half ago, he was thinking the same things about Alana.

"Well, I saw a very attractive young maiden sitting next to you at dinner. I've seen her grow from a pig-tailed ruffian and transform into a lovely over the past few years. She's no changeling," Phillip smiled. "And she's not a figment of your imagination, but I dare say she doesn't affect me quite in the same way she obviously does you."

"I am equally surprised she is not married... or at least promised," John said very seriously.

"I gather she's had plenty of offers, but she refuses them all. Could be she's just been waiting for you, John," he teased, triumphantly amused to see his unflappable, sophisticated, know-it-all sibling thunder struck.

"Do you think that's possible?" John asked quickly and very seriously. "Do you believe in... fate?"

"John, I have no idea. I mean, that's something you'll just have to find out for yourself, isn't it? And knowing you, brother, you'll manage quite well," he slapped John on the back now as a gesture of encouragement.

"I can't think when I'm near her," John confessed in quietly voiced embarrassment. "She's so... breathtaking. My thoughts evaporate and all I want is to..." he stopped himself short. He saw no reason to verbalize to his brother all the things he wanted so badly to do. Gather her to him, kiss her, hold her, touch her, keep her, protect her, make endless love to her... all the things he once had with Alana but with one thing more, with Freyja he had the chance for a very long future and children.

"Welcome to the club," Phillip said with an audacious grin that smacked of vindication, "I think you've just discovered *love*... and why I found myself married at seventeen."

John stopped and looked at his brother for a long moment. Phillip had no idea how hard John had fallen for another young woman. No one here knew he was really a widower. "Did Caroline affect you that way?" he asked quietly.

"Pretty much, more or less. Even now, she can still make me feel a bit muddled. When we're alone," he added, "and she looks at me a certain way... moves a certain way... does certain things..."

John was not interested in his brother's bedroom secrets, not that he expected Phillip to elaborate anymore than he just had. But it was time to change the subject. After all, Caroline was Phillip's wife and so, such talk made John uneasy. It wasn't like trading casual tavern stories about some common strumpet. John saw Caroline as a sister and the mother of his nieces. He drew himself together and forced a calm he didn't feel while turning once again to the matters at hand. "Father isn't going to be happy about this," he mulled.

"With you falling in love?" Phillip questioned in disbelief. "I should think he'll be very pleased."

"No-no, with this whole situation up here. My God," he gasped suddenly, "do you realize *she* could have been hurt?!"

"Anyone in the family could have, in fact, Sven was a little more than just hurt," Phillip replied with sudden seriousness. "I can't believe it, myself. Sven shot to death by renegades! We've never had any trouble with the natives."

"On second thought... on second thought," John grew more pensive, "perhaps it's best we don't tell him, at least not right now."

"Who?"

"Father."

"What?!" Phillip looked at his brother in surprise.

"If we tell him there's a renegade band up here stealing and killing just what do you suppose he's going to do?"

"But we can't lie to him!" Phillip protested.

"I'm not saying we should lie. We just don't have to tell him exactly every-thing... right now."

"Oh, come now, you know Father. He's going to know something's not right if we don't return home shortly. We never could keep things from him."

"Speak for yourself, little brother, you may not have but I've done my share," John grimaced.

Phillip snorted. "You only *think* so. I'll wager Father knows just about every-thing you've ever done, whether you realize it or not. And its undoubtedly no more than what he himself did at our age. He didn't marry Mother until he was twenty-six and somehow I have never pictured him as tending toward monkish-ness."

John paused for a moment. He would have to take a different tactic with this brother of his, he decided. "Do you want to see him heading up a search party him-self?" John's expression had grown dark again. "At his age, he should stay close to home. If anything ever happened to him, it would kill Mother. Do you want that on your conscience? Well, do you?"

"Of course not!" Phillip squirmed.

"Listen to me."

"I'm listening!"

"Good!" John said, with a certain elder sibling satisfaction. "The easiest lie to get away with is one that is close to the truth. So, we'll send a message back and only say that Sven was killed accidentally when a musket discharged unexpect-edly. That is pretty much the truth, you know. At least according to Sonya, she said the savage looked as scared as she felt when the shot was fired and he dropped ev-erything and took off running."

Phillip nodded.

"But you are going to have to stay at the camp to keep things running smoothly until you can figure out who is best to take Sven's place," John added.

"Awwh, naw, not on your life," Phillip shook his head in protest. "Don't think you're going to confine me to camp and take off on me!"

"I'm not planning on *taking off* on you. But someone does need to keep the camp running and see to the fortifications. Besides, you do have a family to think of, don't forget. There will be enough to go with me, you won't have to."

Phillip gave his brother a long sideways look.

"I agree to send a half-truth to Father to keep him home but that's it. Need I re-mind you, brother, that it was you who didn't duck the branch? I'll be damned if I'm going to let you go off after a renegade party of Indians on your own and leave me behind."

"But the camp..."

"The camp will be fine. I already know who should take over. But I can use in-decision as my excuse for not returning. What's your excuse going to be?"

"Oh, you know me. I've never needed much of an excuse to take off. So, who do you figure on replacing Sven with?"

"Sven Junior. He knows lumber as well as his father did. And he's another gentle giant like his father. The men look up to him, figuratively as well as literally."

John nodded. He agreed with his brother's choice for camp manager but not for wanting to be part of the tracking party. Philip was a businessman not an Indian fighter. And he had a wife and three children to take care of and for which to be responsible. John could see no reason for Phillip to expose himself to unnecessary danger fighting savages. But John knew it was useless to argue with Phillip once he had made up his mind on something. Phillip was strong-willed and stubborn. The Olafsons had four sons old enough to be part of their father's avengers. He and Phillip would make the count six. He was certain they would find at least two or three more volunteers. That was enough to go after the renegades. Now, all they needed was a clue as to where they were to be found.

"That's a damn big frontier out there," mused John looking out into the night.

"We have no choice. Stealing and getting away with it is one thing, but killing and getting away with it...?" Phillip shook his head. "Even if the killing was not intentional, still, someone must pay for the deed."

John nodded his agreement. "I'm going by the barn and check on the horses. I'll see you later," he said as he strode off.

Sonya's eldest daughter had helped to clear the table, wash up the dishes, and put the food away in the pantry. Then, she took their littlest sister up to the sloped roof upper room which they shared at the back of the house. After brushing out Skadi's hair and replaiting it, Freyja helped her change into her bedclothes and tucked her in for the night. Skadi begged for a story from her big sister. She loved to hear Freyja's stories about the old heroes and gods, mighty Odin who ruled over Valhalla, naughty mischievous Loki, and the beautiful but dangerous Valkyries who served Odin. But Freyja refused tonight, pleading fatigue.

The truth was Freyja was too distracted, thinking of the refined and gallant Power brother who had sat by her side at the supper table. She had already admitted to herself that he was extremely good looking but it wasn't his looks that caught her attention and held it so closely. There were other good looking men to be found in their camp, although none so neatly groomed as he. No, it wasn't just his looks that appealed to her and made him so different. It was, perhaps, the way he carried himself with a grace that did not speak of weakness or womanish-ness but of strength and power, like his name. An animal grace. Or was it something in his eyes, as clear as river water made remarkable with their rims of black, and the intensity with which he looked at her.

She found the controlled timbre of his voice exciting, and she admired and appreciated his diction and fine speech. In truth, he and his brother were very similar in appearance and refinement but she had no attraction to his brother. Freyja's train of thought halted at her own revelation. There *was* attraction, basic, elemental, undeniable, unexplainable, and as powerful as nature itself. An instant and over-whelming attraction that wove its way like growing tentacles through her being and stirred her blood in an age old way.

"Freyja?" Skadi called to her big sister as she turned to leave.

"What is it?" Freyja replied softly.

"Do you think Papa has gone to Valhalla to be with Odin? He died bravely, didn't he? He would be admitted to Valhalla even if he didn't have a weapon in his hand, wouldn't he?"

"Oh, Skadi," Freyja came back to sit on the bed beside her little sister, stifling her own desire to cry. "Those are only myths and stories… like fairy-tales. We are Christians, we know the pagan gods are not real. Papa is in Heaven with the Lord Jesus now."

"What's the difference?" the younger girl asked innocently.

"Not now, please. We'll talk about it another time." Freyja stroked her younger sister's brow tenderly. "For now, just know that Papa is in Paradise and we will all see him again someday."

"Good night, Freyja," the child murmured, closing her eyes.

"Good night, Skadi."

"I love you."

"I love you, too."

Unbraiding and brushing her own hair, Freyja continued to sit by her sister, lending security and comfort until the younger girl fell asleep. As she continued to sit in the quiet room, Freyja realized she could hear the sounds of sobbing, very quiet, muffled but still there. She got up and walked to Snotra's bed in the far corner.

"I miss him, too," Freyja said softly, putting her hand out to caress her other sister's shoulder as she lie turned to the wall. "Do not weep so, Snotra, you'll make yourself ill. Papa wouldn't want you to make yourself ill. Think of all the happy times. And remember, from Heaven, perhaps he can look down on us all."

"I... miss... him… so… much," came a half-choked sobbing reply.

"I know, I know, shhhhhh, it will be all right," she soothed and smoothed the sheet over Snotra's shoulders. "Now, go to sleep and have happy dreams. Remember, Papa will always be with us in our hearts, always. And he would want you to smile."

The young girl had calmed and grew quiet. Freyja turned and silently walked out the door.

Freyja had been born after four sons. From the moment Sven Senior had held her in his large awkward arms and she had given him a crooked little lopsided smile, she had commanded his heart and there was nothing he could deny her. He named her for the Norse goddess of beauty, love, and enchantment and she was all of that and more to him. He had admonished her brothers to look after her, watch out for her, protect her, and include her in their play. She ran and wrestled and swam and kicked and climbed trees right along with them. Then, when Sven arranged for reading and writing lessons from the wife of one of his crew, little Freyja had been taught along with her brothers.

Sven Junior had spoken fairly at supper that night. She had over a half dozen men from around their frontier community paying her court despite her repeated refusals. Her unwillingness to choose one of them gave them all continuing hope. They were for the most part good men, basically decent, the salt of the earth, some were boys with whom she had played and grown up around. All were of good health, some were quite tall, none were ugly, and working in lumber they were all in prime physical condition, but they were also all rough and coarse and crudely mannered. Some had a few more serious faults. A temper quick to kindle a brawl, an excessive love of spirits, a weakness for gambling away everything. None were literate much beyond the ability to write their own names. Grooming, a desire for education, and an appreciation for finer things simply was not part of their frame of reference. They were clumsy, rather dull witted and ignorant, and in all, Freyja did not feel the slightest attraction to any one of them. She had never before felt the primal excitement that comes from a strong and powerful attraction to a member of the opposite sex.

More than once her brother Sven had sighed at her and questioned whether their father had done her any favor ensuring that she could read and write and gifting her with books. She had read too much, knew too much, and in his opinion a wife who has more schooling than her husband is never content with her lot. Not only was Freyja extraordinarily beautiful but she was educated and that certainly did not bode well for a life that was to be spent on the wilderness frontier with a lumberjack or woodsman for a husband. Her father had hinted at taking her back to civilization to find a more suitable match for her among the townspeople although he was heartsick at the thought of losing her. Now he was gone. And Freyja, herself, still hadn't really accepted that her papa was dead.

In the quiet of the late evening, the young maiden sought a few moments of peace and solitude in the fresh night air to be alone with her restless thoughts before retiring within the room she shared with her two sisters. She silently made her way to the big old oak behind the cabin and sat absentmindedly on the swing hanging from one of its huge limbs. Her papa had fashioned the swing many years ago, and the heavy ropes had been changed often. He had taught her to pump with her legs and dare the heights. How many times, when she was small, had she hung on and cried, "Push me, Papa, push me! Higher! Higher!"

On impulse, the young maiden stood up and set her feet upon the swing. Giving herself a push, she began to pump, the swing climbing into the sky. Her long soft skirt clinging to her as the air pushed against her, cool and exhilarating. Holding on, using the action of her long slender legs to pump herself even higher, the air rushed at her face as she rose up toward the star filled heavens in an ever increasing arc. She wished she could just let go and fly out over the earth. She remembered how she would let go when she was very young and sail into her father's protective arms. He had always been there to catch her, had always returned her safely to the ground. His big arms had been her protection. He had been the rock about which they all had anchored their lives.

"Oh, Papa!" she cried out to the night sky as she stopped pumping and just held on, swinging backward and forward, back and forth, while the tears ran unhampered down her lovely cheeks and fell to the ground below.

Deep within the shadows John watched, spellbound. At first he just wanted to enjoy the sight of her, flying through the air, her hair streaming wildly about her, her dress clinging to her lithe figure. Then, he heard her plaintive cry and realized to his embarrassment that he was intruding on a very private moment of grief. As the swing began to slow, he saw the glistening ribbons down her cheeks and guessed them for what they were and was ashamed that he was eavesdropping on her sorrow. And yet, the desire to hold her and give comfort was so overwhelming he could not back away.

At last the swing was barely moving. She had wiped her tear stained cheeks with her hands, keeping her balance by holding the ropes in her bent arms. She continued to swing very gently and to silently look out at the night sky.

John was concerned to think she might discover he'd been spying on her. He was immobilized at first, not daring to reveal himself. Then, when enough time had passed for it to be reasonable that he might not have heard or seen anything, he forced himself to speak out and prayed he sounded appropriately impromptu.

"They're very beautiful tonight," he called out softly, stepping forward and he saw her start. He noticed her hands sneak to her face as she turned from him quickly wiping her eyes again, and then she turned back. "I'm sorry, I didn't mean to startle you. I just saw you looking at the stars." It was a harmless half truth.

"Oh. No... it's... it's all right. They seem very close tonight," she replied, no hint of her sorrow in her clear voice. She couldn't tell him that she more than welcomed the diversion from her painful thoughts.

"Aren't you a little afraid to be out here alone after dark?"

"Afraid?" she echoed.

"What with the renegades and all."

"Ohhhh. No, they have always come much later at night."

"But if they have any idea how beautiful you are, they might come just to steal you away."

She looked at him but couldn't see his face for the shadows.

"You put me in an awkward circumstance, sir," she replied with poise.

"How so?"

"If I ask if you think they would really think of such a thing you will think me vain of my looks, but if I protest your opinion of my looks, I cannot learn if you really think such a thing is possible."

John reached out and lifted her down from the swing. She let him. She was so light and slender, it was like lifting air despite her height. He did not take his hands from her small waist when she stood securely on the ground before him. Her full, flushed lips, so near, beckoning to be kissed.

"That you are exceptionally beautiful cannot be disputed," he said with quiet tension in his voice. "Don't even try... I abhor false modesty. That you could become the object of marauders is not to be doubted at all. Since marauders have carried off women only half as fair as you, don't you think there is a possibility of your own danger?" John saw her slightly slanted eyes open wide and fear fill them. And suddenly his arms were around her, drawing her to him. He hadn't meant to make her fearful and now he just wanted to make her feel safe.

Freyja did not understand why, but the tenderness of John's embrace touched the depth of her sorrow and she began to weep again while grasping his arm and clinging to his shoulder. Here was someone she didn't have to pretend with, didn't have to appear strong for, someone who wasn't suffering as she was suffering and who could give her solace. Deep cleansing sobs racked her lovely body.

John was at first startled and then understanding when Freyja began to weep again. She was hurting. Her father had just been violently wretched from her life and John was glad that he could provide the shoulder for her to cry upon. He was more than glad. He was pleased, very pleased that she should choose to share this with him. He held her gently, cradling her as they stood, stroking her back, much as one would a child. He encouraged her to vent her grief and relieve her pain. He could smell the fresh sweetness of her and gloried in the wondrous feel of her hair as his hand glided over it. She smelled like flowers and soap, baked cherries and sun warmed meadow grass, with an under note of clean feminine skin. As the moments passed, John became increasingly aware of the feel of her entire body pressed against his. Lord, but she felt wonderful. She had grown still, quiet, and although he was reluctant to break the spell, he reached within his pocket and pulled out his clean, white handkerchief.

"Here," he said quietly. She accepted the cloth and pulled away, wiping her eyes, her tear streaked face, her delicate chin. She blew her straight little nose daintily.

Thank you. I will wash this and return it," she said, keeping hold of the handkerchief.

"It's of no matter."

"It is very kind of you to... you are very kind," she looked at him and feeling a rush in reaction to the feel of him holding her she lowered her eyes. "I still cannot believe this is real," she said softly. "I never imagined a time when Papa would not be here." She took a deep breath to still her ragged breathing. Then she leaned forward and kissed him quickly on the cheek. "Thank you, John Power," she whispered and began to break away, intending to go back into the house but he caught her arms and pulled her back to him. Before Freyja knew what was happening his lips were on hers like soft, warm silk.

He had caught her by surprise and he felt her confusion before she relaxed with his kiss. But she did relax and her lips were soft and pliant. As his lips covered her mouth and felt her warmth, he knew he couldn't stop there. He drew one full lip gently into his mouth and grazed it with his tongue. His fingers dove into her cool, heavy hair and held her head as he pressed harder, his tongue now demanding full entrance to her mouth. She uttered a little gasp and pulled away with surprising strength.

"Is that decent?" she whispered innocently, her hands pressed against his hard chest.

"Between two willing adults, most assuredly so." He saw a fleeting look of indecision. "Have you never been kissed before?"

"Never like that," she replied honestly.

"Then you have never really been kissed by a man, not *really* kissed," his warm breath fanned her face. "I assure you it is decent and harmless in itself. But I am glad I am the one to teach you," he whispered and brought his lips to hers again, covering them lightly, brushing, caressing, feeling her sigh and relax before he pushed passed her lips and tasted her. She was every bit as sweet as he had imagined. He sought out her tongue and felt it come alive with his attentions. He felt her body give over to settle closer into his. He felt her velvety presence in his own mouth, exploring hesitantly, even timidly. She was igniting a fire within him which he was hard pressed to control. He grabbed her tongue with his lips and sucked powerfully, feeling her yield as her body clung to his.

When their lips parted, she found herself gasping for air as he bent into the tenderness at her neck, nuzzling her earlobe, his breath in her ear. She grew so weak she could barely feel her legs beneath her. His kissing created feelings within her she had never experienced, feelings she was having a hard time dealing with. For a moment she let him hold her, while she felt her pulse racing with a kind of madness and her breath growing ragged again but for a very different reason. When she felt his hand move lightly over her, she sighed and allowed herself to enjoy the thrill of his touch, down her back, around her side and up toward her breast.

John caressed the soft roundness of her beneath the thin muslin of her bodice. Her young breast filled his hand perfectly and the warm sensuality of that caress lasted several long moments before she pulled back like a startled fawn made suddenly aware of danger.

"John, you mustn't," she pushed his hand away, the darkness hiding the hot flush which had sprung to her cheeks. "I must go now."

"Please, don't," he grew insistent.

"John," she said with a quiet determination. He pulled his hands back from her in a little gesture of surrender and acceptance and looked so contrite she felt herself unfair. "Put your hands behind your back," she demanded softly and he did. "Now, promise me you will keep them there until I leave. Promise?"

"I promise," he agreed. Then, to his surprise she placed her hands on his cheeks and she reached up to him with her mouth. Its soft warmth covered his while she practiced what she had just learned from him, to his delight and his discomfort. He gripped the rope of the swing behind him, forcing himself not to let go, struggling against every instinct that was demanding he embrace her. Suddenly she pulled away on her own looking flushed and slightly disoriented.

"This I think I should stop," she cried out breathlessly, fearful for what she felt, fearful of wishing John would touch her. "Good night," was all she said before she turned toward the big log house.

"Please don't go yet," he called after her in a muffled voice but it was of no use, she melted into the shadows of the house and he was left with the sound of the tree frogs and his own rapidly beating heart.

That night John and Phillip shared a bed that was infinitely more comfortable than the chairs of the evening before. By half past ten, the entire household of twenty-one had retired. Nineteen were peacefully sleeping, two still lie awake. John had no excuse for not sleeping well other than the images of the willowy Nordic beauty with desire in her eyes which haunted him until almost midnight. He could taste her for hours after their kiss and he wanted so much more of her.

Freyja, alone in her bed, was also having trouble sleeping. She could think only of their kisses and his hand on her breast. She remembered every sensual moment, every sensation, every feeling and relived them over and over again. She had no idea she could feel the things she had felt and she wanted to feel them again. But at the same time she was afraid to feel them, afraid of what she might do, afraid of what she might be led to do. John Power was unlike any of the men of her acquaintance, she thought, her heart still racing at the memory of his kisses. Those kisses! Good lord, what kisses! Until that moment she'd never known what a real kiss could be. She'd felt like melting into utter abandonment in his arms. He was so very thrilling. His masculinity was intoxicating and that made him more than just a little bit dangerous. Yes, *dangerous*, that was the word. He was dangerous because when she was with him, she felt things she'd never felt before with anyone. For the first time in her young life Freyja felt desire, she fairly burned with it. She had more to fear from him, she told herself, than from any renegades.

# *Chapter 8*

Tracking Bear was a rheumy Indian of thirty-five winters who had left a third of his adult body weight in the bottom of a rum barrel. Yet, when he was sober he had wits enough to be of service as he proved when Sven flushed him out of the small cove where he lived and told him about wanting to track the renegades. The older Indian was fishing when the young giant, followed by his younger brother, Regin, came upon him. The savage calmly tilted his heavily pock marked face to look up at the hulk standing over him and remembering when the man had been a lad half Tracking Bear's size. Now he was half of Sven's size.

Tracking Bear had outlived two wives and six children when his body had successfully won the battle against the dreaded white man's disease that had left his face badly scarred. His loved ones had lost their battles. Scars did not distress him. He was a man of heavy, rugged features, who had only been concerned with his prowess in hunting, fighting, and bedding his females, not in his physical appearance. Scars were the marks of living, like tattoos, they told stories of life's adventures. He was proud of the bear claw scars which stood out pale upon his leg, the mountain lion teeth marks purple on his shoulder, the knife scars on his arms, cheek, and chest. The pock scars however, when he bothered to see them, were a reminder of his losses - his two wives, his children, his parents, his two sisters and their children, and his brother and his brother's entire family. It was a great many losses for one man to bear and he sometimes could not. At those times, he sought forgetfulness with the white man's drink. But forgetfulness had a price. His flesh sagged and his teeth were rotting. Two in front had been knocked out when he had taken a bad fall while drunk and no females wished to spend time with him anymore. He had no one and so he lived alone and earned his keep by tracking for the lumberjacks.

"Shadow scare the fish away," Tracking Bear observed bluntly without emotion to convey a certain resentment that Sven's shadow stretched out over the fishing hole like a huge oak tree.

"We need your help," Sven said respectfully, unable to hide his shadow. The Indian only grunted. "You've heard of father's death?"

"I hear."

"It is right that the killer should pay for his crime. Do you agree?"

The skinny frame shrugged.

"We have decided to seek out the killer. Will you track for us?"

The Indian laughed roughly. It turned to a high pitched wheezing sound. "Who can track a trail gone cold these many days? I have no magic."

Sven's brow was knit together and he bit his upper lip in frustration. "We must find these renegades before their lack of punishment makes them even bolder. Our families no longer feel safe. I thought you were our friend, Tracking Bear. Can you offer no help?"

"This I did not say."

"What do you suggest?" It was Regin that spoke out.

"Renegades not drop from sky. Someone know who these thieves are. I will ask around villages. Someone must know of them and what habits are. This is way to find them."

"That's good advice," replied Sven. "I would hope that you could begin your travel before the sun sets on this day. My brother will go with you."

The Indian grunted and nodded his head in agreement.

Sven had to be content and keep a lid on his mounting displeasure that the Indian did not jump up and run to do his bidding instantaneously. The large man had learned that you could not force an Indian to do anything, you had to wait for them to progress in their own time. He held his tongue, nodded farewell to Regin, and returned to the settlement.

The Power brothers understood the reasoning behind the message Sven conveyed upon his return and that of necessity it delayed departure. Personally, John was quite pleased for the purely selfish reason of being able to stay close to Freyja and continue his wooing. But he and his brother watched Sven Junior pick up the mantle of leadership and stand strong within the small community. It was perhaps the hardest for his own brothers to understand the delay. There was a great deal of discussion, some argument, short tempers, frustrations. Finally, everyone did resolve themselves to the necessity of waiting.

Phillip immediately saw the opportunity for everyone to lend a hand in the construction of the stockade. The more hands involved the quicker the wall would go up. And the better they would feel in leaving the community to hunt the troublemakers.

They dug in and set to work. A perimeter was established after due consideration. All the existing homes could not be included within the defense wall but most were. Trees of the proper size were marked out from within the surrounding forest. As the task of felling the trees and hand stripping their limbs began, an assembly line was established to bundle logs together and lead the horses pulling them down into the settlement itself. The settlement took on the look of an ant hill abuzz with activities.

John and Phillip stripped down to their breeches and joined the rest of the lumberjacks in the tasks to be done. Neither brother was of a size or height to compare to the Olafson brood of full grown males, but both acquitted themselves more than adequately. Everywhere one looked a sweating tan back could be seen bent to deliver the powerful strokes of an axe. The sound of those axes biting into the trees echoed through the river valley.

The sight of men stripped to their breeches working in the sun was a common one in the lumber camp but even so, Freyja found herself seeking out glimpses of John Power for when she looked at him she felt something very different than she had ever felt before. She was drawn to him. He might not be so large as her brothers but he was finely put together, this man from the harbor. None could find him lacking in an appraisal for his was a body of excellent proportions and well toned. But it was more than that. More than watching his lean muscles ripple through his back and chest as he wielded his axe that mesmerized her. It was the way he moved, so differently from the lumbermen. There was something powerful without being gigantic or hulking, smoothly graceful without being weak or un-masculine.

A quiet strength radiated from him as he hefted the tool over and over with seemingly little effort. She was spellbound. Feeling somehow wanton, yet somehow incapable of helping herself, her eyes followed the line of his taut stomach as it dipped into his tight breeches. Her cheeks burned but yet she smiled inwardly with admiration. A burnished gold triangle of hair lightly covered his chest and she noticed his skin had begun to flush out in a deepening hue that promised to turn to a golden tan as the days went on. Yes, John was most pleasing to her eye though she would let no one know she watched him.

John caught glimpses of the maiden as the day progressed. He pretended to be pausing for a breath or wiping sweat from his brow, but Phillip who was his work partner merely grinned knowingly. If she was anywhere around, John just couldn't keep his eyes off of her. Balancing buckets filled with water, her golden glory done up in two thick braids which swayed seductively at her hips as she walked. Hanging wash upon the rope lines, her arms outstretched, her breasts lifted high as the breeze blew her skirts against her slim figure. Shepherding children, several clinging to her skirts demanding her attention. She patiently addressed them, settled their disputes, kissed their bumps, and gave laughing hugs to turn tears to smiles. Later, when he saw her with the buckets again heading once more for the river, he made an excuse and left his work. Wiping the sweat from his face with his handkerchief, he hurried to catch up with her.

Snatching one of the buckets from her hand he said loudly enough to be heard, "Let me help you fill these and perhaps you won't mind bringing the crew some water to quench their thirst."

"Oh, of course," she said immediately, "I had no idea you were out of water." She looked almost guilty as she followed him around a small bend toward the river eager to assist the workers however she could.

"Perhaps not out," he replied moderately, "but what is there will now be very warm and not refreshing."

"You're burning," she observed with concern. "You'd best put your shirt back over your shoulders. You'll need a salve to get through the night..." No sooner were they out of sight when he pulled her to him and stole a kiss. "John," she admonished in a good humored fluster, "you must not."

"Why not?" he laughed and kissed her again.

"Someone will see... my brothers..." she was gasping, giggling, trying to avoid his mouth and then she stopped avoiding him and they were locked together and soon quite breathless. She felt her heart racing as his lips claimed her again and her arms went around him, her exposed forearms and hands feeling his naked skin burning hot beneath her touch. When he released her mouth, it took a moment for Freyja to think. "You... really must... protect... yourself... tie... something... around your shoulders... at least."

"The only thing I need protect myself from is you," he replied lightly, shrugging off her concern for his sunburn and holding her with his eyes.

"I must... get... the... water. I will be missed," she tried to push herself free but there was no strength in her arms at that moment, the clean sweat male scent of him holding her faster than bonds.

"Promise to meet me at the swing again tonight."

"John..."

"Promise and I'll let you go now."

"Someone is going to see..."

"Promise."

She couldn't free herself from his embrace. "I'll bring something for your burn," she finally agreed and he let her go, taking up the buckets. He filled them for her, took up the heavy containers and carried them back to within everyone's sight. If anyone noticed them, no one said anything.

"You carry these full?" he asked looking at her and marveling as though just registering their weight.

"Of course," she laughed.

"These are heavy," he grinned. "I'll take them to the house for you."

"You needn't, you have your own work to do."

"I know... but I want to."

She smiled and said nothing more. In a short time, Freyja was going about offering water to all the workers and John had returned to his labors on the stockade.

Phillip watched his brother in restrained amusement. He had to admire the way John had managed to steal a few moments with the young beauty in broad daylight. Oh, he knew what that help-you-with-the-water playacting was all about, it was very transparent to him. Surely her brothers saw it, too. Phillip kept his chuckles to himself and said nothing when John returned to their work station.

When John observed some of the men bantering with Freyja as they refreshed themselves from her water bucket, his hammering became so erratic he struck his own thumb but Phillip knew better than to say a thing. At lunch when several of the bachelors gathered around her at the serving trestle, vying for her attention, John became restless and short tempered and Phillip simply shrugged. After lunch John was so preoccupied watching Freyja move about the construction site, he stumbled over a stack of timber and rather gracelessly fell sprawling to the ground. Phillip couldn't help but laugh which gained him a deadly look. When Freyja went once again to the river, John watched to see that no one else accompanied her. So intent was he that he missed his footing on the short scaffolding and almost took Phillip with him as he fell to the ground, scraped but unhurt.

"I must say that was very neat," Phillip observed dryly. "Thanks for not taking me with you. I'd not realized how clumsy you're becoming in your *old age*. You'd be hard pressed to explain to Caroline that you made her a widow by breaking my neck." The only reply was a string of soft cursing.

At day's end, the men all went to the river with bars of homemade soap and washed the day's sweat and grime away. The married men knew their suppers and the comforts of home awaited them and wasted no time. John's sunburnt skin was beginning to repay him for its abuse and he had acquired a number of knocks, bruises, and scrapes but he hardly noticed. What everyone else noticed were the dark scowls he gave to every man whom he had seen talking to Freyja. The bachelors avoided eye contact with this other Power brother who appeared not to be such an agreeable sort now that the formalities were over. They knew, respected, and liked Phillip but his brother had them hurrying off to the mess hall as quickly as they could.

At the Olafson home, the table was laid tidily and full of good food. John appeared, his hair wet but combed and tied back neatly at the nape of his neck. He'd donned his other pair of breeches and a fresh shirt which was left casually open at the collar. He and Phillip were no longer "visiting guests" but part of the family work crew and after the day's labors together, everyone assumed a great deal less formality than the night before.

John sat as he had the evening before and found it difficult to mask his disappointment when Skadi sat down next to him where Freyja had sat before. Freyja ended up sitting several seats further down on the same side of the table, surrounded on either side by her brothers and John couldn't see her at all. The young man contented himself with appeasing his growling belly and making the best of his growing discomfort.

When the relatively quiet meal was over, the brothers went out to have a smoke and discuss the progress they had made that day. John did not want to smoke. And he was not yet ready to retire. He wanted to be alone with Freyja but she was busy with the other women clearing the table and doing the dishes. He stood around rather uncomfortably and wandered into the parlor where a lamp had been lit against the failing light.

It was a cozy room furnished with hand carved chairs and a love seat all upholstered with animal skins. It wasn't the least bit feminine but the clean lines made it neat and attractive. Several tables of various sizes and a small glassed cabinet against the side wall completed the sparse furnishings. John's eye was caught by a magnificent vase stored protectively behind the glass of that cabinet. He hadn't really noticed anything about the room the night before when they had had their meeting. Now, he walked over to take a better look at the piece. He opened the glass door carefully and picked up the vase for closer inspection. It was perhaps twelve inches in height and decorated with a painting of exquisite detail and craftsmanship depicting a beautiful and voluptuous, bare breasted young woman with streaming red gold hair and a fine looking, beardless blond warrior in golden armor. They were linked together in a most immodest and sensual embrace. John smiled to himself thinking wickedly of Freyja and himself.

Young Peter saw John from the doorway looking at the valued family treasure. "Don't let Ma catch you touching that," he warned and John looked up quickly. "It is very beautiful, isn't it?" Peter asked, smiling proudly as he walked over to John.

"Yes, very. It is an exquisite piece of work. Who are they?" John asked holding the vase with proper care.

"That is Sigurd and Brynhild."

"Quite a happy pair," John grinned, the names meant nothing to him.

"Oh, no, they are tragic lovers. It's really a very sad story." John raised an eyebrow in curiosity and Peter went on. "Brynhild was a fallen Valkyrie."

"Valkyrie?"

"*Ja*, in Norse legend, Valkyries are virgin warrior women who serve Odin in Valhalla. Valhalla is where all worthy and brave warriors go when they die, *if* they die bravely in battle. In Odin's great hall the Valkyries serve the brave at an endless feast. But they are more than just serving girls, they ride over the battlefields with Odin and gather up the men he decides to take with him."

John thought about that for a moment. "You said she was *fallen*?" he asked, looking back at the painted beauty.

"Brynhild disobeyed Odin and spared her half-brother Sigfried from death, allowing him to continue living after Odin said he should die. Odin was furious with her for her disobedience and he banished her to a mountain top where," the boy blushed and lowered his voice, "she could be had by any man who came along. When Odin's temper cooled, he took pity and surrounded her by a protective ring of fire where she would remain sleeping until someone brave enough to breach the fire came for her. Sigurd was a mighty warrior and he came and dared the flames and woke her with a kiss."

"Why, that's rather like our Sleeping Beauty story," John smiled at the boy.

"A sleeping beauty, *ja*, and when they saw each other, they fell in love. Sigurd pledged her his love but there was a curse. He was bewitched into marrying another and Brynhild was tricked into marrying someone else as well. When she discovered what she thought was Sigurd's betrayal of her, she went a little mad and cried out for vengeance. He was slain upon her urging and when she saw his glorious body laid out in death and realized what had really happened, she killed herself and threw herself across him so they could lie side by side for all eternity."

John had watched the boy's animated face. "That is very tragic," he nodded with sober attention, vaguely wondering if some tiny kernel of fact centuries ago had been the start of such a tale. "Well, this vase is certainly a fine work of art."

"My father bought it for my mother as a courting gift. He told us he paid what amounted to three months wages for it, but he did it to prove to her father that he would always be able to take care of her."

John looked back at the vase in his hands. "I can see it is very special," he said as he carefully put it back in its place and closed the little glass door. Just then Sonya stuck her head in through the parlor door.

"Peter, time you go to bed," she said briskly. The youngster bid John good night. Tomorrow would bring another day of the same grueling activity for there was an unspoken pressure to finish the work before Tracking Bear returned with any news of where they could find the renegades.

Freyja assisted her sisters-in-law in getting the small children into bed. The large house grew progressively more quiet as one by one the brothers, wives, and children said their good-nights and retired. Finally, Freyja saw her youngest sister to bed.

Washing her own face and brushing out her hair, the young woman wondered if John would remember their rendezvous by the swing. He had said nothing to her all evening although she had seen him talking to Peter. Perhaps he had forgotten. She should not be surprised, she told herself, he had worked hard and long and was no lumberjack to be used to such labor. He would be fast asleep, she told herself, if that sunburn allowed him to sleep. She picked up a large jar of ointment, thinking of his discomfort and because it made her feel less shameless to carry a useful salve to him, if he was there. Gliding through the quiet house, she slipped silently out through the back door. Going to the swing, she experienced a pang of disappointment. There was no sign of him. She sighed deeply and told herself she should have given him the salve right after supper. How thoughtless of her and now he would suffer through the night. She set the heavy jar down on the grass and sat swinging slowly. Taking a deep breath, she savored the fresh air of the late evening and let her mind drift as young maidens are apt to do.

Suddenly warm hands covered hers as she clung to the ropes. And a soft deep voice was at her ear.

"I missed you at supper."

She smiled in the dark. He hadn't forgotten. Her heart was skipping beats she was so pleased and she tried to keep the tremor from her voice.

"I was there."

"But so far away."

"I could hear you talking." She felt her hair being lifted aside and soft lips bent to her exposed neck and kissed her. The feelings that streaked through her body made her deliciously weak and her head rolled over giving him greater access to plant kisses along her sensitive flesh.

"John..." it was a sigh of wanting, of needing and he was around her, drawing her up from the swing seat and into his arms. His lips were on hers and all those confusing, wonderful, and powerful feelings were wrenching through her body. Suddenly, Freyja's heart was beating so hard she could feel it pound against her rib cage. And she was trembling violently. She reached out to him as much to steady herself as anything else only to discover that when her hands touched him her body could not help but follow. She was pressed into him, feeling his hard lean body against hers, his strong shoulders beneath her hands, his tongue entwine with hers. Her fingers dug into the lose curls of his hair, registering its fine texture. She was struggling for breath, feeling the heat of his body through her clothing when the scent of him registered with her, clean yet masculine and overwhelmingly powerful to her. She breathed deeply and the smell of his skin was as a stimulant to something within her that was helpless to deny him.

John felt the fire within and without as his hand stole up to embrace one soft round breast. His thumb teased the nipple through the cloth of her bodice and it immediately grew hard against his fingers. He heard her gasp, then stiffen and pull back. She looked at him, her slightly slanting eyes fixed upon his face, his eyes, his lips. He saw his own desire reflected in her eyes, then confusion, and finally embarrassment. She turned to run but he caught her wrist and drew her back, holding her wrists to clasp around him.

"You can't go," he cried. "Not yet. I won't let you," he breathed against her ear and he heard her moan softly before her full sweet lips were again on his.

Locked together, she felt the power of that kiss and the power of his presence and knew she would lose all control of herself if she did not break away. She pulled from him again, putting the swing between them. "Please John, everything is happening so fast. Too fast. Please... I beg you."

John took a deep breath and looked at her in the moonlight. His body was aching with need. "If you only knew how difficult it is to look at you and not touch you." He was trembling himself. He took another deep breath, willing himself to a state of restraint.

She stood perfectly still, feeling her blood pound in her ears. He would think her a terrible tease. She had come out here to be with him, hadn't she? What had she expected? Suddenly, she remembered the salve.

"I... I brought... something... for you, for your burn." She was having difficulty getting the words out and she stooped and bent to retrieve the jar on the ground. "It's a salve... it's very good." Her voice had come back from a weak whisper as she focused on the ointment. "Mama makes it from finely rendered fat and healing herbs. It will sooth you and help so you can get some sleep." John took the jar from her, he'd totally forgotten about his superficial discomfort.

"If I fail to sleep tonight, it will not be because of the sun."

Freyja said nothing but averted her eyes.

"So tell me, my little Nordic goddess, how can it be that you are not yet promised to any one?"

She smiled softly at his address. "Papa would not force me to marry against my wishes."

"Have you no wish to marry?"

"Of course, but there has been no man here that I have had any wish to marry," she replied. He had kept his distance and she was finding it easier to breathe and to talk. "I think I worry brother Sven." She smiled broadly and her voice had the tinkle of laughter in it. "He never approved of all my reading, said it makes a woman dissatisfied. Papa talked of taking me back to civilization to..." she stopped suddenly realizing what she was saying and blushed, grateful that the shadows hid her hot cheeks. "He thought I should meet more people." He had stepped closer to her again, his hand raising her chin.

"What was meant to be will be, no matter," his voice rumbled from far back in his throat. "Do you believe that?"

"You mean fate?"

"Yes, fate."

"Perhaps."

"And you and I were meant to be. I knew it the moment I saw you." He lifted her lips to him, those full, flushed, warm lips. He couldn't stay away any longer and he swiftly lowered the jar to the ground taking her shoulders in both hands. Softly his lips brushed hers, tenderly, teasingly, his mouth captured hers again and she felt the hunger rise within.

Somehow his hand had snaked passed the neckline of her bodice. He was holding the bare flesh of her breast possessively, his warm fingers sensually caressing her and her body was tingling in a heated response, her mind swimming in an overload from her senses. "No.... I...I.... oh.. oh... John, I cannot think. I can't breathe, you confuse me so. No one has ever made me feel this way and it frightens me."

"You have nothing to fear from me..."

"You bewitch me…" she gathered all her resolve and pushed away from him quickly tugging up her neckline. She willed herself to think what her mother would say if she saw her. "No..." she said more strongly but keeping her voice hushed as she took several steps back from him. "I cannot stay unless you promise not to touch me. Please, stay there." She pointed a finger at him in warning.

John sighed again but was still. "Don't you know I spent this entire day looking to the moments I could have with you tonight."

"I am not without education but I am not sophisticated. We live a simple, straight forward life here. I am not equipped to deal with... with... I... don't know... how to play these... games of... seduction," she said a little warily.

"Games? Oh, my sweet darling, I play no game with you..."

"I have no experience to prepare me. Your touching my body... it is... more than... I can bear..."

"I want you. Do you know what that means? My body is crying out for yours, the need is overpowering. I want you desperately."

"I... I can't... don't say that. You overwhelm me, John. I am resolved to go to my husband on my wedding night a virgin. You would take that resolve from me," she cried softly and bolted away.

"No, please, don't go," he cried out after her in a restrained voice but she was gone. John looked down at the jar she had left him, and with a sigh, he picked it up.


The next day the activities in the camp continued and the wall progressed. But John was most unhappy. Thanks to the salve Freyja had thoughtfully provided to him, he slept better than he would have without it, but it was not lack of sleep or sunburn that was making John unhappy. It was Freyja's absence. All through the day, he looked for her. Whatever the girl was occupied in doing, she was not doing it anywhere he could see her. Snotra brought them water. Even at lunch time, when he felt certain he would see Freyja at last, there was no sign of her. Phillip chuckled as John's mood grew more irritable as the day progressed.

At supper that night within the Olafson home, Freyja could avoid John no longer. He made certain he waited until she took her seat at the table and then, he sat directly across from her. The intensity of his looks were very disconcerting and she was flushed and concerned that someone would notice. She blistered under his gaze though he said little, and she knew he knew she had purposefully stayed out of his sight. As she helped to clear the table at the end of the meal, he managed to catch her and whisper a request to meet him later at the swing. Since he would not leave her until she agreed, she finally consented.

That night when Freyja went out to the swing, she did so warily. Her hair was still done in thick braids and although the evening was mild she wore a stiff jerkin over her simple blouse and skirt. She saw John sitting in the swing and as she approached she kept her distance.

"Freyja, whatever I did to make you angry, I am truly sorry. I meant no offense, no insult, no dishonor. Please forgive me, please do not be angry with me," he said as soon as he saw her, his intense eyes looking to her, tinged with sadness.

"But... I am not angry," she replied with a little confusion, she had expected him to be angry. "Why do you think that?" she asked.

"Do you deny that you have avoided me all day?"

"No," she replied weakly. "But it is not because of you, it is because of me." She looked down to the ground. "I cannot trust myself around you, John Power."

"Freyja, I can't help what I feel and I know you feel it, too." He stood up and stepped to her, causing her to step back from him. "I want you but I do not toy with you. I can't help myself."

"You must. What I feel when you touch me is too powerful. It is like a liquor that takes away all my inhibitions, all my restraint. John, you affect me like no man I have ever known," she spoke with innocent honesty. "I have so little control." He stepped toward her again but she warned him off with a small voice. "You must not take advantage of me." He stopped and dropped his hands to his sides.

"My God, you're right. What am I doing? Just because we are on the frontier, I have no right... I don't know what's come over me," he said and added with a tinge of bravado, "or where all my good manners have flown. My mother would be ashamed of me," he grinned ingratiatingly and was contrite. "I'm acting like a seducer of innocents. Forgive me, Freyja. I will have restraint for both of us." He stretched out his hand and she hesitantly put hers into it. "I love you, Freyja Olafson. I want to have you and hold you for the rest of my life. To protect, to honor, to cherish. Do you think you could spend the rest of your life with me? Do you think there is a possibility that you could grow to love me as well?"

There was a silence in which John could hear his own heart beating in his ears as he waited for her answer.

"I already do," she said softly and stepped to him. The moon reflected in her eyes, her dewy skin glowed and the shiny strands of her hair reflected silver in the moonlight. She leaned up to kiss him with modest gentleness and when she stepped back he was beaming at her, his teeth white within his smile.

"Freyja, my love, you make me a very happy man. I can't believe I've found you up here in the midst of a lumber camp. I shudder to think I might not have come up here with Phillip, I might never have known you."

She said nothing but kissed his hands as they held hers.

"I suppose the proper thing to do is speak to your big brother."

"I believe so."

"Your family is in mourning but when a proper amount of time has passed, we will wed."

She beamed a smile at him.

"Then we'll travel a bit and see some of the world... would you like that?"

"Oh, yes," she responded flashing her dimpled smile.

"And when we come home I'll build you a fine house and we'll have great fun making many babies."

"Oh," she blushed and her dimples were dazzling.

"My darling, darling Freyja, I am completely... totally... madly in love with you! It has hit me like one of your Nordic thunderbolts and I shall never be the same!" He laughed and spun her around before drawing her lovingly back into his arms for a much more gentle embrace.

# *Chapter 9*

John rose early and had made himself comfortable in the large Olafson kitchen by the time Sven walked in for breakfast. It was still very dark out and Sven didn't contain his surprise to find the lamps already lit and John already up and dressed. Grateful to find the kitchen fire going strong and the coffee pot hot and full of fresh brew, the giant of a man poured himself a large steaming cup as he inhaled the aroma appreciatively.

John watched the big man seat himself at the table and down half the cup in two gulps. "Sven, I have something of great importance to discuss with you," he stated directly.

"*Ja?*" Sven replied rubbing the sleep from his eyes with fingers the size of sausages. "I'm more awake than I look. What is it?"

"With your father gone, you are head of this family. So, it is fitting that I ask you. I wish to marry your sister."

That opened Sven's eyes very quickly.

"Freyja?" he asked in what was more shock than surprise.

John nodded. "I know this is sudden, but I know what I want when I see it. I have been a very lonely man and I need her. She is everything I could want and I love her deeply, Sven, and will cherish her forever. You know I have the means to take care of her and our children. I ask you for her hand."

Sven had listened intently and broke into a wide grin. "I always wondered who Freyja would marry. Papa let her be educated and she is too refined now... you know what I mean, she doesn't fit the roughness of the frontier, she is too..." he groped for the right word.

"elegant..."

"*Ja*, elegant. Too elegant for a lumber camp and I could not imagine her married to one of our lumberjacks. And what says she to you?"

"Our feelings are mutual and she has agreed."

"Then, you have my blessing," and with that the huge man stood and shook John's hand soundly. Then, he grabbed him into a big bear hug. "Welcome to the family, little brother," he said slapping him soundly on the back. John winced despite his best efforts not to. It wasn't just the sunburn, it was the creak of his bones within the paralyzing embrace.

"What's this?" Sonya came into the kitchen. "John joins our family... how?" she questioned.

"Freyja and John are going to be married, Mama. I have approved the match."

"Freyja? My Freyja? She is only a ba..."

"She's eighteen and a woman fully grown. It's time she had a husband and some babies of her own. But not until nine months after the wedding," he added with a pointed look at John.

"Have no fear, Mistress Sonya," John looked the older woman in the eyes. "I intend on making Freyja very happy for the rest of her life." And if that meant putting off making love to her until a few vows were publicly witnessed, he could wait, he told himself, and he would wait. Freyja wished it and her wishes were what he now lived for.

At supper that evening, Sven announced his sister's betrothal to the rest of the family. He couldn't deny he was very pleased that the two families would be connected henceforth by blood, sharing grandchildren and making cousins ever on. As they passed about several jugs of homemade liquor to moderately toast the occasion, Sven found himself wondering if their father had not died, would Freyja and John have even met? Might she have finally accepted one of the lumberjacks or was it destiny? John might have come with Phillip to the camp at any time just for the ride. He could have met Freyja a year from now with the very same results. Papa could have taken her with him into the town and met John. Well, there was no sense trying to second guess the Fates. Papa had died. They had met. And soon, retribution would be extracted from those savages.

Phillip was the second to give John a congratulatory handshake and manly hug. "You might have told me yourself," he miffed, then socked his brother in the arm with a grin, "not that it's any surprise. She's a beauty, John, may you be as happy as I am."

"Thanks, little brother," John grinned back. "Actually, between Mother and Father and you and Caroline, a man's hard pressed not to think of marriage as the state of absolute bliss."

"Believe me, sharing my bed with Caroline is a damn sight more agreeable than sharing it with you," Phillip laughed.

In the days that followed, John and Freyja received the personal well wishes of every man and woman in camp. The younger bachelors saw a much more agreeable John, now that he had won Freyja. They should have known. And how did they let him come into their camp and steal the very prize from under their noses, they asked themselves? Well, it wasn't as if they hadn't tried. Everyone of them had been turned down at least twice and some even more. They commiserated with each other and discovered that being partners in their loss was a bond that drew them closer together.

In little more than a week's time, the simple stockade wall was completed. From that day forth, it would take a great deal more effort to randomly steal from the lumber camp. During the day they could go out to the forests and do their work, during the night they would swing the large gate shut and be secure. At least more secure than they had been. Now they needed only to wait for Tracking Bear and Regin's return.

These were precious days filled with sunshine for John and Freyja and their love, even when the rain fell from the sky. They spent as much time together as possible and suffered the nights apart while looking forward to the day of their wedding. John could have patience now, looking forward to the consummation and a whole lifetime together just like his parents. In his heart he said his good-bye to Alana knowing that both she and Huffsmeier would wish him well for love was everything.

Every hour John spent with the young maiden, his heart and mind rejoiced in fuller and fuller gladness. Finding another woman of such rare beauty was good fortune beyond his wildest dreams but he was discovering so many other facets to her. Beneath that beautiful surface he knew existed a warmth and depth of caring and thoughtfulness but her wit caused him delighted mirth. Her intellect was capable of keeping up with him. Her innocence and lack of sophistication were not just charming but an appropriate backdrop to her honesty and he felt he could talk to her about anything and trust her with his every secret.

"They say I look just like my father," he said as he sat back against the tree. Freyja was amusing herself making daisy chains at his side. "I guess I can see the resemblance except he is much older than I."

She saw the muscles of his jaw tighten. It bothered him, she could tell. If it didn't bother him he wouldn't have brought it up.

"Just as Sven looks like... much like our father did," Freyja replied.

"Yes... I suppose."

"But Sven is not Papa. They were similar in many ways and they looked much alike but they were not the same person at all."

"I don't even think we're similar."

"People do that, John. I don't believe they mean anything by it but it seems to be human nature, when people look alike. I remember reading a story about identical twins. They looked exactly alike and everyone treated them as if they were the same person but they were not, they had very different personalities, feelings, likes and dislikes, thoughts, ideas. One was more quiet, one was more outgoing, and they had different tastes and favorites and skills but the world only looked at the surface and treated neither of them like a complete and whole individual. It caused them a great deal of anguish they said. They hated it. They even went through a period of time when each resented the other for not allowing the one or the other to be seen as a unique person unto his own."

"That would be terribly frustrating," John murmured thoughtfully.

"Even more frustrating than being mistaken for your father, perhaps?" she said softly.

He looked at her. "It's not that I'm mistaken for him."

"But yet you are perhaps compared to him too much? I know if it were me I would be a little resentful."

"It's just that... I don't know. All my life... he's been so perfect. He's done everything and accomplished everything."

Freyja chuckled and smiled. "Surely not, John. You only think so because you have been a small boy always looking up at him. But you are a man now. I'm sure your mother could tell you of some human failings."

"My mother worships him. I've never ever heard her complain about him, not one small fault... ever. He's a paragon of virtue, a god in her eyes. She makes one feel she was the luckiest woman on the face of the earth for all time..." Freyja leaned over and kissed John's mouth, cutting him short.

"Perhaps she was for her generation," she said softly looking at him, her sea-green eyes quiet and alight with a sparkle like sunlight dancing on gentle waves. "But I can assure you that I am the luckiest in our generation. You are your own man, John, you cannot doubt that. It is up to you to decide on whatever you choose to do. And you will accomplish many things your father has never even dreamed of doing."

John looked at her and saw the belief in those beautiful eyes and he believed it, too. He could hardly wait to bring her home, introduce her to his family. They could not help but love her but not nearly as much as he did.

Suddenly, John felt himself a giant among men. She made him feel like a conqueror, a king. He would accomplish things, do things, achieve things. For the first time in his life he really believed that. There was nothing he could not do, no obstacle too high or strong or wide that he could not overcome and master. Together they would build a life, a place, a presence, a family and with her at his side, he would be the best doctor the Jersey colony had ever seen he was certain of it. If Freyja believed in him he knew he could do it. She inspired him. She fueled a new desire in him to stand out and make his mark. He wanted her to be proud of him.

"Freyja, there's one more thing I want you to know. Something I have told no one else."

"What is it, John?"

He took her hand and she gave him her full attention. "Freyja, you know I am a physician?"

"Yes."

"Three years ago I went to France to study. While I was in Paris I read a paper written by a very intelligent doctor. Some other time I will share that with you but... the important point is I wrote to him and asked if I could study with him. There was so much he could teach me."

Freyja nodded and did not interrupt.

"He lives in Switzerland. I traveled to meet him. He invited me into his home to study and learn and... and I met his daughter. She was also a doctor. She was brilliant and she was beautiful and we fell in love. And we married even though I knew she was not going to live."

He heard Freyja take a quick small gasp as her eyes looked at him intently.

"Her mother had died very young of a blood disorder. Her father spent years researching trying to find a cure because he feared his daughter might have inherited it. She did. The same as her mother. We were married far less than a year when she died." He steeled himself to look into her eyes. "I loved her very much, Freyja, and watching her waste away was the hardest thing I have ever done in my life. And you are the only person I have told this. No one else knows I am a widower. Not even my father."

Somehow she was suddenly close. Her free hand stroked his head as she kissed him softly, tenderly, lovingly. "John, I am so sorry," she breathed. It was barely more than a whisper. "You have carried the burden of your sorrow all alone. I understand. It is too private. But you have shared it now and any burden shared becomes only half as heavy. What was her name?"

"Alana."

"If Alana was as brilliant as you say, and loved you as you say then I know she would want you to have the life she could not have. A full life, a long life, and a life full of love. And I do so love you, John Power."

It was a drizzly overcast day when the skinny Indian appeared out from the forest with young Regin at his side. It had been a fortnight since they had left and Phillip had had to send yet another message back home to explain his delay. He'd hinted that he had to play chaperon while John courted the eldest Olafson daughter.

Sven saw his brother and the scout, and taking huge strides was upon them almost instantly. "What news?" he demanded darkly.

"I think we've found out where they are but can we have a decent cup of coffee first?" Regin replied dropping down from the saddle.

"I'm sorry, Regin. Welcome home. It's been so long, we are all raw with the waiting," Sven spoke apologetically clapping his younger brother on the back.

His brother nodded and continued to speak as they walked. "We had to go to three villages before we could really get anything we could use. I see the stockade is complete. It looks good."

"It should have been built long ago," Sven stated flatly and Regin knew he was thinking if it had, their father would still be alive. Regin had been thinking the same thing.

Because of the rain, the men gathered at the mess cabin after instructing their women to stay home. Tracking Bear and Regin both were served hot food and hot coffee laced moderately with mead against the cold chill in the air.

"The best we can tell," Regin was explaining, "they are a small renegade bunch just like we figured. They've been raiding from the Indian villages as well, mostly food. An odd weapon or two. Nothing that much. The local tribes were surprised to learn they'd spilled blood. The first village told us they came from the south. Second one said they figured 'em for coming from the east and the last village knew a couple of them. It turns out they make their base in Deer Gap."

"Deer Gap!" Bor exclaimed.

"That's only a hard day's walk from here," added Uland.

"Right over Old Man Mountain," Regin nodded.

"Shit. They're practically at our back door!" exploded one of the lumberjacks. And the rest began to mutter.

"All right, quiet down," Sven took control again. "How many?" he looked at Tracking Bear.

"Maybe five, maybe seven, no more," Tracking Bear answered.

"How do we know that?" Sven pressed.

"The last village, the chief that knew a couple of them, told us," Regin answered.

Sven stood. "All right let us be counted. Uland, Bor, you come with me. Regin, you stay here, you've been in the saddle many days and I need you to supervise the camp in my absence." The younger brother began to protest but saw the expression on Sven's face and went silent. "That's three. John, you and Phillip make five. Who else comes with us?" Seven more men stood up instantly and Sven picked five of them.

"Ten is enough," Sven said in conclusion, "the rest stay to continue work and protect the camp. We are working men after all, and we must continue to harvest the lumber. Everyone get a good night's sleep, we leave tomorrow at dawn."

Throughout the camp at the supper tables that night the women learned what had been decided and who was going. In the Olafson home, the table full of people were even quieter than usual. John looked at the beauty of Freyja and saw a cloud of tumult in her eyes, like the seas in a storm. They had been sitting next to each other at meals ever since their troth had been announced and he took her hand under the table. She held his hand fiercely and when he looked at her, he saw tears come to her eyes before she looked quickly away.

Freyja had been having dreams, terrible dreams. John was there but distant, no longer reachable, no longer could he hear her when she spoke. He would look through her as if he couldn't see her. And she would always awake feeling cold and empty, deserted and alone. How could she tell him her dreams were omens of disaster?

As soon as the meal was over, John stole Freyja away for some privacy. The other women understood and no one reprimanded the girl for disappearing with her lover into the quiet of the night as long as she stayed near the house, within easy reach.

"What is it, Freyja? Why are you upset?" he asked tenderly as soon as they were alone on the big porch. He held her delicate hands in his larger one and brushed a finger along her delicate cheek.

"Oh, John, there is a feeling," Freyja said looking at him and pulling one hand free to grip the spot at her solar plexus, "here. A heaviness of weight I cannot make go away. You will call it woman's foolishness but it is telling me you should not go. John, I fear your leaving like nothing I have ever feared before. Please do not go. Find another from the camp to take your place. Please don't go." She was begging in earnest, her high brow puckered in dismay.

"Freyja, darling, I cannot play the coward..."

"It is not cowardice to listen to the omens."

"What omens?"

"There are some who are gifted with second sight. And there are times when anyone may be given second sight. As a warning. This is one of those times, John. If we are parted, I fear... oh, I fear we will never be together again."

"Freyja, Freyja, I will not let it be so," he sought to reassure her. His kisses were gentle and tender, on her fingers, her palms, her wrists, on her nose, her eyes, her cheeks. "Nothing can stop me from coming back to you. And when I return we shall be wed. I promise. It's the beginning of a whole life together. You are exactly what I need. Now that I have found you, you don't think I'd let anything happen, do you? I don't want you to fret. It's only a small band, we're hardly going off to war. We take more than enough men, each with a long gun and short. The renegades will never know what hit them."

She was swept up in his clear gray eyes with those startling black rims. He was so earnest, so warm and she clung to his kisses and wanted to believe all would be as he said. But the heaviness of doom within her would not leave.

"I must go and help with the clean up," she said softly.

"Will you meet me at the tree later?"

"I will be there."

It was much later that night when she finally came to the tree. He had begun to give up hope, wondering what had stopped her, what had changed her mind, or who. He had watched as room by room the lights had been snuffed and the log house had grown dark. Then, he saw her in the moonlight and she was carrying a bundle.

"Freyja," he swept her to him and kissed her sweetly. "It's grown so late. I thought you changed your mind."

She kissed him back and took his hand. "Come," she said and he followed. She led him to the barn and climbed to the loft above the stalls. The moonlight streamed in the windows giving them ample light. The smell of the animals was pungent and earthy. The hay was cool and soft and she spread out a blanket.

"What is this?" he asked.

"John, I want to stay with you tonight. We will hold each other and while Sven would not approve, he cannot be too angry for only this if he finds out. I cannot bear to leave you, John. I cannot give up a minute more with you than I must. Please hold me through the night."

"Oh, Freyja," he held her soft shoulders with his hands and then, brushed down her lithe body. "You ask a great deal of my resolve."

"Is it too much?" her voice was intense and earnest, her face a blur of light coming out of the shadow.

"No. Not too much... just a great deal. You are so very desirable... so soft... so beautiful... the smell of your skin... oh, God, your hair smells like spices! The feel of you, the taste of you... I cannot wait until we are one," he moaned and pressed her close to his body. Her hands stroked his arms, his shoulders, his neck. Her fingers were lost in his curls. A cloud went over the moon and she pulled the neckline of his shirt open and began kissing him gently, sensuously, slowly down his neck and upon his chest. Each kiss making his heart pound.

"Freyja, sweet darling, do you realize what you are doing to me?" his voice had become hoarse. "This is torture if I am not to have you tonight."

"Then perhaps, I should not stop you," she said very quietly.

It took a moment for her words to register and when their meaning struck home John's emotions were impacted from several directions at once. He felt the wild ecstasy of knowing he could claim her, make her his right then, that she was offering herself to him and giving him permission to take her. At the same time, something noble and lofty was reminding him that her wish was to come to him a virgin on their wedding night and he should not allow her to sacrifice that wish. And then, there was a darker thought, fleeting, hardly formulated, but it recognized her fears for his mission. If something did happen to him, she would be left deflowered and shamed. He couldn't do that to her. Nobleness won out. He was not so uncontrollably lustful, not so incapable of self-restraint, now that she had put the decision upon him.

"No, you were right to begin with. We will only hold each other this night." He felt her whole body relax as he gathered her into his arms. And thus, they lie until finally in exhaustion they fell asleep.

An hour before dawn, Freyja opened her eyes and lying there quietly in the predawn light, she watched her lover sleep. He looked very young and incredibly innocent with his face relaxed and smooth. His blond whiskers barely showing. The soft lavender tinged shadows beneath his eyes were covered gently with his long dark lashes. His hair a tumble of curls fraught through with small pieces of hay. He had become everything to her and something deep within her, something too terrifying to face, was telling her they would never be together again. Tears came to her sea-green eyes. He didn't believe her and there was nothing more she could do. She did not want him to remember her as red eyed and sad. She must hide away her fear and put on a brave face. Perhaps, it was just possible that she was wrong, and he would return to her again. *Oh, please, dear God, let it be so.*

She watched him until he finally awoke. Stretching, he became aware of her and gave her a lopsided boyish smile.

"Good morning."

"Good morning, my betrothed," she answered him, her exquisite face radiant with love, her dimples totally disarming.

"Are the others up?"

She nodded slightly. "They are stirring. I am going to go to the privy and then I will go up to the house as if returning from it." She kissed him and left.

When Freyja walked into the kitchen, Anna was there. "Good morning," she said calmly.

"Oh, good morning, Freyja. I didn't know you were up already," the young matron looked at her.

"*Ja...* I just went to the privy."

Saying nothing, Anna continued to look at her. Freyja felt her cheeks begin to warm as she continued through the room to the stairs.

"Freyja..." Anna called quietly. Freyja stopped.

"What is it?"

"Best you brush your hair... you've straw in it," she whispered with a twinkle in her eyes. Freyja's hand involuntarily leapt to her head under Anna's steady gaze. "I wouldn't let Sven see it... or Uland for that matter."

"We did nothing, Anna, I swear," Freyja whispered quickly. "We only held each other through the night and I begged him not to go. I... I'm still a virgin."

Anna nodded and turned back to the cook pots. Perhaps that was true, perhaps not, it was between Freyja and her fiancé. Anna certainly wasn't going to tell anyone. She recalled that she and Uland were hardly in a position to throw stones.

In not much over an hour, those leaving had risen, dressed, eaten, and gathered together. Canteens were filled with fresh water and weapons were secured. There were not enough horses for everyone to have a mount, and so they were on foot. John and Phillip's animals were used to carry bedrolls and supplies. The Olafson women put up a brave front as their men left the compound. Of the ten leaving, not counting Tracking Bear, their menfolk made up almost half. They went out single file and plunged into the Indian forest. The last sight Freyja had of John, he was half turned with a broad smile on his face, leading his horse, his hat in his hand, waving to her with it

Sonya watched her sons leave with the others and refused to cry. It would not do for her daughters, her daughters-in-law, and her grandchildren to see her crying now. She would set the example. She would pretend to be strong. God bless them all and watch over those boys! And when they returned? She was loath to even consider Freyja's marriage. Not now, not so soon after losing Sven. She had nothing against John Power personally, she liked the lad and she greatly admired his family. His parents were the very best of people. But for Sonya's sons to marry meant gaining more daughters, while allowing her daughter to marry John meant losing her. Her young husband would take her away and how often would mother see daughter again? The Power family would want him back in Chartes Landing. It had been years since she and Sven had left the coast, and in all the years since, Sonya had never once been back. Of course, having a daughter there and eventually grandchildren was certainly an incentive to visit she had never had before. Oh, well, she told herself, as she waved her sons good-bye. There was time enough to worry about that. Today's worries were sufficient unto themselves. And today's worries included the well-being of Sven Junior, Uland, Bor, and the rest of the tracking party.

# *Chapter 10*

The trapper was puzzled when he came upon the stockaded camp. He thought it a fort at first but knew of no fort in the area. Then he questioned his own senses. Had he become turned around, lost his bearings? Where exactly was he? Could he possibly have so badly misread the landmarks and fallen so far off track? He walked through the big open gate and was further mystified. He saw no redcoats and no flag but modest log homes along with one huge log structure which was probably the main barracks but certainly had the look of a home with curtains at the windows. What kind of a fort was this?

"What can we help you with, Mister?" Sonya called from her porch.

"Ma'am? Where am I?" the trapper asked in vague bewilderment.

"This is a logging camp, Mister, on the Iwiki River. The coast is that way." She pointed to the east. "Follow the river and you'll come to Chartes Landing."

"I'm much obliged. I thought this be a fort at first an' couldn't quite get myself located. So it's a lumber camp, eh? Guess all th' mens is off haulin' trees, huh? Might ya have some vittles I could buy?"

Sonya looked at the man. He wasn't the most savory looking character but she had never been one to turn down a stranger looking for food.

"Stay there, I'll fetch a plate," she replied and went back inside her home.

"Who were you talking to Mama?" Freyja asked as she pulled fresh bread from the oven.

"It's a stranger looking for food. I'll make him a plate. You stay here, Freyja, I don't like the look of the man." Sonya set about putting together a plate of food. Just then the door opened and the trapper walked in. "Mister, I don't remember inviting you into my house! Now get back out onto the porch or I'll be forced to ask you to get out altogether," Sonya spoke assertively.

"Oh, sorry," the trapper removed his hat and nodded a slight bow to Freyja. "Guess I misunderstood. I'll git, no problem. Thankee."

Sonya finished preparing the plate although the fact that the stranger had been in their house upset her greatly. She noticed she was visibly shaking when she went to pour the hot coffee into a large cup and tried to will herself calm before Freyja noticed. Rationally, Sonya reasoned that looking upon Freyja was hardly a crime or a threat, but it bothered her as many things had begun to bother her since Sven's death. She felt vulnerable and insecure not just for herself but for her family. Sonya pushed back her misgivings with a deep breath, took the tray holding the ladened plate, coffee, and fresh bread and cool butter, out onto the front porch.

"Here you are, Mister," she said a bit roughly and dropped the tray down at the top of the porch steps with a clatter. "You eat and then you'd best be on your way. Our men don't like strangers sitting about," she warned with an ungracious scowl.

The man took the tray up with an automatic grin and nodded his head. He sat down in a spot of shade off the porch and ate his food slowly while his small dark eyes took in everything they could within the camp. When he finished, he wiped his mouth on his sleeve and stood up. Bringing his empty tray to the door, this time he knocked. In a moment, Sonya was opening the door holding a large butcher knife carelessly in her hand.

"Yer tray ma'am, much obliged, thankee agin," the trapper smiled.

"Godspeed," Sonya nodded curtly taking the tray and shutting the door again. From the window, she watched him recede to the gate and disappear.

Sonya still felt uneasy about the stranger later and told her son, Regin, about the visitor they had had that day. "I just had the funny feeling," she said that night at the supper table. "He looked like a no good."

"You women stay close to home for the next couple of days. The boys and I will keep a look out in the forest. Maybe one of us should stay here during the day. With so many away, I don't like to leave you completely alone." Regin replied thoughtfully as he mopped his plate.

"Why don't we close the gates?" Peter asked.

"We can't go closing the gates," Freyja argued. "Next we'll be prisoners in our own camp. Why soon the berry season starts, how are we to pick the fruit if we are to stay locked up here?"

"I forgot about berry season," Peter murmured. The boy loved the jams and jellies, pies and cobblers his mother and sisters turned out. He certainly didn't want anything to keep them from gathering the berries in season.

Regin frowned. "You let me know when you go to pick the berries and that day for sure two of us will stay back to escort you," he pronounced.

"One thing I never thought of," Sonya complained. "That stockade wall keeps us from seeing out and about from the houses into the wilderness. Last year the girls could pick berries and I could see them from the back yard."

"Well, we'll just have to work around it now. The stockade wall is here to stay, at least for awhile," Regin pointed out. "We'll manage."

§

The trapper sat at a campfire with his companion who was a deserter from the army. "We should watch for a couple days, kinda get the lay of how things goes, ya know. The routine. I tell ya she's worth a raid all herself but once we're inside, if th' mens is all gone, hell, we could scoop up th' whole litter of young'uns 'n' sell them off, too."

"Jinglo, damn it all, I don't know what you'll come up with next. First, it was robbing trappers, stealing from trading posts, now it's white slavery? Anything to make a living, huh?" the ex-soldier mocked.

"You didn't see her, Shark. I know a brothel in Charles Town what will pay a real hunk of money for th' likes of her. But my friend Salazar in Jamaica, he has a standin' order fer virgin beauties. He'll pay a small king's ransom 'n' once we get her on th' seas 'n' to th' islands, she couldn't make no complaint to th' authorities."

"Perhaps, you have something there," the ex-soldier's interest becoming more genuine. "If I'm going to go into the slave trade with white women, I don't want to do it on the mainland. Ending my life on the end of a rope isn't what I'd call my ambition. White slavery is a touchy business. But I'm due for a trip to the islands. All those fair breezes and native women. Maybe that's just what I need. So tell me again, what did the place look like."

"It's a lumber camp is all, but they put this here stockade around it. The mens all goes off into th' forest all day an' leaves all them skirts alone with a few kids. The blonde beauty lives in th' biggest house right near the gate. There's a couple of cabins outside on th' west, but none on th' east. We could walk right up from th' east an' nobody would see us, slip over th' wall 'n' grab th' girl at th' first opportunity. Depending on how it went we could go on 'n' take all th' rest."

"Hold on, now. We were *two* last time I counted and jist how many women and kids do you think we can handle?"

"They're only women 'n' kids."

"You git a bunch a white women together and they kin be as ornery as cats and jist as hard t' handle. Git 'em with their young'uns and I think they'd be more trouble than they'd be worth. Ain't passive like the injun gals or the niggers."

The trapper said nothing but grumbled indistinctly.

"Now, *one*.... that's a different story," Shark added and the trapper's eyes lit up again. "So tell me, Jinglo, exactly how much money is a *small king's ransom?*"

"I saw him give two hundred pounds sterling for a skirt that wasn't half as good looking as that one back there."

The ex-soldier gave a soft whistle. "Are you shittin' me? 'Cause if your shittin' me and I go along with this thing, yer goin' t' find your own balls stuffed down your throat."

"I'm not shittin' you," the trapper answered in quick defense. "I swear. I think we could get double that for this one 'specially if she's a virgin."

"Why in the hell would a man pay four hundred pounds for a woman, any woman... don't care how much of a looker she is? This friend of yours must have more money than brains."

"Yer most likely right. Money don't mean much to him but he has some very peculiar tastes an' no woman's gunna voluntarily go along with him. Even whores won't."

The ex-soldier raised his eyebrows. "Whores will do most anything," he said.

"But they do draw the line at some things. Why do you think Salazar is always looking for new stock?" Jinglo grinned slyly.

Shark wouldn't admit it, but the thoughts this conjured up turned his stomach.

§

They had taken their positions carefully. Being lumberjacks they could climb trees that an ordinary man or Indian might think unclimbable and they had done so with the quietness of a tree snake. John and Phillip had taken positions in the rocks on either side of the trail leading into the small box canyon which was more like an over-sized ravine. Sven Junior was with them. Everyone was waiting for Tracking Bear to return.

Tracking Bear had gone into the renegade camp under the sign of peace. They were demanding the life of Sven's killer and the return of various stolen goods. If agreed, the renegades would be allowed to leave the area in peace. Now everyone was waiting to hear whether their demands would be agreed to or whether they must fight and probably kill the entire band.

John saw Tracking Bear first and knew by the look on his face that their terms had been rejected. Phillip and Sven joined him when they sighted the scout.

"Killer of Big Sven is son of leader, boy of eleven winters," relayed Tracking Bear. "Not give up boy for white man's justice. Say killing was not meant, will give all horses to you. They have five."

"Did you explain to them that in our world we do not trade a man's life for horses?" Phillip replied coldly.

"Would you give up your son who is not yet fully grown to be hanged?" Tracking Bear replied without emotion.

"I wouldn't have taken that son on a raiding party to begin with," cut in John, "or put a gun into his hand against a human being."

"That was the father's responsibility," said Sven Junior, his face was taut, his eyes inscrutable. "Go ask the father if he is willing to trade his life for the life of his son. A father for a father. Go talk, tell the leader if he surrenders to our death penalty and returns the stolen goods, we will let the rest go in peace."

Two hours later a stocky Indian male of approximately thirty years was hanging from a tree, slowly strangling to death, his face turning dark beneath his copper skin, his eyes bulging, his tongue protruding. He made no sound but his feet kicked and danced wildly in the air. His hands were tied behind his back. The struggle stopped, the body went limp. Dark stains appeared on his breech-cloth as urine and feces ran down his legs, the total relaxation of muscles causing his bowels and bladder to evacuate.

John turned away unable to watch. He told himself it was justice, but somehow justice did not taste sweet but stank foully. Phillip had already turned away. It was justice, he told himself. An eye for an eye. The body would be left to hang as a sign to by-passers that lawlessness would not be tolerated. It was something that had to be done, but it was a damnable business.

Sven, Uland, and Bor watched the body silently. Each surprised that there was no real satisfaction. A father had given his life so his son might live. A son who had not meant to take Sven Senior's life. If he had been white, would they have insisted on this kind of retribution? That was a question no one dared to ask himself and no one could answer.

The rest of the men divided their time between watching that the savages didn't decide to attack them, and holding the horses they had received. They didn't give the hanging Indian much thought. It was retribution. An eye for an eye. Even the Bible sanctioned such justice, they told themselves.

Under his breath Tracking Bear was faintly humming a prayer chant asking the Great Spirit to take this warrior's spirit to be with him. He had died bravely for his child to pay a debt that was owed.

§

Bor's wife Sasha had just put her two year old down for his afternoon nap when the first cramping pain shot through her underbelly. She continued her work wanting to finish the chore of canning the strawberry jam before she became completely incapacitated. Although she tried to ignore them, the spasms were coming more frequently, and suddenly, her water broke.

"Snotra, go fetch your mother," the young woman said calmly after the spasm was over.

"What is it, Sasha?" The girl turned and noticed the puddle on the floor. "The baby?" she exclaimed with excitement and saw the other woman nod as she grimaced again.

"I think better she hurry. Tell her the pains are only minutes apart now."

Snotra took off running. She knew she would find her mother in the barn for it was milking time.

Sonya wasted no time getting to the house.

"Clara! Anna!" she called out as she entered the house. The young women appeared almost immediately. "You help me get her to bed. Kristen..."

"I'll stay in the kitchen, Mother Sonya, and heat some water and make some coffee," Kristen replied quickly. She was a timid girl, only sixteen although married to Regin. She had never helped with a birth and was afraid she might faint although she would not admit it.

"I can help you, Mama," Freyja offered.

"You can help by finishing the milking for me. Elsa isn't empty yet and Delsa hasn't been touched."

"But Mama.."

"No. You know I don't approve of young girls in the birthing room."

"I'm not a young girl, Mama, I'm older than Kristen and soon to be married."

"But not married yet." Sonya was firm. It was her opinion that virgins shouldn't see the trials of childbirth. She thought they might pick up an unnatural fear of what was the most natural result of marriage and become cold before their husbands could warm them up. "Snotra, you and your brother on the babies keep your eyes. They nap now but will wake soon. Take Skadi out back and keep her amused. Forget not to feed the chickens. I be very busy for a while, you understand?"

"*Ja*, mama," the girls replied in unison.

Freyja went to the barn, picked up a milking pail and brought it to Elsa's stall. Only then did she see the half filled pail set to the side.

"Poor Elsa, Mama wasn't able to finish you, was she, girl? Don't worry, I'll take care of you now. And you, Delsa, will be next," she tossed over to the next stall. "Good girls, good bossies." She talked quietly to the cow knowing that it had a calming effect and made the animal easier to milk.

When Elsa was properly drained, Freyja took both pails with the milk to the outside entrance of the spring house beneath the pantry. There she found a clean milk-can and emptied the fresh, creamy milk into it from the pails. When she was finished she brought the covered milk-can into the spring house and set it in the icy water. She returned to the barn to take care of Delsa.

Between the sound of the milk spraying into the empty pail and her own soft humming, Freyja did not hear the shuffling footfalls behind her. Suddenly, she was being wrenched up off the milking stool by strong hands while other hands stuffed a gag in her mouth and tied it so tightly she thought she would choke. A rough, smelly bag was thrust over her head, coarse hemp ropes tied her hands and feet biting into her tender skin, and within seconds she knew she was being carried away from everyone she knew and loved. The women were all at the far end of the house with Sasha, the children were in the inner yard within the wings of the log house. Freyja tried to scream but no sound came, she bucked and struggled and jerked but was immobilized. She was being bounced on a hard and bony shoulder and she couldn't breathe. Everything went black.

The upstairs bedroom where Sasha had been taken to be delivered was growing unbearably hot. There wasn't a single breeze getting past the drawn curtains and the lamps which had been lit added more heat to the room. Clara was trying to make her sister-in-law more comfortable by wielding a large fan but the poor girl was sweating rivers as her damp hair clung to her face in lank strings. It didn't help that she wore a heavy bed-gown for modesty's sake and lie on a bulky thick sheepskin, waxed on the underside in an effort to protect the mattress from the birthing fluids. Otherwise, the labor was going well. Sasha was fully dilated and Sonya knew it wouldn't be long. Having one child already, Sasha knew what to expect and controlled her outbursts to groans and grunts.

"Anna, go ask Kristen for some cold water from the spring house," Sonya told her daughter-in-law. "We can't let you drink any now," she said softly to Sasha, "but a cold compress on your head and wrists should make you feel a little more comfortable." She smiled encouragingly just before Sasha went into another heavy contraction. Anna went out to the landing and called from halfway down the stairs.

"Kristen, can you bring me some cold water for Sasha?"

"Of course, of course," Kristen was more than happy to do anything as long as it was out of the birthing room. She went into the spring house from the pantry and brought out a small pail of icy water.

"I heard Sasha is having her baby," Regin said as he walked into the big kitchen. He was home with the rest of the men from their day's work. Word had already spread through the camp that there was a birthing going on, so it was no surprise to find the household disrupted. Nor did he question the fact that Sally McGuffee, wife of Ginnus McGuffee, was there in their kitchen cooking with Kristen. She had volunteered to come over and help fix the evening meal. Regin was the only lumberjack in the family to feed that night, but everyone else needed to eat as well, even if they did it in shifts.

Kristen returned from bringing the cold water to Anna and ran to greet her young husband. He was six foot four, built like a bull, and hoisted his little wife up into the air before swinging her around with a kiss and a hug. Sally McGuffee was *tsking* teasingly at their hi-jinks which set Kristen to giggling and Regin only smiled.

"So where is everyone?" he asked looking around the big empty room.

"Everyone?" Kristen was back at the kettle she had been stirring with Regin close behind her poking and sniffing. "You know where your brothers are, Regin. Stop!" she giggled and turned red. His hand had pinched her bottom affectionately and she tried to make it appear her admonishment was for something else. "Mama's upstairs with Sasha, so are Anna and Clara. Ouch! now see what you've made me do?" she scolded looking at a spill she'd just made while she blew on a burned finger.

Regin moved off to some of the other cooking pots and tried to peek in and Sally slapped him away.

"Where are my sisters? he asked, grinning at Sally.

"Your sisters are helping with the children," Kristen answered. "I think Freyja's still in the barn. We had to get Mama for Sasha before the milking was done. I saw one new can in the spring house, so she's working on another. Regin, call the children in, will you? We might as well get them fed."

Regin called in Peter and Skadi who brought Clara and Anna's older children with them. Snotra was swinging with Sasha's two year old and heard her brother's call. As she walked to the house she heard Delsa mooing and making a fuss and assumed that Freyja was still milking. And so when Regin asked if she'd seen Freyja, Snotra told him she was still in the barn milking.

Getting all the children fed and washed and put to bed was a time consuming chore, interrupted frequently by requests from upstairs and progress reports. It was almost ten in the evening when Sasha finally birthed her second son. The baby was healthy and exercised his lungs properly before taking to his mother's breast and falling asleep. Sonya, Clara, and Anna cleaned up the bedroom, changing the bed linen while removing the sheep skin which had served its purpose. Sonya took the afterbirth out in a pail to bury it. She was too exhausted to notice the faint mooing coming from the barn. Sonya went back inside, scrubbed up, and finally dropped into her chair with a weary smile on her face.

"I guess we should wait for the father to return before we have a full toast," said Regin as he took a bottle of liquor from the shelf and poured some into a glass. "But I think you could use a nip, Mama."

Sonya smiled. "Just a little one or I'll be asleep before I find my bed. Ahh, but he's a fine looking boy. Bor will be proud. Sasha did well."

"They should be home soon," Regin said encouragingly, knowing his mother worried without saying it. He patted her arm as he brought her the glass.

"*Ja*," she nodded, "soon." Just then the clock on the mantle chimed half passed the hour and Sonya looked over at it. "Good Lord in Heaven, it is almost eleven! Why are these youngsters still up?" she asked looking at Skadi and Peter. "Freyja, come see the children to bed," she called but no one answered. "Freyja? Where's

Freyja?"

"Just sit Mama, I'll find her," said Regin and he began to make the rounds. It was finally determined that the last anyone had actually seen Freyja she had been going to the barn. Regin ran with a lantern to the barn with a sudden feeling of uneasiness and, to his horror, discovered a spilled milk pail, a tipped milk stool, and a very unhappy cow with a full and pressing utter.

"My God, my God, my God," Sonya sobbed, near hysteria, as she methodically milked the discomforted cow. Her state of exhaustion gave her a very poor foundation from which to handle the news that her eldest daughter had vanished. Milking Delsa was Sonya's way of staying sane. Regin may have been a small giant but he was still only a young man of twenty and he was now in a state of absolute anguish and self-condemnation. That this should have happened was unbearable, that it should have occurred while he was charged with watching over the family only served to drown him in an ocean of personal guilt. His equally young wife shared his guilt because she had not given any attention to her sister-in-law's long absence. And Snotra was torturing herself because she had assumed Freyja's presence in the barn and deflected Regin's concerns when he'd asked about her before supper. Peter offered silent childish prayers promising he'd never eat another berry pie if only God would return his sister safe and sound. The boy agonized that he had thought more of berry bakery than his sister's safety, blaming himself that the gates had not stayed locked.

It was agreed that the news should be kept from Sasha who deserved the appearance of serenity lest her mother's milk go bad. Clara and Anna were in a state, worrying who might be next. Guard over the children was elevated to watchful paranoia.

Regin instructed that no one was to go anywhere, not even to the privy, alone. A buddy system was established, especially with the women and children. And before dawn, the news was spread through the rest of the camp. Parties were organized to make a search for the girl and the gate to the stockade stayed closed.

# *Chapter 11*

The ride home was a very quiet one. With the extra horses received from the Indians they could all ride after a fashion, but there were no saddles. Each man was occupied with his own thoughts, no man was willing to discuss them. Killing a hundred Indians wasn't going to bring Sven Senior back. There had been no real satisfaction in it all. The most they had accomplished was to make the statement that crime would not go unpunished. Murder would not be tolerated with impunity. They had to be satisfied with that.

It was late morning when they caught sight of the stockaded encampment with its gate closed. Sven, John, and Phillip looked at one another, none said anything but each nudged his horse to quicken its pace and the others followed.

Peter was standing watch and when he saw them, he jumped down and opened the big split log gate.

"What has happened?" were the first words from Sven's mouth and at the same moment he saw the tears in his youngest brother's eyes.

"Freyja is missing," the young boy blurted and John blanched, feeling his own heart crash against his ribs in an earthquake of panic.

"The renegades!" John gasped, a sickening turn in his stomach; had he not feared they would be starting a cycle of revenge?

Everyone crowded into the Olafson kitchen and Regin quickly relayed the facts such as they were known. Sasha had gone into labor, Sonya had been called from the barn in the midst of milking to assist with the delivery. Freyja had been asked to take over the milking. There was evidence that she had brought one can of milk to the spring house. Sasha had delivered her son about ten. When Freyja was missed, Regin had gone to the barn. There was evidence that she had been abducted in the middle of milking Delsa. Logical deduction had brought them to the conclusion that this was probably as much as an hour before the lumberjacks had returned from their day's labors. They had searched the entire compound. They had searched the surrounding area for clues. Now that the rest of the men were back, they would search some more.

Congratulations to Bor on the birth of his son were sadly muted in the wake of Freyja's disappearance. Regin added that Sasha was still being kept ignorant of the abduction.

"What time did you return yesterday?" John spoke for the first time since they had arrived. He had withdrawn into a deadly calm and Phillip was watching him with grave concerns. He had never seen his brother like this. There was something feverish in his eyes and it was unnatural and terrifying.

"It is early autumn, we get home about five," Regin replied quietly.

"So you're saying that you think she was taken at perhaps three or four, and no one knew she was even gone until almost eleven, is that right?" the cold calm in John's voice was more accusing than any words of accusation could have been.

"That is correct," Regin said simply. He didn't try to explain that the household had been a veritable circus with the baby coming, with all the women involved in the delivery, with all the other children to attend to. He didn't try to hide behind the misinformation he'd been given. He didn't try to sidestep the blame. The quiet in the room was so tense everyone had ceased to breathe. Finally, Regin broke. "It was my responsibility and I would gladly cut off my arm to bring her back," he choked out.

"Would that it was that easy," John said coldly.

Regin bolted from the room. Phillip turned to his brother.

"John, for God's sake! You want someone to blame, but it's not that easy either!" he said compassionately. "The man is bleeding, you can see that. It's not Regin's fault. It's not fair for you to put this all on his shoulders. It's the world we live in, John, women get abducted on the frontier."

John swung to Phillip with a look of pure fury. He brought a fist up as if to swing at Phillip's face, caught himself, pulled back and turned away. The brothers had had their share of physical confrontations through-out their childhood but never before had John held murderous hatred in his heart.

"John," Phillip said more softly, "I'm not trying to trivialize this. I'm only saying these are the dangers of the world we live in, it's like dying in childbirth, being struck by lightning. No one wants it to happen but it does. That doesn't make the loss any easier but it is no one person's fault."

"It wasn't lightning that struck Freyja, it was those damnable renegades! And God help the devils when I get my hands on them! We should have killed them all when we had the chance. Ohhh, God, why didn't we?" he moaned slamming his fist against the log beam wall. "Let's stop wasting time and go after them," he snarled as he stalked to the door.

"Wait, John!" Sven's voice boomed forth. John spun back from the door, clearly in his face was etched a look of disbelief that Sven and his brothers weren't ready to race out into the forest with him for their sister.

"What do you mean *wait*? There's still a chance we could get to her before they have a chance to do any..."

"No sense does it make, John! Stop man and think! How could they have gotten ahead of us? We took their horses. We rode, they are on foot. How could they have been here before us....? And no way they could have walked here yesterday by three in the afternoon."

John stopped and looked hard at Sven. "Then who?"

"That's what we need to find out. Uland, Bor, question everyone in the camp. Perhaps someone saw something, anything. I must find Regin."

Out in the barn, Regin was sobbing. It wasn't manly but he was broken. John's words had sliced through and exposed all the guilt he had been feeling, the anguish of not protecting his sister, their sister, his mother's daughter, and, yes, John Power's wife-to-be. Regin couldn't hold it in anymore and he crumbled against an empty stall, impotently pounding it with his fist.

"I should have made them lock the gate," he garbled through his tears, "ohhhh, God in Heaven, why did not I make them lock the gate? God, why? Why? I should have made them lock the gate."

Sven came upon his brother and reached out to him, awkwardly trying to give comfort. "Regin, Regin, no one blames you. John didn't know what he was saying. He is crazy with fear for her and angry. Take it not to heart. I understand what he feels. If I could get my hands on the villain who took her, I'd rip him limb from limb with my two bare hands. There wouldn't be enough of him left to recognize as human! Come now, Regin. It's not fitting you should bawl. You must pull your-self together like a man."

"I... should have... made them... lock... the gate." Regin kept sobbing.

"What are you saying? Why would you even think of locking the gate in broad daylight? Had something happened?"

"Mama said there was someone she didn't like the looks of who came sniffing around," Regin choked out.

"She did?" Sven was surprised. No one had even mentioned this up until now. He looked at his young brother. "You're exhausted. You have not slept. You cannot even think. You stay here and stretch out in the hay, come now. I'll go talk to Mama."

"No, no," Regin said finally shaking off his sobs and bringing his breathing under control. "I'll go into the house."

"All right, but to bed." Sven accompanied his young brother into the house and saw him to his room. Pushing him onto the bed, he helped take off his boots. "I think maybe Kristen will appreciate you leave these on the floor. Now, that's it. Get some sleep so you can help us think. I insist. I head this family. I am in charge now. I tell you to sleep."

Regin stretched out and accepted the blanket his brother tossed over him. Sven quietly walked out and shut the door.

When Sven reappeared in the kitchen it was to ask Sonya about the stranger who had been there. He asked her to describe him and made her repeat every detail of his conversation and actions. John, on the front porch, could hear it all through the open window.

§

As Shark ran out of the stockade with Freyja over his shoulder, he felt her go limp. Twenty yards out in the underbrush, he dropped her to the ground, pulled the bag from her head and realized she wasn't breathing. Pulling the gag from her mouth, he smacked her cheeks until he saw her take a breath.

"What ya doin'?" Jinglo asked at his heels.

"What does it look like I'm doin'? She's no damn good to us dead, is she? Couldn't you see she wasn't breathing?"

"Oh. No."

"The gag was chokin' her. It was too damn tight, you idiot!"

"Well, I didn't want her t' scream. She gunna be all right now?"

"Yeah, she'll come around," Shark muttered taking a long look at the girl they had just abducted. She really was a stunner, he appraised. Almost unnatural, she was so pretty. This Salazar was going to get himself one hellava prize. He damn well better make it worth their while. He hoisted the girl over his shoulder again and continued to trudge off into the forest to where they had a canoe hidden along the river. They needed to get to the coast and on to the first ship they could find headed for the islands. He had the means to keep her drugged and insure her cooperation. All they needed was to find that ship and get on board.

§

Cedric Hegred brought his wife and four year old daughter, Asta, over to the Olafson house. He carried his daughter in his iron muscled arms as his wife walked quickly to keep up with his long stride.

"I think you should talk to them first, Cedric, warn them if they frighten her, she's like to say nothing," the young woman implored of her husband who nodded a brisk agreement and put his daughter into his wife's arms when they reached the bottom steps of the Boot's front porch.

"Stay. I go talk," was all he said. They watched him mount the steps two at a time and knock on the door. When it opened, he went inside but the door never shut. After only a few minutes, he returned with John Power and Sven Boot immediately behind him. Phillip was on their heels.

"Gentlemen," Phillip said quickly, pushing ahead of them on the porch, then turning to stop them with his own body. "A moment, please. Let me talk to her. Sven, you're bigger than her Pa and like to scare her just by your size. John, pardon my saying so, but right now you scare even me. Let me talk to the child." Without waiting for their consent, Phillip lightly descended the porch steps and smiled pleasantly at the little girl clinging to her mother's neck.

"Hello, Mistress Hegred, your daughter is growing up very quickly. Now, let me see if I can remember... Asta, isn't it?" He grinned at the child and she nodded quickly with a smile. "Do you know I have three little girls of my own? But you are much bigger than they. Two of mine are only babies. When they grow older perhaps I shall bring them with me some day to play. Would you like that?"

"I like to play dolls," the little girl said shyly as her mother put her down to stand on the ground. Phillip immediately hunkered down to the child's level.

"Yes, dolls, that is a favorite for any little girl, isn't it?"

She nodded her head.

"I must remember to bring you a doll from town the next time I come up. Would you like that?"

The child looked quickly at her mother, who smiled faintly. It was enough of an encouragement for her to reply honestly. "Ohh, yes. Will she have a satin dress?"

Phillip's eyes smiled at the child. "She will have a satin dress if that is what you would like. What is your favorite color, Asta?"

"Pink."

"Ahhh, we must have a pink satin dress, with pretty ribbons all about," he grinned and she smiled back at him. "Tell me something, Asta. Your papa says you saw a strange man the other day. Do you suppose you could tell me about him?"

The child looked over at the ingratiating young man and smiled with a nod and held up her fingers. "Two," she said shyly.

"Two? Two strangers. Are you sure?" Phillip asked mildly.

She nodded.

"What were they doing?"

"One was carrying a sack of flour over there." She pointed to the stockade gate.

"How do you know it was a sack of flour?" Phillip asked patiently. The child stopped all movement and was obviously thinking over his words.

"Maybe potatoes," she finally replied.

"So he was carrying a big sack?" She nodded. "How? Was the other man helping him?"

"No, he was carrying the sack alone."

Phillip turned his head and called back over his shoulder to the adults behind him, "Someone get a small bag of beans, please." Then, he turned his attention back to the girl. "Can you tell me what the man looked like?"

She shrugged her tiny shoulders. "A man... he had whiskers. He wore a hat like that," she pointed to John's tricorner. "And his britches were very dirty."

"How do you know they were dirty?" Phillip asked quietly.

"Because you could see the dirt. I think his ma should have washed his clothes," she added primly. "And his jacket was torn. It was probably pretty when it was clean."

Just then someone handed Phillip a small sack of dried beans.

"Here, Asta, pretend you are the man and this is his sack. How was he carrying it? Show us." He gave the bag to the child and she immediately hoisted it over her shoulder. Behind them, John moaned softly.

"That's very good," Phillip told the child and took back the bag of beans from her and gave it over to Sven. "Now, I wonder if you could tell us what the other man looked like."

Sonya was on the porch now, listening, and heard the child describe the trapper with his animal skin hat and buckskin clothing.

"That was him!" Sonya cried out. "Well the child describes him."

"So tell me, sweetheart," Phillip coaxed, "when they left which way did you see them go?"

"I couldn't see them once they left the gate," she said almost sadly.

"And if that is the truth it is just what I want to hear. You are a very good little girl to remember so much. It will help my friends and me if you tell us only what you saw. Is there anything else you can think of?"

The child cocked her head to the side and itched behind her ear. "I think his coat used to be red," she replied softly.

"Yes, child, you may be right." Phillip drew the girl over and gave her a kiss on the cheek. "Take good care of her," he said to the father as he again stood up to his full height. "And I shall not forget that doll," he added with another smile at the little girl.

"What do you make of it?" Uland asked as they all gathered again in the kitchen.

"It would seem apparent that the trapper happened in, saw Freyja, then went back to his companion. They decided to abduct her, came back and did so. Does anyone else get the feeling his companion was perhaps a deserter?" Phillip asked.

"What makes you say that?" Bor asked.

"The child said she thought the clothing he wore used to be pretty. Think of the English dragoon in his white breeches and red coat, very attractive to a child. She also said she thought his coat used to be red, and even she was able to note that his clothing was very filthy. What looks dirtier than soiled white breeches, eh? Complete with the tricorner hat. No one thing says soldier but altogether? And a deserter would be just the sort of companion to join in such a venture."

"So where does that leave us?" John spoke out, the suffering evident in his voice. "We have a trapper and an ex-soldier coming along and abducting a white woman. To what end? The Indians abduct women as slaves and mates. But why would they? Surely not just to rape her. If a man has rape in mind, any woman will do, they don't go out of their way to find one particular woman milking a cow in the barn."

"A slave?" queried Sven as though loath to say the word.

"Freyja doesn't have the look of strength to make a good slave," John replied quickly, shaking his head.

"There are other kinds of slaves, John," Phillip noted grimly. "Not all horses are work horses, some are for show." He regretted his last words when he turned to see his brother looking as if a knife was twisting in his belly.

"We have no wealth for ransom," Sven almost growled. "It makes the only sense. We must assume they have taken her for white slavery. She is much too fair for her own good."

"If that is true," John came to life. "Then they must take her to the coast. Take her to a city where there is a market. A brothel. We have to get to them before they can leave the area. We're wasting time. Phillip, we need to follow the river, are you with me?"

"I'm right behind you," was Phillip's quick response.

§

When Freyja regained consciousness fear prevented her from moving a muscle. She continued to lie as she was and allowed her senses to gather information for her. She was conscious of smooth movement and the lapping of water and deduced that she was in a craft on the river. Since she did not try to move she could only guess that she was still bound. She could feel the breeze on her face and the moldy smell of the rough textured sack was gone. The sack must be off of her. She continued to lie there, motionless and quiet, hoping to hear something that would help her to understand what was happening to her.

"Will you stop raping her in your head and pull your weight back there?" Shark snapped at Jinglo. "I have no desire to have that bunch catch up with us."

"I'm doing no such thing, I told you she's worth a whole lot more if'n she's unspoiled," Jinglo blustered defensively. He had in fact been getting hard looking at the girl. "Jist a little worried why she's takin' so long to come to..." he muttered half-heartedly.

"Hell, she's probably playin' possum."

"I don't think so, ain't seen a muscle twitch..."

"Well, there's one way to find out," Shark whirled around and assaulted Freyja's breast with one hand. She jerked and struggled. Her eyes flew open as he laughed and turned back to his paddling. "Now you know. Now paddle, damn you, and next time I take the rear."

Freyja's brief struggle awoke a multitude of aches and cramps in her body and she moaned despite herself. The rough hemp ropes were rubbing her flesh raw.

"If you can behave yourself, you can sit up," Shark tossed over his shoulder. "If you can't behave yourself, you'll get a whole lot more trouble than you'd have to," he added threateningly.

Freyja understood and struggled to rise up, taking care with her balance. If she wasn't bound, she'd throw herself into the water. She had learned to swim with her brothers but she couldn't swim with her hands and feet tied up. Her efforts increased her breathing and her throat was so dry she began to cough.

"Here," Jinglo swung his canteen into her lap. "Go ahead, take a drink."

With difficulty Freyja managed to uncork the top and raised it to her lips but the smell was strong and sweetly pungent. Rum. She handed it back to Jinglo who took it with a laugh and swigged down a gulp.

"What'sa matter, Pretty Face, you don't like good ol' Jamaican Rum?"

"Water," Freyja croaked out the words. "Please, may I have some water?"

"Well, you shore are a well-mannered little thing, ain't ya, Pretty Face? You're a real little lady."

"Give the girl a goddamn drink of water, Jinglo, before she dies of thirst," barked Shark. "And then paddle, damn it."

"All right," Jinglo grunted grudgingly and got a second canteen out and gave it to their captive. Freyja opened it and took a long drink. She licked her dry lips and then took one more swallow before she spoke again.

"Where are you taking me?" she asked softly.

"Now there's no need for you to worry about that, missy.... or are you a miss'es?" Jinglo asked slyly.

"Miss," Freyja replied. Jinglo grinned.

"Well, now ain't that nice. So, miss, we're jist goin' on a little trip together is all."

"Shut up, Jinglo," warned Shark. As far as he was concerned the less she knew the better and the easier it would be to handle her. It irritated him that his partner didn't seem to realize this.

"Why?" snapped the trapper.

"Just shut up."

"But my family, they will be searching for me," Freyja said desperately.

"But they ain't gunna find us," Jinglo smiled in satisfaction.

"They will never give up searching!" Freyja tried to sound convincing.

"Doesn't matter, Pretty Face, 'cause we won't be here," Jinglo laughed again.

"What is it you want? Money? My fiancé has money, he will give you money," Freyja offered in panic.

"Fiancé, huh?" Shark spoke up. "He been sniffin' up your skirts?"

Freyja was repulsed and embarrassed by the crudeness of the question. "How dare you say such a thing to me," she replied tartly.

"I can dare a whole lot more than that," Shark muttered quietly under his breath but concentrated on his paddling.

Hours later they finally pulled over to the shore to make camp for the night. Freyja was trying to keep the mosquitoes away as the canoe was pulled up onto the bank.

"Be still, unless you want to stay there all night," Shark barked at her, then he pulled her up and lifted her over onto the ground, his hands taking liberties over her body as he did.

"Please untie my feet," she pleaded, the water she had drunk earlier was now pressuring her bladder. "I cannot keep my balance."

"Don't need to keep your balance, you ain't goin' nowhere," Jinglo laughed.

"But I do need to relieve myself."

With that Shark gave a barking laugh and undid the binding around her legs and feet. Then he tied the rope to her waist and held one end firmly. "All right now, you just pick yourself a spot there and *relieve* yourself." His tone mocked the word.

Freyja looked at him in horror. "But... I ..."

"It's dark, go do it."

She walked as far as she could which was little more than six feet, stepped behind the underbrush and spread her feet beneath her skirts. Tears of shame were rolling down her cheeks. Only the darkness saved her pride. Jinglo was rushing to build up a fire for light so he could look but before he could achieve his goal, she had finished and came back.

"That wasn't so hard now was it?" Shark smirked and tied the end of the rope he was holding to his belt. "You can watch me piss, I don't mind," he said, undoing his breeches and urinating into the dark. Freyja averted her face and closed her eyes while Shark and Jinglo both laughed out loud.

The ground was hard and damp and Freyja was trying to flick insects away as her companions both snored. She couldn't sleep, didn't want to sleep. She could sleep tomorrow in the canoe. Now her mind was churning, trying to think of some way to escape before they traveled even farther away from the camp. By now her family would know she was gone but they would think the Indians had taken her and the Indians would never carry her down river toward the white man's settlement. That meant they would be looking for her in the wrong direction, she had to get back to them.

Supper had been some hardtack and dried venison. Then Shark had tied her wrists with a rope thrown over a small tree limb and kept the waist rope tied to his own foot. She couldn't completely lower her arms, so she couldn't reach the knots at her waist to undo them. And she could not walk to any point where she could break the tree limb or create enough slack to work at her wrist knots with her teeth, without pulling his foot. She was neatly trapped and the elevation of her arms was making them feel numb and heavy.

Something big and flying buzzed by again and she recoiled automatically inadvertently jerking the rope connected to Shark's foot.

"Any woman that twitches as much as you do must have a powerful itch that needs scratchin'," Shark's voice came to her out of the pre-dawn gloom.

"It's the insects," she tried to apologize, fearing his displeasure, regretting that she had wakened him.

"If you weren't so sweet, you wouldn't attract them. A woman like you is used to a much better bed, I know," his voice had gone oily. "I'm sorry we have to put you through this."

"But you do not *have to*, no one is forcing you to," she whispered back.

"No, but it seems like a right good thing to do... just like kissing you right now seems like a right good thing to do," his words ended as his mouth covered hers and she struggled to pull away. Her lips were so tightly compressed they were like steel and Shark gave a light laugh. "I don't have to kiss, honey, it ain't that important." His hands went to her skirts and traveled up her legs at lightning speed, then he was under her shift. She started to scream but his hand was over her mouth, gripping her jaw like an iron vice. "I wouldn't scream if I was you," he rasped harshly into her ear. "What we do is jist between us, there's no one to hear you but Jinglo and if he knows he'll just want to take his turn after I'm done. So unless you want to pleasure him too, you best be quiet."

Freyja's heart was pounding in fear and loathing. She could feel his finger inside her, rough and prodding.

"So now we'll find out if that fiancé of yours just sniffed or did something more." Shark's only experience with women had been with whores. He had no idea what a virgin really felt like and didn't realize the impediment he'd only heard of was not as he pictured. Not feeling any impediment to his finger, Shark was certain the girl was no virgin. "Just like I thought," he leered, strangely happy that although the girl's price would be less, it would make no difference to that price if he took her or not. Her price would be what it would be, no matter, and he could have her in the meanwhile all he wanted. He acted on that decision by unleashing his need and rammed his hardened flesh into her in blind lust and without hesitation. Too late did he feel the resistance in his path, too late to stop. What was done was done. Grunting to his climax, he could hear her crying and Jinglo's voice behind him.

"What the hell are you doin', Shark, you jist cost us four-five hundred pounds!"

"She was no virgin," he lied defensively.

"She weren't?"

"If you was betrothed to a gal what looked like her, could you keep your hands off of her?" he challenged as he got up to close his breeches.

"Then, we'll only tell Salazar that we *think* she's a virgin. Then he cain't get mad at us when he discovers she ain't." Jinglo looked down at Freyja, her exposed white flesh evident in the growing dawn. The scent of sex was in the air. His own member was now fully erect and sprang out of his breeches as he tugged on them. "And that means I kin have some, too," he asserted and ignoring her weeping protests, he overpowered her and pushed himself into her. Shark's semen made her easy to enter.

Against the sounds of the girl's continued weeping and Jinglo's grunts and shudders, Shark built up the campfire and tried to mask his anger. He'd just cost himself half of the bonus they could have gotten selling a virgin. It made her the most expensive whore he'd ever had or was ever likely to have and he now intended on getting the most he could for his lost money. He wasn't very pleased with the idea of having to share her with Jinglo. But then, he couldn't very well prevent Jinglo from having her. It was his money that was lost, too, he just didn't know there had been a choice. *Well, damn, how in the hell was I supposed to know?* he thought bitterly. *It ain't as if I ever had a real virgin before.*

As the two men drank their chicory brew, Freyja had lapsed into a withdrawn silence. Shark let her go to the river and wash herself. He intended to take her again, much slower this time, before they got back into that canoe. The first time it had ended too quickly. When they had everything packed and loaded, Shark told Jinglo to get lost for a while and Jinglo just grinned.

Freyja didn't struggle now, she only wept quietly. She had heard enough to realize they had no intention of ever returning her to her family and she was in shock. They were going to sell her! Sell her to someone who was going to use her as they used her. Perhaps even turn her into a whore to be used by many. John was lost to her forever now. She would never see him again, and even if she did, she could no longer claim his love. Perhaps his pity, but not his love. He would never want her to be the mother of his children now. Freyja felt hollow, filled with a great nothingness. She didn't even notice the man grinding into her, his breath panting over her turned cheek. She was resolved. She knew what she must do and from that she took strength.

All that day she was compliant and subdued. And that night when they made her strip and each took her again, she was submissive and obedient, closing her eyes to the shame of not just being so ill used but of providing entertainment for the other who watched. Jinglo wasn't especially trusting but Shark had decided the girl knew there was no use to try and get away, her bridges were burned. He was certain she was beginning to like it. In a few more days, she'd be begging him to bed her now that she'd had a taste of it. She just needed her appetite whetted was all, her pump primed, after all she had been a goddamn virgin. But that didn't mean they wouldn't keep her tied at night. He wasn't that trusting.

While Jinglo and Shark snored softly in their sleep, Freyja carefully stood without making a sound and without disturbing the rope that bound her to Shark who slept closer than the night before. From her standing position, she stepped up onto a large tree root that had buckled and grown out above the ground. She had maneuvered getting herself tied to this particular tree. Taking all the slack she had created in the rope, she gave no thought to trying to loosen the heavy knots, her will to live no longer existed. Straining on tip-toe, she silently looped the rope around and around her slender white neck. She had thought it all out. She said a short prayer, then gave a quick jump upward drawing her feet back up behind her. For a brief split second she felt herself falling downward and then a crack registered in her ears. Freyja had fallen far enough to break her neck and save herself from slowly choking to death.

As dawn approached, Shark awoke and opened his eyes, he jerked up at the sight of Freyja's body gently swaying above him, her toes just dangling above the ground.

"Holy hell! Damn! shit! Jinglo! Jinglo, wake the hell up!"

"Wh... what? Oh, gawd! What the hell happened?"

"I don't know... I never heard a thing... Holy Mary, what she do that for?! What the hell did she do that for?!" Surprise turned to anger, then disgust, and then to fear and an unreasonable panic. "Get your stuff and get in the canoe. We're gettin' out of here."

"You sure she's dead?" Jinglo asked, unwilling to give up on the money she'd have brought them.

"She's cold as ice and stiff as a board. Look at her goddamn neck, for damn sake... come on, I say, let's go."

"Well, hell, fergit th' river. We ain't got no reason t' go back t' civilization now. Shit! They'll be lookin' fer us on th' river. Let's get into that forest before her people comes," Jinglo said practically.

The two picked up their gear as though being pursued by the hounds of hell. They threw everything into the canoe and then, shouldering it, they pushed into the forest leaving Freyja's body hanging as it was. They weren't thinking much about the young girl's life but they thought a lot about the opportunity that had just slipped through their fingers. A split on the price she could have fetched would have set both of them up in the islands for a long time. Of all the damn lousy luck. They should have tied her down completely.

John saw her first. He never knew exactly what he saw, perhaps a glint of sun filtering through the leaves and reflecting off that amazing hair. They had ridden all night and suddenly he was there, on his knees, on the ground, weeping without control but not uttering a word. Phillip came up behind him and stared in horror. It was such a helpless feeling. The only thing they could feel good about was that they had found her before the animals did. There was nothing they could do for her except cut her down and take her home. The odd thing was with her neck quickly broken, her face was still so unbelievably beautiful with a peace and calm on it like she had wanted to die. It made no sense that they should kill her. But she hadn't seemed to struggle at all. And that's when the realization hit John that Freyja had taken her own life.

John studied the ropes silently before he cut them off her. Then he cut a lock of her hair and put it into the lining of his hat band. Using a blanket as a shroud they took her body home, neither brother saying a single word the entire trip back.

A subdued hush settled over the lumber camp when the riders arrived at dusk. Sven took the body and brought it into the house. Uland set up a trestle in the rear bedroom and Sven gently set the corpse upon the boards. Sonya stayed up the night, washing the body, anointing it with oils and dressing it in one of Freyja's newest frocks. Out in the barn, the sound of carpentry could be heard as Uland and Bor built the wooden coffin with loving care.

During her ministrations, Sonya noted the rope burns around her daughter's fine white neck, delicate wrists and ankles, and the bruises on her breasts and between her thighs. They told the story plainly enough. There was nothing John or Phillip needed to say. As Sonya worked she remembered the day she had birthed her first daughter and how many times she had bathed and cleaned her little body since then. It had been many years since she'd bathed her last although she'd often helped her wash her lovely hair. She washed it now, a last time, then brushed and brushed until it was a dry satin sheet. Tears silently flowed down Sonya's cheeks. There was no body heat to evaporate the clinging droplets. With towels she carefully dried her daughter's flesh for the last time.

When the mother had finally finished, she came out to her kitchen looking ten years older and found Sven with John, waiting for her. Sven's eyes asked her the question he couldn't bring his mouth to speak. Her quick nod answered what her tongue could not say. And John saw it too.

As dawn broke, Sven and Regin began digging the grave in the meadow. At noon, everyone in the camp gathered for the burial. It was a gloriously beautiful day meant to mock the sadness of mourning. The gentle winds blew the golden leaves on the nearby tree. The skies were a soft blue without a single cloud and birdsong could be heard throughout the tree tops nearby.

As the solemn figures stood about the grave site, each member of the family said something in the way of a good-bye to their loved one, their little sister, their big sister, their sister-in-law, their aunt. Then Sonya said good-bye to her daughter. Sven read from the Bible, a passage meant to give hope of meeting in Paradise. Phillip heard Skadi ask Snotra if Freyja was now one of the Valkyries serving Odin.

Through it all, John remained silent and dry eyed. He had shed his tears in the forest at her feet. He had no more to shed. He felt hollow, empty and yet filled with a rage he didn't know what to do with. He stood back, as everyone else turned to go to the house, and he watched her brothers, Sven, Uland, Bor, Regin, and Peter, begin to shovel the dirt over her. He watched while the six foot deep hole was quickly filled and each brother said his last good-bye and left. Phillip was with John all the while, not speaking, not touching, just there.

Finally, they were alone, just John and Phillip and her.

"She begged me not to go," the words tore from John's throat. "She knew something was going to happen and I wouldn't listen. We both thought she meant to *me*. If I had listened, she'd be alive. I would have been with her. None of this would have happened!"

"John, you can't say that. You don't know, it could have happened anyway. You wouldn't have been with her every moment. You can't think that way," Phillip reasoned softly but John just shook his head.

His brother was loyal and trying to ease his pain but there was no real denying it. Cowards that her abductors were, his presence would have deterred them. It would have saved her, he was sure. Freyja would be alive and smiling right now if only he had listened to her. They would have had a life together and made a family.

The hollowness grew within John, and the anger. All the anger. You cannot be angry with a woman who fights to her last breath against a disease that is killing her, but he found he could be angry, very angry, feel himself consumed by unquenchable anger for a beautiful, innocent young woman who just chooses to end her own life. People who commit suicide were cowards! He had always thought that. They did not have the passion to fight, the passion to live!

There was no way to take it back, no way to change time, no way to bring her back. He could not help but feel she had hated him for leaving her to this, the abduction, the brutality, the raping! And she had taken the easy way out. And she had left him behind to his life of nothingness.

It was quiet again. The wind blowing their clothing and the rustling of the tree tops were the only sounds now. The birds had grow still.

"Go home, Phillip," John said flatly. "It's time you reported everything to Father."

"What about you?"

"I can't yet."

"What are you going to do?"

"I don't know but I won't be doing it here."

Phillip opened his mouth to speak, then closed it, then opened it again and said, "John, please listen to me. Forcing Mama and Papa to lose a son isn't going to bring her back. They love you, John, we all love you, don't forget that."

John turned with a small twitch on his lips. "I won't. I just have to deal with this in my own way." Then his lips pulled tight before he asked. "What would you do if you lost Caroline... if she killed herself because she'd been shamed and she couldn't wait for you to find her and tell her it didn't matter?"

"I'd..." Phillip stopped. He had been going to say he would have to be strong for their children. But John and Freyja had never gotten that far. Phillip thought hard trying to imagine how he would feel. For the woman you love to die was bad enough, but to *kill herself?* He'd be crushed. "John, you have to let us know where you are. At least that much, big brother. Think of Mama's face if I return to say you've taken off, but I don't know where... and we'll all see you again sometime... maybe, but I don't know when. Come on, John, have a heart."

"In a month. Within a month, I'll send word and let you know what I'm doing."

"Your word?"

"My word."

"All right," Phillip sighed. "Take care of yourself."

The two brothers embraced, Phillip trying to give comfort and convey sympathy, John mechanically receiving. Phillip walked slowly back toward the new palisade while John sat down on the ground beside Freyja's grave as immobile as stone.

No one saw John after that. The next morning his horse and gear were gone. But within the month, true to his word, he sent a letter home. He had volunteered to join the British Colonial Army at the frontier.

# *Chapter 12*

## Somewhere in Indian Territory

"Come, my little brave," Singing Wind called in a coarse guttural voice to her young son as he squirmed deeper into the furs of his travel pallet. But the delicious smells of food had already tweaked his nose and set his stomach rumbling in an empty hollow response. He squinted his eyes open and crawled out. His mother stood stout and plump, a sturdy presence by the cook fire, stirring the corn mush porridge with a broad cooking stick. She had already served her mate, Red Elk.

She gave the boy his bowl as he squatted near her feet, naked. His hair was rumpled and a dirt smudge from the night before lingered on his baby soft cheek. He ate with his fingers and plucked chunks of warm cornbread up from the serving board, shoving them into his eager little mouth and grinning upward in appreciation. His mother smiled back and, then, looked over at his sister.

"Come, my daughter, you eat too," Singing Wind motioned her daughter to join them. Morning Light had rolled up her own bedroll and like a dutiful daughter, had begun on her small brother's. Her long single braid of warm brunette hair hung down her straight slender back keeping it out of her face, a face of gentle features.

Morning Light was already as tall as Singing Wind but as slender as a reed. Her mother thought that had to be the white blood in her, just like the fine silkiness of her warm dark hair which was not coarse like an Indian's, nor as black, and did not fall straight but in soft gentle waves.

Singing Wind's mother had spoken of her maternal grandmother being a full blooded white woman as tall as her husband, slender and with silky golden hair and eyes like a summer sky. Singing Wind was short, dark eyed, and black-haired. But it was not hard for Singing Wind to believe that her maternal grandmother, *Naxàti*, had been half-white. Singing Wind vaguely remembered as a small child seeing her. She had been a tall woman even in old age with pale skin and gray hair the color of sand mixed with ashes.

*Naxàti* had given birth to six children who had lived and two very pale children who had eventually died. Her surviving children had looked very much like the tribe except softer featured, lighter skinned, and with telltale brown hair except for Singing Wind's mother who had been the youngest of the brood. She had kept the blue eyes she was born with and blonde hair that had darkened as she grew older. All her siblings had been born with blue eyes as well, but they had turned brown later. Singing Wind had never believed that story until the birth of her own daughter who also had blue eyes that slowly turned the color of wet clay.

When her parents had mated, her father had brought her mother to his tribe who had lived by the sea for many generations. But there were too many white men there and their diseases continued to ravage the native peoples. Finally, when their numbers had fallen to no more than what could be counted on fingers and toes, Singing Wind and her parents had migrated in fear with two other families. They had gone west and south until they had discovered a new and fertile valley untouched by the white man or his diseases. The land was rich for growing corn and hunting was excellent. They had thrived and expanded through intermarriage with a neighboring clan.

Now as Singing Wind looked at the first child of her union with Red Elk, she saw traces of the white heritage she had been told of as a child. A heritage she had never discussed with her husband or children, it seemed unimportant. But her daughter did look different. It wasn't just her hair or her height but something in her face. A peculiar tilt to her thin nose, the lightness of her skin when it wasn't exposed to the sun. Singing Wind knew Morning Light was going to be very handsome someday.

Morning Light's soft doeskin garments fit her loosely, allowing room for her childish figure to fill out as time passed. She was six winters older than her young brother and was on the brink of becoming a woman, her parents said. Jokingly, they had started to talk of her marriage but Morning Light always scowled at the very mention of the word and pouted in resistance to the idea. The teasing was gentle but meant to condition her into acceptance of the future for all young girls. In truth, it would be several more winters before they could expect to lose their daughter to another's hearth but eventually they would trade her for the alliance and extended kinship she would bring them.

The morning air was chilled and the boy shivered as he dipped his fingers into the bowl and ate rapidly. He had no time to appreciate the birds singing loudly in the tall trees. No thought for the fine morning it promised to be. His expectation was of another long day of walking, seeing new sights, and sharing an adventure as they traveled to the white man's fort.

The white man had come up the river and built his forts. He brought with him metal knives and pots, fine cloth, beads of brilliant colors and asked for skins in return. Beaver skin was in high demand. The brothers joked amongst themselves that the white man did not understand the value of things. He traded fine knives that rarely broke for only a few animal pelts. He also brought something called "firewater" to which the boy had only heard vague references made.

White men were not threatening in small numbers but when their numbers grew, as they had on the coast, then disease became a stealthy enemy that could always rear its evil head. The four year old had never actually seen a white man but in his mind they represented a vague threat, something fascinating that was also to be feared.

"You are hungry," Singing Wind observed, "Here, my little warrior, have some more and grow strong."

"My little brave", "my little one", "my little warrior", even "my little baby" were all terms of endearment which his mother used in addressing him. They were softer, more personal and affectionate than the "Son of Red Elk" or "Son of Singing Wind" that his uncles and aunts and cousins called him, which were also better than the more formal and less friendly title of "Red-Elk's-Son-Who-Has-No-Name." But none of these were proper names. The young boy was only four and still his mother's child. He had no proper name of his own, not yet.

In his seventh winter, his mother would give him to his father, Red Elk, in a formal ritual ceremony and he would begin to learn to be a man. He would attend the meetings with the men of the tribe. He would be taught ancient secrets, partake in mysterious rituals, and learn what was taught and carried down from father to son. When the tests had been passed and the signs were right, they would have a naming ceremony. Then, and only then, would he be given a proper name.

Girl children were different. They were the delight of their father's hearth and their mother's right hand until the day they were given to another. They received their names when their fathers were inspired to name them. It could be when they were first born but usually it was much later when they did something to distinguish themselves. Morning Light had been a very happy toddler who could always be found in her hanging basket cooing at the very first rays of dawn and so Red Elk had named her his *Ajappawe Waseleechen*, his Early-in-the-Morning-Light. It was well suited. She had a sunny and bright disposition despite her scowl at the mention of marriage. Proper formal names were verbalized with discretion amongst the natives, however. It was never considered very polite to over use another's proper name.

As they traveled to the fort, they were a small family of only four but the boy's uncles were with them. Fleet-of-Foot had left his young wife back at the village with her new baby. The young brave ate at the campfire of his eldest brother, Bending Branch, who had brought with him his new young wife, Mist-On-Moon, as well as his young son, Yellow Rock. Bending Branch's two daughters by his first wife had been left back at the camp in the care of their future husbands' families. Bending Branch's first wife had been one of the victims of the epidemic.

Yellow Rock was twelve winters old now, old enough to have his own name, old enough to be counted a warrior and he was disdainful of associating with Red-Elk's-Son-Who-Has-No-Name.

Together they numbered eight, three braves, two squaws, one girl, and two young boys of which one considered himself fully grown. The boys were there to learn. The squaws were along to cook and because they had wheedled permission from their mates. In order to obtain a bit of peace and quiet, Bending Branch and Red Elk had both agreed to allow their wives to accompany them. Morning Light was there because her mother would not leave her behind. They were traveling to the white man's fort where they would trade beaver pelts for supplies and cloth and wampum.

When everyone had finished eating, they broke camp and continued on their journey. Red Elk and Bending Branch carried a large bundle of pelts attached to a carrying pole. Fleet-of-Foot carried a pack of pelts on his back. The squaws carried the camping gear and supplies on their backs while the young boys were allowed to run free and Morning Light carried the boys' bedrolls on her back as well as a basket in hand into which she foraged berries as they walked the forest path leading to the fort.

The small party moved at a steady unbroken pace never pausing, as the sun climbed its way up into the spring sky and then, reaching its zenith, began its gentle decent. Bending Branch knew well the way and finally turned to say that they would stop when they came to the stream. The thought of cool running water made the boy lick his dry lips in anticipation. He longed for a deep cool refreshing drink but he knew better than to complain. No one complained. It was not the Indian way.

At last the travel party came to a small brook as it bubbled out of the forest and cut down and across a small glade. The boys were the first to run up to the water's edge, drop down upon their bellies and stick their faces into the water to drink deeply. Pulling out after a long moment, they gasped for air in unison and then, returned to drink some more. The females scooped up water with their hands, daintily, and drank their fill. The braves, after taking in their surroundings in a complete three hundred and sixty degree turn, finally dropped to their bellies and drank as well.

Refreshed by the sweet water, the women proceeded to make camp. They drove short, thick, sharpened sticks into the ground and draped skins over them for a temporary tent-like shelter just in case it rained in the night. The sleeping furs were quickly arranged while the light was good and then food was prepared. Fleet-of-Foot and Red Elk had flushed a wild turkey earlier and now the women set upon it. In only minutes it was plucked, gutted, and ready to roast.

As they sat around the fire waiting for the turkey to crisp up, each was occupied with his own thoughts. Bending Branch told them it would only take one more day of travel to reach the fort. Mist-On-Moon and Singing Wind had been promised they could personally select from the white man's cloth, cloth enough to make each member of the family something new. They were prickling with anticipation. The white man's cloth was finely woven and sewed together with great ease. Some had the silkiness of water, some the softness of fine moss. And some was so light it could float on the air. The white men seemed to like this for their shirts.

For generations, clothing amongst their people had been something one put on and took off in harmony with the seasons. When it was cold, one bundled in warm furs, when it was chilly, leathers were sufficient, and when it grew warm there was simply no need to carry extra skin upon one's back. It was logical and it was natural. In those days, it had been common place for both the women and the men to abandon their heavy tunics and go naked in short skirts and breech-cloths much as the men did in the summer heat. But the white man's holy men had come to teach that this was not proper. Their parents had been taught that they must cover themselves and hide their bodies in the name of decency. Even a woman's life sustaining breasts were treated as something she must hide in shame. And if women had to cover their breasts, then, the lightness of the cotton cloth was a blessing. Mist-On-Moon and Singing Wind both looked forward to the new clothes they would be able to sew.

Fleet-of-Foot stared into the campfire and thought longingly of his young wife. Having been celibate for several months because of the new baby, he itched to share a pallet with her again. His need was growing strong.

Bending Branch felt a twinge of arthritis in his joints and wondered how many more years he would be able to trap and trade. The day would come when his usefulness would be limited to sitting before his hearth making tools and sharing stories with his grandchildren and their playmates.

Red Elk looked from his graceful daughter who he knew he would soon lose to another's hearth to his growing son and decided Singing Wind should have another baby. Secretly, he would not be displeased if it was a girl-child although he could never admit that to his companions.

The food was cooked and they ate without ceremony. As Bending Branch finished, his son called over to him.

"Tell us a story, my father," Yellow Rock entreated as the shadows grew longer. "Tell us the story of how the stars came to be in the sky."

Bending Branch grunted. "You have heard the story many times," he teased as if reluctant to tell it again.

"Please, Father, please," Yellow Rock begged.

"Oh, yes, I love to hear that story, too," Mist-On-Moon encouraged him and he grunted again, secretly pleased as he readied himself. A hush fell over the campsite as his audience waited in silent anticipation.

"Once, long ago, further back in time than anyone has any counting for, the Great Spirit walked the face of the earth creating its many wonders. Mountains were formed and trees grew taller than an eye could see, sparkling fresh waters burst forth from the mother earth teaming with fishes. The sun was created to rule the sky of the day and the moon, its lesser sister, was made to rule the sky of the night. All was beautiful, all was peaceful. Then, a great tree grew up from the giant turtle's back and from it sprouted men and women. This was a time when the wolves played with the bear cubs and the cubs played with the deer, and the deer played with the mountain lions. And none were afraid.

"Then, there came to be a beautiful princess, daughter of the mightiest and wisest chief in the land. With a perfect woman's body combining strength, softness, and grace, her eyes were the color of birch smoke, her teeth as white as the moon, and her long shining hair which hung to her ankles put the night sky to shame. The princess was so breathtaking to look upon that brothers from the four corners of the world came to bring tribute and offer for her hand. But the beautiful princess begged her father not to marry her away to anyone for she loved him dearly and did not want to leave his fire. The chief of the tribe loved his daughter well and gave in but when her sixteenth summer came, he told her the time had come for her to wed. He told her he wanted to see her joined with a worthy husband, to be a happy wife of her own hearth with children of her own. The old chief expressed his desire to see his grandchildren before he left for the spirit world.

"A contest was devised wherein the strongest and bravest of all the suitors would be rewarded with the hand of the beautiful princess. The birds took the message to all in the land and brothers of all sizes and ages came seeking to try to win this beautiful princess for their own. The braves competed with each other for three days, and in every event, the same strange beastly looking brother took first place.

He was of such unbelievable ugliness, such repulsiveness that the princess shuddered to look upon him. But no one could deny he had won the right to claim her, fairly and justly, and the old chief had no choice but to give his daughter to this ugly brave.

"The beautiful princess begged one last night in her father's wigwam. 'Give me this last night,' she begged her hideous new husband, and tomorrow I will come to you willingly.'

"The monstrous looking husband agreed and went away vowing to return at sunrise to claim her.

"That night, the maiden sought out the most powerful medicine man in all the land and asked him to use his powers to keep the sun asleep and make the night last forever. The medicine man made powerful magic and the night went on as the sun continued to sleep. But the maiden did not realize that without the sun to warm it the earth would grow very cold and everything would die. As the long night stretched on and on, the plants could not grow, the food ran out, the animals turned on each other, and the peoples grew ill tempered and began to fight amongst themselves as the winds grew colder and colder. The maiden cried for the tragedy she was causing and her tears turned to ice and the wind blew them into the sky where they were caught forever. The maiden looked around and saw death was ready to take the earth and she could not allow it. She asked the medicine man to stop his magic. And when he did, the sun awoke and rose, the earth warmed again, and all returned to normal.

"The ugly brother came to claim his bride and the maiden went with him meekly as she had promised. That night she entered his wigwam and bowed in submission before him. She submitted to his will and slept beside him without protest. In the dark she could not see his ugliness and she found that he pleased her, giving her much pleasure in their joining."

At this point in the narration the wives smiled slyly and the young boys giggled. Morning Light only kept her eyes averted and blushed.

"In the morning, upon rising," Bending Branch concluded, "the beautiful princess found herself lying beside the most handsome brave in all the forest for her obedience had erased the magic of an evil shaman. But always in the night sky you can see her frozen tears sparkling forever as a reminder to all."

The group was quiet, each taking his own reminder from the ancient story. They sat watching the crackling fire. The landscape had grown completely dark and night sounds replaced the sounds of the day. Crickets and tree frogs, owls, and the occasional howl of wolf song. Then, out of the darkness, came the sound of a strange human voice.

"Ho, there! *Winkalit! Elangomat!* Friend! We are friends," cried out a stranger as he slowly appeared out of the darkness into the faint circle of light.

"*Winkalit!* Friend!" echoed a second, slightly behind the first.

"What we got here, this is right cozy, now ain't it?" said a third as each approached the fire and grew more visible.

Coming into the brighter light of the fire, the natives saw a trio of white men not knowing these were bushlopers. Bushlopers were so called for their habit of hanging out in the bush around a fort and praying upon unsuspecting Indian traders. These three were dressed in peculiarly unique apparel. One had on what had been a uniform at one time, now shabby, threadbare, missing any insignia or braiding, and its few remaining buttons grown dull long ago. The once red jacket had become so soiled and stained the color had dulled to a brown and no one could have placed it for a uniform any longer. The second wore large drab colored pantaloons with billowing legs and cuffs fitted just below the knees. With the pantaloons, the owner wore an odd little short jerkin that hardly met the tops of his trousers. The third was wearing breeches with a buckskin shirt, a pistol jammed into his waistband and an animal skin hat. They weren't carrying weapons in their hands but had muskets slung over their backs. The three led pack animals but held their hands out and open in a universal sign of friendship and peace.

"So, I don't s'pose ya'd mind us sharin' a bit of warmth from your fire now, would you?" the one in pantaloons grinned showing a broken tooth and gaping hole where another was missing in the front of his mouth. The others grinned as well and Red Elk and Bending Branch grinned in reply.

The white men sat down, rubbing their hands together and holding them to the fire.

"Ahhh, now that feels real good, it does, real good," said the one in an old uniform. "And does anyone here speak English?" he smiled broadly.

The natives smiled in return.

"Oh, I guess not... not a bloody word do you, huh, no, I guess not," he continued to smile and nod his head as he talked. "So, I guess we're gunna have to communicate in another way, ain't we now? See, that, Jinglo, just grin as broad as you please and smile and keep your voice real pleasant like and you can say anything you want and the stupid bastards don't understand a word. It's bad manners for an Indian not to share his campfire and even his food with a stranger, any stranger... unless we were formally at war with each other."

"It'd seem we has us a little party goin' t' trade at the fort. Notice them piles of beaver?" said Jinglo with a broad smile while giving a little bow to the Indians. "Do ya think we could manage t' convince them t' trade with us instead?"

"I sees more than beaver skins over there," Pantaloons grinned. "Did ya spy th' little savage over there in the shadows? Pretty little piece, ain't she?" He bobbed his head and smiled.

Red Elk knew a little Swedish but the words the white men spoke were totally foreign to his ear. But he smiled and nodded agreeably.

"Yer right, by gawd, she's real sugar that one, ain't she, Shark? Bet she's tighter'n a drum, too. I could have a lotta fun openin' up her little honey pot and plowin' her deep..." Jinglo's eyes had grown flinty.

"Now, you just watch your mouth," Shark said, almost sing-songing, "they may not understand our words but you'd have t' be a complete idiot not t'understand the lechery in your voice. Let's not be stupid, boys, let's not spoil a real good opportunity here."

"Well," exclaimed Pantaloons rubbing his hands together. "I think we ought t' loosen up here 'n' have a little drink. Would you like t' share a little libation, sir?" he asked the natives in a hospitable tone. "Bring us a jug, Jinglo, that's a good fellow!" he called to the one in buckskins.

Jinglo took a jug off one of the pack mules and uncorking it, he pulled a swig first and then, handed it to Pantaloons.

"Thank ye, kindly." Pantaloons pulled a long swig and passed the jug to Bending Branch who hesitated but then accepted for it would have been unfriendly not to do so.

The Indian drank deeply and felt the mellow fire spread down his throat and into the pit of his stomach creating a warm comforting sensation. He passed the jug to Red Elk who also took a long swig. Then, Fleet-of-Foot reached for the jug.

"Well, I think this is goin' just fine, now ain't it? Yessir, just fine," Pantaloons grinned again. "We're all friends now, ain't we? Yes." He gave another exaggerated nod toward Bending Branch and Red Elk. "Jinglo, get another jug in circulation or we'll be here all night."

Singing Wind and Mist-On-Moon looked at each other and Pantaloons detected the universal expression of a sourly disapproving female. He took the fresh jug and pulled the cork and pushed it toward Mist-On-Moon who was younger and looked more easily convinced.

"Here, my little dove, a fresh jug just for you. Go ahead, try it, I guarantee you'll like it, c'mon now," he insisted pleasantly.

"Take it," commanded Bending Branch in *Lenni Lanape*. "It is inhospitable to refuse."

Mist-On-Moon accepted the jug and tipped it to take a small sip but Pantaloons reached out and kept the jug tipped upward, forcing the squaw to drink several gulps before he allowed her to lower it and breathe. She gasped as the fiery liquid bit her tongue and splashed down her throat and he laughed. After the initial burning subsided, she felt the warmth all the way down to her stomach. It tasted good, she decided, and smilingly she took more. When she had downed another gulp or two, she passed the jug to Singing Wind. Singing Wind knew she, too, must join in and tried to take only a little but Mist-On-Moon began to laugh and tipped the jug farther causing Singing Wind to gulp several times herself and dribble down her front.

The strangers joined in the laughter and soon everyone was laughing except the children who had retreated into the shadows of the tents. They heard their parents laughing louder and louder, they were starting to talk strangely, their tongues growing thick. The white men continued to laugh and pass the jug back and forth.

In less than an hour, everyone had grown drunk and the laughter was unceasing. Shark was paying special attention to Mist-On-Moon who was thoroughly intoxicated. Under the pretense of helping her hold the jug she drank from, he ran his hand up under her tunic top on the side away from the fire and view. Rubbing her breast, he tweaked her hardening nipple.

The young squaw's response was natural and uninhibited. It was, after all, her mate who had told her to join in. And it was not unheard of for Indians to give their second and third wives over to visitors. She drank deeply, she was doing as Bending Branch wished and the man in uniform was looking more and more appealing to her. She did not mind his roaming hand and squirmed against him.

"I couldn't help noticing, friend," began Pantaloons a few feet away.

"*Fer-end...*" Bending Branch enunciated the word, elongating the sounds.

"Yes, friend. *Winkalit.* Friend. We are all friends now. So, let's talk a little business. I couldn't help noticing that you have a nice pile of beaver pelts. And, I suspect you would like to trade," Pantaloons continued to the Indians, pantomiming as he went.

"Trrrrade," Red Elk repeated.

"Trade," said Pantaloons again.

"Trrrade," mouthed Bending Branch.

"Trade," nodded Pantaloons.

"Trrrra-ade," repeated Fleet-of-Foot, belching as he did.

"Yes, yes," Pantaloons bobbed his chin. "I think ya got the idea. You have many furs. We have much rum, good." He held up the jug and smacked his lips.

"Good." Bending Branch repeated in a bleary agreement.

"And I have wampum for beaver pelts."

"Wampum?" Bending Branch questioned, recognizing the word.

"Yes, wampum."

"Wampum."

"Here wampum... for you, my friend!"

"*Winkalit.* Ferrr-end!"

Bending Branch was presented with a stack of wampum that was poorly made and had many broken shells but he offered no resistance in being convinced to trade his entire portion of skins for the wampum. And he considered himself a rather skillful bargainer when several more jugs of fire water were thrown in as a bonus.

Then, Pantaloons began to negotiate with Red Elk and Fleet-of-Foot. Fleet-of-Foot was close to passing out when they struck their bargain, which was no bargain at all for the drunken Indians. And still the drinking continued and everyone was very happy.

Morning Light was on her stomach, her arm around her brother. "I am afraid," she said softly. "Our parents are not themselves, the white men's drink has done something to them."

Yellow Rock also lay watching, trembling at the transformation in his father and uncles, even in Mist-On-Moon and Singing Wind.

"This is not right," he whispered to Morning Light, "the white man has confused their minds, they are giving away the pelts for practically nothing!"

"There is nothing we can do," Morning Light replied in a hushed whisper.

Pantaloons was laughing hard but knew exactly what was going on. "Watch yourselves, boys," he warned in a jovial tone, "it wouldn't do to let yourselves get drunk. If we want to keep the upper hand here, we have to play along but hold back how much you swallow, hear now?" And he rolled in laughter again. "They're so pie-eyed stupid I bet we could swive their women in exchange for another jug," he roared with congeniality. "You see the thing about an Indian is once you get them drinking, they just don't know how to stop, do you, you ol' sod faced pile of donkey dung? Do you?"

Red Elk bobbed his head agreeably while Bending Branch slumped down. Singing Wind and Mist-On-Moon were in a dizzy haze of inebriation. Pantaloons and Uniform gave each of the braves another jug of their own and pointed to the squaws making several obscene gestures. The Indians nodded. It was understood that in exchange for the fire water, the women could be "borrowed." The white men turned their attention to the squaws who had seen their mates agree.

In wild-eyed fear, the children watched. Singing Wind was amiably on all fours, her tunic bottom riding up around her plump waist and Pantaloons was on his knees behind her. His white buttocks high-lighted by the firelight as he slapped up against her accommodating rear. Uniform was grunting and sweating on top of Mist-On-Moon. How could their fathers let this happen? Why didn't their mothers resist? Had everyone lost their mind? Then, Morning Light saw the third white man look up from the coupling bodies and look straight across the campfire into the shadows at her. She shivered and ducked her head trying to make herself small and invisible. The man stared and then, carrying his jug with him, he stood and stumbled slightly. He was walking toward her and she uttered a small cry of despair.

He was upon her, then, and grabbing her by the braid, he pulled her to her feet. Since the Indians had no problem sharing their women, Jinglo saw no reason not to have the little one. Yellow Rock and the boy both began to protest, beating at the man with their small hands but with a swift movement of his more powerful arm he cuffed them off into a state of stunned consciousness. Dragging Morning Light out of the furs, he pulled her down on his lap and tried to make her drink. The liquid burned and she stubbornly let it spew from her mouth.

"That's a waste of good rum, but have it yer own way," Jinglo said gruffly, throwing her down and pinning her to the ground. Wiggling and fighting to get away with all her strength, she could hear him laughing at her. She didn't want him touching her, he had no right. He was ugly and loathsome and smelled bad.

All her blows were no more than a fly's buzz to him. He continued to laugh as he grabbed at her doeskin skirt, pulling it up to her hips. With a forceful snap, he broke the thong about her waist and the small suede breech-cloth fell away exposing her to his lust-filled eyes. She continued to squirm and fight, kicking and bucking, trying to keep him away. He teased and laughed and held her tightly.

Morning Light felt herself growing tired. She wreathed and cursed, twisting and turning as he continued to laugh but his eyes looking down at her had no laughter in them. Now, she was gasping for air and her limbs felt leaden even as his hands spread her slender legs apart. She no longer had the strength to resist.

He had played her like a fish on a line, watching her grow exhausted, hearing her breathing become ragged as his strength overcame her childish resistance. Then, with his knees between her legs, he opened his breeches and lifting her slender hips with his harsh hands, he drove himself into her.

Morning Light screamed. She could feel him tearing her apart. He had impaled her upon his angry organ and she'd felt her tender flesh burning like fire. He didn't stop with her scream but holding her tightly he continued to move savagely in and out. There was more painful ripping. In and out, back and forth, fire and agony burned through her female flesh and she continued to cry out, begging mercy.

Red Elk was in his own world of oblivion clutching his jug of fire water. Flames danced before his eyes. It was like a dream and everything had lost substance and floated about him. Uniform had finished with Mist-On-Moon and was encouraging Bending Branch to drink more while Fleet-of-Foot was rolling with his brother's squaw himself. The white man had not satisfied her and she was eager to entice her well endowed young brother-in-law to pleasure her. Red Elk found that very amusing, perhaps he should also assist in satisfying his older brother's young mate. She had often smiled at him invitingly.

Singing Wind was panting as the white man leaned into her, hard. Then, Red Elk saw her roll onto her back. She lay with her legs open, inviting the one with the uniform to join her. He poured from the jug into her open mouth, the brownish liquid splashing against her tongue and teeth. She gulped greedily. Shark next straddled her chest on his knees, and put himself into her mouth. Red Elk looked on without ire, everyone was having a good time in this dream. The spirits of pleasure surrounded them. Red Elk himself had now grown stiff and erect under his breech-cloth and was lustfully waiting for Fleet-of-Foot to finish with Mist-On-Moon. Bending Branch was raising no objection. And Red Elk admitted to himself that this was not the first time he had desired his young sister-in-law. Then, suddenly, he heard a scream. His daughter.

Red Elk struggled to get up. The earth was rocking beneath his feet and his legs felt like water. He fell and grazed his head. It stunned him but he tried to stand again. He wobbled as if riding the back of a giant snake and fell again. Now, he crawled on his hands and knees in the direction of the scream. His daughter, his little Morning Light... where was she? What was happening to her? Why was she screaming? What was hurting her? Who was hurting her?

To Shark's frustration, Singing Wind immediately disengaged her activity and twisted around to look in the direction of her daughter. Morning Light had screamed.

"Husband! Help her! Help our daughter!" she cried out and struggled to get free of the weight upon her chest.

Hearing his mate's voice, Red Elk struggled on. Help her, she had said. He must help...

Jinglo was not ready to give up his prize. "Keep him off me," he shouted out as he saw the Indian crawling toward him. Jinglo's breath was ragged, he was almost there, had almost reached his climax and wanted no interruption to his pleasure. The Indian was crawling closer. Thrusting and grinding, faster and faster, Jinglo suddenly arched and grabbed the pistol in his waist band. At the same moment as he spewed his seed deep into Morning Light's immature womb, he mindlessly pulled the trigger of his pistol and blew off Red Elk's face. Bits of flesh and bone and brain sprayed out, landing harmlessly about the ground around him. Some flew out far enough to spatter upon Morning Light's face.

Singing Wind was screaming now and Fleet-of-Foot staggered up to lunge at Jinglo only to be tripped by Pantaloons. Shark, realizing the whole affair had turned nasty beyond saving, drew his own weapon and shot Bending Branch in cold blood. Pantaloons took his knife and slit Fleet-of-Foot's throat, leaving him gurgling on the ground, his blood gushing forth onto the dry earth.

In a matter of seconds everything had gone quiet, the women frozen in sober horror.

"What are we gunna do now?" asked Shark soberly.

"A slight change in plans," replied Pantaloons, after several deep breaths, his heart thumping in the aftermath of the mêlée. "Start diggin', we'll bury the bodies."

"Then what?" demanded Shark.

"Then nothing," said Pantaloons. "We just got our goods back, along with the pelts, 'n' we have some slaves t' sell in the bargain. Not a bad turn of events, my friends," he said encouragingly. "Not bad a'tall. They was just some lousy injuns. Now, tie them brats together along with the squaws and let's get workin' so we can get some sleep. Tomorrow, I'll go to the fort myself and sell these pelts and then, we'll head north. We can continue to trade and capitalize on these squaws at the forts along the way. They should be good little money makers." He forced a laugh. "There's a randy soldier or two what will give a week's pay for a short half hour with a good whore. And these are some good whores. Even that young one there. And eventually, we can sell 'em off to the highest bidder."

Jinglo got up from his position over Morning Light and hitched up his breeches, hardly looking at the girl who was lying stiffly upon the ground in a state of shock. Her father's blood seeping into the earth inches from her head.

In the morning, in the merciless daylight, without shadows or the fog of rum, the squaws passively submitted to being sexually taken by the men in front of their children. This was done to shame them and break their will. Singing Wind and Mist-On-Moon, both in shock over the sudden death of their mates, told Morning Light to submit as well and do as the white men said if she wanted to live. There was no sense in fighting. Surviving was what was important and perhaps some day, if they survived, they could escape and go home. But Morning Light was stubborn. She resisted. She screamed out at her mother that she didn't care if she died. Then, Shark handed Singing Wind a small switch. As she stood staring at him wondering if he really expected her to beat her own daughter for him, he walked to the fire, picked up one of the wood branches which had burnt to a glowing tip of red ember. He carried it over to her young son, grabbed him soundly and held the glowing stick a scant inch from the tender flesh of his babyish arm.

The boy felt the heat of the glowing stick as the white man held it. It burned without touching and he stared at it in frozen fear clamping his mouth shut like a warrior, making no sound. He would not scream before his enemy, he thought proudly. Then, the white man pressed the glowing stick to his skin and the sound ripped from his mouth. Singing Wind understood then, all too clearly, and begged him instantly to stop. Shark lifted the branding stick off of the boy and threw it back into the fire. An ugly red blister raised under the blackened skin of his tender little dusky arm. He sobbed with the pain. "Daughter, you must submit or they will hurt your brother. Do you not see?" his mother cried to his sister. "You cannot resist. They are too strong. It is for your own good. We must survive. They will hurt us all if you resist," her mother pleaded with her, tears streaming down her cheeks as she lightly flogged her own daughter in a symbolic beating. After only a half dozen light strokes, Singing Wind withdrew. And then, Morning Light, too, allowed herself to be taken by each of the white men in front of the others. She had submitted without a struggle and clenched her teeth through the excruciating pain their acts inflicted on her flesh. The last to take her was Jinglo and he had done so with violent savageness, as if he had wanted to make her scream out but despite his brutality she had bit her lip bloody and refused to make a sound.

Pantaloons then went to the fort alone and sold the pelts while his companions stayed to guard their captives and when he returned, they headed northward to the next fort.

# *Chapter 13*

"You on guard or you sleepin' soldier?" came the gruff challenge. The young private immediately recognized the approaching voice as that of the sergeant on duty.

"I'm on guard, Sergeant," the private replied with just a hint of irritation in his voice.

"Then ya better look like it before I get my ass chewed," the sergeant replied, not without a small note of understanding. "Pretty damn dull, ain't it?"

"I'd say that describes it only by about half," snorted the private dryly, shifting his weight and adjusting his grip on his musket. He stood on the upper walk of the wall where he'd stood all night looking out at a sea of green forest which began about five hundred yards from the stockade walls of the fort.

"I know," grunted his superior, "but look at it this way. It's better than the alternative. Let's enjoy this respite and relative quiet, it's guaranteed to change soon enough." The man walked on continuing his rounds and left Private Power to his thoughts.

John had taken on a new identity of sorts. No one here knew him as the first born of a wealthy founder. He had not sought to purchase a commission with his personal wealth. Part of his penance was accepting this humble station, taking orders from those far less educated than he, and being barraged as a new recruit by a plethora of unflattering but impersonal epitaphs such as "dregs of scum pond," "worthless coxcomb on a she-goat," and "witless son of a dung bellied jackal" hurled impersonally until they rang of affection from a drill sergeant who had spent some time with pirates from the north African coastline.

Telling no one he was a trained doctor, he was just a common soldier now, with his hair shorn to a cap of curls and with that station he answered to a new personal name. His buddies started to call him *Jack*, he had accepted it and let it stick. Almost every common soldier had a nickname and his could have been far worse. Jack Power was a career soldier and far removed from the John Power who had loved, married, and been widowed by the incomparable Alana Huffsmeier or who had allowed tragedy to befall young and innocently bewitching Freyja Olafson.

Standing watch, the young soldier slipped back into his own thoughts. His mind had been wandering back to some of the wild times he'd spent in the Amsterdam tavern with the serving lasses who were so generous with their charms. He could use a mindless night with an accommodating wench right now. Superficial, easy, no strings, no attachments. No emotional costs. Had he really been so stupid as to sign into the King's service? Stupid indeed, he thought mockingly of himself. He was in the only home he'd ever known, the colonies of America, yet he was soldiering for a country halfway around the world in which he had never lived. A country which was often at odds with the country his parents came from although that country had not treated them fairly. And he was serving a king who was a German and couldn't even speak English. He almost laughed aloud. The irony of life and politics was too perverse. But he knew why he was here, standing in a British uniform, peering out into an emerald green sea of wilderness until his eyes ached.

He was here because he had needed to get away from everything and everyone that was familiar to try to come to terms with his anger. Fighting savages face to face in the wilderness seemed a good way to vent the burden of rage with which he'd had to deal. Of course, killing did not fit well with his oath to preserve life so he had set aside his doctor's mantle and the Hippocratic Oath. Only problem, there hadn't been any fighting of late but there was always the threat. It was the threat that worked on one's nerves. The threat hanging over every waking moment and creeping into every dream. It was harder to bear than an all out battle.

"Hey, Jack!" a voice again broke into the young private's thoughts and he recognized his fellow recruit without looking around.

"Ben," he acknowledged calmly.

"Yer due to git off duty soon, ain't ya, same as me, right?"

"Guess so, not that it makes one whole helluva lot of difference." His tone was tired and bored.

Ben almost giggled in glee, his big, broad, freckle filled face split into a grin, ear to ear. "Ya ain't heard, have ya?"

"Heard what?" John cocked an eyebrow at his companion.

"Some traders got some young Indian whores outside th' gate." Ben could hardly contain himself.

"Ahhh, please," John snorted. "Like the pigs that were here last summer? I really don't..."

"No, no, no," his friend interrupted. "These is young, and I hear tell they be pretty good to look at, too."

"Like they're all good to look at if a man's drunk enough."

"Ah, c'mon, Jack, don't be sour. It ain't gunna hurt nothing to take a little peek, is it? Won't cost ya nothin' t' look. If theys pigs, forget it... but if theys like I hear'd we kin have us a fine time this morning soon as duty ends, they should be set up by then and ready," his eyes glinted as he grinned. "Don't tell me ya ain't jist as randy as th' rest of us."

John looked at his buddy and then smiled. "Little Johnnie's been yearning for a warm place all damn winter."

Ben slapped his friend's arm with a laugh. "Then I'll see ya as soon as we git off duty." He bounced away almost doing a jig and Jack had to shake his head in amusement despite himself.

Corporal Ogden was behind them as they left the front gate. The two privates didn't particularly like the man although they had no choice but to tolerate him.

They were all after the same thing but it didn't surprise Ben or John that the corporal pulled rank to have first choice. He liked the look of Mist-On-Moon and tossed the greasy looking pimp his money as he disappeared into the makeshift tent.

"Gentlemen," Pantaloons' gaping smile was solicitous toward his first customers. "You can consider yer money well spent today. I believe we have just what you need. Yer money, please?" he thrust his dirty hand out and Ben gave up half a week's wages when he saw Singing Wind's half-naked body peeking out from the tent flap.

"She's not bad at all," Ben said enthusiastically. "Didn't I tell ya," he added poking John in the ribs before he, too, disappeared within.

"Guess, I'll wait," John muttered.

"Oh, no need to wait, my friend. I have a special prize in there," he nodded to what John now realized was a third shelter, taking one of its walls from the fort wall itself. "Fresh as new mowed grass," he grinned salaciously, holding out his hand for money.

"Sight unseen? I don't think so," John grinned back without warmth.

Pantaloons snapped his fingers and Shark, holding the boy by his unmarked arm, opened the flap and motioned with his hand to Morning Light. She saw her little brother. His blistered wound had torn open that morning and was seeping and raw. She understood the threat and because of it she walked to the disgusting white man meekly. As she gained the outer air she stopped and looked to see a young man with hair the color of pale sunflowers looking across at her. She looked back at her brother and closed her eyes, then felt Uniform push her back into the enclosure.

John didn't say another word but parted with his money and walked straight to the third shelter. Inside, the light was dim but he had no trouble seeing the young girl who was now sitting obediently on the pallet on the ground.

John hesitated for a moment, suddenly feeling a little awkward.

"Can you speak English?" he asked softly, and saw the girl look at him with large luminous eyes, unblinking. "Guess not. You are a pretty thing..." he walked over and reached out his hand to stroke her cheek. Was she trembling? "I have to admit, I never expected anything like you. I don't suppose it matters much that you can't understand me. I guess every one probably says the same things anyway. And it's not like you don't know what we want, right?" he smiled with a chuckle and started to undo his breeches.

Morning Light's expression was unfathomable. The hate she felt for the white men burned within her but she dared not show it lest they torture her small brother again. She did not know his language. Did not know how to tell him of the injustice she had suffered. Did not know how to ask for pity and help. And she had finally concluded that she would never lower herself to ask for the white's pity or help. Instead, she did as her mother had told her. She remained quiet, closed her eyes, laid back upon the pallet and spread her legs. She would let the white come into her and she would take her mind to another place and ignore the pain it gave her.

John saw the girl open her legs and he felt himself go hard as a rock. *Merciful heaven.* He fumbled with his breeches, feeling an ache in his loins that begged for release as the pressure mounted. He didn't bother taking his breeches off completely, that would have meant he'd need to take his boots off first. It wasn't necessary, he could lift her skirt and.... Suddenly, he drew back in revulsion.

In a former life he had been a doctor, a reasonably accomplished lover, and a husband, all of which gave him a better than the average grope-in-the-dark acquaintance with the female anatomy. But this female had been monstrously abused.

"Good lord!" he gasped, "Who did this to you?" He looked up at the girl's face. It remained expressionless or did it? It was hard as granite, her teeth clenched. Suddenly John noticed something he couldn't believe he hadn't noticed before and he lifted her tunic exposing her flat, childish chest. "You haven't even got tits!" he cried softly. "You're just a baby." John thought of his own little sister, Izzy, she was about this one's age. *Johnnie* had gone limp but John was taunt with anger. He pulled the girl's skirt down to cover her nakedness and stood up himself. Lacing up his breeches with amazing speed, he bolted out and grabbed Pantaloons by the throat.

Shark and Jinglo both jumped in to pull the strong young soldier off of their partner.

"You sick piece of shit!" John growled at Pantaloons as he yanked and jerked and worked to throw off the others.

"Wh..what is it? If the girl didn't please you, you can have another... she'll be dealt with, believe me," Pantaloons cried out rapidly in defense. "We don't want trouble."

"I'll just bet you don't!"

"What is the problem, Private?" Corporal Ogden appeared. He was fastening his breeches and looking more relaxed than he deserved.

"They've got a child in there, Corporal," John replied with heated indignation. "She's no older than my baby sister, she doesn't even have tits and they're whoring her out!"

"If it's tits you want, Power, let me assure you this one has nice firm ones," he replied with a nonchalant toss of his head in the direction of the tented room he had just come from. "I'm finished. Go ahead and help yourself."

"You don't understand," John stepped in closer, lowering his voice. "The child's ripped clean up and needs a doctor."

Corporal Ogden calmly turned to Pantaloons with a lifted brow and air of self-importance. "It's bad business to try and sell damaged merchandise. Certainly you should know that. Personally, I don't care about your business. I don't care about your merchandise, now that I'm finished with it," he gave a tight smile. "But you might want to ask the doctor to see the girl. Of course, he has a right to treat who he wants and he may not want to touch an injun. But I could ask..." his blasé expression coming to rest upon Shark.

"Where's Doc Wicke?" John asked as he approached what served as a surgery. The young soldier on duty shrugged.

"Probably sleepin' it off, don't usually show hisself 'til lunch time."

"Go get him."

"Go git 'em yerself," came the belligerent reply.

"Fine." John opened the door to the back room and almost gagged at the stale smell of vomit, whiskey, and human sweat mingled with the underlying acrid smell of mold. He shook the lumpy pile on the cot. "Doc? Doc Wicke?" he repeated until at last his efforts were rewarded.

Doctor Wicke was at the frontier because he couldn't keep a practice anywhere else. He almost always reeked of cheap whiskey or rum and the patients he attended generally got well of their own accord despite his attentions or they died. The fort, however, was glad to have him on retainer if for no other reason than appearances. They could at least say they did have a doctor on staff. A good, experienced doctor with a healthy practice, however, was not likely to attach himself to the military in most circumstances and could hardly be expected to accept a post at some frontier wilderness fort.

"W...what is it?" a grizzly, bewhiskered face turned to squint up at the form hovering over him.

"Doc... I got someone for you to see, someone who needs your help."

"W..what?" The lumpy pile shook his head in a conscience effort to clear a fog, coughed, and cleared phlegm before rising and spitting into a bedside spittoon. More throat clearing, a groan, while hands went to the messy nest of hair trying to smooth it back, then the eyes blinked repeatedly and squinted again. "Someone's hurt, you say, are they in there?"

"No, Doc... it's a young girl."

"A young girl?" the voice was growing more forceful and intelligible. "Where the devil would a young girl come from in this God forsaken place?"

"She's a young Indian girl. Someone's hurt her badly."

Doc Wicke put his hands to his face and rubbed the loose skin back and forth. Then, rubbing his eyes and sitting straighter, he began scratching his cheeks and chin. Finally, he lifted himself off the cot. "All right," he sighed, shuffling over to a small chest and taking up a whiskey bottle.

John stayed his hand. "Doc, you need to be clear headed on this now. She's just a young girl. A pretty young girl. And she needs a good doctor."

Wicke looked at the young man and set the bottle back down.

"Then you had best look elsewhere, my young Samaritan. I ceased being *good* fifteen years ago."

"Doc, dammit, she needs help," John heard himself growl.

"All right. Give me some time to piss, wash my hands and face and find my wig. Then, I'll see her."

By the time Wicke had finished and changed his shirt, he was shaking with the need for a drink and he took one, but only one. It calmed him and he called for black coffee.

Shark had accompanied Morning Light into the fort. She was terrified at the sight of so many white men all in one place and the panic in her eyes was obvious. They had separated her from her mother and brother, everyone she knew. Did they expect her to lie with all of them? Her heart was beating as rapidly as a young bird's.

John went out and brought them around to the surgery.

"This is the doctor's office," he said trying to control the loathing he felt for the stranger. "Doc Wicke, here is the girl I told you about," John said walking in. He was glad to see Wicke had cleaned himself up some. He almost looked respectable.

"Hello, young lady, and what might your name be?" Wicke asked congenially.- Morning Light only stared.

"What is it?" he looked at the other two. "Can't she talk?"

"She can't talk nothing but injun talk," Shark responded. "Found her an' a couple of other squaws down at th' last fort sellin' themselves," he lied. "Didn't have no one to protect them an' they got into some rough stuff. We kinda came to a mutual understanding that we would look after 'em from now on, so they travel with us."

"And you came to this little *understanding* without even being able to talk to each other?" John's disbelief was obvious.

"That's right."

John knew the stranger was lying through his teeth but he had no proof, so he didn't challenge it.

"I guess you just didn't realize how badly hurt this one was, did you?" John almost snorted at his own sarcasm.

"Why, no... I, ah... my tastes ain't partial to 'em that young, if ya know what I mean. I didn't realize... none of us realized. But we'd be glad for you t' take a look at her, Doc, an' see if you can help her."

"What seems to be the problem," Wicke stifled a belch. "I don't see any injury."

"Doc," John leaned into Wicke's ear. "It's her... her privates."

"Oh. All right. Well, clear out and I'll examine her."

Shark left, taking up a position outside the door while John hung back. He was concerned with what the rheumy doctor with obvious shakes would do.

The other had left her with these new ones and Morning Light was puzzled when he motioned for her to get up on the smooth wood structure in the center of the room. Then, she noticed strange weapons setting around. Instruments of torture perhaps? Did they wish to torture her? What had she done? And what could be worst than the torture to which she was already subjected?

Morning Light heard her blood pounding in her ears until she couldn't stand it anymore. It didn't matter, she told herself over and over in her mind. It was all the same. It didn't matter. She would take her mind to another place. Or perhaps the Great Spirit would take her spirit and it would all be over.

The white man motioned for her to lie back on the hard wooden surface. His touch was firm but she saw no lust in his face. He spoke sounds, not harsh... almost soothing but she could not understand and she did not trust him. She felt his hands on her legs. She had been wrong, she barely stopped herself from groaning in the expectation of more pain. He was like all the rest.

Morning Light tensed, then she remembered her mother's words and let herself go limp. He opened her legs, he pulled back her skirt. She felt him grasp her ankles and push her knees up and back toward her stomach. The movement set the entire area between her legs on fire. She whimpered softly before she could stop herself. He was staring at her, and her shame and humiliation was more than she knew how to bear. She heard him speak words to the other and then, he lowered her legs, pulled down her skirt and patted her gently on her knee before he turned away.

"What do you think?" John asked. "Do you think you can help her?"

Wicke's hand rubbed over his face and his eye strayed to the whiskey bottle on his desk. "I might have done twenty odd years ago but today..." he held out his shaking hands to demonstrate without words. "I fear I'd do the child more harm than good, best leave her be."

"Doc, they're going to whore her out again. I can only imagine the pain she has been in."

Wicke, his feelings of guilt and ineptness obvious, went to the bottle and gulped a long swig.

John stepped over and snatched the bottle away. "Enough of that! If you can't help her then I will but you are going to help me!" he said fiercely. Startled, Wicke stared at John. "I'm going to tell you something," John kept his voice down but his face was contorted into a scowl. "And this doesn't leave this room, you understand?"

The old doctor nodded his head.

"I used to be a doctor myself, and a pretty damn good one..."

"Why... ?"

"That's my business but I have not shared this with anyone and I choose not to... understand?"

Wicke barely nodded.

"I have my reasons. But I can't stand by and allow this child to go untreated. Sewing was my special area of expertise. I have a delicate touch and leave a minimum of scarring. Now, I can do the job but you will have to front for me so no one else knows. You got that?"

Wicke shook his head vigorously in agreement.

"Go out there and explain to her pimp that you must do this operation or his *merchandise* will soon be no good to him as she is open to a bad infection and will die. Then you are going to help me set up; you're going to pretend to do it and take credit for it. Do I make myself clear?"

"Of course." With the pressure off, Wicke was actually feeling much better. He would be happy to assist and get all the credit.

"I'd like to get my hands on the fella who did this to her," John growled.

Wicke echoed that sentiment as he opened the door and walked outside. Shark was half sitting on the porch railing. "Do you have any idea how much pain that girl has been in?" he looked at Shark accusingly.

"Hey, it wasn't me. Some customer I expect," he said uneasily, knowing very well that Jinglo had done the initial damage.

"But you've been selling her!" Wicke said rather righteously. "Expecting her to take a man before she heals is like expecting her to sit willingly on a knife blade. How would you like a blade up your ass, sir, or perhaps your *dickie?*"

Shark visibly paled.

"I cannot imagine how she's done it without screaming her head off," Wicke exclaimed.

"I have a pretty good idea," John said from his position behind Wicke "There's a young boy down there, probably little brother, and he has a burn on his arm that doesn't look like any accident."

"Since when do white men go in for torturing children?" Wicke snarled.

"That's an insult, sir!" Shark protested indignantly. "These whores attached themselves t'us. We protect them. Nothing more. An' it's nobody's business but ours. Now, can you help her or do I take her an' leave?"

"She is not going anywhere until I say so. But I am going to need some help," Wicke said harshly, warming to his role.

"Jack," Wicke said with a tremor as he leaned on the door frame while John stood near Shark, waiting. "I'm gunna need you to help me. If there were any women here I could communicate with, I'd make them my nurses. But there ain't and I judge you to have brains a step above the others so you just got the job."

John nodded. "I guess I'm up for whatever needs to be done, Doc," he said following the elder man back into the surgery and shutting the door on Shark.

Back inside, John gently encouraged Morning Light to sit up and Wicke began giving her watered down whiskey. "She's going to need something," Wicke said, sneaking a sip from the bottle for himself.

"But no food, she can't have food for a while," John said frowning as he proceeded to set water to boiling on the stove in the corner. After he dumped all the instruments he could into the boil, he began scrubbing down the examination table. "Do you have a clean sheet I can use once I'm done?"

Morning Light grew more and more puzzled as the time passed. She could not imagine what they were going to do to her. They gave her water which tasted strange but no food and her belly growled. She remembered hearing someone tell her mother once that pain was easier to bear on a full belly. She was frightened and she wanted her mother.

"We must purge her bowels. You have a chamber pot in here?" John asked.

Wicke nodded.

"Get it. Rinse it out. Then you hold her while I administer the flush. She'll be busy eliminating for a time. We can give her some more whiskey, maybe a little stronger but I don't want to make her sick to her stomach. Do you have any laudanum?"

"Yes."

"Good. This should be the easiest part, at least she'll understand it. But everything is going to hurt like the devil. Now, let's get on with it."

"All right," Wicke said and swallowed hard.

While Wicke went to fetch the chamber pot, John looked at the girl. She looked scared to death and he stroked her head like one would a frightened animal. He proceeded as delicately as he could as he set her into position to administer the flush. He could tell it was very unpleasant, perhaps painful but she made not a sound.

They had her get down from the table and as she sat on the chamber pot she watched as the yellow-haired white man began scrubbing the table top again after which he spread a cloth on the top. Then the yellow-hair began to scrub his hands. He scrubbed vigorously with a small brush all the way up to his elbows. He scrubbed his hands and nails again. He smiled at her. She did not trust a white man's smile but she looked to his eyes. They were gentle. Then he took something, she saw it was a needle, and he made motions like sewing. He pointed to between her legs and made sewing motions.

Suddenly, Morning Light thought she understood but did not understand. She thought he was telling her he was going to sew up her entrance but why would the others allow him to do this? They wanted her to whore for them, how could she take in a man if this one sewed her closed? Morning Light's head ached from the confusion and from hunger.

"It would help greatly if I could tell this child what I was going to do to her. Chances are she's going to think we're out to torture her. It isn't a pleasant thought. I thought of showing her some of the pictures in your medical book, then I realized they were cut away sketches and she might think we were going to cut her up like the pictures."

"I see what you mean," Wicke nodded and admitted only to himself that he would have never even considered that possibility.

"If I could knock her out, it would help but we can't just bash her over the head. Maybe the laudanum will do the trick. We are going to have to tie her down to the table. Tie her legs back and open. Got to keep her still.

John did the finest job of sewing he had ever done and when he finished he mopped the beads of sweat off his face and treated himself to a double whiskey. Mercifully, the girl had passed out as he had swabbed her bottom with alcohol and begun to reconstruct her anus. By the time she had regained consciousness, he was finished with everything else.

"I've never seen anything like that," Wicke said with admiration, helping himself to a shot. His nerves were frayed just imagining the pain the young girl had endured. "You have a rare gift young man and it seems a sin not to use it."

John said nothing. There was a knock on the door.

John opened the door. Ben had come by to see how things were going.

"Jack, you been tied up in here forever, everything all right?" he asked hesitantly and craned to see the girl neatly resting on a cot.

"Ben, glad to see you." John tried to sound appropriately shocked and amazed. "Took that long for the doctor to fix her. Now doc says he wants cold creek water brought in here every thirty minutes, can you see to that for us?"

"Sure," Ben nodded agreeably. "Is she gunna be...?"

"I don't know but we're doing our best. Now go fetch the first delivery."

"Yes si.. ahh, sure Jack."

Withdrawing into the surgery again, John added to Wicke, "We need to keep cold towels on her bottom, it will help numb her. She's got to be in a lot of pain, but hopefully the worst is over."

"Then, what?" Wicke asked.

"Then what? God, I don't know *then what*. We hope she doesn't develop an infection, hope she doesn't get a fever. Hope she heals. Hope God has mercy on her. Hope someone else doesn't do this to her again. Hope she doesn't lose her mind from the savagery of it all!"

"That's an awful lot of hoping, young man."

"I've done the best I can, Wicke. The rest is in God's hands."

"When do you suggest we allow her to eat again?" Wicke asked after a moment. "She hasn't had a thing to eat all day."

"And we have to keep it that way for as long as possible without starving her," John replied. "We can tell the cook to render up some clear broth. That's all she can have along with water. The first time this child moves her bowels she's going to feel like knives are in there carving her up... but, if she's healed enough before then, she'll only *think* she's dying. And she should be all right."

They opened the door and stepped onto the porch together where Shark still sat waiting. "She's resting but she cannot leave the surgery." Wicke said wearily.

"How long?" Shark asked.

"We must keep an eye on her until she has her first bowel movement," Wicke replied.

"Excuse me Doc, did you not say something about it taking three weeks before you might be able to remove her stitches?" John interjected in what he hoped sounded like a subservient way.

"Oh... yes, of course. How stupid of me. I am tired. I have to keep watching her for signs of infection."

Shark grunted, obviously not terribly happy with that news.

"I suppose I'd be a damn fool to think I can persuade you to stop selling her?" John said. He immediately put his hand up to check the protesting response the bushloper was about to make.

"Look, I'm going to tell you straight and then, you can judge for yourself, mister," Wicke went on. "Give this girl the time she needs to fully heal clean and proper and she'll be able to continue her business as usual. But, if you *allow* her," he chose his words with a certain diplomacy, "to start taking customers before she's healed, she will most likely develop a fever and die."

"Can't make any money for you that way, can she?" John added ominously.

"I hear ya, Doc," Shark said with a dark look and ignoring John, he turned to leave. "I'll go tell the others how she's doin'."

"Yes," the doctor looked after the stranger with loathing as he left the porch, "you just do that."

In the days that followed, Mist-On-Moon and Singing Wind continued to service a series of paying customers. As she lay beneath the grunting men, Singing Wind thought constantly of her daughter. Why did she feel that Morning Light was being cared for? Something about the yellow-haired one. She had understood the facial expressions if not the words. He had been angry at their captors and it was he who had taken Morning Light away. But to where, to where and why so long? Those were the questions and she asked them of herself in time with the rhythm of the customer she was with.

The boy shrank back into the shadows, trying to keep out of the way, nursing his painful arm and wondering what had become of his sister. He missed Morning Light. She had looked out for him when their mother was with the white men. First, their father was gone, now she was gone. He peeked now and then into his mother's tent, not knowing what else to do, wanting to reassure himself that she was still there, still well, still alive. He saw her coupling with the strangers, the white men, like she had coupled with his father. Why did she do this? He did not understand.

Yellow Rock watched at times also and came away muttering a string of curses upon the white men. And where had they taken his cousin Morning Light? But he, too, was aware of the boy's ugly scar and did not wish him to be injured again which was bound to be the result if any fuss was made. What cowards the white men were, Yellow Rock raged quietly with the boy. To make war on a boy with no name in order to keep everyone else in line. Yellow Rock hated them with venom and loathing. They had no honor. But the boy hated them even more intensely.

"It's time we was leavin'," Jinglo said one slow afternoon. They had been there a month and had drained pockets and purses of the recently distributed monthly payroll. "I think we about played out this gold mine. When is that damn little bitch gunna be ready to travel, anyway?"

"S'pose there's nothing keepin' us from takin' her now," Shark responded as he gnawed on a turkey bone. He wiped his greasy mouth on his sleeve. "No reason she shouldn't be able to move on, but remember what I told you. No sense permanently damagin' the goods. No money if the moneymaker is broken. We just have t' leave her be for a spell."

"Yeah, I heard. Jist git in there and tell that doctor we're leavin' first thing in the mornin'. Tell him she better be ready."

Wicke protested when Shark came in and told him they were leaving in the morning and taking the girl with them. But, the doctor knew he was powerless to stop them.

Shortly after she had gone, John came by the surgery as he had done everyday since she had arrived.

"How could you let them take her?" he protested when Wicke told him where she'd gone. "You should have stopped them, you should have... you said yourself her stitches might be out but she wasn't completely healed yet."

"I'm sorry, son, there just wasn't anything I could do. She's their property and they wanted to leave."

John gave the wall a backhanded pound with his fist.

"C'mon now," the doctor admonished, "let it go. We did everything we could."

"She reminded me of my sister, Doc. If anyone did that to my sister I'd.... I'd..."

"I know, I know. But she's not your sister. She's an injun, don't forget that. Next month we might be at war again and you might be wishing we'd let her die."

John shook his head. "If we have to make war on women and children, we have no business being here."

The doctor said nothing. Obviously the young man was still very naive. It was a gallant and chivalrous way to think in the white world but here on the frontier being a woman or child didn't mean the same thing if you were injun. They could and would cut your throat as soon as any brave.

# *Chapter 14*

From his perch atop the pack mule, the boy watched his sister force herself to put one foot in front of the other. She looked footsore and bone weary. He felt guilty riding but the white men put him there because he could not keep up. He did not understand what had been done to Morning Light but when she had returned to them, he had rejoiced at the sight of her. He had thought she was dead. At first, they had let her ride as well because she could walk only slowly but she had begged to walk, telling them it hurt too much to ride the animal but they did not understand her words. Finally, they had thrown her across the mule on her stomach and she had remained quiet. Sometimes they, too, rode the pack mules and sometimes they walked but the women and Yellow Rock always walked and now, they would no longer allow Morning Light to ride.

It was days since they had left the fort and the boy wondered where they were going. He looked at the ugly wound on his arm. It was healing and didn't hurt anymore but it was a reminder to him of the hatred he felt for the white man. He almost wished it did still hurt for it had given him a focal point for the rage living within him.

After that horrible night when his father and uncles had been murdered, he had come to realize his young life had changed forever. They all seemed to belong to the white men now. They would never see their village again. Would they never again be free? He could not believe that. He would not accept it. Some day he would grow to be a strong warrior and he would kill the white men and, then, they would be free. When he was strong enough, he told himself, he would kill all whites. Men, women, children, he would drive them from the land.

They walked along the bottom of a small valley. The sun was high and it was getting very hot and the boy felt his eyelids growing heavy in the quiet monotony. Insects buzzed in their ears. Suddenly, out of nowhere a warbling cry of chilling fierceness split through the air. Arrows whistled by and one caught Pantaloons in the shoulder from the back. Another hit Jinglo in the ribs but did not sink in deeply; it fell out, leaving a bloody hole. Shark fell to the ground, just avoiding an arrow coming at his head. Singing Wind grabbed her son off the mule and joined the others trying to find refuge in the shelter of a large tree.

Three powerful bucks came swooping in like lightning, war clubs in hand, and Pantaloons was the first to crumple as a powerfully swung stone club cleaved into his skull. The fiercely painted faces of the warriors were horrifying to behold. Several more had run in at them and without the time to reload their single shot muskets and pistols, Jinglo and Shark were overwhelmed and rendered helpless.

The women didn't know whether to be glad or not. They had never seen warriors like these and wondered what their fate was to be now. They knew the white men were all but dead. What was in store for them and their children? That they could not predict.

Jinglo and Shark were tied and led on a leash by their captors. The women followed submissively, their children in hand. Others led the pack animals along. Behind them, Pantaloons had been left unceremoniously on the ground, food for the carrion scavengers, only a top knot of hair removed with a bit of bloody scalp to hang from his vanquisher's trophy belt.

Before long, Morning Light stumbled and fell, there was a fire raging within her loins, and she was flush with fever. One of the largest and fiercest looking of the warriors barked out something and another of his braves, the one closest to her, pulled her up onto her feet. Then, in a blur of movement he grabbed her long doeskin skirt at the side, reached under with his razor sharp flint knife and split the skirt open from thigh to hem, exposing her length of leg. He repeated his action on the other side and then tossed her up on the back of the pack mule to ride astride, her knees and thighs able to grip the animal beneath her. Morning Light said nothing, looked down only at the mule's neck, afraid to look at the brave, but she was grateful to be off her feet and found it no longer so painful to sit astride.

Next, the boy found himself riding in front of his sister. And before long his mother and aunt were each riding one of the pack mules. Jinglo and Shark continued to be led along by their captors, suffering the pokes of sharp sticks if they lagged. Yellow Rock walked quietly beside his stepmother, his hatred growing with the humiliation of now being another tribe's captive.

In time, they reached their destination, a village protected all around by a palisade made up of young tree trunks lashed vertically into a wall. More than two dozen cylindrical shaped huts of bark construction stood within the palisade walls. Each hut had a door opening on one short end and a window on the far opposite side. The Indian captives huddled together silently while the white men were half dragged away and strung up on a tree by their wrists so that only by stretching on tiptoe could they touch the ground. There they were ignored and left to await their fate.

A small group of squaws came up to Singing Wind and her company, guiding them to a shelter which was little more than a cleared place under a thatched roof of branches braced up on poles. The people of the village, men and women alike were dressed much like her people had dressed before the white man's holy men came. Many of the men wore only breech-cloths, as the weather was already quite warm. Most of the women wore short wrapped skirts that covered their hips and thighs. And the little children ran naked. Some of the older braves and squaws wore intricately woven bead and shell necklaces which draped over their bare chests and breasts, denoting their wealth. The younger men and women generally had fewer such decorations.

The squaws looked the captives over with curiosity and gestured for them to sit. When they complied, they were given bowls of corn mush and water flavored with fresh berry juice. There was nothing solicitous or sympathetic in these actions. The women would not have expected it to be so. But then, there was nothing overtly hostile in their treatment either. They were simply prizes of a raid and until their fate was determined, they were treated indifferently but fairly, much as the captive mules were treated.

Singing Wind was discovering there were similarities in their languages and they knew a few words in common. It was sketchy communications, awkward at first, but Singing Wind's heart grew more fearful at what she thought she had understood herself being told. These were the *killers of men*, a fierce and feared tribe of whom she had heard. They were also said to be *eaters of men:* cannibals! She quaked within and considered whether or not to tell the others.

After they had eaten, they were led out of the palisade under the conspicuous guard of several strong bucks, and down to a small river where they were able to wash the dust and grime of their forced travels from their faces and bodies. Without inhibition, the squaws dropped their doeskin garments to embrace the cooling water.

Morning Light gladly dropped her torn clothing and joined the others. For a time the white men had left her alone but then the one in buckskins had taken her again, and once he did they began passing her around amongst themselves and each night she had been forced to share a different bed. Now, she wanted nothing more than to scrub the smell of the white men from her body with the fine sand of the river bottom and to sweeten her skin with fresh herbs. She scrubbed and scrubbed until her flesh was almost raw and still she thought she could smell them on her.

Singing Wind approached her daughter, concern in her face. She worried about Morning Light. She saw the young girl scrubbing herself violently. How quickly she had had to grow up. It was not what any mother would want for her daughter, but they were still alive, that was the important point. She handed Morning Light some soap root plant. The girl nodded gravely and beat the fat root upon a river stone and used the lathery pulp to begin to wash her hair. Singing Wind took over massaging her daughter's scalp affectionately, wishing she could wipe out all the memories from her daughter's mind. As Morning Light laid back in the water, the water felt cool and soothing as it passed over her scalp.

Singing Wind also made certain her son was washed, taking special care with the boy's angry looking arm. She showed no pity, however. For a warrior was never to be shown pity, it was the greatest insult. She knew her son, small as he was, took pride in showing his courage and even a certain disdain for his injury.

When they had finished bathing and dressed again in their soiled garments, the captives were led back into the Council Circle. One particular squaw, with coarse skin and heavy features, seemed to understand them better than any of the others and so she acted as a translator as Singing Wind and Mist-On-Moon told their story. Leaving out the details about their willing debauchery, they told how their husbands had been made drunk and then easily slain, how their goods had been stolen, themselves raped, and Morning Light's maidenhead brutalized. Singing Wind pointed out the boy's scarred arm, showing the dishonor of the white men in torturing a small child to gain power over a couple of women and children.

Shark and Jinglo couldn't understand what was being said but they had a pretty fair idea. Neither man could feel his hands anymore, the circulation had been cut off for hours. They grew weary, unable to stand on their toes and the ropes cut deeply into their wrists under the strain of their body weight.

"I'm thinkin' none of it was worth it," Shark said quietly in a mournful sigh. "I'm thinkin' we could'a just taken the bloody pelts an' left them all in their drunken stupor... I'm thinkin'..."

"Yer thinkin' it's all my fault for grabbin' th' little savage bitch," Jinglo hissed at his comrade.

"Why'd ya have to go after th' girl?" Shark asked with a sudden burst of remorse. "You could'a had either of th' squaws... both'a them, ready an' willin'... why'd you have t' take th' girl?"

"Because I wanted to," Jinglo responded belligerently. "Because I ain't never had me no virgin before."

"But ya didn't have t' shoot her old man! He was too drunk to do any harm," Shark continued accusingly.

"Like you didn't shoot the second one..."

"Sure, after you blew off the first one's face. What else could we do?"

"And you didn't enjoy pumpin' her yourself the next day!"

"Oh, shut up!"

"Admit it, Shark. You'd never had anything that tight and sweet, had ya? E'ceptin' maybe that golden hair'd gal what hung herself."

"Yer disgusting, Jinglo! We're gunna die an' all you can think of is cunts? Ya better be making peace with yer Maker."

"Least-wise I'm no whimperin' hypocrite. I did what I did an' I enjoyed it. So did you. You even burned th' little pup so you could pump his sister. Yer jist sorry now 'cause we got ourselves caught an' strung up. If we hadn't you'd be pumpin' that one agin tonight, tonight would'a been yer turn 'n you'd a been lovin' every minute of it."

"Shut up, damn you, jist shut yer ugly face!"

Jinglo's sneering reply was cut short as drums began to beat around the blazing fire in the ring before them. A fiercely painted warrior with malevolent eyes approached them and almost before they realized what was happening their clothes had been deftly cut from them. They heard jeering voices as they stood stretched and as naked as the day they were born.

"Ughhhh! Look at the pale skin, like slug worms!" shouted one squaw.

"And all the hair, like a beast!" shouted a second.

"See their manhood shrivel!" shouted another, and laughter followed.

"With pellets so small, no wonder they must torture a small child!" shouted a fourth.

"Let the mother of the burned child take her revenge!" shouted someone, and murmurs of approval followed.

The coarse-skinned squaw called Okonhsa translated to Singing Wind. "They say you have right to take your revenge. Make the white feel your son's pain."

After a moment, Singing Wind understood what she was being told and she walked up to the fire and pulled out a branch about half as thick as her wrist, its tip red hot and glowing. It was the size of the one he had used on her son. She approached the naked white men slowly, watching their faces, watching Uniform's face as he registered understanding. He knew she was going to burn him just as he had burned her son.

Singing Wind stopped before Uniform, reaching out toward his arm. Then, slowly she moved the branch downward. Burning a man's arm was nothing, his flesh was not tender like a small child's. The squaw moved the burning point down from his arm, down over his pale scarred chest, mottled and covered with a light scattering of hair. No, she would not burn his chest. She continued to move the hot tip down, down, over his soft white belly... then suddenly, she knew what she wanted to burn. His tenderest flesh! She looked up at his face and in an instant he, too, knew what she was thinking. She saw the sweat break out on his forehead. Singing Wind deliberately focused on her objective and brought the hot poker down, slowly, steadfastly, and then, at last making contact as the white man screamed in agony and then fainted from the pain.

Jinglo cringed beside his comrade, sweat pouring from him in empathy. The other's scream had ended abruptly when he had passed out. The smell of burnt hair and flesh was in the air. The crowd cheered in approval and Singing Wind looked at the other. This was the one who had raped her happy, innocent daughter so savagely. She called to her daughter. "Daughter! What would you do to him? Come. It is your revenge," she said. "Come, take your revenge."

Morning Light walked into the circle, looking around at the crowd. They were speaking in a strange tongue but she could tell they were encouraging her to take her revenge. Then, she spied the fierce brave who had split her skirt so she could ride astride the mule. She walked over to him and held out her hand.

"Your knife," she said but he did not understand her words. "Give me knife." She pointed to the razor sharp blade stuck in a sheath on a thong at his lean muscled waist. He followed the line of her finger and realized she asked for his knife and he grunted and gave it to her.

Taking the knife gingerly in her right hand and picking up a flaming torch from the fire with her left, she walked slowly to Jinglo. Here was the man who had stolen her maidenhead with so much brutality, who had impaled her in two places. The man who had laughed at her heartlessly as she had struggled to keep him away. The man who had completely overpowered her and laughed at her was now, not laughing. He was stretched naked and helpless and she would show him all the pity he had shown her.

She could still feel the tearing of her flesh, the burning agony that he had started and that had plagued her for days as they all used her repeatedly and now, she burned with hatred. This was the man who had blown away her father's face for no reason but his lust. Her father had done him no harm. Her father had only been coming to help her and for that he had died. She had felt her father's flesh and blood spatter her face.

Morning Light looked at the white man and enjoyed seeing the sweat running down his dirty face as she brandished the knife threateningly, circling him with menace. She thought of everything she had experienced since he had ripped sav-agely into her. How would he ever know what she had felt, what she continued to feel? Even after the yellow-haired medicine man had sewed her, this one had sav-agely taken her again. And she wanted him to know exactly what she had felt.

He was gasping and straining to back away from her as she teased at first, and made several fake lunges. His fear made him stiff and his offensive flesh grew erect before her. She turned to Okonhsa.

"His legs must be spread," she cried out with a gesture. "I want his legs spread wide and bound."

The large woman nodded and translated to the others. Three husky braves came forward, two each grabbed a leg while the third bound it to a stake. In mere mo-ments, Jinglo was hanging spread-eagled, immobilized, and totally vulnerable.

"Now, you will feel what it was like, white man," Morning Light growled as she approached with deadly concentration. He couldn't understand her words, but as she looked into his eyes she saw the terror and she was glad. "Now, you will know the pain you gave me. Now, it is I who will take pleasure!" His erection was quivering before her and with hardly any effort she laid the tip of his manhood open, cutting the flesh more cleanly than she had been ripped. The sound of his scream was pleasant to her ears. Then, her wild glittering eyes lit upon a thick stick and dropping the knife upon the ground she grabbed it up and pushed the end sav-agely into his rectum, mimicking his thrusts and grunts when he raped her also like this. His screams intensified as blood and excrement oozed out. She dropped the stick when he passed out and set fire to his pubic hair which did not burn well be-cause of the wetness of the blood but it cauterized the flesh and stopped the bleed-ing.

The boy saw his sister drop the torch to the ground, then stand back and turn slowly. The crowd gave way to her as she walked stiffly back to the shelter she had been taken to earlier that day. Her face was proud and impassive while she passed them. Only after she had reached the shelter did the tears begin streaming down her face. The boy ran to her. They held each other and cried until together they fell asleep in each others' arms upon the skins on the ground.

The villagers had been entertained and felt justice had been served in allowing the new captives to seek their own revenge upon these whites. But they were not finished with the white men by any means. They were a blood thirsty people who dealt very harshly with their foes and this made them admire the young girl greatly.

In time, the screams of agony grew monotonous as the two white men had their flesh removed strip by strip through the next days. Raw and bleeding, they were force-fed water to sustain them for further torment. Souvenirs were collected by anyone wishing one in the form of toes, noses, ears, fingers, pieces of scalp. The small wounds left nerve endings raw and exposed, the blood letting was slow and agonizing, nothing serious enough to cause a quick death.

Finally, on the fourth day when the bushlopers appeared to be so weakened they would permanently slip into unconsciousness and death, their hearts were cut out and the warriors passed the warm slippery prizes around, each taking a bloody bite. Then, the squaws came up and took their turn by cutting off the symbols of the dead men's manhood, skewering the flesh onto a stick and setting it up to roast. When toasted to satisfaction, the tidbits were daintily passed around. Thus, they believed they gained the life essence of their victims, whatever small amount of bravery, strength, wisdom, and fertility these strangers might have possessed.

Singing Wind found Morning Light doubled up in pain as she tried to pass her morning water at the back of the hut they had been told to shelter in.

"What is wrong?" the plump squaw asked, anxiety in her voice.

Morning Light shook her head, grimacing. The squaw placed her hand upon her daughter's brow, smoothing back the loose wisps of hair now plastered to her skin. She was running a fever and her smooth brow felt hot and dry, then flushed with sweat turning clammy.

"How long have you been this way?" Singing Wind asked in bewilderment.

Morning Light bit her lip in pain. "Ever since we leave fort and white men force me again... it grows worse each day."

Her mother took the vessel up and brought it into the light, there was a bloody tinge to the liquid contained there.

"Do you bleed?" she asked.

"Only when I pass water," the girl moaned.

"That is not the cycle of a woman or the bleeding of a wound. It is something else. Lie down. I will seek help." The mother went off in search of Okonhsa, the woman who could understand her words.

The captives had been given the freedom of the palisaded village. The boys had quickly found other children their respective ages with which to play. The women were supervised by the village squaws until their fate was to be decided. Okonhsa of the coarse skin was the go-between who was assisting them in learning the language. At this time Singing Wind found her bent over the cooking pots outside her own hut.

"Okonhsa," Singing Wind bowed respectfully, "I wish to speak with you."

The older woman sniffed at the wooden ladle, let it slip back into the pot and looked around. "Good morning, Singing Wind. You frown. What is wrong?"

"It is my daughter. She is ill. She passes blood in her water. She has a fever and much pain. Know you what could be wrong?"

Okonhsa pursed her lips in thought, her eyes narrowing. "When did this start?"

"She says it started after the white men took her and it grows steadily worse."

"I will talk to the shaman and come to see you."

A short time later, Okonhsa walked into the hut sheltering the captives and found Singing Wind on her knees beside Morning Light who was on all fours poised over a vessel, stifling a moan of pain.

"Let me see the water," Okonhsa asked gently.

"There is none," Morning Light fell onto her side. "I feel I must pass water but nothing comes but burning pain."

"The shaman said I should examine you. Will you allow me?" Okonhsa looked at the girl patiently.

Morning Light was caught off-guard by the request and looked straight at the woman. Tears stung unexpectedly in her eyes though she fought to hold them back. Ever since that fateful night of her father's death, no one had asked her permission to do anything to her body. She had been violated and used and left with little doubt that she no longer was in command of her own person; even the white men who had tried to help her had done so as they wished, not with her permission. Okonhsa had just given Morning Light back a small sense of dignity. The girl nodded.

When the examination was finished, the older woman told Singing Wind to make a warm poultice. Okonhsa then gave her an amulet and instruction for the girl, telling her that when the poultice was ready she was to put it, along with the amulet, between her legs, snug up against her womanhood and lie quietly. Then, Okonhsa motioned Singing Wind to follow and walked outside the hut.

"Your daughter's wound reminds me of another. I remember a birth many years ago when mother was torn in such a way. She has been in much pain, I have no doubt. But she is healing."

Tears came to Singing Wind's eyes. "She is tall but only ten winters old, she is not even fully grown."

Okonhsa nodded. "I saw no sign of infection and yet, she has the fever and blood in her water. I must go consult with the shaman again."

Some time later Okonhsa appeared once again and motioned Singing Wind aside. "The shaman says to make her drink cranberry tea, and much water laced with these herbs." She handed the mother a small leather sack. "All day long, at least," she held up her hands, palms out, and spread her fingers, "this many bowls of water and this many bowls of tea."

Singing Wind nodded.

"If she does not get better," the woman stopped for a moment before uttering the last, "he says, if she does not get better then she must have the white man's disease and none can help her."

The mother gasped and clutched at her heart.

Singing Wind had two pieces of colored leather lacing to wrap about her short strong fingers. One tinted with the stain of blueberry was for the herbed water, one rubbed with red clay was for the cranberry tea. She watched over her daughter and with each bowl Morning Light drank, the mother moved the leather lacing to another finger. Thus, she diligently kept track of the count. The cranberry tea was strong but the girl liked the tart taste and drank it willingly until the sudden ingestion of so much liquid caused her to urinate more frequently, which meant she endured the pain more often.

Morning Light argued and balked at drinking anymore but her mother insisted. As the day drew on, the girl began to notice it was growing less painful to pass her water. But still, Singing Wind could tell the fever remained.

When the boy, sweaty from his running play with some of the smaller children, joined his mother and sister in the hut, along with Yellow Rock and Mist-On-Moon, he came to understand that his sister had been on her pallet all day. He felt remorse that he had not noticed her absence outside before this. He should have been with her to see if he could help her. As their closest male relative, it was his responsibility to watch after them, he thought solemnly, his dirt streaked little face cast in a sober look.

"What is wrong with my sister?" he asked of his mother with authority.

"A fever," Singing Wind said without betraying emotion. "But it is better. It is time now for you to rest."

In an instant he went from the male head of the family to just a little boy being sent to bed. With a slightly haughty air he considered whether he felt like resting. He realized he was actually quite tired from his long day of running and jumping and showing off amidst his new companions. He crawled onto his sleeping furs without protest and watched the shadows play upon the wall from the firelight outside the hut. He had not yet dozed off when he heard his sister whimpering. He opened his eyes and saw her sitting on her knees over a vessel, cringing in pain.

"It is worse, mother," he heard her strained voice.

"Hush .... it will get better," Singing Wind replied but she didn't sound as certain as she would have liked.

Three of the six warriors in the raiding party were arguing their claims for the captives. These three each wanted Mist-On-Moon who was young and healthy and easy to look upon. They had to be satisfied with drawing lots and Quick Panther, a husky brave with no wife, gave a snort of pleasure when he drew the long twig that settled the matter. She was his and would be brought to his hut that night.

The others immediately laid a claim to Singing Wind and her young son but the leader of the raiding party who was the sachem's brother cited his status. "As leader of this raid," Five Beavers growled, "I have the right of first choice. I did not lay claim to the other. I choose the one with the boy as mine."

Five Beavers was a seasoned warrior. His large coarsely featured head was set upon a thick muscled neck rising out of heavy shoulders spanning a barrel-like chest. His leg muscles were equally thick which made his small rather flat buttocks look almost incongruous and unbalanced as though he had nothing to sit upon as the tops of his legs joined to a slight belly rising over his loin cloth. He kept his head shaved except for a thick fanning spread of hair, like a coxcomb dressed stiff with urine and clay, running down the center of his skull, front to back. The standing hair made him appear just that much taller and a nose ring completed a look that was successfully intimidating. No one dared to grumble or argue his right to his claim.

"I heard the young one is diseased..." said one gaunt faced brave with an upper lip so thin it seemed to not exist at all.

"If she has the white man's sickness, she will be no good. If she lives, she will be barren, and could infect her mate," said Five Beavers and the others grunted and muttered in agreement. They knew something of the white man's mating diseases. Females could give it to the men they coupled with and render them impotent and ill. Afflicted males could give it to the females they coupled with and render them ill unto death or forever barren. It was a plague.

"She should be killed swiftly with mercy," said one of their number and Five Beavers held himself back from agreeing. Even the most formidable warrior wants peace at his own hearth. And Five Beavers was well aware that the young one was the daughter of his new woman. If he was to bring the mother to his hearth without the threat of constant disharmony, he could not appear to sanction any decision to dispose of the daughter. He indicated that he did not want to be the one to make the decision.

"No!" Came a strong straight forward contradiction. The speaker was the same young warrior who had loaned Morning Light his knife. He had said nothing until then, not squabbling with the others over the captives. He had shown no interest in pretty Mist-On-Moon. Singing Wind was much too old for him. But now he spoke with quiet strength. "I will take her. I will provide for her. She will be my slave. If she dies, it will be my loss." His low resonant voice spoke with dignity.

Five Beavers looked around at the rest but none raised an objection or a challenge. Then, he nodded in agreement. "The youngest female belongs to *Atakenhrohkwa Okwaho:* Gray Wolf," he proclaimed.

Then, the oldest in the group who had remained rather quiet until that moment, spoke. "Last year I lost my son of ten winters. I have only daughters now and my wife is no longer fruitful. I would take the tall boy to raise as my own son." His companions all nodded in agreement. Yellow Rock would be adopted.

Through Okonhsa's intercession, Singing Wind and the boy were allowed to stay in the small hut and continue to nurse Morning Light. The woman was told that she now belonged to the leader of the raiding party who would have her for a second wife and adopt her boy as a son.

"What of my daughter?" Singing Wind asked.

"Gray Wolf has asked for her," Okonhsa replied smoothly.

"But she is only a child, she has not yet reached womanhood. Does he know he cannot bed her?"

Okonhsa looked at the woman without expression. "She is his to do with as he pleases. But it is his wish that you should be allowed to nurse her."

Singing Wind sighed in acceptance. "You are right and I am grateful. Please tell him," she gestured, "my daughter and I, we both are grateful. I will tell my daughter when she is better."

Okonhsa nodded.

Mist-On-Moon was brought to Quick Panther immediately. The pretty young squaw accepted her fate. She would do as she was told, try to get to know her new husband and adapt to his will. Things could be worse. The other women had conveyed that her new master was a decent warrior, not the most handsome but young and proud and fair-minded, and they would not expect him to beat her unless she deserved it. She was the first and only woman in his hut which gave her status as first wife and Mist-On-Moon was certain she could please him in the furs.

Morning Light grew steadily better under a faithful regiment of strong cranberry tea, plenty of water, and rich meaty stews. The boy helped to amuse his sister, keeping her company when their mother went out to do chores or gather herbs and food.

"When I am grown, I will have revenge upon the whites for all we have suffered. I will kill them for what they have done to you and to our mother. I will kill them for killing our father. I will kill them for the pain they have caused you, my sister. This I swear," he said gravely, his black eyes alive with feeling. His messy tangle of hair fell into his dirty little face. He had dodged the attempts of his mother and sister to comb and groom him, he was a man-child and they could not tell him what to do.

Morning Light looked at her young brother with sad eyes, then her face grew grim as she thought of the white men strung up on the tree. "We have had our revenge, little one. You are just a boy, you do not even have a name yet. You are too young to swear anything. We must accept. It is over."

"No, I am not too young," he scowled fiercely, his small brow puckering tightly. "I have a warrior's heart," he argued with a gesture that brought his small hand to thump upon his small chest.

She smiled and took comfort in his presence. "I am very sleepy now but stay by me, little warrior, and I will not fear to sleep."

That evening, after her daughter had eaten, Singing Wind told Morning Light their fate. The girl was beside herself with anxiety.

"No, it cannot be," she cried out in disbelief. "Why? Why must they separate us? I am your daughter. I am not a woman yet. I need my mother. Please, do not let them take me from you," she begged and Singing Wind was distraught with upset on her daughter's behalf.

"I am told he is a good man," she offered, trying to find something positive. "He is very young and wants to care for you. Do not anger him by rejecting him. Oh, my daughter, I believe he will not touch you until you are of age. I believe he has honor. If I did not believe this, I would fight for you."

"You believe what you want to, mother," the girl replied bitterly. "I want nothing to do with men, ever again." Then she turned once more to beseech her mother piteously. "Please. I would work by your side. Help to raise my brother and care for you and your mate in your old age. Please, mother, speak for me. Please do not let another take me. Please...." she begged, growing hysterical. "Why can't they just leave me alone? All I want is to be left alone."

Singing Wind held her daughter and rocked her in her arms. Her young son silently beat his fist against the ground and re-swore his oath of revenge silently to himself for his sister's sake.

Okonhsa stopped by the hut early the next morning to see how Morning Light was progressing. She found Singing Wind looking exhausted with dark shadows under her eyes and Morning Light was fretting upon her pallet as though in another fever.

"What has happened?" Okonhsa exclaimed, "She was doing so well. I was certain she would be up on her feet today and could go to the river to cleanse herself before going to her new home."

Singing Wind got to her feet as quickly as she could and she motioned the older woman outdoors.

"The child was doing well until I told her she is to live in Gray Wolf's hut. Now, she frets herself sick again."

"Bah! Does she wish for all to lose patience with her?" the woman asked, impatient herself. "Gray Wolf has every right to expect her today and she must clean herself. Look! He has sent a present. Garments in the fashion of our tribe." Singing Wind looked down at the clean soft garments over Okonhsa's arm. "Perhaps I should have told you, the others were in favor of killing her immediately because she is sickly and perhaps carries the white man's plague. Only Gray Wolf spoke for her!"

Singing Wind's eyes opened wide in startled disbelief. They had been ready to kill her daughter? "They think she has the white man's disease?!" she gasped.

"Tell your daughter to calm her face and go to the river to cleanse herself. She goes to her new home today and you go to yours. You should both be grateful!"

The mother nodded and turned to see her son watching in silence.

At the wide river, Morning Light scrubbed herself and then her hair in the refreshing clear water. She sunk slightly into the soft river bottom and she could feel water grasses at her feet. As she moved naked through the cool liquid caress, she couldn't help but notice the slightest change in her nipples which used to look exactly like Yellow Rock's. Now, they were slightly swollen and pink like bee stings upon her otherwise flat boyish chest. As she rose from the water and went to her waiting mother's arms, she shivered and continued to tremble even as the sun warmed her. Her mother rubbed her with a soft absorbent chamois and toweled her hair. Singing Wind helped her daughter into her fresh garments, a skirt wrap that fell to her knees and a tunic top that fell over it. These were more suited to cold weather wear but Morning Light was grateful for their coverage. After combing and drying her daughter's long thick hair, Singing Wind plaited it into the single braid Morning Light was fond of wearing down her back. Then, they returned with their escort to the palisade.

Morning Light hugged her mother and her brother in a sad farewell as they stood outside the small hut which had been their temporary home. Okonhsa had come for the girl and to tell Singing Wind to go to Five Beavers.

"We are still right here," Singing Wind encouraged her daughter. "I go only to Five Beavers' lodge. We are not going far. We will see each other often."

Morning Light nodded and silently followed Okonhsa to Gray Wolf's hut. He was not there and the older woman told her to make herself useful and do some cleaning, for surely the young brave's hut could use a woman's touch. Then, she left.

The girl slipped noiselessly inside and looked around her. It was a smaller hut than most of the others and without a rear window. The inside was gloomy but light streamed in the entrance as the opening flap stood tied back. A thin, sharp beam of light cut through from the smoke hole at the top. As her eyes grew used to the light, or lack of it, she saw there were two sleeping pallets, arranged with soft furs, one on each side of the hut. The cooking ring in the center had been recently cleaned up and showed little signs of fire. It was summer and having a fire inside was not desirable because of the heat. Most of the cooking was being done outdoors now, either in front of the individual huts or at a main cook fire sheltered from rain by a thatched roof on poles.

There was little else in the hut. A few weapons hung on the wall along with a pair of snow shoes that had seen considerable wear, a dwelling talisman hung over the doorway. Various vessels were stacked to the side. She would have to ask which were for water and which were for relieving oneself in the night. There were some containers that held meal and dried fruits. A larger lidded basket that she guessed might hold his clothing. A leather bag hung by the weapons. She shrugged. There was nothing to do, everything was quite neat.

Morning Light reflected on what her mother had told her. They had wanted to kill her for being sickly and he had spoken for her. She wasn't sure if that was good or bad. There had been many times in the past weeks since that fateful night the white men had stumbled into their camp when she had thought hospitably of death.

So, they thought she might be diseased... forever. If they thought she carried the white man's mating plague, she would be *taboo*. No one would ever touch her like that again. Was she diseased forever? Was she slowly dying? And if she was, then why did he want her?

She tried to remember what he looked like. She had a vague recollection of a very fierce and terrifying face painted in hideous designs when he had pulled her to her feet and split her skirt before setting her astride the mule. He had lifted her without any effort. True, she weighed almost nothing, but she weighed more than her little brother and many grunted to lift him into the air. He had lifted her like she was no more than a feather.

Then, she remembered, she had asked for his knife. What had he looked like? She couldn't recall. She thought he had still been painted, that was how she had known it was him. All she could remember was his knife. She had pointed to it as it hung at his side. The muscles of his stomach were taut and sharp, that she remembered. She could have traced each one of them with her fingers. Not like the white men who had had soft rounded bellies like grub worms. She shuddered remembering her last sight of them and closed her eyes. She did not see the change in light as the figure passed through the doorway of the hut.

Gray Wolf had entered silently and saw the little female standing with her back to the door, seeming to look at his weapons and tremble at the sight. That amused him.

"You are here."

Morning Light spun around and saw the figure against the light from the doorway. Her eyes opened wide in startled surprise. She could not make out the face which was in shadow and she was uncertain what he had said but she immediately bowed her head in a sign of submissive meekness.

"Come outside so I can look at you," he said arrogantly, but she only looked at him until he gestured, pointing from her to the door and then motioning with his hand. She responded and moved quickly through the door. He followed her and when she stopped and looked at him, she saw him clearly for the first time.

Outside the hut, he stood tall and straight, his bare torso covered by a bear claw necklace and a quill bib. A breech-cloth and leggings covered his lower body while his tall moccasins reached high up on his calves. He did not fashion his hair into a coxcomb but wore a single, thick, blue-black braid from the top center of his shaved head which ran down to his shoulders. His face, without the fierce paint, was not harsh but was held in an arrogant expression. His skin was smooth over high, full cheekbones and a straight firm nose. His black piercing eyes were spaced wide and a high forehead balanced a strong firm jaw. His lips were thin and sometime later when he laughed, she saw his teeth were white, straight, and even. But now, he just looked at her with a haughty curiosity.

"You look well. I was told you were ill. Do you feel better?" He saw her eyes look at him searching for meaning. "Uhhh," he grunted in realization, "you do not understand our language yet. I will teach you."

And this he proceeded to undertake at once. For several hours, despite his haughty appearance he patiently repeated words and pointed to objects. He saw her concentrate on learning and begin to relax. Only at bedtime did he recognize nervous fear and apprehension which he quickly put to rest when he pointed to her sleeping pallet. More vocabulary. He pointed and said the words. She repeated them. Then, he told her to go to bed and turned his back on her. Taking off his quill vest and necklace and removing his moccasins and leggings, he crawled onto his own sleeping fur on the other side of the hut.

Gray Wolf would have been more appropriately named Lone Wolf. He had no kin left among his tribesmen. His parents were killed in the same Huron raid in which his sisters were stolen, and his older brother had died in a retaliatory raid a year later. His mother had been an only child and his father's brother had died of a fever before his wife had conceived and she had gone to another. When Gray Wolf's paternal grandmother had died seventeen moons ago, he had lost the last person on earth who was blood kin to him. No uncles, no aunts, no cousins, just him. And now, it pleased him to have the young female in his hut... to be a little sister? No, that would imply they were of equal status and they were not. To be a servant? That was the excuse but he really did not need a servant. To be a companionable pet? Perhaps that was closer to the truth. He did not know for certain but just to be there and belong to him was enough.

It had taken very little to get the story from Okonhsa who liked to talk. Like everyone else at the Council Circle, he had heard of the brutality this one had suffered at the hands of the whites. But Okonhsa had been able to supply even greater detail when alone, and had even let slip the facts of the little one's brutal wound and inner scars. Then, Okonhsa had begged him not to betray her loose tongue. He also knew the little one was not yet a woman but was, understandably, close to hating all men. He could hardly blame her. A man should not lust after children and she was only a child. But he did admire the way she had survived, the way she had faced her enemy and taken her revenge. There had been nothing squeamish in the torture she had extracted as her right. She had a warrior's heart and therefore she was worthy of his protection. She would share his lodging and he would provide for all her needs. And if he died, thought the sixteen year old, there would be at least one person to mourn for him.

# Chapter 15

## Three years later

The camp elders met in council to listen to the words of the sachem, their leader, who had been communing with the *manitous*, the spirits of all things. He had sat in the sweat-lodge for many hours. He had fasted and had smoked tobacco. He had invoked the Great *Manitou* to make His wisdom known. Then, the sachem had slept and seen the Great *Manitou* who had showed him a new land, a lush green valley into which he was commanded to lead his people. He had asked the Great *Manitou* for direction and had seen an eagle take flight into the sun which had become the star of the North. A band of braves must go out, he would lead them and they would find this land.

After an appropriate amount of thought and discussion, smoking and consulting, the elders all agreed. This was a good dream and it was time to move the camp. The tribal sachem led his small party out northward and in ten days they returned with the news that the valley of the sachem's dream had been found. Offerings were burned first to the Great *Manitou* in thanksgiving. Then, offerings were made to all the *manitous* lest any be jealous.

Spring had come early and the sachem decreed it time for the entire village to move to a new location. The omens were right. After seven years in the same spot, the wood of their structures was starting to rot, the soil of their garden plots was not producing as well as it might, and the human and animal refuse strewn about was creating a stench. The waste pits where they went to move their bowels were so fowl and such a breeding site for flies that no one wanted to go there anymore. And this was creating even more of a problem. No one could doubt that it was time to move on and start fresh.

Each household was responsible for its own possessions. The women gathered up the vegetable seeds, pots, bowls, baskets, sleeping furs, and such foodstuffs and herbs as had survived the winter and were worth taking. In short, the women were responsible for everything necessary to set up housekeeping elsewhere and plant the family garden. At the same time, they were also responsible for herding and carrying the small children.

The sachem, hereditary leader of the village, and his household were in charge of the corn seed which was a communal property and the most valued possession. This was the wealth of the tribe and from this seed would come the life sustaining corn which was a staple to their diet. The older men took charge of the tools as many had become skilled tool makers and they also supervised the older male children while the younger fully grown braves were held accountable for all the weapons and the defense of the entire village. A few of the strongest, were attached to the shaman who had no family and they carried the tribal totems and large baskets filled with the sacred things hanging on poles between them, but most of the warriors stayed relatively unencumbered, weapons within easy reach, prepared to defend the group in the presence of any encountered dangers or hostility. The sachem and his scouts prepared to lead the way.

The shaman, dressed in short robes decorated with many quills and feathers, stood before the people. His head was smoothly shaven except for the tall ridge of stiffened hair running down the center of his skull to his neck like a gray-white coxcomb. He wore a multitude of beads and shells and animal bones about his old neck, piled upon each other in a multitude of necklaces. The exposed skin of his head was colored with red clay, his face was divided into patches by blueberry stain, and the patches colored with yellow ochre. Many years ago, his ears had been pierced and carved bone inserted, stretching the flesh each year with a new decorative piece until the lobes touched the necklaces about his neck.

Now, with a steady hand defying his years, the shaman took coals from the sacred fire into a modestly sized clay pot of intricate decoration. Air holes laced the upper half. Tossing bits into the pot causing the smoke to rise out in colors, he said words of placation to the spirits of unhappiness, discontent, sorrow, jealousy, greed, envy, illness, laziness, disobedience, and infertility as well as the spirits of those who had died. He bid them to stay in this place and not follow. He circled gravely around the gathering, letting the colored smoke rise up and fall out upon the air. It was to come in contact with every man, woman, child, and possession and render the unhappy spirits incapable of attaching themselves and therefore unable to be carried along with the migration.

Next, the old man added something else which turned the smoke very white. This, then, he held high in the air as he slowly turned full circle before the people and chanted a prayer asking the good spirits of love, joy, happiness, contentment, fruitfulness, respect, courage, wisdom, strength, health, prosperity, and industry to follow them as they left their old home behind and established a new one. Then, the pot of coals was fastened very carefully to an intricately carved walking stick which the shaman always carried. Elevated above everyone's head, the pot was as a beacon for the good spirits to follow. As he walked forward just behind the sachem to lead the people, it was imperative that the coals not be spilled and not be left to die out. This was a sacred trust. And four of the strongest braves, walking two on each side, served as the honor guard for the sacred fire. From this fire every hearth in their new location would get its first light. And the braves were watchful and protective of the pot and their shaman.

Singing Wind had watched the proceeding with great curiosity while holding her new infant tied into the folds of her short pliable carrying robe. From this position, she would be able to nurse him easily as they traveled without stopping. The plump squaw looked around for a glimpse of her daughter. She caught sight of her then, standing behind Gray Wolf with a huge basket on her back. It was not difficult to pick Morning Light out of the crowd. The girl had grown tall, at least a full head taller than Singing Wind, and strong. She did not bend beneath her burden. She also was wearing way too much clothing, Singing Wind sighed, she would become too hot and exhausted before half the day was through.

Most of the younger women wore simple folded skirts in anticipation of the heat of the journey even this early in the spring. They were proud to show off their healthy bodies and nubile breasts, symbols of their womanly status. But not Morning Light. She always hid behind folds and layers although Singing Wind could tell there was a woman's figure beneath the large loose garments her daughter chose to wear.

Morning Light had never admitted to having a monthly cycle like the other girls her age, not even to her mother. She had never been formally recognized as having become a woman.

"What is the point?" she would shrug her shoulders. "I am diseased and therefore of no use that way."

"I do not think you are diseased, my daughter. You look healthy enough to me and if you have monthly cycles you can have children."

"I am not normal," was all she would say when Singing Wind hinted around the subject.

"You are normal," her mother would insist. "And you have become very pleasing to look upon."

"Do not say that," Morning Light's eyes flashed, "or I will take the shells of the river mussels and scrape my face, scarring myself to make myself ugly." Singing Wind had gasped in disbelieving horror at the very idea and pressed the subject no more.

Now, as Singing Wind stood in the organized confusion of their departure, she wondered about the very tall, well-muscled brave standing near her daughter in his simple breech-cloth and bear claw necklace. His feet were shod in thick moccasins, his bow and quiver were on his back, and a waist thong held his knife and war club. He stood almost arrogantly aloof and a full head taller than her tall daughter. He continued to wear his hair in one long top knot and his ears were decorated all around their edges with a multitude of silver rings pierced into the flesh.

Gray Wolf was a very handsome warrior of nineteen winters, Singing Wind pondered, and had yet to take a wife. He had lived within the small hut with her daughter for three years. Surely, he was not blind to her beauty. Was he not normal? Singing Wind shook her head. Life was not the way it used to be, she thought to herself. She didn't understand young people anymore. Those two could enjoy all the pleasures the Great Spirit had given unto men and women and there they were, hardly looking at each other and never seeming to smile.

Singing Wind was not unhappy with her own life. She rarely thought of Red Elk anymore. Five Beavers, her present mate, gave her an adequate share of his attentions and provided well for all of them. His first wife was not hateful toward her, they both had healthy new sons and Five Beavers had now given her older boy a name of his own. She thought of her older son's name, *Wakuwéskwani Atatswvhsera,* and translated it into her old tongue. The translation was rather odd. The closest she could come to was "One Who Loves to Hate" or "I Enjoy Hatred". That didn't have a very friendly sound to it. She adopted the habit of calling him *Wani* for short. She didn't have time to bend her tongue around all the sounds in his full new name she thought to herself with a grunt, and neither did the rest of his family. By the time she finished saying his whole name formally she might forget what she wanted to say to him in the first place.

"Hello, Singing Wind," a voice speaking her old tongue disrupted the squaw's thoughts. She looked around and saw Mist-On-Moon approaching, her toddler at her side. "I have yet to hear anyone explain why the elders are making us move like this, do you know?"

Singing Wind shrugged. "I know for these people it is not unusual."

"My mate tells me nothing but says only 'pack, we move'. Do you realize how much work we will have to do when we get wherever it is they are leading us? New gardens to prepare, new fields to clear..."

"But all will be fresh and clean."

The younger woman looked at her, a hint of disgust in her face. "All they needed to do was fill in those revolting pits and dig some new ones. It would have saved a lot of work. Now, a whole new wall must be built as well as constructing all the huts."

"Perhaps you did not notice the rot setting into the wood of our shelters. The palisade itself was growing weak from insects."

Mist-On-Moon shrugged. "I don't know who we have to be afraid of anyway. No one attacks us. All are too afraid of us. The Mahicans are too weak," she sneered, "and the Cayuga, Oneida, Seneca, and Onondaga are all our brothers. Oh, well, I must go and take up my pack. There's nothing I can do about it, I suppose." She tugged at the hand of her toddler and pulled him along. The child's bare little buttocks made Singing Wind smile. Nothing was quite so adorable as the clean cheeks of a little baby bottom.

They had been marching for half the day when Gray Wolf came up beside Morning Light and asked how she was bearing up under her burden.

"I will be glad when we stop for the night," she replied honestly and gravely, "but I am not overburdened." Just then he saw a small animal scamper into the brush and thinking of supper, he grunted acknowledgment of her words and went off after it.

Left alone, Morning Light continued to put one foot in front of the other without complaint, her mouth set in resolute obedience. The last time she had walked so far for so long was when... and suddenly in an instant, it all came flooding back to her again as if it had been yesterday. A cold chill gripped her and in the warm sunlight she felt clammy and shuddered. Her heartbeat raced and her stomach churned. The rape. The blast of the gun. Her father's face disappearing before them, wet bits of his flesh and blood hitting her face. She looked quickly around her, momentarily disoriented, but nothing had changed. She knew these people. She had grown to know them over the past three years and for three years she had been safe. Still her stomach had suddenly knotted into a tight ball beneath her ribs and she felt almost sick as her own heartbeat thudded in her ears. Despite a sudden chill, sweat broke out on her forehead and she felt it running down her back and between her breasts. Her breasts, she thought with loathing. If she did not have breasts she would take off her stifling tunic and go bare chested like the braves and feel the breeze upon her skin. She clenched her teeth as her heartbeat settled back to normal and she continued to put one foot in front of the other.

The leaders halted the migration by mid-afternoon when they came to a narrow but deep river at the base of a beautiful small waterfall around which the foliage was already rich and green. Camp must be set up, food prepared, babies and small children tended and put to sleep for the night. Everyone was weary and the spot by the water was the best they would encounter this day. Seemingly out of nowhere, many of the young braves produced freshly killed turkeys, pheasants, rabbits, squirrels, even a deer. Fires were started, roasting pits arranged, spits set up and the smells of roasting meat had everyone's stomachs growling. While some watched the spits, others, in a large mixed group of young people, children, even some of the elders had tossed aside their meager clothing and jumped into the river to bathe away their weariness and the dust of their travels. Laughter, mingled with the sounds of the river falls, could be heard drifting out over the encampment.

Gray Wolf staked out a spot for himself and Morning Light beneath the gently sloping branches of one of the huge evergreen trees. The needles would give them a very soft bed for the night and the huge branches draping to the ground provided a natural enclosure and privacy screen. But when the tall dark brave took a moment to observe Morning Light, he was not pleased with what he saw. She had set down her pack and, then, almost collapsed to the ground. Her hair, pulled in disarray and loose from her braid, was stuck wet to her head. Her thick shapeless tunic was soaked with her sweat. She looked as if she had been caught in a rain but not a drop of moisture had fallen from the sky that day.

"*Eksáa,*" he said sharply, and her head snapped up to look at him in obedience. He called her *girl*, which was more pleasant than *slave*. He had the right to call her anything he wished and he had never asked her what her name was. "Where are the garments I gave you this winter?"

She looked startled, not knowing what to say. Was he angry with her? What had she done? "I..I have them."

"Where? Get them now."

Dutifully she set upon her pack and began digging through it looking for the soft chamois garments he had presented to her as a gift in anticipation of spring.

She had loved the soft feel of the garments and their fresh leathery smell but when she had tried them on she had been horrified to wear them. The top was sleeveless and short with fringing and a deeply cut neckline decorated with quill work to keep it from stretching. It had clung to her breasts and when she raised her arms, the skin above her waistline showed. The skirt was also very short with a deep fringe leaving her legs completely exposed from the tops of her moccasins to her mid-thigh.

She could not wear them. She would have felt naked and exposed. Everyone would have seen her woman's figure. But she had appreciated his gesture. She had not thrown them away which would have been an insult to him. Why did he want her to bring them out now? They were much too fine for anyone to wear on a dirty journey.

At last, she had the garments in her hands. She stood and held them out to him with both hands but he simply turned and commanded her to follow him which she did.

Despite the day's march Gray Wolf walked with brisk energy, climbing up the steep slope to the top of the waterfall. Morning Light followed in obedience but she panted as she did and grimaced in exhaustion. At last, they were at the top and he cut a path upstream to a pooling in the rocks of the river. The sounds of the laughter and voices below them had grown dim, even the sound of the falling water was lessened. He stopped.

"Here," he said gruffly, pointing to the sheltered spot. "You stink. Bathe. And when you finish, you may wash these," he pointed to her shapeless tunic and leggings, "but you wear these."

He had never criticized her person before and when she heard him say that she smelled bad, she felt a flush of humiliation that distracted her from any other fears. For a moment she thought of nothing but scrubbing herself clean and sweetening her skin with herbs. During that moment, he turned and walked away, taking up a watchful vigil farther downhill to guard her in her privacy. Morning Light could do nothing but obey. She searched around and found wild mint and fennel, and then spied soap root growing along the banks. Taking everything to the large rock, she slipped from her smelly leathers and plunged into the river pool.

The water was pleasantly warmed by the sun, just enough to take away the icy chill yet still cool enough to be refreshing. Standing, the waters were only deep enough to come to her mid-thigh, but squatting down she could submerge her whole body and with a little effort she submerged her hair for washing.

Wasting no time, she first scrubbed at her soiled tunic and leggings, knowing they would dry stiff and unwearable until they were reworked with wood ash and fat. Then, she scrubbed herself. The soap root lathered through her long soft black hair and she found herself very glad that Gray Wolf had insisted she bathe. She *had* smelled bad, she thought. And now she felt much better. As the water outside the pool rushed passed her she reached out into the fast flowing stream and drank.

Her thirst was great after so much sweating. Then, ducking beneath the water of the pool for a final rinse, she rose up only to realize she had nothing to dry herself with.

The water coursed over her smooth lightly bronzed skin, running in rivulets to the rock she stood on and streaming at her feet. Morning Light grasped her heavy hair in her hands, twisting and squeezing it while the water from it splashed below. She shook herself then, like a dog will shake its coat when it comes out of the water, and in doing so she shut her eyes. When she opened them, she was startled to see Gray Wolf standing only a few feet from her. He was looking at her but she could read no expression in his face, his black eyes were inscrutable. She froze like a wild animal caught in sudden light, the vein pulsing at her throat her only sign of life. He stretched out his hand holding a length of chamois, and then, as if impatient, he shook it slightly at her. She leaned out from her stance on the rock and took it; he immediately turned his back and walked away.

Shivering, Morning Light dried herself and slipped into her fresh garments. She would need help combing through the snarls of her hair, she thought. She would seek out her mother, she told herself. Carefully drying her feet, she re-laced her moccasins and wrapped her hair in the length of chamois before gingerly picking up the wet leather tunic and leggings. She worked her way back down the steep slope and when she turned around a heavy bush, she found Gray Wolf waiting for her. He immediately began to walk back toward the camp and she followed without a word.

Singing Wind did a double-take when she caught a glimpse of Gray Wolf returning from the river, her daughter following behind him. As she watched, Singing Wind's gaping mouth spread to a broad grin. It was the first time her daughter had worn anything to show her body to its full advantage and she was obviously the most beautiful young woman in the camp. Long lean legs. Small tight buttocks. A slender waist, smoothly formed hips and a flat belly. Just how flat was easy to see in the garments she now wore as she stretched to hang her old garments over the tree limbs. With her arms now empty, one could see the softness of the cloth she wore sculpting to the high upward curve of her full young breasts. Singing Wind was very proud. Her daughter had finally come out of the darkness and showed herself to be a prize beyond all the others.

Morning Light tried not to appear self-conscious for instinctively she knew it would only draw more attention to her. With most of the women bare breasted, she was still modestly covered by comparison. Gray Wolf had been considerate enough to think of that when he had designed these clothes for her. She went to her personal grooming bag and removed a large wooden comb.

"I must comb out my hair before it drys," she said softly, "I will ask my mother's assistance." She was asking his permission to leave but had no doubt he would give it.

"No," he said in response which caused her to look up at him in surprise. "Your mother has her own family to care for. I will comb your hair this night."

Morning Light didn't know what to say but couldn't refuse his offer. Within their enclosure, she simply sat quietly back upon her feet, her back straight, and gave him her comb. He was surprisingly gentle as he took her hair, a small strand at a time, and worked the comb through it.

The smell of the crushed mint she had used to sweeten her hair filled his nostrils as he gradually worked from the bottom to the top. Carefully pulling the comb through the lowest portion of the strand until it combed smoothly, he went farther up its length, and farther still, until the comb could be drawn from scalp to end without snag. Her hair was like the silken tassels of ripe corn in his fingers and he used his hands to dis-entangle and work out the larger snarls without pulling her tender scalp.

As he worked, his fingers often touched the back of her long graceful neck. She grew used to his touch and found it reassuring, almost comforting, as it became familiar. Like a restive horse grows calm under its master's touch, so, too, did she grow calm.

"I should be preparing your supper," she said softly as he continued to comb and stroke.

"Singing Wind prepares the turkey and pheasant I caught, we will eat that. She was also roasting several ducks... there is plenty. The Great Spirit provides well."

Gray Wolf continued combing long languid strokes through her hair, fascinated that as it grew drier it drew up into gentle waves. After a time, Morning Light began to find his attentions disconcerting. His touch was pleasant but it was the touch of a man. Why was he doing this? She remembered how he had looked upon her naked body at the river, and she grew uneasy again.

"Does it not shame you to groom me?" she asked quietly. "It is woman's work. Do you not care what others will say?"

"What a man chooses to do for a..." he hesitated and decided against using the word *woman*, "...another is a matter only for him alone."

The sunlight was now streaking through the trees in a few small shafts as the fiery ball made its way to its nightly resting place. The last bird song was growing quiet. Morning Light felt the need to move away from Gray Wolf's undeniable masculinity. She should help to do something, she thought restlessly, if not prepare food, then watch children or organize their sleeping pallets. She withdrew from him.

"Th..thank you, Gray Wolf, for your kind assistance. I will plait my hair now and go help the others."

"Leave your hair hang free until it dries," he said more softly, his eyes slightly hooded. "You may braid it before you sleep."

She nodded and was instantly glad as she realized the long cloud of hair would help cover her body from view. That had not been Gray Wolf's intent, he thought only of the pleasure he took at looking upon the thick, shiny, soft, dark mass.

That night the air grew chilled and Morning Light snuggled into her sleeping furs beneath the tall pine tree. It took no time for her to fall into an exhausted sleep. Only a few feet away, Gray Wolf was not as fortunate. His memory kept replaying the sight of her, wet and naked, fresh from the river. His fingers still felt each strand of her silken hair. His loins responded to a primal need as ancient as creation, but in his mind he could still see the haunted look of fear in her eyes.

She had lived in his hut for three years and he had thought long before this, time would have healed the wounds to her spirit. She was quiet and obedient, never gave him the slightest cause for upset or rebuke. She worked hard, was quick to learn, was kind of heart and thoughtful. And if she lacked affection, she was totally thoughtless of herself. She never asked for anything, made no demands, never complained, and did not gossip. In fact, his only grievance against her was that she could not forget the brutality she had suffered at the hands of her white captors and it crippled her from being the woman he knew she could be, a woman above all others. The woman who, piece by piece, was stealing his heart but who had never asked him to call her by name.

At last, in the quiet darkness of the camp, sleep came to Gray Wolf and in his dreams he made love to Morning Light.

Before the camp could see the first rays of dawn, the birds of the forest had begun their song anew and the inhabitants began to stir. Morning Light woke before Gray Wolf and she paused for a long moment to gaze at his sleeping form. She had never watched him sleep before, had never seen him asleep by outdoor light, outside the shadows of the hut. As it grew lighter, she continued to watch him, amazed by how young he looked without his attitude of arrogance. The planes of his face were softened with his black lashes just touching the flesh above his high cheek bones on either side of his straight nose. His strong jaw was slack in relaxation, his mouth appearing not quite so thin. She watched in fascination as his steady breathing moved his hard, smooth chest up and down. Up and down. Morning Light was tempted to touch him. He looked like river rock, hard stone, and yet she knew his flesh would have to feel like flesh, not stone. Would he be warm or cool to her touch? Would his skin feel as smooth as it looked or have a tougher texture? Surprised at the direction of her own thoughts, Morning Light turned suddenly and moved out from under the tree. She strode forth to join the other squaws who went down to the river to fetch up water and relieve themselves in the bushes.

At the sound of her fading footfalls, Gray Wolf opened his eyes. He had felt her studying him and had known by the soft sound of her breathing that she was there, the soft female scent that was hers alone confirming her identity. He had willed himself to do nothing to alarm her, nothing to disrupt her attentions and had found himself forced to think of other things to keep his body from wantonly reacting to her and his desire to pull her down beside him.

The entire encampment was on the move before the last mists had disappeared.

Gray Wolf took note of Morning Light as she walked unfettered by the heavy clothing she had worn the day before. She looked more comfortable even while carrying the heavy basket upon her back. She had a long stride with a natural grace and was obviously growing used to her scantier clothing. He grunted to himself in a pleased manner and then looked around to see Tonoaki approaching him.

"I do not understand why you make her cover herself all the time, Gray Wolf. I see nothing to be ashamed of in her looks. She is a pleasing looking bitch, for a slave. Or is it because she has proved barren? Did her disease leave her barren?" he asked boldly. The remarks and questions were personal, crude, and impolite but the younger brave was very bold.

Tonoaki and Gray Wolf had little to say to each other in the daily life of the tribe. Gray Wolf was a year older than Tonoaki and had always bested the other in any competitions when they were growing up. That rankled the younger brave who jealously resented the elder's superior skills. Gray Wolf considered Tonoaki belligerent and ill mannered, and jealousy was not an admirable trait.

"You talk foolishness," Gray Wolf replied disdainfully, attempting to discourage further comment.

"Surely after three years, she should have grown fruit... she must be barren. Or is your spirit too weak," Tonoaki snickered.

Gray Wolf's face had darkened and Tonoaki was pleased.

"There is nothing about her which causes me shame. You assume too much and you have no manners. Perhaps you need someone to teach you some!"

Tonoaki laughed. "You are too touchy, Gray Wolf. You'd think I was talking about your wife. I've not heard that you have taken her as wife, so she is only a slave, and one without a name. No better than a Huron dog. And one that, it would seem, you do not even have an interest in using properly. If you are afraid to mate with her because of the white man's plague, then why do you hide her from the rest of us? Or are you afraid she might prefer one of us?" he laughed and walked off in another direction. Gray Wolf hid his fury beneath a stoic mask.

That day the migration followed the course of the river, a slow meandering downhill hike into a small valley. At first the women perked up, calling back and forth to one another. "Here we are!" "This must be the place!" "Finally, we have arrived!" But this was not the valley the sachem had seen in his dreams. This river was too small and threatened to dry up in the late summer. They all pressed on.

Through the day more than one young buck had taken sudden notice of Morning Light and found reason to walk near the tall young girl as they looked at her boldly in her provocative attire. Being lightly clothed was more enticing than being naked. All around them walked bare breasted young women carrying their loads but they were of no interest. Morning Light wore just enough to cover what they now judged to be well worth looking at. Some of the young warriors ran ahead, only to stand at rest against a boulder or tree and watch her, without appearing to watch her, as she moved by. Some criss-crossed around the perimeters of the migrating line, but always cutting through near her.

And one of these braves was Tonoaki. He had been in the same raiding party that had captured Morning Light and taken the white men. At the time, he had listened to the others speak despairingly of her sickness and he had thought her of little value and certainly of no attraction. Now, he wondered if Gray Wolf had not tricked them into thinking she was worthless. If Tonoaki had known she would recover and grow up as she had, he would have made a claim on her himself. He could have challenged Gray Wolf and perhaps, by lot, he might now own her and she would be his to do with as he pleased. The virile young brave knew exactly what he would do with her and growing resentment took hold as he convinced himself that Gray Wolf had somehow cheated him.

As they marched along, Morning Light became aware of Tonoaki's presence and it made her vaguely uneasy. He was always coming into view and his looks grew longer and more intense. She pretended not to notice but looked straight ahead of her. When her brother happened by she hissed a whisper to him.

"Wani! Walk with me a while!" There was a desperate touch in her voice.

"Morning Light," the soon to be eight year old came to his sister. "Is something wrong?"

"No," she tried to keep the emotion from her voice. "I have not seen much of you, my brother. I wish only for your company."

The boy grinned. "It will not be long and we will be at our new home. I heard the others talking. In our new home there will be much game and I shall go hunting," he said proudly.

"Be careful what you hunt, make sure it isn't bigger than you or you'll have trouble getting it home," she teased lightly.

"I can feel myself growing taller every day," he countered assertively.

She was going to tease again but her gaze fell upon his scarred arm and she stopped herself, growing solemn. "I do think you have grown again," she said sincerely. They walked side by side for some time and she noted with relief that Tonoaki stayed away.

Word spread through the marchers that there was a small marshy lake they had to skirt around and, once on the other side, they would proceed westward and camp on high ground that night. As they passed through the marsh grasses, Morning Light began to gather as much in her arms as she could hold. Subconsciously, she was hiding herself with it. Hiding from the frequent stares of the young bucks. But she told Wani it would make excellent padding that night against the hard ground.

"How do you know the ground will be hard?" he asked her as she harvested the tall grass.

Morning Light did not know and paused for a moment before looking to the higher ground they were walking toward. "Can you not see for yourself, my brother?" she smiled then at him. "We are headed for the rocks. No evergreen forest of soft needles tonight." He was satisfied with her answer and began gathering up grass himself.

The entire migration stopped again about mid-afternoon. Many of the women were grumbling in a low undercurrent of complaint although Gray Wolf noted proudly that Morning Light was not one of them. They had come to a rocky out-cropping that jutted high into the sky and the leaders had decided this was where they would make camp for the night. Two of the braves climbed to the pinnacle of the rocky formation to establish a look-out. From the summit, the entire landscape stretched out before their eyes. They could see far and they saw a lush green river valley beyond. Their new home was only two more day's march away they cried down to the others.

Morning Light approached a natural alcove within the rock wall and dropped her arm load of grass before removing her pack. Taking the pine branch she'd car-ried with her from the forest, she swept at the ground removing all small rocks and sticks. Wani watched her in amusement. Then, she spread out the marsh grass be-fore laying Gray Wolf's sleeping furs on top. She was pleased with the effect.

"Not so strange an idea, was it, Wani?" she smiled. "Do you want yours or do you wish me to put it to use?"

"I will keep it," he grinned back and went off looking for Five Beavers and his mother.

Morning Light looked around her for more long grass or straw for her own bed. Not too far from her she saw a clump of dried grasses standing brown from the year before. She walked over to them, broke them off and moved on to another. Putting them in her arm she spied another patch and went on to do the same. She wandered farther than she had intended.

She had not yet filled her arms when she looked up and gave a start. Tonoaki was standing on a small ridge above her. He made a sound intended to attract a young maiden and let her know his interest. Morning Light was terrified and took off walking back toward the encampment as fast as her long legs could carry her, not wanting to give away her panic by breaking into a run.

The young warrior wanted to see what would happen. She might only be a slave but she was a fine looking female and he no longer believed she was dis-eased. She looked very healthy to him and he would not mind a tumble with her. He pressed the thought and ran up behind her. Most females played hard to get and loved the chase, the young warrior thought to himself as he grabbed playfully at the firm small buttocks beneath her skirt.

Morning Light dropped the grass and like an arrow springing from a bow she took off at full speed, pumping hard to outrun her pursuer. She heard the young brave laugh as his feet were momentarily caught up in the clump of fallen grasses. Then, he also took off running in pursuit.

Gray Wolf looked up from where he was cutting a small sapling to use as a roasting spit. He saw Morning Light flying like the wind toward the rock where their pack was and he knew she was running too fast to be able to stop. Looking then to see why she would run so, he saw Tonoaki running after her. Gray Wolf bristled, hatchet in hand, and took off running himself.

She reached the rocky wall at such a pace she could not keep her body from slamming into it. Her heart was racing, there was no hut to go to, no place to hide. She rebounded off the wall and fell on the pack basket. Digging into it, her hands searching desperately for a weapon. Her fingers fell upon her cooking knife and she pulled it out and brandished it before her. She did not raise it above her head, where it could be easily wretched from her arm. Instead, she gripped it out from her body and held it low and menacing where she could thrust, slice, and jab swiftly at her attacker's belly.

Tonoaki slowed immediately when he saw the knife in her hand and the glare of wild-eyed hatred on her face. He knew better than to corner a wild animal with only his bare hands. And she was just like a wild animal, a wolverine or a badger, her back against the wall, baring her fangs and claws.

He raised his hands in mock surrender and began to back up with a snort of embarrassed laughter just as his competitor arrived.

"What are you doing?" Gray Wolf snapped at the other.

"I meant no harm. I was only teasing. After all," he turned, his gaze raking insolently over Morning Light's body, "she's only a nameless slave."

Having had enough of Tonoaki and his attitude, Gray Wolf dropped the hatchet to lunge at him with his bare hands. Gray Wolf's accelerated body mass took Tonoaki to the ground. They rolled several turns, each trying to get the other at a disadvantage. Gray Wolf outweighed Tonoaki who was the more wiry and slippery. At first Gray Wolf was on top but Tonoaki used leverage and ended up astride the other's chest while producing a knife of his own from his side sheath. With all his weight behind him, he was trying to drive the knife into Gray Wolf while Gray Wolf was using both hands to keep the blade away from his own flesh. In a lightning like movement, Gray Wolf bucked and wrenched to the side, while simultaneously ceasing all resistance to the knife. Caught off-guard, Tonoaki plunged with his blade to the ground where the flint broke beneath the pressure. The broken knife still presented a jagged danger as Gray Wolf sprang up and came down on Tonoaki's back, pushing the younger brave's face into the hard surface barely missing the wicked points of his own broken knife blade. Pulling Tonoaki's head up by his hair, Gray Wolf again slammed it into the ground. The younger warrior was now dazed and had ceased to struggle.

"Enough!" called out one of the elders who had been observing, ensuring that no real harm would come to either young brave. A good clean fight helped to hone skills, a bloody or broken nose never really hurt anyone but they did not have so many warriors that the tribe could afford to have them kill each other off in their private, hot blooded quarrels. Gray Wolf ceased. He stood, one foot on either side of his opponent looking down at his face, twisted to the side and now covered with blood and dirt.

"Let all know, she is to be treated with respect!" he roared, "Or they will answer to *Atakenhrohkwa Okwaho*!" Then, he moved away from Tonoaki with disdain, and the other slunk away quickly.

Those who had stopped and gathered to watch, turned and went back to their own work, giving Gray Wolf and Morning Light a modicum of privacy in their own little niche of the rock.

He turned slowly to her. Her breasts were rising and falling rapidly in agitation. "It is over," he lulled, motioning for her to put away the knife but his eyes lingered a moment too long on her sensuously heaving chest and her eyes went wild again. She turned the knife on herself. Gray Wolf saw the razor sharp tip draw blood as she poised the blade treacherously over her left breast.

"I will cut them off and then no man will want me," she cried hoarsely and would have done herself serious injury if he had not been too quick for her. Grabbing her hand in an unrelenting grip, he swiftly twisted her slender wrist until the sharp blade dropped to the ground. She stood rigid and silent, too proud to cry, but trembling violently. He was shaking as badly as she from the adrenaline pumping through his body.

"No," he croaked gruffly, "you will not! I forbid it!"

She stared at him.

"And from this day forth you shall have a Mohawk name, you are *Ohronkene Hahser*," he said firmly.

Slowly the wildness left her eyes, they calmed as she looked at him. He had given her a Mohawk name but he had let her keep her own. *Ohronkene Hahser...* Morning Light, a person, not just Gray Wolf's slave or girl. She lowered her head before him.

Gray Wolf wanted to take her into the protection of his arms and hold her gently, cradle her until all her fears fled and she grew soft and pliant to his touch. But he did not. To fight for his property was acceptable. But to show emotion to his slave was much less acceptable. And, if he had tried to gather her to him tenderly and she had rejected his touch, it would have cost his dignity much in the eyes of his clansmen who he knew were watching every move, without seeming to watch. Then, he would have had to take her by force to bend her will to his and re-assert his superiority over her. And taking *Ohronkene Hahser* by force was something he would never do.

That night, he insisted she sleep on the softer pallet and she had no choice but to obey. Morning Light curled up in the furs. Her back pressed against the hard wall of rock. She was exhausted and her body radiated a dull ache from its slam against the rock. Finally, she dozed off only to dream.

Her father came to her and was calling her his Morning Light, his little treasure, and she looked away and he was gone. She saw him across a wide meadow of brown grass and she started running to him. Then, she knew someone was chasing her, she could hear them breathing they were so close and her heart was pounding like it would burst. Her legs were like tree stumps, so heavy she could hardly lift them. Big hands grabbed her and the white man fell upon her and when her father tried to save her, his face disappeared in an explosion of blood...

Morning Light was whimpering and moaning. Gray Wolf was not asleep. He had never touched her while she slept, had never crossed over to her side of their hut. There had been many nights when he had heard her whimper in her sleep but tonight was different, she was actually sobbing, violently. Finally, he could stand it no longer and quietly, swiftly he moved to her side.

Gently, like one tames a wild animal, he stroked her hair and cooed tender words of gentleness. It was dark and the encampment slept and there was no one to see him. Softly, he called her name and when she began to whimper again he shook her soundly to break through her dream. She started awake and went rigid with fear when she realized fully his presence, right there, right beside her. But he continued to do nothing more than stroke her head and softly coo a faint humming sound. Minutes went by and he did nothing more. Her need to sleep was warring with her fears and she began to relax. He was comforting. His gentle masculine touch reminded her of her father, soothing, but strong and protective. He was her protection and she was safe from the rest of the world. And as he continued to stroke her gently, she finally drifted back into sleep.

It was almost dawn when Morning Light awoke. It took a moment for her to realize the warmth and comfort she felt was due to Gray Wolf's body being next to hers as they shared the same soft cushion of furs. Then, she remembered. He had come to her in the night and had stopped her horrid dream. He had made her feel safe and had been there when she had yet another terrible dream. He had stayed with her all night, holding her. Giving her something to cling to. New fear hovered over her as she speculated on what changes would now take place between them.

Gray Wolf was a good man, she realized, like her father had been a good man, and he had given her a name, her own name back to her. But if he now tried to force his physical claim on her, she did not think she could survive it. She had to make him understand. She did not want anything to change between them. She did not want his body in hers. But he still had the right to do whatever he wanted to her, even slay her if that would please him. She was, despite having her own name, still his slave.

She moved abruptly to leave the furs but found her body stiff where she had impacted against the rock the day before. Gray Wolf woke and she tried to mask her aches as she moved away. "I must get the fire going," she said flatly, "and fix our morning meal. We will be leaving soon."

Gray Wolf said nothing but he understood all too well.


The encampment seemed to be on the move more quickly than ever. The long line of women, children, and elders, carrying, dragging, and balancing belongings, dutifully followed the sachem and the shaman with his sacred fire. The younger braves continued to keep a sharp lookout for dangers, wild animals, or hostile raiding parties. The entire village had only a few stolen mules to assist in their migration.

Everyone's spirits were high that morning for they knew the journey was almost over. At the bottom of this high rocky valley there were two crests to traverse and the new valley lay beyond. The look-outs had described it repeatedly. All had been assured a view of their new home the next day. Toward noon, the sky clouded and grew threatening. Morning Light saw Gray Wolf coming toward her.

"Get the robes. We will need them," he said. And she fell out of line and put down the pack basket, hunting within it for an unusual seal skin robe Gray Wolf wore in the rain. He had bartered it from a trading party from the far north. Water ran off it like magic, no matter how hard it poured and yet it was exceedingly soft. She found the robe and handed it to him. The air was gusting now and she shivered as she pulled on her old tunic. It was very stiff and uncomfortable but it was a shield against the wind and would serve her in the rain. Then, she quickly put on her leggings as well.

Gray Wolf hated to see her put on the old garments again but didn't stop her as the air grew chilled with the threat of a downpour. She used the robe he had given her to cover and protect the pack basket. When she picked up her pack again he left her to continue his patrol of the travelers and urge the stragglers to catch up with the main body. Suddenly, the skies opened and water came sheeting down in force. The sounds of children's squealing laughter and adult commands to youngsters could be heard all around. Mothers with papooses on their backs threw skin ponchos on over their heads which protected their precious baggage. Everyone but the warriors scrambled for the shelter of the trees until the sachem called out an admonishment. They would never make their destination if they did not continue and ignore the bothersome rain. They were not to hide from a little water. And so the marchers continued and in a few minutes everyone was drenched. Water streamed off their faces and hair as they continued to plod along through the wet grasses and muddy paths.

It rained off and on for the rest of the day and the marchers grew grim in their determination. What had looked easy from the perch atop the rocky outcropping, was taking a great deal more time to traverse. Pushing themselves through the mud, they went farther than any other day and were exhausted by late afternoon. Very small children whimpered for their food and parents tried to keep their tempers in check. Singing Wind felt her years and Mist-On-Moon was in a bad temper, pouting as badly as her toddler.

"We should have stopped when it started to rain. We might have been able to get some decent fires going then. Now, what are we going to do? Everything is soaked. There isn't dry brush or kindling to be found anywhere. They will be fortunate to keep the sacred fires going," she fumed as she worked with the other women to weave fresh green branches into canopies under which they hoped to start a cook fire. The rain soaked branches flicked more water at them, further adding to their discomfort. "What is the sense of walking until you are too tired to go on the next day? What was the sense in walking in the rain? We can all sleep in the wet and the mud and catch fevers and die!"

"Hush, Mist-On-Moon," Singing Wind admonished with a no-nonsense tone in her voice. "No one is pleased with our poor luck but complaining only makes it worse."

Mist-On-Moon was about to snap that it was all well and good for Singing Wind to act so infuriatingly patient but she didn't realize how difficult it was to deal with very small ones during such tribulations. Then, Mist-On-Moon remembered that Singing Wind herself did have a small one. But Morning Light didn't, the young mother's mind leaped onto that recognition. No, Morning Light didn't have anyone but herself to think of and it was all well and good for her to smugly stomp along like one of the men.

Morning Light, in fact, wasn't stomping along smugly at all. The girl was chafing from the wet leathers and felt chilled to the bone but she made no complaint. She wanted a fire more than anything in her life and after putting down her pack, at Gray Wolf's direction, they both began searching everywhere for dry kindling.

Everyone that wasn't assisting in putting together rough shelters was searching for dry kindling. Many quick lean-tos were constructed using the low hanging, long needled pine limbs in plentiful supply around them. But trying to maintain any fire outside of the sacred pots was futile. Acceptance fell over the mass, it was as it was and they could do no more than to bear it. Family groups huddled together to share body warmth. Even energetic young Wani gave in to exhaustion and finally chose to eat his supper cold before falling asleep curled up between his mother and one of his stepbrothers.

Under the corner of a shared lean-to, Morning Light curled into a tight ball against the large basket she had carried all day. She, too, was exhausted but she shivered violently and dozed only fitfully. Waking nervously with every sound of movement, she feared Tonoaki might come up on her in the dark. At last, Gray Wolf came to stretch out on the furs beside her and share his body warmth and his protection. He pulled the rain repellent seal skin over them and she found she was glad for his nearness. Morning Light curled up against him and slept soundly.

# *Chapter 16*

When dawn came, the sun rose into a clear sky. It was a good omen, the rain was gone. Building fires was still useless so there was no delay in continuing the march once more. Babies were nursed but everyone else had to content themselves with cold travel cakes and plain water.

They avoided the meadows which held the moisture and circled around within the forest. Morning Light noticed that the heavy carpet of pine needles and fallen leaves dried rather quickly, at least on the surface. Despite their detour, she was certain they were making better time than if they had slogged through the tough wet grasses. This was a different forest they marched through now. There was no need to cut a pathway. There was very little underbrush as the trees rose so high she could not see their tops. Only small plants along with mosses and lichens could grow in the gloom where sunlight rarely came through the thick canopy over their heads. Only where a massive tree had fallen, split and charred by lightning or rotted in old age, was there an opening to the sky above allowing sunlight to shaft down brightly. And in these infrequent puddles of light, small brush and thickets sprang up, whose dormant seeds and roots had been awaiting the kiss of the sun.

Mid-afternoon, they reached their goal. It was a beautiful valley and everyone was almost giddy with gladness. The ceremonial drums were brought out and the shaman walked about and chanted in a stirringly rich voice, singing to the *manitous* of all living things and asking for the Great Spirit's blessing on their new home. A serious ceremony of song and dance, in which most participated, continued in an effort to placate the evil spirits and ask them to retreat and leave this place for only the tribe. The shaman used more smoke of various colors and chants and finally the new village site was properly cleansed.

In the next days everything was painstakingly marked and roughed out. Where the palisade would be constructed, where each family hut should stand, where the Council Circle was to be placed. The shaman marked where his dwelling would be in accordance with the path of the sun and corrected it by the stars that next night. Several scouted the locations suitable for the latrines, one for men and one for women, on land draining away from the encampment. Trees not used for construction would be girded and over the course of time they would die, be burned, and finally felled with stone axes. Thus, vegetable gardens would be established amongst the blackened stumps. There was more than enough work to keep everyone busy that spring.

Morning Light enjoyed helping Gray Wolf construct their new dwelling. It was going to be larger than the one they had had before and she assisted in holding the bent saplings used to construct the framing as he lashed them together securely with rawhide bindings. It would be a strong shelter. He had used two live growing saplings to anchor the structure to the ground. Bark and skins were used to cover it completely except for a door, a smoke hole and a high window left in the back wall for light and venting.

Something had changed in their relationship. Morning Light could feel it. Despite Gray Wolf's arrogant attitude, she was a little more relaxed around him now and found herself smiling upon occasion only to have him smile back at her. They had slept side by side and he had not pressed himself upon her. She knew she was his slave, but he never threatened her.

She was getting used to wearing the garments he had given her and when he brought new skins to her and instructed her to make new clothes, she made them along similar lines. She had to admit they were more comfortable in the heat of summer. Besides, she knew he could have forced her to go naked if he had so wished. And, that he did not, was something for which she was very grateful. She did not wish to shame him. He was good to her. To comport herself like a crazy woman would have been to his shame. And only a crazy woman, she realized, would wear heavy leathers all through the heat of summer.

He had spoken for her when they would have killed her. He had come to her defense. He had given her her own name back. He had comforted her at night. He protected her. He made no demands upon her body. And her heart was warming to him.


Now that they were settled in their new home, some of Mist-On-Moon's good humor returned. She had to admit the new encampment felt and smelled cleaner and fresher than the old one. She was pleased with their new hut which Quick Panther had constructed directly across the grounds from Gray Wolf's. The palisade was now finished and gardens were going in. It had been a lot of work, but she had avoided much of it, finding excuses in having a small child to tend.

As Mist-On-Moon sat on a mat outside the hut grinding some of the last remaining corn of last year's stores, she looked across the way and saw Gray Wolf working intently over a new weapon. She watched him just as intently, taking in his proud carriage, his corded muscles rippling in response to his movements. He was fashioning a new bow and the wood was thick and strong. She saw the tight muscles of his stomach contract even tighter as he applied the obvious strength it took to bend the bow enough to string the rawhide tautly from end to end. Drawing the string back in a practice gesture, the muscles of his arm thickened into distinctive knots. Eventually, her eyes fell to his narrow hips and the lean muscular thighs of his sturdy legs, naked beneath his small simple breech-cloth. There was little of his flesh that was not observable and she watched him with growing lust.

Mist-On-Moon had been a very young second bride to Bending Branch and he had not been a vigorous lover. She remembered the night of his death with mixed emotions. Secretly, she relived the pleasure of Fleet-of-Foot mounting her like a wild stallion, giving her an intensity of pleasure she'd never known before. Red Elk had lusted for her that night, also, just as the white men had, and that had excited and pleased her. That the evening had ended badly was unfortunate. It was only because of Morning Light, the skinny twig. What had the third one seen in her? She, herself, would have coupled with him willingly. Instead, he had gone to the little twig who had screamed and made a fuss and gotten her own father killed, as well as Bending Branch and Fleet-of-Foot.

During the weeks that had followed, Mist-On-Moon had not been entirely un-happy as the white men's whore. She had quickly learned to find her pleasure by the time her customer did, for she would not get it after. Once they had had their pleasure, they were always finished with her. Well, that was over and done with. Quick Panther was her mate now. He had been eager in the beginning, eager for her and eager to give her pleasure. But, of late, he was much less attentive to her and her eye was beginning to wander.

She watched Gray Wolf closely and felt the heat rise in her body as she imag-ined the energy of his coupling, the size and shape of his *ohnoru*, the feel of it as it drove inside her with the powerful thrusts of which she knew he would be capable. Mist-On-Moon caught herself trembling and realized she was wet with excitement. She quickly glanced about her to assure herself no one was aware of her thoughts. Then, she attacked her corn meal with renewed vigor.

As the weeks went on, Mist-On-Moon made opportunities to flirt with Gray Wolf. She looked at him through her lashes. She thrust out her breasts which she knew were full and pleasing, and swung her hips seductively whenever Quick Pan-ther was not around. But Gray Wolf took no notice. This irritated her greatly. Surely she had not lost all her appeal. She could almost swear the skinny twig was not in his bed. She was diseased and odd in her mind, she went crazy if any man looked at her. Mist-On-Moon, on the other hand, could appreciate those looks. But she wasn't getting any looks these days. And that made her dissatisfied and deter-mined.

It was a warm summer evening and Morning Light was hot and tired and dirty. She longed for a refreshing swim in the river and waited for Gray Wolf to return from the Council Circle to obtain his permission to venture outside the palisade alone.

At last with the sun already setting, he appeared.

"I am so glad you have returned," she said in quick but subdued excitement. "While it is still light, may I go to the river to swim."

"Alone?"

She nodded.

"You cannot go alone," he said and saw the look of disappointment cross her face. She did look hot and weary. Her hair was sticking to her face and sweat stains marked her garments. "Get your things, I will go with you," he said and immedi-ately she brightened.

It was twilight as they reached the river. A soft wind kept the mosquitoes away.

Gray Wolf led Morning Light to the water's edge and then, feeling the need to bathe himself, he walked in, seeming to take no notice of her. She left her clean garments at the water's edge and followed. When the water was deep enough to hide her she shed her chamois clothing and washed it with a soft mixture created from wood ash and fat. It had grown darker and she was bold enough to walk back up toward the shore and toss her garments in the grass. Then, she returned to the depths of the cool liquid that felt so refreshing as it ran over her entire body.

Silently, they swam together for a time. Then, they undid the plaiting of their hair and washed it in the darkness using some of the soft soap.

Mist-On-Moon had slipped out of the palisade. Her baby was asleep and her mate was at the lodge of his friend gambling with several others. She hurried to a small grassy clearing and waited with anticipation in the sultry breeze, her heart thumping in her chest. She heard a rustle.

"Who's there?" she whispered softly.

"Who else would you expect to meet here?" came a sly reply in a deep masculine voice.

Mist-On-Moon turned in expectation and opened her arms for an embrace. Eager lips brushed her skin as rough manly hands groped over her ripe, mature body. Her hands were hot as embers as they grasped his hard, broad back, then went down to his breech-cloth, slipping within. She sighed as her bold stroke brought him instantly alive and turgid.

With a groan of desire, he pushed her down to the soft ground where she poised on all fours, her knees spread open and inviting. She was wearing no breech-cloth and all he had to do was lift her short skirt. He reached around to squeeze her plump breasts, still swollen with mother's milk, then grabbing her hips he thrust into her like a stallion.

The sound of crickets was almost deafening as they grunted and panted and finally they fell upon the cool grass with mutual satisfaction. As they lie there under the dark sky strewn with stars, the sound of splashing and laughter drifted to them.

"Who is it?" she whispered, quickly using her elbows and hands to push herself up.

"Hush..."

They strained to hear. Picking themselves up, they cautiously crept closer to the river. The moon was rising and in the distance they saw two figures playing in the water.

"Who are they?" whispered Mist-On-Moon, a trace of demand in her voice.

"I am not certain." Then, he saw the female turn her face in his direction and by the moon's light he saw, to his surprise, that it was Gray Wolf's slave, *Ohronkene Hahser*. "Quiet, or they will see us," he said, stilling Mist-On-Moon who being shorter could not see over the brush they hid behind. He continued to watch as the tall lithe beauty rose up out of the water, her firm young body sparkling as the moonlight reflected over her wet skin. She dried herself quickly and put on her garments. Then, he saw her companion walk up out of the water. Gray Wolf. He wrung out his breech-cloth, readjusted it, and, then, followed.

"Are they gone?" breathed Mist-On-Moon still unable to see and afraid of being seen.

"Yes," he replied savagely. His anger and envy and lust had made him stiff again and he grabbed Mist-On-Moon, holding her against a tree while he tugged down the flap of his breech-cloth and entered her roughly.

Mist-On-Moon quietly gasped in delight. She wrapped her legs around his narrow hips and caught his rhythm with abandonment, wedging herself between him and the tree trunk. Grabbing a low branch above her she arched and thrust and rode the crest to satisfaction and then grew quiet trying to still her own panting breath. He grunted and let her down.

"I have to go back now," she whispered, pressing close for one last embrace. As she sought to compose herself and smooth her skirt she gave a gasp.

"What is it?" he whispered.

"My back!" Her fingers flew around and then up to the moonlight and then to her nose, she sniffed, to her mouth, she tasted. "It's blood!"

"What blood?"

"My blood. My back was scraped on the tree! Oh, no, how can I explain it?"

"It is not so hard to explain. You fell back against a tree. Your child caused you to stumble back against the wall of your hut. That's it. Easy enough to explain," he said, without further concern.

But when? she thought to herself. Her mate had seen her before he had left and she had not been bruised then. The baby had been sleeping, how could he have caused her to fall against a tree or a wall? No, she would have to think of something better than that if Quick Panther should notice.

Morning Light felt completely refreshed as she walked with Gray Wolf back to their hut. But she also felt something else that she did not fully understand. There was something different in how she felt in his company now, something special about the moments they shared together alone. She was not certain what it meant. She had not always hated men. She had loved her father, she had liked her uncles, there had been many young braves in their old home village that she had looked up to and admired. It was only after that night that she had laid the blame for all the horror, all her hurt, her loss and her pain on all men. But, in truth, it had only been a few men who had caused her pain. Those were the men who had killed her father and uncles, those men had taken her and her mother and Mist-On-Moon and sold them to be used by others. But the white man with the hair of gold had been kind to her. And Gray Wolf had done nothing to her but good.

Inside their hut by the dim light of a fat lamp, she sat while he groomed her long beautiful hair. When he finished, she turned to him and began to comb through his hair. It was coarser than hers, completely straight and only allowed to grow out of the top circle on his head. She was careful not to get tangled in the rings decorating his ears. As he sat still and relaxed, she grew bold enough to ask his permission to ask him a personal question. He grunted his consent.

"Master," she asked softly. "Why have you not taken a woman?" She hoped her question was not offensive.

"I already have a woman," he replied in a steady voice.

"B..but I cannot be a woman to you in e..every way," she stuttered. She continued to comb his hair, trying to maintain an uninterrupted stroke.

"I have no wish for any other woman," he said at last neither confirming nor denying her last statement.

The air hung silent between them.

"I..I think I am glad," she said softly then commenced to plait his hair. When she was finished she withdrew and went to her pallet for the night.

The next day, Morning Light went to see her mother. The woman was bent over a new deerskin stretched taut on the ground. Using a very strong mixture made with the animal's brains, she was scraping away the hair and softening the skin. It was tedious and hard work but the squaw was used to it. Morning Light fell in along side and helped.

"Mother, do you ever think of my father?" she asked quietly at last.

Singing Wind stopped and looked over at her daughter. "Why do you ask?"

"I am trying to understand. You have accepted a new mate. You have a new child by him. How can you go on as you do? Do you wipe all the past from your mind?"

"If a tree falls in the forest killing your mother, do you then hate all trees and stop living? If a dog goes rabid and bites its owner, we kill it. Do we then hate and kill all dogs? The white men we met were very bad, very evil. They did us much harm. They did you the most harm, my daughter, but you should not hate all men because of it. You should not even hate all whites because of it. Was it not a white who mended you?"

Morning Light thought for a long moment and then said almost as a challenge. "It does not seem like you even remember my father."

"My first husband has gone to the spirit world. Would you have me beat my breast and turn away from all men? Would you have me mourn him until I, too, would soon end up in the spirit world? Then, I would not be here right now talking with you. Is that what you would have?"

"No, I would not want that."

"You were wounded. To lose your maidenhead in such a way is a terrible thing. But you have life. You can heal. You can go on. The men who did this to you.. to us... they are dead now. And they suffered much as their punishment. Do not let them continue to make you suffer. You have suffered enough, my daughter."

There was a silence between them as they both scraped at the skin held down by long pointed pieces of bone pressed into the ground.

"I still have bad dreams," Morning Light admitted after a time. Her mother nodded in understanding. "Sometimes I wake up crying out. I live it over and over."

"A woman's lot has never been easy," said the older woman, her face placid. "We are smaller and weaker, but we can endure more suffering. I have a new mate who is good to me. I have a new son. I am content. I would only that my first son and daughter put this from their thoughts and live full lives."

"Thank you, my mother. I will think on your words."

Life in the village settled into a comfortable summer routine. Fishing was good and the fertile earth was producing excellent crops from the small patches under cultivation interrupted by tree stumps. After the initial clearing of the land and felling of the trees, gardening was woman's work. Hours of hoeing and weeding, and carrying water if the rains did not come often enough. The men made excursions out in several directions from their new village once the palisade had been completed. They refused to trade amiably with the white men and raiding parties were an acceptable way to gain goods and take more slaves.

Morning Light noticed Mist-On-Moon's boy was growing quickly and learning to talk. Singing Wind's new baby was beginning to walk. And she caught herself yearning to have a baby of her own. Her mother had said if she had moon times, she could have babies. Morning Light had never told anyone but she did have moon times and one had just ended. But she was diseased, taboo. Or was she? Was it possible that she did not have the white man's disease? She did not feel diseased. She felt well and strong. Her insides had never burned like fire again. Her flesh had healed. Her mother had said she was not diseased. But in order to have a baby, she would have to mate. And that was more than Morning Light could bring herself to even imagine. The thought was so repulsive it made her stomach knot up and churn.

The men gathered around the council fire in the open air. It was too hot for a fire but it gave them light and the smoke kept the insects away. The sachem was there to preside over the discussion.

"The *Lenape* are fools," Tonoaki was saying, "they give their land to the whites for nothing. Without the land, how can they live? Without the land, they will have nothing! They are women, afraid to fight, afraid to stay independent!"

There were many around the fire who agreed with him and indicated so with their grunts and nods of approval for his words. Gray Wolf said nothing but he, too, agreed with Tonoaki on this. The whites were a scourge that needed to be eradicated from the land and yet, they grew more abundant with each passing year.

"There is truth in these words, but there is another truth," said an older warrior sitting next to Quick Panther. "The last raiding party encountered steel knives and iron tomahawks. They were fortunate to return to us alive. Our stone weapons are no match for the white man's iron ones. In order to defend ourselves against the iron, we, too, must have iron. How is it that we should get this iron? How can we, the brave men of our tribe, own steel knives and iron tomahawks like our enemy? There is only one way. We must trade with the white man for these things."

Again there were grunts of understanding and agreement with these words of another view.

"My brother, Many Leaves, speaks well," said Quick Panther, "But perhaps this is the plan of the white man, to arm us both with stronger weapons so that we can kill each other off and leave the way clear for him."

More utterances of frustration and rage were heard.

"Whether this is the white plan or not," said the sachem in the strong unmistakable voice of leadership, "the truth is our enemies have superior weapons now and we must have weapons like these before we find ourselves enslaved."

In their fierce dignity, this small branch of the tribe had maintained an independence and disdain for the encroaching white man with his plagues and greed. They tried to pretend they could ignore him, coming in ever greater numbers into their land. But he killed them with his diseases and he took the spirit from their brothers with his fire water, and he squandered and stole and horded the gifts that the Great Spirit had given unto all of them, the land, the game, the waters. And he armed their enemies with weapons superior to their own.

Somewhere deep within his heart, the sachem knew that the day would come when they must learn to live with the whites or be driven out of existence. And perhaps, this latter would happen even if they did try to live in peace. But that day was not yet come. A trading party would seek the white man, then equally armed they would increase their raids and steal the white man's superior weapons from him and others.

Morning Light sat waiting for Gray Wolf. She wanted to go bathe and purify herself. Earlier that day, Wani had stopped by to see her and ate some of her fresh cornbread and she had missed seeing the women collect up to go to the river. Her brother was growing up. He would soon be nine winters old and he spent most of his time following the older warriors around and practicing his hunting skills. She always enjoyed his company when he thought to stop by Gray Wolf's hut. They shared a bond from that brutal time and they would always be close. He had joked with her as he stuffed his face. Then, he had demonstrated his hunting prowess and growing ability with the bow and, finally, he had left. Alone, she realized she had missed the opportunity to go with the women to the river and so she waited for Gray Wolf's returned so she could ask his permission to leave the village.

Gray Wolf was hot and sweaty from sitting around the council fire and looked very tired when he entered his lodge. Morning Light dutifully served him his food and waited patiently and quietly at his feet with her shins and feet tucked under her as she sat on her knees. As he ate her tender cornbread and stew, she saw his good spirits returning and, at last, she cleared her throat. He looked at her.

"I would ask a favor," she said softly. He grunted and nodded slightly as a sign for her to continue. "My little brother came to see me today and I missed going to the river with the other women. I would wish to go and purify myself with your permission."

That she wanted to go for a swim did not surprise him. He felt like one himself. But it was the phrasing of her words that caused him to pause for just an instant. The words she had used were the words women used to tell their mates that their monthly cycles were over and once purified they were no longer taboo. With only the slightest flicker of his eyes he remained expressionless and nodded his agreement. On seeing it, she rose with a happy smile and gathered her things.

All the way to the river, Gray Wolf wondered if she had really meant what she had said the way she had said it. If so, it was the very first time she had ever admitted to being a fully matured woman. She always wore a breech-cloth and although he suspected she had moon cycles, she never gave any indication of it... until now. But it may have only been an accident of words, she might not have realized what she had implied. His language was not her first tongue. He must have patience.

By the time they reached the river, heavy twilight had fallen. Gray Wolf went into the water first as always, keeping his back to her. Morning Light, secure in her privacy, slipped off her garments leaving them on the bank taking only her own breech-cloth to be washed with the mixture of soft soap. It lathered well and she scrubbed out the remnants of her menstrual blood. When she was finished she tossed the cloth to the shore and swam out to Gray Wolf.

They played in the moonlight as they had before. And after a time, both were ready to seek the shore. The moon had hidden behind a cloud and when it reappeared Morning Light gave a short gasp and reached for Gray Wolf's arm.

"There," she pointed with the other arm in a whisper, "someone is there." He looked in the direction and caught only the briefest glimpse of a human form disappearing into the brush. "Someone was watching us," she murmured in agitation.

They were standing on the river bottom, the water not much above Morning Light's waist and as the moon disappeared again he took her shoulders in his hands in a gesture of protection. "I am here, you have nothing to fear."

"Who would want to watch us?" she asked with a shiver.

"I do not know. Let us go back now."

Silently, they dried themselves and dressed. And when he took her hand to lead her back, she gave it willingly. She did not notice the stone tomahawk he held in readiness in his other hand.


Back within the protection of the palisade, Morning Light's fears melted away but she kept hold of Gray Wolf's hand and followed him to their hut. She hung her wet breech-cloth up to dry before she sought his comb and her own. This time she combed Gray Wolf's hair first and was aware of her own desire to stroke the clean skin of his muscular shoulders and arms. She felt affection for him and it was growing stronger. She no longer saw him as a man grouped with all men whom she feared, but as a unique individual who was not just her master but her protector and friend. She felt safe with him.

Gray Wolf felt the soft touch of Morning Light's fingers on his skin as she carefully combed out his hair. Were these more signs that her demons were retreating? Stoically, he denied the effects her gentle feminine touch was having on him. He thought of her hand in his, small and trusting, as they had walked back to the protection of the palisade.

When it was his turn to comb out her long glorious waterfall of sable black hair, he worked at it diligently with concentration. But he found himself following her silken strands down over her shoulders, her back, her arms and savoring the smooth soft flesh beneath his touch. He thought he felt her tremble as he stroked again following her hair all the way down to the small of her back. Finally, he was finished and there was no more excuse for further contact. He sat still watching her back.

Morning Light had felt the gentleness of Gray Wolf's touch and it had been pleasant and pleasurable. It was several long moments after he had stopped stroking her hair when she realized he had stopped but was not moving. Was it her imagination or could she feel the heat from his body so close but not touching her? Slowly, she turned to face him. In the faint dim light of the fat lamp, she could see his eyes and they looked at her tenderly from a face which was inscrutable but held no aggression, no harshness, no arrogance now.

As if drawn by some invisible cord, her hands rose up steadily and reached out to touch his face, her fingers softly caressing his brow, tracing gently over his eye lids, feeling his eyelashes, his cheek, his lips, tracing along his jaw. There was pleasure in the contact, a hypnotic sensuality that drew her in. He remained still and immobile under her feather light touch. His skin had grown warm as her fingers stroked across his shoulders, traced over the sculpted muscles of his arms and finally found one hand. She picked up his hand with hers, then for a moment she met him palm against palm. With her palm heel even to his, his fingers stretched out above hers by almost a third again her length, dwarfing her hand in comparison.

Gray Wolf watched her in fascination, remaining completely still. When she put her palm to his it was a poignant reminder to him of how fragile she was compared to his own size and strength. He watched her study his hand against hers and then she slowly brought it to her own cheek where he instantly took command of his own movements with slow controlled fluidity. He held her jaw gently and slowly she turned into his hand, drawing her lips across his fingers. The sensuality of this moment made him inhale sharply. His fingers continued to stroke her cheek softly as his thumb drew back and forth over her soft full lips. Her eyes, large and trusting, looked into his and then she lowered her gaze. His touch feathered over her in the same quiet non-threatening manner as she had touched him. Her eyelids were growing heavy and holding his hand to her arm she crumpled slowly to the sleeping pallet drawing him in to lie beside her.

Holding her, he continued to stroke her softly, gently, slowly without hesitation and without intimidation on her arms, her back, her head, her silken hair. He felt her relax completely against him and fall asleep.

He uttered no sound as the air passed through his lips and his heart thudded in his own ears. It was torture to lie beside her, smell the subtle scent that was distinctly hers, feel her warm skin beneath his fingers. He clenched his jaw in the darkness as his body cried out for hers.

The next morning, Gray Wolf awoke feeling the heat of Morning Light's backside tucked up against his groin and what was at first pleasurable turned almost immediately into considerable discomfort. She stirred and he withdrew from her quickly, knowing he must restrain himself and get away. He rose and left the hut in haste.

Gray Wolf threw himself into the most strenuous activities he could find all day. He stayed away from the hut and away from Morning Light. He tried to forget about her and think of other things but his mind kept coming back to images of her and his desire for her was growing unbearable. At the end of the day he went to the sweat-lodge with several others, then took a long swim in the river. Finally, he ended up at Quick Panther's hut gambling with several others, staying up very late. By the time he returned to his own hut, Morning Light was asleep and he fell onto his own pallet, exhausted, yet unable to sleep until it was almost dawn.

Morning Light sat quietly at Gray Wolf's feet attending him as he ate. She had seen little of him for several days. He left early, he never returned until after she had fallen asleep. She missed him and concerned herself that somehow she had offended him. She had gone over and over the last evening they had spent together and could see no reason for any upset. Today, she had taken great pains to fix his favorite dishes and it was a sufficient enticement for him to eat his evening meal with her.

He ate, saying nothing, but she could tell he was pleased. As he finished she dared to speak.

"I have heard talk," she said softly. "I have heard that there is to be another raiding party."

It was barely perceivable that he acknowledged her words.

"I have heard that you are to be a part." She looked up into his eyes. "Is this true?"

He nodded again, more obviously.

"When?" her voice was small.

"We ready our weapons, when all are prepared, we leave."

"I will not know peace until you return."

He found himself tensing slightly. Did she know peace now? It certainly did not seem so. He would have thought she would be glad to see him gone for some time.

"Have I done something to displease you?" her voice remained soft and quiet, her gaze downcast.

"Why do you ask?" he answered with a question of his own.

"I have seen so little of you these past days. I ... I..." she stumbled then, realizing that she was going much too far in assuming he cared at all for her company. Just because she had begun to enjoy his? It was foolish of her. She was only a slave, his hearth-tender. She flushed and was tongue tied and wished to slink away. His hand reached out and with his fingers he lifted her face upward. "I...I am sorry," she stammered, unable to meet his eyes, "I have no right to complain. I take back my words."

"Are you saying that you missed me?" he asked evenly.

"I have no right..."

"Are you saying that you missed me?" he repeated firmly.

"It is not my wish to displease you."

"Then, answer me truthfully," his eyes bore into her.

"It is very lonely without you." He continued to hold her chin, forcing her to look at him. "Yes. I have missed you. I will miss you even more when you join the raiding party. I will be anxious for your safe return. I care."

Gray Wolf put his hands on her shoulders and caused her to rise off her heels to match his level, face to face. Gently pressing his forehead to hers he whispered, "I care as well."

She didn't remember how they got there, but she was aware that they were together on Gray Wolf's pallet. She held him in her arms, his warm strong body, her comfort, her protection. She heard him inhale the scent of her, deeply, before he released his hold upon her to tug at her garments.

"Master, please..." the note of panic in her voice was clear. "Can we not just hold each other? It is such pleasure just to hold you."

He pulled back and stroked her cheek tenderly. "I have no words for the beauty I see when I look at you," he said softly. "The strength of your spirit, the courage of your being." Then, his fingers began moving lightly over her once again. "Let me look upon you."

She was his to do with as he pleased and that he was seeking her permission to look at her, touched her immeasurably. She lifted and allowed him to remove her short tunic. She lay back. Her small breasts stood high, firm, and perfect. He grazed the petal soft nipples with his fingers and she felt them contract into stiff peaks while something very pleasant stirred in her depths.

He looked upon her and she saw a hard edge, a hunger, in his eyes as he drew her close and his tongue went to the barely visible scar on her breast, a memento of the day she had threatened to disfigure herself. He licked it softly and the feel of his tongue upon her flesh pleased her. He moved to take in her nipple, sucking on it strongly and the sensations shooting through her body set her hips to stir. Her legs were locked together as his hand came around her hips and loosened the wrap she wore, tossing it aside. She thought she heard him gasp ever so softly before she felt his lips on her flat firm belly. His mouth was hot upon her skin, his breath, a sultry summer breeze.

In smooth stroking movements, he caressed her body until his hand reached the apex of her legs and slipped beneath her breech-cloth. She willed herself not to recoil but she stiffened. He probed her gently, but her fear sat upon her, blocking all sense of pleasure. Her eyes were tightly closed. He continued to move upon her. She tried to breathe evenly and willed herself not to pull away, not to betray her fear to him. She had no right to stop him. Then suddenly he stopped.

She opened her eyes. Gray Wolf lie beside her, his face contorted as though he was in agony. He was trembling, beads of sweat upon his brow and then she saw his *ohnoru*, fierce, stiff, swollen, almost purple and bursting from his breech-cloth.

"Tell me what to do!" she whispered disparately, wanting to give him release, wanting to help, knowing he had stopped himself from driving into her as the others had. "Tell me what to do," she begged and instinctively her hands flew down to caress him, to hold him, to rub him. It was only moments until Gray Wolf's seed splashed across her belly.

Lying side by side, facing each other she heard him take a deep breath. In curiosity she pulled back just a little to see the expression on his face. It stirred her deeply.

She was his property. He had the right to do anything to her. And yet, he had forced himself not to satisfy his need in her. The entire experience was overwhelming until with sterling clarity she knew she loved him. Did he love her? Surely only love could have exercised the restraint he had shown unless...

"Do you think I am diseased?" she asked quietly.

"No," she heard him say, his lips had barely moved but his hand came up to stroke her cheek.

On a basic level Morning Light understood that spilling himself outside her belly was not going to give her the child she now craved.

"I am ashamed," she said, her eyes downcast.

"Of what?"

"I am ashamed of my fear," she admitted softly and met his eyes again. "It is not worthy of being Mohawk. It is not worthy of you. You are a most worthy warrior and I am an unworthy slave."

"Do you trust me?" he asked just as softly.

"Yes."

"Do you trust me... completely?"

She looked him in the eye and held the gaze. Something inside her told her she could indeed trust him completely. "Yes."

"Then trust, and we will conquer this fear together," he said as he continued to stroke her cheek. He had been to see the widow five years ago and she had told him his patience would someday win him a prize above all others.

He raised up and pressed his forehead to hers. Then, with patience and tenderness, Gray Wolf began to caress her again.

The reactions coursing through Morning Light confused and surprised her. She liked all the sensations and there was an ache growing within her. She was pressing against him until she felt the hardness of him at her belly and she stiffened in fear.

"Not yet," he cooed softly, swinging her up over him and bringing her attention back to his hands and tongue and the pleasure they were giving her. He drew her body down upon him to reach her lips and her graceful neck. His gentle breath in her ear caused a deepening reaction within her.

Morning Light was losing herself in these feelings and found her hands moving over Gray Wolf's broad chest and hard belly beneath her. The desire within her was growing stronger as she moved against him. His hands stroked her backside, caressing her and then, freeing her from her breech-cloth.

He gently lifted her in place over him so she could control their joining. She felt his *ohnoru* patiently awaiting her command. The need within her was growing as he continued to caress her. Need was now consuming her until she knew she wanted him inside her. No sooner had the thought flown through her mind when, as if he'd heard her, he began to press into her very slowly and she received him with painless hunger.

Morning Light shuddered with unbearable pleasure and responded fiercely to take him in deeper. He was buried within her, she marveled, a smile of joy upon her face. Her body answered a primal call to run free and wild, and climb to heights untried. She was bounding like the mountain lion, then soaring like the eagle until at last she could bear no more and cried out in one last convulsive shudder as he rode out his own explosive crest.

# *Chapter 17*

When Morning Light stepped out of the hut the next day her smile was like a second sun beaming out at the world. She embraced her existence with joy and felt true contentment in her life for the first time. Her love for Gray Wolf and the complete oneness she felt with him in their coupling had forever changed her. She would never be the same and her happiness knew no limits.

Mist-On-Moon was outside her lodge in the midst of making corn cakes for her mate and child. She looked across the way and was the first to see Morning Light. Instantly, she knew and the hot jealousy that coursed through the young matron's veins turned her virulent and poisonous.

So, now the little twig smiled! After all these years of drawing attention and sympathy to herself, making herself seem so special and delicate, invoking pity from all because a few men had opened her thighs. Hah! She had succeeded in attracting a virile young brave like Gray Wolf with her antics because she played the victim! Well, now she willingly opened her thighs just like every other female, didn't she? So what made her such a prize?! What made her so special now? *Without all those ploys for sympathy Gray Wolf would have spoken for me,* she told herself savagely. She was only a few years older than he and she would have known how to make him happy in the furs from the very beginning.

Bile and loathing filled Mist-On-Moon with venom against Morning Light. She watched the younger woman, buoyed by an inner lightness, set about her work. Then, Gray Wolf came out of the hut and Mist-On-Moon ducked her head down to her work as he looked quickly around. Thinking no one was watching, she saw him run his hands quickly over Morning Light's body and the other laughed and playfully slapped him away. If Mist-On-Moon had not been certain before, that little scene removed all doubt. The jealous squaw silently screamed in hot blooded fury.


"I wish to make a marriage with *Ohronkene Hahser*," said Gray Wolf respectfully. He had sought a private audience with the sachem to discuss his personal affairs. They sat together cross-legged upon skins in the leader's hut. The sachem drew slowly on his pipe.

"This woman is yours already, she has nothing more to bring you. Why do you wish a marriage ritual?" asked the tribal leader gravely. "You do not even know if this woman can be fruitful."

"This is the woman I want."

"And you have her."

"I wish to give her the gift of her freedom, so she knows she has a choice. It means much to me for her to choose me of her own free will," the young brave spoke gravely in moderate tones.

"Hmmmmm," the sachem replied thinking of his youth and remembering the craziness of young love. "I would speak with you now not as the father of the tribe but as your own father since you have none to council you. It is your right to free your slave. No one can deny this. But are you certain you know her heart?"

"It is because I seek to know her heart that I must do this thing."

The older man grunted and continued to smoke his pipe. "If you would truly know her heart then she must be free in the eyes of all. Free to choose from any other offers which might be made for her." The older man had struck a cord of fear in Gray Wolf. "To go from being your slave to being your wife while never leaving your hearth, will not tell you what you seek to know, my son. She must be free of your hearth to choose you over all others."

This was not what Gray Wolf wanted to hear. He knew that there would be many within the village who would now want her if they learned that she was free. Tonoaki for one, although he had no fear of him gaining *Ohronkene Hahser's* favor. She loathed Tonoaki. But what of the others?

"I will think on this," Gray Wolf said quietly. "Thank you for your council, my chief. I would leave now to ponder your words," he added. The sachem nodded his approving dismissal and Gray Wolf left the hut.

That night Gray Wolf made love to Morning Light with great tenderness and gentle manifestations of his love. He willed her to know how much she meant to him for he had no words to express the deep feelings of his heart. Sated and happy they lie in each other's arms afterward and he knew if he did not speak then he would never again have the courage, so fearful was he of losing her.

"I am going to set you free," he said softly as he stroked her silky cheek.

"I do not understand."

"Free... you understand freedom," he replied almost sharply.

"Yes," she pulled back straining to see his face in the shadows. "I understand freedom. I do not understand what this means to us. You do not want me any more?" she questioned in a very small voice.

"No," he said quickly pulling her to him again. "I want you always and forever. I want you to be my wife."

"Oh, Gray Wolf," she cried out his name rubbing her lips against his lean face repeatedly, nuzzling.

"Wait... I must explain," he said gravely, reaching out to still her caresses before they took his total attention. "Tomorrow before all of the village, I will declare that you are free. You will no longer belong to me. And you will move into the hut of the shaman. In three moons, after the harvest is in, if you still want me over any other, we will make the marriage vows."

"But why must we wait? If this is what you want we will make them now."

"This is what I want more than my life," he replied almost fiercely, bearing his heart, "but the question is what will *Ohronkene Hahser*, the free woman, want three moons from now?"

She rolled over and pulled up then to lean on her elbow, her hair falling luxuriantly around her naked shoulders. "I will want the same thing I want now... to be your mate forever and share your lodge and have your children...and to make love whenever we are together."

"I pray this is so, but you will not know for certain until you have been free for three months. You will have other choices."

"Other choices?"

"Are you unaware that others look at you with desire? When I declare you no longer my property any warrior in the village will have a right to offer for you."

"But I want no other," she said nervously. "Can they promise me to another?" Panic was in her voice.

"Not if that is not your wish. The sachem has spoken. You will be free to make your own choice."

"Then, I still do not understand why we must wait. I know who I want, my heart will not change."

"It must be so," he said and pressed his forehead to hers signaling the end of the discussion.

The next day Gray Wolf went to the sachem with his decision. The village gathered together around the Council Circle in response to the call of the tribal drum. Singing Wind was there with her mate and his first wife and all their children. Morning Light had gone to her mother and told her what was going to happen and Singing Wind had felt great joy for her daughter. Morning Light was not just pleased or content, she was in love! And her lover was setting her free as a token of his love for her. This was indeed an occasion.

The sachem stood in the midst of the Council Circle and spoke.

"I have called you together, my children, so that you may bear witness to very important words. You all know Gray Wolf."

The crowd murmured acknowledgment.

"Three springs ago, Gray Wolf took part in our last raid to the south before we made peace with our brothers, the Lenape. From that raid he took the girl-child, *Ohronkene Hahser*, as his slave."

Another murmur of acknowledgment.

"Gray Wolf will now speak." The sachem stepped back and Gray Wolf stood facing his people. Although the weather was warm, he wore the new tunic and leggings that Morning Light had just finished for him with quill trimming running down the arms and around the neckline and down the outside of the legs. He looked extremely dignified and handsome.

"I took the woman *Ohronkene Hahser* as my slave when she was just a small, frightened and sickly child," he began with great solemnity. "This was the time when there were those who thought she would not live. Now, she has spent more than three cycles of the seasons at my hearth. She has kept it well, done my bidding and never given me cause for complaint or anger. I have never had to raise my voice to her or discipline her. I have never found her wanting in any virtue. She has always worked hard and has never complained. She has grown into a woman and it is my wish to reward her by giving her freedom from this day forth."

There were more than a few murmurs and several gasps of surprise that rippled through the attentive audience. Within the small band of villagers, there was very little to vary their existence from day to day. This was high drama being lived out before their eyes. No one wanted to miss a word.

Gray Wolf was certain he could see the young bucks visibly take greater interest in the young woman off to his side. Trying to quiet the wild beating of his proud heart, he stepped over to her and led her out in front of the crowd.

"*Ohronkene Hahser*," he said commandingly, "let all witness that this day I give you your freedom. And now, I turn the free woman, *Ohronkene Hahser*, over to her new adopted hearth." With these words he brought her in front of the old shaman who nodded his head in acceptance.

"You shall be the daughter of my hearth and live with me until you go to a home of your own," the shaman proclaimed soberly and Morning Light bowed her head in a sign of respect and obedience to the old man. Next, he turned his attention outward to the gathering. "Since *Ohronkene Hahser* is now free and of suitable age, she shall be married in three moons to the husband of her choice. Let any who wish to offer for her know this." And with that, the little ceremony was over and Morning Light followed the shaman to his hut, but not before she looked back longingly at Gray Wolf.

Singing Wind was beaming and yet, her eyes were moist. In a round about way, her beautiful daughter had finally been recognized as a fully grown woman, and thus, of marriageable age. Gray Wolf had just demonstrated to everyone his profound love for her in giving her up in order to give her the freedom to choose him as her husband. It was extremely touching. The Great Spirit was indeed kind and just. Morning Light had suffered much and now, it was fitting that she should have happiness equal to her past suffering. She would have that happiness with a warrior such as Gray Wolf.

The older mated warriors of the tribe were wise enough to realize it was not worth the bad feelings at their hearth to try and court the slender young beauty. She and Gray Wolf undoubtedly had an understanding between them and all an already married brave could hope to reap if he offered for her was rejection from her and rejection for some time in his own hut. The unmated warriors, however, each in proportion to how highly he thought of himself, considered himself a worthy and viable contender for the free maiden's hand. That she had been used by the whites made no difference, that she almost assuredly had been used by Gray Wolf only meant she was well broken in and trained. He had spoken highly of her temperament and virtues, and she was the most exotic looking female in the entire village. Many lusted for her.

"You can not really think you have a chance with her. Do you?" joked Walking Bear as he gave Crooked Arrow a friendly shove on the top of his head. "She towers above you and will not want a man she must look down upon." He laughed at Crooked Arrow's expense. The shorter brave looked appropriately humbled. In fact, he was several inches shorter than Morning Light and only the extreme height of his coxcomb tufted hair put him at equal stature.

"She was always so shy and quiet, I never really took notice of her before," commented a third in their group, a husky brave with a rough, scarred face and broken nose called Moose Horn.

"She has changed," stated Walking Bear.

"She has changed greatly," added Crooked Arrow.

"I do not understand why Gray Wolf is giving her up," said Yellow Rock musingly. As the young woman's first cousin by blood he was considered the same as her brother and so, any intimacy between them would be incestuous and taboo. He was, therefore, the only grown male who had absolutely no interest in mating with her at all. "I think it is obvious he cares for her, and my sister has certainly grown beautiful."

"Yes, she is beautiful and if she is as pleasant and dutiful as he claims... it makes no sense," muttered Moose Horn.

"I think it has something to do with her now being a woman," put in Walking Bear.

"That is crazy. Now, that she is a woman, he should want her more to get strong sons off her," said Moose Horn.

"It is because of her virtues that he is setting her free," said Crooked Arrow. "It is a gift."

"He is stupid," grunted Moose Horn, "now is when I would want to keep her and ..." he made a provocative gesture indicating coupling with a woman.

"Do you think maybe Gray Wolf is... different?" asked Crooked Arrow.

"Different? In what way?" asked Yellow Rock.

"Different..." Crooked Arrow grimaced. "Perhaps, women do not excite him."

This made the two eldest laugh uproariously and Yellow Rock looked puzzled.

"If that is true... you better watch yourself, little man," Moose Horn guffawed at Crooked Arrow.

Yellow Rock remained puzzled for a moment and then began to understand what they were saying and pulled a face. "Not Gray Wolf," he said with a shake of his head in an almost stunned manner.

"I never thought... Gray Wolf?" Walking Bear was now puzzling seriously. "But it would explain why he has taken no interest in any women over these past years. Not since his initiation with the widow."

"He spent much time with her," offered Moose Horn.

"True enough, but who can say how they passed that time," reasoned Walking Bear cynically.

"And now that he has a real woman in his hut, he gets rid of her," Moose Horn snorted. "Maybe she made demands he could not fulfill," he laughed again. "If she is wanting a real man, then, my *ohnoru* is just the answer to her maidenly prayers."

They all laughed.

"Not with your face!" exclaimed Walking Bear. "I have the more pleasing appearance!"

"But I have a bigger *ohnoru*!" retorted Moose Horn boastfully.

"And I doubt that either of you know how to use them for anything more than pissing!" Crooked Arrow got in a final barb before dodging into his family's hut.

Yellow Rock just laughed. He had also *been to see the widow*.

Within this Mohawk clan, by the time a warrior reached his fourteenth winter (and sometimes before), he had *been to see the widow* which was a phrase describing a rite of passage more than a person. It was a ritual privately arranged by his parents in a reciprocal agreement with another village. The woman was usually a widow but one no longer grieving, somewhere between the age of his mother and his grandmother, old enough to command respect for her knowledge but not so old as to be unattractive or lack interest in the lessons to be taught. Sometimes she might even be a younger second wife desiring a child but wed to an older warrior who through age or injury could no longer perform his husbandly duties. With his permission, she could anonymously fulfill the role of the widow. The woman was never a relative and the young warrior was allowed two unrestricted days with her, no more lest an unhealthy bond form fomenting jealousies.

During those two days the young warrior was sexually schooled and practiced in how to please a female. What he took from those lessons, what he kept and what he chose to disregard was up to him. Usually a village had two or three qualifying women and through this rite of passage, the tribe insured that there was no excuse for a female mate to be left unsatisfied. The male may have the last word in the home but the female was the giver of life and if she was left unsatisfied, might not the future generation be in jeopardy?

A warrior was expected to join with a female soon after his sexual awakening and if he found himself without a mate or slave and in need of sexual gratification, widows could be most accommodating. Forcing a woman or *rape*, was an act of violence never seen within the tribe. It was only associated with warfare, a way to terrorize, demoralize, and demonstrate conquest to an enemy. No warrior would ever force a female of his own clan or brother clans. Such an act and such an accusation would stain his reputation for life and leave his sense of honor and self-worth in shreds for it would be viewed as warring against his own people. He would become an outcast.

Tonoaki prided himself on his skills in wooing and his many virtues. He was confident that he was one of the most desirable bachelors in the village. He was strong, had great physical endurance and had never been sick. His hunting skills were excellent, he was far above average with the bow and knife, was an excellent toolmaker, and he could provide well for a family. The tattoos across his chest told of his deeds and accomplishments, and his prowess in pleasing a woman was well tested upon many. He considered himself just as pleasing to look upon as Gray Wolf, his teeth were straight, strong, and white, his eyes sharp sighted, and he was clever. He did regret that he had chased and frightened Morning Light that one time, only because he did not want it to prejudice her mind against him now. He had the advantage of being someone new and exciting while Gray Wolf had undoubtedly become common place and routine after three years of sharing the same hut. Women were just as inconstant as men. He knew this from experience. They might pretend to be more virtuous and loyal but he knew better. He would know how to keep his woman in line, however, and she would learn immediately what to expect if she ever so much as thought of being unfaithful to him. But first, he must woo her and win her away from Gray Wolf, and this he was determined to do.

"You make me sick! You are like all the rest, mooning over that one. What makes her so special? She has hated men for years!" Mist-On-Moon tried to pull away but he caught her by the wrist and pulled her toward him. They had met behind the corn field in the late twilight, shielded from view by the tall ripening stalks. He easily overpowered her, bringing her down to the ground. Her strength was no match for his and although she struggled he knew her heart wasn't really in it. He reached down and grabbed a breast, nipping at it gently and then, taking it deeply into his mouth he suckled on it hard. Mist-On-Moon groaned, her struggle losing all energy. His hand went between her legs and they parted easily allowing him unencumbered access to her. His fingers teased her and he released her breast.

"You are just jealous but there is no need. I will not forget you. I will always want you," he lied in a husky whisper. "But you are another man's wife and I cannot make you my wife. But her, I can take from Gray Wolf. It would be the greatest victory! The ultimate victory over him! That is the only reason..." he was between her legs now, his strong tongue darting over her. He knew this was one of her favorite pleasures and he was going to use it to gain her agreement.

It was only a short time before she was moaning and thrashing and begging him to enter her. But still he continued, overloading her with addictive, pleasurable frustration. She was almost in tears, pleading with him. Then, he pulled back and proudly displayed his fully swollen erection before her.

"Will you help me?" he asked, watching her writhe beneath him, panting in expectation of his entrance. "Swear you will help me!"

She clutched the air trying to reach him, trying to bring him to her, wanting to slide him into her. But he avoided her and continued to taunt her.

"Please," she begged, her eyes smoldering with frantic desire.

"Swear!"

"Yes, yes, all right..." and she gasped then, feeling him glide into her.

They had worked all day in the gardens, weeding and hoeing, and now the women and older girls looked forward to a refreshing swim in the river. The small children were with them and a few braves stood as a watchful guard outside the palisade.

With her son running ahead of her, Mist-On-Moon fell in close to Morning Light.

"I feel like I am covered in dirt," she complained although she had worked only half as many rows as the others.

Morning Light nodded pleasantly. "The water will feel good. Did you ever wonder how weeds can grow so much faster than our vegetables?"

Mist-On-Moon forced a little laugh. "It is true. If our plants grew as quickly, we could have several harvests in one season."

"But then, what would we do with all that food, it would be far more than we needed. I would be content if only the weeds grew not so quickly."

They were at the river now and the small children were splashing and laughing.

The women dropped their skirt wraps. Some wore breech-cloths which often signaled they were in their cycle. Morning Light still wore her abbreviated top and now pulled it off over her head.

The sight of her perfect body, devoid of stretch marks and fatty dimpling made the jealous bile rise in Mist-On-Moon but she fought against it and tried to sound pleasant and friendly.

"So, in three moons you will marry," she observed casually as she lapped the water over her own arms. "Tell me, what do you most admire in a husband?"

Morning Light stroked the water around her and thought seriously. "Tenderness."

"Tenderness?! Tenderness will not save you when the enemy is upon you. Or kill the meat to fill your belly. Do you not admire strength and skill with weapons and... muscles?" she added lasciviously.

"Of course," Morning Light answered, a serious look upon her face. "All these braves are worthy warriors. You and mother and I know well that their fearsome reputation is far reaching. But, if one is fierce and formidable, it is very admirable to be able to express tenderness as well."

Mist-On-Moon paused for a moment seeming to attentively watch her child at play on the river's shallow edge. Tenderness was not something for which she had a great deal of reference. "Well, I certainly think it was kind of Gray Wolf to give you your freedom so you could marry your own choice. I hope you choose wisely, Morning Light. Life can be very difficult if you choose the wrong partner. Men are so fickle. They pay attention to you for a while and then they develop other interests and forget about you." She moved off to pull a cattail and used it to scrub her back. "I think sometimes it is better to mate without your heart. If not given, it cannot be broken."

Morning Light said nothing.

"I saw Gray Wolf with Robin Song this morning. But then after last night I should not have been surprised. She was struggling with her basket and he couldn't rush in quickly enough to help her. Have you ever heard Robin Song sing? Her voice is very sweet and soothing. It is the clearest voice I have ever heard."

"What about last night?" Morning Light couldn't stop the question from popping out of her mouth.

Mist-On-Moon was very pleased the other had leapt to the bate. "Oh, well... nothing except... Well, Robin Song was at my hut showing me the beautifully worked moccasins she had just finished. She stayed for quite a while. Quick Panther was off gambling again and I thought she meant to keep me company but then I noticed how often she looked across the way at Gray Wolf, I might just as well have not been there." Mist-On-Moon feigned an innocent lightheartedness. "When she started to sing, Gray Wolf seemed to find more and more reasons to be outside near us. It really was quite funny... and so obvious," she sighed nonchalantly looking slyly back and feeling very pleased with herself when she saw the frown on

Morning Light's face. "I suppose it is only natural that he would eventually look in the direction of one of his own kind."

Singing Wind was coming toward them with her little son and as she approached, Mist-On-Moon moved off toward her own child.

"Mist-On-Moon, Morning Light, I haven't seen you yet today," she greeted them warmly and then frowned at her daughter. "Are you feeling not well?" she asked cautiously.

"No, my mother, I am well," Morning Light responded but avoided her mother's eyes.

"Something has upset you," Singing Wind pressed.

"No, nothing."

"I thought perhaps it was Gray Wolf's leaving."

"They have left already?" Morning Light blanched.

"Yes," her mother replied, then smiled patiently. "Do not worry, he will be back before you know it."

Morning Light turned and dove into the water swimming several strokes away. Her heart felt as though a fist was squeezing it and her stomach turned inside out. He had not even sought her out to say good-bye. Mist-On-Moon was insensitive and self-centered and often spoke without considering another's feelings but if the truth is not pleasant, it is still better to know it. He had purposely not come to her to say good-bye because he wanted her to look elsewhere perhaps? Because he preferred another?

She felt the hot sting of tears and dove again into the water to wash them away and hide. She would not have her mother and Mist-On-Moon know she wept.

"I also want to wish you congratulations," Singing Wind was saying as Morning Light surfaced again.

"For what?" Mist-On-Moon replied in surprise.

"Oh. I thought... well, perhaps I am mistaken..."

"What are you talking about?" Mist-On-Moon demanded briskly, she was in no mood for guessing games.

"I just assumed when I saw you... are you not expecting another baby?" Singing Wind asked earnestly.

"I..." Mist-On-Moon was startled at the thought and then, recovered. Thinking quickly to herself she realized she had not had a cycle since the spring planting and she supposed Singing Wind was right. To keep from appearing ignorant she replied, "Yes, I think so, I wanted to be certain before saying anything."

"That is what I thought. Congratulations."

"Thank you," she replied a bit flatly and went after her little son not particularly looking forward to carrying another child and then having to watch after it as well.

"Let us wash each other's hair," Singing Wind said to her daughter when Mist-On-Moon left. "Then we will comb it out for each other like we used to. Would you like that?"

Morning Light smiled faintly. She remembered fondly the times she and Gray Wolf had done this together. It bothered her terribly that she had not seen him for several days and now he was gone. Was he really more interested in Robin Song? Morning Light thought of the girl. She was very pretty with huge deep dimples when she smiled and a small dainty body that tended toward soft plumpness. She was like a soft bunny one could almost scoop up in their hand, thought the tall young woman ruefully, suddenly conscious of her own height and long limbs. Gray Wolf most certainly must think Robin Song pretty, any brave would think her pretty. Perhaps, he was having second thoughts about marriage after all. Had he only given Morning Light her freedom just to clear her out of his hut? That was what Mist-On-Moon implied. Perhaps she was right. Did he prefer to have one of his own kind? Someone small and plump with large dimples and a beautiful voice? Now that the words had been said, Morning Light could not get them out of her mind.

The women had gone to the field to pick ripe ears of corn in preparation for a feast. It was late summer and the sachem's daughter had safely delivered twins, two healthy sons, equally perfect and strong. This was a rare and auspicious event which bode very well for the future of the village. Everyone was to join in on the celebration, a neighboring village of the tribe was invited and there would be prayers to the spirits and much feasting and dancing.

Morning Light walked back from the end of the row with her arms full of corn ears. Her sack had been nearly full and now it was brimming over. It was much too full. Even for her strength it was extremely difficult to move and she was struggling with it when Tonoaki approached her.

"*Ohronkene Hahser*, please, let me help you," he greeted her warmly but a bit formally.

She started back in reflex to his voice and quickly glanced around, trying to see if there were others around within view. She could see no one.

"Please do not trouble yourself, I will manage," she said guardedly. It was not customary for men to assist in the harvest and she was suspicious of his intentions.

"No, please," he coaxed gently, "be not afraid. I mean you no harm. I want only to help you. It gives me an opportunity to say something that has weighed on my mind for many months." He picked up the full sack easily and swung it over his back. He did not make a move to leave, however, and stood to speak with her.

The raiding party had just returned and all Gray Wolf could think about was finding Morning Light. He was still upset with Crooked Arrow. The brave had come by Gray Wolf's hut, told him to grab his things, Five Beavers wanted to see him at once. He had not dreamt they meant to leave out on the raid at that moment. No drum beating, no preparation. It had been a total surprise. Five Beavers had been convinced they needed to leave without further delay and Gray Wolf had not even been able to say good-bye to Morning Light. Now, out of habit, he went to his hut first, then remembered she lived with the shaman. He strode quickly to the shaman's hut. The old wise man chuckled at the young man's eagerness and explained about the feast and that the women had gone to gather corn. Gray Wolf crawled up on a small ledge upon the palisade wall to look out over the corn fields. While he meant to give her the freedom to speak and relate to others, he did want the pleasure of seeing her himself as well. He had been gone for half a moon. Did he not have the right to press his own offer for her? He smiled to himself and then, his smile froze and disappeared. He saw her standing with Tonoaki. Of all the braves, he was the last one Gray Wolf would have thought her to tolerate and yet they continued to stand together for some time. Gray Wolf stood spellbound watching but could hear nothing of what they said.

"I wanted you to know," Tonoaki spoke, "I am very ashamed for the way I behaved toward you when we were traveling here." His tone had lost all traces of his former arrogance and Morning Light thought she saw true contrition in his eyes. "I have meant to apologize for a long time but I never could find the opportunity to speak with you alone. It is not easy to admit one is wrong but I regret my behavior. It was foolish and I would like to ask for your forgiveness."

Morning Light was momentarily speechless. For a proud brave to apologize was rare but to apologize to a woman was almost unheard of.

"I... of course, I forgive you."

He seemed to breathe a sigh of relief.

"I did things and said things I am ashamed of and I do not want you to hold them against me. I meant no harm."

"Consider them forgotten," she said quickly and lowered her eyes against the intensity of his gaze. "I reacted too strongly, perhaps."

"Will you press cheeks with me as a sign of forgiveness?"

"That is not necessary."

"Then, you really do not forgive me." His expression turned downcast and mournful. "You do not believe me."

"I do forgive you," she assured him. "I believe you."

"Prove it with the embrace," he coaxed.

She looked around and did not know what to do. She was a free woman and could embrace him if she wanted. And it was, perhaps, the only way they could get on with things.

"No tricks?" she raised her brows at him.

"No tricks."

She stepped to him and placed her cheek against his quickly. He continued to hold the sack over his shoulder. "And now I return the embrace as a sign of friendship," he said softly and leaning over to her, he held his cheek against hers for several long moments. When he retreated she lowered her eyes and flushed. She was very surprised to discover Tonoaki capable of such gentleness and humility.

"I think we should bring the corn in to the roasting pits," she said quietly.

"You are a truly beautiful woman, *Ohronkene Hahser*," his voice had become like velvet as he spoke her name. "While you belonged to Gray Wolf, I could not say the things I have long felt in my heart but now that you are free... I want you to know of my feelings." She shook her head. "Do I not have the same right as any of the others to court you?"

"I..."

"Come, let us bring in the corn. I do not want to frighten you again. I will always regret that. But I want you to promise you will not close me out without a fair chance." He had started walking but continued to look at her. She could only nod.

From the palisade, Gray Wolf had seen it all and his heart wrenched, burned, and raged. He had seen something he was not meant to see but he could not get the image out of his mind. The one he thought he had least to be concerned about was the one she had embraced. So what had been going on in his absence? The dark look on his face warned everyone who saw him to say nothing as he jumped down from the ledge and stormed out into the countryside seeking to vent his jealous anger.

He ran until he could run no farther and then, he dropped to the ground heaving, every breath burning in his lungs, his sides aching. Despite his efforts, he had not been able to run away from the image of *Ohronkene Hahser* rubbing cheeks with Tonoaki. And accepting the same from him. He thought of the times they had made love together and wondered if, in fact, it had meant so little to her. Had she only been doing what she thought he had expected of her because she had been his property? Had it only been more of her unwavering obedience? Gray Wolf would not shed tears. It was not the warrior's way, but his heart was crying. How could he go back to a celebration? He could not. He was not fit company and could not bear the thought of seeing her with... with any of them. Her suitors! Why had he freed her? While she was his, no one could approach her. No one had dared except Tonoaki!

Blood was in Gray Wolf's eye, while murderous thoughts went through his brain. He would challenge Tonoaki. They would fight to the death. If he lost, his suffering would be over. If he won, Tonoaki would be out of their lives forever. But he would forever have to live with the thought that she might have picked Tonoaki, she might have preferred him. Gray Wolf beat his hands into the ground, unmindful of scraping and tearing his knuckles on the small rocks and sticks.

At the celebration that evening, Morning Light looked for Gray Wolf among the crowd of visitors but did not see him anywhere. She had heard the raiding party had returned. She had hoped that he would seek her out. As the evening wore on she realized she did not see Robin Song either. Her suspicions grew. She tried not to think of the two of them together but seeds had been planted and the weeds were impossible to be rid of now. And whether he was with Robin Song or not, it was a certainty that he had not bothered to come and see her upon his return, just as he had not bothered to say farewell to her when he had left.

Morning Light was looking very withdrawn when Tonoaki came along and pulled her to her feet. He brought her out into the circle to join with the other dancers. It was a well-known dance in celebration of life which then led into the traditional corn dance. Morning Light went through the motions and kept perfect step, but her mind was elsewhere and her heart was not in it. She never stopped scanning the gathering, searching for Gray Wolf, hoping she was wrong, unable to stop herself from seeking some glimpse of him.

Before she realized what was happening, Morning Light found herself in the midst of a traditional courting dance along with a number of other very young women of their village and the visiting village who had just reached marriageable age. The females were together in the center of the circle. Tonoaki had been joined by Walking Bear, Moose Horn, Yellow Rock, even Crooked Arrow as well as many of the more prominent young braves of the visiting village as they danced around the females in a circle. The purpose of the dance was to give the male an opportunity to strut before the females, displaying his body, his strength, his prowess and agility, and in a rather suggestive manner, his implied sexual potency. If any was receptive, she, in turn, responded with a demonstration of her own of grace and interest in a manner that was left very much up to her own ingenuity.

The drums continued to beat a solid driving pagan rhythm conjuring primal emotions of lust. Morning Light was growing more and more uncomfortable as each young man went to strenuous lengths to attract her yet she didn't know how to escape, how to leave without causing insult. If only Gray Wolf were here, she would follow his lead and do whatever he led her to do and she would know that it was right.

Her eyes went out to the crowd of watchers. She saw her mother smiling pleasantly as if all was perfectly naturally. One of the maidens had stepped forth in response to Tonoaki's raw sensual display. Thrusting her body to within a scant finger's width of distance from his sleek and sweat covered one, she moved slowly in a carnally driven response, ungulate her hips so close to his there was no mistaking her invitation. But Tonoaki was looking at Morning Light. The heat of his look, even from a distance, was enough to make her flush out and grow uncomfortably warm. She must do something in response, all the young women were starting to move off of dead center in response to the warriors dancing around them. She was left as the only figure in the center and she felt the pressure to move, to show response in some fashion.

Then, inspiration came to her and she began a steady movement lacing her steps between and around each one of the warriors in turn without hesitating with any one of them in particular. In this fashion she made her way all the way around the circle and when she'd done one complete turn, she left quickly to seek the hut of the shaman without looking back.

With his hunter's instinct in play, Gray Wolf had found a defensible position in the midst of the thick forest. He chose to have no fire. It was a warm evening and he preferred the darkness, the stillness and to stay away from the celebration. He had nothing to celebrate. The moon had risen and was sailing across the starry sky. It was a full moon. Only two more moons were left and she would be married. But to whom would she be married?

Gray Wolf shuddered violently. With sad realization, he felt a terrible loneliness. He was again alone. He had not felt this lonely for...? He thought. Not since she had come to his hut. She had become the reason he hunted, the reason he sought the most beautiful skins. She was his reason to return to his lodge. She was his reason for existing. Without her, there was nothing but emptiness and he knew he would continue to love her forever whether she loved him or not.

But could he live with this loneliness? It was worse than anything he had ever known before she had come into his life. He remembered when he had first seen her, frightened, perhaps terrified, and exhausted but making no complaint. Dirty, footsore and in a fever but stubbornly ready to drop in her tracks without a word. He had admired her then, felt something then. He sensed she, too, felt a terrible loneliness, even with her own people and she and he were kindred souls.

He had admired her fierceness in dealing with her enemy, facing them with a warrior's heart, taking her just vengeance without female squeamishness. And when they had talked of killing her in fear that she carried the white man's disease, he had been alarmed. He knew how feared the white man's plagues were and was terrified that they might truly kill her. And when he spoke for her, he also had been apprehensive that Tonoaki, who was ever at his elbow trying to challenge him in every way, would demand a right to have her as well. But Tonoaki had not challenged him, no one had cared and she became his without contest. He had prayed through those next days that the Great *Manitou* would heal her and the prayers had been answered. His heart had been delighted when he had found her in his hut.

He remembered his joy at spending time with her, teaching her to speak their tongue. He savored the hours, the attention. The fleeting looks of delight upon her face when he rewarded her with approval in her lessons. And so she had woven her way into the fiber of his life and the fabric of his heart.

It had been a long process, gaining her trust. He could have killed Tonoaki for almost pushing her to the point of self-mutilation. He had been so afraid when she had turned the knife upon herself. But he had kept her trust and finally he had been rewarded. She had finally opened herself to him as a woman and his love for her was now beyond measure.

But had he only been a teacher? Just as he had introduced her to their language, had he only been the teacher who had introduced her to the pleasures of coupling? It was something he knew many could indulge in vigorously without deep sentiments. He had felt the emptiness of loneliness for too long before her. And now he felt it again.

Morning Light was crying as quietly as she could although the noise of the drums and revelers effectively drown out her sobs even to herself. The drink of fermented fruit had loosen inhibitions and the courting dance had given way to a mating dance which had dissolved into a frenzy with unmarried couples of all ages seeking scant cover in the shadows of the night. The widows were happy to accommodate the young bucks. Only the very young maidens were off limits, being assiduously watched by their families.

She felt safe in the hut of the shaman, for no one, no matter how bold, would dare to violate his hut by entering without his permission. She trembled at the strength behind Tonoaki's blatant gazes and raw sexuality. She did not understand why on some level her body had felt something in response. It terrified her. At the same time ugly visions of Gray Wolf making love to Robin Song somewhere out there burned in Morning Light's brain and she felt powerless to do anything about it. Why had he stayed so faithfully at her side all these years? He had never had another woman while he owned her, she was sure of that. Why now? Why had he waited until she had become so completely trusting in his love? Until she had fallen so irretrievably in love with him she could not bare to live without him? Until she wanted him and only him and was sickened at the thought of his having another? Was this just more of how men tortured women?

Mist-On-Moon had said men were fickle. They grew tired of what they had and wanted something new. So, no matter who she chose, she could only expect that after a time, he, too, would drift on to someone new. So, what was the point in getting married? She would never marry, she would be independent... no, she thought with sudden realization. The sachem had said she MUST marry. Only two months left and she must pick a husband to provide for her. Maybe it was better to pick one she did not love so that when he grew tired of her, she would not care. With such thoughts, despite the din outside, Morning Light sobbed herself to sleep.

Tonoaki had a need that would be satisfied. The dance had worked him into a fine state and he had never lusted so openly for anyone as he did for Morning Light. He willed her to come to him, his brain burning the path before her and for just a moment he thought he had won. Then, she slipped by and sought shelter in the shaman's hut. He would have pursued her anywhere else, even into a den of mountain lions so great was his need to have her but not there. Bad medicine would follow him the rest of his life even into the afterlife if he violated the shaman's hut to pursue a woman.

The mating dance brought a handsome widow before him. She was still firm although the bloom of youth had faded. She was of the visitors. Her mate had died a little over a year ago in a moose hunt when he had slipped from a precipice and fallen, breaking his neck. Now, she danced seductively before him, aware of the fine erection beneath his breech-cloth. It only took one graze against his *ohnoru* by her wide undulating hip and he took her hand and pulled her off into the shadows.

Singing Wind was not unaffected by the rhythm and the frenzy. She was pleased when Five Beavers' first wife suggested the three should celebrate together that night, sharing pleasures, which they did while the children all slept.

Mist-On-Moon was seething with the display of lust Tonoaki had exhibited for Morning Light. If she could have she would have clawed the girl's eyes out but instead she had to sit in Quick Panther's presence and pretend to be enjoying herself. Then, she saw Tonoaki pull the youngish widow off into the dark beyond the light ring of the fire. Torches burnt here and there and she saw them duck beside a far hut. There was no need for them to go far. There was nothing taboo about what they were going to do and no one but she to care. The visitor was a widow who had needs but no mate. Tonoaki was a free single male who could couple as he wished with any free woman. They could rut all night to their hearts content and no one would think twice about it.

Mist-On-Moon turned her attention suddenly to Quick Panther.

"Will you dance with me, my husband?" she asked seductively.

"It is unfitting for a married woman to do the mating dance," he almost growled in response. "Do you wish to flaunt yourself in front of all?"

"No, of course not. Only in front of you," she smiled. "It has been a while and I grow hungry. Do I not please you anymore?" she purred.

In response his hand dove under her skirt and she squealed and squirmed. He felt the wet running down her inner thighs and it triggered his own response. He glanced around. They were sitting at the edge of the shadows and everyone was occupied in their own pursuits of pleasure, drinking, gambling, coupling. This was a celebration of life and fertility, after all. The *manitou* of fertility appreciated healthy lust. Quick Panther undid his breech-cloth exposing his *ohnoru* and set his wife upon him where she worked to satisfy them both.

# *Chapter 18*

Gray Wolf watched the sky turn from a pewter gray to a light robin's breast orange and finally to blue. He had not slept all night. He thought briefly of going off and hunting for a few days but quickly realized he had not brought any weapons except for the sturdy knife at his side. He dreaded the thought of returning to the village. He could only imagine what might have happened during the long night of celebration. Then, as his stomach rumbled in protest of having had no food for almost twenty-four hours, he told himself he was being foolish and womanish in his wild imaginings. He was a warrior not a squaw, and he would win his prize. Gray Wolf got up and began his long walk back to the village.

There were few regrets as the camp stirred awake late that morning. Only those who had drunk too much fermented juice or lost too much in gambling were sorry for anything they had done. Most everyone else recalled the night as a rather pleasant evening. And some, like the visiting widow, would remember it as very memorable.

Yellow Rock would remember it always as the night he made his first conquest since seeing the widow. She was a squaw old enough to be his mother although she surely did not seem so at the time.

Crooked Arrow, smarting under the ridicule of Walking Bear and despondent of ever being able to attract a maiden, had danced with a little sprite he found very attractive but more surprising to him, *she* had seemed to find him attractive. He had spent the rest of the evening with her under her mother's watchful eye.

Morning Light awoke with swollen eyes and a headache. As she stirred, the shaman spoke. "Are you well, my daughter?" The old man had seen much in his life. The evening's revelries were bound to bring a full spectrum of human reactions. Good and bad were always dependent upon how one viewed things. "You disappeared very early in the evening."

"I came here to sleep."

"Sleep?" he replied with a hint of astonishment. "Last night would not have been a night to sleep when I was in my youth."

Morning Light sat up and he watched her hand go to her head.

"What is it?"

"My head... it aches."

He grinned. "You drank."

"No, Father, I did not. I had much to think about and came here to be alone."

He observed her face then, and realized her eyes were unnaturally puffy. "You have been weeping. Why?"

"My thoughts were not happy."

"Hmmm," was his only response. He was not one to waste words on the obvious. This young maiden knew she had many to choose from. Choice was often a difficult burden. Perhaps she would share the reasons for her unhappiness in her own time.

"Excuse me, Father, I have a need to go out," she said and went off to the latrine. No sooner had she reached the women's latrine when Robin Song approached for the same purpose.

The girl was glowing and in such high spirits she was unaware of anything else.

"Was it not a wonderful night? I am too happy to think of anything else. Surely, today is not a day for work," Robin Song laughed, "I won't be able to concentrate on anything. I am glad the celebration with our visitors continues. I will share a secret with you," she continued to babble, "last night I truly became a woman," she giggled, "and it was wonderful! Perhaps I shall also marry when you do, oh, don't repeat that," she gasped, slapping her hand across her mouth and giggling. "I... he... well, he hasn't actually asked me to join with him. But I am hoping... especially after last night. My legs feel bowed with contentment!" she giggled again and was gone as quickly as she had arrived, leaving Morning Light in a wake of confusion.

Had Gray Wolf been with her all night? She had not seen either of them. Robin Song had obviously been with someone and there was no mistaking her words. They had coupled. And she was expecting to mate with him. Tears sprang to Morning Light's eyes and she brushed them away with anger. She was finished with tears. Robin Song would be the one crying next when she discovered he was no longer interested in her either.

Mist-On-Moon had just settled her baby with a corn cake when she saw Gray Wolf walking back toward his hut. She had not seen him all night. Where could he have gone and why would he have missed the celebration leaving Tonoaki such a broad field with The Twig? Just then, she caught a glimpse of Tonoaki and to spite him she walked over to Gray Wolf, flirting with him coyly.

"Gray Wolf, we missed you at the celebration. Everyone had a wonderful time. You should have seen *Ohronkene Hahser* dancing, Tonoaki had her on her feet in no time and... ohhh, the courting dance," she fanned her face. "Very exciting."

It was not what he wanted to hear and he stopped for a moment to scowl at her.

"But the mating dance was even better," she laughed, knowing she was implying that Morning Light had danced this provocative dance with someone, perhaps Tonoaki. "You should have been there, Gray Wolf. I wish I could have danced with you," she murmured now in an invitation and boldly she ran her hand along the outside of his thigh. "Perhaps tonight? Our visitors stay and the celebration continues."

With one strong hand he stopped her advance and pulled her hand from his flesh. "Mist-On-Moon, you have a husband who awaits you."

It took a moment for the salacious smile to leave her lips and for her to realize the meaning of his words. She turned, and seeing Quick Panther standing at the door of their hut, she uttered a tiny gasp of surprise. Then, composing herself she walked back to her own home.

Quick Panther had decided to spy upon his wife. He had suspected her for a long time. There had been so many little things, like the scrape upon her back suddenly appearing in the night; the way she really did not pursue his attentions anymore; the times he had awakened to find her creeping back into their hut. None would have been enough to create suspicion but all together...? He would have to be stupid to not realize she was cheating on him. Last night it had been obvious that she had been lusting for Tonoaki and when he had run off with the widow, Mist-On-Moon, wet and ready, had turned to her husband as a substitute. And now she was brazen enough to put her hand on another man's thigh in broad daylight, right in front of him and their child. At least, he had always assumed it was his child but this next one? He didn't think so. He had spent some time thinking and she had been careless with this one. Nine months from the time she said the baby was due he had been on a hunting trip. And he remembered he had not touched her for weeks before, conserving his essence for the hunt, nor for a full moon after in sacrificial thanks. The child growing in her belly was not his but in order to give her the punishment she deserved he would have to have proof. He resolved to catch her in the act.

Gray Wolf entered his hut. It felt lonely and stifling. He was suffocating, he couldn't breathe. He left again and went down to the river for a swim. The image of Morning Light dancing with Tonoaki was almost more than he could bear. The dances of celebration were one thing, but the courting dance? And, the mating dance? He dove into the water and swam and swam. Far beneath the surface he pulled himself along in strong strokes against the current, until he felt his body screaming for air, his lungs threatening to burst, and he continued to deny himself the surface. Then, in one swift powerful stroke he vaulted into the air and gasped his lungs full again. He still wanted to live.

Upon returning to his hut, he gathered his hunting gear, wrapped a suit of warmer clothing around his quiver filled with arrows and took off telling the sachem he was going hunting for a few weeks. The sachem grinned, certain it was bridegroom's nerves.

The depression that fell over Morning Light was like a heavy boulder that weighed her down and let her see nothing but sorrow. She had set aside the shell she had built around herself and trusted a man. She had opened her heart and now the pain she suffered was more than any physical pain she'd ever felt. When the physical pain became too much, she passed out. When the pain of her heart became too much there was no such respite, nothing to keep her from knowing the hours and days passing by without him. He did not come to see her. He was rid of her. She should have died long ago. It would have been better. To slip into a black slumber and never awake. This is what she now yearned for.

Singing Wind audibly gasped when she saw her daughter by chance coming back from the latrine early one morning. Morning Light did not look well, in fact she looked like she was starving. Her face was thin, the skin stretching over her fine bone structure. Her body was gaunt, the bones protruding from her shoulders while her arms looked like they could be snapped in two. She had been avoiding everyone, even her own mother, and hiding within the hut of the shaman ever since the first night of the celebration. That had been many weeks ago, Singing Wind thought as tears gathered in her eyes. Little Smoke, her mate's first wife, saw her tears.

"What is wrong?" she asked immediately for Singing Wind had never been a tearful person. Morning Light had slipped back into the shaman's hut and when

Little Smoke looked in the direction of Singing Wind's stare, she saw nothing unusual.

"Have you seen my daughter?" Singing Wind asked aghast.

"Not for some time, now that I think about it. What has happened? She should be getting married soon, in only a month, right?"

"She may not live that long."

"What?"

"I must go see the shaman. Please, ask Five Beavers to obtain permission for me to visit the shaman. I must find out what is wrong."

Little Smoke knew Singing Wind to be a stable woman not given to hysterics. Something was indeed upsetting her but surely she was exaggerating.

Singing Wind's visit was granted.

When she approached the shaman's hut she waited outside the door and he came out to meet her.

"Wise One," she bowed low before him.

"Sit," he gestured to the furs on the ground beside the door.

"Please let me see my daughter."

"Sit," he said again firmly.

Singing Wind sat down impatiently. The shaman took a seat near her, his old limbs amazingly agile as he sat cross-legged upon the ground. "Now, what is it that concerns you, my daughter?" he spoke softly in a thin reedy voice, nothing like the voice in which he sang.

Singing Wind looked at him as though he were crazy. Was it not obvious to anyone but her?

"Morning Light..."

"Who?"

"*Ohronkene Hahser,*" she said in quick impatience, "I have not talked to her in many, many days, more than a moon."

"She does not wish to speak to any right now."

"What has happened to her?"

"Nothing has happened to her."

"But... she looks like she is starving!" Singing Wind finally gave voice to her concern. "Does she not eat? Is she sick? She is so thin."

"She has been fasting. She seeks a vision."

"A vision?!!" Singing Wind tried not to shout. "But one does not need to starve to seek a vision."

"But this one has become the daughter of my hearth."

"Forgive me, Wise One, I am only adopted myself and do not mean to offend. All I know is my mother's heart. She is my flesh and blood, I remember the day I birthed her, the pain that gave way to rejoicing. I have been very proud of her and now I see her wasting away, I do not understand. Please help me understand. Help me to help my daughter."

The old shaman sat quietly for many moments allowing the tears falling from Singing Wind's cheeks time to stop.

"She drinks a broth I have prepared. She will not starve. But your daughter must find her own answers from the Great Spirit. In less than a month, she is to be wed. You cannot help her. She must make her own choices."

"But if only she would talk to me, tell me what is troubling her heart. She loves Gray Wolf. He loves her. What is so hard to decide?"

"Each has his own eyes and must see for himself," the old man answered cryptically and then rose to signal the end of the meeting. "Your daughter knows of your concern. She will speak with you in time."

"Please, promise me you will not let her starve to death?"

He nodded. He had thought Gray Wolfe loved the girl as well, but where was the young brave? He was nowhere to be found and certainly he had shown no attention to the girl since giving her over to another's hearth.

§

Gray Wolf had been gone several weeks for he had had much to think about. He had stayed to himself, avoided crossing paths with others and in his solitude things had become more clear. Except for that embrace which had by no means been passionate, he had seen *Ohronkene Hahser* do nothing to cause him pain. Mist-On-Moon was a trouble-maker, one he had long suspected of being jealous of *Ohronkene Hahser* and he had been a fool to let the woman fire his imagination. That he had not been at the celebration to observe and participate for himself was his own fault. In fact, he should have been there. How he would have liked to have done the courting dance with his love. They had spent three years together and professed their love for each other and how easily he had become a fool. He had no right to accuse her without evidence or hearing. And might not have she, herself, misinterpreted his absence?

Soon after coming to this conclusion, he had spotted the white deer. It was like a sign from the Great Spirit that all would be well. There were legends and stories about a pure white deer but no one he knew had ever seen one in their lifetime, nor did they have parents or even grandparents who had seen one. He had only one thought, its rare and precious hide would be his wedding gift to his bride. He had tracked the white deer farther and farther into the forest. Then rains had washed all tracks away and he had floundered in frustration and prayed to the Great Spirit. The very next day he caught sight of it again and continued in pursuit. It had been a night of singular celebration when he had finally dropped it with his arrow. A shot guided by the Great *Manitou's* hand, directly into the eye, killing instantly without harming the fine skin.

For many days he had worked on the skin and eaten of the meat. Stretching the leather, working it, scraping off the hair and rendering it, finally, as soft as a baby's tender flesh. And he had rejoiced. He would return to her with his rare gift, and he would fight for her if it was necessary, but they were meant to be as one for all time.

Time! Time had escaped him. The moon told Gray Wolf that he had been gone more than a month. He hurried his pace on the long walk home. Finally, knowing he was close he broke into a trot. He would be there tomorrow.

Wani was the first one to see Gray Wolf and he ran as he gravely approached the warrior. Gray Wolf had carefully concealed his gift beneath other skins he had collected.

"You have been gone long," Wani said, his eight year old face looking old for his years, his voice accusing.

"I have been hunting," Gray Wolf smiled. "It has been good hunting!" When Wani said nothing the smile faded from Gray Wolf's face. "Why are you so grave? What has happened in my absence? Your sister! Has something happened?"

Wani's face could not hide the despair he felt.

"Is she well?!" Gray Wolf frowned.

"My mother does not think so."

"What?!!"

"No one has seen her for over a month."

"Where is she?" Gray Wolf demanded in sudden panic.

"She stays with the shaman day and night and sees no one, not even me," he added with a sad forlorn note. Gray Wolf hurried to Singing Wind's hut. Wani slipped inside as Gray Wolf called.

"Singing Wind. It is Gray Wolf. I would speak with you."

In only a moment, the squaw came out looking thinner, older, and worried. "Gray Wolf! I thank the *manitous* you are back! Why have you been gone so long?"

"What is Wani telling me? *Ohronkene Hahser* is ill?"

"The shaman says she is fasting. I caught a glimpse of her and she looks starved to near death. He says she is on a vision quest. A vision quest? For this she has not eaten in over a month? I do not understand, Gray Wolf, she will speak to no one, she sees no one. You must talk some sense into her."

"I will leave my things here and go to the shaman," he said and took off without seeing her nod of agreement.

With great discipline, Gray Wolf stopped at the door of the shaman's hut and called. "*Ohronkene Hahser*, it is Gray Wolf, I have returned and wish to speak with you." He heard nothing at first, then a rustle and shuffle and at last the shaman poked his head out.

"Humpf," he grunted and stepped out, closing the flap behind him.

"Where is she?" the young man demanded with impatience. "I want to see her, old man, do not try to stop me."

"Calm down," the shaman said with great authority. "You do no one good by losing your head."

"I will calm down when I know she is well."

"She is NOT well, Gray Wolf, and I must prepare you for that. Each day she sinks deeper into the darkness. The first night of the celebration she left early and fled to my hut. She has not eaten solid food since. I have been able to sustain her only by adding herbs to the broth I make her drink. And she drinks that only because I have convinced her it will enable her to have a vision. A vision which will give her the wisdom she seeks. Gray Wolf... what happened between you?"

"Between us?!!" he replied in shock. "Nothing!"

"You have long been absent."

"I was hunting." The shaman continued to look at him, almost an accusation on his face. "I went hunting," he repeated.

"She has only known your absence. It had the appearance of a change of heart. If you no longer want her, you should tell her so directly."

"I... I must see her."

The old man nodded and Gray Wolf went in. A small fire burned in the center of the hut giving it a comfortable warmth. Several fat lamps gave additional light along with the light coming in from the smoke hole and a pair of small vent holes. It took a moment for his eyes to adjust to the dimness but he saw the pallet off to the side with a figure on it buried in furs.

"Why?" he cried out softly and fell down on his knees beside her. "Why?"

She opened her eyes slowly and looked at him, her eyes seemed to burn brightly from deep within her head. It pained her to see him for she loved him so, then she thought of Robin Song and closed her eyes again shivering with cold.

"No!" he shouted. "I will not let you shut me out. *Kunoruhkwa!* I love you! If you die, I will die with you and we will be buried together in each other's arms. I will not let you go. I will not."

She opened her eyes again and as she looked she saw the tears falling down his cheeks. "Gray Wolf..." she whispered and her thin arms tried to reach out for him but fell back with no strength. He bent to her, forehead to forehead. He caressed her cheek on cheek. She tasted the salt of his tears as they coursed over his cheeks and near her mouth. Gray Wolf, her Gray Wolf, so proud, so reserved, so arrogant... was crying. "Why did you free me?" she whispered sadly. His face was inches from hers, his eyes dark pools.

"I wanted to know you choose me of your own free will, I told you this. I want nothing more than a lifetime with you."

"Then why... Robin?"

"Robin...?" his brow wrinkled in puzzlement.

"As... your slave... I... would have... accepted. As a free... woman... I... cannot," she said but the effort seemed to exhaust her.

"I do not understand... Robin who?" he asked but she had slipped into unconsciousness. "Something is very wrong," he said desperately, shaking her and seeing no response. "Who is this Robin?" he cried out, then he turned and saw Wani who had crept in unnoticed. Gray Wolf quickly wiped his face to remove any trace of tears. "Do you know who this Robin is?"

"Perhaps Robin Song," Wani offered, a stricken look upon his face as he looked at his sister.

"Why does your sister think there is something between us?"

Wani shook his head.

"Please, get her to eat something," Gray Wolf pleaded to the shaman who just shook his head.

"She is dying of love," the old man said quietly.

"NO!" Gray Wolf shouted in a sudden roar of defiance. "No, I will not allow it!" He scooped her up, appalled at the feel of her weight in his arms. Like dry leaves, he thought, she felt no heavier than an armful of dry leaves. "Wani, fetch your mother. Tell her I take *Ohronkene Hahser* back to my hut. She is my responsibility. Tell your mother to cook food, rich food, her favorite dishes. Run." And he strode off to his hut, carrying Morning Light's motionless form tenderly.

When Morning Light opened her eyes again she recognized Gray Wolf's hut and tried to rise.

"Why am I here?" she asked weakly, falling back on her pallet.

"If I must make you my slave again to order you to eat and be well, then that is what I will do. I forbid you to die! Do you hear me? I forbid it!"

She nodded.

"I have been a fool," he said resolutely, deciding to confess while they were still alone. "The day the celebration began I saw you with Tonoaki and I saw you allow him to caress you, cheek on cheek... and I ran from the village. I stayed away all night when I should have been here to dance with you and court you as a maiden should be courted. I came back and let Mist-On-Moon pollute my mind with stories of how you danced with Tonoaki, how you did the courting dance and the mating dance together. I thought I wanted to die. I went away to hunt and to think and I realized I must fight for you to be worthy of you, I could not let Tonoaki just take you away from me without a fight. And I came back to find you... like this."

She had listened and the slow realization that Mist-On-Moon had tried to poison his mind made her realize it was Mist-On-Moon who had first said something about Gray Wolf and Robin Song. And if he had been gone all night then he couldn't have been with Robin Song.

"Oh, my love," she barely whispered. "I, too, have been a fool. Mist-On-Moon told me... you and Robin Song...." A slow surge of fight began to ebb through her body, the will to live, the will to fight, the will to choose life over death. "You did not make love to Robin Song during the celebration?" she asked with more strength in her voice then he had yet heard since returning.

"No. I have no interest in Robin Song. I was not even here."

"As I have no interest in Tonoaki. The embrace was a token of forgiveness, nothing more. Oh," she cried softly, "forgive me? Forgive me and hold me, please."

He bent to her and gently pulled her into his arms where she clung to him, drawing strength from him to continue breathing. And this was how Singing Wind found them when she arrived with a platter of food.

The smell of the food was tantalizing but even with her best efforts, Morning Light could eat only a few meager bites before her stomach tightened in pain. Gray Wolf soothed her and praised her and told her he was pleased and she would eat again soon. She slept then in his arms and when she awoke she ate a few more bites. And so they continued through the night. He never leaving her side, holding her, cushioning her bones from the hardness of her pallet.

As the days passed, Wani watched love cure his sister and restore her health. By the fourth day, she was sitting up on her own and feeding herself. On the seventh day she was up on her feet with Gray Wolf's arm around her walking slowly around the hut. The next day, he carried her to the river and she bathed while he held her. Shortly after that she walked outside with him, within the palisades.

Quick Panther held his breath as he stood absolutely still within the thicket. He had followed her and saw them now rutting in the leaves. The sounds of their passion echoed through the quiet forest in the still autumn night. He was certain that it was Tonoaki she was with and Quick Panther was not about to challenge the younger warrior who was larger, stronger, swifter, and more skilled than he. He had no intention of risking life, limb, or injury in fighting over the slut he had made his wife. He would not interrupt them, he would not intervene. He could wait until she was alone. Then, he would exact the punishment of the tribe for an unfaithful wife. And she would bear the mark of it for the rest of her life.

Under the naked tree in the stark moonlight, Moose Horn grunted in satisfaction while Mist-On-Moon giggled on their bed of leaves.

"It takes a long one to reach beyond your belly," he said proudly.

"You are much bigger than he is," she panted as he began his stroking. "And much better than he is, too," she added knowing how competitive these braves were.

Tonoaki had blamed her because Morning Light had closed herself away with the shaman and almost starved herself to death. And then Gray Wolf had returned and whisked her to his hut, closing the door on any more courting. Tonoaki had turned on Mist-On-Moon viciously and dared to call her ugly names. Well, he wasn't the only fish in the river. He lusted too much for The Twig and Mist-On-Moon wasn't going to be a second choice.

Instead, she had concentrated on Moose Horn who had been sulking around that insipid little Robin Song. It was Mist-On-Moon's guess that Robin Song had been holding back on him in hopes of marriage and so he had been ripe for a good roll in the leaves.

Despite her growing belly, Mist-On-Moon wiggled and squirmed and arched in demanding delight while Moose Horn did his best to erase any memory of Tonoaki she might still have. Then, she climbed on top of him and rode him like a bucking bull without any interference from her protruding fertile belly. When, at last, they had finished she had tumbled over in exhaustion where they lay for several minutes.

"Help me up," she demanded, and with a groan he stood up and helped to get her on her feet. "There are some negatives to being big with child," she commented dryly as she pulled down her large tunic. "And one of them, my great fine bull, is trying to get up off your back. Now, you stay here and I'll slip back inside first."

"When will I see you again," he asked quickly, playing once again with her full heavy breasts.

"We'll see," she chuckled. She liked them eager and Tonoaki had become too complacent. She walked back toward the palisade wall.

They all heard the scream, blood curdling and terrifying. Morning Light looked up at Gray Wolf. Together they rushed outside. The fires and torches were burning brightly in the autumn evening. Others were coming out of their huts armed with weapons, mutters and questions flew through the air. Was it a raid? Was it an animal attack? No one came out of Quick Panther's hut Gray Wolf noticed, and he wondered if this was something Morning Light should even see.

"Come," he said authoritatively, and turned her back in the direction of their hut.

"I want to know what has happened," she said quickly, resisting. "I've had my taste of being a free woman. You cannot make me feel like a slave again until I am a wife," she found herself teasing him despite the fearful sound they had all heard.

"Then, I must first prepare you," he looked at her solemnly, speaking quietly. "There is an old law in our tribe. If a man discovers his wife has been unfaithful to him he does not have the right to kill her, but he can punish her in another way."

"How?" she asked, her eyes wide.

"He can cut off her nose so no other man will look upon her, and the whole world will know her shame."

She cringed while her hand flew to her own nose. "Why do you tell me this now?"

"I think Quick Panther has invoked the old law."

"Mist-On-Moon?!" she cried out in pity. "Oh, no... has she...?"

"Did you not know?"

"No," she said and then recalled sudden images of that night, over four years ago. How Mist-On-Moon had thoroughly enjoyed coupling with the white men and Fleet-of-Foot. "But I think I am not surprised."

"There are several who have bragged of having her. She even threw herself at me," he said softly.

"You!" Morning Light felt a pang with this knowledge of betrayal. "While she tried to drive us apart. My uncle's wife... one of my old people," she was aghast not disbelieving yet finding it hard to believe as she watched from the door of the hut. "I have every reason to hate her, but... I can not. I must pity her," Morning Light said sadly as Quick Panther dragged Mist-On-Moon back to his hut. The pregnant squaw's hand was covering her face as she wailed and blood covered her hand and had soaked her tunic over her large belly. "I must go to help," Morning Light said compassionately but Gray Wolf's grip stayed her.

"They must work it out for themselves. He will care for her." It had grown quiet and they could hear Mist-On-Moon's sobbing cries from within Quick Panther's hut.

"My husband-to-be... would you ever do that to me?" Morning Light asked, thinking of the horror people inflicted upon one another.

"Would you ever betray me?"

"I asked my question first. Whether I did or not... if you thought I did, would you... could you do that to me?"

He looked at her for a long moment, his pride fighting with the truth. "No," he said at last, "I could never harm you no matter what. I should not admit this to you," he smiled earnestly, "but between us there will be no secrets."

"This is why I love you," she said softly and he took her into his arms and caressed her cheek with his own. The tenderness which started this embrace changed to passion as he tasted her and breathed in her subtle female scent. The need for her was rising strongly within him. "I have one more thing to ask of you," she said breathlessly.

"Woman... do your questions never stop?" he said in mock annoyance.

"Can you swear to me... upon your honor as a warrior... that you will never take another woman while I live?" She looked at him now unblinking with the calm dignity most associated with braves. "I have learned something these last months. I have learned that I could not bear to share you with another woman. I have learned that I would rather die."

"This is easy for me to swear," he replied hoarsely, touched so by her words it made him tremble. Feeling a rush of emotion that filled him with warmth and drove away every shadow of loneliness he'd ever felt, he embraced her face with his hands in extraordinary delicacy.

"If ever you have need to put me aside for another, kill me, Gray Wolf. Promise you will kill me, so I can have peace."

"I will spend my whole life loving only you," he said fiercely his eyes daring her to disbelieve him, his heart thudding at the horrifying image of ending her life. She met his gaze with her own, the golden flecks in her eyes giving them warmth and softness. Then he saw the corners of her mouth begin to turn up.

"Only me as your woman..." she said, breaking the tension, "but you can love

our children, and their mates... as a father," she smiled, "and our grandchildren..."
He grabbed for her and chased her back into the hut.

"I will show you how I love you, woman," he threatened playfully and she raced to the furs and threw herself down, rolling over to stretch out her arms in a welcome. He fell down beside her and began nuzzling her all over again. He felt the passion rising, his need for her was almost paralyzing. They had been almost three months without each other. Then he pulled back and drew himself up onto his knees.

"What is it?" she asked softly.

"We will wait. You are no longer my slave. You will soon be my bride. It is sweet torture that we should wait and you shall gain back all your strength."

She smiled at him.

"Then lie with me," she begged softly. "Just hold me while I sleep."

And this he did.


Gray Wolf had gone to Okonhsa and bartered with her, settling on a price to make a wedding dress for Morning Light. He had then produced the splendid white deer-skin and the woman had been astounded.

"It is magnificent! In all my years, I have never seen anything like it," the older woman said as she admired the skin.

"It is a sign that our union is blessed by the Great Spirit."

She nodded. "There is only one problem," she added.

"What is that?"

"Even though your bride-to-be is slender and not a large woman, she is tall. This piece makes," she shrugged her shoulders, "a fine skirt, or a fine tunic but there is not enough to make both."

"But is there not enough to make the garments that we are so used to seeing her in, the short skirt, the little tunic?"

"Yes, there will be enough for that," she nodded thoughtfully.

"Then, that is the kind of garment she should have, all in white, with beads like the sunset meeting the water around the neck. And white fur around the sleeves and bottom." He handed her a bag of white fox tails he had been collecting his entire life.

"She will be a breathtaking bride," Okonhsa said taking the bag from him and looking through the fine white tails.

"Yes," Gray Wolf agreed with pride.


She went with the women to the river to be purified. Her moon cycle had just ended and her wedding day had dawned. They scrubbed her skin with herbs and washed her hair in the oils of wild flowers mixed with soap root. He went to a more distant section of the river with the shaman, her male relatives and his closest warrior companions. He scrubbed his skin with the river sand and washed his hair in a mixture of wood ash, fat, and herbs. As he came up out of the water the shaman cleansed him with the sacred smoke. As she came up out of the water, her mother brightened her lips, earlobes, finger tips, and nipples with sweet red berry juice.

The women plaited the hair at her temples in two thin braids woven through with wildflowers and used them to form a crown atop her remaining mass of shiny, sable black hair, flowing in a thick undulating sheet over her shoulders and past her waist. The men shaved his head smooth leaving only the thick top-knot. Then they wrapped the hair at its roots in bands of shells and beads so it would stand high upon his head and the rest would flow downward like a waterfall. The shaman gave him a new chamois breech-cloth made of the palest yellow doeskin and invested with a blessing of fertility while her mother gave her a small new chamois breech-cloth, petal thin and soft, invested with a blessing of fertility.

His friends dressed him in her gift to him, a new pair of leggings, a finely beaded tunic, and golden fur lined moccasin boots all of the palest yellow doeskin. They girded his lean waist with a fine large belt of wampum, the sachem's gift to him. Then, they led him back into the palisade and to the middle of the Council Circle to await his bride.

The women dressed her in his gift to her, a pure white skirt and a short tunic top both made from the albino deerskin and edged in winter white fox tails. The reds and yellows and blues of the beading around the neck looked, indeed, like the sunset hitting the water. The fringe of tails swayed seductively beneath her breasts and at her hem above her pale fur lined boots as she walked. Chanting a lyrical tune, the women led her back into the palisade. They threw wild rose petals in her path which finally came to a stop before her bridegroom in the Council Circle.

The sachem spoke the words and bound their wrists symbolically with a length of wampum symbolizing their joining together and being blessed with prosperity.

Gray Wolf looked with pride upon Morning Light's glowing beauty, now fully restored, and his eyes shown with such love and tenderness it softened his starkly handsome face and transformed his arrogance into dignity. The pure white was a sharp contrast to the dusky gold of her skin, the soft brown-black of her hair, the deep golden brown of her eyes. He fought the urge to suck the juice off her berry stained lips while they stood publicly in front of the village.

Morning Light gazed at Gray Wolf with all the trust and love it was humanly possible to have in another human being. They listened to the sachem. They listened to the shaman. They took their vows solemnly, before their tribe, before the Great Spirit, and before all the *manitous* of nature. At last, Gray Wolf and Morning Light were recognized as one in union.

The celebration went on all night, long after the bride and groom had slipped away to their own private bower which had been filled with autumn arrangements of colorful leaves, flowers, bittersweet, and sweet smelling herbs. With the sounds of the chants and dancing and drums, Gray Wolf tied the door flaps securely against any mischievous intrusion. Morning Light added more sticks to the little fire and lit the fat lamps. The air was heavy with the herbal smells.

Silently, she began to undress him, carefully folding and arranging each item, his belt, his boots, his tunic and leggings, everything down to his small soft breech-cloth. Her fingers ran fires over his flesh, her lips seared trails as she moved her mouth over him. She fingered his breech-cloth shyly. They were mated now, she was his wife. How bold did he wish her to be? She caressed him and he struggled within himself to withstand the immediate reactions she caused in his body. In self-defense, he turned his concentration upon her. Her boots came off first and he nuzzled her toes and stroked the little arches of her feet, at first it tickled, then a shiver of desire raced over her for her handsome brave, her dark and fiercely tender warrior husband.

He withdrew the tunic top from her and his gaze fell upon her berry stained nipples peeping out from her cascade of hair. The intended response was immediate and his *ohnoru* strained against his breech-cloth. Pushing her hair gently aside, he grasped her breasts, licking the sweetness and suckling hard. The moan he heard escape her made him thicken with an ache. He grasped her berry stained lips with his own. He breathed in her breath, soft as a spring breeze, fresh as new grass, his tongue licked her cheeks and neck. Then he sucked on her earlobes. His breath in her ear made her shiver in expectation as the heat of his lips burned down her neck, trailed past her breasts and went on to her belly, smooth and warm. He groaned in appreciation of the silkiness of her skin. He released her skirt and drew it aside. Hot and wet, his tongue traced its way up and down, finally circling her navel while removing her breech-cloth.

In response to her passionate cries, he drew her onto her back and she immediately reached out for him, hungrily drawing him down onto her.

"I give myself to you," he whispered hoarsely. "My heart, my soul, my life essence are my gifts to you, my wife." Then the heat of her flesh folding around him tightly, made further words impossible as they moved together, slowly, rhythmically. He drove into her and brought her to the peak of pleasure, as simultaneously she felt his seed shoot into her womb.

He collapsed against her, his head resting beside her neck while her legs continued to grip him tightly, unwilling to allow him to move from her.

"Oh, my husband," she sighed softly at last. "May your spirit rise up strong within my womb. It is my wish to bear you a son."

"You shall bear me many sons," he replied softly, raising his head to look at her as he continued resting on his forearms. His lips curled into a smile. "And I shall take great pleasure in giving them to you."


Across the way in the hut of Quick Panther, Mist-On-Moon was living on hatred. She had not joined the celebration. Had not witnessed the wedding. Even if she was not loath to be seen, she would have been too embittered to see Gray Wolf marry The Twig. Those who are unhappy cannot find joy in another's happiness. Quick Panther had gone and she had stayed home with her toddler, her big belly, and her mutilated nose.

As she was alone she relived again the night of her undoing. She had left Moose Horn. She had been heading for the trail to the latrine, so that any who might see her would think that had been her business. He had suddenly appeared out of nowhere. It had happened so fast. Quick Panther had cursed her and she had seen the flash of his knife. But she had not realized what he had done until she felt the blood gushing forth and she had screamed. They had all come running, everyone. But when they had seen, they had backed away. There had been no word of reproof for Quick Panther. No sympathy for her. This barbarous tribe! How could they approve of this? But then, had they not approved of the barbarous acts The Twig had committed against the white captives? She should not have been surprised. She had forgotten their blood lust. Not one of her lovers had said a word. She would spend the rest of her days hiding her face from stares and pointing fingers. She, who had been a pretty woman, who was still young, who men had found desirable. One husband had died. What if Quick Panther were to die? Who would want her then? How could she get another husband? What would become of her and her children?

She gingerly touched her healing flesh. It was scabbed over and stiff and caused her to whistle when she tried to breathe through her nostrils. There was no way to tell what she would really look like until the scabs were gone and the flesh was healed.

How could he have done this? How could he? She asked herself over and over. He would have to look at her everyday. It was a constant reminder to him of his own brutality. It would also be a constant reminder of his authority, his power over her. And a constant reminder of her having made a fool of him with half the unmarried men in the village. He would never forget, how could he… when every day he would see her ruined face and be reminded? He would never forgive her. Oh, how could he have done this and to a pregnant woman, the mother of his children, how could he? Of course, only the first one was his and this one? She rubbed bear fat into the stretching skin over her belly. This one was Tonoaki's, not that he deserved a child. If he hadn't been rutting with someone else, then she wouldn't have sought out Moose Horn and Quick Panther would never have caught her and this would never have happened.

Mist-On-Moon crawled into her sleeping furs alone. She hated everyone around her. And that hatred was becoming a fire in her brain that seemed to move to her belly. After a time she realized she was having regular contractions and she knew her baby was coming. She was alone, wanted no one to see her so she sought no help.

It was almost dawn when Quick Panther returned from the revelries, his mind thick with fermented drink and tired from hours of gambling. The smell of fresh blood permeated the hut and he looked to Mist-On-Moon and found her sleeping with the new infant beside her. Impersonally, he opened the wrapping about the infant to discover it was a female. A daughter. Tonoaki's? Someone else's? It didn't matter. It wasn't his. But he was feeling magnanimous as he looked upon the tiny baby. He would provide food and shelter for the next twelve years and then marry her off. She would bring him more kinship and be no problem.

# Chapter 19

## Spring 1720

Gray Wolf's blood quickened as he finished the last of his preparations. His quiver was filled to capacity with his best and straightest arrows, each handpicked for their perfection. His bow was restrung with well-seasoned rawhide. And in his belt he now carried an iron tomahawk. The blood-lust was rising like a tide within him. It had been long since he had joined a war party. He spared a last moment of thought for his wife. His only regret was to leave her but a woman was an unneeded distraction to a warrior going to battle. And he had done his duty in making provisions for her safe keeping.

She was the adopted daughter of the shaman and it had become her habit and her mind set to watch after the old wise man, bring him food, clean his hut, see to his needs. He was there for her but Gray Wolf could not imagine the old shaman being able to defend beautiful *Ohronkene Hahser* from the aggressive hot bloods of their camp of whom Tonoaki topped the list. Since the wedding, Tonoaki had kept his distance, disdainful of even speaking to her, but Gray Wolf was not fooled into believing for a moment that his lifelong rival did not still want her. And it was conceivable that he would be troublesome if he had the opportunity and Tonoaki was not part of the main war party.

Two weeks ago they had learned that the Algonquin and Huron were pressing down from the north. It was *wateriyo!* War! Gray Wolf knew he would be leaving soon to fight and he did not hesitate to speak with Yellow Rock who was now sixteen winters old, a man, and first cousin to *Ohronkene Hahser*. It was fitting that Gray Wolf should ask Yellow Rock, her only male blood kin of age, to keep an eye on her in her husband's absence. Gray Wolf had no family upon whom to bestow this responsibility of trust. It was especially fitting since Gray Wolf knew Yellow Rock would not be in the main war party with him this season whereas Five Beavers would.

Shortly after this, Yellow Rock went out with a small group led by Tonoaki. They were to scout the surrounding valleys, lay traps for intruders and return to protect the main village while the larger band of which Gray Wolf was a part would seek out and strike the enemy.

The drums had begun the primitive rhythm at the Council Circle, the steady percussive call to war, to violence, to blood, to feats of bravery and daring, to counting coup, to victory. The powerful warrior in his prime, at his peak of strength and agility was not alone as he painted himself with the colored clays, turning his handsome face into a face of terror and aggression. The drums grew louder, quickening their pace. Women were forbidden at the circle. The warriors gathered on their feet and began the ancient chants. *Kateriyos! Keriyos! Tewatatèkv wateriyo!* The drums beat faster. The rhythm was moving their bodies, making their blood surge through their veins, hot and vengeful. The power of the drumming was like a giant heartbeat growing faster and louder, permeating their brains as they began a frenzied dance around the circle. The chants increased.

*Kateriyos! Keriyos!*
*Kateriyos! Keriyos!*
*Tewatatèkv wateriyo! Tewatatèkv wateriyo!*
*Kateriyos! Keriyos!*
*Kateriyos! Keriyos!*
*Tewatatèkv wateriyo! Tewatatèkv wateriyo!*

The drum beat increased, the frenzy increased until in a crescendo of whoops and yelps, savage cries and murderous pantomimes, it climaxed in a cacophony of warbled shrieks. Thus, they surged out of the village, grabbing their weapons and jogging out into the forest.

From within their hut, Morning Light heard and shivered. The savage sounds echoed through the village. "I fight!" "I kill!" "We are brothers in war!"

Mist-On-Moon peeked out of the hut and saw no one. It had been an entire winter. Quick Panther had brought everything to her, had fetched the water, fetched the wood, only drawing the line at burying the afterbirth which Singing Wind had come and done while Mist-On-Moon had lain in her furs covering her face.

She had refused to go out before she was healed but now Quick Panther had gone with the war party. And she must fend for herself. She could feel that her skin was healed but she had been afraid to look. She had to go down to the river and look in the water for herself before she could allow anyone else to look at her.

As she made her way to the river her heart thumped with hope. Perhaps it wasn't so bad. A little nip. Hardly noticeable. After all, Quick Panther said he cared about her. He wouldn't want to make her really grotesque, would he? Mist-On-Moon finally reached the river bank. The sun was rising and in a side wash the water was still. A good reflecting pool. She crawled upon several boulders to look over the edge at her reflection.

Mist-On-Moon would have screamed but no sound came out. She stared in horror, in disbelief, in shock. The space in her face where a well formed nose had been now looked like a miniature snout! She was grotesque! The stuff nightmares and spirit stories were made of. It was worse than she could have imagined. The young woman crumpled in tears. She could hide no longer and this was how she must face the world.

§

"As far as I'm c'cern, th' only good injun's a dead 'un. Ya cain't tell one from th'other, no-how," Private Surly McQuin was complaining as he shucked his ruck-sack from his back and flopped down on the ground.

"Hush up, Surly," admonished his buddy, Craigy Withers, also a private. "Ya want so's th' scouts kin hear ya?"

"Awhh, damn th' scouts. More injuns!" scowled Surly. "Somebody wanna tell me why we'rn here fightin' injuns an' then lettin' injuns tell us what t' do?"

"But th' scouts is th' good injuns, ya know that. Ain't likely we're gunna have one of th' king's men t' tell us which way t' go."

"Th' whole thing stinks!" Surly growled.

"Well, hell, Surly, ya ain't gunna get no argument outa nobody 'bout that. Shit, when was soldierin' ever a bed o'rosebuds? But at least we don't hafta fret none 'bout thems attacking at night."

"Shit yerself. I wish I wuz as shore 'bout that as you'uns."

"Well, now ya hear'd Ernie. Injuns is afear'd to war at night, thinks if they die their spirit cain't find its way to th' happy huntin' ground or some such."

"Aren't you men tired enough to sleep or do you want to pull first watch?" a deep voice of calm authority broke into the grumbling.

"No, Sergeant. Thank ya anyway, I thinks we's right tired enough. Goin' right t' sleep now," Craigy replied with an ingratiating grin.

"All right then, lights out." It was perhaps a silly thing to say, thought Sergeant Jack Power, a matter of habit. There were no lights here to extinguish, not even campfires. But his intent had been communicated and his men knew what he meant. Time for them to pipe down, shut up, and get some sleep. Sounds traveled far in the dark.

John settled himself down at the foot of a large old tree. He pulled his pipe out and filled the bowl with fresh tobacco, the one luxury he allowed himself in the field. He enjoyed a relaxing smoke before going to sleep.

They were on a three week mission to scout the area and report any movement of hostiles into the valleys they patrolled. It was a thankless job and a matter of pure luck if they should actually be able to see any movement but the reports had been coming in that the Huron were on the move with the Algonquin prodded by the French to make war against the Iroquois and the English. With only a small de-tail of men, they were under orders not to engage the enemy. Orders *not to engage*, John shook his head to himself. Hell, only a stupid Pink Cheek would think to en-gage the enemy with only a detail of men.

*Pink Cheek* was the name they gave to newly arrived officers, no matter the rank, fresh from the Royal Court, with a newly purchased commission and no practical experience in the wild. They could study traditional battle strategies all they wanted but over here on this side of the ocean, they might as well throw their damn books away. Indians didn't fight with traditional battle strategies and surely didn't give a good goddamn about any white man's rules of waging a so-called *honorable* war. The only rule here was that there were no rules.

John was focused on his strike box, catching a spark to light his tobacco when the raiding party attacked. There had been no warning war cry but since being converted to Catholicism, the attackers no longer were afraid to fight and perhaps die at night. In fact, they found the surprise of their attacks usually rendered them the victors.

Surly's throat was slit before he knew what was happening and he blacked out when the oxygen rich blood could no longer get to his brain. The crush of a tomahawk between the eyes took out Craigy. The only thing that saved John was the tree he sat against. An oddly protruding piece of heavy bark in a most strategic place took the majority of the blow that otherwise would have crushed his skull. Instead, he sustained a nonfatal blow that knocked him backward off an embankment where he rolled downward about thirty feet and remained unconscious... for nineteen hours.

John felt a hammer beating on the inside of his skull before he even opened his eyes. It was a warning he heeded and he moved very slowly. With his eyes open he could tell he was lying on uneven ground and that it was daylight. His body felt disassociated from his head and he had to concentrate before he could get anything to move. When he did move, thunder and cannons went off inside his skull and he groaned pitifully before he could stop himself. The aching stiffness of his body and paralyzing numbness of his limbs were minor difficulties compared to the blinding pain in his skull. When he was able to get his hand to respond to the orders his brain was giving it, it reached for his head and his fingers felt the flesh gingerly. It felt crusty and sticky. Blood no doubt. But it was solid, no holes, if there was a crack at least it wasn't big enough to spill forth his brains. He felt a laceration of the skin and dried blood. That was a good sign, he thought.

His legs were finally responding and he pulled his knees to his stomach, not all the way just enough to assure himself his body and back seemed to be intact as well. But the little blacksmith inside his head was hammering relentlessly on an inner anvil and he soon found out, contrary to his first opinion, it could get worse and immediately did when he tried to raise his head off the ground. His head screamed so badly it was making him violently sick to his stomach. He could not quell the nausea and the intensity of pain caused by the pressure of his vomiting made him pass out again. Fortunately, he'd turned to his side which kept him from choking to death.

When John opened his eyes again it was dark night and he decided it was better he not try to move. It was too damn dark to see where he was going anyway, he thought. He managed to roll onto his back before he slipped back into unconsciousness.

It was getting light when his eyes opened suddenly. He remained still, trying to remember. The fog in his brain cleared and he was cognizant of where he was and that he had been injured. It was dawn. It was over twenty-four hours since he had had any water. He must have water. For some reason that thought came to him very clearly. He thought again although the effort seemed to sap him. He had a canteen. The canteen had been in his pack. He had dropped the pack by the tree. He began to grope with his hands, reaching out, exploring the ground around him, trying to feel out the pack. Where was the tree? He had to orientate himself. It was then that he realized, he wasn't anywhere near the tree, in fact what little he saw of his surroundings told him they were unfamiliar and he was alone. Alone? What had happened? Without lifting his head he turned it. It was very painful but he realized he was on a hillside, a slope, and the markings above him seemed to indicate he had fallen down that path. He began to crawl upward. He stifled the groan which came up from his throat, his head hurt too badly for any noise.

The instinct for self-preservation is strong. He needed to get back to his canteen. He needed water. Laboriously pulling one knee up, one hand up, and then the others, he crawled slowly on his belly back up the embankment. How long it took, John didn't know. He stopped or rather passed out at several points, then, came to and continued on. Finally, he breached the crest. Looking out from his lower position he saw his tree and his pack. He also saw the buzzards picking at the bodies of his men but he really didn't pay any attention. His feet pushed him up onto the leveler ground. His head was little more than a blinding mass of searing pain and he reached out blindly, groping. Finally, he felt something. A strap. His fingers grasped the material and pulled. It was heavy. It was difficult but he had moved it closer. His fingers set about exploring again, his eyes shut against the light. Now he could feel the pack, his fingers flew over it, redefining it in his mind. His hand worked to open it and reaching in he made contact with his canteen. He almost smiled he was so relieved.

Dragging the canteen to him, John carefully removed the stopper and drank. His mouth was dry, his throat almost strangled with constriction. The wetness of the water was like a small bit of heaven as it slid down his throat soothing the acid burn created by his vomiting. Only a few swallows. He must pace himself. He carefully recapped the canteen. He would have more in a few minutes, he told himself and he passed out again.

When he regained consciousness the sun was high overhead. The first thing he did was uncap the canteen and drink deeply. As a doctor he knew the standard treatment for a serious concussion but he wasn't at home with someone to watch over him and bring him sustenance and water. He had to get to his feet and back to the fort before he died of starvation and exposure, he told himself. It had been...

How long was it? A day, no, two days since the attack? Two days. At least he thought it was two days. Two days laying on the ground without food. No wonder he was feeling weak. And his head, it was still pounding. Could he get up? He had to try, he had to start moving.

He dragged himself to his knees using the tree to steady himself when the ground started to pitch and roll like the deck of a ship. He clung to that tree and willed the earth to stop moving beneath him. He stood feet spread, letting his legs get used to his weight and his heart to pump blood up to his brain. Sweat broke out on his brow. The ground beneath him steadied but his head throbbed fiercely. Squinting with the pain he surveyed the scene. What was left of his men turned his stomach and he forced himself to take deep breaths as he looked away. The Indians had taken their scalps. He reached suddenly to feel the top of his head. His hair was there. Why hadn't they taken his? They had missed him but they hadn't missed his men. And neither had the scavengers. They hadn't bothered him when there had been easier, surer pickings nearby. They fed on the corpses.

John felt his legs begin to shake beneath him and he sat down, leaning against the tree. With trembling hands he opened his pack, found some hardtack and jerky and tried to eat. Chewing did not make his head feel any better but he forced himself. The noise of the hardtack crunching between his teeth was like a battalion of musket fire in his ears. But he had to eat as much as he could, he told himself. As the energy from the food began to ebb through him, his headache eased somewhat. He would sleep tonight and by morning he should be able to travel, he thought. He must be able to travel. Back to the fort. Back to some protection while he recuperated. He continued to gnaw on the jerky and drank more water. His canteen was almost empty now. He looked over at what remained of Craigy. His pack was there. His canteen. He wouldn't need it anymore. John crawled over to it and dragged it back to his place beneath the tree where he curled up around it and again fell asleep.

Yellow Rock watched the white man stumbling down the forest path. He was staggering like he was full of firewater. He mumbled talk to himself from within the grizzly looking whiskers on his face. The other members of the scouting party were beginning to walk out of their hiding places. Then Yellow Rock realized why. The white man carried no weapons, he was harmless. There was no need for caution. They stood watching him as he stumbled toward them. As he drew nearer, the large swollen purplish knot on his forehead became obvious along with the caked dry blood in his matted yellow hair. He was injured. Perhaps that was the reason for his crazy behavior. He walked straight at them, his white man talk becoming more excited. Yellow Rock wondered what he was saying. His voice became louder and was accompanied by many gestures. He pointed back the way he had come. He went from one to the other, not in fear but in agitation. Talking to them, gesturing, until he began to weave and collapsed upon the ground, motionless.

"We will bring him to the village," said Tonoaki. "There is no honor in killing an unarmed man who walks up as a brother."

"Brother? What brother? The white is no brother of mine!" said Yellow Rock, spitting upon the man lying at his feet.

"I have no love for the whites," said Tonoaki, then looking at the others he added, "You all know this. But we are not Huron dogs to kill a man who walks up to us without fear and unarmed. He is injured, we will take him to our shaman. Let him be healed and grow strong and become a worthy enemy. Then, we can kill him with honor."

"Tonoaki is right," said another. "We can wait until he is well before we kill him." And with that they each grabbed a limb and carried Sergeant Jack Power back to their village.

Morning Light was nearby when the party returned to the palisade carrying the white man with them. They went straight to the shaman's hut and dropped him carelessly on the ground. There was something about the man that caught her eye and caused a twinge of familiarity to ripple through her. His hair beneath the blood and mud and dirt was yellow. She moved closer to hear.

"We must allow him to grow well," Tonoaki was saying. "Then I will fight him fairly and when he loses, our people can do with him what they like."

The shaman nodded. "You had better bind him. I do not want him to destroy my hut," the old man wheezed. Several of the braves produced rawhide roping and a strong length of wood to which they bound his ankles, hobbling his steps. They trussed up his hands, anchoring his lashing to a sturdy stake outside beneath a canopy along side the shaman's hut. He wasn't going to go anywhere and the shaman would be able to see to his health.

When John opened his eyes he discovered he was lying on a pallet under a canopy of branches and a young squaw was sponging his head with a rag.

"So, I'm still alive," he mutter to himself in a hoarse whisper and the squaw jumped back. "Sorry. I didn't mean to scare you," he said immediately, then moaned with the pain in his head. "Where am I?" he gasped at last.

The squaw continued to stare for a moment and then, brought a bowl of water to his lips. He drank eagerly. When he finished he cleared his throat and took several deep breaths. Then he noticed his shackles.

"What the...? I guess someone is afraid I am going to do some damage. Well, I can't say I blame you. I can't even remember how I got here. Oh, man," he reached for his head with one hand which brought the other with it and Morning Light pulled them back down, away from the wound. "I still have one real beaut of a headache, I can say that." He looked at the girl again. "I don't suppose you can tell me where I am?" He paused but she gave no reaction. "No, I didn't think so. Does anyone around hear speak English? English? No? *Anglais? Parlez vous française?* No French either, huh?" Just then his stomach growled and he pointed to his belly and then to his mouth and made eating gestures.

Morning Light certainly understood that and really hadn't needed the pantomime. She went off and brought back a bowl of pea soup and a wooden spoon.

"*Onekwa?*" She offered. The white man tried to sit up and cringed in pain. She gestured for him to stay down and she began to feed him herself. He ate eagerly at first, then pushed away.

"Oh, God, I think I'm going to be sick again," he groaned. Something universal in his sounds made Morning Light bring a large empty bowl to him and he grabbed it and vomited. After a few moments he lay back panting and moaning, holding his head. She gently tugged his arms down again and washed his face. The cool, clean, wet rag felt soothing and John lie quietly for a time.

She continued to sit with him and soon he was looking at her intently. "I could swear I've seen you someplace before," John said after a while and then, despite his pain he gave a half chuckle and half grin. "I wouldn't be surprised if a lot of men tell you that," he joked, it was the oldest pick-up line since Adam had daughters. Then he took another deep breath and was still. "But you certainly are beautiful."

He raised his finger and pointed to himself, "Jack," he said looking at her. "Jack. My name is Jack." Then he pointed to her. She lowered her eyes.

"*Yukyats, Ohronkene Hahser,*" she responded and he tried to repeat her name.

"Yuk-yats-o-run-keenee-hahs-er," he said and he saw her laugh softly. "I guess I didn't do to well. Let's try again." He pointed to himself. "Jack. Jack."

"*Sak,*" she repeated passably.

John bobbed his head in exaggerated acceptance, then moaned with the effort. "*Sak,*" he repeated weakly, pointing at himself. Then pointing to her he said, "Yuk-yats?" She giggled again and shook her head. Then she pointed to him.

"*Sak.*" she stated firmly. Then she pointed to herself and said, "*Ohronkene Hahser.*"

"O-ron-keenee-hah-ser," he tried. It was a passing effort and she gave him a small smile of encouragement and nodded her head. "O-ron-keenee-hah-ser," he repeated to himself. Then he looked up at her. "Yuk-yats?' he asked in an obvious question. "What is 'Yuk-yats'?"

She pointed to him and made her voice very low, "*Yukyats Sak,*" she stated.

John looked at her for a moment, thinking and then broke into a small smile. "My name is Jack," he said softly. "I get it. *Yukyats Sak,*" he repeated pointing to himself and he saw her nod.

"*Yukyats ... Ohronkene Hahser,*" she said pointing to herself.

"Your name is ... O-ron-keenee-hah-ser," he repeated and saw her nod in approval. He felt exhausted already and wondered if he should try and eat a little more food. He motioned to the bowl and she eagerly brought a spoonful to his mouth. This time, she slowed his pace, however, and wouldn't let him gulp. The food stayed down. It didn't take much for his belly to feel full and he was becoming sleepy again, his eyelids drooped and he slept.

Morning Light took the food bowl and left.

Since Gray Wolf was away, Morning Light saw no reason not to help the shaman with the prisoner. She had an understandable revulsion for white men but this one was different. The hair that covered his face obscured his features but there was something about those gray eyes and the sound of his voice that drew her to him.

She thought about the other white men that had been dragged in when they were all brought to the village. They had been guilty of murder and rape and torture. They had deserved their fate. But what had this one done? She had caught only part of what Tonoaki had said but it sounded as if this one really had done nothing. That was why they had not killed him. Why was he alone? And why were they waiting for him to be well only to torture and kill him later? She wished Gray Wolf was here to explain this to her.

Morning Light continued to tend the white man and watched him slowly grow stronger. The purple lump on his head was getting smaller and turning yellow green, and his appetite was improving. Then, one day he confused her. He began moving his fingers over his face and fingering his hair.

"I've never liked a beard," John said, "I really would like to shave. Shave. My beard. Can I have something to shave my face?" He looked at the squaw in mild frustration. "God, I wish someone here could speak English or French."

Morning Light looked at him, concentrating, trying to understand. What did he want?

"Shave... like this," he pantomimed shaving but Indians did not shave their faces. His movements meant nothing to Morning Light. The shaman came out to check on the prisoner's progress and John noticed the old man's shaved head. He pointed to it and then to his face and Morning Light made the connection.

"He wants to remove the hair from his face," she said to the shaman.

"I should not wonder. It is a disgusting thing these white men are cursed with. Hairy faces, like beasts."

"What should I give him to remove his hair?"

"I use a sharp flint edge to scrape the hair from my head, but that could be a weapon for him. He could cut through the ropes that bind him."

"If a few stood guard?"

"I suppose it would be all right."

The next day Morning Light brought a flint edge and two warriors with her. John wondered what was going on but the warriors simply stood on each side watching him. Then, she gave him the flint and motioned to his face as he had done. He understood. With more pantomiming, he managed to convey a desire for hot water which she brought to him.

Without a mirror to see by or soap to lather with, John did his best to shave his beard without cutting his face to ribbons. The spots of blood were proof that he'd nicked himself up a bit but at last he felt smooth and he looked up at the squaw and smiled.

Morning Light was staring. Could it really be him? But she could never forget his face. This was the yellow haired man who had been kind to her, who had taken pity on her, who had taken her into the fort and sewed up her wound. He did not recognize her. Of course, he could not recognize her, he had seen her as a child in agony. Now, she was a woman blooming with health.

The young squaw suddenly realized that she could not let this man be tortured. She simply could not allow it to happen. She secured the flint edge from him and left to seek out the shaman.

"Wise One," Morning Light called, standing before the door of the hut. "May I enter?"

"Come."

She stepped inside. It was very warm. Despite the mild weather he often complained of the cold and he had been sitting contentedly before his small fire.

"Wise One, I need your advice," she said as she sat submissively before him.

"What is it?" he asked continuing to sit upon his cushion in quiet dignity.

"Remember when I came to the village? The white men who had been so evil?" He nodded.

"Before the raiding party caught us, we had been at the white fort. There was one man who took pity on me. Who helped me. It is this man who is now our prisoner. I cannot let him be tortured. I owe him much."

"You are a woman." he said simply, implying that since women owed everything to men, they could never be expected to think about owing a debt or repaying debt the way a man did.

"But he is not one of our kind," she reasoned. "I owe a debt that needs to be repaid. Father, I was badly wounded by the evil ones. This one is a medicine man who sewed me so I would be like other women again. Please do not let his kindness be repaid with torture. That would be evil on our part."

"He is Tonoaki's prisoner," he wheezed.

"But Tonoaki would have to listen to you."

"I will think on this."

Morning Light lowered her head and left.

Outside the shaman's hut, she breathed deeply of the fresher air but could feel a great heaviness in her heart. The white man was getting better each day. Soon Tonoaki would challenge him to fight. It was almost a certainty that the prisoner would not have the strength to beat the healthy young brave. Then, he would be tortured like the others had been and finally, killed. The shaman gave her no hope. She sensed that he did not want to intervene. She did not understand it. If only Gray Wolf were there to help but she had no idea when he would be back. There was only one thing left to do. She would have to speak to Tonoaki herself.

"May I speak with you?" Morning Light approached the proud brave as he stood outside his hut watching her approach.

He acknowledged her with a nod. "You honor me," he replied in a softer voice.

She felt his gaze upon her lingering over her body, and did not raise her eyes to look directly into his. "I must ask a great favor of you."

"Really? This is good for I am in your debt. You are responsible for the fast recovery of my prisoner. Your beauty affects even the white dogs."

"This is what I must speak to you about..." she faltered.

"Go on."

"You know I have no love for the whites."

He laughed. "So, you want first blood."

"No... please. While I have no love for the whites, I also could not kill them for no reason."

"They give us many reasons," the brave sneered.

"But I know this one." He looked at her saying nothing. "This was the one who took pity upon me. Before I came to this tribe. He is a medicine man. He saved my life. I would ask you to spare him."

"He did not save my life."

"No... it is my debt."

"And what do I get out of it?" he asked in a soft seductive way.

She flushed uncomfortably, his look was intense and she knew too well what he wanted.

"Please, have pity. I am not a man, I cannot challenge you for his life."

"No, you are not a man," he said softly and then reached out with the speed of a serpent, grabbing her arm, pulling her closer. "You are a woman who sets my blood on fire," he rasped with quiet intensity. "Do you want him? He is yours... just give me one night, one night in your arms. Gray Wolf is gone. He will never know."

"He would know!" she gasped, flinching from his grip. "I would know! Do not ask this of me. I cannot betray my husband!"

"Then the white dog dies."

"Please," she pleaded. "To repay his kindness with torture would be evil on our part. We must not do this."

"He is white. He has done no kindness to me! He is my sworn enemy!"

Tears brimmed in Morning Light's eyes and now overflowed.

"You cannot give me one night, but you cry for the white dog. What would your husband think of that?"

"He would understand the honor involved," she sobbed out. "I am begging you. Ask anything of me except to betray my husband, anything that I can give you and it is yours."

Tonoaki hardened his heart and with a grunt of disgust he went into his hut leaving Morning Light standing outside alone.

She decided she had no option left but to go to the Council of Mothers. Although the Council was not a body with overt leadership power, they were a forum to hear a just complaint, sit in judgment on disputes and give support. They dealt most commonly with issues involving domestic justice and fairness and although the sachem was the top authority of the tribe, any issue the Mothers strongly supported was an issue the sachem gave consideration. Ignoring the Council of Mothers was to invite domestic strife into one's own hearth. Now, with the men off to war, the Council of Mothers was the strongest tribal authority in camp.

Morning Light sought out Okonhsa and asked to speak to the Council of Mothers. Her request was granted.

"It would not be just to give back evil for good," she explained, as she had with the shaman. "He showed me mercy. We cannot repay mercy with treachery."

"He showed you mercy," repeated a very fat gray-haired squaw, who headed the Council. "You have shown him mercy. He could not keep you from your fate. You cannot keep him from his fate."

"But Mother," Morning Light addressed the woman with extreme deference, "if it were not for him, I would have died."

"You were close to dying when you came to our camp," Okonhsa interjected. "If our shaman had not helped me treat you, you would have died. This white did not save you from that."

Morning Light felt her hopes sink. The Mothers were not seeing her point of view. "But the white nursed me back to health so I would have the strength to fight off the fever the evil whites gave me again."

"And so you have nursed the white so he has the strength to fight Tonoaki," the Head Mother spoke.

Morning Light grasped at this last thread of reasoning. "Yes, Mother, this is almost true. But Tonoaki would fight the white before he is well. This would not be a fair fight. There is no justice in a fight with an opponent who is still not recovered. Please, can you not require Tonoaki to wait until the white is truly recovered."

"This is only fair," pronounced the Head Mother as she looked around the gathering of squaws. "Do we agree?"

Every squaw nodded her head. Although none had any love for the white, there was no honor, no justice, no fairness in challenging an enemy who was handicapped. Morning Light gave a very small sigh of relief. The Council of Mothers would make Tonoaki be patient and give *Sak* time to heal.

# *Chapter 20*

Gray Wolf made the cry of the Night Bird and heard a similar cry in return. They had the trading post encircled. The warriors were in position and they would attack as soon as the first ray of sun showed itself. The trading post was quiet in the pre-dawn light. Then the door opened and a white man in a long tailed shirt and breeches came out rubbing his eyes and walking in a slow stagger to the little building they had learned was a white man's latrine. Moose Horn was closest to this little building and it would be his task to kill that one.

They had watched the post all afternoon of the day before. A fat Frenchman and his wife lived there. There was a young boy, perhaps their son. Several traders were there at the moment, which was their poor luck but the raiding party's good fortune. They all slept inside.

The first sunbeam streaked through the trees and the warriors gave a blood chilling warble of challenge and sped through the clearing, descending upon the post. The man in the little building opened the door and Moose Horn slit his throat before he could pull up his breeches. Four warriors burst in the door while others crawled in the windows. There was little challenge in the fight.

Gray Wolf found the fat Frenchman in his bed with a musket in his hands. A small brown haired woman hid behind him. The native faked a lunge into the room, the man fired and missed. Before he could reload, Gray Wolf leapt upon him and slit his throat. The woman was screaming hysterically as he pulled her off the bed, tearing the neck of her garment as he did. Then, he saw the wild look in her eyes and thought of Morning Light and the rapes she had suffered. In a moment of compassion, he slit the woman's white throat, watching the blood immediately begin to spurt out and down, mingling with her brown tresses which grew sticky and matted. In a moment the life left her eyes and with it the fear. He noticed pearl earrings on her ears and plucked them off thinking to bring this present to his wife. Then, he dropped the woman's corpse and left the room.

Later as they were taking what they wanted in booty, Five Beavers, Moose Horn, Quick Panther and the others complained profusely that he had been overly hasty in killing the woman. They had been many weeks without a woman, they snarled, and would have made good use of her before ending her life. Gray Wolf simply shrugged that he had reacted instinctively and had dispatched the enemy before he thought of her as a woman. He carefully wrapped up the earrings and put them into his pouch.

"You are still a bridegroom, too newly married to think of any but your wife," grumbled Quick Panther. "Leave the females to us next time."

Gray Wolf gave a nod of agreement.

The young boy would have been taken for adoption if they had been going home but that prospect was too far in the future to have to drag around a young captive. So his throat was also slit quickly. Before they left, they set fire to the post and its outbuildings. They grabbed up the chickens, tied their feet together and brought them along for supper.

§

With increasing agitation, Morning Light watched John grow more animated each day. She anguished to see him push himself to regain his abilities. If she could talk to him, if she could make him understand her, she would tell him of the death challenge that awaited him. She would advise him to disguise his returning strength and feign continuing weakness, at least until he was truly fully recovered. She would tell him who she was and that she wanted to help him. Tell him that her mate would want to help him because of what he had done for her years ago. But Morning Light had no words to communicate any of these thoughts.

The cool of the evening had come when she brought a bowl of meaty stew and freshly baked cornbread to John. She was adept at adding savory herbs to her cooking and the aromas wafting in the air immediately caught his attention. She found him sitting bent over, rubbing his legs.

*"O-ron-keenee-hah-ser,"* he grinned looking up at her, glad for her company, silent though it was. "I wish I wasn't trussed up like the family goat," he complained with a touch of humor knowing full well she didn't understand a word he was saying. "This wood really is bothersome, it's rubbing my legs raw." He pointed vigorously to his shackles. "Off? Take away? Remove?"

She understood what he wanted well enough but she could do nothing. She gestured for him to receive his supper and handed him the food. He inhaled the smells and made appreciative sounds that made her smile.

"I see your sick-ling is growing well!"

She turned around quickly and saw Tonoaki standing a short distance away, his feet spread, his arms crossed, staring at her with a tight smile on his lips.

"He gets better but he still is not well enough to be a match for you," she said smoothly.

"He will never be a match for me," he retorted arrogantly.

"But you must give him a fair chance..."

*"Must?!* Now you tell me what I *must* do, woman?"

"I... I am sorry," she bent her head immediately in submission. "I did not mean that as it came out."

"Tomorrow I challenge him! I have been forced to wait long enough! He is ready."

"Noooo," the word came out as a moan. "Tonoaki, please..."

"I told you, you may have him," he replied softly, his eyes narrowing upon her. "Is his life not worth one single night to you?"

"It is not mine to give or I would gladly give it to repay my debt to this man, but

I have made my vows."

Somehow she had just made the act of sharing intimacy with him seem as impersonal and trivial as giving him a bowl of soup or a kettle that was also not hers
to give.

"Tomorrow!" he bristled and stalked away.

Morning Light looked back at John. He had been watching the exchange and
his face had grown serious. He wasn't sure about the relationship between the warrior and the squaw but he'd heard men proposition females before and there was a
familiar tone in the Indian's voice.

"He doesn't seem like a very friendly fellow," John said dryly. There was a
sound in what he said that struck a cord of remembrance in Morning Light.

"FFerrr-enn," she said cautiously.

"Yes. *Friend!*" he responded eagerly. "I am *friend*." He pointed to himself. She
pointed to herself then pointed to him repeating the sound, the word.

"Friend. Friend."

John nodded and smiled. "Well, it's a start. If you understand that I am friend,
then you know I mean you no harm."

"*Sak*," she said pointing to him. "*Ohronkene Hahser*," she pointed to herself.
Then, she pointed at the empty space the brave had occupied. "*Tonoaki*."

"Oh, I get it. It's his name. *Toe-no-ah-kee*."

She nodded. "Friend," she repeated again and then shook her head exaggerat-
edly. The universal sign of a negative. Instinctively, a baby knows the meaning of
a head shake and John knew it also.

"No friend, huh? Well, now how come that's not a big surprise?" he replied
with a dry chuckle.

Encouraged, Morning Light tried to pantomime as she spoke. "You sleep
tonight, tomorrow you wake up. Tonoaki come. Make fight. You win, you go.
Tonoaki win, they torture you. You must act sick. No well. No strong." She
watched his face and he was studying her gravely but she had no idea how much if
anything he really understood.

John lay awake on his sleep pallet long after Morning Light had left. She was
upset about something, that much he understood, and it had to do with that *Toe-no-
ah-kee* character. He couldn't make sense out of the scramble of gestures she had
made other than it had something to do with him and the scowling brave.

Wani had been spending his nights with his sister ever since Gray Wolf had
left. It had been Singing Wind's idea. She knew very well her daughter's experiences with Tonoaki and would not have put it passed the arrogant brave to creep
into her hut and threaten her in the night. Singing Wind expressed her concerns to
Five Beavers before he had left for war, and Five Beavers had told Wani to sleep
in Gray Wolf's hut with his sister until her husband returned.

Now Wani was waiting for her. "What is wrong, my sister?" he asked when she
came back to the hut. He was finishing the stew she had left near the fire outdoors

for him. Her face looked solemn and her look was distant.

"I am sorry, Wani, I have much on my mind," she said distractedly and set about readying herself for bed. She picked up her comb, and undid her braid, combing out her hair and then, plaited it again.

"Tell me, I will help you," the boy said seriously.

She gave him a rueful smile. "I wish that you could."

"Tell me, sister. We can ponder your problems together."

She looked at him then and he saw tears welling in her eyes. "If I were a man..." she started to say and then stopped herself. "Wani, do you remember the yellow haired man who took me into the fort?" She saw her young brother tense with the reference to a time he did not wish to remember. He shook his head. "You do remember that someone took me into the fort and helped my injury?"

"No! Don't think about those times. I do not wish to talk of them. When I am older I will make the white pay. I cannot wait until the prisoner is made to pay."

"Wani!" she gasped and then exhaled softly. "Oh, Wani. I am tired of all the hate. This prisoner has done nothing wrong."

"He is white! He is like all the rest."

"But he is not like all the rest! This is the man who took pity upon me when the evil ones were ready to sell my body to everyone. This was the man who helped me."

"How do you know?"

"I recognize him."

"Does he recognize you?"

"No, I have grown up since he saw me."

"You may be wrong."

"Wani, I am not wrong. This is the man. And he has done us no harm. It is not right to repay his goodness with torture and death."

"He is a soldier. He kills our kind," the boy pointed out.

"Does he? Or does he kill the Hurons who are our enemies?" For the first time she saw a flicker of doubt cross Wani's face.

"He is Tonoaki's prisoner, there is nothing you can do," he said flatly.

"You asked me what was troubling me, now you know. I have asked Tonoaki to spare him, set him free... he will not. We are about to return evil for good and we will curse ourselves."

Wani scowled, then laid down on his sleep pallet and turned his back to his sister, signaling that he did not wish to talk anymore.

Morning was long in coming as large dark thunderclouds rolled in through the night. They obscured the sunrise and as the rain fell on the village, Morning Light wondered about Tonoaki's threat of a challenge.

She was exhausted, having slept very little, tossing, turning, and trying to think of a solution all through the night. If only Gray Wolf would return. He could challenge Tonoaki on her behalf. Hand to hand combat but not to the death. And if he won, as she was certain he would, they would free the man named *Sak*.

But Gray Wolf was not here and she had no one to be her champion. Tonoaki was determined to kill the white and only by bending her to infidelity would he relent. And if she agreed to Tonoaki's terms and he turned *Sak* over to her, how could it be explained? The very act would point out her guilt. Everyone would know. And what would be Gray Wolf's reaction? Would he understand that she had been put in a position of having no choice in a matter of honor? But could one dishonor be justified to prevent another dishonor? What was the difference?

The difference did not escape her. The difference was *Sak's* life. She might gain her husband's wrath or even lose her nose but *Sak* would keep his life. It was his freedom compared to a slow agonizing death through torture. The difference was she could not allow it to happen no matter what it cost her. The sachem was gone, Five Beavers was gone, even Quick Panther was gone. There was no one to turn to and the Council of Mothers did not see it her way. And then Morning Light had a thought that surfaced with the clarity of a sunbeam cutting through a clouded sky. She would cut *Sak* loose. Set him free! And pay whatever consequences she must.

She slipped a knife into the top of her moccasin before she draped the skin over her head and held it out with one hand to protect the bark holding the food from the rain. Swiftly she avoided the standing puddles and made her way to the shaman's lodge and the covered lean-to where the prisoner was tethered. He was awake and looked pleased to see her.

John sat up when he saw *Ohronkene Hahser* coming and pulled the skin he'd been given closer against the chill of the damp. She had been so upset yesterday, he couldn't help but have a certain sense of uneasy expectancy. He grinned his usual greeting but was aware of a heightened tension in her movements. She looked at him to give him his food but her eyes kept darting all around the empty grounds.

"Not many out this morning," he observed conversationally.

"*Inseks!*" she said with urgency, motioning him to eat and he got the impression he was to eat quickly. He began shoving his breakfast into his mouth when he saw her slip a knife out of her boot and attack the rawhide cording that bound his feet to his wooden brace.

"What are you doing?" he exclaimed in a low whisper. She drew the skin cover around him to hide his feet.

"*Raeks!* Eat!" she said and motioned, knowing he would need his strength. Looking quickly around again to assure herself the way was clear, she cut his wrist bindings. Then, she slipped the knife into his boot and pointed in the direction from which he had been brought. "Come quickly! We go now. You must run for your life!" she spoke low with agitation and there was no mistaking her meaning. She motioned him to follow her. She would lead him to a place in the palisade where there was an opening covered by brush.

He stood to follow her and suddenly realized his feet would not respond properly. After weeks of being trussed and shackled to the wood brace the muscles of his ankles had atrophied badly. He fell on his face only inches from his pallet.

Morning Light saw John go down and in frustration she tried to lift him as he sat helplessly rubbing his ankles, cursing his own inability to command them. Then, they both looked up and in the direction of sardonic laughter.

Tonoaki stood with his hands on his hips, oblivious to the pelting rain. "So you would help the white dog escape!" he growled accusingly, a hard grimace on his face. "Do you know the punishment for traitors?!!" he barked, enjoying being able to threaten her, having something else with which to leverage his desires.

"What escape?!" she replied back defensively, thinking quickly as she jut out her chin. "I only wished to prove the man incapable of defending himself. A man cannot fight you without his feet. He has lost all the feeling in his feet. I knew this. I have seen him rubbing his legs for days. You cannot challenge a man who cannot walk! The Council of Mothers will not allow it!" she said defiantly.

Tonoaki scowled at her and raised his arm in a threat to strike her for her disrespect but he pulled back at the last second, mastering his temper. She was no longer a slave but another warrior's wife.

"Watch the dog, woman!" he barked unnecessarily. John was not going anywhere. Tonoaki rushed off to get rope and came back to tether the prisoner by his neck, like a dog. With rawhide, he bound John's hands to his waist so he could not raise them but his feet were left free to walk. "Make certain he exercises well in the time I give him, woman! Two sun rises, no more," Tonoaki glared before he walked away.

Morning Light's heartbeat returned to normal and her breathing eased. They had gained two more days. But when Crooked Arrow appeared and took up a post nearby from where he did nothing but watch them, she knew they had also gained a watch guard.

She went to her hut, got more food and some salve and brought them back to the prisoner. She started to give him the food and then realized, trussed as he was, he could no longer feed himself. She set the food aside. They both knew the knife was still hidden within his right boot and together they managed to remove his boot without betraying the small weapon. With his boots removed, Morning Light began to massage his feet and ankles which, with his current binding, John, also, could not reach for himself. Her hands kneaded over them to get the blood flowing and work the muscles. She used the salve on his raw skin.

In time, with Morning Light's help, he was on his feet, barefoot. With John leaning heavily upon her for balance, she walked him around and back and forth within the boundary of his tether. As he grew more confident, she made him walk on his own. Then, she began to feed him as he walked. He walked to her, took a mouthful, walked away to chew and returned for another mouthful.

They kept at it all day despite the rain, taking short rest breaks during which John managed to relieve himself in her absence. He did not understand the squaw's compassion but he knew very well she was the only friend he had in this village. He was also beginning to sense that a confrontation with the big buck called Toe-no-ah-kee was coming and John cussed his lack of ability. His legs felt weak and his footing was stiff, his ankles cramped and inflexible.

The next morning John groaned with frustration. If he had thought his ankles were stiff yesterday, they were like wood today. Morning Light saw him try to walk toward her and she rushed to begin massaging again. She worked more salve into his muscles and they began again to exercise. As he walked he felt his ankles begin to flex.

She stayed with him all day but this time when it grew late she saw him settled down upon his pallet and placed his boots within hands' reach. He did not miss the significance of her action.

In the quiet of the night, John waited until he heard the light snoring of his watch guard. Then, he reached for the knife and began to cut at his bindings. There was only a sliver of moon and even that was hidden by many clouds. He had just cut through the last of the binding when he heard a distinct *thud.* Something fell.

"*Sak?*" it was a female voice whispering to him.

"Here," he whispered back. Then she was there, beside him, as he pulled on his boots.

"*Oksa!* Hurry!" She tugged at his arm and he followed her, stepping over the unconscious guard.

She led him to the hole in the palisade, gave him a water skin, a food packet and another knife and pushed him out. He didn't know how to thank her. He didn't understand why she was defying her people to free him but she did communicate clearly by her body language that he was to get away as far and as fast as he could. John paused for a moment, bent in to kissed her cheek and then took off. Morning Light slipped silently back to her hut where Wani was sleeping.

John considered that he had only until morning to cover as much distance as he possibly could before he would have pursuers. Possibly not even that long. When the guard came to, he would alert the village. But most likely, they would not try to track him until it was light. The girl had indicated the general direction he needed to go in. He moved as rapidly as he could, wasting no time, hoping and praying he would recognize some land formations as daylight came. He needed to spot something that would give him his bearings and help him to return to his fort.

Back in her hut, Morning Light lay sleepless waiting for indications that the escape had been discovered. Crooked Arrow would not remain unconscious forever. Then, she heard the shouts and saw the light of the torches reflected in the small window at the back of the hut. She knew Tonoaki was coming but she did not expect him to burst into the hut and drag her out. Wani, startled from his sleep, was no match against the fierce full-grown brave and he slipped out and ran for Yellow Rock.

"What did you do with him, woman?!" he shouted as he dragged Morning

Light by her hair from her sleep pallet out into the mud outside. She tripped and fell to her knees but he continued to drag her along the ground, her scalp burning from the pulling. She said nothing knowing her denials would only make him more furious. "He was *my* prize! Mine! How dare you help my prisoner escape! You shall regret this, woman. I will make you pay!"

"Tonoaki!!" Yellow Rock stood with his bow half drawn, an arrow notched into place. "Why do you threaten my sister?"

"The white dog is gone! Someone cut his leash and knocked out his guard."

"Someone? And do you accuse my sister?"

"I know it was her. I caught her trying to help him escape two days ago." Tonoaki roared back.

"I did not hear this. Who among you heard this?" Yellow Rock asked of the gathering crowd of women, half grown children, old men and the few braves left to guard the village.

Crooked Arrow walked up rubbing his head. "He told me to guard the prisoner so he could not escape," he muttered shamefaced.

"Did he tell you my sister had tried to help the prisoner escape?" Yellow Rock demanded.

Crooked Arrow shot a brief look at Tonoaki and then answered truthfully. "No," he grunted.

"Do you know who attacked you?" Yellow Rock persisted.

"I... it happened so fast. I did not see," uttered Crooked Arrow, not wanting to admit he had fallen asleep.

"So, you know not who attacked you. What proof have you that my sister is guilty, Tonoaki?"

Tonoaki pulled Morning Light to him roughly, his fingers biting into her arm. "Do you deny you helped him?" he hissed. Before she could say anything Yellow Rock shouted again.

"Take your hands from her, brother, or I will put an arrow through your heart!"

Tonoaki let go of Morning Light with a shove and she fell to the mud again.

Singing Wind came to pick her up.

"Look at this! Dragged from her sleep! Covered in mud! The girl is frightened out of her mind. And you expect her to answer your wild accusations? You brute! You would not dare do this if Gray Wolf was here. Do you like to frighten small children, too? I am taking her to my hut," the mother said resolutely. "We can sort this out in the morning. Come, Wani. This is enough. Thank you, Yellow Rock. Stay outside with Wani until I get some clean garments on her and then we would be pleased for you to stay the rest of the night with us."

Tense with rage, Tonoaki sputtered off in frustration.

Inside the hut, Singing Wind helped her daughter remove her muddy clothing and wash her face and hands as well as her knees and legs.

"I do not know if you are guilty or not," she whispered to Morning Light, "I do not want to know. But say nothing. Admit nothing, deny nothing. Say nothing until Gray Wolf returns. Do you hear me?"

Morning Light nodded.

The next morning under the threat of more rain they met in the Council Circle.

"What matters this white man?" the shaman was saying. "He is only one man. He stumbled unarmed into your presence. And now he has disappeared. Perhaps the Great Spirit allowed him to come here and now the Great Spirit has taken him back."

Tonoaki clenched his teeth. The old man was growing more tedious every day. But the brave could not deny the argument the others had presented. It made no sense for the remaining braves to go out to track down one lone white who had done them no harm and leave the village defenseless with the threat of the Huron and Algonquin very real.

In reality, the white meant nothing to him. He had, in fact, been willing to let the prisoner go himself in exchange for *Ohronkene Hahser's* favors. It was only because of her ability to thwart him that he felt such rage. And he had no proof of her duplicity although he knew as certainly as he drew breath that she had helped the prisoner escape. And, he knew that she knew that he knew this and yet she was safe from his retribution and this enraged him further. Oh, what he would give to have just one hour alone with her. He wanted to master her, conquer her, force her to accept him. He wanted to spend himself between her thighs. Pound her into submission. He wanted to feel those long legs locked around him as he ravished her with his mouth. It didn't even have anything to do with his rivalry with Gray Wolf anymore. She had become an obsession, a fever in his blood.

# *Chapter 21*

The French commander of the small fort realized it was hopeless. Under a white flag of truce he agreed to surrender with no other condition but that his wife and two children be allowed safe escort back to Quebec, a short trip over land, and then a longer but more comfortable journey by river.

The English commander being a gentleman of honor, agreed. *Madame Augine de Marron*, a striking woman in her early thirties with auburn hair, and her young daughter Gabernette and son, Édouard, bid a tearful goodbye to *Le Commander Monsieur de Marron*. *Le Commander* had successfully convinced his wife that he would join her in due time. He must surrender the fort. He must submit to being a prisoner of war and eventually, there would be a prisoner exchange. The English would trade him for some officer they had lost and he would see them all again in Quebec. Because Pa-pa said it, because Ma-ma believed it, Gabernette and Édouard believed it as well. Little ten year old Édouard was to be the man and look after his ma-ma and fourteen year old sister, his pa-pa told him. With a noble air of composure the small party left the fort with a half dozen French soldiers as escort.

It had only just been decided that the warriors had pressed north far enough. A scout had told them the French fort was already taken and they had decided it was time to head southward again. They had no notion of the pact made at the fort, the agreement for safe escort to the *de Marron* family. They only thought of easy booty when they saw the carriage slowly progressing over the rough road.

Overwhelming the six soldiers was almost ridiculously easy and when they found the women in the carriage it was to them as if a gift from the *manitous*. They were ripe with lust. Then, there was a pistol which appeared out of nowhere. As Moose Horn reached into the carriage and struggled with the red-haired female, the pistol went off, and the shot hit the sachem full in the chest. He sank to the ground, his brother Five Beavers ran to his side. In shock that she had actually killed someone, Madame grew silent and still, making it easy for Moose Horn and everyone else to turn their attention to the last seconds of the dying warrior.

"You are sachem now, my brother," he rasped, and then looked like he wanted to say more but didn't. With a final exhale, he was dead. Five Beavers looked to the woman. She would die for that but not before they had their revenge. Pulling the hysterical *Madame De Marron* from the carriage to the ground, Five Beavers ordered Moose Horn and Gray Wolf to hold her while he dragged out young Édouard before her. The child was too startled to say a word. Five Beavers saw the wild roundness of the red-haired one's dark blue eyes as he clutched the boy by the throat, lifting him so his toes barely touched the ground. Nimbly, Five Beavers produced his razor sharp knife and gutted the boy with one hand, leaving his limp body to drop to the ground in a puddle of his own blood and viscera. The boy was still moaning as his mother screamed madly, thrashing against her captors. The screams increased when Quick Panther dragged her daughter out of the carriage next. The fair young girl was cringing and made a pathetic attempt at fighting the warrior off. She was crying hysterically, looking weak and without dignity as he ripped her clothing from her thin body just blossoming into a woman's figure. Striking her into submission, he mauled her over and took her violently. In the frenzy that followed they all raped the two females, some more than once. Even Gray Wolf avenged the death of his sachem upon the red-haired woman in an act that was nothing more than a vengeful punishment with no association to normal lust or mating. When, at last, the warriors had finished their frenzy of rape, the females lay moaning upon the ground. Their faces were puffed and swollen, red, blotched, growing black and blue, streaked with small lines of blood where the skin was split, and becoming more and more unrecognizable by the minute. Five Beavers bent quickly and slit the females' throats without a single thought to the lives they were ending. Then they all turned to mourn their dead sachem.

§

The women and children were at the river bathing and washing. It was customarily a time for relaxing, for gossiping, for visiting, for exchanging remedies for common maladies like poison ivy and bee stings. For the children, it was an opportunity to practice their swimming skills and expend energy in exercise. Since war had been declared, however, trips to the river outside the safety of the palisade for other than fetching up water had been reduced to once every four or five days and the time spent there was shortened to only the time necessary for the actual tasks of washing and bathing quickly. The old men who were there to guard them, were too nervous to allow the women and children to linger.

"It won't be long now," Singing Wind said as she scrubbed her plump form then bent her knees to submerge lower into the river and rinse off. "Five Beavers and Gray Wolf and the rest of our men will come home soon."

Little Smoke agreed. "I saw a yellow leaf yesterday. Summer will be leaving us in another moon."

"And you think they will come home then?" Morning Light asked anxiously as Little Smoke resurfaced from dunking her head under the water to rinse her hair.

"Of course," replied Little Smoke, squeezing the water from her mass of hair and turning her attention to her small bundle of laundry. "No one stays out in the winter to fight. It is not a good time and it is too easy to be seen in the naked forest."

"Besides, the men know they must help with provisions for the dead season. A warrior does not leave his family without provisions," Singing Wind said reassuringly.

"I never thought it would be so long. They have been gone almost four moons," Morning Light replied quietly. Her mother nodded. They didn't like to dwell on the fact that they had not seen their men for so long. The last message received had been over a moon ago when a runner had come simply to tell all that they were going north and everyone was well. Morning Light herself had ducked beneath the water's surface and upon coming up she looked up and out and caught sight of Tonoaki watching her from a distance. He was not part of the detail entrusted to guard them while bathing and he should not have been where he was. She said nothing but kept her body below the water's surface and swam around so her back was to him.

"But the winter to come will be full of pleasure," her mother smiled at her. "And what a gift you are preparing for your husband," she added conspiratorially.

Morning Light then smiled herself, all thoughts of Tonoaki leaving her as she instinctively brought her hand to her belly beneath the water. It was no longer as flat as it always had been but compared to other women she was still slender and no one had yet guessed that she was with child. It was a secret only her mother knew. The child would come in the month of the Long Nights when the days were shortest. How she longed to see Gray Wolf and share her good news before the entire village knew it.

"She still keeps from everyone," Singing Wind sighed and Morning Light followed the direction of her mother's eyes to see Moon-On-Mist bathing alone with her two children, apart from everyone. "She was too vain about her looks and now she cannot bear the thought of any seeing her as she is. But such aloneness is not good. It is poison to the spirit. I will try again tonight to go to her and share some time. I will reassure her that she is welcome to join us."

Morning Light worked out in her garden when all the other women were working in their gardens. She bathed with them. She always had company going to the latrine. She kept to their community and never went anywhere even within the limits of the palisade without the company of others. If there was not another woman, then Wani was her companion, and at night Yellow Rock was always there to check in on her and Wani as they stayed in her hut. Tonoaki was finding it impossible to catch her alone. As his frustration grew, it took him beyond seeking retribution for his prisoner's escape. He never even thought of the white anymore. His thoughts, his dreams were filled with Morning Light. And deep within his secret heart he prayed for Gray Wolf's death.

Morning Light awoke. She was very thirsty and as she arose from her sleeping furs she noted the chill in the air. She squat over the large covered bowl used for such purpose and passed her water. She needed to eat quickly to stop the nausea that still arose within her each morning. She took a piece of yesterday's bread then she groaned quietly when she saw the water-bag. She had asked Wani to fill it yesterday evening and he had forgotten to do so. It was empty.

Wani was still sleeping. She stepped out of the hut. The mists of the morning lay thick in the air of the village and all was very quiet. Everyone slept. She went back into the hut, pulled on her moccasins and picked up the water-bag. She would slip down to the river, fill it and return. No one would know. The mists would hide her.

It was a peculiar feeling to be alone and by herself after so long a time. Morning Light savored the feeling as she held the water-bag beneath the surface of the running water and watched it fill. Not even the birds were awake. The birds were a calendar unto themselves. All knew that until they began to gather in flocks and head southward as they did each year, summer was still in its fullness. Morning Light inhaled deeply, smelling the scent of the forest, the water, the rich earth around her and offered up a small prayer to the Great Spirit to see her husband safely home. Then, she picked up her water-bag and turned to bump solidly into Tonoaki.

A small startled cry escaped her lips before she stepped back a short step. She could retreat no further without going into the river itself. Her heart was pounding in fear of what he intended to do.

"Please let me pass," she said softly forcing a calm but he said nothing. He took the water-bag from her and she released it immediately. He dropped the bag to the ground beside them and grabbed her to him. "Noooo," she struggled but his mouth was upon her's blocking all sounds.

She was afraid to fight, afraid of what harm might come to the child within her and he mistook her limited struggle for a token. His tongue licked her cheeks. She was as food to a starving man, water to a desert, air to one who is drowning. He was in a fever of desire, nurtured by months of frustration and yearning, months of sensual dreams and coveting her body, of catching glimpses of her perfect curves from a distance. His hands flew over her, grasping, touching, squeezing, and although she struggled it was no more than the struggle of a bird.

He almost laughed. She wanted him, too, he told himself. She was a woman of passion and had been without a man for many moons. But she must give a pretense, a show of defense, something to sooth her pride and salve her conscience. He understood. She did not want to think of herself as an unfaithful wife. He would overcome her struggles, he would give her no choice, and she would be glad. She would be his at last.

Morning Light felt him pushing her to the ground and she struggled but lost her balance. Only his arms kept her from falling, and she had gripped them instinctively to stay her fall. Then she was down and his weight was upon her, his legs pinning her legs down, his body heavy upon hers, heavy upon her belly. His hands bruised her tender breasts.

"No, Tonoaki, you must not. Please, you cannot do this. No, no...please, I ... I..."

He wasn't listening. He sucked fiercely at the lushness of her breasts. One hand covering her mouth, one jerking away her tunic skirt, exposing the perfection of her thighs. He yanked away his own breech-cloth and was tearing hers from her.

It was Buckskins all over again! Too powerful to struggle against and he was going to tear her asunder without mercy, without care! Morning Light relived the blinding streaks of pain before Tonoaki even entered her, she screamed but his hand was again covering her mouth, she could not breathe. Then, her body went limp as she lost consciousness.

Tonoaki wanted only the relief he could find within her. After months of lustful yearning, she was suddenly his to have and hold, to plummet and rub against. He felt her scream into his mouth and mistook it for a scream of pleasure, his response was to thrust into her deeply. He felt her go limp but he was now too involved, too driven as he stroked back and forth immediately transported by the mindless wave of pleasure into a swirl of sensations building rapidly toward the explosion to come. Again he buried himself deeply within her as he felt his seed burst powerfully into her. It was over very quickly and slowly his senses returned. He was drained but so pleasantly drained, and he pushed himself back to look at her. It was then that he realized her mind was not there.

He pulled back quickly. His first fear was that she was dead. He listened for breathing, heard nothing, but his panic was stanched when he noticed the blood vessel at her neck pulsing. She was alive. His eyes moved to her thighs, the triangle between her legs, he bent to kiss it reverently but noticed then the bulge at her belly. What was this bulge? He had not seen it before. His hand moved over it and he felt a hardness within the softness of her relaxed muscles. He drew back from her, self-revulsion creeping over him. He replaced her breech-cloth. He quickly tugged on his own.

She was with child! Was that why she had not fought him like the wildcat he knew she could be? But what had happened? Where had her mind gone and how long would it be in returning? Tonoaki sat back and pulled down her tunic top and re-wrapped her skirt. His heart was beating fiercely as panic took hold of him and he thought of what her family might do to him. He stood. He could not carry her back. Her people would see. He must leave her as she was. She had come to get water and she had passed out. All else had been a dream, a dream she would not want to admit to. When she came to, she would come in on her own... or someone else could find her. He backed away and silently crept back into the palisade via the hole behind the brush. The fogs were still thick as he made his way to his own hut and crawled into his furs pretending to sleep.

Time seemed to crawl by. It had not been his intent to leave her beyond the defenses of the palisade, exposed to dangers. He wanted to hear some sign that she was missed, that someone was looking for her. That she had returned. He strained to hear but heard nothing but the quiet of the fog.

There - now he heard the sound of voices. A child's voice... Wani, perhaps. Wani had awakened and missed his sister. He would be telling her mother, running to Yellow Rock. They would look for her now.

In a short time, Singing Wind had the entire village roused and looking for Morning Light. Yellow Rock ran to Tonoaki's hut and called to him.

"Tonoaki! I would speak with you."

"What is it?" he staggered slightly pretending to be roused from sleep.

"Have you seen *Ohronkene Hahser*?"

"No... is something wrong?"

"She is missing."

"She is not here," he held his door flap open for Yellow Rock to see inside. "How long has she..." but Yellow Rock was already gone.

Little Smoke and several other mothers stayed to watch all the young ones. All others searched. Tonoaki joined in the search, how could he not? It would have been too suspicious for him not to. In a short time, it was determined she was not within the palisade. Every nook and cranny had been scoured. The latrines had been checked and the search parties proceeded outside the palisades into the woods, down to the river.

It was Yellow Rock and Crooked Arrow who found her, lying on the ground, her water-bag beside her. It seemed pretty clear that she had gone to get water and fainted. Her mother explained *Ohronkene Hahser* was with child and so it did not seem so strange. But it was a deep faint, for she was still unconscious. They carried her back to her hut and laid her softly onto her sleeping furs.

Singing Wind shooed everyone outside and then went back to examine her daughter. She wanted to make certain Morning Light was not bleeding, that nothing had happened to the baby. The older squaw tugged aside her daughter's breech-cloth and was disturbed by the evidence she found there of a man. The smell of his seed was still strong and clinging to her daughter. Singing Wind wiped her daughter clean.

The older squaw could not believe that her daughter had willingly done this. And if not willingly, then she had been raped. Had she been struck unconscious? Singing Wind felt her daughter's head. There were no lumps, no bumps, no bruises until she saw Morning Light's breasts. Purple markings from rough handling or what one might have called "love bites" appeared on them. She had been raped! And the experience had left her unconscious. Who could have done this?!

There were only a few young men left in the village. Tonoaki hated her for his prisoner's escape. Crooked Arrow had a young woman of his own and was working hard to accumulate the bride price to conclude the arrangement for marriage. Yellow Rock was her first cousin, her protector. That left only Swimming Turtle. Could Swimming Turtle do such a thing? But he was the only one possible. Singing Wind was stunned at her own conclusions.

She went through her reasoning again. She knew her daughter. Morning Light loved Gray Wolf deeply, rejoiced in carrying his child and would never be unfaithful to him. But it was also obvious that a man had taken her very recently. That meant she had to have been forced... a violation of all the ancient laws. No warrior could retain his self-respect if he took a free woman by force, and to take another's wife by force was a blood crime. Oh, by the *manitous*, it was hard to accept that one of their own could have done this thing. And Swimming Turtle was so young, younger than Yellow Rock, and seemed such a shy and awkward youth. She would have never imagined him to be capable of such a thing. Did he not realize his life would not be worth dandelion seed when Gray Wolf returned? Singing Wind shook her head and covered her daughter again. When Morning Light awoke certainly she should be able to tell them exactly what had happened. There was an outside chance a stranger could have done this for it was not the Indian way to rape and leave one of their own. But would she not have been taken as a prisoner, a captive, a slave by a stranger? Yes, it had to be one of their own.

It was early afternoon when Morning Light finally awoke to find her mother sitting at her side.

"What is it, Mother?"

"How do you feel, my daughter?"

"I feel fine. Why are you here? What time is it? The hour grows late. Why did no one wake me? I have much to do," she said as she started to get up. Singing Wind's hand stayed her.

"Do you remember this morning?"

"This morning?" The young squaw smiled sheepishly. "Have I slept through the entire morning?"

Singing Wind was shaking her head. "No, daughter, you were up very early."

"I was?"

"Do you not remember?"

Morning Light frowned. "No, are you certain?"

"You went to fetch water. You were found by the river."

"I was found?" her puzzlement deepened. "Why do I not remember this?"

"I was hoping you could tell me. "You were not conscious. You fainted and lay on the riverbank. But you have no injuries."

Morning Light gasped, her hands flying to her stomach. "The baby?"

"All is well," her mother reassured her. "But it disturbs me that you do not remember going to the river. Wani awoke and you were gone. Everyone was searching for you. We found you by the river and carried you back here. Are you certain you can remember nothing?"

The girl quietly nodded her head. "I am very hungry, Mother, please... I must eat something now or my stomach will be ill."

Singing Wind decided if Morning Light did not remember what had happened to her then it was a thing better left buried. There was no reason to tell her she had been raped if she did not remember it and could not identify her attacker. Singing Wind hurried to ready a bowl of stew for her daughter.


"Yellow Rock," Tonoaki called out to the young brave as he saw him going to the latrine. He fell in along side him and asked as casually as he could, "How is your sister?"

"She seems to be well. My father says women are prone to many strange things when they are with child," he laughed. "She cannot even remember going to the river this morning. She awoke and thought she had slept late."

"Hmmm" Tonoaki grunted, not allowing his relief to show. "Well, it is good that she is well."

Yellow Rock nodded.

Tonoaki left Yellow Rock to his business and wandered into the forest to be alone. So she had revived none the worse but did she really not remember? Was that possible? Or was she just claiming not to remember? He hoped she really didn't remember. He felt shame. Never had he had to force a woman. He was Tonoaki, and women had always found him attractive. His women all came to him willingly, ever since he had first become a man. He remembered the lusty widow who had first led him to her bed and taught him how to please her. She had told him women would always want him.

He had thought *Ohronkene Hahser* had wanted him, he told himself, or it would not have happened. Then, he felt his conscience respond that she had never given him the slightest encouragement, not even when he was trying to court her. He must be honest with himself above all things. The truth was he was too blinded by his own lust and need to know if she wanted him or not. No, that was not truth either. He was too blinded by his need and lust to *care* if she wanted him. He had wanted her and that was all that had been important to him. He had been wanting her for so long and she was the only female who had ever rejected him. He had grown impatient with the rejection. He had not even been able to blackmail her into accepting him. His pride had smarted with the rejection. He hadn't been able to accept that she didn't want him. And now?

Now, he hoped and prayed that she would never remember what he had done for he felt very small in his own eyes and knew that he could not but become exceedingly small in hers if she remembered.

§

Lieutenant Power crawled on his belly, Indian style, using his elbows to propel himself. He carried his musket in the cradle of his bent arms. It wasn't the proper way for an officer to move about, but then he had been promoted from the ranks when the former lieutenant had been shot threw with six arrows walking *properly*. So much for what is proper in Indian country.

Steady effort brought John to the crest of a hill and very slowly he peered over. He saw nothing with his naked eyes and then quietly took out the spyglass he had inherited from his luckless Pink Cheek. With patience he surveyed every inch of the countryside through the glass. Foliage was dense, creating a thick canopy that was almost impossible to see through. Then, he saw them, snaking along the rim at the far side of the valley.

John continued to study them for awhile, then pulled back from the rim and scrambled down to report to his captain. As he walked back toward the grove along the small creek where Captain Greeley had chosen to bivouac what was left of their company, he couldn't help but notice how many of their men were wounded in one fashion or another. Head wounds, legs, arms, chests. They were one damn pitiful sight and hardly up to fighting off an attack of fifty fresh warriors.

"Spotted the hostiles, sir," John said, saluting as he did. "Directly across the valley, Captain."

"How many?" asked Greeley who himself was nursing a lacerated hand that had been caught by a warrior wielding a knife before John had shot him in the head.

"My best guess is about fifty."

"Fifty..." the captain sighed softly.

"They seem to be heading straight for us, sir. Once they get into the grass it might take them all day but eventually they'll be here. Of course, the sea of grass is perfect cover."

"Of course," Greeley grunted. "Any suggestions, Power?"

"Only that we better act fast."

"Tell me something I do not know, Lieutenant," he replied irritably. Just then a corporal came up to the captain's tent.

"Sir?"

"At ease, Corporal," replied Greeley, wearily returning the salute.

"Yes, sir. I was sent to advise you that Captain Kipling is arriving with two dozen friendly hostiles to assist, sir," the corporal uttered this last in such a mechanical manner as to say he had almost certainly memorized his message.

"Friendly hostiles! Now what the blessed... what is that supposed to mean?" growled Greeley.

"Sir, I think it means these injuns are on our side," whispered the corporal.

"To be sure, to be sure," sighed the captain. Obviously, the young corporal didn't understand the irony. "But why not *allies* or *friends*? If they aren't hostile to us, then they should not be termed *hostiles*!" he barked.

"Yes, sir. But beggin' your pardon, sir. These is the fiercest of the Five Nations and they don't much like us even though they are treaty bound to be on our side right now."

"Great! That's exactly what we need, Indians who resent having to keep from slitting our throats and taking our scalps." Greeley turned in disgust. "Two dozen more men, Power. Can you use them?"

"We can use every single one, sir," John replied.

"All right. Of course, you do realize you cannot *command* an Indian, don't you? You simply explain what you want to accomplish and suggest how they might assist you in doing the same. If they agree and have a mind to help they will and if the omens or the spirits or the *manitous* or the signs are against it, they won't lift a finger. The moral to this is... don't count on them. They are only extra help... maybe... hopefully… understand?"

"Yes, Captain."

"All right. Dismissed."

"Captain?" John said hesitantly.

"Yes? What is it?"

"Begging your pardon, sir, but who's looked at your hand? Has Wicke seen it?"

"If Wicke isn't drunk he has enough men to look after. This is nothing," the captain said dismissively as he waved his injured hand with its filthy bandage.

"Sir, an injury like that is never *nothing*. If you get a bad infection, gangrene can set in and you could lose your hand altogether or possibly your life. I am assuming you are right handed? It would be a terrible loss. Could I look at it?"

The captain looked at John curiously and nodded a mute approval as he held out his hand.

John carefully unwrapped the dirty rag and inspected the wound seeing the captain wince.

"Sir, you already have the start of an infection. If I may, I would like to dress this for you properly." The other nodded. "Please sit down," John suggested, then called for one of the men outside to run to his tent and bring his bag, a black bag stored under his cot. "And someone bring me a pitcher of boiled water, not boiling hot but thoroughly boiled."

Deftly John scrubbed his hands thoroughly as he waited for his medical bag. When it arrived, he poured out a modest shallow pan of alcohol from the bottle within. After rinsing his own hands, and feeling the alcohol bite on a torn cuticle or two, he said, "I am sorry, sir, but this is very necessary... and it's going to hurt like hell." Without hesitation, he took the captain's hand and pushed it into the pan. Captain Greeley reacted somewhat violently and swore profusely.

"I'm sorry, sir. We will flush it as soon as that water arrives." Just then a private arrived carrying a pot of water. "Has that been boiled?" John barked.

"Yes, sir, cook says it were on the fire this mornin'."

John lifted the hand out and proceeded to clean and flush out the wound with the boiled water, scraping pus and causing fresh bleeding. When he had assured himself that the wound was clean, he paused. "This needs to be stitched, sir, to keep the dirt out." Assuming permission, John fetched his needle and silk thread, threaded the sturdy needle and then soaked them both in the bowl of alcohol.

Compared to the throbbing of his alcohol bath, the stitching was nothing. Greeley poured himself a drink from his personal flask with his left hand.

When John finished stitching the wound, he bandaged the hand in clean linen. "I'll need to check that every day," he said at last.

"Where did you study?" Captain Greeley asked.

"In Europe... France... Switzerland," John responded flatly.

"So what the hell is an educated... I could tell you were raised a notch above our average frontier recruit... an educated sawbones doing getting his ass shot at on the front lines?"

"It's *physician*, sir, or *doctor*... not *sawbones*."

Greeley downed his shot and with a laugh he poured himself another.

"My question remains the same, Power. Why did you not tell us? There was no need to work yourself up from a private... yes, I've seen your records. And why the hell have you not been taking care of the men from the start? You've been wasting yourself!"

"It's personal, sir, but for a long time I just didn't feel like a doctor."

"Well, start feeling like one because you are taking over the surgery. As soon as we're over this next challenge, Wicke works for you. Understood? I will inform him. He's lucky I haven't kicked his ass out long ago... but some help is better than no help."

John left the tent with mixed emotions. He couldn't accept the thought of doing nothing while the captain's hand became gangrenous and in need of amputation. Not when he knew about the microbes and what needed to be done. Did that mean he could devote himself once more to helping people to heal?

That he had spent a good many weeks being nursed back to health by an Indian woman too beautiful to describe, did not keep John from remembering that she had helped him escape because the others in the tribe were ready to kill him off as soon as he had been declared well. It was a strange code these Indians had. It was all right to torture and kill a man as long as he was in basically good health. The unit scout had explained that to him upon his being reunited with his company. John wondered if he'd ever understand the Indians. How had his mother made such good friends with them? Or were the different tribes so very different from each other? Perhaps he never would understand them but they certainly were intriguing.

He thought of all the men he had seen with injuries; men who needed to heal so they could go out and take another chance at being killed. It was ironic but there was a difference.

Gray Wolf sat sharpening his iron tomahawk with a whet stone. He had acquired several muskets over the summer, during the very first skirmish they had had with the Algonquin who had been given muskets by the French. But when one was in the thick of the fighting there was no time to reload a musket and the tomahawk was indispensable. Gray Wolf sat patiently sharpening and waiting.

They had had a very busy two months encountering enough Algonquin and Huron to satisfy their blood-lust and add significantly to their scalp belts. They had also added to their personal wealth. Gray Wolf alone had acquired several steel knives, an additional iron tomahawk, several muskets, powder, shot, a pony, and a pack mule loaded with other things taken during the raid on the French trading post. The spoils had been divided up equally, others in his party from their village had very similar booty and horses from the carriage they had stopped. They were all ready to go home.

The tall and virile brave thought more and more often of his young wife and longed to return to her and share the pleasure they had with one another. He had special gifts for her. The pack mule carried several bolts of white man's cloth in vivid shades of colored calico. *Ohronkene Hahser* would like this, he was sure, and he could not wait to see her eyes light up in delight. He also had the pearl ear-rings which he wished to see dangling from her delicate ears. They would glow against her golden skin and warm black hair. He smiled to himself as he thought of her.

John had a talk with the leaders of the "friendly hostiles." He was thankful that the company scout could interpret for him as he had no talent with these heathen tongues. He explained the Algonquin had been spotted on the other side of the valley and were likely on their way over.

Five Beavers, who was the recognized sachem now that his brother had been killed, suggested immediately that they fire the meadow grass. By shooting flaming arrows simultaneously they could start a fire ring that would trap the enemy.

Captains Greeley and Ripley agreed it was worth a try. And with two dozen more hands to help they just might pull it off. This was the last group of Algonquin who had not left to return to the north. If they could wipe out this group, or so demoralize them that they went packing for home, it would be the end of the fighting for another year. And they could all hope that with the new year might come a new treaty.

The soldiers had the horses which could cover the perimeter of the valley far faster than a man on foot. The problem was the horses stood tall above the grass and any rider would be exposed as a target for anyone in the grasses.

John asked for six volunteers from his own men. "I want good horsemen, men who can ride hanging off the side of the horse if necessary and control a horse dragging fire. You're going to be exposed up there on a mount, make no mistake."

Six men stepped forward.

"Good," he said quickly, and turned to the scout interpreter. "Explain that I need their fastest runners," he turned toward the warriors. "We'll send runners down each side of the valley. They won't be so exposed as the horsemen and, up on the hillsides a man on foot will make better time than a horse. They will need to run close enough to the far end of the valley to be within range so they can torch the far end using flaming arrows. Once the runners are within reach of the end of the valley and start their fires, we will send the horses dragging burning bales to ignite the sides. Three riders on each side so if one is downed the others can keep going.

"It's important we ring the enemy as quickly as possible. Once the sides and end are burning the only way they can come is this way," John explained, "and before they can reach us we will start the fires here. They should end up in a fire ring."

"It's a good plan, Power," Greeley nodded his approval as the scout explained the plan to the warriors. "With luck it will work."

"Thank you, sir," John saluted, "we need to begin immediately."

Gray Wolf and Quick Panther were among the fastest runners of the tribe. Both were lean, strong, and well conditioned. Each took a different side of the valley and left immediately along with the other runners. They took all the fire-starting paraphernalia they could possibly need. They chose their paths amidst the cover of small trees, bushes, and tall grasses.

John crawled back up to monitor the valley. With his spyglass he could see the runners making their way down the sides of the valley. So much depended on good timing and the element of surprise. He searched the grasses for some sign of the hostiles. He couldn't detect a thing. They had to be on all fours which would make their progress slow but he didn't doubt that they were making better time than one might expect. After twenty long minutes he lost sight of the runners. After, perhaps, twenty more minutes John saw a series of flaming arrows arc up toward the far end of the valley.

"It's time to send the horses," he rasped to a sergeant waiting beneath him.

"Yes, sir," the man promptly responded and gave the signal.

John watched the horses and riders take off, three in each direction, running the perimeter of the valley. The burning bales they dragged ignited the tall dry grass quickly and soon smoke was making it difficult to see. Arrows began flying at the riders who rode low on their horses, urging their mounts to greater speed. Then one of the riders fell and his mount took off unguided and panicked with the smell of wildfire in its nostrils. The animal began to climb the hillside, dragging the burning bale with it, continuing to ignite everything in its path until the bale became caught and the animal with it. Screaming in fear, the horse pulled at its tethers until fire ate through the roping and set the animal free. It galloped off out of sight.

John saw that the far end of the valley was now enveloped in flame and smoke. The runners had done their jobs well. It was time to start the fires at their end of the meadow. John backed off from the ridge and ran down to the remaining waiting Indians. With flaming arrows they ignited the last side of the valley, the closest side. The entire meadow was now encircled in a wall of flames.

The Algonquin warrior smelled of rancid bear grease and snake venom but he was so used to the smells that they did not bother him. He scratched absentmindedly at his crotch as he sat in the fork of a large maple tree. He envied his brothers who were crossing the valley for the scalps they would take. He prided himself on the variety of color he had on his scalp belt and was not pleased to lose this opportunity to add to it. The whites on the other end of the valley were weak and wounded. It would be a memorable end to the season of killing.

He had been left behind on the ridge to watch for enemy coming from the rear. To signal if he saw any and to intercept any runner from fellow bands come south this season. As he sat in the tree looking out over the valley, he saw the runners working their way around toward him but did not immediately comprehend why they came. They were too few to launch an effective attack from the rear. The Algonquin scouts had reported this pocket of enemy too few in able bodied numbers to be much of a challenge at all. It made no sense that they should split up their warriors and diminish the numbers left to stand against the attack. Surely they knew the attack was coming.

Then, he saw the fire arrows launched into the meadow grass and he understood. He was helpless to do anything to prevent it when suddenly the wall of flame was growing between him and his comrades. A wall that once completed would consume all the braves of his war party and leave him alone to return in shame to his tribe.

In frustrated rage, the Algonquin warrior sat rigidly in his perch and when he saw one of those responsible for this circumstance he dropped to the ground and drew arrow in bow, waiting and aiming to let the Mohawk dog see who would take his life. The arrow left the bow and hit its mark sinking deeply into Gray Wolf's chest.

Gray Wolf felt the burn in his flesh at the same time as he saw the Algonquin step from the tree and show himself arrogantly, defiantly. Knowing he had just received a mortal blow, Gray Wolf had no thought but to strike back. With strength that denied his mortal wound, he hurled his tomahawk and took satisfaction in seeing it embed itself in the Algonquin's skull. The startled expression was frozen on the face of the enemy warrior. He was dead before he hit the ground and Gray Wolf was left with his life slowing oozing from his own body.


The fire burned for hours sending billows of black smoke high into the air. The horsemen came back grinning out from behind black sooty faces. Their smiles vanished for a moment when they lifted down the body of their fallen comrade. Several arrows protruded from his shoulder and one from his leg but he was still alive.

"Good work men," Captain Greeley said in gratitude. "Someone tend to that man's wounds."

"Thank you, sir," responded the rider whose buddy had fallen.

"Did you see the runners?" John asked immediately.

"Sorry, Lieutenant. I didn't see anything moving," responded one.

"I didn't either."

"Neither did I."

"Well, like as not, they're holed up in the forest where they could find some decent air to breathe," John replied. "We'll go out looking for them just as soon as the wind blows some of that away.

When the fire had completely burned itself out, John gathered a detail to search for survivors and get a body count. He took eight men, a scout and a couple of the Indians, all mounted. They rode the right perimeter of the valley as the middle ground had yet to cool off.

At the far side of the valley they began looking for the runners. Quick Panther had retreated in exhaustion after torching his part of the valley floor. When he heard the riders coming, he showed himself.

"Quick Panther! It is good to find you. Have you seen Gray Wolf or the others?" Five Beavers asked authoritatively.

Quick Panther shook his head. "I have seen nothing since we torched the grasses," he replied.

"We must continue to look," said Five Beavers.

The riders eventually picked up all the other runners with only Gray Wolf left unaccounted for.

The Indians jumped down from the horses and began to look on foot, searching for signs and watching for tracks. They spread out in a widening area and it was Quick Panther who finally came upon him.

Gray Wolf was sitting up against a tree. He was so still that Quick Panther thought for a moment he was dead, then decided he was sleeping. It was just like Gray Wolf to be confident enough to catch a nap after toasting the enemy.

"Brother!" he called smiling and waving, and saw Gray Wolf open his eyes. But as he came closer, Quick Panther saw the blood seeping out from the warrior's chest and his smile vanished. An arrow was embedded deeply, much too close to the heart. Quick Panther said nothing but dropped to his knees beside the dying warrior. "Brother," Quick Panther stated simply but the one word said everything. It was a cruel irony that Gray Wolf should now be mortally wounded when they were ready to go home but a warrior must always be prepared to die. A show of pity would be the gravest insult. Quick Panther gave an Indian cry that echoed through the forest and let the others know he had found their comrade. After inspecting the body yards away with the tomahawk wedged in its skull, Quick Panther sat with Gray Wolf waiting on the others to arrive.

"We will take you to camp," said Five Beavers when he approached.

"No. I will die here," Gray Wolf said quietly. His body had grown very cold and he was feeling light headed. Five Beavers nodded. "See that my wife gets my share."

"Yes."

"Here..." Gray Wolf reached for his waist pouch. "This is for her. Tell her... tell her simply that I died with her name on my lips and her love in my heart." Then Gray Wolf gathered his remaining strength and shouted "Ohhhhhronnnnkene Hahhhhhhsssser!!!!" with his last breath.

"What did he say?" asked John who had arrived upon the scene.

"He called his wife's name," responded the scout. "*Ohronkene Hahser*."

"O-ron-keenee-hah-ser?" asked John. "Find out if these warriors are from a village over on Possum Creek. Ask if this person is unusually beautiful, very tall for an Indian girl, slender with wavy soft hair, instead of straight?"

The scout spoke briefly with Moose Horn and Five Beavers. Then he turned to John. "They want to know how you know Gray Wolf's woman."

"She is the person who saved my life!"

With the aid of an interpreter, John described how he and his men had been set upon by the Huron earlier in the season. How he had stumbled into the group from the village and how a warrior by the name of Toe-no-ah-kee had claimed him and left him in the care of the squaw to recuperate. John wasn't too sure how far he should go in telling the whole story and held back on the details of the squaw actually helping him to escape. He didn't want any retribution to fall upon the young woman.

"I would like to go with you," John added, waiting for the interpreter to translate. "I would like to pay my respects concerning her husband's death. I would also like to ask her a question which is personal to me."

Five Beavers nodded. He was not looking forward as keenly now to going home himself. His second wife, Singing Wind, would be in sorrow for her daughter. Her daughter, Gray Wolf's wife, would be stricken with grief. Perhaps, if she had shown such interest in the white man, there would be some good in his coming with them.

Gray Wolf's body was placed across one of the mules and they traveled several days without more than short rests to get back to the village before the body began to decompose. The first person who saw them spread the news. But it was a moment of joy and sorrow. That they were back was a matter of great joy, that several of them, including the sachem, were no longer with them was a matter of great sorrow and loss. That Gray Wolf's body was coming back focused attention and emotion immediately upon him and Morning Light.

Morning Light was weeding in her garden when she heard the commotion. Her heart danced with joy. They had returned! Her hand went to her belly. He would probably notice immediately and she would not have the fun of telling him in surprise. But his seeing would be surprise enough. Who cared how he learned? She just wanted to be in his arms again, to feel his strength and protection. To know his passion and his love. She cleaned the soil from her hands. She smoothed her hair.

Suddenly, her mother, Wani, Yellow Rock, Little Smoke, even Five Beavers were all there standing before her, looking at her in a strange way. Her heart was beating wildly. No. NO. NO! NO!! And she knew... she knew. She knew but she did not want to believe. Her mind denied it and refused to accept even as she pushed passed them. Behind them, she saw his body laid out upon the ground, rigid and cold, his blood dried to his skin and his breech-cloth. His bow laid across his chest. The arms that had held her so gently, rigid at his sides. She could deny it no longer.

"AAATAKENHROHKWAAA OKWAHOOO!!!!" the cry of his name tore from her throat as she dropped to his side and beat her fists against the earth. Mother Earth, giver of bounty, was taking back Gray Wolf, her Gray Wolf, her husband, and Morning Light impotently railed against it. She beat and beat as if pounding on the gates of the spirit world, demanding entrance to take him back out. She keened in howls of grief, until her arms felt like lead and her fists were numb. Then, she rocked back and forth, back and forth. Desperately she sought an outlet to relieve the overwhelming misery she felt welling up inside her, pressuring to get out until she felt as though she would surely explode. She tore at her hair and undid the braiding. Then, pulling out her small knife, she began viciously cutting long silky hunks and dropping them over his chest. When she'd hacked the last of her hair off, Five Beavers stepped in at the prodding of Singing Wind who was fearful lest Morning Light turn the knife on herself and begin mutilating herself or severing her fingers. He removed the knife from Morning Light's hand and gently scolded that Gray Wolf would insist she take care and live for their child and that she remember him to the young one.

She stiffened at this and was still. Quietly, she stayed at the side of her husband's body for the rest of the day and through the night repeatedly singing the song of grief. Yellow Rock came and built a fire for her, to keep her from the dark. He tended the fire for her, but let her remain in solitude beside her husband's body, moaning and crying. In the morning, Gray Wolf's funeral pyre was constructed outside the palisade.

Five Beavers and Yellow Rock were among those who carried the body out on a blanket. As Morning Light walked with it, she could not even feel the earth beneath her feet. She watched as the first flames quickly sped through the dry brush and enveloped his body. She continued to watch as the very last of the structure crumbled in ashes. Her eyes had glazed over in disbelief. Her short chopped hair blew about her face in thick uneven curls. She had eaten nothing and drunk nothing since the day before. She continued to sit upon the ground, her voice hoarse as she intermittently broke forth into more keening and wailing. None who saw her could help but be filled with pity.

Tonoaki's guilt hung in his belly like a rock. He had been jealous and he had wished his brother dead. He had given no thought to the pain it would cause her. Now, he would wish to lift this pain from her but it was too late.

As the sun set, Yellow Rock and Singing Wind went out and brought Morning Light back inside the palisade. They took her to her hut. Singing Wind insisted Morning Light eat for the baby's sake but food would not go down her throat. She tried to swallow but the lump was too large and finally she spit it out.

"At least some broth, please, daughter, some broth."

Morning Light sat dumbly. Then Singing Wind did something out of pure instinct. She slapped her daughter across her face.

"He loved you and trusted you to have his child. To care for it and raise it. To be a good mother." Singing Wind avoided saying the name of the dead, it was not good luck. It disturbed the rest of their spirit.

Morning Light was shocked by the slap more than hurt. The hurt within her was more than anyone could have inflicted upon her physically. "He never even knew about the child," she stated flatly.

"Do you not think he knows now? The Great Spirit knows all things and where his spirit has gone, he now knows you will have his child."

Morning Light stared at her mother for a long moment. "Do you really think this is so?"

"It is so," she said emphatically.

Morning Light took the broth and drank.

# *Chapter 22*

"Woman," was the only greeting and acknowledgment Quick Panther offered as he stepped into his hut and saw Mist-On-Moon hovering in the shadows. She bent her head in a silent acknowledgment. She had not come out to greet him. He had not really expected her to. She was well shamed by her appearance and he ignored her as he hung his new scalp belt upon the wall like the trophy it was. Next, he bent and picked up his son who was clinging to his mother's skirts. The boy was growing fast and it pleased Quick Panther to note how the child looked at him in bold curiosity, silent but unafraid. The stocky warrior exhibited a pleasant expression to match his mood as he set the child down again. He ignored the little female in her carrier other than to note she appeared healthy. The warrior was feeling good. He had much booty and only minor flesh wounds for his troubles. And he was now home again.

As Quick Panther sat eating the food his wife obediently served to him, he considered his increased wealth, his improved status and his life in general. If he had been a cuckold husband and a laughing stock before, he had been most fortunate this summer. Unlike Crooked Arrow, Silver Fox, Moose Horn, Smooth Water, and several others, he had no serious wounds. Silver Fox had had to be carried back on a litter. His tendon severed, his foot flopping. He would never run again, he would most likely never walk again without a crutch. This was a bad thing for a warrior for it meant he could no longer hunt. At least the sachem, Gray Wolf, and three other brothers had left for the World Beyond as true warriors, they had died with honor.

A twinge of envy passed through Quick Panther as he thought of Gray Wolf. Strange to envy a brother who was dead when one still had much life. But Quick Panther realized the source of his envy. How well Gray Wolf's widow mourned him. Would that he, Quick Panther, had a woman who cared for him so deeply, showed as much respect, mourned so gloriously for him when he finally died. He sneered slightly to himself when he compared Mist-On-Moon and *Ohronkene Hahser*. Mist-On-Moon fell very short in the measure.

A thought occurred to Quick Panther. He was wealthy enough now to take a second wife, a good wife, an honorable wife, a pleasant looking wife. Someone of whom he could be proud. *Ohronkene Hahser* was such a woman. And as he continued to think of her, he felt his loins stir with lust. She would have her time of mourning and then she would be ripe for re-marriage. There was no reason why he should not offer for her, no reason at all.

Later that night Quick Panther stretched out upon the sleeping furs and Mist-On-Moon stripped off her tunic and timidly lie beside him. She was aching for a man. Not since the night of her disfigurement had she shared pleasures and her need was great enough to risk rejection as, naked, she snuggled up against her husband and slipped her hand into his breech-cloth.

She didn't know that her husband's thoughts were of another woman as he mounted her in the darkness and she climaxed almost immediately. She didn't know that he was only interested in getting another son off her, now that he knew the child would be his. But once he took a second wife, a younger wife, a prettier wife, Mist-On-Moon would be relegated to watching over the nursery and working in the fields.

Mist-On-Moon climaxed again as Quick Panther rode her quickly and after his final thrust, she would have come again if he had only stayed in her for a few more strokes. Despite her pleas, he rolled off her and turned his back to go to sleep.

She was an insatiable whore, he thought to himself, but if she was very good and if she was very obedient, once he had his second wife, he might go to this one's pallet once a moon just to reward her. And then she could not complain to the Council of Mothers that he ignored her. In the dark he could remember her as she had been. He need not disgust himself looking at her as she was now.

The dung colored dog sat nervously twitching and licking its chops as it watched John eat the meat from a good sized rib bone. John noticed the dog, its eyes bright and alert, watching every movement he made. The animal was an unattractive little beast, gaunt and with matted hair and fleas, but it offered some diversion to the soldier who was hunkered down alone by a cook fire. John refrained from pulling the last of the meat off the bone and chose instead to throw the whole greasy mess off to the side. Before the meaty scrap had left his hand, the animal had sprung up in attention and jumped at the tidbit, catching it before it landed.

The mutt retreated a distance as if afraid the human might want to reclaim the prize. Then, it settled down to gnaw on the bone and John's gaze shifted over to the hut again. He had seen the older squaw go into it early that morning and the boy had come out. After a considerable time, the boy came back and the squaw had left. Now another young buck had gone in. They were apparently unwilling to leave the young woman alone to herself for an instant and this had been going on for several days.

So far, John had not been able to do anything to express himself to the young widow to whom he owed his life. Not that he really thought he could ease her grief but he had hoped to be able to offer her some words of respect and condolence. He knew from experience that comfort was beyond her grasp at this time. As things had turned out, however, it had been five days and he doubted that she was even aware that he was there. But John discovered she had had a tremendous effect on him. As all others who had witnessed her grief, he had been profoundly touched. He had consciously empathized with her, recognizing in her someone who knew and felt the same depth of grief he had felt. Unconsciously he experienced a sympathetic catharsis, a purging of his own tortured soul. She expressed his own grief so much better than he had been able to do, and it drew him to her.

Since the burning of the funeral pyre, she had retreated into her hut and it had been impossible to speak with her. He did not know he longed to talk with her because he felt she of all the people on the face of the earth would understand what he felt. He only knew that he had a burning question to ask of her. The solving of a mystery, a loose end for which he had to get an answer before he could move on. He had to ask her why she had helped him in the first place. Spurred by the knowledge that he could not stay forever, John got up and sought out the scout who was his interpreter. He found him several yards away, dozing against a tree.

"Charlie-One-Claw," John called firmly.

"Ugghh," the scout grunted.

"It's coming on a week now and we're going to have to be leaving. I want you to come with me again. We'll go speak to the mother."

Charlie-One-Claw got up from his contented repose and followed.


Morning Light knew her family cared about her. They were afraid she would harm herself but she knew she would no longer do that. Not since her mother reminded her of the need to protect the baby growing within her. Gray Wolf's baby. *Gray Wolf. Oh, Gray Wolf!* Without him this world was terrifying in its emptiness.

She only wished to be left alone, left to struggle through this pain and blackness. The ache of it welled within her, pressing against her nerves, threatening to consume her. If she allowed the pain to have her without fighting it, then soon it must kill all feelings within her. Like a raging fire it must be allowed to burn itself out and leave her cauterized, empty, hollow, and dead to any more feelings. This was preferable to living with a controlled pain that would eat away at her for the rest of her life. Better than an aching grief that simply smoldered on forever and ever.

*Oh, Gray Wolf!* she cried out to herself silently, unaware that Wani had returned again to relieve Yellow Rock. This baby was the last little bit of Gray Wolf left to her, she realized. But would it also not always be a reminder? Without it she might convince herself that their love, their passion, their time together had all been a dream. That she had lost only a dream and to have it again she need only dream. But the baby would be living proof that it had not been a dream. It had been real. For a short time, she had known such happiness with a man who had been so patient, so understanding, so tender, and so strong that he had made her whole again and had stopped all her hurting.

How could she watch his son, for she somehow knew she carried a son, how could she watch this son grow up, a copy of the warrior she had lost, constantly rubbing the pain within her soul with the reminder of what she had lost? Morning Light began again to rock back and forth, back and forth, back and forth. Her eyes were closed and all she could think was to will the pain to kill all her feelings, to burn them out of her heart forever. Leave her to feel nothing. It was better to feel nothing. Right now she felt so much it was going to cause her heart to explode. Yes, it would be better to feel nothing.

When Singing Wind entered the hut she found her daughter rocking again, a low soft moan escaping her lips. She sighed shaking her head and looked at Wani. "You should have told me she started that again," she said almost accusingly.

"She hurts, we must let her hurt," he said with surprising maturity. "A wound must bleed to be cleansed and grow better."

"It sounds like you have been listening to the shaman again," she sniffed before sitting down by her daughter. "My daughter. I have come to talk to you. Will you listen to me?"

The young woman opened her eyes and stopped rocking.

"The yellow hair that was our prisoner has come back as a guest. He also fought the Hurons," she added by way of a simple explanation. "He wishes to speak with you. At one time you did much for him," she said cautiously, "will you agree now to speak with him? He has an interpreter."

Morning Light nodded in agreement simply because it was easier than having to endure repeated requests from her mother.

When John stepped into the hut, hat in hand, with Charlie-One-Claw, he saw the young boy bristle and send a hostile look his way before leaving the hut. John did not see the large circular scar on the young lad's upper arm. As John's eyes grew accustomed to the darkness, he saw Morning Light sitting, knees bent, with her lower legs tucked under her, her thickened middle announcing her coming motherhood. Her mother was sitting beside her in a similar fashion.

John sat down cross legged upon the ground. The young woman looked so different. Her beautiful hair was hacked off leaving rebellious curls that made her look even younger. Like a street urchin, he thought, ashes and dirt dusted her hair and lovely face, a face that was now dull and drained of expression. He noted her apparent condition. She was just far enough along for her husband to have left her pregnant before going off to war. John was almost certain her warrior husband would not have known she was carrying his child. *Poor bastard,* he thought sympathetically.

"O-ron-keenee-hah-ser," he said her name awkwardly. "Jack," he pointed to himself. She stared at him, not moving, then, finally gave a slight nod to indicate she did recognize him. "I... I never was able to thank you properly for what you did for me," he began and paused frequently for the scout to interpret. "Your loss deeply saddens me... I was proud to know your husband," John said diplomatically, he really hadn't known Gray Wolf beyond passing. "We fought together." This was true in a sense. "He was a very brave warrior. He helped to kill an entire war party of fifty Algonquin... and he killed the one who killed him." John paused and felt agony in empathy for her as he watched her receive his words from Charlie-One-Claw. What could he possibly say to make it any better, he asked himself and his response to himself was *nothing*. He knew what it was like to lose to Death the one you loved and cherished. He had gone through it twice and could do nothing but be honest in his feelings.

"My heart is very heavy for you," he said when Charlie finished. "After what you did for me, I would have done anything to have spared him for you if I could."

Her face remained motionless, her eyes distant.

"If there is anything I can do for you now... anything you can think of... anything... at all, please, let me know. I am in your debt."

When Charlie-One-Claw finished this time, John saw her eyes flicker. Then, they actually focused on him.

"No. We are even now," she said. He puzzled when he heard the scout say the words.

"I don't understand."

"It was I who was in your debt."

"How could you have been in my debt?"

"Did you not recognize the scar on my young brother's arm? He will never forget his hatred for the whites. I grew tired of hatred and chose to leave it like an empty husk to blow away in the wind. Still, I would not have helped you, white man, if I had not owed you a debt."

"I still don't understand," John frown in puzzlement, trying to remember what the scar should have meant to him. He had seen so many injuries and wounds during his years of warfare, too many.

"Four summers ago you sought a woman and found a young girl. You took pity on that girl and acting as medicine man you sewed her back together after your kind repeatedly forced her."

John looked questioningly at Charlie-One-Claw when he said *forced*. "Taken by force," Charlie-One-Claw elaborated, then thought of the English word. "Raped."

The look of puzzlement changed suddenly to comprehension, then surprise, and finally to disbelief. "You?" John asked softly as though he had to be misunderstanding. She didn't need an interpreter for that. She nodded her head.

"Then you did heal well?" he asked and immediately grew uncomfortable, thinking the question was much too intimate even to ask an Indian woman. He had, in fact, seen her intimately while doing reconstructive surgery.

She understood he was referring to her old wound. She nodded as she said simply, "I am whole again. I will have a baby in the winter."

"That is good news," he said relieved to focus on something else. Then, he relaxed a bit and slowly shook his head. "Well, it all makes a little more sense now. All the while I was here I could never understand why you alone were kind to me, why you helped me. And then, why you risked setting me free. Talk about casting bread upon the water..."

At this last, Charlie-One-Claw turned to look at Lieutenant Power as though he hadn't understood him properly.

"It's from the Bible," John answered the scout's unasked question. "It says when you cast your bread upon the water it will come back to you ten fold. That means when you do good, you get good back more than you give."

"Ugh," he grunted and gave the shortened version.

"Not always," Morning Light responded. "Often good is repaid with evil." She remembered vividly how her parents and uncles had opened their camp to the white men and had been repaid with treachery.

"Well, I guess that's true, too, when you're dealing with evil people."

"In my experience, the whites are evil people. You were an exception."

"I'm very sorry you feel this way because it isn't true. There are many who are good. I'm even more sorry for what happened to you to make you think this way." John replied, a little frustrated at having to wait on Charlie-One-Claw to repeat everything. However, the hint of patronizing condescension which had crept into his voice needed no interpreter.

"Go," she said abruptly, "I am in mourning and wish to speak to no one," and she turned her face from him.

"You must go now," Singing Wind added, "leave her in peace."

When Charlie-One-Claw finished interpreting he added, "Come, we must leave her now."

John looked at him and back at the girl, then at the mother and nodded his head in agreement.


As the days passed, Tonoaki said little but listened closely to pick up tid-bits relaying information on *Ohronkene Hahser's* progress. He arrogantly ignored the yellow haired man who had come back into their village. The white had entered under the protection of Five Beavers and Tonoaki deigned to spend no time thinking about the former prisoner, allowed himself no feelings about his former captive. He only shrugged when he heard the man was part of that group of whites with whom they were in alliance against their ancient foes, the Huron.

Tonoaki harbored no grudge that the yellow hair had escaped. Would not the warrior have been compelled to do the same if their roles had been reversed? He nurtured no resentment that the white had played upon the sympathies of a weak female. She was soft to him because of the past. In fact, Tonoaki did not view John as having committed any personal affront or grievance to him and therefore, bore him no harsh feelings. At the same time, he felt no guilt or remorse at almost having taken a hand in killing the man who was an ally. Such were the fortunes of warfare and life. There was a strange logic to the Indian code, strange to the whites, perhaps, but perfectly understandable to the Indians.

John Power had to get back to his company but he was very dissatisfied with his interview with *Ohronkene Hahser* and was reluctant to leave. He was disturbed.

All night he had been dwelling on the memories of the little girl who had been so savagely used. The little girl had grown up now, and out of all the hurt and anger and fear she had been able to show him mercy. But what was it she said, she viewed all whites as evil? And why not? What else did she know? He wished there was some way he could change her opinion and then again, the more he thought on it, the more he could find little to support an opposing argument. *We come, we see, we conquer. Just like the bloody Romans,* John thought to himself in disgust. It's always been the same, and one can't blame the conquered for not liking it. These natives weren't completely conquered yet, but the day would come, John had no doubt, they just didn't know it was coming. But then one couldn't really blame the conquerors for doing what men have done for centuries, through all the histories he had ever studied. Even in the Bible, God had instructed His people to conquer others.

John saw *Ohronkene Hahser* step out of her hut and take the path to the latrine. He signed to Charlie-One-Claw and went to her hut to wait.

"Get the white dog away from our dwelling," Wani scowled at Charlie-One-Claw from the doorway. "He has no more business here. Take him and go back to where you came from, we do not want you here. You, too, smell like dog, you have caught his fleas."

"Being too small to challenge, it is easy for you to be insolent and ill-mannered. You have the stature of a hyena," Charlie said to Wani in his own tongue and the boy looked stunned and then indignant. Charlie turned to John. "He does not welcome us," he said simply.

"You know, Charlie, I couldn't help picking up on that myself," John replied dryly. "Tell the little fellow that we're leaving just as soon as I speak with his sister one more time."

Charlie-One-Claw conveyed the message and Wani stomped away while John hunkered down to wait.

Morning Light saw John and his interpreter waiting for her at the hut. She felt no anger in her heart toward this white man. How could she explain? This meeting would have been very different if Gray Wolf had been here with her. She would have sought to make them friends. Gray Wolf would have honored John for how he had helped her. How she missed her husband. Everything was ashes in her mouth, bitter and dry, and the pain was still too fresh. She nodded a silent greeting as she approached the waiting men.

"O-ron-keenee-hah-ser," John said softly to the tall young woman. Her short curls lifted in the slight breeze, framing her delicate features. As a man, he couldn't help but respond to her loveliness, her vulnerability, and her pain. It brought every protective instinct out in him, feelings he had never been able to demonstrate with Freyja. Feelings he had felt for this woman when she was only a child. "I'm leaving now," he frowned softly, "but I could not go before I saw you one more time. I wish it was in my power to right all the wrongs which have been done to you. I wish I could thank you by giving you back your husband. I wish I could find a reason for you not to dislike and distrust all of us. I cannot. I can only tell you my name, Jack Power. I can only tell you that if you ever need anything, send a message to Jack Power. I will answer if I am there."

When Charlie-One-Claw finished, John reached out slowly and took her hand, bringing it to his lips, he brushed a kiss onto her knuckles. She stared at him, watching. She did not resist. She did not react at all. Then, after he released her hand and looked into her face, she gave a brief smile and said in thickly accented English, "Sak Pow-er, Fur-end."

John smiled broadly. "O-ron-keenee-hah-ser, Friend," he responded.

# *Chapter 23*

It was late in the month of October, but the sun was hot, the air was still and Morning Light asked Wani to come down to the river with her. She wanted to bathe. She carried a small knife. Wani sat on the rocks with his back to his sister. He kept a look out and enjoyed the warmth of the sun. It would turn cold soon enough. The leaves were all down and frost was on the ground every morning.

As the lad sat quietly he could hear his sister splashing in the water behind him and then it grew very quiet. He turned briefly to make certain she was all right, her belly was big and she was not as nimble as she used to be. He stared for a moment when he saw that she was cutting her hair again.

He turned back without saying anything. Amongst these people it was common practice for a young woman to cut her hair when she lost a husband. The time it took for her hair to grow out was her time of mourning. When her hair was again its full length, she was eligible for re-marriage. But if Morning Light kept cutting hers, it would extend her period of grieving. Wani was already aware that there were those who wanted to offer for his sister and take her to their hearth. They would grow impatient. Then he smiled to himself. Let them be impatient.

Morning Light did not realize that because of her unusual hair what was supposed to be defacing and a loss of beauty, was instead, on her, yet another attraction. Shorn of its weight, her soft silky tresses bobbed into curls. Her look created a stir. Some of the women were envious, most were curious. The tribe had never seen one of their own kind with a tousled head of curls. Their hair was thick, heavy, coarse, and straight. Tonoaki was only one of many who found her more beautiful than ever in her mourning.

Singing Wind couldn't help but be proud. Even in mourning and pregnant, her daughter was more attractive than any other female in the camp. The young bucks could barely contain themselves and would soon be quarreling with each other over her. She could recognize the signs. Many were impatient to see the mourning period over. Once the baby was born, Five Beavers would most certainly want to see her settled again to quell the competitive disruption. But Morning Light had truly loved Gray Wolf, thought Singing Wind. Who was to say how long it would take before the heart would heal? It would not be fair to push her too soon. Her daughter had already had enough tragedy in her young life.

She was out with the others who were gathering wood in the snow. Her huge belly made it impossible for her to bend well so she was there simply to help carry and because not having anything to do would have only increased her impatience. Suddenly, the first pain enveloped her body. Morning Light marveled at the feeling. It was not really pain as she had known pain in her life, but she knew instinctively that the feeling signaled the coming of her baby, Gray Wolf's baby. She dropped her wood and stood silently, riveted to the spot while caressing her belly.

Tonoaki saw her. She was never far from his sight these days. He was at her side in an instant and for the first time that he could remember she actually had a smile for him.

"Are you well?" he asked anxiously.

She nodded.

"I will carry you back."

"No, no," she said gently. "There is no need. I think I should walk. It will be a long time yet." He helped her pick up her wood and when she had finally bundled it all into the carrier on her back another spasm took her.

"I... you... I'll get your mother," the brave said finally and hurried away.

Morning Light stopped to consider the moment. Gray Wolf's child was coming. Soon he would be here. *Do you know this my husband?* she thought to herself. *Can you see us now? Are you here? Oh, Gray Wolf, I wish that you were here to share this. I wish I could feel your hand in mine. If only we could have one last day together, this day, the day your child is born. Gray Wolf, I need you. I need your tenderness, I need your strength, I need your love. Please stay with me.*

Quick Panther came out of his hut and casually walked over to join Tonoaki, Yellow Rock, Five Beavers, and Wani at the fire they had built outside of Gray Wolf's hut. It was the end of a cold winter day and without seeming to, without acknowledging it, the braves kept their vigil, pulling their furs around them. The mere birth of a child was not something to which warriors normally gave too much concern. It was women's business. Quick Panther had ordered Mist-On-Moon to serve his friends food and she followed him a short time later with her fur pulled up over her face allowing only her eyes to be seen.

Although they pretended not to be, all including Tonoaki, were too involved in listening to pay Mist-On-Moon any attention. They could hear the sounds from within the hut of Gray Wolf, grunts, soft groans, pants but never screams or cries. Morning Light had been in labor all day. Little Smoke and Singing Wind were with her. Their women had no time for them now, but they understood. New life must come first. They received the food from Mist-On-Moon as their due. Then, they heard the crying bawl of an infant and the braves smiled amongst themselves.

"It is a son, my daughter," Singing Wind said happily from within the hut as she tied off the umbilical cord. She wrapped the baby in a soft chamois and handed him to his mother.

Morning Light was exhausted but happy. She fell back upon the furs and gathered her son to her breast. His little mouth moved to suckle but he fell asleep. She smiled.

"He looks just like his father," she said joyfully. *Gray Wolf, do you see... your son. We have a son... a son*, she murmured silently and went to sleep herself.

Singing Wind took the baby back and cleansed him. After washing, she wrapped him in a warm fur and brought him outside where everyone was waiting.

"It is a boy," Singing Wind proudly announced, "Gray Wolf has a son."

"Son of Gray Wolf," Five Beavers said looking at the child with an approving nod. "Gray Wolf's Son shall be his name. It is good the father's blood lives on in his son. He is a fine boy."

Five Beavers, the sachem, had sent for Morning Light. Gray Wolf's Son was standing now and Little Smoke took the toddler from his mother and went outside as soon as Morning Light arrived. The sun was warm and bright on the crisp autumn day.

"Sit, my daughter," Five Beavers motioned.

Morning Light sat obediently. He looked over at her hair which was just touching her shoulders.

"Either your hair grows very slowly or you have been assisting it," he said dryly. Morning Light looked up at him briefly and then lowered her eyes. "You have been mourning long enough, daughter. You need a man to provide for you and protect your hearth."

"But I have my brothers, they provide for me and my child," she started to protest.

"You are a young and healthy woman and we have young and healthy braves who need mates," he interrupted. "It is not right to stay alone too long. It is not natural."

"Please, my chief, do not compel me. My heart still weeps for my husband."

"It is time to stop weeping," he said sternly. "In spring you shall choose a new husband. Your first husband left you a wealthy widow. Your bride price shall be high. I will allow you to make the final decision."

"I am not ready," she said with quiet stubbornness.

"I have been too lenient, do not test my patience. Because you have had Gray Wolf's Son to care for I have ignored the wishes of the others. I have allowed you to remain alone but it is now too long, spring will be the sixth season. It shall not continue more."

She looked at the sachem and knew there was no sense in arguing. She had known this would happen eventually. She was sixteen summers old, too young to be allowed to remain a widow. She was of child bearing age and had proven her ability to produce a healthy son. But Five Beavers was being very generous to allow her to make the final decision. Morning Light nodded her head and silently left.

Tonoaki's heart skipped a beat in joy when he heard the announcement that Morning Light had been told to marry in the spring. At last, after years of yearning, years of waiting, years of wanting, he was going to make her his. He sobered then to think of his competition. Swimming Turtle was so undistinguished one almost forgot he was around. Crooked Arrow? Tonoaki didn't consider him to be competition. Moose Horn had mated with Robin Song. Quick Panther had been too interested in her of late but he was married also. There was no reason for Morning Light to accept status as a second wife. She was wealthy now in her own right as well as young and beautiful. The woman did not have to take second place at any man's hearth and Five Beavers was sure to insist on a high bride price. Confidently, Tonoaki decided he would spend the winter gathering furs and courting his wife-to-be.

"Okonhsa?"

"Yes, Tonoaki." The large squaw looked up from the stew pot before her hut and smiled at the virile young brave.

"I have need of your counsel," he said with a pleasant grin and a winsome wink.

"Now, why would the most handsome brave of our village need counsel?" the coarse skinned woman continued to smile at the young brave's attentions. "Might this have to do with winning a woman?"

"Ahhhh, wise woman, you read my mind."

"I keep up with things," she grinned back as he came up close to her and bent to her ear.

"What is a sure way to win a woman's heart?" he asked softly.

"Ahhh, but that depends on the woman," she teased.

"I think you know," he said slyly giving her a hug.

"For you, I should think only the most eligible young woman will do. Am I right?"

"You are always right. You are very wise. This is why I come to you."

The woman was not above being partial to flattery and although almost old enough to be his grandmother, she fairly giggled under Tonoaki's attention. "If you seek to mate a woman who already has a child, you must woo the child. Win the child and you will win the mother."

"But the child is only a baby."

"Which makes it even easier. Pay attention to the baby. Show love and caring for the baby and the mother's heart will soften toward you."

"I understand," nodded Tonoaki and then he bent his head to touch forehead to forehead with the woman. "Thank you, flower of wisdom. You are wonderful!"

She watched the young brave walk away smiling. She herself was smiling wistfully. She would have preferred to have his appreciation take a more intimate path. As she watched the lean muscles of his back and buttocks, she could only imagine how pleasurable that might have been.

Tonoaki sent presents to Gray Wolf's Son. He inquired after his health and suggested outings where he carried the child on his broad shoulders to the toddler's delight. With Tonoaki's attention so focused on her son, Morning Light grew more relaxed in the brave's presence and even found herself laughing at his antics. He had a tender side, she discovered. A side rarely seen. Much as Gray Wolf's tenderness had been hidden from the world. These braves made such a show of being fierce and aloof, they were reluctant to show a tender side but it was there. Tonoaki had matured, Morning Light observed. He could be thoughtful and caring and when he left to go hunting, she found she actually missed his company.

In Tonoaki's absence, Swimming Turtle pressed his own suit for Morning Light's attentions. He was a very shy young brave and not as large as Tonoaki who had filled out in the past year and gained breadth in the chest so similar to Gray Wolf. But for some reason Singing Wind did not like Swimming Turtle and was not opposed to letting Morning Light know it. She fairly loathed the young brave which Morning Light did not understand at all. Her mother had a generous nature and was usually tolerant of others. Morning Light couldn't help but feel there was something negative about Swimming Turtle she did not see.

Because they were neighbors, Morning Light could not avoid Quick Panther but she gave him no encouragement at all. Being a second wife in itself, Morning Light did not object to. After all, her mother was a second wife. Morning Light's passion for Gray Wolf had been too strong to share him. But if she had no passion, then she could see where it might even be advantageous. But certainly, Mist-On-Moon was not someone with whom Morning Light would want to live. The older squaw had lied. She was a trouble stirrer. Morning Light did not come right out and say this to Quick Panther, however, as she did not want to create problems for Mist-On-Moon. She also feared a man who could slit his own wife's nose. But she did not say this either as she did not want to make an enemy of Quick Panther.

And there were others. Many young and old hopefuls sought time with the young mother but seemed to ignore her child and she could not warm to any of them. The only young men not interested in her were Yellow Rock, her own close cousin, and Tonoaki's younger brother who knew better than to even think of challenging his brother for the woman's hand.

By spring, Morning Light had decided to accept Tonoaki as her husband. She did not love him but she had grown fond of him. He treated her son so well and he had shown her his tender side. She told her mother. Singing Wind approved and told Five Beavers who was pleased.

Five Beavers decided to have some fun at the young brave's expense. This was his first joining, after all, and he deserved some teasing. He sent Wani to Tonoaki with a message to come and see him. When the brave arrived Five Beavers beckoned him to sit.

"How have you been?" Five Beavers asked innocently.

"Well," Tonoaki replied in confusion. He had not come rushing over to talk about his health.

"*Yànere!* Good!" Five Beavers sat quietly puffing his pipe.

"You asked to see me."

"*Hv.* Yes."

Tonoaki waited expectantly and when Five Beavers said nothing more he finally urged him on. "About what did you wish to see me?"

Five Beavers looked at him darkly as if it was a difficult topic to pursue. "As you know, my wife's daughter is to remarry."

"*Hv.* I know."

"Many seek her hand."

"*Hv.* I know. I am one of them."

"It is difficult to know what is right," Five Beavers muttered.

"*Hv?*"

"We have come to a decision."

"*Hv?*" Tonoaki betrayed his hopefulness.

"I decided it was best to talk to those who have not been accepted, individually." Tonoaki was silent. "It is better to learn these things in private, don't you think?"

Tonoaki felt his heart stop. This could not be. Who had they chosen? Who could they possibly feel was better than he? Had all his efforts to woo her gone unheeded? Had she really rejected him for someone else? Did she not realize how strongly he felt about her?

"Of course, that also means he who is accepted has no audience to gloat over," Five Beavers could barely keep himself from laughing out loud. The expression on Tonoaki's face was still frozen in a stare. "Knowing you, my son, since you were a little pup, I would say you would rather have a group of rivals to gloat over."

Tonoaki still didn't know what to say. He didn't know what Five Beavers was saying.

"She has accepted you, son. Congratulations!"

Tonoaki felt his heart start to beat again and he grinned in relief.

"Well, have you nothing to say?" Five Beavers grinned.

Then, Tonoaki broke into a chuckle. "You had me, old man. My heart went still in my chest."

"Watch who you call *old man.*"

"You are lucky I do not call you worse. You really had me for a moment." Tonoaki beamed. "When will we wed?"

"Why don't you go ask your bride-to-be?"

Tonoaki leapt to his feet and was out of the hut before Five Beavers could say another word.

When he reached her hut, Tonoaki stopped and called out to her. Wani opened the door and beckoned him in. Singing Wind was with her daughter and took her grandson as the young brave entered.

"*Ohronkene Hahser?*" he beckoned her.

She walked out with him.

"I have just come from the sachem," he stroked her cheek with the back of his hand. "Is it true? You have agreed to join with me?" She smiled and nodded. "I am a very happy man," he grabbed her slender waist and lifting her. He swung her around. She laughed at his impetuousness and before she knew it, his cheek was rubbing hers. He held himself back. He wanted to devour her but he told himself his goal was in sight and he could be patient. He gave her a caress of controlled gentleness instead. She was willingly going to be his. He could hardly believe it. "He asked me when we will wed."

"When would you like, my husband-to-be?" she asked softly, a gentle smile lingering on her lips.

"I am eager, my bride-to-be. You know this. I would wed tonight."

She laughed softly. "I am in my moon time. Give me five days to purify myself."

"Five days. Not a heartbeat more," he spoke softly and caressed her again.

Morning Light didn't want her wedding to be anything like the first one but then she told herself it was Tonoaki's first wedding even if it was not hers. He deserved to experience all the ritual. She had made a soft buckskin suit of clothes which she sent to him. She received a soft long tunic dress in return. Both were decorated with unique designs in quill and beading. Again she went to the river to wash and purify herself. Again her mother stained her lips and finger tips, earlobes and nipples with sweet berry juice. Morning Light almost broke down and cried.

Singing Wind grabbed her daughter soundly and shook her once. "He would want you to continue on with life. You have many years ahead of you. Years of happiness, of more children, of pleasure. You have another fine strong young husband. Be happy, daughter. Be happy and do not think of the past."

Morning Light nodded soberly, bit back her tears and hid her heart. They walked her to her waiting husband. He took her hand and they were symbolically bound. Then he led her to his hut which had been filled with spring flowers.

Tonoaki could not believe he was nervous. He had had many women, small, large, young, old. He had even had *Ohronkene Hahser* before although it was now something he preferred to forget. But at this moment he felt like an inexperienced and untried youth. He loved her greatly in his own arrogant fashion and he knew deep down that she didn't really love him. He would make her love him, his pride said. He would make love to her and pleasure her. He would be strong and provide well. He would be temperate and patient, and soon, she would love him, she would have to love him.

"I would look upon you, my wife," he said in a voice grown husky as he untied the lacing at her shoulders and let the tunic fall to her feet. Morning Light stood obediently before him as his hands slowly reached out glazing over her shoulders, down and up her arms, hovering over her full round breasts, down her sides, her hips. It was as if he was memorizing her by touch. "You are so beautiful!" The words came almost as a whisper. Finally, his hands held her buttocks and pulled her to him.

She felt awkward as she moved to him and began to remove his tunic. He helped to shrug it off. She went on to his leggings and she heard his quick intake of breath as her hands moved timidly over his skin.

"Do you know how long I have dreamt of you touching me like this?" he whispered.

She shook her head slowly. "No," she replied.

"Forever," he sighed. He grabbed her then, trying not to be harsh, and sucked berry juice off her earlobes. His tongue ran over her cheeks, smelling and caressing as he went. He felt her give way and then respond. Her hands were caressing him. Her body became pliant and soft, molding against him. She was his and his heart soared as he laid her back upon the pallet and his *ohnoru* sought her heat.

Morning Light gave way to all the need her healthy young body felt. He was so like Gray Wolf, she could close her eyes and almost believe. She reacted, drawn into the sensuality. His hands, his fingers, his mouth all assaulting her senses. She felt all the desires and responses she had experienced with Gray Wolf. Her skin tingled, her loins ached. Arching up to him with her breasts begging to be fondled. Then her hips thrust upward taking him in completely. She reveled in the feeling of being loved and desired, being caressed and being filled. She cried out in pleasure and began making demands of her own. Her insides were wound up like a coil ready to spring in release as he thrust within her again and again and she rode the wave and felt the release wash over her. She cried out.

At last he crumpled on top of her, panting and drained. Then, he shifted most of his muscular weight to the side. They lie in the stillness. The only sound filling the sweet smelling hut was their ragged breathing growing slowly more quiet. Finally, Morning Light opened her eyes and saw Tonoaki looking down at her. She could not read what she fleetingly saw in his eyes before they became impassable black mirrors reflecting back to her. He raised up resting his forearms on either side of her shoulders, his large hands holding the top portion of her head. "Someday," he whispered, pressing her head between his hands without hurting her. "Someday." But she knew not what he meant.

Tonoaki had heard her cry out Gray Wolf's name in the midst of her ecstasy. He had heard it and she did not even know it. Her eyes had been closed and he had been Gray Wolf to her. It was a bitter taste in his mouth and he vowed to drive out Gray Wolf's memory someday. Someday, she would think only of Tonoaki when he made love to her.

If he was to be truthful, Tonoaki would have to admit that he rather enjoyed the teasing although he pretended to ignore it and maintained a rather haughty air. He was a new bridegroom. It was expected that he should prefer to stay at home and make love to his young bride. But still his companions joked and teased. He never came to gamble and drink anymore. His brother, father, and uncle complained they never saw him anymore. He rarely sought out their company except to hunt for food. Tonoaki was getting lazy, they jested. Tonoaki was bewitched by a woman. Tonoaki was becoming spoiled. At times he could not help but smile. They could but wish they could be spoiled in such a way as he.

Each night his only desire was to lose himself between her thighs and make her cry out in pleasure. When he felt her wrap her long legs around him it spurred him on. Love, lust, desire, need were all rolled up together with this woman as they never had been for him before. He discovered he wanted nothing more than to please her and her smiles were priceless to him.

She had not called out Gray Wolf's name since that first time. He told himself it was not really so unexpected that she should do so on their first coupling. After all, had she not been Gray Wolf's wife first. Was not her first pleasuring connected with him? Tonoaki didn't want to think on this too long. But it seemed reasonable and nothing to dwell on now that she no longer cried out for Gray Wolf.

Tonoaki could take satisfaction in the fact that she was *his* wife now. It was his hut she kept neat and tidy. It was his food she prepared with such care and attention. The leathers he wore were worked by her lovely hands and sewn with her needle. She was obedient, she was beautiful, she was his. And he was the envy of all the bachelors and many of the mated braves for having this prize. So why was he discontent?

She never denied him. She never put him off. She never lacked responsiveness to his lovemaking and yet... Tonoaki realized he wanted to hear her cry out *his* name. He wanted to have her come to him first sometime, to see desire and passion in her eyes before he brought her body to its uncontrollable and natural response. He wanted her love.

Since his suit was refused, Quick Panther was glad he had said nothing to Mist-On-Moon about his intentions. The last thing he wanted was to give the slut something to mock him over. But now that *Ohronkene Hahser's* fate had been decided, he realized he still was of a mind and mood for a second wife. There certainly had to be other available maidens in the village. At the wedding gathering, Quick Panther took notice of the young sloe-eyed daughter of one of the elders. She had a generous smile and an equally generous sweep to her hips beneath her small waist. She was in her first nubile bloom and their eyes met several times in the crowd. She was petite and made the stocky brave feel quite tall. *A much better choice*, thought Quick Panther. He decided he wanted a woman who would have to look up to him. And this young maiden looked to be born for breeding. Quick Panther smiled and saw her return his smile before she looked modestly away. His eyes went down to her naked and firm young breasts before he looked up and saw her father looking at him with a stony expressionless face. Quick Panther decided he would speak with her father that evening and he did. Now the bride price had been set and met and he was soon to be wed.

Mist-On-Moon went far from the other women beating their wash on the rocks. She found a secluded curve in the river and as she worked she wept. Everyone in the village, except her, had known of her mate's intent to take a second wife. Why hadn't he told her? At least he could have warned her so she wouldn't seem a complete fool in her ignorance.

It was his right to take another wife as long as he could provide for her but in a considerate relationship the man at least advised his wife to prepare her. In a truly considerate relationship, he would even be sensitive if she had strong objections to his choice. Not only had she not been consulted, she had not even been told.

At this moment Mist-On-Moon was crying as if her heart would break in two. It wasn't for love she cried, it was for angry disappointment, for embarrassment and shame, for frustrated impotency. He had made her ugly to look upon and now he would set her aside and there was nothing she could do about it. She could turn no brave's head now. Bend no warrior to her will with lust. The squaw's hot salty tears fell into the cold fresh water but no one saw as the river carried them away.

Tonoaki sat watching jealously over his wife and her child as they bathed in the river. He wanted no other brave to see her. He remembered well how he had covertly watched her, many times, when she had thought she had her privacy. He knew how it could be. He was glad now for her habit of wearing short tunics in the summer rather than going bare breasted like the other young women. And he encouraged her to make soft light cotton tunics from the materials they had captured from the whites.

This morning he had brought *Ohronkene Hahser* to the river early just to avoid unwanted onlookers. She had just finished her moon time and needed to purify herself so he could again make love to her. He had made love to her every night since their mating except for her moon times and the thought struck him that his seed should soon take root in her belly.

"Husband," she called laughing and he turned quickly in the direction to which she was pointing and saw her child crawling naked up the river bank. "Catch him before he wanders too far," her voice was musical. "I still must rinse my hair."

Tonoaki got up and quickly crossed the distance between himself and the toddler. He picked up the slippery naked body and the child giggled and laughed. This was Gray Wolf's child but Tonoaki could see *Ohronkene Hahser* in his facial features. And for this reason he warmed to the child.

As he held the laughing baby in his arms, the mother rose up out of the river, sleek and wet and sensual. Tonoaki felt his *ohnoru* rise as well, hard and hungry, after five days of abstinence. Despite the feisty toddler in his arms, Tonoaki's loins throbbed and his eyes smoldered as he watched the mother approach.

Morning Light saw the swelling movement behind Tonoaki's breech-cloth. He was so good to her now and to her child. She felt guilty that she had not been outgoing enough. She was guilty of lacking the spontaneity she had felt with Gray Wolf. She was not as demonstrative to Tonoaki. Now, she saw her husband's desire and wanted to be the first to initiate their lovemaking for a change. She did not stop to pick up her clothing but walked up to him and gently moved her naked thigh against him.

"Do we have anything to tether the little one?" she asked softly, one hand stroking down his back and buttocks while the other rested on her baby. Her hip undulated against her husband. She heard the air escape his lungs.

"I will find something," he barely whispered as his tension increased and immediately his mind whirled to think. He took his own waist thong, causing his breech-cloth to fall to the ground, and tethered the child by his foot to a sturdy bush back from the river. The child was happy enough to sit upon the grasses and pick up pretty wild violets and stick them in his mouth.

Tonoaki had barely finished when he felt her hands upon him again and her caresses on his back. Oh, how he had longed for this! She had come to him! He reached backward and ran his hands down her hips, savoring the satiny skin beneath his touch, feeling her wet bare flesh against his buttocks as he pulled her closer. She had reached around and was caressing him gently and he had to pull her hand away with a groan.

"I...I will lose my seed too quickly," he cried out in a low growl and turned around to hold her at arms' length. Then, he fell on his knees before her, his arms around her hips, his face buried in her smooth flat belly as he began to trail caresses over her. His hands grasped her firmly rounded bottom, pulling her flesh to his mouth almost knocking her off balance at his onslaught to her loins.

"I am falling," she cried out softly.

His response was to pull her down on top of him, his tongue continuing its assault upon her as her knees dug into the dirt on either side of his head. She shuddered and convulsed as he stirred the desire in her, her body wantonly accepting the pleasure he gave. She was moaning as he looked up and saw her eyes closed again.

In a swift movement, he positioned her beneath him. "Look at me!" he rasped at her. Her eyes opened to his. He had become harsh, his lips came down on hers, bruising, biting. Some old memory flitted through her mind so quickly she didn't even recognize it but it sent fear racing through her and in a mindless reflex she pushed against him, tried to push him away. He was unmovable and had entered her harshly.

She gasped, consumed in the unexplainable panic, all pleasure now gone. Suddenly, with shocking clarity, memories returned of another time along the river, a time more than two years ago. A time when he had come upon her, when she had been Gray Wolf's woman but he had forced himself upon her. How could she have forgotten?! How could the memory have disappeared when she remembered it so clearly now? He had taken her when she was Gray Wolf's mate! He had forced her!

Tonoaki was unmindful of *Ohronkene Hahser's* change in mood, so consumed in his own desires was he. With brutishness, he ground his hips into her. He was beside himself in his own arousal. Thrusting into her, he was lost in the rush of ecstasy. His seed shot forth but he did not stop, he was still able to thrust again and again sustaining the wild rush of pleasure. Morning Light had gone cold but she pretended satisfaction so he would stop.

They lie quietly together. Morning Light turned to see her child playing harmlessly a few feet away, innocently entertained by the adult coupling. After a brief time, Tonoaki rose up on his elbow and looked down into her face. She studied his black eyes. She didn't know what she was seeing there but her own face had become a mask. She could not let Tonoaki know what she was thinking until she had had time to consider her thoughts. Consider her new memories and what they meant to her life now.

"I have longed for this day, the day when you would come to me," he said in a hoarse whisper. The irony of his words struck her dumb and she made no response. "I do not expect you to ever love me as much as I love you but now I know you love me a little."

"Oh... Tonoaki," she whispered, her eyes welling with tears. Before the return of her memory she might have loved him a little but now she could only feel pity and try to let go of any resentment. She took his face in her hands and drew him to her. She caressed his cheek gently. She didn't know what else to say or do and he accepted her gesture as love, not as the pity it was.

Pity was the very worst insult one could give a warrior.


The raid came swift and harsh and was over almost before anyone was aware of it happening. In the wake of the onslaught two of the women of the village were carried off and the corn fields had been burned. Morning Light had not been in the field that morning. Gray Wolf's Son had been feverish and she had stayed at the hut and soothed him. She saw the smoke outside the palisade and heard the screams.

They had come on horseback and a small party of braves on horseback had gone out to pursue them and try to rescue the squaws. They were unsuccessful. Three-fourths of the corn harvest was lost and it was going to be a very hard winter.

Shortly after this, the sachem received a message of a new treaty to which the brothers of the Long House, or what the whites referred to as the Five Nations, had agreed. The elders were angry and the young braves gathered around the council fire to hear their discussion. They had just sustained a crippling raid and were in no mood for another treaty. The white man loved his treaties but he never abided by them. Now they were trying to dictate where the tribal hunting grounds would extend and where they would be free to roam and where they would be restricted. And this was supposedly from the friendly whites, the English whites who fought the Huron enemy.

Eagle Wing spit in disgust. "What are our brothers of the Long House doing to us? They are no better than the *Lanape*. We should raise the war club against them for the disrespect they show us!"

A loud murmuring of voices was heard and Five Beavers stood.

"*Tewatatèkv!* Brothers!" he said in a conciliatory tone, "We should not war against our brothers of the Long House and we cannot expect them to war in the winter against our enemy. Which of you wishes to make war in the winter? Which of you wishes to leave the warmth of your hearth, your wives, your young ones to wage war against an enemy in the frozen north? Ask yourselves if our pride is blinding us. It is time to move camp anyway. Were we not speaking of moving our village to a new fresh location in another year or two? Are we not ready for fresh huts and new gardens? Do not let pride blind you to the truth. This treaty means little to us. We move anyway. We will seek our own hunting grounds in our new location. What matter is it to us?"

Five Beavers sat down and his words were followed by quiet. He had made his point. Declaring war against their brothers over a supposed slight that really was no slight nor of any consequence to them would be absurd. And trying to maintain a grievance over winter against an enemy just because they had struck the harvest fields in their last raid was impractical. Going to war in the winter time was a fool's game.

Tonoaki stood and Five Beavers silently groaned. He feared the young hot-head was going to stir everyone up again.

"I agree with our sachem," Tonoaki said, and the older brave could hardly believe his ears. "With the corn harvest destroyed, it will be more important that ever for us to hunt well for our families. In spring the village can move. We will seek a fresh location where the waters are clear, the earth is fertile, and the smells are again sweet. This treaty means nothing to us. We should forget it." He sat down. His father nodded at him.

"My son grows wise," the elder spoke with calm pride. "I think marriage has been good for him. He grows an appreciation for things other than the blood-lust of a battle cry."

There was a rumbling twitter of grunts and agreement among the elders while the younger braves, still stiff and proud, disdained of such homely sentiments. But it was agreed. There would be no declaration of war. They would weather through the coming winter as best they can and as soon as spring showed itself, they would move on. As sachem, Five Beavers would go to the shaman and seek a vision for their new location.

Tonoaki was pleased with his father's approval and the praise he had received. It was true. Marriage had changed him. He was thinking more conservatively now. He thought more about the future, about what was best for his wife and their children. Their children. They had yet to have any indication of a child. He wanted his own child. As he walked to his hut, he also knew that he had a selfish reason for wanting to move. He would be pleased to get *Ohronkene Hahser* away from this place. Gray Wolf's hut still stood, a strong dwelling and a constant reminder of her old life, her old love. It would be small of him to tear it down and eventually someone else might use it but he would wish it gone from sight.

As Tonoaki entered the hut he shared with *Ohronkene Hahser* he saw her giving suck to her son as she readied him for bed. He paused, looking at her.

"The child is almost two winters old. Too old to need his mother's breast," he said coming up behind her and kneading her free breast with his fingers.

"You sound jealous, my husband," she teased.

"I am jealous. I do not wish to share you with anyone." He dropped down behind her and began licking her neck with his tongue.

"The child is almost asleep," she begged off nudging him away.

"So, I will wait," he said without humor and turned to add fuel to the fire in the center of the hut. Then he settled back impatiently to watch her as she finished with the child and put him to bed. She came to him then.

"What occupies your thoughts, husband?" she asked quietly as she sat beside him.

"I was just thinking... a woman rarely conceives while she gives suck."

Morning Light considered this. "You think the child keeps me from conceiving your child?" she asked bluntly.

"Is it not possible?"

"Perhaps. It would be the Great Spirit's wisdom to understand that one young one at a time is more than enough," she tried to add humor to the mood. Tonoaki did not laugh with her and she looked at him. "You are upset?"

"I want a son, like any other man," he answered a little petulantly.

"I understand," she spoke softly trying not to let her anger show. "If Gray Wolf's Son were your son, you would not have this impatience to deny him his mother's milk. This is what comes of marrying a widow with a new babe." Her voice sounded tight.

He looked at her stonily but she wouldn't meet his eyes and suddenly he was feeling ashamed. "You are right," he agreed. "I am impatient. We have not even been mated a full year."

"Let me have this winter with him, husband," she offered in compromise, now looking at him. "My milk will help him be strong against the cold. In spring, I will wean him and we shall see if you are right."

He nuzzled her while his hand unlaced the other side of her tunic top. It fell from her, exposing her to his gaze. "Will your milk keep me strong against the cold?" he asked before teasing her nipple with his tongue, then pulling her breast into his mouth.

Her breath caught in her throat as the sensation so unlike nursing her child aroused an appetite within her own loins. Despite her deeper feelings, her body could not help reacting to his touch. "I do not think it is my milk you want," she murmured as he drew her down onto the furs.

# *Chapter 24*

## Spring 1723

The snarling *takoskowa* screeched a warning growl. The blood ran cold in Morning Light's veins as she stood rigid, legs apart and feet firmly on the ground. She had pushed Gray Wolf's Son behind her and held only a small knife in her hand as she faced the hissing feline on the rock before them. She did not know that they were only a few steps from the den where the mountain lion's kittens were nestled. Given the opportunity, most mountain lions ran from human encounters but this threat to the lair was an exception.

It was spring and the village was migrating as planned. They had struggled through a sparse winter with little corn, the mainstay of their diet. Now, they were on the trail and Morning Light had gone to fill an extra skin with water before they broke camp and continued on their march. As she filled the water skin, Gray Wolf's Son had wandered away. He had been naughty in not listening to her admonishments to stay and as she rushed to catch up with the child, she suddenly found them both facing the angry wild cat.

The two mothers continued to eye each other. The compactly powerful cat hissed vociferously, baring her lethal fangs. Morning Light suddenly spat out an imitative hiss, baring her teeth with a deep guttural growl while raising her arms to appear larger. The wild cat pulled back in confusion. The sound did not correlate with the scent of human. Morning Light began to back away but Gray Wolf's Son was clinging to her legs in fear and she could not move easily. The cat jerked and leaned forward. Morning Light saw its muscles contract as it poised to spring. She cried out loudly while she braced herself to take the impact of the animal's weight hoping somehow her son could run to safety, hoping that the small knife would find a vital spot, hoping that someone would find her son before the cat was finished shredding her with its vicious claws and fangs. Time had slowed to almost a standstill. Perspiration had beaded up on Morning Light's forehead. Then, a musket shot rang out and the animal immediately pulled back with another snarl and disappeared in retreat, hoping to lead the danger away from the den.

Morning Light spun around in the direction of the sound and saw a white soldier on horseback coming toward her. In panic, she grabbed her son and began to run.

"Wait! O-ron-keenee-hah-ser!"

She recognized her name although it was pronounced very poorly. When she stopped to look again she recognized the white man she knew as *Sak Power, Friend.*

Captain Power was out on a scouting expedition, checking on the migration of the village. According to the recent treaty they were supposed to move west of the Tuwok River and he had been given the task to assure that they did. By shear chance he had woke early that morning, unable to sleep, and roused his companions out on the trail before daybreak.

"O-ron-keenee-hah-ser! Are you all right?" He jumped down from his horse to approach her. She smiled a greeting in reply, pleased to see him and thankful for his intervention with the mountain lion.

"*Sak! Sak* Power, Friend," she grinned at her awkward English and observed the man coming toward her. He was fully matured now at thirty-one years of age and he had the look of a toughened frontier soldier and Indian fighter. Still extremely handsome with a solid, hard muscled body, he had, however, lost everything youthful in his looks and manner. His hair had mellowed to a burnished gold and lines were beginning to etch character in his sun weathered countenance but his smile came very easily in Morning Light's presence.

"Friend," he replied and took her hand, bowing over it and kissing it gallantly. She looked vibrant and alive, much different than the last time he had seen her.

Through the interpreter they spoke to each other.

"This is Gray Wolf's Son," she introduced her boy.

"He is a very fine looking boy."

"He looks like his father, I think."

"He looks like you." She blushed when she heard this. "It is difficult to believe it has been this long..." he gesturing to the growing youngster, "since I last saw you. Has life been good to you?" he asked sincerely, noting that her hair had grown long again.

"I have re-married," she said quietly, almost as if it was a slight to Gray Wolf's memory.

"You are too young and too beautiful to stay alone," he heard himself say and then felt the blood in his gaunt cheeks. He had never spoken this way to her before but it was the truth and he didn't ask Charlie-One-Claw not to repeat it.

She lowered her eyes not admitting to herself that his words pleased her. Then she told him how she came to be there with the mountain lion. In return, she learned that he was looking for the tribal leader. She led him back to the encampment and brought him to Five Beavers.

Tonoaki had been looking for his woman and was surprised to see her emerge from the forest with three white men and their scout. As he strode nearer to her, he recognized the one she called *Sak* and bristled perceptibly.

"What is he doing here?" Tonoaki demanded curtly of her.

"He comes to see the sachem. Please, my husband, for my sake, greet him in friendship. He is a friend." Morning Light looked up into her mate's eyes. She could see blatant hostility for no reason and she was reluctant to relay that *Sak* had just saved her life for fear that Tonoaki would be angry with her for going off without him. The defensive brave slipped into the arrogant stance he reserved for adversaries and he stiffly greeted Power. But he did greet him, in a civil fashion, more or less, just to please *Ohronkene Hahser*.

Since her mother was mated to Five Beavers, Morning Light and her mate were asked to stay. Thus, Tonoaki was a witness to the conversation and the news which John brought regarding the migration and the need to move west of the Tuwok River. It was agreed that John and his interpreter would stay with the tribe to help them find the right area to settle in. Then, the captain released one of his men to report back to the fort.

Traveling was not nearly as difficult this time for the tribe. Many had horses and mules captured during the war raids and these were used as pack animals. Tonoaki and Morning Light each had mounts and often she took her son and rode the pony Gray Wolf had left to her while her mule was laden with their household goods. Her place was close to the front, she was a daughter of the shaman's hearth and her mother was the second wife of the sachem. Tonoaki was one of the young braves who rode up and down the traveling line, keeping watch for anyone in difficulty, keeping watch for animals and raiders, and encouraging the stragglers to keep up with the main body.

The shaman was now so old he sat comfortably on a *travois*, but still was painted in colored clay as ceremony required, with the sacred fire now being carried by his honor guard. One young brave named Quiet Waters was at his side constantly. This was his acolyte, training to someday take on the responsibilities of the ancient medicine man. The old man's mind was still sharp and clear but his legs were giving out on him. It was his reminder that even a shaman did not go on forever.

Five Beavers, the sachem, sat nobly on his horse at the very front of the caravan. He had his animal walk at a pace no faster than those who were walking could maintain. In his wisdom as the tribal leader, he accepted John's guidance in seeking a new location for the tribe. Five Beavers was no longer eager for war, that was a young man's game. He was thankful he had gained the wisdom to accept a certain co-existence with the whites. There seemed to be no end to them and unlike the young hot-bloods, Five Beavers was coming to an understanding that they would never be able to push the whites back into the waters. He did not like to think of what that really meant for his people or their future. It was enough to live one day at a time.

John had been riding at the front for most of the day with Five Beavers. They did not speak much. Everything that was said had to be said through an interpreter but John felt comfortable with the tribal leader. They had been in battle together and they had a bond now. And he was aware of *Ohronkene Hahser*. She rode behind them a short distance but when John turned he could see her off his left shoulder. She radiated dignity in her carriage even on her mount, he observed, she just stood out in any crowd. It was her height, he decided. Even off a horse, she towered above the other Indian women and many of the men. No, it was more than that. She was a damn fine looking woman and his eyes couldn't help being drawn to her repeatedly. Finally, he pulled over and rode beside her for a while just to enjoy her silent company and occasional smiles.

Tonoaki came back to the front and was not pleased to see the white riding beside his woman and John could feel it. Perhaps it was just a trifle small minded of him, he considered, but John couldn't help but take a tiny bit of satisfaction in irritating the brave. He still remembered being tied and shackled, awaiting a fate for which no man would wish. As they rode along John thought long on this.

The Indian psyche. They could be ready to skin you alive one minute and then suddenly everything was forgotten, or was it? He'd been given to understand Indians never forgot a grudge. They could wait years to settle a score but eventually they would get their revenge. If that was true then how safe was he really? How safe was any white out on the frontier? How many months of peace to lull everyone into a false sense of security before the war paint went back on and they turned on you just like a rattlesnake? But he had not known an Indian to capriciously turn on anyone. They did have rules they lived by. When you came to them as a friend, they had to treat you... well, if not exactly like a friend at least they wouldn't harm you. They believed in honor. And just because you were fighting each other one day didn't mean you couldn't be friends the next as long as you weren't a sworn enemy. But if you did them a personal wrong, that they would never forget. And John then realized he had never done Tonoaki a personal wrong. He had been captured as a general enemy and had escaped but he had not done anything to personally offend the arrogant brave.

John thought longer about this and realized he could understand. After all, didn't kings bring men to war on opposite sides of the battlefield that might have sat down as brothers at another time? His father and uncle had trapped and traded for years in the wilderness and never had any real problems with the Indians. It was the British and French fighting each other that caused the mess. But then, the native tribes weren't all innocent. Some of them were pretty damn blood thirsty and they were never at peace long amongst themselves. They had their sworn enemies and never truly made peace with them.

A call shook John from his thoughts, and he looked up to see the Tuwok River glittering ahead like a gold ribbon in the sun.

The tribe crossed the Tuwok and traveled along a tributary until they reached the perfect location for their village. In ceremony, Quiet Waters dispensed the sacred smoke while the ancient shaman sang the prayer. The signs were good, the omens positive, and Five Beavers and the ancient shaman were both pleased.

Everyone went to work to erect new housing and a new palisade. As John employed his horse to help haul logs, he couldn't help but wonder if the signs were really all that good or if it had been good diplomacy to make them seem to be. The elder leaders realized the military wanted them there. It would have led to a terrible dilemma if the signs had been against it. John chided himself for his jaded but realistic thoughts.

As the days went by he shared meals with the leaders and took the time for frequent conversations with *Ohronkene Hahser*. He was picking up bits and pieces of the language and had learned a simple greeting.

"*Shékuiksha!*" he greeted her each day.

"*Shékuorye,*" she would respond with a smile but from there they would have to depend upon Charlie-One-Claw to interpret. John could not help but ask things as they came to his mind.

"Why do you wear the clothes you do?" he asked one afternoon as the sun grew very warm. "All the other women wear only skirts."

He saw her face flush as the words were interpreted. Was she blushing? John suddenly realized he had for all intents and purposes just asked why she didn't expose her breasts to the world. He would have never asked a white woman that kind of question. In the midst of his own chagrin, she answered.

"My mother's people were converted to the white man's god and taught to cover themselves. We were taught shame. Since then I have learned it is better to cover myself, not for shame, for this tribe does not think this way, but because of my experiences with... in the past."

"I'm sorry," he found his tongue by the time Charlie-One-Claw finished, "my question was ill mannered."

"No, *Sak* Power, Friend. Nothing you should ask me is an offense. You have been too kind to me. You are very kind to my people. I see you with the elders. You show them respect. I see you with the children. Your heart is warm. You were treated very badly when you first came here and that is our offense. But you have forgiven, have you not?"

"I hold no grudge," John replied sincerely.

She nodded. "This is good."

"I don't think your husband much cares for me, though," he added noting that Tonoaki had just seen them talking and was scowling when he thought he was unseen.

She smiled. "Tonoaki knows without your aid, I would not be here. He is jealous even of my small son, so I think it is good for him to learn tolerance."

On another day, she approached John as he was assisting in the struggle to right up a portion of the palisade. He had given up wearing his uniform jacket around the encampment, dressing only in his breeches and a loose belted shirt. His musket and sword were generally with his horse and he carried only an Indian style knife on a sheath in his belt. Morning Light stopped and offered him freshly drawn water from the cold river. "Thank you," he replied automatically as he accepted the water vessel and drank deeply, the raw masculine angle of his throat moving up and down as he swallowed. She watched him. When he finished he blotted his mouth and then his sweaty brow with his sleeve. He paused in handing her back the clay bowl and smiled, his sun tanned face making his eyes and teeth very white. She nodded and for a few long moments their eyes beheld each other but they said nothing and she went on her way leaving him to return to his labors.

Later that evening as the camp relaxed she approached him when Charlie-One-Claw was there.

"Hello, *Sak* Power, Friend," she began in English and then continued in the Indian tongue. "I have just put my young one to sleep for the night. It is a good evening is it not?"

"It's a very beautiful evening."

"The wall is complete."

"Yes."

"And soon you will go?"

"Yes, soon I will have to go," he nodded.

"Have to? Do you not want to?" she asked softly and he did not answer. "Where is your family, *Sak* Power?" she asked abruptly, but then he had learned much about her and her life and she knew so little about him.

John frowned and looked off into the distance before he replied. "My parents are alive and well... back on the coast. I write to them... occasionally. I should write to them more often. I'm not much at writing," he said a little defensively, trying to excuse the fact that he had in fact not written to them in several years. As she stood silently looking at him he felt the strangest prodding to somehow explain himself to her. "I joined the army to get away for awhile and it's rather become my way of life."

"Away? From your parents?"

"No... I love my parents very much."

"Your mate? Do you have a family?"

"No," a frown crept over his forehead. "I have no one."

She only nodded and smiled gently. If he had not left to get away from his family then there could only be one other reason a young man would run off so far from home for so long. Morning Light guessed it was a woman. As she now knew Jack Power, she could not imagine a woman not being proud to be his. Who would reject such a man, she asked herself, not knowing the tragedy in John's life.

"Your parents have the right to be proud of their son," she said and he looked at her, unable to speak. He couldn't think of anything he'd ever done to really make his parents proud, not since he was a small boy at his slate and lessons. Phillip was the one who ran the mill and had given them grandchildren while he had almost given their father a stroke when he'd learned his eldest son had joined the army.

He still had the letter Phillip had written describing their father's anguish, their mother's tears. He was sure he was a vast disappointment to them. He knew he'd caused them sorrow when he'd run away and he missed them more and more, knowing they were growing older.

Morning Light saw the feelings race across Jack's face with the speed of lightning and then fade beneath a controlled facade. Because she didn't understand his words, she felt rather than heard. And her woman's inner sight enlightened her more about Jack during that brief minute or two than all their years of acquaintance had before. And she was aware that she felt something for him that she knew she should not feel. It was more than friendship. She cast her eyes down and murmured good night as she left.

Weeks had passed and John knew he needed to return to the fort. His mission was accomplished and he held high hopes for even more. He hoped that he had established some trust with this tribe that would lead to a stronger alliance. But he could only hope. He did feel he had had some meaningful conversations with Five Beavers and the other elders and, therefore, hope wasn't completely fanciful. At last, he said his farewells and left the peaceful new village with his aide and his scout.

"The fort is only one hard day's ride," he told Morning Light. "If you ever need anything, get word to me." He stood hat in hand before the young squaw, realizing he was going to miss her a great deal as he stared into her soft brown eyes.

"Be safe, *Sak* Power, Friend," she replied with a smile and let him take her hand and brush a kiss onto her knuckles. "You will come back again." She said it as a statement and he nodded, clearing his throat.

"You can count on it. It may not be until next spring, but I'll make it a priority." Charlie-One-Claw had a little trouble trying to translate that last and settled on the word for *important*.

She watched him mount his horse and leave. He had no sooner ridden through the gate of the palisade when Tonoaki was by her side.

"What is that he does, taking your hand to his mouth?" he asked suspiciously. Morning Light turned to her husband innocently and shrugged.

"It is a greeting between the whites."

"I do not see him greet anyone else like this."

"I think it is only between men and women. Man friend presses lips on hand of woman friend in greeting and parting, young, old, makes no difference. It means only a sign, recognizing I am not a warrior," she added diplomatically with a feminine intuition that told her she needed to dispel her husband's concerns.

Tonoaki didn't know if he could accept this but decided he was so glad to have the white man gone from his village that he would say no more to bring the soldier to his wife's mind.


Morning Light worked hard helping to clear a plot of land for the family garden, while Tonoaki along with the other strong braves went on to clear a larger field for corn. Once the men had the land cleared and planted, it would go to the women to continue to care for the crops. Weeding and hoeing and watering were a daily occupation not only in the larger communal fields but in the small individual family gardens as well.

As she worked in the gardens, tenderly encouraging all the young plants to flourish, she taught her young son to play nearby without trampling on the objects of her endeavors. And she had a great deal of time to think. She was surprised to realize her thoughts often ran to the white man named *Sak*. As he had stayed to help them, they had often spoken together. She had even begun to pick up a few of his strange words. And he had become a man to her, not a *white* man. She could not help but admire his willingness to help and assist her people, as well as his wisdom and strength. His kindness she had known for many years. But what surprised her more than anything was that secretly she was beginning to wonder about his personal life. What was a man such as he doing so far from his people? She intuitively recognized a difference between Jack and so many of the white soldiers. Had it really been a woman who had driven him away and into the wilderness? And if so, what was she like and where was she now? Morning Light would have never dared to ask such personal questions. But what of his family? Now she wished she had asked what they did, how they lived.

Had his father been a soldier? Was soldiering all *Sak* knew? Was it all he wanted of life? Did he not want a family of his own? Surely all men wanted a family eventually, or didn't they? Were the whites so different that they could not want families like her people did? Every man wanted a son, at least, every man she had ever known... except...

Her stomach actually knotted for a brief moment as she thought of the horrid white men who had killed her father. These were men she could not imagine ever having a family. These were men who seemed born of an evil spirit and would only pass along that evil spirit so it was better they never have a family. She forced herself to turn away from these memories which had been fading from that time in her life.

Jack was the very opposite of those men and Morning Light found herself thinking of him again and again, daring to appraise him physically, now that he was gone. His gold-yellow hair was beautiful against his tanned skin and his eyes were as light smoke at times. At others they reflected the colors around him. His appearance was most pleasing when you became used to the differences between his people and hers. Hair on the face and chest was strange to her but his body looked to be the equal of any well made warrior. In the white world he surely must be thought very handsome. His face had strength as well as warmth and pleasing looks. But above all, he had never been anything but decent to her, even when he was a prisoner, treated no better than a dog on a leash. And the first time she had seen him, he had come to her for pleasure. What would it have been like if she had not been such a child and wounded as well?

Suddenly, Morning Light stopped these thoughts and reproached herself. Why did she spend time thinking of another man? If Gray Wolf were alive she would not be thinking of another man or what it might be like to couple with him in pleasure. She felt the blood rise in her face at the guilt she felt. It was because she did not love Tonoaki as she had loved Gray Wolf. But that was no excuse. She was Tonoaki's woman now, his mate and he deserved her loyalty. Guiltily, Morning Light forced herself to concentrate on her plants.

As the young squaw worked in her garden her skin darkened with the exposure to the hot bright sun. To the casual observer her skin tone looked much like everyone else in the village. As a child running naked in the sun, she had looked much like everyone else except her skin was more golden and less coppery in hue. But now after many years of covering her hips and breasts, the tendency to a slight paleness which was an inheritance of her white blood grew sharper in contrast. Tonoaki did not realize this. He only knew that his wife's womanliness had always seemed to be highlighted, all the erotic parts, and it drove him wild. It had been attracting him since the first time he had spied upon her nakedness in the moonlight, bathing in the river with the water glistening over her skin and making her breasts, hips, underbelly, buttocks, and loins seem to emanate light.

It was a soft, sultry summer eve and twilight hovered like a caress upon the earth. Singing Wind was watching Gray Wolf's Son and Tonoaki took his wife to the river to bath away the sweat, dirt, and toil of the day. He always enjoyed watching her at this ritual and tonight he slipped into the inviting water with her. She glowed like a goddess, he thought, it was a wonderment. Of all the women he had known, only she looked like this. All the enticing curves of her body reflected the moonlight and radiated a glow of their own that never failed to excite him. He moved in closer to take her in the water.

He was pleasantly surprised at the intensity of her response to him and when at last they lie together on a rock still emitting the warmth of the day's sun, he cradled her tenderly.

"You complete my world," he whispered quietly, gently stroking her hips and belly. "I used to envy your first husband. I admit we were rivals and I burned because he was always better than I. But now I am grateful to him. I pray to the Great Spirit that he is well in the Spirit World." Tonoaki was superstitious and was careful not to say Gray Wolf's name aloud.

Morning Light was still, not certain what Tonoaki was leading up to but uncomfortable thinking of Gray Wolf now, after she and Tonoaki had just shared pleasures.

"He spoke for you when others would have..." he didn't finish. "For this he deserved to have your love first but I am grateful to have your love now."

Morning Light was struck by the tenderness in his voice and reached out to caress his cheek. It was wet. He was crying. This was Tonoaki of whom she had once been so terrified and he was weeping before her in the darkness, baring his soul. Braves did not weep, ever. She knew she was seeing a side to this proud defiant brave that no one else had ever seen and would never see. It was a moment that drew her to him like no other; it was not love but she was giving. She pulled him to her and began to caress him gently, tenderly, like a butterfly nuzzles a branch. She touched him in all his most sensitive places, igniting his skin and quickening his pulse. Her warm breath lingered on his face, his chest, in the palms of his hands, between his loins, until his *ohnoru* was rigid.

As he stretched back in the moonlight, she brought her body over him, her knees on either side of his hard torso, her hands gently guiding his flesh into her. He watched as her smooth firm body undulated in what was almost a dance. She stretched and moved provocatively, seeming to embrace the moonbeams with her arms while always her hips kept her gliding upon him. He was fascinated, beguiled, unable to move or speak. He trembled and gasped as her slow sensuous rhythm tortured him with its promise. Her soft silky hair floated out about her shoulders as it dried in the gentle evening breeze. A long, thick curl wound around her breast. She was like the earth mother, the bringer of all pleasure, the one who captures a man's soul, totally sensual and capable of draining away the very essence of life from a warrior. He watched her, mesmerized as she moved upon him, riding him with such a slow intensity until he could take it no longer and still he held back and watched her, spellbound, his body grown so sensitive he felt it would ignite. He could feel her molten essence drench him again and again. Then, unable to contain himself any longer he grabbed her hips and began guiding her faster and faster until at last the pent up pressure exploded from within him. Totally drained, completely sated and feeling euphoric in his happiness, he drew her upper body down to hold her on him for a long while, her softness molding to him.

At long last they took another quick dip into the water, toweling themselves dry this time and dressing. As they walked back Tonoaki had a thought.

"Did you have your moon time when we were traveling?" he asked.

"No, I had it just before," she replied quietly.

"But you have not had one since..."

"Not yet," she said and then stopped realizing how long that had been. "You are right, my husband, my moon time is overdue."

His hand slipped down gently to her belly. "Perhaps you will not be having one for many months."

She smiled. "Perhaps."

Tonoaki's heart was full to bursting.


The gardens were growing well in the fertile soil and the vegetables were ripening. Morning Light was out pulling the ever present weeds when she found she couldn't help herself from nibbling at the fresh raw peas. Plucking pod after pod, she greedily chomped on the peas, pod and all, throwing out the stringy cellulose hull. They tasted so delicious, like nothing else she had ever had and they were exactly what she was craving. Suddenly she stood back in the realization she had actually devoured an entire row. She stopped herself and puzzled at her own actions. Then, she shrugged. They had tasted perfect, what more could she say.

Singing Wind stopped by the garden plot on the way back to the palisade. She observed the plucked row and discarded hulls. "When I was expecting you I used to eat raw squash and river oysters. I couldn't get enough of them. Today a raw river oyster would make me puke." She grinned. "So when is the baby due?"

Morning Light looked at her mother and smiled. "I think in the time just after when days are shortest, the month of the big cold."

Her mother nodded. "I welcome another grandchild."


Tonoaki endured the friendly teasing with proud pleasure. His wife's belly was getting as big as a mountain and she sent him out daily for some strange tidbit of one kind or another. Finding strawberries in the fall was impossible but he did have the good fortune of uncovering a hibernating nest of snakes and was able to bring home fresh snake for her. Finding blueberries was not easy until he was lucky enough to discover a patch in the hills which were frozen on the bushes. He came home delighted with the way his treasure made his wife's eyes light up. She munched the berries down, staining her hands and lips and teeth like a small child, and he laughed and nuzzled her for it.

In her jealousy and misery, Mist-On-Moon found the whole thing absurd and disgusting. Who would have thought Tonoaki could play such a fool over a pregnant wife? Quick Panther certainly didn't make that kind of fuss over her. In fact, he treated her more like a breeding dog. He entered her only from behind so he would not have to look at her face. He had pleasured himself until they knew she was pregnant and then he rarely touched her. She had been five months pregnant during their last march and he had no sympathy for her aching back and swollen feet. He had his new wife now and Mist-On-Moon had to listen to their love making in the night. There was little she could do about it. She was stuck with another squalling brat and he spent his evenings gambling and then crawled in to sleep with his new wife. The only satisfaction Mist-On-Moon could take was that he did not get the son he wanted off her this time, this last child had also been a girl and he had not touched her since.

It was bitter January, the month of the Big Cold and a storm was raging outside. The wind blew viciously making the huts shudder and the palisade creak. Snow had been falling for several days and was drifted up close to the roofs of some of the huts, burying wood stocks and food keeps. Inside the hut, Tonoaki kept the fire burning brightly and listened to his wife's ragged breathing. Her water had broken in the middle of the night and he had gone to get her mother. It was not customary in their tribe for a father, especially a new father, to witness his child's birth but with the winds driving the snows straight across the earth, there was no place for Tonoaki to go. He refused to go to another hut. He refused to leave *Ohronkene Hahser's* side.

Morning Light tried to joke and smile but finally the pains were becoming too strong for her to keep up a pretense. "Please, husband, go to my mother's husband, eat something. Drink something. This is going to take a while and I must rest. Take my son with you."

"Go," Singing Wind grunted in agreement. "Nothing is going to happen for a long time. The baby is not yet in position to enter the world."

"But..."

"Go... tell Five Beavers to give you some of my newest batch of drink. Perhaps it will help you gain patience." She shoved him out the door with her grandson bundled against the cold and quickly fastened the flap behind them.

Tonoaki carried Gray Wolf's Son and ran to the sachem's hut. There he was greeted with a knowing nod. Didn't Five Beavers have two wives and seven children born to his hearth? "Come, my son," he offered the hospitality of his warm fire. "Let the women do their work, I have found it is better to stay out of the way."

It was the longest day of Tonoaki's life. He thought he heard *Ohronkene Hahser's* screams but Five Beavers assured him it was only the screaming gale outside. The hut was too far removed to hear anything. By mid-afternoon Five Beavers agreed to send Wani over to bring back a progress report. The boy returned ashen and solemn saying the baby had not yet come but that his sister suffered greatly.

After Little Smoke had seen to everyone's supper, she wrapped up in her thickest robe and went to Tonoaki's hut to see if she could help. She found *Ohronkene Hahser* struggling through a breech birth. The baby's legs were out and *Ohronkene Hahser* was biting down on a small piece of thick leather to contain her desire to scream out the pain. Her face was twisted. Her body was bathed in sweat. Singing Wind was trying to free an arm where an elbow was caught.

"Here, let me help," Little Smoke offered and deftly brought the child into position just as Morning Light gave another mighty push and delivered both shoulders with a deep primal groan that set the framing of the hut to vibrating. At last, the head appeared.

"It is over, my daughter," Singing Wind choked back her tears. "You have a daughter of your own now."

Morning Light gasped for breath, grateful the worst was over, and looked at the child through a haze of weariness. "Tonoaki wanted a son," she rasped in a whisper of disappointment.

"A son, a son, they always want a son. You have a son, now you have a daughter. He can get a son next time," Singing Wind fussed.

"At this moment," the new mother gave a weak crooked smile, "I do not want to think about a *next* time, my mother."

After Singing Wind tied off the cord she delivered out the afterbirth while Little Smoke saw to cleaning and washing the infant. Laying the baby girl down next to the fire she paused over her, looking at her closely.

"What is it?" Singing Wind asked in a whisper, her daughter finally slept and she did not wish to disturb her.

"The skin... it is so pale. Do you think it is sick?"

Singing Wind examined the babe now that the membrane had been washed away. "She seems to be all right," she observed. "It is perhaps the light. And she is very bald." She smiled. A girl with no hair, she mused. Every baby she had ever seen had always had at least a dark fuzz over its head if not a full head of hair. This one did not have even a shadow and looked like a plucked turkey. "It will grow fast enough," she said with more confidence than she felt.

The grandmothers wrapped the child up snugly against the cold drafts and put her into her mother's arms.

"Well," sighed Singing Wind, "I suppose it is time to put the father out of his misery and let him know he has a daughter. If you will stay with her, I am going to get something to eat."

"Of course," replied Little Smoke. "There is plenty of *onekwa* in the pot."

When Singing Wind entered the hut, Tonoaki looked up expectantly. Suddenly she felt sorry for the young brave. "Your wife is well but it was a very difficult birth. You have a healthy baby girl." She saw disappointment in his eyes but he covered it quickly.

"They are resting?" he asked.

"They sleep. They are exhausted."

"But she is well?"

"She will be fine. Next time it will be a boy." Singing Wind smiled warmly and Tonoaki nodded.

Singing Wind sent him home with extra of the thick pea soup and when he arrived Little Smoke left. He went to his wife's pallet and looked at her. He said a silent prayer of thanksgiving for her well being. Then he looked at his daughter. He didn't know much about babies. He saw the puckered up little wrinkled red face and was not impressed. She looked sickly but he told himself he had to accept the grandmothers' assurances that she was perfectly healthy. He supposed a few days would make a great difference. He could not remember ever having seen a baby that was only minutes old before. Then, he looked to *Ohronkene Hahser* again. Her face was smoothed out, placid and peaceful again. He was glad and his heart swelled with his love.

Tonoaki put more wood and peat upon the fire and stretched out on his pallet. It had been an exhausting day for everyone.

# *Chapter 25*

Through the next days, word spread around the village that *Ohronkene Hahser* had given Tonoaki a daughter. But the storms continued and everyone stayed in their own huts. Mother and child remained bundled up deep in furs. The days old infant did little more than eat and sleep. Morning Light was bleeding heavily after the rough delivery and Singing Wind insisted she remain still in her bed as much as possible. Singing Wind, Little Smoke, Wani, and Five Beavers had managed to trample a path to Tonoaki's hut. They visited the snowbound couple and helped with the infant and Gray Wolf's Son.

The weather continued to be harsh. Another storm blew in and it snowed like a whirlwind. The winds were so fierce that no one went outdoors unless it was unavoidable. Singing Wind and Little Smoke took turns watching over their grandchildren and cooking for both their lodge and for Tonoaki's. The wise older women kept Morning Light inside with her infant. After her difficult delivery, her rest was earned, they said. But even after she was up and on her feet, the baby rode in a fur skin carrier tied to Morning Light's bosom where her body's warmth was shared with her child.

Tonoaki paid little attention to the baby. In his mind a girl-child was something to gain alliances with later, but that would be years from now. At present, she was just a squalling, wetting, messing, little wrinkled creature with a disgusting pallor in the firelight and no hair. He was concerned with his wife's recuperation however, and found himself chafing with impatience. With the grandmothers fussing about they had no privacy anymore. He wanted his wife well and purified and able to satisfy his hunger for her and so he was willing to give the grandmothers the room to come and go and help *Ohronkene Hahser* in her recuperation.

By the time the baby was almost two moons old, warm winds had come from the south and all but completely melted away the deeply drifted snow. Everyone was out and about within the village and Morning Light brought the baby out for the first time, bundled in her carrier.

As the women came to greet the mother and see the baby, they grew strangely quiet and subdued. Morning Light was aware that her daughter's eyes were blue but then Singing Wind had told her of their white blood and how she herself had been born with eyes of blue which turned a soft brown later. Morning Light was now used to her child's pale skin thinking of how the sun would warm it in the summer and soon it would have a healthy color. But the people of the village were seeing this baby for the first time and did not know what to say. It was apparent to them that something was very wrong with the child. It made "congratulations" seem like hypocrisy.

Mist-On-Moon was loath to see Tonoaki's child by another woman but Quick Panther had insisted she go out to give her congratulations to the new mother. She had no wish to congratulate anyone. Tonoaki had been her lover and because of him, she had been punished for adultery she told herself. He had cast her aside and now he had his beautiful wife and his baby. Mist-On-Moon saw the infant and her eyes widened as she held her own fur over the lower half of her face. She grinned broadly and had to stop herself from laughing out loud. The child was *white*! It was so obvious, was no one else going to say it? The sun caught the golden fuzz on the top of the head, *gold* hair. The eyes were *blue*! Great Spirit, its skin was as pale as...

Mist-On-Moon made the appropriate mumbles of congratulations then, and walked away. She went straight to the horse corral where she had seen Tonoaki go. If she hurried she could catch him there before he decided to set off hunting or fishing. She saw him and as she watched the tall arrogantly handsome brave grooming his horse, all the bitterness rose up in her and her smile beneath her fur was filled with hate.

Keeping the fur skin up to hide her face, she spoke, "Tonoaki?"

He barely grunted an acknowledgment of her presence and did not spare the time to look at her.

"I have just seen the new baby," she purred maliciously, "I must say I admire your tolerance. Of course, it is only fair, as many men as you have helped to cuckold, it is right that you should not mind being a cuckold yourself."

"What are you talking about?" he snapped, looking at her sharply.

"Well, to raise the boy is one thing, after all you did marry his father's widow but to accept a bastard is really very remarkable, especially when it is so obvious that it is another's. Quick Panther accepted your bastard but at least she looks like us. If you really want to see what a daughter of yours looks like, come and see my oldest girl."

She had his attention then. He stared at her, his black eyes burning into hers. "Speak plainly woman, what are you saying?"

"We all know whose company Morning Light was constantly in last spring, and now the baby looks just like him. How could you miss it? No one else has. Yellow hair. Light eyes. White skin. What was his name? *Sak*? Was that it?"

Tonoaki leaped at her with murder in his eyes. Grabbing her so roughly he bruised her arms, she continued to clutch the fur to her face and began to laugh. A mocking laugh.

"You lie, woman. You are nothing but lies!" he spit out fiercely.

"See for yourself. Go look at the baby and this time open your eyes."

Tonoaki pushed her back and took off for his hut. When he burst through the door he startled Morning Light who was about to begin nursing. His eyes were wild and his face was dark and twisted.

"What...?" she wasn't able to get the words out before he snatched the baby from her arms.

"I want to see this child outside," he said as his only explanation. He took the infant outdoors. It was the first time he had really seen her in the full light, with her eyes open and now there was some hair growing on her head. Tonoaki stared in horror. Her eyes were blue! Her hair was coming in soft and golden! And her skin. This sickly pallor was not sickness, it was the skin of a WHITE!

Morning Light had followed him outside and saw the revulsion in his face. She didn't really understand the full meaning yet but her instincts told her to take the baby from him at once. She did without any effort as Tonoaki stood as a man in a trance. But the rage was building within him. He was too proud, too arrogant to be made mock of in this way.

"What is it, my husband?" she asked beginning to feel panic and clutching the infant to her. When he came at her she had no place to go except back into the hut.

Inside the hut, Tonoaki lashed out at her. The full force of his hand landed on her delicate face. She fought to keep her balance and held tight to her child. Another blow fell on her.

"What?" she cried out. "Tell me? Why?"

Her questions amounted to a denial. They said to him that she was still trying to deceive him and his temper was beyond his control as he went after her. Morning Light thought he went for the baby and she felt hatred rather than fear. She fell on her arms and knees over the infant, protecting her daughter with her own body, rather than trying to run for escape. Tonoaki continued to pummel her with his fists shouting obscenities and accusations, calling her names for coupling with the white dog and trying to pass his bastard off as their child. She felt the blows on her back, her kidneys, her head.

What was he accusing her of? Her mind ran in a whirl of speed disrupted by the blows raining down upon her. He didn't believe the baby was his? He thought she had betrayed him with... with... *Sak*?

"Nooooo, no, my husband, no," she cried out but her words were muffled and disjointed. "She *is* your daughter. I am the one who is part white. It is me. I have white blood..." she tried to speak between blows.

His response to her words was to take a thick length of rawhide and begin lashing her with it. Her heavy buckskin tunic was saving her skin which infuriated him more and he found the loose lacing she had untied to nurse her infant and he tore back the top to expose the flesh of her back. Venting his rage with full force, each blow meant to cause her the fullest pain, he continued to beat her until her back was swollen with red welts and still he continued until her back was bloodied. Then, he grew still as if suddenly seeing for the first time what he had done. Morning Light was cringing, sobbing, broken and bent over, huddled to the ground, bruised and covered in angry welts and bloody stripes. What had he done?! He threw down the rawhide and ran from the hut.

Tonoaki ran blindly out of the palisade, away from the eyes of the village and into the forest. The shock of what he had done to her reminded him of his love for her. But the hurt he felt was burning away that love. The shame to his proud spirit was unbearable. The confusion of emotions held him in a maelstrom he tried to outrun. As he ran his love drained away and fertilized hatred of the most malevolent kind that sprang up to consume him. It was hatred born of a jealous rage mixed with the unbearable disgrace of having been publicly humiliated and made a cuckold for all to see.

He had loved her. He had adored her. He had fairly worshiped the very ground she walked on, the air she breathed. He had spoiled her and revealed himself to her as to no other person on the earth. He had played the fool hunting and fetching for her ridiculous whims and cravings while she nurtured the white man's bastard in her belly. She had made him a laughing stock of the highest order. No different than Quick Panther in the eyes of the tribe, but worse. She had deceived him the very first year of their marriage and had the audacity to think she could get away with it. And her blatant deception was with the enemy, a white man! She might as well have coupled with a beast. Had he not been man enough for her? Had she not found enough pleasure in his arms? How had his manhood been lacking to send her into the arms of a white? What made him less than Gray Wolf?!

The terrible slur this implied against the young brave's dignity and very identity was more than his mind could stand. The new rage building in Tonoaki slipped beyond the limits of reason and became blindingly insane. Cutting off her nose was not enough! Besides, he worshiped her beauty and would not live with her ugliness. But to betray him with a white was something he could not live with either. He would kill her and her bastard half-breed. It was not allowed to kill her for being unfaithful, but he would exact the punishment for betrayal with the enemy! She had become worse that filth in his eyes for she was filth packaged in the pretense of innocence, a poisonous serpent in the guise of beauty. Tonoaki finally turned to go back, his reason gone, his mind filled with white hot blinding rage. He must kill her. He should have just killed her to begin with. Then she would be out of his life, out of his heart, out of his mind, and he could forget it all forever. He would remove the scourge and take back his life and his dignity.

As soon as Tonoaki left the hut, Morning Light, sobbing and in agony, pulled herself up off the ground to assure herself her baby was well. Sheltered in the hollow between her knees and chest, the infant was unharmed but screaming for her interrupted meal. Morning Light uttered an involuntary gasp and cried out. Her back was on fire and the pain was making her weak and sick. Her left eye was starting to swell shut and she could taste her own blood as it ran down her face from her nose and mouth. Her tongue gingerly felt her lips. She grimaced but as she touched her teeth, she noted they were all still in place. She looked at her daughter and tried to hush her.

Mother's instinct told Morning Light that Tonoaki was not finished. He was lost to her and the passion that consumed him now was hate not love. At the very least he would come back to slit her nose. At the worst, a fleeting image crossed through her mind's eye of him dashing their baby's head against a rock, throwing it off a cliff, or pitching it to the wild beasts. She must flee to save her baby. Her mother could not help her against his rage. Even the Council of Mothers could not protect her. He would find a way to catch her, to harm them before anyone could stop him. Then, it would be too late. She could not stay. She had to get away.

Stumbling and gritting her teeth to stifle her cries, she awkwardly began stuffing a sack with essentials. Every step sent waves of agony to the point of nausea through her beaten body. But the adrenaline rush from fear drove her on. The baby continued screaming as Morning Light strapped it in the carrier, grinding her teeth through the pain as she tried to strap it to her back. She almost lost consciousness, the pain was so intense, and she stopped. It was stupid to try to use her back. She wasn't thinking. She wished the baby would stop screaming. She tied the infant into a sling across her breasts, bared one to give her suck, and was relieved at the sudden quiet. Then, she grabbed a water-bag, a knife, arrows and Gray Wolf's old bow, along with two robes she knew they would need to sleep on. Taking her three year old son, who had sat quietly crying through the savage scene, she fled to the village corral where she picked out the horse Gray Wolf had left to her. Putting the robes upon the horse, somehow she managed to pull herself onto its back where she had already placed her son to ride in front of her.

Those few who saw her leaving did not question, did not interfere. They could tell by Morning Light's bloodied face and blood stained clothing that there was domestic trouble. They were shocked but not interfering was the code they lived by. They sought to spare her shame by trying not to look at her. Singing Wind did not see her daughter leave or she might have tried to stop her. She knew her daughter carried white blood.

With the adrenaline influx born of panic, Morning Light urged the horse out of the palisade at a gallop. She clutched the horse tightly with her knees, each jarring hoof beat making her jaw ache and biting into her back. Her head felt like it was going to split open. But she would not slow down. She held tightly to her son, her baby and their sack of supplies as they traversed into the forest and then took a course following the tributary to the Tuwok River and the fort. She desperately needed a friend and Jack Power was her friend. She didn't think of what she would do when she got there. She was not thinking beyond the moment and the moment was totally absorbed in panic-riddled fear for her baby's life.

"Why do we leave the village?" Gray Wolf's Son spoke.

"Not now, my son. We must not talk. Save your breath for riding," she said finding it more and more difficult to speak.

"I have plenty of breath."

"I do not. Now hush, everything will be all right."

She heard the sound of water and followed it. She was certain that by following the river down stream they would come to the fort. Would *Sak* be there? What would she do if he was not? What would she do if he was? These were questions she could not deal with rationally. It was all she could manage just to hang on and ride blindly following the sound of the water without having to think.

Morning Light had never seen a map and was not one of the warrior-hunters to know the lay of the land by experience. She knew the tributary connected to the Tuwok. She knew the fort was on the east side of the Tuwok to the south. What she did not know was that the Tuwok River did not run a true north and south but flowed in such a weaving westerly direction as to run somewhat parallel to its tributary for almost twenty miles. In fact, the fort was located due south of the village as the crow flies only a full day's ride across a small mountain range. Subconsciously, one of John's remarks that the fort was only one hard day's ride away was in Morning Light's memory. She just did not know it was a ride to the south and not the east. Holding on by sheer willpower she urged the horse onward believing they would make the fort by nightfall, and then she could collapse.

She had reached a state of numbness and was developing a fever. She could not think of anything but reaching her goal, the fort. The fort and the man called *Sak*, Jack. Jack Power, Friend. He had helped her once before and she could only believe that he would help her again. She had nothing else to cling to. The sun sank, her baby slept, and she slumped over her three year old upon the horse which now walked along the water's edge.

At last, they met the Tuwok River. Morning Light roused herself from her stupor to search the horizon for a fort. There was none. It must be here, it must be only a short distance down the river, she thought desperately. She did not know that the fort was now over thirty miles southwest as the river flowed.

It was growing dark and she could go on no more. She slid from the horse, tethered it to graze and dropped the robes on the ground. She pulled food for her son from the sack and gathered wood for a small fire. Then, she collapsed upon the robe next to her children and pulled the second robe over them. She was shaking with shock and fever but despite her injuries or because of them, Morning Light fell into a deep sleep.

§

When Tonoaki arrived back at the hut he was in a cold mad rage. He was thwarted in venting it because no one was there and he was more angry with himself when he realized he was also just a little glad she was not there. He was almost blind from the blood in his eye and had been prepared to kill her with his bare hands, to break her neck, to choke the life from her, to bash her head against a post and the adrenaline surging through him found no outlet.

"Where is she?" he howled as Quick Panther ran out of his hut.

"She took a bundle and went to the corral," he volunteered.

Tonoaki took off to the corral and saw Morning Light's horse was gone. She had left to go to *him*, he thought murderously and jumped upon his own horse to take off for the fort.

It took him all night to get there but just before dawn he saw the lights of the fort across the river.

"Lieutenant, there's a rider coming across the river." Private Smally had been sent down from his perch in the lookout hut by the sergeant to report to the officer on night patrol.

"Friend or foe?"

"Cain't tell, sir."

"Well, go back and look. Give the challenge."

"Yes, sir." Smally hurried back to climb up to his post.

As the rider came closer, the lookout could tell he was a native.

"It's an injun," Smally said aloud and his near-sighted sergeant stopped chewing to listen. "He's stopping just out of range. But he's just sitting out there, big as life, like he's waitin' for something."

"What's he doin'?" his sergeant asked peering out into the growing light but unable to see anything.

"Nothing."

"What the hell does he want?"

"Cain't tell, Sarge, he's just sitting there."

"Ohhh, damn," the sergeant spit the juice of the tobacco he was chewing, then decided he better spit the whole wad before he approached the lieutenant. The sergeant lumbered down from the look-out hut and paced quickly to the officer's station.

"Sir," he said saluting as he approached the officer.

"Yes," the lieutenant replied.

"Beggin' pardon, sir, but I think we better report this to the commander on duty. There's something kind of strange about this. Captain Power was real involved in settling that village a while back and this looks like one of them injuns, maybe. He's alone and he's jist sittin' there."

The junior officer was quiet for a moment, contemplative even. Then he nodded. "All right. Back to your post I'll report to Captain Power. He's on duty tonight."

John Power went himself to the lookout box and peered out into the graying landscape. He pulled a spyglass out and confirmed his suspicion. He recognized the brave pacing his horse back and forth. It was *Ohronkene Hahser's* new husband. What the hell was he doing here? By treaty he shouldn't be on this side of the river. Then the thought came to him that something had happened to her and his stomach turned over in dread.

"Get Charlie-One-Claw out here fast," he commanded and the lieutenant turned to the sergeant.

"Go fetch Charlie-One-Claw for the captain, on the double," he said curtly.

The sergeant snapped to and went off for the scout in a rush. To the first private he caught he barked, "On the double to the bunk house, get Charlie-One-Claw and deliver him to the captain before I finish reloading my weapon or you'll wish you'd never been born!" The private paled and raced to the bunk house shared by the scouts and found Charlie-One-Claw fast asleep.

"Come on, Charlie," he shouted thumping his leg in agitation. "Get your sorry ass out of that bed on th' double. Captain Power wants to see you, right now."

Charlie-One-Claw uttered a string of oaths, after which he asked gruffly, "What for?"

"How should I know what for? But he wants you now and it's my ass if you ain't out there!" the private paced impatiently.

The scout rolled up from his pallet but he wasn't going to run.

Power and Charlie-One-Claw went out of the fort gate to meet with Tonoaki who was still sitting on his horse staring at them as they approached. "I want my woman, White Dog! Hand her over to me!" he shouted.

"He says he thinks his woman is here and he wants her back," interpreted Charlie-One-Claw diplomatically.

"His woman?!" John exclaimed in surprise. "O-ron-keenee-hah-ser? Ask him why he thinks she is here."

The scout hadn't the chance to finish when Tonoaki leaped across from his horse to take Power flying to the ground. John was caught off guard but quickly recovered. The two men rolled around on the ground for a bit before struggling to their feet. John was more clear headed than the brave who was lashing out in blind fury. When Tonoaki tried to fly at him again he ran right into the soldier's fist. John got in a solid punch to the gut that doubled Tonoaki over. He took advantage of it and landed an upper cut to the warrior's jaw, snapping his head back. The brave recovered, shaking his head for clarity and suddenly there was a knife in his hand. They circled around slowly, John wary of the knife while Tonoaki slashed out. The soldier ducked and nimbly avoided the blade. He caught the Indian's hand from behind, twisting it so he could hammer the offending wrist down upon his lifted knee until the knife dropped harmlessly to the ground. He drew back and flattened the brave with a combination punch that knocked him out.

"Tie his damn arms together behind his back and then throw some water on him," John said panting as much from adrenaline as from exertion.

Charlie-One-Claw grunted taking rope from his saddle and proceeded to truss Tonoaki up. "Do you have water?" he asked with a grunt.

"No, I didn't bring any water," John snapped. He was worried about *Ohronkene Hahser* and couldn't appreciate the scout's humor.

"I come from sleep. I have nothing to carry water in. How I get water from river? By magic?"

"Oh, for Christ's sake..." John bent over to pick up his hat, marched to the river's edge a few yards away and scooped up a hat full of water. He brought it back and threw it on the brave's face. "There," John said in exasperation. "Now, slap his face. Get him conscious again."

They heard the brave moan and saw his eye lids flutter.

"Now tell this horse's ass he better tell me the whole story right now before I really get mad," John barked.

With questioning, Tonoaki admitted to having had a quarrel with *Ohronkene Hahser*. He would not tell the white man that it was about him. He would not let the white man know that Tonoaki now knew he had lain with his wife. And he did not tell John that he had beat her. He did tell them she had had her baby and had run off. He had assumed she had run here. He had been mistaken, he said as he gathered his wits realizing the white man had not seen the woman. She must have gone back home by now. He must return to the village, he said with furious dignity.

John finally allowed Charlie-One-Claw to untie the brave and let him go but the whole incident set Power on edge. Something about it wasn't right. This hot headed buck who was once going to skin him alive or worse, was suddenly there demanding to see his wife, demanding as if he fully expected her to be there. And attacking him as if he had a personal score to settle. Why? A quarrel? No, John told himself, *Ohronkene Hahser* wouldn't just run away because of a simple quarrel and if there had been a quarrel, how was he involved? He wasn't the fort. If this brave thought his wife had come to the fort, why attack John? No, it didn't make sense. After everything that girl had been through, she wouldn't run away with a small child and a new baby unless... Too late did John realize that the brave must have beaten her for her to flee from him, from her family, from the entire village. And knowing the strength of the hot tempered brave, John scowled, she could be badly injured.

Upon reaching this conclusion, John was very angry. They waited only until it was fully daybreak before he and Charlie-One-Claw headed out for the village to see for themselves whether *Ohronkene Hahser* had returned and in what condition.

§

Morning Light awoke and almost passed out when she tried to rise. She was dizzy with the pain. Her head was pounding and her left eye was completely sealed shut. She should have put cold compresses on it last night to reduce the swelling, she chided herself. She had been too racked with misery and exhaustion to think of it. Then, for a panicky moment she thought she could not move until she realized her children were pressed close against her and slowly her body began to respond to her demands. She felt the ache in her kidneys from the punches she had received and her back was a flame. She crawled on all fours to the water's edge, leaving her children asleep under the robe. She washed the dried caked blood from her face. The cold water felt good against her swollen skin. Her lip felt huge and stiff. Her whole face burned and ached with the least movement but then so did her back. On impulse she drew off her tunic and went into the cold water, the icy fingers were a soothing balm to her tortured flesh and aching muscles. She was shivering violently but went deeper, the cold numbing the pain. At last she withdrew, thankful for the small reprieve the numbing cold had given her from the fiery throbbing. She hurried into her garments. She knew it would be agony to eat and chew, but she must try. She must keep her milk flowing for her infant, the daughter Tonoaki would kill if he could.

Fear spurred her on, overcoming all else. She stood still for a moment, looking at the river. Where was the fort? Morning Light looked suspiciously up and down the river banks, fear still strong within her that Tonoaki would suddenly appear and harm their child. They must cross the river and continue on.

She woke her son giving him dry meat to chew on. She could not chew any herself and sucked on a handful of dry corn. She changed the baby's swaddling, wrapping a fresh chamois cloth around her, washing her soiled one and letting it hang from the horse to dry. Then, she tied the infant into the pouch so she could nurse. Morning Light fetched the horse. They must cross the Tuwok here before it grew any larger, before it grew deeper or wider. The fort was on the other side, she knew, and they must cross now. Again putting the robes over the horse, she held on to her son and daughter and urged the animal across the water at a shallower spot. Morning Light was grateful that the water never got any higher than just above the horse's hock. The animal went across easily.

By treaty, Tonoaki was not supposed to cross this river. None of their village were to cross. Why did that not make her feel relief? She realized, by treaty, she was not supposed to be on this side of the river either. But that had not stopped her and she did not think it would stop Tonoaki either. She pressed on.

In the full light of a bright day, Morning Light asked herself what she expected when she found Jack Power. She would tell him of her plight, of course, but what did she really expect him to do about it? Did white blood of four generations ago give her any right to seek the white man's protection? Perhaps in time, Tonoaki would listen to reason and come to his senses. Perhaps in time, she could go back. The tears that came unbidden told her she did not believe this would ever happen.

After riding half the day, her son was asking for food and her baby was crying.

Morning Light found a soft grassy clearing at the edge of the river and stopped the horse. Sliding off its back, she grit her teeth to keep from moaning aloud as she lifted her young son down and bid him to sit.

"I must pass water, mama," he said quietly and moved off to the side to relieve himself. The horse grazed on the tender grass shoots it found in the small meadow.

Morning Light pulled dried cornbread from her sack and laid it out for Gray Wolf's Son before taking up the baby again. Her baby daughter had messed herself and the young mother took her to the water's edge to wash her. When the baby was clean, the young squaw wrapped her in another fresh chamois cloth and drew her to her breast to suckle.

She hobbled back to the pine tree, carrying the nursing babe in her arms and sat down with Gray Wolf's Son. The young child sat chewing vigorously on the corn bread.

"Where are we going?" he queried in a baby voice.

"We are going to find the white man's fort," she replied trying not to wince at the pain it caused her to speak.

"Why?"

"Because mama has a friend there," she mumbled.

"We're going to see your friend?"

"*Hv.* Yes."

"*Sak* is your friend?"

"*Hv.*"

"Why are you crying, mama?"

"Because I am sorry this is happening?"

"What is happening?"

"Never mind, hush. We will talk of it another time."

Morning Light patted her son's head tenderly. She knew she, too, should eat something although she had no appetite and the swollen split on her lip made it difficult and painful to chew. She still could not see out of her left eye. It remained swollen closed. She would need strength to continue on and to heal. She stretched out on her side with her baby and nodded off into oblivion.

§

By the time Tonoaki returned to the village again it was late afternoon. Still Morning Light was not to be found and neither were her two children. He stormed about in a rage, questioning everyone, even Wani. Where could she be? Who was hiding her? It would be the worse for anyone who dared to keep her from him, he shouted and threatened and bellowed, his face contorted. Feeling thwarted and frustrated, he began to tear up the hut. Throwing mats on the fire, cooking utensils, baskets and pots. Child's toys. Blankets. All the things she had used, things she had touched. He roared his rage and with his bare hands he torn into the walls, rent up the roof, and left all in the growing blaze of the cook fire gone wild. Soon the dwelling site was an inferno of destruction.

"WHERE IS SHE?!" he demanded of the wind. "WHERE IS SHE?!"

Mist-On-Moon watched from the cracks in the walls of her hut, a smug smile on her lips. The flames from Tonoaki's hut rose high for many minutes and she could see them dancing and shooting above the roofs of the huts blocking her vision. It served him right, she thought and then absently itched at the scars in the center of her face. Slowly she became aware of what her fingers were really feeling and hot tears filled her eyes. The bitterness was still there. His misery did not make her life any sweeter and she had not even been with him the night Quick Panther had caught her. But why should he be happy when she was not? She jerked away from the wall and shushed her children in their clamor.

Singing Wind was beside herself over her daughter's disappearance. Now, she saw the hut going up in flames and ran for Five Beavers. Five Beavers was already calling upon Tonoaki's father and brother for assistance. They must bring the young brave to the Council Circle. They must talk. He must listen. Enough was enough. Next, his jealous anger would be responsible for burning down the whole village.


"I always knew she was different," Singing Wind was speaking to the gathering of family in the neutral space of formality known as the Council Circle. She spoke with a certain air of formal dignity that she hardly felt. Her knees were shaking and she quivered as she stood before the others. She was suffered to speak in the circle only because she was Morning Light's natural mother and her only living parent. "Her hair was never the hair of our people," she stated in her usual coarse voice. "And then there is her height, the look of her face, her paler skin. As a baby she was barely darker than her infant daughter. I became so used to it, I never thought of it. Everyone in our tribe knew our family history. I never thought something like this would happen. And I never spoke of it here. Perhaps I should have."

"You lie, woman, to protect your own!" Tonoaki accused with a sneer. "You are a mother. You would say anything to protect your child."

"I do not lie!" Singing Wind shot back sharply, her anger quelling her fear. "There is no need for lies when the truth speaks for itself. My mother's grandmother was a full-blooded white woman! She had yellow hair and eyes like the summer sky. She was stolen by my mother's grandfather at a time when there were not enough women in his tribe. Her people brought her back but she chose to return to her warrior husband. My mother's siblings had soft hair like Morning Light. I was told some were blue eyed when they were born, eyes that later turned to the color of wet loam. I was told my own eyes started out the color of the sky. I do not know who has poisoned your mind against my daughter, Tonoaki, but you are wrong. You are wrong! You do her great injustice. She is a faithful wife. She is good and decent. The child she bore could be no one's but yours!"

"Does it look like mine?!" he spat out and turned his back to her. Tonoaki did not hear. He did not want to hear. If he was wrong then what he had done was unforgivable. If he was wrong then he had allowed all his love to turn to hate unjustly. He could not accept this. If this was true, then, for nothing he had driven the greatest prize in his life away forever. She was the only woman he would ever love so completely that he had dared to share his secret self with her. If what Singing Wind said was true than he had caused his own loss. But how could it be true? Did not Gray Wolf's Son look normal? His pride rebelled and he remained stiffly in denial. No. Morning Light had deceived him, her mother now tried to deceive him, but his own eyes did not deceive him. The girl-child was obviously from the seed of a white man. And he would not be taken for a fool a second time.

Twelve year old Wani had been listening. And the revelation stunned him. "If what you say is true, my mother," he said in horror, "then I, too, am part white?" He stared in horror at his own flesh.

"*If?* If? Now you dare to question my truth as well?" she looked at him scowling. His head snapped up to look her in the eyes and he said nothing. His face a startled blank. "Yes, Wani, you, too, have white blood," she said more reasonably, her shoulders slumping with sudden weariness, "through me, through my mother, through her mother... perhaps someday your mate will bring forth a yellow haired baby with blue eyes, the image of your ancestor. Will you beat her for it? Will you be ready to throw your child to the wolves? It will still be your child. It will still be your blood. What will you do? Accuse your mate of being unfaithful like this... this ignorant back-end of a..."

"Enough!" Five Beavers stated with authority, then turned to the young husband. "Tonoaki, now that you know that your wife has white blood and is capable of bringing forth a child of that blood, you would be wise to reconsider."

"No," the brave stated flatly.

"Who accuses her?" Five Beavers asked, surprised at the young brave's stubbornness. "Who? Who has witnessed her in the acts you accuse her of? Who has witnessed anything to make you suspect her faithlessness to you?"

Tonoaki thought and realized it was only because of the words of Mist-On-Moon that he had believed. He stiffened. "It matters not. She is gone... forever."

"If she had not left, you would have killed her before you heard reason." Singing Wind could not be still.

"Perhaps," his voice was much quieter now, "but she has left me all the same."

"You must go after her," Five Beavers growled. "She is alone with two small ones. You are responsible for her safe keeping. You must bring her back here *safely.*"

The younger man looked up then. Was there any chance he could bring her back? His mind replayed the images of the confrontation in the hut. Her face covered with blood beneath his fist. The look of horror in her eyes as he struck out at her to make her hurt as badly as he hurt. The hatred he saw in those eyes when she saw him go for the baby, a baby he could never accept as his own. He had laid open her back, her beauty would be scarred for life... if she was even still alive.

"No. It is over. She has left me, and I have burned our home," Tonoaki repeated and walked away from the council fire tight lipped and stiff necked. No one heard him say, "She will never forgive what I have done."

Singing Wind was very unhappy and the agitation was obvious in Five Beavers' hut. Her only daughter and her grandchildren were gone. Fled. Driven out. They were on their own in the forest and subject to all the harm and tragedy which can befall the unprotected. She wrung her hands and fretted. She wanted Five Beavers to gather a group of braves and hunt for her. But her mate thought Morning Light would come back on her own when evening fell.

"You do not know her, my husband. She is not a silly girl playing a game. She does not flee from guilt. Morning Light has been through much in her life, she has much inner strength. She flees now for the life of her daughter and sees no hope in returning. She will die out there," the elder squaw said as she wrung her hands, "or she will survive but I will never see my daughter again unless you bring her back."

Five Beavers still was not moved to interfere, he maintained the position that Tonoaki and Morning Light must work out their own problems. In despair, Singing Wind went outside of the hut and fell to her knees on the ground. She poured ashes from the dead cook fire on her head and began to keen and wail. She was in mourning for her loss and Five Beavers was not certain what to do next.

§

Morning Light awoke with a start. She chided herself for losing good daylight and wondered how long they had slept. Gray Wolf's Son was still sleeping, so was the babe at her breast. Her face felt very hot and tight. She hesitantly touched the side where Tonoaki's blows had fallen the most. It felt strange and not like herself. She still could not open her left eye. Her throat was dry and she took some water but her lip burned when she moved it. Her back had stiffened to inflexibility, every movement spoke of her abuse. Strapping the baby back into the carrier, she nudged her small son awake. Painfully, she managed to throw the robes up over the horse again before she tied the top of the papoose carrier to the sack of supplies. They counter balanced each other as she dropped them on either side of the animal's withers. She wished she had thought of this before. It allowed her aching body freedom from the small added weight of the infant.

"Come, my son, we must continue," she slurred through her swollen lips. The three year old was still in a sleepy stupor and looked at her with curiosity. This was his mother but she did not look like his mother, she did not even sound like his mother. She led him to the horse and lifted him without a sound although the effort cost her much, then she managed to crawl up upon the sturdy little animal herself.

They continued to travel downstream.

That night she heard the howl of wolves and built three fires in the outline of a triangle. The air had turned very cold. Spring had suddenly disappeared and snow crystals were in the air. She and the children slept within the center of the fire points. She didn't sleep well. She woke repeatedly, feeding the fires to keep them blazing. The fires did more than warm them, they kept the animals away as well. But perversely they also kept her in fear that the light would lead Tonoaki to them. What little sleep she stole was riddled with nightmarish dreams of the white men who had come into her parents' campfire circle those many years ago. But the white men turned into Tonoaki who beat her and wanted to murder their child.

§

When Captain Power and Charlie-One-Claw arrived at the village, the two men immediately sought out the sachem to inquire after *Ohronkene Hahser*. They found Singing Wind sitting outside the hut wailing in mourning for her daughter. John recognized the posture and signs, his heart jumped within his chest. It seemed like an eternity for Charlie to relay the information that the young woman wasn't actually dead, at least not to anyone's knowledge, but that she had never returned to the village.

In short time John's suspicions that Tonoaki had beaten *Ohronkene Hahser* were confirmed. She had been beaten very badly according to the witnesses who had seen her leaving the village with her children and her horse. John was seething with contempt for the very people who claimed to be her family. That they had done nothing to protect her was unforgivable. But then wasn't her mother the same woman who let her daughter be sold out as a whore? They saw the contempt in his eyes before he was able to mask it. Then, he told himself he had no right to judge. Deep down he also knew he wasn't being particularly fair. In white society were not women often beaten and some even killed by abusive husbands and fathers while friends and relatives looked the other way?

"She has fled," Charlie told him simply. "They do not know where. Five Beavers thinks she will return soon."

John stood looking around him in frustration. "How could they let him do that?" the disgust in his voice was obvious.

"That is nothing. Among these people a husband has the right to cut off the nose of an unfaithful wife."

"Good God, that's barbaric!!" John stormed. The scout said nothing. "Is that what she is accused of? Being unfaithful? That's ridiculous," he turned to march off to where the hut used to be, seeking Tonoaki. Nothing but black ash remained at the spot. His hands kept making fists. He should have killed the arrogant savage long ago for making him a prisoner. This would have never happened then. It was just as well the warrior couldn't be found. No one had seen him since the fire. John was afraid he might have killed the savage on the spot if he were there and let the devil take the treaty.

John returned to where Charlie-One-Claw stood with the horses.

"Tell her mother I'm going to look for her and I won't stop until I find her," he growled as he checked the cinch around his horse's belly. "Tell her... tell her... never mind, come on, let's go."

"It is almost dark. We wait 'til dawn," the scout reasoned.

"No. I can't wait. Not here. I want to get away from here. We'll get some riding in and make camp soon."

The scout only groaned, then spoke to Singing Wind.

John's mind was racing as he sat upon his horse outside the palisade gate waiting for Charlie-One-Claw. She had taken two babies and a horse and she'd been gone for two days now. Where the hell had she gone? Visions of *Ohronkene Hahser* with her two helpless children being attacked by wild animals in the midst of the forest spurred the man on.

"Where did she go, Charlie?" he demanded as the scout appeared along side him. "Why didn't she come to the fort?"

"Maybe she not know where fort is," the scout replied.

"But I know she knew there was a fort..."

"Yes," Charlie nodded.

"and that it was only a day away right straight over these mountains."

"Are you certain?"

"I told her it was only a day away," John snapped back. "I remember that distinctly. Don't you remember?"

Charlie-One-Claw nodded. "But you never say what direction."

"I didn't?!!" John gaped and the scout shook his head. "Then... do you think she followed the river?"

Charlie-One-Claw shrugged. "She know fort on river."

"Good God, Charlie, if she followed the river, it'll take days. Come on, while we still have some daylight," John spurred his horse down to the tributary and on.

# *Chapter 26*

**M**orning Light foraged as they continued their journey the next day. Her supplies were running out. She had only thought it would be a day, two at the most to get to the fort. She had made meal cakes for their breakfast with the last of her corn flour. She walked and found tuber plants which were edible raw. She gave them to Gray Wolf's Son. She could not chew them herself. Then she remounted the horse and urged his speed. The fort had to be close. She knew it was on the Tuwok. How much farther could it possibly be?

By afternoon she was exhausted, aching from the jolting ride and happy enough to sit quietly at the river's bank and fish. She caught two good sized trout and after cleaning them, she baked them in wet leaves for supper. Carefully, gleaning the trout flesh free of bones before giving it to Gray Wolf's Son, she fed the child first then attacked what remained herself. She was famished and craving the fatty oils of the fish. She had to eat to be able to satisfy her baby daughter's appetite and the fish did not take much chewing. When she had cleaned up every morsel, she rubbed her fingers in the fish oil and gingerly spread it on her facial cuts hoping it would make the skin more supple.

They had stopped near a rock face and two good fires protected them from unwanted visitors. None the less, Morning Light kept Gray Wolf's bow at her side with an arrow poised in its string. Exhaustion overtook her and she slept soundly through the night finally waking near dawn to the cries of her infant.

Snow began to fall and Morning Light was the most frightened she had been since they had left the village. It was the fourth day and still they had not come to the fort. How far had they traveled? She did not know. Even in her fever, she realized that traveling alone with two children meant she could not make as good a time as a soldier but surely after four days they should have reached the fort. It was nagging at her that somehow she had become confused and turned around in the wrong direction. But she followed the flow of the water on the Tuwok, and the flow remained the same. She traveled with the flow, she traveled down river. Had the fort really been up river? No, no, she told herself. From what she had heard the fort had to be south. What direction were they going? The sky was a thick overcast and it was impossible to tell where the sun was.

She watched for river caves, any kind of shelter. If the snow did not stop they would need a good shelter. At this time of year, it was not unusual to have a late storm. It would be over quickly and the sun and warmth would return but they must survive it. The snow was falling faster and Morning Light knew they must stop for she must build a shelter.

She halted in a grove of pine trees when she spied a huge fallen tree. The trunk had broken in two. The roots, torn from the ground, created a small cavern. Working in the growing wind as quickly as her stiff and pained body would allow her, she pulled together several smaller fallen logs, bracing them against the large rooted one. Then, she piled thickly needled pine branches over them. It was so crude, she thought, a really stiff wind could blow it all away. But, in fact, the ground was depressed and it was sheltered from the prevailing wind. She put one of the robes in the hollow made by the unearthed roots and put her babies on it, covering them with the second soft, thick robe. With her flint, she started a small fire against the upper fallen trunk and continued to drag up dead-fall to feed it until the trunk itself took hold and began to burn. That would last for days, she thought, even in the storm.

Morning Light took their water-skin and the horse to the river. When she returned, she tethered the animal in a close thicket. She checked on her children who were both sleeping, set the full skin near them and, then, she staggered out into the forest quietly with Gray Wolf's bow.

She didn't know what she expected to find. With the storm increasing the animals would all take shelter. But she was so hungry she was feeling weak and was afraid if she did not find food now, tomorrow she would not be able to and after that, it would be too late. She must eat to keep her milk or her daughter would die.

Tears of frustration fell silently from her eyes and she realized how stupid she was being. Her vision was already hindered by her swollen eye, tears just blurred it further. But then her stomach growled and she felt even more desperate. Patiently she stood, silently, waiting, hoping. She grew cold and numb, the wind biting at her already painful flesh. She could no longer feel her fingers. If only a deer would come along, a pheasant, a rabbit, even a squirrel. There was nothing. The snow was falling harder and she knew she should go back and tend to the fire. She needed to warm herself. But how could she return empty handed? She was leaning her shoulder against a tree, her head ached and her back was tormented with any but the shallowest breathing. Her kidneys felt bruised and the riding had not helped.

Then she heard it, the distinct sound and her heart beat sped up. She drew the arrow back as she pulled the string. She waited and prayed. *Please Great Spirit, guide my arrow.* Then, she saw the big bird walking along, clawing at the ground for insects, scratching aside the rotting leaves from last autumn. It was a wild turkey and Morning Light took careful aim before letting the arrow fly. It sank deeply into the bird and it screeched and ran and staggered and finally sank to the ground. Morning Light hurried to it, ignoring her aching body. It started up again and she grabbed it and slit its throat letting the hot blood run over her cold fingers, warming them.

Picking the dead bird up, she hastened back to the camp site, sighing in relief to find her babies still sleeping. Poking at the fire and putting additional kindling on it, she settled down stiffly to prepare the bird for roasting.

§

John frowned in the growing wind and turned his collar up. They had reached the Tuwok and turned south. If this was the way she had come then he hoped they'd find her before it was too late. The storm was growing and the temperature had dropped below freezing. Snow swirled around their heads and it was becoming impossible to see.

"We stop and shelter," Charlie-One-Claw raised his voice above the howling wind.

"We can't stop, she's out here somewhere and we've got to find her," John yelled back.

Charlie-One-Claw reached out from atop his own horse and grabbed John's arm. "We must stop. Horses cannot continue. If horse breaks leg, we never reach her," he said looking straight at John.

John knew the scout was right. The night was upon them getting blacker by the minute and he was being unreasonable. But how could he stop, knowing she was out there, somewhere, with two small children? John suddenly realized how much he cared about this woman and it frightened him. It did more than that, it terrified him. He had cared for someone... twice before and he hadn't been able to save either of them.

Without a word, John dropped from his horse and led it to a thicket on the leeward side of a ridge. He squatted to start a fire with some tinder and Charlie followed him.

§

Morning Light awoke to her baby's cries and struggled to take her daughter to her breast. She had the remains of the turkey within reach, along with the water-skin. Gray Wolf's Son was still sleeping after having his stomach filled for the night. As the mother nursed her child she tried to assess their position although her fevered brain had now lost the ability for fully rational thought. The snow had fallen heavily and it was in fact insulating them from the wind. But she was shaking with chills. She had forgotten all about the horse and wondered how she'd get back to the village. They were stranded in a storm but soon it would be over. The wind seemed to have grown quiet but it was not yet light and she could not see anything, especially pinned down as she was with her infant. Morning Light had to turn to bring her infant to her other breast and she stifled the involuntary cries as her body sharply reminded her of her wounds. No, not the village, she was running away from the village she reminded herself in her murky fog of consciousness before she once again fell back asleep.

§

John was up at the first light. He and Charlie-One-Claw had taken turns through the night staying up to keep the fires going. Now it was time to move on. A thick blanket of cold white snow covered the landscape deadening the sounds, making everything seem eerily quiet. Somehow it made the sound of the river water only yards away more distinct. No one could have guessed that only a few days ago it had been warm spring.

"Come on, Charlie, we'll eat in the saddle," John snapped in his anxiety. He had his bedroll on the horse before Charlie-One-Claw could get up. "Come on, let's go."

"I come, I come," the scout protested, pulling his fur robe around him.

"We've still got a good fifteen miles left to cover."

"Don't have to remind me," the scout grumbled and saddled his horse.

The wind had died down but the snow was still falling as the sun hid behind the clouds. There was no hope it would warm this day.

§

It was almost cozy within their little shelter and Morning Light convinced Gray Wolf's Son to remain quiet and inside while they finished the last of the turkey. She had crawled out of the shelter earlier. The baby had to be cleaned of her mess and Morning Light had washed her and her chamois cloths in the icy river. She had hung the cloths near the burning log to dry. The huge log was a massive burning ember as she had thought it would be, despite the snow. Its heat radiated to the horse on one side and the shelter on the other. Now, Morning Light brought her baby to her own flesh to warm. The young mother had a vague perception that she was in a fever for her baby's cold body felt soothing to her own. Her son had eaten his fill. Her baby suckled. For herself, she had no appetite any longer. Tomorrow, she thought irrationally, tomorrow the sun would appear and melt off the snow. The earth would be muddy but the animals would return and she would kill something and they could eat again. Today she only wanted to sleep.

It was the smoke from the burning tree trunk that led John and Charlie-One-Claw to the trio. They saw the smoke from a distance on the other side of the river and immediately crossed over the icy water. As they approached, John saw a horse tethered in a thicket, neighing for attention. Charlie-One-Claw slid from his own mount and took the little pinto to the river to drink.

As John surveyed the site he wasn't sure what he was looking at. A huge tree had fallen and split in two, its roots heaved out of the earth taking mammoth chunks of loam and clay with them. Part of the formation was covered in fresh branches creating what looked like a crude shelter over what had to be a cave-like hole. The second part of the trunk was in a slow burn that glowed and radiated heat from beneath the deceptive light ash. Everything but that burning trunk was covered in snow and there wasn't a sound.

"O-ron-keenee-hah-ser! Are you there?" he cried out in a frenzy and went forward floundering through the snow to look in. As he pulled the branches aside, snow fell in on a bear skin robe. He saw the three bodies curled up together, as peaceful as if they were asleep and tears sprang into his eyes as he choked out a groan of protest.

"Nooooooo. God, oh, please, nooooooooo." Falling to his knees with his cries he continued to push the branches aside unwilling to accept what he feared. The waste of it all. The completely incomprehensible waste of it all! She had taken the wrong direction and been caught in a freak storm. Driven out without the proper preparation. Terrified for her child because of that insane, jealous mate of hers. And the storm had taken them. John was blinded by the hot tears filling his eyes as memories of another tree at another time with another young woman flashed through his brain with horror. His heartbeat raced in his ears. His chest felt as though it would explode. His stomach was drawn tight and painful in overwhelming dread.

He choke a sob once, then fiercely wiped at his eyes. Out of the corner, he thought he saw movement. Movement? Had he really seen it? His grief riddled thoughts were interrupted as he crawled farther in under the branches to peer more closely in the gloom. A pair of black eyes were peering back at him with a grin.

"Gray Wolf's Son!" John cried hoarsely. "Charlie! Charlie! Get over here."

John carefully crawled on and was leaning over Morning Light's body when he discovered the baby was also alive, clinging to the smooth, light honey colored breast of her mother. At that very moment, Morning Light, herself, moaned softly and John gasped. He stripped the glove from his hand and felt her head. She was hot, too hot, and only semiconscious. But she was alive! John would have shouted for joy if it hadn't been for the distorted features he next caught sight of as her head moved toward him. The sight of her battered face made him suck in his breath sharply.

After giving the boy and baby up and over to Charlie-One-Claw, John carefully and gently lifted Morning Light out from under the robe and into the stark light of day. She was a tangle of hair and blood and dirt. He was horrified when he saw her face. He had seen men die in battle, faced the gore of war but not since the sight of Freyja hanging from her tree had anything affected him this strongly. He agonized for this young woman just looking at the angry black and purple and blue discolorations of the too taut skin. Swollen flesh distorting her fine and delicate features beyond recognition. The crusts of blood running above her eyebrow and in two vertical slashes on her upper and lower lip told of the splits in her skin. Pity and tenderness quickly turned to hatred and rage as John cursed softly under his breath and tried to quell the overpowering urge to ride breakneck back to the village and reduce Tonoaki to a pulverized mass of jelly. But that wouldn't help *Ohronkene Hahser* now.

Her own husband had done this to her, John thought darkly. How could he? There was nothing she could have done to deserve this. Nothing! Not her, not any woman, but especially not her. Then, he disciplined his mind to think only of getting them all back to the fort safely.

Charlie-One-Claw spread a robe out onto the snow covered ground and as John laid Morning Light out onto it he noticed the blood stains on the back of her tunic. The suede leather had grown hard, stiff, and inflexible with so much dried blood. He bent and leaned to look down the back of her neck and then cried out again.

"Oh, my God! Charlie, look at this! Look... oh God, oh, dear God!" Her back was a bloodied mass of stripes and welts now angered by the constant abrasion of the coarse hardened leather. At some points the leather was sticking to her skin and she cried out when John pulled the tunic away creating fresh bleeding.

"We've got to clean this up," he said hoarsely, while he gently turned her so she was resting half on her side, half on her stomach. His own stomach churned. "She's burning up with fever and infection could kill her." John looked fiercely at the scout. "It's time for some of your Indian magic, Charlie. What can you come up with to help her fight the infection and heal?!" he demanded crossly. Charlie-One-Claw was not the enemy but at that moment John saw himself pitted against the world to save this one young woman. He had not brought his doctor's bag but over the years he had come to rely on Charlie-One-Claw's native medicinals more than once.

Charlie-One-Claw grunted a nod and went off into the forest scraping aside the snow and hunting mosses and wild herbs. John was left to watch over the woman and her off-spring. The baby was content in the carrier and Gray Wolf's Son was quiet and wide-eyed as though sensing his mother's peril. The small child watched the white man boil up water, cool it in the snow then take a clean white handkerchief and dab ever so gently at his mother's face and back.

John washed Morning Light's back as carefully and as best he could then he did something he knew he had to do but something he was loath to do. He fetched a flask of whiskey from his saddlebag and with a corner of his handkerchief he dabbed at the first stripe. Morning Light rose up suddenly in a gasp of pain.

"Oh, God! I'm sorry! I'm sorry!" he moaned but pushed her down and continued dabbing. "I have to do this. I have to. It's going to help. Please forgive me. Please." She writhed around to look at him, agony in her eye, bewilderment. Her one open eye shouted the question, *why... why are you torturing me?* Then she saw the tears from his own eyes rolling down his cheeks and she grit her teeth and slumped back to the ground. It was something that had to be done, just like years ago when he had sewn her. She trembled and shivered and tensed but from then on she made no sound.

By the time John had finished dabbing every open wound with whiskey, Morning Light had lost consciousness again and he was able to dry his own eyes. Charlie-One-Claw reappeared suddenly with his hands full. He had a peculiar moss he had gathered. Washing it quickly, he next pounded it between two rocks to form a poultice which he applied directly to her skin, covering her back. John pulled a clean shirt from his saddle bag and wrapped her in it, threading her arms through the sleeves to keep the moss in place. Finally, they had to pull her dirty tunic back up over her for warmth before wrapping her again in the robes.

The two men left the baby wrapped up and John put the carrier on Charlie-One-Claw's back, covering the bundle against the cold. Then the scout helped John take Morning Light, wrapped in the warmth of the robe, into the saddle with him while her horse was tethered behind his mount. Gray Wolf's Son was more than happy to ride with Charlie-One-Claw when the big scout gave him a hunk of hardtack to chew on. The child acted as if he was starving.

"How long do you think it's been?" John asked, with a nod to the boy while holding the young woman tenderly and with the greatest care.

"I saw fresh bones in shelter," the Indian said. "Could not be long." They began to work their way more directly to the fort.

Morning Light slipped in and out of sleep or unconsciousness only stirring to whimper when John shifted her weight in his arms. She opened her eyes for a moment of recognition. "*Sak* Power, Friend," she mumbled softly reaching for him and then fell against his neck, slipping back into oblivion. That simple gesture of reaching out in trust went to his very soul. With his gloved hand, he continuously scraped snow from the tree branches to hold to the young woman's fevered brow as they rode. When the baby started crying, she awoke again and somehow took it to her breast while riding facing him in the saddle. Keeping his eyes averted, John helped her hold the infant so it could suckle while he kept the heavy robes wrapped around mother and child.

Upon finally reaching the fort, John immediately carried Morning Light himself to his quarters. Charlie-One-Claw followed with the children. The captain's quarters were small and spartan, comprised of a modest sized room which served as both sitting room and bedroom, but it was clean and private and ran above the surgery. John would make his report and explanation to Major Greeley, the post commander, later.

When Major Greeley was given orders to take over as commander at this outpost he had brought John with him. There had been no doctor, drunk or otherwise, at this fort. John became the official post doctor as well as the senior captain only one rank beneath Greeley and therefore his second in command. They had a strong relationship of mutual respect and dependence.

John wrestled with the idea of sending Charlie-One-Claw back to the village for *Ohronkene Hahser's* mother. But his anger continued to spill over onto her family. *They* hadn't gone out looking for her, *he* had. If it had been left to them, she and both her children would be wolf bait by now. Why should he tell them where she was and invite that damned hot tempered brave to come storming back here?

"Sergeant?" John snapped at a gawking soldier outside his door snickering at Charlie-One-Claw carrying a papoose.

"Yes, sir." The man smoothed his uniform and came to attention before Captain Power.

"Who around here is fit to take care of a couple of children?" John asked. "Their mother is very ill and I don't want anything to happen to them, understand?"

"Yes, sir, but I don't.... I mean, there's no one... "

"You a married man, Sergeant?"

"Yes, sir."

"Any children?"

"Five, sir."

"Five?" John eyed him suspiciously.

"Every time I go home, sir."

"Then I am going to assume you know something about children. I'm making these two your responsibility and remember, I don't want a single hair on either of these heads to see harm."

"No, sir, I mean, yes, sir, I mean, begging your pardon, sir, but it's my wife what knows about babies, sir, not me."

"Learn! Now, help Charlie off with that baby carry thing and then get someone to bring me lots of hot water and fresh clean rags and make that on the double, and take these children with you."

"Yes, sir." The seasoned soldier was in shock.

"And I want a bucket of clean snow up here every hour, starting now."

"Yes, sir."

"And sergeant, get a couple of old summer weight blankets and tear them up to make nappies for the little one. I'm sure the cook can help." John added lamely.

"Yes, sir." The sergeant winced as he took up his new charges and worked his way down to the mess hall where the first private he saw was sent running to do the captain's errands.

Alone, John motioned to Charlie-One-Claw.

"Help me, Charlie. We have to get her out of these clothes and into bed."

The scout grunted and together they cautiously set about removing Morning Light's soiled, torn, and blood stained garments to settle her more comfortably, keeping her off her back but not completely on her stomach. John untied his shirt from her and pealed away the mosses. The angry look of the welts had been reduced remarkably but it was obvious there was still infection.

"What do you think, Charlie? Should we put the mosses back on or leave the wounds to the open air?" he asked.

"Good has been used. Now clean again and leave to air. I prepare something more better now we back. It take time to make but take infection away like magic."

"Right," John agreed.

"All marks are on her back," Charlie-One-Claw said as he stood back observing the woman.

"Why yes, they're on her back, he beat her, that's obvious. My God, he must have beat and beat on her. Why didn't she run?"

"No... see," the scout pointed to lash marks on her arms. "Only on back of arm here, no here or here." He pointed to her forearms. "And blows," he pointed to the purple, blue, black, and greenish pallor of her skin from fist pummeling. "None on front of body."

"What are you trying to say?" John asked taking a better look at the pattern of the lash marks and the hideously colored bruises.

"She has no mark on front of body except on face. Man who beats wife usual punches all over body, not just back."

John looked at the scout and back at *Ohronkene Hahser*. "She wasn't fighting him... why? Why didn't she run?" Suddenly, John gasped. "Do you think he had her tied up?" Charlie-One-Claw examined her wrists and shook his head. "So, she wasn't tied up but she didn't run. She kept her back to him and stayed... because she was protecting something maybe... like her children? He was going to beat her children? Good God, what kind of a monster is he? She was afraid for her children."

The scout shrugged.

"He was going to..." John went on, "or she thought he was going to hurt them and she was hiding them, not hiding... sheltering. She was bent over the baby, maybe, protecting it and just let him beat on her," John was dark with anger. "I'm surprised he didn't kill her, kill them all. The bastard! The ass! The insane, barbaric, bloodthirsty, Philistine asshole!" John vented, then stopped and gathered his composure. "Well, that's not helping her now. Where's that damn snow?!"

John packed snow around Morning Light's swollen face while Charlie-One-Claw went off to render down a pitchy syrup made from tree tar. The scout knew from experience it made a powerful topical infection fighter but it took time to brew.

Watching over his patient, John saw the girl begin shivering violently as chills took over. He drew the sheet up over her and covered her with blankets. The melting snow was creating a wet mess and John used towels to keep the bed from getting soaked. Her skin was dry and hot although she continued to shiver. Finally, Charlie-One-Claw returned.

"What is this stuff?" John asked, frowning at the small pot Charlie-One-Claw thrust at him. The pot was still very warm and the liquid within was dark and strangely pungent though not unpleasant.

"Spread over whole back," was his only reply.

John cleaned the raw infected wounds again before applying the decoction liberally over them. Then, for modesty's sake, he tucked the sheet up as far as he could without getting it into the dark syrupy liquid spread over her back.

"It's too cold, Charlie, we can't leave her uncovered."

"Better. Easy to put on medicine," he rebutted.

"Help me move the bed closer to the stove." And together they brought the bed closer to the small iron stove set in the corner.

The scout left the room and John threw more wood in the stove. He had to make the drafty room warmer. She was exposed and he didn't like the sound of her breathing. He ordered extra blankets to be brought to him along with a hammer and nails. When they arrived, he proceeded to nail the blankets over the drafty windows. Then, John sat back to wonder how any man could do this to a woman. And for this to happen to her of all people, after everything she'd already been through in her life? At the hands of a husband who was supposed to protect her!

He shook his head silently. Despite everything she had been through she still had the will to live. Thank God for that, John thought, and then he realized he was proud of her for that very reason.

She was such a gracious creature, warm and gentle. He sat looking at the young girl draped on his bed. His eyes following the long line of her slender legs outlined easily beneath the covering. Then his gaze went up over her softly rounded rear end. His eyes slid up her tortured back covered with the dark medicine and noted the paleness of her breast, honey colored he thought, barely visible as she lie on her stomach, and a contrast to her brown arms. Had he really never noticed what a truly beautiful body she had? Would she now bear the scars of this beating for the rest of her life? She was young, she'd heal he was certain, but even if there was some small scarring, it couldn't detract from her natural beauty. He knew she was a female of intense passion. He remembered when she learned of her first husband's death, the passion of her grief. And John suddenly found himself wondering if she made love with that same kind of passion?

He hardly believed his own thoughts. He was stunned. Then admonished himself for the direction of his thinking. Hardly a direction worthy of a gentleman assisting a lady in distress. Totally unprofessional of a doctor. But a perfectly understandable direction for a lonely soldier out on the frontier.

And what would happen now? She was in his room and in his bed. If that damned husband of hers was jealous before, he'd kill her for certain after this. No, by God, he would not! He wasn't ever going to get the chance. It was at that moment that John unconsciously made the decision that *Ohronkene Hahser* was never going to go back to Tonoaki. He'd see the brave dead first.

John stood and walked back over to the bed to stare at the brutalized young woman stretched out against his pillows on her side and naked. The sight of her was intensely disturbing for several reasons far beyond her flesh wounds. He thought back over his own feelings when he went searching for her, when he had found her and when, for one heart stopping minute he'd actually thought he had lost her. That *he* had lost her? But she had never been his to lose. Disturbing wasn't the half of it, John realized. Involuntarily, his hand went out to adjust the pack of snow at her cheek and gently stroke a small patch of forehead that wasn't bruised atop the swollen face. Then he went on to stroke her smooth unmarked forearm with decided tenderness before tucking the blanket at her waist and around her chest.

"Dear God," he whispered to himself. "What am I going to do with you?"

# Chapter 27

It had been over ten hours and Morning Light began to cough. After several applications of Charlie-One-Claw's topical decoction, John had placed a piece of fresh, clean sheeting over the young woman's ravaged back and covered her with the bed sheet and blankets. Now, he noted a sweat break out on his patient, her body was covered with it, making the sheeting cling to her. Her fever had broken perhaps, he thought hopefully. He brought a hand to her head, with the cold snow he couldn't tell and resumed his seat. Then, suddenly her eyes bolted open causing an involuntary cringe and then panic. She moaned as she pushed herself up, wincing as pain shot through her body.

"My children!" she cried and John was up out of the chair again in an instant.

"It's all right," he spoke softly, trying to sooth her as one might sooth a dumb animal. "You are all right. Stay quiet. You're safe."

She had begun to pick up a little of his English and when her mind cleared enough to realize she was with Jack Power, her friend, she visibly relaxed but not before she turned to her other side and pushed the snow pack and oil cloth from her pillow.

"*Sak*," she sighed softly, then her head sagged back down.

"Here, I'll get you a fresh pillow," he said, tearing his focus from the sight of her naked breasts, full and round. He took the sodden pillow away and replaced it with several fresh ones but now she had begun to shake with chills and he pulled the sheet over her tightly.

He pulled the blanket over her again as well and threw more wood on the fire. Suddenly she pulled herself up into a sitting position, she was sweating again, the sheet caught damp at her waist. He handed her a cup of water and helped to steady it and found his own arm trembling.

Morning Light drank uneasily and was aware of the pressure in her breasts telling her that her baby had gone too long without nourishment. Unconsciously she brought her hands gingerly to her hard bosom, took her breasts in hand and looked to John. "I am so full with milk," she said, "I must feed my baby. Bring her to me."

He didn't understand a word of it. He only saw her hands holding her swollen breasts and his masculine appendage was reacting with a will of its own that made him ashamed of himself.

"I....I'm sorry I don't know what..." he said hoarsely. Just then he was aware of the sound of a baby crying, followed by a rap on the door and Charlie-One-Claw called out.

"Come in," John said, pulling his jerkin down self-consciously while he stood in front of the bed to block its view from the door. The scout entered with Morning Light's children, the infant screaming in frustrated hunger. "I'm glad you're here,"

John said, trying not to look at the Indian woman sitting naked on his bed. "She's just woke and I don't know what she's saying."

"Give me my baby, I must feed her," Morning Light cried out to Charlie-One-Claw and extended her arms. He did just that, only too glad to be relieved of the bawling infant. She immediately gave the child her breast and it became quiet and content, the milk coming so quickly it overflowed the babe's mouth, running in blue white rivers down its cheeks. John followed the action and found himself flushed again, hot, uncomfortable, yet fascinated, feeling he had no right to witness this intimacy but unable to look away. He glanced at Charlie-One-Claw and was surprised to note that the scout didn't appear to notice anything unusual about the scene at all and was busy with Gray Wolf's Son.

"She knows baby hungry. Mother always know. Milk come plenty. We try to feed from goat but could not. This one," he laughed at the little boy whom they had bathed and given a makeshift change of clothes, "he eat everything Cook have in kitchen, then start on supply shed."

John had barely given a chuckle in reaction to that when another knock came swiftly at his door. He jumped to stand in front of *Ohronkene Hahser*, once again blocking her from view at the door. "See who it is," he told Charlie-One-Claw and the scout opened the door to the cook who handed in a tray with broth, tea, fresh bread, roast venison, and baked apples.

"It's for you and your... ahh, patient, Captain," the cook said gruffly, his eyes cast down. "Needs to eat. And here's more snow but its about the last of it. Everything is melted." The tray was handed to Charlie-One-Claw, the bucket of snow was taken from an anonymous pair of hands on the other side of the wall and dropped on the floor inside the room. The cook turned quickly and left as if embarrassed himself. The sounds of his footfall as well as his assistant's disappeared.

"Well..." John said when they were again alone. "It was good of him to think of food." Charlie-One-Claw said nothing. "Ask her if it bothers her to talk while... you know."

"It better she eat than talk," the scout grunted.

"Right... yes, of course. See if she can eat," John almost stammered.

It soon became apparent that Morning Light was not really of a clear mind. The scout was able to get a few spoons of broth in her but even though she seemed to know she was nursing her infant, she was growing delirious and incoherent regarding everything else. John encouraged her to accept more water and realized without the snow pack she was still burning up in fever. With the baby fed, the children were put down to sleep. The baby went into one of John's bureau drawers and Gray Wolf's Son was content with a pallet on the floor. John again packed snow in cloths around Morning Light's head.

The scout put his head to the young woman's chest and listened to her breathing. When he stood up again he shook his head.

"What?!" John exclaimed.

"No sound good," the scout said gruffly.

"What doesn't?"

"Breathing."

"Charlie, we haven't come this far to lose her now! I won't lose her, do you hear me? I won't! What can we do?" John looked at the scout with wild desperation in his eyes. He was a trained physician but he felt so helpless. At least he knew enough not to bleed her, he told himself. "What native wisdom do you have up your sleeve?"

"Baby drain her energy," the scout grumbled as he proceeded to put a pan of water on to boil and begin the process of rendering down a vile smelling concoction made from things he pulled from his pouch. "She eat almost nothing, but feeds baby. Has nothing left to heal her body," he continued to remonstrate as he worked.

A sweat broke on John's forehead. "Are you saying it's a choice between her or her baby?" he anguished. "Can't we find a wet nurse? Isn't there some woman out there," he gestured broadly, "who could feed that baby?"

"Maybe, but you no want village to know she here."

"Oh, God!" John slumped with his head in his hands, his elbows resting on his desk top. Suddenly he sat bolt upright. "Red Fox's village! Why couldn't we take the baby to Red Fox's village, surely in the entire village there must be at least one nursing mother we could pay to keep the baby."

"Maybe, but too far. Who feed baby for three days it take to get there?"

"Charlie, I'm not giving this girl up to her husband so he can kill her. We have to work around it. We have to figure a way to save them both."

The scout simply shrugged. "Maybe husband sorry now."

"Maybe," John said curtly. "And maybe next time she won't be so lucky as to escape. Any man who can beat a woman once can do it again. It's her choice if she wants to go back to him but I will not hand her to him on a silver platter. She came to us for help, for sanctuary."

"What mean this, *sanctuary*?

"It means protection, safety from pursuers," John explained dully, his mind frantic to find a solution and occupied in a desperate attempt to think of alternatives.

When the new syrup Charlie-One-Claw created had been sufficiently cooled, he began spooning it down Morning Light's throat. One spoonful each hour. It was two in the morning when John noticed her fever had broken. He toweled the sweat from her brow. The snow had melted long before. She awakened enough for him to get some more broth into her and even a little of the baked apple and venison. Then she lapsed into a deep sleep.

She continued to cough through the night but Charlie-One-Claw thought this was a good sign and found it hopeful. When her baby woke she heard it and in-sisted on having it in the bed with her to nurse. Charlie managed to get another spoonful of his vile syrup down her and John urged some meat. She took two bites before she fell asleep, the infant pulling contentedly at her breast.

By this time Gray Wolf's Son had awakened, the baby was completely soaked, and John demanded the sergeant he had assigned nanny duty take back his charges. With the children gone, John told the scout to get some sleep while he continued to watch over his young patient.

John sat listening to every rasping breath with a sense of complete frustration. He didn't know what else they could do. She was in God's hands now. Either her body would be able to fight off whatever it was and heal or it wouldn't. But she was strong, he kept telling himself. She was young and healthy and she had a will to survive. God, what a will to survive! She was a fighter. If anyone could survive, she could. Look what she'd been through in her life and she was still so young. Seventeen or eighteen, he was guessing. No, he told himself, if anyone could come through this, Ronnie could. *Ronnie?* When had he started thinking of her as *Ronnie?* He couldn't answer himself. It just sounded right. He was tired of stumbling over her Indian name, even in his own thoughts, and saying it badly. Besides, after everything they had been through together, didn't he have the right to give her a nickname of his own? Didn't she call him *Sak?*

The clock ticked on his desktop hypnotically and John dozed.

It was late morning when Morning Light woke again. She couldn't sense what time it was for the window light was blocked by blankets. The candles had burnt out but in the gloom she could see John sitting at his desk, his head on his arms. He looked so uncomfortable, why did he not lie down? Then she observed that she was on the only sleeping platform in the room while Charlie-One-Claw slept on the floor. As she looked at John, she tried to remember. It was so very hazy. She was in the snow with her children. And now she was with *Sak*. Had he found her? He must have. He had found her and... her children? Her heart began to beat rapidly until she remembered vaguely that she had suckled her baby. Unconsciously her hands went to her breasts to verify this fact. She was not painfully gorged. So her baby had drained her. Then her hand went to her face and she could only imagine what she looked like. One side of her face was numb and yet it throbbed. It was so swollen the skin felt stretched uncomfortably. There was no forgetting how she had gotten this way. Tonoaki had beat her.

Tonoaki! It flooded back like a bad dream. His anger, his accusations, his rage. She had been right to run away but the fort was not where she had thought. Yes, she had been right to run away but what would happen now?

She tried to adjust her position in the bed and fire leaped across her back causing her to suck in her breath sharply which set off more coughing. John's eyes flew open and he sat up straight.

"Ronnie?!" he said quickly getting up to help brace her as she coughed. When she finished he helped her to sit upright, propping pillows behind her and draping a blanket over her shoulders. Then he saw her mime eating. "Food? You want food?

Thank God! You're hungry! That's got to be a good sign." He was so delighted he laughed out loud.

John had fresh food brought up and when it arrived he helped her to eat. A subsequent rap on the door, through which they could hear a baby squalling, woke Charlie-One-Claw. He got up and took the infant bringing it to the mother who put it to her breast again.

"Now," said John in a relieved tone as he began to take the blankets down from the windows. "I guess we can take this down and let some light in here. Her fever's gone, her appetite is back. This is good. Very good. Time will heal everything else. Charlie, thank you. For all your help, I mean. I don't know what I would have done without you. I don't know what she would have done without you," he added earnestly.

The scout only grunted but he was pleased.

"Now, would you please ask her if she feels up to talking a little?"

After a brief discourse, Charlie said, "It not bother her."

"Then, for God's sake, find out from her what happened," John said authoritatively, then he stepped to the stove and listened vaguely to the ensuing discourse as he tended to the fire.

The scout and the squaw spoke at some length. She told him candidly of everything that had happened, pausing at one point to switch her infant to her other breast. John waited impatiently, watching the small fire in his stove through the grating. Finally, when they stopped speaking, John's curiosity got the better of him and as he turned back to face the bed he saw Morning Light opening the wrappings around her baby. John found himself staring at a naked pale skinned baby girl with white blonde fuzz and bright blue eyes who was lying in the path of a shaft of sunlight.

"Whose child is that?!" he asked in astonishment without thinking. "Has she stolen it?"

"It is her child."

"But that's impossible," John gasped, then scowled. "Ask her if she was raped by another white man."

"She..."

"Ask her," John demanded.

The scout shrugged and did as he was told and John saw Ronnie's eyes seek his and fill with tears. She bent her head and shook it slowly.

"Then how...?" he mumbled in confusion.

Charlie then explained what she had already told him, "One of her ancestors was a white woman, she says. The blood has shown itself."

"That's incredible!" John looked from child to mother and back again. "So, she is part white?!" he referred to Morning Light.

Charlie nodded.

"And that's why he beat her?"

Charlie shook his head.

"Then why?"

"Because he did not believe. Her husband accuses her of being unfaithful to him..."

John turned with a snort of disgust.

"... with you."

"With me?!!" John stopped cold and looked incredulous. "That ignorant bastard!" he said tightly, trying to keep his temper under control. "She's innocent!"

"You sure?" asked Charlie dryly.

"Well, she certainly has not been unfaithful with me and that's who he accuses her of being with. And I know that's the goddamn truth. Don't look at me that way, dammit. I've never touched her, ever. I... Why would he think such a thing?" John demanded indignantly.

"Because baby looks white," Charlie replied deigning to state the obvious. "And you were the white man she was around, same yellow hair."

Charlie went on to relay all that Morning Light had told him of her great, great grandmother just as her mother had told her. A tall, blonde, blue eyed woman kidnapped after the first devastating plagues of small pox and measles had been visited upon the natives by the white explorers. Plagues which were still wiping out so many of their population. A woman stolen to make up for a wife lost. A woman whose blood Morning Light had inherited and that white blood had suddenly made itself known. Because of John's presence last spring, he was the most likely candidate for the child's coloring since Singing Wind had never bothered to share their family history which in their old tribe had been common knowledge.

John said nothing for a long while but watched the mother change her baby daughter, carelessly tossing aside an ammonia reeking piece of blanket onto the floorboards. As Morning Light bundled her infant back up, John automatically scooped up the soaked diaper, depositing it in a bucket outside his door. When he turned back into the room he saw Morning Light was again exposed as she sat upon the bed. John found himself going over and silently taking the extra blanket and tucking it over her chest, covering her nakedness. As she clutched the blanket to her, she could not look at him. He had made her feel shame, he realized. He hadn't meant to. He simply had to cover her for his own comfort. He stood for a long time looking from mother to child.

"Ask her... ask her if there's anything she needs right now. Ask her if her back pains her very much."

They spoke and Charlie said, "She says she wants nothing, only the shelter she came seeking. Your protection."

"Tell her she must eat more and rest," he said nodding, then he turned suddenly to leave. "I'll be back later."

John arranged for bath water to be heated and scrounged a fresh change of clothes from the company drummer who he judged to be about the young woman's size. It would be awhile before she was well enough to be allowed up and in the meantime he had several shirts she could use for bedclothes. After he supervised the delivery of the hot water, he set out his personal tub and a fresh shirt along with a comb, towels, and soap.

"Charlie, tell her if we had a woman here I'd send for her to help but there is none until the commander's wife returns. Ask her if she thinks she can manage alone or if she'd like... help," John spoke hesitantly. "Tell her I just thought she might like to freshen up, wash her hair and so on. If she's too weak to hold the rinse bucket, you can stay and help her." The scout did as he was told, after which there was a brief exchange and John was poised with his hand on the door latch ready to leave the room when Charlie spoke to him.

"She say wants help only from you."

John groaned inwardly. He wasn't strong enough for that. "Tell her I can't... tell her... I have to go on duty," he flung back as he escaped the room. He was trembling within as he stalked down the stairs. She was sick and beaten, bruised and battered and yet he couldn't keep himself from wanting her. She was a temptation he was finding impossible to ignore and he needed some distance.

John decided it was time to report to his commander. He walked steadily to the major's office and knocked on the plain, rough hewn door.

"Come," a voice responded. John stepped in and saluted.

"At ease, Captain Power. I can't say I haven't been expecting you. You certainly took your good sweet time about it," came the gruff but friendly greeting.

John frowned. "So you've heard. I was hoping to..."

"Heard? Hell, it's been days. Or has time gotten away from you?" the middle aged man who sat at the desk had a deceptive fatherly look about him. But he was a toughened Indian campaigner and no one's fool. His stout figure and ruddy complexion gave no hint of the eight arrow scars at various points on his body as well as the scar from the hand laceration John had tended some time back.

Greeley detested wigs and wore his own hair neatly clubbed at a moderate length. His face was always freshly shaven and his rooms, like his dress, were scrubbed clean and presented neatly even when his wife wasn't there.

"I'm sorry, sir," John replied, his handsome tanned face bearing the burden of unsettled responsibility and exhaustion. "I really am. It's... well, it's taken some time to sort out what exactly has happened."

"So, why don't you tell me. Sit down... want a whiskey?" Commander Greeley asked hospitably. He watched the younger man. He liked John, had promoted him up from the ranks. He had recognized in the younger man an air of authority, an ability to command and lead that was officer material being wasted. And he was pleasantly shocked to discover John was a trained physician.

"No, thank you... well, maybe a small one," John conceded as he took a seat in a very firm, horsehair cushioned chair.

John proceeded to relay the entire episode as he knew it, leaving out no details, except that he was the accused father in Tonoaki's mind. But that was a detail that didn't alter the fact that an Indian woman had come seeking help after being beaten severely. When he was finished so was his drink and a second besides.

"Is this going to cause an incident?" the commander asked at last.

"We're not the ones who've beat her, sir. I don't understand how..." his voice trailed off suddenly as he realized. "You mean for assisting her?"

The commander nodded.

"Sir, right now, I don't believe anyone even knows we found her or that she is here or alive. I can't believe they didn't even go out looking for her, her own family!" he suddenly exploded clenching his hands into fists as they rested on the heavy chair arms. "I suppose in time they will hear but I don't believe Five Beavers will be ready to go to war with us because we helped a stepdaughter who was lost in the wilderness. As far as that Toe-no-ah-kee is concerned, he may threaten but he has no power behind him."

"And what do you propose to do with her, now that you have her here?" There was something in the older man's eyes that John found disturbing, almost accusing.

"I don't know, sir. I guess I'll have to ask her what she wants to do. She's been delirious with fever until now. But she has told us she was coming here to seek sanctuary when she was caught in the storm."

"I should think so."

"Excuse me, sir?" John looked at him questioningly.

"The husband obviously is going to see this as his wife running off to you. John, I expect you to be candid with me, completely candid. Have you left something out?"

John swore silently. So, somehow the rumor had already gotten to the commander.

"Well, I guess you mean the reason for the beating to begin with. It seems that Morning Light has a white ancestor. Once you see her, after she heals, you'll be able to note how different her appearance is from the other natives. Anyway, her new baby is very light and the hot head she married thinks it's not his."

The commander said nothing but allowed John to continue uninterrupted.

"So, it seems he's taken it into his head that since I was with the village so much last spring... and the baby is light... that it's... my child. But it's not, Commander, I swear on the Bible, I've never... there's been no such conduct. And I believe her when she says it is only her white blood appearing."

For a long moment the commander said nothing and then, with a slight nod saying he accepted John at his word, he spoke. "You have to admit, John, it does seem a bit far fetched. But, it would seem that whether or not it is true, you now have this very same young woman living with you. As a matter of perception it becomes increasing difficult to argue the difference. The appearance is that she is your mistress."

John felt the blood rise in his face and knew he was turning beet red. He felt guilty and he didn't know why. He hadn't done anything! He was going to say "to hell with appearances" but he caught himself and stopped because the fact was, after experiencing the emotions of the passed forty-eight hours, he realized that it could have been true. That it was not true was really to her credit, not his.

"Get yourself temporary quarters, John, or for God's sake move her into the surgery." This came not harshly but with a certain benevolent exasperation and John nodded in agreement.

"She has been very ill, sir," was all he said before saluting smartly and leaving.

When John left the commander's office, he made a point to find the sergeant he had assigned nanny duty.

"Now that the woman is conscious," John said bluntly, "and we know that she will live, I will be needing temporary quarters until she's completely recuperated and it's determined what she intends to do. I want a cot set up in my office."

"Yes, sir," the sergeant agreed holding back the smile he felt tugging at his lips despite the wriggling little mass in his arms. Having a young woman in the captain's bed, beat up squaw or not, is likely to be a bit disconcerting even for him, now weren't it? No wonder he needs fresh quarters. Of course, it takes no genius to put two and two together. There she was running to him fresh from a beating from her ol' man and carrying a little white baby what looks just like the captain. And back nine, ten months ago when the little half-pint was only a glimmer in her daddy's eye, it were the captain what was the only *white* man to be camping with the Indians. No, it certainly doesn't take no bloody genius to add two and two together, the sergeant thought as he ambled off snickering under his breath.

# *Chapter 28*

As the days passed, John insisted Morning Light be given English lessons by Charlie-One-Claw. The young officer realized the common gossip about the fort was that his mistress had brought his bastard to him and he caught himself resenting *Ohronkene Hahser* for it. His career in the military had been going along quite well up to this point but officers who became laughing-stocks did not progress. If she was going to be such an influence on his life, she damn well could learn to speak his language so he could really talk to her without a third person always being there.

Almost three weeks had passed since Morning Light's arrival when John told himself he was being childish and ill-mannered not to have been to see his "guest." What kind of a friend was he anyway to ignore her like this? And when he put the stodginess of public opinion aside, he knew how very much he missed her company and wanted to see her himself. He sent word by Charlie-One-Claw to request permission to pay her a call for dinner and was told she would be most happy.

"*Most happy?* Is that what she said?" he smiled faintly. The scout grunted. "How does she look?"

"She heal fast now," was all the Indian deigned to volunteer.

Gray Wolf's Son had already been fed, having, under the sergeant's watch, been made into something of a kitchen mascot. Now the little boy played until bedtime within the outer yard with the company dog. John had sent a request to the cook and they both arrived at his old quarters along with a tray laden with food. The tray was placed on the large desk where there was room for several people to dine. The cook set out two place settings and retreated quickly. Morning Light was standing shyly in the corner.

Morning Light had been nervously awaiting John's visit. It had been a long time since she had seen him and she had missed his company but she understood why he had stayed away. Men did not like to look upon ugliness in a woman. Weeks ago when she had pulled herself out of bed to use the chamber pot and wandered over to the small mirror that hung upon the wall, she had seen her ugliness. For the first time, the pain and discomfort she had been feeling were given a visual image in her mind and she had been horrified. It was no wonder at all that he did not choose to gaze upon her. She did not recognize herself. In a lapse of weakness she had actually asked Charlie-One-Claw when they were alone if he thought she would ever look like herself again and she had been surprised by the scout's tenderness toward her. He had touched her cheek gently and had told her not to be concerned, that it would all go away.

She had clung to those words of encouragement and each day when he came to give her lessons in the white man's talk, he had conveyed encouragement without saying another word directly regarding her fears. She had tried to be a quick student. She had meekly stayed within the confines of the room to spare everyone the ugliness of her appearance. She played tirelessly with her children and tried to eat the food. And she watched as slowly her face did return to normal. Still Jack Power did not come to see her. She asked about him daily. She knew he was close by. And she had been overjoyed when she received his message.

"*Shékuiksha*," John greeted her in an effort to make her feel comfortable.

"*Shékuorye*," she immediately responded.

"You look much better," John smiled warmly, his eyes took note of the form fitting clothes he'd borrowed from the drummer. "You certainly do something to those clothes Leedes never could," he joked. "Can you understand me?"

She nodded. "If you talk no fast."

He smiled again. "Very good. I heard you are doing very well in your lessons. It's probably time you had a better teacher than Charlie," he said lightly. He saw the color heighten in her cheeks at the praise. Going to her he drew her gently into the light and took her perfect chin tenderly in his fingers. Tilting her head one way and then the other, he scrutinized her bruises in a very professional manner. The flesh had returned to its normal shape. Only a yellowish tinge remained of the bruising and the splits had healed leaving no scars. "Truly, you look much better. I think you were hurt more than you were harmed, thank heaven. You are very fortunate, that husband of yours has one hel... ah, one very bad temper. How is your back?" he asked.

She looked at him a bit blankly and he realized despite his good intentions, he had spoken rather rapidly.

"How does your back feel?" he repeated and gestured.

"Oh... It feel no bad," she answered quickly.

"May I look?" he tried to maintain a clinical attitude.

He motioned for her to turn around while he gingerly lifted her shirt tail. Her flesh was pinker and tender looking where the lash marks had been but the lacerations themselves were healing clean. John momentarily forgot everything else as he pulled the shirt up even higher. "Amazing!" he exclaimed softly. Whatever the scout had brewed up and put on the ulcerated flesh, it had worked wonders. All signs of infection were gone without leaving any ugly scar tissue. "I dare say, you may not even be left with scars," he said with wonderment evident in his voice. "Your skin is beginning to look like satin again..." his voice trailed off as his finger tips registered the intimacy of touching her. That was not a doctor's touch. He stopped himself immediately and drew away, quickly lowering her shirt. She was another man's wife, he reminded himself.

When she turned back to look at him, he saw a question in her eyes and tried to avoid it. "I can remember there was a time he wanted to fatten me up for the kill," John said softly with an uneasy chuckle, "but thanks to you, I am alive. I cannot forget that. I will never forget that. I will do anything possible to help you square this up." Then, John motioned to the food. "Here, sit. You must be hungry."

Morning Light was not accustomed to sitting at a table, albeit a desk makeshift table, on a chair. It was very strange but she did as he asked. She watched him and tried to imitate what he did. She became frustrated trying to use a knife and fork to eat chicken. Soon she dropped the utensils in favor of her fingers. John laughed.

"You are absolutely right. I could never understand trying to eat fried chicken with a knife and fork, myself." He smiled and picked up his chicken with his fingers. He saw her relax.

John sat across the desk trying not to stare but he was unwilling to look away. It had been too many days since he had seen her. And those clothes clung too revealingly. He should have made Charlie stay. What was he doing here alone with her, anyway? The major would be furious.

"You anger me?" she finally asked haltingly in a faint voice. John looked at her for a moment trying to decide what she meant.

"Am I angry with you?" he asked slowly and when she nodded he replied quickly. "No. Of course not. Whatever would make you think that?"

"You face."

John relaxed his frown and smiled. "Sorry, I have a lot on my mind."

"I not see you many day."

"..days," John corrected automatically.

"Days, many days. I not mean to..." she pantomimed a bit. "hold?... give?... many troubles to you."

"You mean *bring* many troubles... no, Ronnie, no," he reached out for her hand and she gave it to him. "I told you if you ever needed me, I'd be here. I meant that. It is just that," he sighed. "I am having a little difficulty explaining your white baby to the rest of the fort. I don't want them to think you have done anything improper."

She withdrew her hand and actually gave the appearance of withdrawing from the food and table by pressing herself back into the chair. He had worded it so politely but she knew what he really meant. Suddenly she realized his people also thought the baby was his and she was shaming him.

"Don't you like the food? Is something wrong with it?" he asked.

"No," she said in a small voice, shaking her head. "*Sak*, I did not know. I have brought shame to you." Tears welled quickly in her eyes. "I sorry. I much sorry. I should not come."

"No... no, don't think that! It's not important," he rushed to refute her claim suddenly seeing himself as very selfish. *God, that was stupid,* he told himself. *She's got troubles enough of her own and you whine about yours which are nothing in comparison. Shut up, John!* "Look, first of all, you did not come here. Remember that. I brought you," he smiled infectiously. "If I did not want to help, I could have brought you back to the village. Right? Now. Is that settled?"

She nodded and tried to return his smile.

"And I think you have been cooped up in this little room for too long. You need to get out of here for a while. I have an idea. Next Sunday, if the weather's good, how would you like to go on a picnic? We'll get out into the countryside. Take a ride. We will bring the children and Charlie and have a great time, all right?"

She looked at him in puzzlement and he realized he'd done it again. She probably hadn't caught half of what he had just said. He laughed at himself and slowed down. "In four days. Go for ride, eat, have good time, pick flowers... all right?

She laughed then as well, and despite the slight discoloration remaining on her jaw and eye and the faint scars on her brow, her face lit up and she was beautiful. Too beautiful, thought the lonely soldier, much, much too beautiful.

John sat alone on the corral railing at the back of the fort, smoking his pipe. The sky was so clear he felt like he could pick stars by the handful just by reaching out. But no matter where he was or what he was doing, his thoughts were not long away from Ronnie. *So, she was part white. No wonder she looked so... unusual. She never really had looked like any of her people. Not only was she taller, but she was softer, no, not exactly softer. She looked strong enough but... more delicate...*

*finer boned. That was it. She lacked the broad course-boned look of the other women and now he understood why. It made sense.*

He contemplated life in general and wondered why some people in this world seemed to have such a difficult time while for others, everything just seemed to come so easily. This girl had been through hell. What was she now? He considered how many years it had been since he had first met her. He'd known her since she was about ten, that made her all of maybe eighteen years old. She'd been used, abused, sold out, widowed, and now the young buck who had her was ready to... God, would he really cut off her nose? With a face like hers that would be more than a travesty, it would be almost sacrilegious. And it seemed she was more afraid for her baby than for herself. Afraid Tonoaki was going to kill the baby all because he thought it was a white man's baby. John's baby. Yet, in fact, if John was to believe in Ronnie, and he most certainly did, the Indian would be killing his very own flesh and blood, his own little daughter. Was life so bloody cheap to these people?

John got down and walked back to his office and temporary bedroom. He went in and readied himself for bed by the light of the half moon and stars, never bothering to light a candle. He had to put her out of his mind until Sunday, he told himself. If he didn't put her out of his mind, he wouldn't get anything done. But it wasn't that easy to do and sleep didn't come for many hours. Hours of mulling over what to do about Ronnie. He finally fell into a light sleep without ever coming up with any answers.

Sunday dawned sterling. No more traces of snow or cold, only verdant greens and multicolored flowers. Trees were blooming into full leaf, a perfect late spring day. As promised, John took Ronnie for a ride and a picnic. Beyond the walls of the fort to the east, up a particular high hill he knew, where the horizon stretched out in four directions from the summit. After they had eaten, Charlie-One-Claw took Gray Wolf's Son down to a nearby stream to fish and Ronnie was picking flowers while John carried her baby.

As he walked along with the child in his arms he had an opportunity to really look at her. She was a sweet little thing. Damned if she couldn't be his daughter with those fair pink cheeks and pale silky blonde hair. There were no blue eyes in his family but then her eyes might turn some day. He vaguely remembered his mother saying all white babies are born with blue eyes. His had turned gray, like his father's, like his father's mother and like his baby sister. And his mother's were a changeable hazel that darkened and lightened with her moods. Half of his siblings' eyes had turned brown, like their mother's father but Louise's were hazel just like Mother.

John had let the little hands take his finger and she was sucking on it, happy drool running down her cheeks and he couldn't help but smile. He stood thus for some time and then became aware of Ronnie standing only a small distance away watching him intently. He looked up and grinned rather boyishly at having been caught so, a bachelor soldier with a small infant in his arms sucking on his little finger. And he saw a look he couldn't define in her eyes as she returned his smile.

"Do you still love him?" John asked her as they sat in the shade enjoying the quiet and the bird song together. She had just finished nursing the baby while John, being a gentleman, had turned his back. Her daughter now lay quietly sleeping on a corner of the blanket. He didn't believe he'd just asked that but it was a question that had been burning in him for weeks.

"When you young you no can stay... mmm," she struggled.

"A widow?" John offered.

"Widow... yes," she continued. "Because I love Gray Wolf much, I make long time of... of..." she groped in her newly acquired vocabulary.

"Grieving... sadness after someone dies?" John supplied.

"Yes, long time grieving. But finally, tribe say I must marry. Many offer. I have choice. Must make choice. I think Tonoaki best choice. He strong warrior. He good hunter. He accept Gray Wolf's Son and... he say he love me much," she added shyly.

"Not a surprise," John said softly under his breath, more loudly he added, "He had a strange way of showing his love."

"Was not always so," she replied quietly. "Until baby born he perfect husband, much more you can think. He honor me. He tell me things most men never say to woman... never..." she groped for the word, then said something in her tongue in frustration. "Tell feelings, open his hide, no... heart to me... He believe I betray him," she said solemnly.

John was looking at the young woman. "You sound almost sorry for him."

"Maybe yes, I am."

"Why?" he asked incredulously; he was looking at her intently and her gaze rose to meet his. "How can you feel sorry for a man who beat you like that?"

"Tonoaki want my love more than anything and I not have to give. I not love him. I think he always know. It wrong me do this. He deserve mate's love. He try so hard to please. Maybe, if I really love he trust... believe baby his... believe I no betray him..." there was a quiver in her voice but her eyes were dry.

John had heard what he had wanted to hear. She did not love her husband. It was like the bursting of a dam of restraint. He reached out, unable to stop himself, his hand drawing her head to his, drawing her mouth to his. She did not shrink away from his touch.

From the first moment his lips brushed hers they both felt the inexplicable current flowing between them. She was not familiar with what the European world called a *kiss* but she found it exciting and followed John's lead.

She tasted ripe, warm, and sweet, and she was intoxicating. He held her head with both hands, his tongue pillaging her mouth tenderly. When he finally released her full soft lips, he moaned slightly. "I cannot help it," he whispered. "I want you.

God help me if it's wrong but I want you." Then, his hands were under her shirt cupping those perfect breasts firmly, turgid nipples grazing his palms and he thought he heard her moan softly. He'd been wanting to caress her like this for weeks. He marveled at the heavy silken fullness of her. His lips carried kisses across her face to her neck and her earlobes, while he breathed in the scent of her. A shiver passed through her body as he pulled the bugler's shirt up and over her head.

Morning Light ached for John's touch even as she allowed herself to seek out the warm strength of his body. She saw desire darken his eyes and she gave free reign to everything she was feeling for him. No sooner had he dropped aside her shirt, when her own savage passion burst out of its restraints. Her arms were around him as she rose up on her knees. Her fingers dove into his silky hair, pulling him to her, her mouth demanding, her tongue fiercely tasting him, plummeting him into wild excitement. She tugged his shirt from him, barely waiting to undo the laces and they pressed their bodies together, rubbing, writhing, groaning, drowning in the feeling of their flesh burning against each other.

She was grasping, sucking, licking, nipping, grazing him with her teeth in a frenzy just barely under control. It took no time to remove the bugler's breeches from her hips and she kicked them wildly from her legs. His boots were gone, his breeches were off and he was stretched out over her long slender body. Her hands sought out every part of him, memorizing him by touch, stirring his blood to an inferno and urging him on.

She knew where to be gentle and where to bite and rake and grasp harshly. He looked down at her and she was staring up at him. Their gaze was locked as they read the need, the want, the passion between them. Her eyes suddenly became sultry and soft, half closed as her fingers traced down his back to his hardened buttocks. He felt her hands squeeze his flesh and pull him to her in an unspoken demand. He had been wanting her and he realized she had been wanting him just as much.

"Oh, dear God," he groaned as he slid into her. She was incinerating heat and tight slippery wetness and he had to hold his breath and pull himself back to not ejaculate instantly like a half grown boy. She let him pause, her eyes half closed, her own body humming to the feel of him within her. Then, he began to move and she met him move for move, thrust for thrust, and with each soft cry, he could feel her essence like liquid fire drowning his own flesh. John could hold back no more and she lurched up covering his mouth in primitive passion to receive his explosive cry and feel it vibrate down her throat.

He rolled over then onto his back, taking her with him, never parting. She clung to his chest, her skin was faintly lustrous with perspiration beneath his fingers, her hair a tangle around his arms and hands. After a brief moment while she slowed her breathing, she sat upon him, still holding him within her. He could feel her, hot and pulsating, close around his own flesh and he was growing hard again as her body stretched and moved with a feline grace above him. Her fingers ran slowly through his golden curls, then, she was mapping the ridges and planes of his face with her fingertips, light as a feather. Her soft brown eyes meeting his clear gray ones.

"Lord, woman, I want you all over again." His voice was a husky rasp. "I feel like I want to live in you. I haven't had enough. Ronnie, I want more! I need more, more of you!" His hands molded her beneath them as he ran them over her smooth supple flesh. She smiled wantonly while she continued the pulsing of her muscles around him until he began a very slow sensual thrusting from beneath her. When his mouth released her breast, she licked his lips, then his eyelids and his earlobes, working down his neck to his chest where his hair tickled her when she sought his nipples. They had become uncoupled as she wiggled on him.

He heard her giggle faintly as she nipped at him again. He felt her teeth, not harshly painful but just sharp enough to make the hairs stand up all over his body in a surge of uncertain expectancy. He had grown very still as he felt her continue her path downward, across the hard muscles of his abdomen which tensed involuntarily when he felt her warm hands embracing him. Then, every muscle grew taut as he endured the alternate heat of her mouth and chill of the air upon his moistened flesh. Her teeth still making their presence known even on his tenderest parts, his mind alternately trusting and apprehensive. At last he could endure no more. In one swift movement, he rolled her back under him while his mouth reclaimed hers, sucking at her flush lips until he realized he tasted blood. Whether his or hers he didn't know, but he heard her moans and felt her body quivering in urgency as she arched her hips up to meet him, silently begging him to take her, enabling him to sink into her completely, deeply, fully at every stroke, pubic bone meeting the pressure of pubic bone. John had never experienced the like before. Over and over he thrust into her, finally burying himself in one last deep plunge while they rode the elongated wave of fulfillment together.

After a sweet sublime suspension of time during which they just held each other, reality finally returned to the new lovers. Morning Light rose to check her baby and put on her clothing. John wondered warily how long it would be before Charlie-One-Claw returned from the stream with Gray Wolf's Son. He hurriedly put on his breeches and shirt. He took more time with his boots. Then he stood, looking toward the river. There was no sign of anyone yet. He turned back to look at her.

His emotions were in a whirl. He was staring at her profile, the high smooth forehead, straight nose with just the slightest hint of an upturn, the full lips slightly swollen from his bruising kisses.

What had he just done and when had he ever experienced anything like it? He was asking himself silently and repeatedly. And what would be the repercussions? She was a married woman not a whore. He couldn't expect to just take her whenever it pleased him. And yet, now, now after what they had just shared he couldn't bear the thought of not having her again and again and again. Had she just become his mistress? He wasn't certain she even understood the concept of a mistress. What was she thinking about all this? What did she expect? Did she expect anything?

Morning Light sensed John's sudden pensiveness and was puzzled by it. She did not know the ways of the white man but she did know herself. She was in love with this man. He was much more to her than just a friend. And what they had just shared was much more to her than just lust. She thought she should tell him so.

He had walked up behind her and bent to kiss the exposed flesh at the back of her neck before she laced up her shirt.

"*Sak,*" she said softly, turning to him. She tied the shirt lace. He gave her a little smile.

"Your hair. Here, let me pull the grass from it," he offered and reached out for a small grass stalk in her soft curls. She stopped his hand, taking it into hers and pulling it toward her cheek. She kissed it and caressed it.

"*Konoronkhwa, Sak Power,*" she said simply and then repeated herself slowly in English. "I... love... you, Jack Power. Perhaps Tonoaki feel before I know. I only know I love you," her hand and arm gestured in a graceful movement to the horizon, "all time."

He heard her and grabbed hold of her slender arms and pulled her to him, his kiss was hard on her mouth now. His emotions were reeling. He wanted her, to hold her, to have her, to keep her always in his arms, to share what they had found but how could he do that? When he released her there was a note of bitterness in his voice. "But you are married to Toe-no-ah-kee. You are his wife."

She looked at him with a little frown and slowly shook her head. "No more. I leave him."

"Left yes, but..." he looked at her, puzzling. "I don't understand. Are you saying this dissolves your marriage?" he asked and she looked at him without comprehension. He sighed in mild frustration and repeated. "Man," he put up one hand, "woman," he put up a second hand. "Come together, married, mated. Have babies, make family." She nodded in understanding.

Then she put up her two hands. "Married," she repeated and then separated her hands, holding them wide apart. "No more married."

John studied her. "Do you mean if you leave...? All you have to do is leave and you are no longer married?" he puzzled.

"Yes, leave... no more married," she confirmed.

John consciously closed his gaping mouth in response to this revelation. This put everything in a totally different light. He had been going on the assumption she was still married which certainly limited their choices. But if he was understanding correctly, Ronnie was, according to her customs, divorced, no longer married. Could she really be a free agent? That easily? That meant if he wanted... John was still mulling over the ramifications of this revelation and what exactly it might be that he wanted when Gray Wolf's Son could be heard calling to them. The child was running up from the incline, a string of fish in his small hand, and a proud broad smile on his face.

Later that evening, when they had returned to the post, John had a chance to get Charlie-One-Claw by himself.

"Charlie, help me understand something," he began. "As an Indian, when you marry, how do you get a divorce?"

"Different tribes, different customs," the scout replied. "Marriage when you say in front of everyone that you take woman to be yours. No more marriage when you say in front of everyone that you no more are together."

"But that's too easy. What's to keep everyone who has a little argument from saying they are now divorced?"

"Marriage not just union of two people, is also union of two families. Do not want to dishonor family. Families work to help keep together if couple wants to end marriage for no good reason."

"You mean to tell me that no one wants to get involved if a brave beats the living tar out of his wife," John snapped, "but if she wants to get a divorce *then* the families will get involved? That's ridiculous!"

Charlie-One-Claw simply shrugged.

"And what about leaving? If you just leave your mate, is that a form of divorce?" John prodded.

"Indian world not like white world. In Indian life a warrior must hunt for his woman, provide shelter and meat, provide protection from enemies. If he abandons his woman, she needs to find another to look after her, so he loses her. She is free to choose another who will protect her, provide for her, give her children. If she could not be free to be with another, then she would be burden on parents, brothers, or she would die."

"And what about if a woman leaves?" John finally got to his point.

"Woman come to man, give sons, keep hut, keep garden, cook, make clothes, robes, all for man. If she leaves, he have no one to do, must find another woman to do for him. But woman usually not go unless she have another lover to take care of her for woman cannot survive alone." he added.

John sat in his office brooding. He kept thinking about Charlie's words especially that last how a woman usually didn't leave unless she had another lover to take care of her. Is that what she had planned, to put him in the position of taking care of her? John jerked himself up from his chair. What was he thinking, he asked himself and felt deeply ashamed.

He had told her himself if she ever needed anything to come to him. Then, she had been beaten and beaten damn badly. No one could have expected her to stay after that. So she had done as he'd told her. She had needed help and she had tried to come to him for it. And she almost died in the process. How could he suspect her of any manipulative plotting? She was what she had always been, an intelligent, sensitive, and beautiful young woman who had once risked everything to save his life. She had become a friend. And now, she was a lover. And, with a sudden surge of emotion, John realized he never wanted to let her go!

His blood was stirring wildly as he thought of her, only steps away, above him in his own bed. He wanted her. He wanted to hold her, and feel her and feel her holding him. He had been alone for too long. He swung his legs from the cot without bothering to put on his boots. Grabbing his shirt and boots in his hand, he padded out the door, up the stairs and tapped on her door lightly.

He saw the door open a crack as she looked at him without speaking. Quietly, she stepped back. The door fell open wide and he saw her standing naked before him in the moonlight. He closed the door softly letting his shirt and boots slide noiselessly to the floor. Then, he scooped her up, carrying her to his bed. In seconds, the rest of his clothing was off and he was joining her, savoring the feel of her smooth, cool skin growing hot against his own.


"Captain Power?" the sergeant snapped to attention before his superior officer who in deference to the heat of the day sat at his desk in shirt sleeves.

"What is it?" John replied as he returned the salute. He had been perusing some maps which were spread out before him. The cot in the corner was well-made, neatly fitted and tucked perfectly. So perfectly it looked the very same as it had the day before, and the day before that and the day before that. In fact, it was starting to show a hint of dust.

"Major Greeley wants to see you, sir."

"Thank you, Sergeant," John didn't even look up, feigning a calm he didn't feel. "Dismissed."

"Yes, sir."

John carefully recapped the ink bottle he had been using so it would not spill. He had been expecting this but he wasn't anymore prepared than he had been a week ago or three weeks ago. It had been almost two months since Ronnie had taken up residence in his quarters and he knew what the commander wanted to know. He rose from his desk and smoothed back his curly cropped hair. Then he slipped into his uniform jacket and hurried to the commander's office.

"Sir. Reporting as requested," John saluted smartly.

"At ease, Captain. Have a seat," the elder man offered, though it sounded more like a command.

"Yes, sir," John sat on the same uncomfortable horsehair cushioned chair. He really must get the major to procure new chairs some day, he thought fleetingly.

"I'd like an update on the disposition of one Miss Morning Light and her two children." Major Greeley had been of a mind to be tolerant of the status quo as long as appearances were maintained and discretion was employed. Far be it from him to deny John a certain degree of emotional fulfillment. He'd known the man for over six years, and a more lonely, more solitary figure, he'd not come across.

They'd never spoken of home or family, but Greeley had made it a point to discover John's roots. He came from position and money. Why he'd come into the army as a mere private and hiding his status as a doctor, Greeley couldn't understand. *Escaping from something* was the older man's guess, and since no crime or dishonor was linked with the name, Greeley could only suspect it was something emotional. To see the younger man finally *involved* emotionally was actually heartwarming. Then, Mistress Greeley had returned from her visit to her relations back east. It only took a day for her to begin wheedling questions and finally offering solutions and warnings. An officer keeping a mistress on post was simply unacceptable, she'd said. Oh, she'd said it in a very sweet, totally subordinate, round about, unspecific way, but he hadn't missed her meaning. And she made a good point, bless her. Keeping a mistress on post *was* unacceptable.

John cleared his throat. "Permission to speak candidly off the record, sir."

"Of course." Major Greeley held his round usually jovial countenance in passive neutrality.

"I have learned that in the culture from which Ronnie comes..."

"*Ronnie?*" the Major cocked an eyebrow in question.

"Sorry... I pronounce her name so badly, sir, I've gotten into the habit of calling her Ronnie."

"I see. You have a difficult time with *Morning Light*, do you?"

"No, sir, I mean her Indian name... I've always used that instead of... well, I mean, it seemed more respectful... anyway, she laughs at how I say it and I just sort of shortened it to *Ronnie*."

"Uh-huh. Yes." The major understood completely. One usually developed pet names for people with whom one was emotional involved. "Go on."

"Well, sir, as I was saying... the fact that she left her husband is equal to a divorce in her culture. She has no one to take care of her and no one to go back to. Her life and her baby's life are in jeopardy from her ex-husband and her home has been burned down."

"Yes..."

"Well... don't you see... I mean, we can't just cast her out," John squirmed uncomfortably.

"Captain, let us be reasonable men. You can't expect her to be allowed to take up permanent residency in your quarters, can you? This is not a goddamn inn!"

"No, sir."

"My reports say the woman is healed and up to full function."

"Yes, sir."

"And she is not a member of this army, nor a dependent there of."

"No, sir."

"Technically we have no responsibility toward her."

"N...no, sir."

"So, what do you propose is the solution?"

"Couldn't we take her on as an assistant to the cook? A sort of civilian employee? She could work for her room and board. Maybe do wash and mending...?"

"John!" Greeley was red at the temples now and the muscles in his jaw were white. "I've caught a glimpse of the young woman and my wife has had more than a glimpse. I have a garrison of ninety-some randy soldiers here and not one of them is going to mistake her for the likeness of his sainted mother. Unless you are suggesting that she can double as the garrison whore, I cannot allow her to be mixing with the rank and file!"

"No," John said darkly, "no, I guess not."

Greeley calmed in response to the younger man's dejection.

"We are not a social good works society here, John. We cannot billet every stray Indian with a problem."

John shook his head in an admission of agreement.

"There is Shanty Town," the major suggested.

Shanty Town was in no way a *town* but a stray collection of discarded army tents pitched around a single two room cabin and located a convenient half-mile from the fort. The proprietor served rum and whiskey when he could get it and took a percentage from the working girls both white, Indian, and half-breeds in exchange for assuring them a violence-free atmosphere.

"No!" John bristled and then modified his response. "I mean, that is no place for a decent woman or her children, sir."

"So, what are we to do with her?" the major asked amiably.

"That's exactly what I have been asking myself, sir. Please, give me one more week to try and figure things out."

Greeley raised his eyebrows sharply. "One week, no more," he agreed.

"Yes, sir. Thank you, sir." John left the commander's office in a despondent mood.

He had known all along that things couldn't possibly stay the way they were. She spent her days watching her children, reading, and sewing in the company of Mistress Greeley and going for walks outside the fort in his company. And at night they lie in each other's arms with him stealing back to his office before dawn. She was balm to his spirit, joy to his life. Her soft laughter warmed his heart. And her warm body and intense passion made him feel... he caught his own breath just thinking of her... like no whore had ever made him feel that was for certain. He was spoiled to her now. He'd spent ten lonely, God forsaken years since Alana's death. Freyja had been a beautiful hope that had been dashed. He didn't want to be lonely anymore. It wasn't dishonor to Freyja's memory, he told himself, anymore than Freyja had been dishonor to Alana. It was life. He was alive and he wanted to feel alive again, really alive but John still had not broken completely free of the guilt.

"Captain Power?" the young lieutenant snapped a salute as he stopped before his captain. It was three days since John's talk with the commander and he was no nearer a solution regarding Morning Light than he had been. But at the moment he was on duty and in the process of double checking surgery supplies with the help of his sergeant.

Ever since John had been put in charge of the fort surgery, he saw to it that it was scrubbed down regularly and the instruments were maintained clean and boiled sterile. Huffsmeier's words still echoed in his mind. "*What they cannot scrub clean, they boil clean.*" During times of peace there wasn't much demand for any real doctoring but he wanted the men who worked beneath him used to the conditions he expected for treating patients when there was a need.

"Yes," John sighed heavily, "what is it?"

"We have an injun woman asking for you, sir. Least wise, it sounds like your name. She keeps saying *Sakpowr Ferend.*"

Power frowned and came out of the small structure. "Where is she?"

"In the compound, sir, she's got a couple young bucks with her."

"See that the inventory is finished, Lieutenant," John ordered the junior officer. "Get Charlie-One-Claw out here," he tossed back at the sergeant and strode away.

The sun was shining brightly but there was a decent breeze stirring the air that kept it from being suffocatingly hot. John walked briskly out to the dusty compound absently thinking they needed a little rain. As he turned the corner of the command post, he was not surprised to find Singing Wind standing in a loose cotton tunic flanked by Wani and Yellow Rock dressed only in loin cloths and moccasins. They were near the front gate and as John approached he was grateful to see Charlie-One-Claw coming toward them as well.

John raised his empty hands in the sign of greeting. They greeted him back.

"My daughter. Have you found my daughter?" the older woman asked through the scout. Her eyes bespoke the weariness in her heart and John thought the woman had aged years in the months since he'd last seen her. It appeared as if she had lost some teeth and her cheeks were sunken.

"Yes, we found her," John spoke grimly. "She went the wrong way and was caught in the snowstorm. When we found her, she was in a strong fever and had nothing to eat. She would have died. She almost did." John didn't spare their feelings. He was still angry that they had not even bothered to look for her.

"Her children?"

"They, too, would have died. But they did not because we found them. They are well." He saw the relief visibly flow into the woman's face.

"We want to see her," the woman said piteously. John considered for a moment. He wouldn't really deny them but he couldn't help but stretch out his approval. Extending their doubt and keeping them hanging was no more than they deserved. If he could have stretched out the suspense for several days, he would have. But he didn't. After a few long moments, with a quick nod he left to get Morning Light.

After a courtesy knock on the door, John entered and saw her bent over a book practicing her letters. Her soft brunette hair fell in waves about her shoulders. She had stopped braiding her hair at his request. The white muslin blouse she wore was modest but clung revealingly to her high full breasts, the skirt, a modified style suitable for the frontier, was nipped at her slender waist by a wide sash. She looked up and gave him a smile that warmed his heart. He wanted to stay in this room with her forever and forget the outside world but he knew they couldn't do that.

"Ronnie..."

She rose and came to him with what he had taught her was a *kiss* before he could say anymore.

"Oh, dear God, I..." he held her close and then put her away from him. He couldn't tell her that he was afraid, afraid she was going to leave him. "You have visitors." His voice had become tight and she searched his eyes but he said no more.

John escorted her down to the compound and over near the gate where he saw a blanket had been spread on the ground although all three natives still stood.

Wani and Yellow Rock had taken places of silent vigil behind the edge of the blanket with their backs to the fort wall. Singing Wind stood in front, her arms open to the figure she almost did not recognize.

As Morning Light walked on John's arm, her mother had time to take in everything about her. Her clothes were in the fashion of the white women. Her hair held back with a bright ribbon, hung in soft loose curls down her back. Even her skin had paled since she was no longer laboring in the fields every day.

"Mother," she cried and ran to Singing Wind.

They dropped to their knees on the blanket and talked for a long while; Wani, Yellow Rock, and John looked on in various stances of arrogance. Wani and Yellow Rock deigned to be disinterested once they had exchanged greetings. John couldn't understand a word of what was said. Charlie-One-Claw's face was a blank.

"I could not wait any longer. I told Five Beavers I would go and find out about my daughter and grandchildren, if he did not want to come, then I would take Wani and Yellow Rock. He did not try to stop me. I have mourned you for months. Why did you not send me word?"

"I am sorry, my mother," tears were slipping down Morning Light's cheeks. "Please forgive me but I was afraid that Tonoaki would find out and come here to find me."

"Tonoaki is gone. No one see him since you leave. He come back from hunting for you in a rage. He burned down hut and all your possessions."

"Yes, Jack told me."

"So, you are his woman now?" her mother asked bluntly.

"He found me and nursed me back to health. He takes care of me. He has been very good to me." Her mother looked at her long and hard and finally she added,

"We are lovers now but we were not before. You know this."

Singing Wind nodded. "And has he publicly acknowledged you as his woman?"

"That is not the white man's way, my mother. But I love him and I am content."

"I want you to come home," the older squaw said, a sad look in her eyes. "You belong with me. With your people. There are many braves who would offer for you. And everyone knows now that we are part white."

Morning Light reached out and grabbed her mother's rough chaffed hands. She kissed them and lowered her forehead to them. Then she began to weep in earnest. "Perhaps, since I now know that Tonoaki is not there, I can come to visit," she said when she composed herself. Her mother looked at her in puzzlement.

"Why do you not want to come home? If he will not publicly acknowledge you and pledge to care for you, why?"

"I cannot," she said softly so only her mother could hear. "I carry his child."

"That means nothing since you have no husband now," The woman raised her voice. "The child is yours. You do not have to stay with a man who will not publicly acknowledge you."

Wani who was pushing his thirteenth year and was growing husky, and Yellow Rock who was in his prime, both heard and understood. They bristled at the white man and John could feel lethal darts coming from their black eyes although he didn't understand why.

What had she said, he wondered. Why was she crying? He looked at Charlie-One-Claw in an expression of bewilderment. The scout's face was an unreadable mask.

"Tell me what she's saying," John demanded quietly of Charlie.

"Mother wants girl to come home. Old husband gone, many braves want her," he replied choosing to leave out the part about the baby.

"What did she say?" John asked anxiously.

"She think about it."

"What?!"

"Says you will not publicly acknowledge her."

"What is that supposed to mean?"

"In white man's world it means you will not marry her."

"Who says I won't?!" John railed, panic suddenly seizing him as he watched the young braves continue to bristle and her mother pleading with her. Isn't this exactly what he had expected when her family arrived, part of his mind reasoned. The major already had set a deadline for change. Ronnie couldn't stay here as things were and hadn't he known if she went back to her village they would force her to marry again. Had he thought she would just sit there waiting for him to visit her so they could make love? How had he expected this all to end? A sweat broke out on John's brow. Marry her to another? "No, by God! She's not going back. She's staying right here. We are getting married and that's final."

The women had stopped talking and Morning Light turned to John.

"What did you say?" she asked looking up at him with a tear stained face.

"I said..." he almost shouted and then, taking a deep breath, he lowered his voice and softened his tone. "I'm asking you to marry me, Ronnie. I'm asking you to be my wife. Forever and ever. But in my world, you cannot just leave. Never. If you say yes, you are stuck with me until death parts us. Do you understand? If we have a fight, we work it out. I promise never to beat you and I'll never cut off that beautiful nose. I will protect you and your children, provide for you and shelter you, and you can have my children and cook and sew and tend the garden." He saw something in her eyes and was relaxing now and smiling, remembering the things Charlie-One-Claw had told him.

For the other's benefit, the scout was translating what John had just said and her mother began to say something to which Morning Light put up a hushing finger. She put her hand out and John helped her rise up off the ground where she had been kneeling on the blanket with her mother.

"Why do you wish to marry me, Jack Power?" she asked directly, composed and solemn, looking into his clear gray eyes.

"Because... because I love you." There was a sense of realization in his words. He did love her. If what he felt wasn't love than he didn't know what love was. "I want us to be together for the rest of our lives. I never want to lose you, never want us to be parted. I cannot stand the thought of you not being with me," he replied never wavering his return gaze. Charlie-One-Claw had withdrawn from them to give them privacy, the others spoke no English.

"Do you know how happy this makes me?" she replied, her eyes shining. "Why have you not told me this before?"

"I guess I did not realize it completely myself. Ronnie, there are things about me I have not told you. I promised myself a long, long time ago that I'd never fall in love again. I did twice and both times the young woman died. It has been many years now, but when it happened it hurt so badly I thought I would never get beyond it. It tore me apart." He sighed looking at her warm gaze of no judgment. "God, I guess I've been a yellow coward. I think of everything you have been through and you can still love, openly, warmly, and be so giving. I'd be the biggest idiot on the face of the earth if I didn't hold on to you with both hands."

"And arms," she added softly in agreement.

"And arms," he agreed.

"And lips?" she teased gently.

He took hold of her, wrapped her into his arms and kissed her soundly right in front of everyone.

"Captain Power, may I see you a moment?" the request was really a command and came from the sudden and unexpected presence of Major Greeley.

John spun around and letting go of Morning Light, he admonished, "Now nobody go anywhere. I'll be right back." He rushed over to his commander and gave a stiff salute. "Yes, sir."

"Explain yourself, Captain."

"Permission to have a wedding, sir."

"Permission granted," Greeley replied at once in what was now a most amenable attitude and then added quietly. "It's about time you made an honest woman of her, John." Then the major turned and left.

John looked after Greeley a bit stunned at first and then his expression broke into a smile. The ol' fox. He didn't miss a thing.

The wedding date was set for a week from the day and the entire garrison was invited. So was the Indian village and coaxed by the promise of a feast about half did attend including all of Morning Light's extended family. Captain Rigby served as the post chaplain and officiated. Major and Mistress Greeley were the official witnesses.

When the day came, it turned out to be cloudless, breezeless, and overwhelmingly hot. Morning Light, on the arm of Major Greeley, walked down the aisle created outside the fort walls under the shade of a tall oak tree. She was dressed in a simple gown of petal soft silk in a peach shade that set off her radiant complexion. The Major's wife had assisted her in sewing the gown as well as a full complement of petticoats and a corset. With her long hair styled atop her head beneath a small veil, Morning Light looked very lovely.

John was there to receive her, standing tall and proud, the image of the handsome officer in his spotless dress uniform, complete with shiny brass buttons and tight white breeches. His gold blond locks had been trimmed to just off his collar and his tanned face crinkled into a loving smile when he saw his bride.

The words were said, the vows exchanged. John used his own ring with his family's crest on it to place on her finger until he could have a more feminine wedding band made for her. Morning Light was overwhelmed with the press of people and the stifling warmth beneath the layers of fabric Mistress Greeley had insisted she wear. When the chaplain gave John permission to kiss the bride, he did and she promptly fainted from heat, nerves, and excitement.

It was a poignant scene. Some of the oldest and most hardened veterans could be detected wiping a tear from their eyes. The groom was handsome, the young bride so exotically beautiful. Then, the kiss and the bride crumpled into the groom's arms. It was like a tale their mothers had told to them in the nursery.

John set his bride down in the full shade of the tree and someone fetched fresh cold well water in a tin cup. They fanned her until she revived and looking a bit chagrined she pulled on John's sleeve. It was time to tell him what she had been waiting to confess. Nursing a baby did not always prevent conception.

"I am going to have your baby, Jack," she whispered in his ear and he laughed with joy, deep, rich, and rumbling. Then, he picked her up into his arms again and swung her around, totally pleased with her and himself and the world for the first time in so many years.

The story continues in

The Huguenot and the Heathen II: The Prodigal Returns

## Book Club Discussion Questions

1. Do you think Elka should have told her family about the rape? Justify your answer.

2. Why do you think Herr Hendrick Huffsmeier is obsessed with time and punctuality?

3. In Switzerland, Dr. Huffsmeier thanks John before he leaves and it says "There was no need to explain for what." What do you think he was thanking John for?

4. Compare the way John grieves and the way Morning Light grieves.

5. What is the guilt John has been living with?

6. Discuss the pros and cons of rigid gender defined roles. Why do you think more primitive societies favor this? Do you think it is a slight to women?

7. Although it is rare, geneticists say Morning Light's situation with Tonoaki's daughter is indeed possible if not probable. Today, we have DNA testing to prove paternity, but just one generation ago this was not so. Discuss what you think some of the reactions would have been if the same situation had occurred within a "white" family 25 years ago. 50 years ago. 100 years ago. 200 years ago.

8. The sons of very successful men often struggle with the long shadow their fathers cast. Each of Jacques' sons deals with this in his own way. Discuss how differently John and Phillip deal with it. Why do you think it seems to bother John the most?

An excerpt from

### *The Huguenot and The Heathen II:*
### *The Prodigal Returns*

For the first time in over ten years, Captain John Power wanted to visit home. He felt whole again. He felt like a part of him that had been missing for a very long time had returned and settled in with a contentment and tranquility that had eluded him for over a decade. He was thirty-three and in the prime of life. His career was established. He had a sensually beautiful wife he loved with a passion and children to bring joy to their lives. Now it was time to revisit the parents he loved and missed and renew bonds with his siblings…………..

John had hopes the soon to be twenty-year-old Isabelle would become close to his wife. John recalled his baby sister fondly and had thought she amongst all the siblings would have the most in common with Ronnie. They were, after all, both women and almost the same age. Isabelle had always had a rather devil-take-the-hind-most attitude toward convention. He imagined that she would see Ronnie for the person she was, not for her race. But Isabelle was not home for their arrival. She was on a chaperoned trip up to Boston, he was told, where she was spending time with her husband-to-be. Staying under the protective care of her fiancé's family, the trip was the concession she had wrung from her parents when they had postponed her wedding out of respect for her sister's loss.

On the day Isabelle was expected to return, John went down to the harbor himself, in his officer's full dress uniform, to surprise her. Standing, feet slightly apart, hands behind his back and with a broad grin on his face he silently watched as the delicate little figure gathered her skirts about her and began searching the wharf for signs of her family escort, her parents perhaps, or the servants. He felt her eyes float over him and saw them focus on the family carriage several yards away. He thought he saw recognition as she continued to look and puzzlement showed on her delicate little face. Then, suddenly the large gray eyes were back on him again and, after an instant, he saw the recognition as she began to run down the gangplank.

"John!" Isabelle squealed in rapturous delight as her tiny feet flew lightly over the uneven footing and she rushed into her handsome big brother's arms. He lifted her into the air much as he used to when she was very young. "You've come home for my wedding! I knew you would. I just knew you would. I told Mother, John will come home for my wedding, just you wait and see if he won't."

John chuckled. "Let me look at you, midget," he teased setting her down and holding her at arms length. She was just as pretty and effervescent as everyone had said with soft almost silver blonde curls and huge dove gray eyes set in a face of very delicate features. Her skin was almost translucent in its fairness and hypnotic black rims circled her gray irises.

"Good lord, how you've grown up. And when is this big event I keep hearing about?" John smiled warmly.

"Oh, John. We had to postpone it," her mouth curved into a delightful little pout.

"When was it supposed to be?" he asked amiably.

"Didn't you get my letter?" she asked quickly.

"No," he shook his head.

"I swear, you can't depend on anything that goes to the frontier!" Then, she leaned forward to whisper in confidence. "It was supposed to be at the end of summer as soon as Rafe and Richie returned. I mean, Hamilton proposed late last summer. It's been almost a full year but now Mother says we must wait until Louise is officially out of mourning. It's not fair. When Phillip decided to marry they just up and married. Helen and Louise only had to be engaged a few months. It seems like by the time it came around to me, they just keep pushing the engagement longer and longer."

"You're their baby," John grinned, giving her a little squeeze. "It's hard to give you up."

"But I'm not a baby. I'm almost three years older than Phillip was when he got married and I'm a woman!"

"But then we know why Phillip got married so quickly," John winked. "I hope you're not saying you've a similar concern?"

"No. Of course, not." She swung to punch his arm with her tiny lace gloved hand. "But Helen got married at eighteen, Louise was only seventeen and here I am nineteen already, soon to be twenty!"

"Tsk-tsk-tsk," John clucked. "A veritable old maid. And as I recall, both your sisters had lengthy engagements waiting *patiently* until their birthdays."

"John," she frowned, trying to exude dignity. "it's just not fair that we have to wait until after the new year. It's so silly. Louise doesn't care. And it's not like she has to stand up for us or anything, she can still wear her widow's weeds, no one will notice. Talk to Mother, John, please?"

"Hey, I didn't just arrive to start getting into your little arguments," he laughed.

"It's not a *little argument*," she stamped her tiny foot, "it's my life. And Hamilton is so disappointed. Of course, he's being an angel about it. I mean, he'll do anything for me. But why does my wedding have to be put off just because my sister married a wandering fur trader?"

"That's a trifle hard, isn't it?" he quirked a brow at her as he gathered her things into his arms and began to walk toward the carriage.

"Oh, you know what I mean," Isabelle sighed.

An older woman, robustly plump and as tall as a man, came up carrying more baggage.

"And who is this?" John nodded to the older woman knowing very well who she was but reminding his young sister that an introduction was due.

"Who? Oh, this is Rachel. The Spanish maidens have their *duennas* and I have Rachel. She's my chastity belt."

John almost dropped the luggage. "Your what?! Never mind, I know damn well I heard you, though I don't believe what I heard."

"Oh, don't be silly," she grinned saucily. "I'm grown up now, John, I know about a lot of things."

He ignored her last remark and hoisted the baggage into the rear of the carriage and then turned politely to the older woman. "Rachel," he acknowledged her with a slight bow, "I'm John Power, this scamp's oldest brother."

"Pleased t' meet ya, Master Power," Rachel said in a distinct Cockney accent and dropped a small curtsy which looked totally out of place. Although her shawl and dress covered her arms discreetly, John had the feeling her biceps could win most challenges at tabletop arm wrestling.

"I understand it is your job to chaperon my sister."

"You 'ave that right, sir, an' pleased I am t' be of service."

"I don't envy you the job. I imagine she runs you ragged," he smiled and helped the older woman into the carriage.

"No, sir. I mean, she h'ain't any real trouble, sir. Just a ball o' energy is all."

"Yes. To be sure." John looked down upon his sister and saw her expression darken. He could tell she was about to protest his talking about her to a mere servant or maybe it was because he had assisted the older woman to her seating ahead of his own sister. "Now, don't get your ruffles up, missy. You're coming up front with me," he cut her off as she opened her mouth. He picked her up and placed her, billowing skirts and all, up onto the front box seat.

"Oh, John," she cried out in surprise and then fell into giggles. "No one's done that since I was a child."

He smiled as he took his seat beside her and flicked the reins. "Sorry, I'm afraid I still think of you as a child. You're hardly any bigger than you were when I left." He saw her look of protest. "But then you've filled out very nicely," he added and it mollified her.

"I wonder if anyone saw us," she mused looking all about. "You really are quite dashing and handsome in that uniform. The tale will go round that some officer has abducted me off the wharf." She giggled to herself.

"I can't believe you're all grown up and about to be married."

"Yes," she sat straighter, "but good heavens, if people were to put off getting married because of non-blood relatives dying, if you had a really, really large family, there would never be any weddings." She smiled at him infectiously.

"Then the family couldn't get very large," he grinned back.

"Oh, John," she feigned exasperation.

"So, it's *Hamilton*, is it?"

"Yes," she smiled broadly again, this time with a faintly distant, dreamy expression crossing her face.

"Hamilton, what?"

"Hamilton... Chadwick... Grenville... Carter. He's so wonderful, John. You'll like him. He's tall... but not too tall... with very dark hair and bright blue eyes. He's very handsome and very smart. Well, he had the good sense to fall in love with me, didn't he?"

"I never heard where falling in love had much to do with good sense or smarts," he teased. "It's entirely other matters."

"John," she slapped playfully at his arm. "That's so naughty."

"Look who's talking."

"Anyway, he *is* very smart and, of course, he's very successful."

"Hmmmm, of course," John murmured obligingly.

"Father brought him home to dinner one night and every time he looked at me I had this melty feeling in the pit of my stomach. I couldn't eat a bite. Hamilton says he fell in love with me the very moment he saw me." Then she gave a high tinkling giggle. "You should have seen Father's face when Hamilton asked if he could call on me. And when he asked for my hand, Mother and I both had to convince Father that Boston is not on the other side of the moon."

"Far enough. The better part of a week by ship, I'd wager."

"Oh, not nearly a week," she replied sweetly, "only a few days on a big ship."

"Well, I hope I get the chance to meet this paragon who has swept my baby sister off her feet."

"Why, of course you will... I mean, why shouldn't you? Oh, John, you're not going to disappear again are you?" She grabbed his arm earnestly. "If you are, then we really must have the wedding before you go."

"And what does Father say?"

"Pish-posh, you know Father, he always ends up agreeing with Mother," Isabelle pouted again daintily but her voice had the clarity of a little bell.

They continued to chat amiably on the short trip to the Power family home. John was still smiling when he drew the horses up in the drive, jumped down and helped Isabelle and Rachel from the carriage. Then, swinging his sister around to face him he exclaimed, "All right, enough about you for a moment, brat, I want you to meet someone."

"Who?" Isabelle asked breathlessly.

"My wife."

"Your wife! Oh, John, you're married?! Why didn't you say so?" She stopped and clapped her hands in childlike glee. "I don't believe it. I was just saying not too long ago that you had best marry soon before you grew so old and set in your ways no woman could stand you." She grinned broadly. "That's one of the reasons I told Mother we had to get you back here for my wedding... so you could meet some nice young ladies. I said to Mother, who could you possibly meet on that horrible frontier where there's nothing but savages and soldiers."

"It's not that devoid of beautiful females," he replied evasively. They walked through the door and Isabelle found herself facing Ronnie in the entry hall.

"Darling, this is my little sister, Isabelle or *Izzy* as we've been calling her since she was in diapers," said John warmly.

"Hello," Ronnie said graciously and extended her hand as John had taught her to do.

"Hello," Isabelle barely touched Ronnie's fingers with her own as she looked the taller woman over. She certainly had an exotic look about her. In contrast to her own milk white skin, the woman looked positively dark. Had John met some Spaniards on the frontier? But she was so tall and Spaniards were supposed to be little people.

"This is my wife, Ronnie," John said proudly.

"Ronnie?" Isabelle smiled mischievously. "What an odd name. Surely that's not your real name."

"No," Ronnie smiled hesitantly, "it is what your brother calls me because my name does not come easily to his lips."

"Can't remember your own wife's name, huh, John?" Isabelle teased with a look at her brother, then she turned back to the taller woman and continued to appraise her. "So, what is your real name, if I may ask?"

*"Ohronkene Hahser."*

"That's very... exotic," Isabelle said cautiously. "So you're foreign."

"Foreign?" Ronnie questioned the word.

"English doesn't seem to be your mother tongue," Isabelle responded.

"Ah, no, your brother taught me English," replied Ronnie with a quick glance at John.

"What is your first language?" Isabelle asked, her eyes narrowing slightly.

*"Lenni Lanape,"* Ronnie replied. "But since I be eleven I speak *Kanien'keha.*"

"Goodness." Isabelle stared for a moment and then looked to her brother in ill-disguised irritation. "I'm sorry, I don't recognize that, is she Portuguese?"

"The Portuguese speak Portuguese," John replied stiffly, not happy with how the conversation was going.

"Oh, I know that," Isabelle huffed, "but I don't know every country in the whole wide world, nor what every language sounds like. What in heaven's sake is *Lenny la nappie*? Where is she from? She's obviously foreign. Not that that's a bad thing," she turned to the taller woman with a small smile. "My goodness, Mother and Father are French and didn't speak any English when they first arrived. Bengt Solinson who is our neighbor has parents who came from Sweden and they didn't speak anything but Swedish when they first arrived. So where did your parents…?

"Is that all you can talk about? Trying to dig up my wife's pedigree? Where are your manners, Izzy? I expected better of you," John was frowning and Isabelle flushed. His upset was intensified because he realized he was actually trying to evade a direct answer to her questions as if he was ashamed. A quick glance at Ronnie made him feel even worse for he saw that she knew it, too.

"I'm sorry," Isabelle said contritely. "Welcome to the family, of course. I guess anything that gets John to come home and visit his family is a good thing. How long have you been married?"

"Actually, it's been a while," John replied, continuing to be evasive while his self irritation put an edge in his voice. "We have several children."

"What?" Isabelle giggled infectiously as she chattered. "I bet that put everyone into a spin. Not only are you married but you already have a growing family before anyone even hears about it. Several children... that's at least several years while we've been thinking of you as this big, lonesome bachelor. And all this time, the whole ride home you never said a thing. Oh, John, you are bad. I'm beginning to think you were on the other side of the world. Is that it? Were you in one of those far off exotic places like... like China or Japan... or Arabia? Is that where you are from, Arabia?" she turned again to Ronnie.

"Ronnie is an Indian," John said softly his eyes locked to his wife's.

"You were in India!" exclaimed Isabelle. "Oh, how romantic. Isn't that where they wear those turban things and sell exotic spices and..."

"I didn't join the navy, Izzy," John looked at her. "I'm in the British colonial army, we stay on the continent."

"But then how did you meet a girl from India?" Isabelle looked at him in puzzlement.

"Ronnie isn't from India, she's from right here," John said in exasperation.

"But you said she was... Oh, my God! You mean a savage?!" Isabelle looked at her brother in horror as realization struck home. "John, how could you? Does everyone know?"

John couldn't believe his sister's reaction. She hadn't even tried to hide it. "I'm not certain what you mean by everyone. I haven't been up on the rooftop lately shouting proclamations to the world. The family knows, of course. What difference does it make? What's the matter with you? Are you afraid she's going to take out her tomahawk and scalp you?"

"Oh!" Isabelle gasped indignantly. "Evidently you left your own manners back in the wilderness! What do you expect a person to say when you give them a shock like this?!" she snapped peevishly. Then, with a tight nod at Ronnie she added, "I'm sorry but I really must go to my room now. I've just returned from a very tiring trip. You'll have to excuse me," and she flounced up the staircase.

Order soon

## *The Huguenot and The Heathen II:*
### *The Prodigal Returns*

by
D.C. Force

www.dcforce.com

***www.Amazon.com/author/dcforce***